Library of America, a nonprofit organization,
champions our nation's cultural heritage
by publishing America's greatest writing in
authoritative new editions and providing resources
for readers to explore this rich, living legacy.

S. J. PERELMAN

S. J. PERELMAN

WRITINGS

Adam Gopnik, *editor*

THE LIBRARY OF AMERICA

Contents

Introduction:
Perelman, the Pearl of Providence

ADAM GOPNIK

S. J. Perelman's reputation rose first in the 1930s, when he became famous as a comedy writer in New York and then in Hollywood, and rose still higher in the forties and fifties, when he became the most admired of *New Yorker* satirists. Perelman (whom everyone called "Sid") then reached a kind of surprising apex of late fame in the 1970s, when the combination of the glamour newly associated with his thirties work as a scriptwriter for the Marx Brothers—not a word he would have used to describe the connection—got coupled with a larger rush of general reverence: Woody Allen's early written work was as straight an homage to Perelman as one writer can offer another. Those offering encomiums to his preeminence —as he might have said, the ill-turned cliché being one of his fascinations—included Dorothy Parker, Wilfrid Sheed, and many out beyond. The British critic Clive James recalls having lunch with the famously shy *New Yorker* editor William Shawn and alleviating the awkwardness by exchanging Perelmanisms at length. When Sid moved to London in the 1970s—he soon came back to New York, complaining of "too much couth"—it was hard news in the *Times.*

Fifty-some years later—well, who knows where anyone's reputation rests now. "Everything is niche," a wise Gen Zer, tells her father, which means both that no writer has a secure shared reputation, but also that in an English-speaking world of perhaps a billion readers, *any* readers at all are enough to create a critical mass. For every niche there is a nosh, and for every nosh a niche, as Sid might have had Groucho say: the smallest bite of writing finds somebody to chew on it. An audience of less than 1 percent of all potential American readers alone is larger than the entire audience in London who saw all of Shakespeare's plays. (I sourced this statistic just now from my imagination, in Perelman's honor, but the general take is surely right: mass audiences make even minor readerships massive.) Certainly, his sentences dazzle a contemporary reader as much as they did Shawn and James. Not sentences alone, but entire paragraphs as beautifully and intricately constructed as a Rube Goldberg machine, with cliché backing into argot flirting with Broadway slang, Yiddish and British pretension side by side. He was one of the best pure *writers* in American English. He still is.

No, what has shifted is not so much the scale of his reputation as the persistence of a tradition in which he can still be seen as a master. The kind of extended rococo, satiric riff that he helped invent, and then perfected, is no longer an entirely living genre, as it was even in the eighties when Allen mastered it. Even in—especially in—the pages of *The New Yorker*, the casual comic piece has become more compressed and less consciously literary. A typical Shouts and Murmurs in the magazine now is scarcely longer than the prefatory quotations that Perelman would use as the straight-man setup of one of his pieces, those eyebrow-raising citations from advertising copy or fashion magazines—or even an instruction manual for an electric blanket—whose inanities or fatuities Perelman would then satirize in a comic sketch. This is, to be sure, a reflection of changing mores as much as changing editors; extended anythings are rare enough these days, so why should comic riffs be different?

If that means that Perelman's voice now flows less naturally into the next literary thing, it also means that we can see it more clearly as *a* thing—not something meant to be quoted and recycled but as a finished form of American literature in itself. Two essential truths about Perelman, as a satirist and stylist revealed themselves, somewhat surprisingly, even to this lifelong Perelman lover in the course of assembling this anthology. First, that Perelman's great subject is singular and simply defined: his subject, as Wilfrid Sheed first intimated, is American vulgarity, flowing up and down like waves of electricity through a cat in a cartoon, exposing its innards even as it shocks our sensibilities. (He said as much himself, simply: "I've sought material . . . in the novels I read in my youth, the movies I saw, my Hollywood years, and in advertising," i.e., the three prime sources of American vulgarity.)

The way that high art on its way down to the many met acquisitive popular energies on their way back up to the prestigious top, both together working to make the astonishing, absurd and yet in many ways still-appealing middlebrow magazine and movie culture of the mid-part of the American century—that was what he saw and registered. Biopics about the life of John Singer Sargent, abstract expressionists caught in mid-cult as their style became décor, hard-boiled pulp detective fiction extending its metaphoric reach into metaphysical dimensions—"she was as dead as vaudeville"—these collisions of sensibility, going on all around him, were his subject. (Of the Hollywood tycoons he despised, the only ones he despised *more* than the cheap cynics were the aspiring highbrows who knew "that Joseph Conrad was a Polack.")

A second essential truth that revealed itself is that Perelman is a writers' writer in the literal sense that his rhetoric—his style—always emerges from his reading. Every sentence written references some earlier, once-read sentence. The matchless Perelman tone is taken over from the pulp literature of his childhood: he is always a Kipling adventurer, a Conan Doyle detective, a Maupassant boulevardier, dressed British and thinking in Yiddish. From childhood on, his experience was almost entirely shaped by reading books and magazines (and secondarily by watching movies and shows) and then comparing the thing imagined with the world he met. Reading left so deep an impress on him as to become not an additive to experience but a kind of substitute for experience; his life forever after is modeled after the thing read more than the thing known. His biographers record a relatively melancholic and mostly parched life of stiff relationships on all sides; his real life lay within the books he fled life to get to. In particular, he was looking at mid-century American vulgarity through the lens of the popular, mostly British, fiction he had read as a boy—seeing Mike Todd through the lens of Kipling—and the overlay is what gives his work its density and heft.

One only has to compare him to the top comic writer who preceded him in *The New Yorker*'s estimation—or in the world's estimation of *New Yorker* writers—to see this clearly. James Thurber, a wonderful minimal stylist, is writing about plain American manners in the plain American manner. He offers us the nightmarish underside of the desperate, pained, austere respectability of WASP Ohio life—the buried craziness, recycled as eccentricity, the cruelties and alcoholism recast as comedy. He shows us life. Some of Thurber's best things do involve reading other people's things, as with his great comparison of Salvador Dalí's memoir with his own, "The Secret Life of James Thurber." But it is the marked, impassable space between Spanish surrealism and Ohio truths that registers. Thurber is, in the old-fashioned phrase, true to life. We read him for his relatives.

With Perelman, parents and relations, his entire childhood in Providence, Rhode Island—where his ne'er-do-well father passed from failure as a grocer to failure as a chicken farmer, both classic Jewish occupations of the period—scarcely register at all, or only as phantoms, passing obstacles to the boy's determination to get safely away to read. But each book he reads haunts his imagination and his writing forever after. He reads junk and good things interchangeably, and never forgets a single turn: Sax Rohmer's absurd Fu Manchu stories, Elinor Glyn's sensual overexcitements, Edgar Rice Burroughs's ornate Tarzan tales are his reading, along with Twain and Conrad, and of course behind them hover the club and detective literature of London. (He rarely directly parodies the Sherlock Holmes stories, but often implicitly alludes to them.) To those one might add, as essential mulch, the silent movies. He once listed his movie loves as "Corinne Griffith, Priscilla Dean, Aileen Pringle, and Nita Naldi"—hardly names to conjure with now, they were hardly names to conjure with then. But the melodramatic movies provided other strata of imaginative support. Thurber's best stuff is "observational"; Perelman's best stuff is critical, a study of reading and viewing habits.

Like many good writers, he was a startlingly long time finding his best voice—he was famous before he was great. Though his contribution to the Marx Brothers became an important part of his legend, what he wrote for the two best of their movies —*Monkey Business* and the even better *Horse Feathers*—is unsettled. Perelman's contributions are hard to define amid the uncertainties of studio-system group-grope writing, but when Groucho says, "Come lodge with me and my fleas in the hills . . . I mean fly with me to my lodge in the hills," or when the college secretary informs him in *Horse Feathers* that the waiting dean is waxing wroth, and Groucho replies, "Is Roth out there, too? Tell Roth to wax the dean for a while," we are surely hearing Perelman at work. In the thirties, as an efflorescence of his unhappy Hollywood years, he did write the single piece that comes closest to being the kind of literary "masterpiece" that would find its way into anthologies, the long, amazing, "Joycean" piece called "Scenario," a surreal representation of what's now called a pitch meeting, in which we find every imaginable cliché of the period's movies, and even of its movie reviewing (James Agee makes a brief appearance). And he never outgrew the appetite for writing a movie or, better, a stage hit. He did win an Oscar eventually for the not-very-stirring 1956 spectacular *Around the World in Eighty Days* and did write one good play, *The Beauty Part* of 1962, doomed to a short run by, of all things, a New York newspaper strike, but sporadically revived ever since.

To this reader, though, it is after World War II, with the growth both of American abundance and of the American analytic culture that went with it—it is no accident that Perelman's single best collection, *The Road to Miltown*, is named after a psychiatrist's pet tranquilizer—that Perelman gets great. And here an odd point arises: though the subject of his satire, American vulgarity, is evergreen, the objects of his satire may seem to have been transient, and now long passed. The manners of the art-house movie theater; the prose style of Diana Vreeland in *Harper's Bazaar*; the decorum of Hathaway shirt ads; the behavior of Greenwich Village dry cleaners; or the imagined behavior of Pandit Nehru . . . all of these things seem long faded as targets. And yet the pieces have not faded at all.

It is the myth of satire that satire is diminished as its objects lose luster. Who now, the argument goes, can even recall the names, much less the styles, of the poets Pope is mocking at such laborious length in *The Dunciad*? In truth, just the opposite is the case for even minimally attentive readers. Great poetic satire brings its field of mockery with it; the objects of satire are *more* evident in the satire than the mockery is, *more* evident than they were to the time supposedly satirized. We enjoy satire more when we *don't* know the things being satirized—and so cannot protest their portrayal—and depend on the satirist for all our information, both for the ground and for the graffiti he scrawls upon it. The satirist acts as a delighted stylist of other people's affectations, with the manners being mocked evident in the mockery. So, we get the affectations and manners as they come at us, presorted through the sieve of the satirist's imagination. Like fossils—or, to use a Popeian metaphor, like ancient flies caught in amber—Hollywood producers or the advertising copy from the 1940s survive *because* they still exist in Perelman. It is not his disgust but his defensive reaction, his spinning webs of silk to weave around the caught objects of his pursuit, that still delights. The particular Hollywood producers whom Perelman hated are long gone— the Mike Todds (who employed him on *Around the World in Eighty Days*, and drove him crazy while getting him an Oscar), the Hunt Strombergs—just as the particular poets whom Pope mocked are gone, too. But the evocation of a show-business world marked by hearty hyperbole, mindless energy, empty promises, and limitless dissembling remains. Knock on any producer's door, and meet a Perelman character. Though we love his stories for their period nature, we know the period best through Perelman, which means, since Perelman is permanent, that they transcend the period.

This anthologist must confess a prejudice in assembling this anthology, but a prejudice forgivably rooted in passionate early attachment rather than a late-arriving judicious pose. You learned reading Perelman, as a kid, that anything post-1945 and pre-1970 was bound to be good, just as, with P. G. Wodehouse, a quick glance at the copyright page told almost all: any Wodehouse title before 1930 or after 1960 wasn't likely to be the real mint stuff.

And so, the prejudice is for the poetic-critical pieces that Perelman wrote in abundance throughout the 1950s and into the 1960s, particularly for the matchless "Cloudland Revisited" series, in which he indeed revisited all of those books and movies from his own adolescence, from the point of view of a more wizened oldster. The collision of sensibility is particularly pure in those pieces, and they seem to offer the essence of Perelman's genius in a way that this other favorite genre of that period, the travel pieces, don't. In the second half of his career Sid often found a kind of shortcut to his subjects by going somewhere exotic and writing about it once he got there.

(There were travel magazines and travel sections of newspapers prepared to pay for these wanderings—no small point.)
He took trips to Timbuktu and Africa and even tried one right
around the world. These pieces fill a couple of what were once
very successful books, and have their fans, but for this lover
of his work, they seem more rote than inspired. They follow a
pattern that tends to dull more than delight: they begin with
false hopes of exotic pleasures, find our hero swindled or suck-
ered by the locals, with the promised exotic ecstasy reduced to
mere tourist-trap torment. Where the narrator, Sid himself, is
the victim in the Hollywood and Broadway and Madison Avenue stories, abroad Perelman is to some extent the typical rich
American tourist, though this is the last thing he wanted to be,
and so it becomes harder for us to root for him. The joke is on
him, rather than on all of us. (I feel similarly about his accounts
of trying to manage a rural abode in Bucks County; the jokes,
though often good, seem also predictable, and their targets,
the bumbling yokels, more familiar.)

Perelman, to be sure, had a generally difficult later period.
By the sixties, the secure sense of disgust that he could share
with his audience had passed. Advertising had become canon-
ized by Warhol and pop art; the Hollywood of the Thalberg
era, perhaps most bizarrely, had become a golden age, not a
tarnished one. (There's a nice moment when a youngster tries
to ask Sid about the Golden Age, and he has to dry him off
behind the ears.) The secure basis of discrimination between
quality and vulgarity that Perelman's satire depended on had
overturned—cracked past putting together again. By the mid-
sixties this secure set of distinctions—and what is called, dis-
paragingly, middlebrow culture, the join between them—was
gone, and Perelman was increasingly lost.

But what Perelman offers us at his best—and he was at his
best for a very long time—is not a parody of a time gone by
or the notebooks of a grump. It is a picture of an entire civilization, the mid-century postwar civilization of American
abundance where advertising reigned and middlebrow culture
flourished.

We try too often to lift the reputations of great comic writers
by insisting that they are not really—or, worse, "not merely"—
comic writers. Beneath the comic surface lurks a darker picture

of manners and society and sex or something or other—phrases
that get written too often (sometimes by me).

What makes a great comic writer is not that they are secretly
serious but that they are entirely so—that the indignation or
even the rage they feel at their subjects all gets sublimated into
shapely sentences, worth marveling at. Poetry, the famous saying has it, is emotion recollected in tranquility; comedy is indignation reanimated with style, pain, and annoyance, forced
to wear a funny hat and perform.

Trying to "raise" Perelman's reputation, we may misplace
it. Many have tried to augment his stature by referencing him
to Joyce, or to Nathanael West—a less talented writer than his
brother-in-law but, with *The Day of the Locust*, the author of
a more assured "masterwork." But Sid was at his most literary when he wasn't being that literary, or not in that way. If
there is a revelatory comparison to be made of Perelman to
a contemporary, it may be in his kinship with his closest literary friend (and double-dedicatee), J. D. Salinger. Although
they seem as different as two writers can be—the mordant New
York satirist and the visionary New Hampshire mystic—as stylists (and writers interest us first as stylists, or they don't interest us) they have an immense amount in common. Both were
born as writers in public libraries—hyper-bright American
Jewish urban boys from unliterary backgrounds, encountering
the classics on their own, without too much presorting, re-
sponding with delight, imitation, amusement, and familiarity.
Salinger's Zooey seeing Jesus as he is reading *Dombey and Son*
while drinking ginger ale and eating saltines could be a more
mystical version of Perelman's poetic epiphanies in Rhode Island. The light irony with which even their straight descrip-
tive sentences are always loaded is part of this acute horizontal
consciousness—always hearing in one's own sentences another,
favorite author's pages. One sentence after another in Perelman's voice is uncannily in weight and wit like those of Salinger, with the same note of wry amusement at an overstuffed
larder or reference.

And both Sid and Jerry, as they called each other, ended
their lives in some bitterness and too much isolation—more os-
tentatious in Salinger's case, of course . . . but both, in their
writing, also landed on an ideal of improvised, eccentric high

style as an instinctive alternative to the dreck of daily life and what we now call the media culture. Even in a niche, salvation by glimpses, and redemption by verbal energy, are still possible. Both Sid and Jerry take quick hits of spontaneous high style —one girl seen with her dog on the Park Avenue median, one genuinely new verbal twist found in a London paper—as the best we have in life, or the best we can get. For all his disgust with what the world was becoming, you can't read Perelman without feeling better about the world we have, because he gave the world he knew to us so fully that it becomes a world we want. You can't ask for more than that from any poet.

Adam Gopnik
December 2020, New York

SKETCHES AND SATIRES

Puppets of Passion:
A Throbbing Story of Youth's Hot Revolt Against the Conventions

D AWN GINSBERGH lay in her enormous sixteenth-century four-poster bed and played tag with her blood pressure.

Oh, it was so good to be alive on this glorious May morning instead of being dead or something. Dawn, you must know, was very fond of being alive. In fact, as she used to remark to Nicky Nussbaum, the most devoted of her lovers:

"I would rather be alive than be Alderman."

Such was Dawn Ginsbergh, impetuous dashing Dawn of the flame-taunted hair and scarlet lips bee-stung like violet pools and so on at ten cents a word for a page and a half.

With a lazy hand composed of five tapering manicured fingers Dawn reached over to a small table by her bed and picked up a dainty chiffon handkerchief. She folded it several times and tied it securely around her eyes. Then she groped about and lit several cigarettes, inhaling long breaths of smoke. Ah, there it was, sure enough—an Old Mould, her favorite brand, which she could distinguish from the others even blindfolded. She removed the bandage and lay blowing thin spirals of smoke at the chandelier. How like a chandelier was her life, she thought; and the familiar lines of the poet came again to her in all their intensity:

> *"I burn my chandelier at both ends.*
> *It will not last the night . . ."*

She looked around at the immense room that was her bedroom. It was, she reflected, large enough for the whole Sixtyninth Regiment. To tell the truth, the Sixty-ninth Regiment *was* in the room, in undress uniform. Dawn was like that, unconventional.

A knock on the door aroused Dawn from her lethargy. She hastily slipped it off and donned an abstraction. This was Dawn, flitting lightly from lethargy to abstraction and back to precipice again. Or from Beethoven to Bach and Bach to Bach again.

It was her mother, Mrs. Wharton Ginsbergh-Margolies, a slim nervous woman, nervous like a manatee or Firpo. She wore her hair piled high on her head, an odd place one must agree. But then the Ginsberghs were all iconoclasts. They never gave a whoop. When Dawn, at five, had come down with the whooping-cough, not a whoop did she give. Perversely, she broke out with the yellow jack. But she lived.

"Dawn!" It was her mother.

"Yes, Uncle Nate," replied Dawn stretching lazily like a great tawny cat. Dawn always called her mother Uncle Nate —ask me why.

"Dawn, how can you lie in bed with those three suitors waiting hours already to propose to you?"

Dawn made a little moue of distaste. It did not satisfy her, so she made another, then still another. She lay there making moues while her mother stood there getting grayer all the time.

"Dawn, stop making moues and get dressed. Remember, time and tide waits for no man."

"What the heck has the —— —— tide got to do with it?" inquired Dawn, "What do I look like, an oyster-dredge?"

"I will oyster-dredge you, you momzer," said her mother. "Come on, get into your clothes!" And she slammed the door.

II

The eyes of her three suitors followed Dawn as she swept gracefully down the stairs into the early Ludwig Baumann drawing-room. She was a slim little thing, mostly eyes. There was even an eye in the middle of her back, not to mention one on her left leg. The three suitors spoke together.

"Dawn!"

She regarded them disdainfully. Nicky Nussbaum, tall, dashing, soldierly Nicky, leader of the Pants Gang; DuBois Moskovicz of the Foreign Legation, and Hastings Berman, the great portrait painter, any one of them an ideal catch. They stood there with worshipping eyes, holding their hearts out to Dawn; and she trod airily upon them with her high French heels. It was Nicky who was the first to speak.

"Dawn, come with me. I will give you villas in Firenze, châteaux at Nice, estancias in the Banda Oriental, shooting-boxes in Scotland, and castles in Wales. I will deck you in cloth-of-gold, drape you with rare jewels. I will——" But the courtly diplomat Moskovicz had interrupted him.

"Do you long to mingle amidst the gay throngs at Ascot, to rub shoulders with England's nobility, to be smart, *smart*, SMART? Do you desire to be amongst those seen at Longchamps, Melton Mowbray, the Lido, St. Moritz, the Danish Duck Shoot? Then come with me on the 'Aquazonia,' sailing July twelfth for Cherbourg!"

"Stop!" cut in Hastings Berman, impatiently. "Throw aside this stifling artificial existence and as my bride share my carefree Bohemian existence, roistering by night in Montmartre and Chelsea, posing as my model by day; we shall dream away our days in some tiny Breton village, or tiring of that, take lessons in basket-weaving at the Barbizon school."

Dawn, heavy-lidded of eye, yawned. How many thousands of times had she heard these same proposals. She reached for another cigarette and three lighters flared. A voice, a cool masculine voice, startled them.

"Pardon me, lady, but I thought this was the kitchen."

They turned around, these three lovers, to behold a clean-limbed young man with laughing blue eyes and wind-tossed hair. He bore a huge cake of ice on his shoulder. Dawn was staring at him, a wild thought forming in her mind. In an instant she had crossed the floor like a livid moonbeam.

"What do you do for a living, buddy?" she asked tensely.

"I am an iceman," he replied simply.

"Are you—are you married?" asked Dawn and there was a catch in her throat.

"No," was the bewildered answer.

"Listen," said Dawn in a low fierce voice, "will you marry me?"

"Why, sure, ma'am, but I'm not very rich—I——"

"That doesn't matter," exclaimed Dawn hurriedly, "I have millions." She turned to her astounded lovers.

"Gentlemen," she said with a satirical bow, "meet my future husband—er, what did you say your name was?"

"Moe Feinbloom," replied the youth, with a pardonable blush.

"Gentlemen, my future husband, Marvin Furbish," said Dawn, her eyes mocky, and she kissed the young man full on the mouth.

"Oh, Marvin, I'm so happy," she breathed. "I knew you were the man when you walked in through that door! And after we're married, I'll go along with you on the route and help you carry the ice into the kitchens, won't I?"

There was a moment of perplexed silence. Moe scratched his head slowly.

"Sure, lady," he replied doubtfully. "But who'll hold the horse?"

Those Charming People:
The Latest Report on the Weinbloom
Reptile Expedition

EIGHTEEN MONTHS AGO, when Lieut. Buster Weinbloom left with his expedition into the lower ramp of Grand Central to add fresh reptiles to his collection, many wiseacres dubbed his project "ramp foolishness." "Fresh reptiles, indeed!" said they, "as if the reptiles he has now aren't fresh enough! We dub his project ramp foolishness." But this criticism only succeeded in irritating Lieut. Weinbloom and he soon began to chafe under restraint. The chafing had been barely finished and the saltines spread with butter when the Dean appeared with the college whip to flay the offenders. Lieut. Weinbloom was overcome with impatience. "You people make me tired," he said; "if you must vex somebody, why don't you go home and vex the floors?" The Dean went home but, as there were no floors in his house, he had to close the act with a blackout and three bends.

The expedition met with small success at first. Three months after they had shuttled over the upper headwaters of the Leblang they captured a small orange drink stand which had gotten separated from its mother. The small but fierce prisoner attempted to gore Lieut. Weinbloom, and when it failed, offered to take him into business on a fifty-fifty basis. But the lieutenant was wary. To quote his own words: "No. I am wary, I am wary wary." His men then took up the refrain:

> *"He is wary, we are wary,*
> *All of us are wary wary;*
> *None of us have beri-beri,*
> *But we all are wary wary."*

At the end of the first half the orchestra plugged the theme song, "Snakes No Difference to Me," and after signing the customary contracts with Hearst, the expedition struck camp and mushed on. Only one member of the party had to be left behind, a colored beater named Cobra Perelman, who had mumbled something about "Hearst by his own petard." His bruises were so numerous that Dr. Dietrick, the medical adviser, ordered him buried up to his neck in rice puddings and set fire to. This was done.

Seven days later pythons were sighted, and the python traps were baited. To lure the tricky reptiles to the snares, a man named Leeds was tied to a tree and smeared with honey. But the cautious pythons refused to bite. Another man named Leeds was smeared with honey and tied to the same tree, but still without results. Lieut. Weinbloom's entry in his log for that day reads: "Gave the pythons lots of good Leeds but without effect. Perhaps we are wrong in using traps and snares? Will try muted woodwinds, tympani, and oboes to-morrow." But the oboes did not do the work either, for it is notorious that oboes never do work. That, kiddies, is why they *are* oboes.

Leaving the pythons to their own devices, Lieut. Weinbloom now decided that the expedition must cross a plateau. Maps were consulted but no plateaux could be found. After some discussion an advertisement was inserted in the *Times* and the following morning found owners of several good second-hand plateaux on hand. The best one was selected and the party then put on its swaddling clothes, in preparation for swaddling the plateau. In a very short time the plateau was completely swaddled, and tired but happy, we pitched camp outside the city walls. Camp had been unruly anyhow and some of us felt that he should have been tied to the tree and smeared with honey along with Leeds. Maybe some of you feel the same way about Cobra Perelman.

And now, exactly seventeen months and five days after starting out, the expedition is reported in the East Baggage Room of Grand Central, being held for charges. It has been there thirty-five days, and at the usual rate charged for expeditions (ten cents a day), there is three dollars and fifty cents due on it. Anybody who has three dollars and fifty cents and feels that he would like to own a nice almost-new expedition can get same by applying there. Nothing like a nice stuffed expedition to hang up on the wall of your den, boys. Do you stuff expeditions? Here's your chance!

Scenario

FADE IN, exterior grassy knoll, long shot. Above the scene the thundering measures of Von Suppe's "Light Cavalry Overture." Austerlitz? The Plains of Abraham? Vicksburg? The Little Big Horn? Cambrai? Steady on, old son; it is Yorktown. Under a blood-red setting sun yon proud crest is Cornwallis. Blood and 'ouns, proud sirrah, dost brush so lightly past an exciseman of the Crown? Lady Rotogravure's powdered shoulders shrank from the highwayman's caress; what, Jermyn, footpads on Hounslow Heath? A certain party in the D. A.'s office will hear of this, you bastard. There was a silken insolence in his smile as he drew the greatcoat about his face and leveled his shooting-iron at her dainty puss. Leave go that lady or I'll smear yuh. No quarter, eh? Me, whose ancestors scuttled stately India merchantmen of their comfits and silken stuffs and careened their piratical craft in the Dry Tortugas to carouse with bumboat women till the cock crew? Yuh'll buy my booze or I'll give yuh a handful of clouds. Me, whose ancestors rode with Yancey, Jeb Stuart, and Joe Johnston through the dusty bottoms of the Chickamauga? Oceans of love, but not one cent for tribute. Make a heel out of a guy whose grandsire, Olaf Hasholem, swapped powder and ball with the murderous Sioux through the wheels of a Conestoga wagon, who mined the yellow dirt with Sutter and slapped nuggets across the rude bars of Leadville and Goldfield? One side, damn your black hide, suh, or Ah'll send one mo' dirty Litvak to the boneyard. It's right up the exhibitor's alley, Mr. Biberman, and you got to hand it to them on a platter steaming hot. I know, Stanley, but let's look at this thing reasonable; we been showing the public Folly Larrabee's drawers two years and they been cooling off. Jeez Crize—it's a hisTORical drama, Mr. Biberman, it'll blow 'em outa the back of the houses, it's the greatest thing in the industry, it's dynamite! Pardon me, officer, is that General Washington? Bless yez little heart, mum, and who may yez be, savin' yer prisince? Honest old Brigid the apple-woman of

9

Trinity, is it? How *dégagé* he sits on his charger, flicking an infinitesimal speck of ash from his plum-colored waistcoat! Gentlemen, I give you Martha Custis, hetman of the Don Cossacks, her features etched with the fragile beauty of a cameo. And I walked right in on her before she had a chance to pull the god-damned kimono together. But to be away from all this—to lean back puffing on one's churchwarden at Mount Vernon amid the dull glint of pewter, to watch the firelight playing over polished Duncan Phyfe and Adam while faithful old Cudjo cackles his ebony features and mixes a steaming lime toddy! Tired, Roy, I'm tired, I tell you. Tired of the rain, the eternal surge of the breakers on that lagoon, the glitter of the reef in that eternity out there. CHRISTIAN! She laughed contemptuously, her voluptuous throat filling with a rising sob as she faced Davidson like a hounded animal. You drove me out of Papeete but I'll go to Thursday Island with my banjo on my knee. Yeh, yeh, so what? We made FOUR pictures like that last year. Oh, my God, Mr. Biberman, give me a chance, it's only a flashback to plant that she's a woman with a past. Sixteen hundred a week I pay you to hand me back the plot of *Love's Counterfeiters* Selig made in 1912! She's who? She's what? What's the idea her coming here? What's she trying to do, turn a production office into a whorehouse? No, Miss Reznick, tell her to wait, I'll be through in five minutes. Now get it, Mr. Biberman, it's big. You establish the messroom and truck with Farnsworth till he faces Charteris. I said Sixth Rajputana Rifles and I don't want a lotta muggs paradin' around in the uniforms of the Preobazhensky Guard, y' get me? Yep, he's on a tear, those foreign directors are very temperamental, did I ever tell you about the time Lazlo Nugasi said he'd buy me a brassiere if I let him put it on? Fake it with a transparency of Khyber Pass. Now an overhead shot of the dusty tired column filing into Sidi-bel-Abbes. Shoulder by shoulder they march in the faded blue of the Legion, fun-loving Dick and serious-minded Tom. Buddies, the greatest word in the French language, flying to the defense of each other like a homo pigeon. Greater love hath Onan. Swinging a chair into that mob of lime-juicers in the Mile End Bar in Shanghai. But came a slant-eyed Chinese adventuress, and then? Don't shoot, Butch, for Gossake!

Heave 'em into the prison yard, we'll keep the screws out of
the cell-block and wilderness were paradise enow. Stow the
swag in Cincy, kid, and go on alone, I'm done for. Too late,
old Pogo the clown stopped it in the sweetbreads. They buried him outside the town that night, a motley crew of freaks
and circus people. What a sequence! Old man Klingspiel told
me he bawled like a baby. Laugh, you inhuman monster they
call the crowd, old Pogo lies dead with only a bareback rid-
er's spangle to mark his grave and a seat for every child in the
public schools! When tall ships shook out their plumage and
raced from Salem to Hong Kong to bring back tea. Break out
the Black Ball ensign, Mr. Exhibitor, there's sweet music in
that ole cash register! A double truck in every paper in town
and a smashing drawing by the best artist we got, mind you.
Take the kiddies to that colossal red-blooded human drama
of a boy's love for his dog. This is my hunting lodge, we'll
stop here and dry your things. But of course it's all right,
cara mia, I'm old enough to be your father. Let me go, you
beast—MOTHER! What are you doing here? I ask you con-
fidentially, Horowitz, can't we get that dame to put on some
women's clothes, a skirt or something? The fans are getting
wise, all those flat-heeled shoes and men's shirts like a lum-
berjack. Get me Gerber in publicity, he'll dish out some crap
about her happy home life. Vorkapich around the room to
Dmitri's brother officers as they register consternation at the
news. Good chance for some hokey bellies on comedy types.
What, sir, you dare mention Alexandra Petrovna's name in a
saloon? The kid takes it big and gives Diane the gloves across
the pan socko. The usual satisfaction, I presume? Drawing on
his gloves as a thin sneer played across his features. Yeh, a
martinet and for Crisakes remember it's not a musical instrument this time. But eet ees madness, Serge! The best swords-
man in St. Mary's parish, he weel run you through in a
tweenkling! Oh, darling, you can't, you can't. Her hair had
become undone and he plunged his face into its fragrance,
unbuckling his sabre and flinging it on the bed beside them.
Hurry, even now my husband is fried to the ears in a low
boozing-den in Pokrovsky Street. Of course it is he, I'd know
that lousy busby anywhere in St. Petersburg. Shoot it two
ways, you can always dub it in the sound track. She shrieks or

she don't shriek, what the hell difference does it make? Told me he was going to night school at the Smolny Institute, the cur. And I believed him, thought Pyotr pityingly, surveying her luscious bust with greedy eyes. Never leave me, my sweet, and then bejeezus an angle shot toward the door of the General leaning against the lintel stroking his mustache. Crouching against the wall terrified yet shining-eyed as women are when men do gallant combat. Throw him your garter, Lady Aspinwall, throw your slipper, throw your lunch, but for Gawd's sake throw something! *Parry! Thrust! Touché!* Where are they all now, the old familiar faces? What a piece of business! Grabs a string of onions and swings himself up the balcony, fencing with the soldiers. Got you in the groin that time, General! Mine host, beaming genially, rubbing his hands and belching. Get Anderson ready with the sleigh-bells and keep that snow moving. Hit 'em all! Hotter on eighty-four, Joe Devlin! Are we up to speed? Quiet, please, we're turning! Chicago, hog-butcher to the world, yclept the Windy City. BOOZE AND BLOOD, he oughta know, running a drug store eleven years on Halstead Street. You cut to the back of the Big Fellow, then three lap dissolves of the presses—give 'em that Ufa stuff, then to the street—a newsboy, insert of the front page, the L roaring by——Kerist, it's the gutsiest thing in pictures! Call you back, chief. Never mind the Hays office, this baby is censor-proof! Call you back, chief. We'll heave the telephone through the glass door and smack her in the kisser with the grapefruit, they liked it once and they'll love it twice. Call you back, chief. The gat in the mesh-bag. A symbol, get me? Now remember, staccato. . . . A bit tight, my sweet? Marrowforth teetered back and forth on his heels, his sensitive artist's fingers caressing the first edition he loved. Item, one Hawes and Curtis dress-suit, one white tie, kindly return to Mister Dreyfus in the wardrobe department. What color do I remind you of? Purple shot with pleasure, if you ask me. Do I have to work with a lot of pimply grips giving me the bird? Papa's in the doghouse and keep up the tempo of the last scene, you looked crummy in yesterday's dailies. A warm, vivid and human story with just that touch of muff the fans demand. Three Hundred Titans Speed Westward as King Haakon Lays Egg on Shoe-String. And sad-eyed Grubnitz by the Wailing Wall demands: What will the inde exhibs do? Let 'em eat cake, we're packing 'em in with 29 Powell-Loys in 1938. Ask Hyman Gerber of Waco, he can smell a box-office picture a mile away. In the freezing mists of dawn they gathered by the fuselages of their planes and gripped hands. But Rex Jennings of the shining eyes and the high heart never came back. Heinie got him over Chalons. I tell you it's murder to send a mere boy out in a crate like that! The god-damned production office on my neck all day. It's midsummer madness, Fiametta! You mustn't! I must! I want you! You want me? But I——I'm just a poor little slavey, and you—why, all life's ahead of you! Fame, the love of a good woman, children! And your music, Raoul! Excuse me, miss, are you Fiametta Desplains? I am Yankel Patchouli, a solicitor. Here is my card and a report of my recent urinalysis. Raoul! Raoul! Come quick! A million dollars! Now you can go to Paris and study your counterpoint! Damn my music, Fiametta, my happiness was in my own back yard all the time and I was, how you say it, one blind fool. The gingham dress and half-parted lips leaning on a broom. But why are you looking at me in that strange way, Tony? . . . Tony! I'm afraid of you! Oh . . . You utter contemptible despicable CAD. He got up nursing his jaw. Spew out your poison, you rat. You didn't know she was the morganatic wife of Prince Rupprecht, *did* you? That her affairs with men were the talk of Vienna, *did* you? That——Vanya, is this true? Bowed head, for her man. His boyish tousled head clean-cut against the twilight. Get out. *Get out.* GET OUT! Oh, mumsey, I want to die. That hooker's gotta lay off that booze, Mr. Metz, once more she comes on the set stinking and I take the next boat back to Buda-Pesth. But in a great tangled garden sits a forlorn tragic-eyed figure; the face a mask of carved ivory, the woman nobody knows—Tilly Bergstrom. What lies behind her shattered romance with Grant Snavely, idol of American flaps? Turn 'em over, you punks, I'll stay on this set till I get it right. Cheese it, de nippers! The jig is up, long live the jig—ring out the old, ring in the new. For love belongs to everyone, the best things in life are free.

Strictly from Hunger

Yes, I was excited, and small wonder. What boy wouldn't be, boarding a huge, mysterious, puffing steam train for golden California? As Mamma adjusted my reefer and strapped on my leggings, I almost burst with impatience. Grinning red-caps lifted my luggage into the compartment and spat on it. Mamma began to weep silently into a small pillow-case she had brought along for the purpose.

"Oh, son, I wish you hadn't become a scenario writer!" she sniffled.

"Aw, now, Moms," I comforted her, "it's no worse than playing the piano in a call-house." She essayed a brave little smile, and, reaching into her reticule, produced a flat package which she pressed into my hands. For a moment I was puzzled, then I cried out with glee.

"Jelly sandwiches! Oh, Moms!"

"Eat them all, boy o' mine," she told me, "they're good for boys with hollow little legs." Tenderly she pinned to my lapel the green tag reading "To Plushnick Productions, Hollywood, California." The whistle shrilled and in a moment I was chugging out of Grand Central's dreaming spires followed only by the anguished cries of relatives who would now have to go to work. I had chugged only a few feet when I realized that I had left without the train, so I had to run back and wait for it to start.

As we sped along the glorious fever spots of the Hudson I decided to make a tour of inspection. To my surprise I found that I was in the only passenger car of the train; the other cars were simply dummies snipped out of cardboard and painted to simulate coaches. Even "passengers" had been cunningly drawn in colored crayons in the "window," as well as ragged tramps clinging to the blinds below and drinking Jamaica ginger. With a rueful smile I returned to my seat and gorged myself on jelly sandwiches.

At Buffalo the two other passengers and I discovered to our horror that the conductor had been left behind. We finally decided to divide up his duties; I punched the tickets, the old lady opposite me wore a conductor's hat and locked the washroom as we came into stations, and the young man who looked as if his feet were not mates consulted a Hamilton watch frequently. But we missed the conductor's earthy conversation and it was not until we had exchanged several questionable stories that we began to forget our loss.

A flicker of interest served to shorten the trip. At Fort Snodgrass, Ohio, two young and extremely polite road-agents boarded the train and rifled us of our belongings. They explained that they were modern Robin Hoods and were stealing from the poor to give to the rich. They had intended to rape all the women and depart for Sherwood Forest, but when I told them that it was in England, their chagrin was comical in the extreme. They declined my invitation to stay and take a chance on the train's pool, declaring that the engineer had fixed the run and would fleece us, and got off at South Bend with every good wish.

The weather is always capricious in the Middle West, and although it was midsummer, the worst blizzard in Chicago's history greeted us on our arrival. The streets were crowded with thousands of newsreel cameramen trying to photograph one another bucking the storm on the Lake Front. It was a novel idea for the newsreels and I wished them well. With only two hours in Chicago I would be unable to see the city, and the thought drew me into a state of composure. I noted with pleasure that a fresh coat of grime had been given to the Dearborn Street station, though I was hardly vain enough to believe that it had anything to do with my visit. There was the usual ten-minute wait while the porters withdrew with my portable typewriter to a side room and flailed it with hammers, and at last I was aboard the "Sachem," crack train of the B.B.D. & O. lines.

It was as if I had suddenly been transported into another world. "General Crook," in whom I was to make my home for the next three days, and his two neighbors, "Lake Tahoe" and "Chief Malomai," were everything that the word "Pullman" implies; they were Pullmans. Uncle Eben, the dusky Ethiopian in charge of "General Crook," informed me that the experiment of air-cooling the cars had been so successful that the road intended trying to heat them next winter.

"Ah suttinly looks fo'd to dem roastin' ears Ah's gwine have next winter, he, he, he!" he chuckled, rubbing soot into my hat.

The conductor told me he had been riding on trains for so long that he had begun to smell like one, and sure enough, two brakemen waved their lanterns at him that night and tried to tempt him down a siding in Kansas City. We became good friends and it came as something of a blow when I heard the next morning that he had fallen off the train during the night. The fireman said that we had circled about for an hour trying to find him but that it had been impossible to lower a boat because we did not carry a boat.

The run was marked by only one incident out of the ordinary. I had ordered breaded veal cutlet the first evening, and my waiter, poking his head into the kitchen, had repeated the order. The cook, unfortunately, understood him to say "*dreaded* veal cutlet," and resenting the slur, sprang at the waiter with drawn razor. In a few seconds I was the only living remnant of the shambles, and at Topeka I was compelled to wait until a new shambles was hooked on and I proceeded with dinner.

It seemed only a scant week or ten days before we were pulling into Los Angeles. I had grown so attached to my porter that I made him give me a lock of his hair. I wonder if he still has the ten-cent piece I gave him? There was a gleam in his eye which could only have been insanity as he leaned over me. Ah, Uncle Eben, faithful old retainer, where are you now? Gone to what obscure boneyard? If this should chance to meet your kindly gaze, drop me a line care of the Railroad Men's Y.M.C.A. at Gloucester, Mass. They know what to do with it.

—II—

The violet hush of twilight was descending over Los Angeles as my hostess, Violet Hush, and I left its suburbs headed toward Hollywood. In the distance a glow of huge piles of burning motion-picture scripts lit up the sky. The crisp tang of frying writers and directors whetted my appetite. How good it was to be alive, I thought, inhaling deep lungfuls of carbon monoxide. Suddenly our powerful Gatti-Cazazza slid to a stop in the traffic.

"What is it, Jenkin?" Violet called anxiously through the speaking-tube to the chauffeur (played by Lyle Talbot).

A *suttee* was in progress by the roadside, he said—did we wish to see it? Quickly Violet and I elbowed our way through the crowd. An enormous funeral pyre composed of thousands of feet of film and scripts, drenched with Chanel Number Five, awaited the torch of Jack Holt, who was to act as master of ceremonies. In a few terse words Violet explained this unusual custom borrowed from the Hindus and never paid for. The worst disgrace that can befall a producer is an unkind notice from a New York reviewer. When this happens, the producer becomes a pariah in Hollywood. He is shunned by his friends, thrown into bankruptcy, and like a Japanese electing hara-kiri, he commits *suttee*. A great bonfire is made of the film and the luckless producer, followed by directors, actors, technicians, and the producer's wives, immolate themselves. Only the scenario writers are exempt. These are tied between the tails of two spirited Caucasian ponies, which are then driven off in opposite directions. This custom is called "a conference."

Violet and I watched the scene breathlessly. Near us Harry Cohn, head of Columbia Studios, was being rubbed with huck towels preparatory to throwing himself into the flames. He was nonchalantly smoking a Rocky Ford five-center, and the man's courage drew a tear to the eye of even the most callous. Weeping relatives besought him to eschew his design, but he stood adamant. Adamant Eve, his plucky secretary, was being rubbed with crash towels preparatory to flinging herself into Cohn's embers. Assistant directors busily prepared spears, war-bonnets and bags of pemmican which the Great Chief would need on his trip to the "Happy Hunting Grounds." Wampas and beads to placate the Great Spirit (played by Will Hays) were piled high about the stoical tribesman.

Suddenly Jack Holt (played by Edmund Lowe) raised his hand for silence. The moment had come. With bowed head Holt made a simple invocation couched in one-syllable words so that even the executives might understand. Throwing his five-center

to a group of autograph-hunters, the great man poised himself
for the fatal leap. But from off-scene came the strident clat-
ter of cocoanut shells, and John Mosher, Filmdom's fearless
critic, wearing the uniform of a Confederate guerrilla and the
whiskers of General Beauregard, galloped in on a foam-flecked
pinto. It was he whose mocking review had sent Cohn into
Coventry. It was a dramatic moment as the two stood pitted
against each other—Cohn against Mosher, the Blue against the
Gray. But with true Southern gallantry Mosher was the first to
extend the hand of friendship.

"Ah reckon it was an unworthy slur, suh," he said in manly
tones. "Ah-all thought you-all's pictuah was lousy but it opened
at the Rialto to sensational grosses, an' Ah-all 'pologizes. Heah,
have a yam." And he drew a yam from his tunic. Not to be outdone in hospitality, Cohn drew a yam from his tunic, and soon
they were exchanging yams and laughing over the old days.

When Violet and I finally stole away to our waiting motor,
we felt that we were somehow nearer to each other. I snuggled luxuriously into the buffalo lap-robe Violet had provided
against the treacherous night air and gazed out at the gleaming
neon lights. Soon we would be in Beverly Hills, and already the
quaint native women were swarming alongside in their punts
urging us to buy their cunning beadwork and mangoes. Occasionally I threw a handful of coppers to the Negro boys, who
dove for them joyfully. The innocent squeals of the policemen
as the small blackamoors pinched them were irresistible. Unable to resist them, Violet and I were soon pinching each other
till our skins glowed. Violet was good to the touch, with a
firm fleshy texture like a winesap or pippin. It seemed but a
moment before we were sliding under the porte-cochère of
her home, a magnificent rambling structure of beaverboard
patterned after an Italian ropewalk of the sixteenth century.
It had recently been remodeled by a family of wrens who had
introduced chewing-gum into the left wing, and only three or
four obscure Saxon words could do it justice.

I was barely warming my hands in front of the fire and
watching Lloyd Pantages turn on a spit when my presence
on the Pacific Slope made itself felt. The news of my arrival
had thrown international financial centers into an uproar, and

sheaves of wires, cables, phone messages, and even corn began piling up. An ugly rumor that I might reorganize the motion-picture industry was being bruited about in the world's commodity markets. My brokers, Whitelipped & Trembling, were beside themselves. The Paris Bourse was begging them for assurances of stability and Threadneedle Street awaited my next move with drumming pulses. Film shares ricocheted sharply, although wools and meats were sluggish, if not downright sullen. To the reporters who flocked around me I laughingly disclaimed that this was a business trip. I was simply a scenario writer to whom the idea of work was abhorrent. A few words murmured into the transatlantic telephone, the lift of an eyebrow here, the shrug of a shoulder there, and equilibrium was soon restored. I washed sparsely, curled my mustache with a heated hairpin, flicked a drop of Sheik Lure on my lapel, and rejoined my hostess.

After a copious dinner, melting-eyed beauties in lacy black underthings fought with each other to serve me kümmel. A hurried apology, and I was curled up in bed with the Autumn, 1927, issue of *The Yale Review*. Halfway through an exciting synthesis on Sir Thomas Aquinas' indebtedness to Professors Whitehead and Spengler, I suddenly detected a stowaway blonde under the bed. Turning a deaf ear to her heartrending entreaties and burning glances, I sent her packing. Then I treated my face to a feast of skin food, buried my sleepy head in the pillow and went bye-bye.

—III—

Hollywood Boulevard! I rolled the rich syllables over on my tongue and thirstily drank in the beauty of the scene before me. On all sides nattily attired boulevardiers clad in rich stuffs strolled nonchalantly, inhaling cubebs and exchanging epigrams stolen from Martial and Wilde. Thousands of scantily draped but none the less appetizing extra girls milled past me, their mouths a scarlet wound and their eyes clearly defined in their faces. Their voluptuous curves set my blood on fire, and as I made my way down Mammary Lane, a strange thought began to invade my brain: I realized that I had not eaten breakfast yet. In a Chinese eatery cunningly built in the shape of an old shoe I managed to assuage the inner man with a chopped glove salad topped off with frosted cocoa. Charming platinum-haired hostesses in red pajamas and peaked caps added a note of color to the surroundings, whilst a gypsy orchestra played selections from Victor Herbert's operettas on musical saws. It was a bit of old Vienna come to life, and the sun was a red ball in the heavens before I realized with a start that I had promised to report at the Plushnick Studios.

Commandeering a taxicab, I arrived at the studio just in time to witness the impressive ceremony of changing the guard. In the central parade ground, on a snowy white charger, sat Max Plushnick, resplendent in a producer's uniform, his chest glittering with first mortgage liens, amortizations, and estoppals. His personal guard, composed of picked vice-presidents of the Chase National Bank, was drawn up stiffly about him in a hollow square. But the occasion was not a happy one. A writer had been caught trying to create an adult picture.

The drums rolled dismally, and the writer, his head sunk on his chest, was led out amid a ghastly silence. With the aid of a small stepladder Plushnick slid lightly from his steed. Sternly he ripped the epaulets and buttons from the traitor's tunic, broke his sword across his knee, and in a few harsh words demoted him to the mail department.

"And now," began Plushnick, "I further condemn you to eat . . ."

"No, no!" screamed the poor wretch, falling to his knees and embracing the general's same, "not that, not that!"

"Stand up, man," ordered Plushnick, his lip curling, "I condemn you to eat in the studio restaurant for ten days and may God have mercy on your soul." The awful words rang out on the still evening air and even Plushnick's hardened old mercenaries shuddered. The heartrending cries of the unfortunate were drowned in the boom of the sunset gun.

In the wardrobe department I was photographed, finger-printed, and measured for the smock and Windsor tie which was to be my uniform. A nameless fear clutched at my heart as two impassive turnkeys herded me down a corridor to my supervisor's office. For what seemed hours we waited in an ante-room. Then my serial number was called, the leg-irons were struck off, and I was shoved through a door into the presence of Diana ffrench-Mamoulian.

How to describe what followed? Diana ffrench-Mamoulian was accustomed to having her way with writers, and my long lashes and peachblow mouth seemed to whip her to insensate desire. In vain, time and again, I tried to bring her attention back to the story we were discussing, only to find her gem-incrusted fingers straying through my hair. When our interview was over, her cynical attempt to "date me up" made every fiber of my being cry out in revolt.

"P-please," I stammered, my face burning, "I—I wish you wouldn't. . . . I'm engaged to a Tri Kappa at Goucher—"

"Just one kiss," she pleaded, her breath hot against my neck. In desperation I granted her boon, knowing full well that my weak defences were crumbling before the onslaught of this love tigree. Finally she allowed me to leave, but only after I had promised to dine at her penthouse apartment and have an intimate chat about the script. The basket of slave bracelets and marzipan I found awaiting me on my return home made me realize to what lengths Diana would go.

I was radiant that night in blue velvet tails and a bouton-niere of diamonds from Cartier's, my eyes starry and the mer-est hint of cologne at my ear-lobes. An inscrutable Oriental served the Lucullan repast and my vis-à-vis was as effervescent as the wine.

"Have a bit of the wing, darling?" queried Diana solici-tously, indicating the roast Long Island airplane with apple-sauce. I tried to turn our conversation from the personal note, but Diana would have none of it. Soon we were exchanging gay bantam over the mellow Vouvray, laughing as we dipped fastidious fingers into the Crisco parfait for which Diana was famous. Our meal finished, we sauntered into the play-room and Diana turned on the radio. With a savage snarl the radio turned on her and we slid over the waxed floor in the intri-cate maze of the jackdaw strut. Without quite knowing why, I found myself hesitating before the plate of liqueur candies Diana was pressing on me.

"I don't think I should—really I'm a trifle faint—"

"Oh, come on," she urged masterfully. "After all, you're old enough to be your father—I mean I'm old enough to be my mother. . . ." She stuffed a brandy bonbon between my clenched teeth. Before long I was eating them thirstily, reeling about the room and shouting snatches of coarse drunken doggerel. My brain was on fire, I tell you. Through the haze I saw Diana ffrench-Mamoulian, her nostrils dilated, groping for me. My scream of terror only egged her on, overturning chairs and tables in her bestial pursuit. With superhuman talons she tore off my collar and suspenders. I sank to my knees, choked with sobs, hanging on to my last shirt-stud like a drowning man. Her Svengali eyes were slowly hypnotizing me; I fought like a wounded bird—and then, blissful unconsciousness.

When I came to, the Oriental servant and Diana were battling in the center of the floor. As I watched, Yen Shee Gow drove a well-aimed blow to her mid-section, following it with a right cross to the jaw. Diana staggered and rolled under a table. Before my astonished eyes John Chinaman stripped the mask from his face and revealed the features of Blanche Almonds, a little seamstress I had long wooed unsuccessfully in New York. Gently she bathed my temples with Florida water and explained how she had followed me, suspecting Diana ffrench-Mamoulian's intentions. I let her rain kisses over my face and lay back in her arms as beaming Ivan tucked us in and cracked his whip over the prancing bays. In a few seconds our sleigh was skimming over the hard crust toward Port Arthur and freedom, leaving Plushnick's discomfited officers gnashing one another's teeth. The wintry Siberian moon glowed over the tundras, drenching my hair with moonbeams for Blanche to kiss away. And so, across the silvery steppes amid the howling of wolves, we rode into a new destiny, purified in the crucible that men call Hollywood.

The Love Decoy:
A Story of Youth in College Today—
Awake, Fearless, Unashamed

"**P**ROFESSOR GOMPERS IS ILL!**"

The whisper spread like wildfire through the packed classroom. A feeling of emulsion swept over me. Kindly old Professor Gompers, whose grizzled chin and chiselled grin had made his name a byword at Tunafish College for Women! Ivy Weiskopf, sauciest co-ed in the class, she of the unruly locks and the candied gray eyes, leaned over to impart the latest gossip.

"That new instructor, Russell Gipf, is subbing for him!" The color drained slowly from my face, entered the auricle, shot up the escalator, and issued from the ladies' and misses' section into the kitchenware department. I remembered Russell Gipf as a lean brown giant in tweeds whose resemblance to Warren William had caused his suspension the year before. It had been an ugly scandal but luckily his nose was broken in an auto accident soon after and the faculty had restored him. Dreamily I recalled an autumn afternoon when I had visited him in his office in ivy-covered Schneider to discuss a theme I had written. Through the half-open windows drifted the mingled smell of wood smoke and freshmen. He confided that he was doing research in dirty limericks for his doctor's thesis and asked if I knew any "Good Ones." In the twinkling of an eye we were in the gutter. At no time, however, did he allow himself the usual indecent proposal, and I returned to my dormitory room raging, determined never to see him again.

An impatient voice summoned me rudely from my daydream. I looked up; Russell Gipf was addressing me crisply from the platform. My feminine eye noted that he was still a spiffy dresser, a regular up-to-the-minute gink.

"Will you please answer the question, Miss Hornbostel?"

"I—I didn't hear it," I quavered. Deep in my heart I hated him for lousing up my revery.

"Well, Miss Sly Boots," he retorted sardonically, "maybe you

23

had better stop galvanizing around nights and pay attention!"
A cold fury welled up in me and I longed to hang one on his
lug for his insolence. I was seething but he could not see it, for
several of my girl chums were seething in front of me. A moment later the bell tolling in ivy-covered Hoffenstein brought
the class to a close. Slipping my pencil box and pen wipers into
my corsage I approached his desk, a plan fermenting in my
brain.

"Yes, Miss Hornbostel?" Russell Gipf's eyes were dancing
with fun.

"Oh, Mr. Gipf," I began, "I hardly know how to say this.
It—it's so personal." His eyes stopped dancing with fun and
began dancing with sex.

"Go on," he urged.

"I—I can't get the cap off my toothpaste," I faltered, a tear
trembling on my nose. "If you could only help me . . ." I
gazed out of my huge bedroom eyes appealingly.

"Well, now—ahem—this is serious," he said slowly. "No
wonder you weren't prepared in class just now. Naturally, you
were upset."

"And you were cruel," I said.

"I'm sorry," he added Quigley.

"Why did you add Quigley?" I begged him. He apologized and subtracted Quigley, then divided Hogan. We hastily
dipped the slices of Hogan into Karo, poured sugar over them,
and ate them with relish.

"Tell me," said Gipf, as he wiped his mouth on the tail of his
shirt, "about this toothpaste: if you could bring the tube to my
office . . ."

I explained hurriedly that it was too heavy to carry and that
he would have to come up to my dormitory room that evening after "lights out." He readily fell in with my wish and
promised. As we walked across the campus toward ivy-covered
Lapeedis, I drew him out craftily. He had been in the north of
Scotland that summer shooting bob-tail flushes, and he was
full of his subject. Although I hated him, I had to confess that
his smile made my pulses sing, and I gladly would have leaped
through a hoop had he asked me to. He must have been aware
of it, for he suddenly reached into his green baize bag and
produced a hoop.

"Here, leap through this hoop, you," he ordered. I did so and he flicked me lightly with his whip. I saw his face go dark with passion. "Dolores—I love you!" he whispered, his hand closing over mine. Mine in turn closed over his. In an instant we had chosen up sides, it was my turn at bats, and I knocked a sizzling bunt to Pipgrass in the daisies.

"Ah, *cara mia*, giz a kiz," panted Russell. I tried to resist his overtures but he plied me with symphonies, quartets, chamber music and cantatas. I felt myself softening, but I was determined to go through with my plan.

"Are you mad, Russell?" I stopped him haughtily. He bit his lip in a manner which immediately awakened my maternal sympathy, and I helped him bite it. Foolish man! In a trice the animal in him rose to the surface again. He caught my arm in a vise-like grip and drew me to him, but with a blow I sent him groveling. In ten minutes he was back with a basket of appetizing fresh-picked grovels. We squeezed them and drank the piquant juice thirstily. Then I blew him an airy kiss.

"Tonight—at ten-thirty, *mon désir*!" I flung at him over my shoulder. Even in my room I could hear him panting four floors below on the campus as I changed to a filmy negligee and began to cold-cream my glowing cheeks.

The dim glow of shaded lamps and the heady intoxication of incense had transformed my room into a veritable Oriental bower when Russell Gipf knocked cautiously on my door at ten-thirty. From my chaise-longue where I was stretched out lazily fingering a trashy French novel I murmured an inviting "Come in!"

"Come in!" I murmured invitingly. He entered swiftly, shaking himself vigorously. There had been a heavy fall of talcum several hours before and as far as the ground could see the eye was white. I offered Russell a dish of soap flakes, but despite my attempts to put him at his ease he seemed nervous.

"The—the toothpaste," he began, looking about suspiciously. I indicated the bathroom with a lazy finger. In a moment he reappeared, his face haggard and his eyes like burning holes in the snow.

"Yes," I shot at him coldly, "I tricked you. No, it's useless to try the door—and it's a four-story drop straight down from those windows, Mr. Russell Gipf. Perhaps you're wondering what I intend to do now." I picked up the telephone, my voice a snarl. "In five minutes the faculty will break in and find you in a co-ed's room. What will your wealthy old father Prosper Gipf, president of the Drovers and Plovers National Bank, say to that?" He backed away from me whimpering piteously. But I was goading him on as only a raging woman can. "You humiliated me in front of all my classmates today. Now—you shall pay." My hand was lifting the receiver when a faint scratching sounded at the door, followed by stertorous breathing. I threw it open. Dean Fothergill, his face that of a man mad with desire, lunged at me.

"Dolores," he implored, "you adorable little witch—I've been following you with my eyes—I . . ."

"You rotter!" I turned in surprise at Russell Gipf's voice as he flashed past me and drove a decisive blow into the aged roué's kidneys. The two men grappled, their teeth bared. Russell's head snapped back as Dean Fothergill, who I forgot to say was once amateur light-heavyweight boxing champion of University of Southern California at Los Angeles, drove a decisive blow to the Gipf kidneys. The noise of fist on kidneys rang out in the still air. I watched the spectacle unmoved. After all, tomorrow I would have to pass my law exam; I opened *Fist on Kidneys* and was deep in it when I heard a groan. I looked up. There, manacled to Russell Gipf, stood Dean Fothergill, a hangdog expression on his face.

"Well, Miss Hornbostel," he admitted shamefacedly, "I guess the jig is up."

"Tell her, you swine!" grunted Russell menacingly, pounding his windward kidney.

"I—I am Jim the Penman," said Fothergill with bowed head. "I forged the notes which sent your father, Harry Trefusis, to the cooler."

"Then you are Rensselaer Van Astorbilt, Russell?" I queried, dazed. He put his strong young arms about me and nodded shyly.

"Now may I ask you that question?" he blushed.

"Yes, Donald," I told him, hiding my scarlet face in his shoulder. Outside, the insupportable sweetness of a guitar cleft the warm summer air and bewhiskered, beflanneled, bewitched, bewildered, bejasused and bejabered undergraduates strolled under the hoary elms. And to this day, as I lie in my bed with the wind howling outside, I ofttimes seem to hear the hoarse croak of Long John Silver's parrot calling "Pieces of eight! Pieces of eight!" and the tapping of the blind man's stick outside the Admiral Benbow Inn.

Waiting for Santy:
A Christmas Playlet

(WITH A BOW TO MR. CLIFFORD ODETS)

Scene: The sweatshop of S. Claus, a manufacturer of children's toys, on North Pole Street. Time: The night before Christmas.

At rise, seven gnomes, Rankin, Panken, Rivkin, Riskin, Ruskin, Briskin, and Praskin, are discovered working furiously to fill orders piling up at stage right. The whir of lathes, the hum of motors, and the hiss of drying lacquer are so deafening that at times the dialogue cannot be heard, which is very vexing if you vex easily. (Note: The parts of Rankin, Panken, Rivkin, Riskin, Ruskin, Briskin, and Praskin are interchangeable, and may be secured directly from your dealer or the factory.)

RISKIN (*filing a Meccano girder, bitterly*): A parasite, a leech, a bloodsucker—altogether a five-star no-goodnick! Starvation wages we get so he can ride around in a red team with reindeers!

RUSKIN (*jeering*): Hey, Karl Marx, whyn'tcha hire a hall?

RISKIN (*sneering*): Scab! Stool pigeon! Company spy! (*They tangle and rain blows on each other. While waiting for these to dry, each returns to his respective task.*)

BRISKIN (*sadly, to Panken*): All day long I'm painting "Snow Queen" on these Flexible Flyers and my little Irving lays in a cold tenement with the gout.

PANKEN: You said before it was the mumps.

BRISKIN (*with a fatalistic shrug*): The mumps—the Gout—go argue with City Hall.

PANKEN (*kindly, passing him a bowl*): Here, take a piece fruit.

BRISKIN (*chewing*): It ain't bad, for wax fruit.

PANKEN (*with pride*): I painted it myself.

BRISKIN (*rejecting the fruit*): Ptoo! Slave psychology!

RIVKIN (*suddenly, half to himself, half to the Party*): I got a belly full of stars, baby. You make me feel like I swallowed a Roman candle.

PRASKIN (*curiously*): What's wrong with the kid?

RISKIN: What's wrong with all of us? The system! Two years he and Claus's daughter's been making goo-goo eyes behind the old man's back.

PRASKIN: So what?

RISKIN (*scornfully*): So what? Economic determinism! What do you think the kid's name is—J. Pierpont Rivkin? He ain't even got for a bottle Dr. Brown's Celery Tonic. I tell you, it's like gall in my mouth two young people shouldn't have a room where they could make great music.

RANKIN (*warningly*): Shhh! Here she comes now!

(*Stella Claus enters, carrying a portable phonograph. She and Rivkin embrace, place a record on the turntable, and begin a very slow waltz, unmindful that the phonograph is playing "Cohen on the Telephone."*)

STELLA (*dreamily*): Love me, sugar?

RIVKIN: I can't sleep, I can't eat, that's how I love you. You're a double malted with two scoops of whipped cream; you're the moon rising over Mosholu Parkway; you're a two weeks' vacation at Camp Nitgedaiget! I'd pull down the Chrysler Building to make a bobbie pin for your hair!

STELLA: I've got a stomach full of anguish. Oh, Rivvy, what'll we do?

PANKEN (*sympathetically*): Here, try a piece fruit.

RIVKIN (*fiercely*): Wax fruit—that's been my whole life! Imitations! Substitutes! Well, I'm through! Stella, tonight I'm telling your old man. He can't play mumblety-peg with two human beings! (*The tinkle of sleigh bells is heard offstage, followed by a voice shouting, "Whoa, Dasher! Whoa, Dancer!" A moment later S. Claus enters in a gust of mock snow. He is a pompous bourgeois of sixty-five who affects a white beard and a false air of benevolence. But tonight the ruddy color is missing from his cheeks, his step falters, and he moves heavily. The gnomes hastily replace the marzipan they have been filching.*)

STELLA (*anxiously*): Papa! What did the specialist say?

CLAUS (*brokenly*): The biggest professor in the country . . . the best cardiac man that money could buy. . . . I tell you I was like a wild man.

STELLA: Pull yourself together, Sam!

CLAUS: It's no use. Adhesions, diabetes, sleeping sickness, decalcomania—oh, my God! I got to cut out climbing in chimneys, he says—me, Sanford Claus, the biggest toy concern in the world!

STELLA (*soothingly*): After all, it's only one man's opinion.

CLAUS: No, no, he cooked my goose. I'm like a broken uke after a Yosian picnic. Rivkin!

RIVKIN: Yes, Sam.

CLAUS: My boy, I had my eye on you for a long time. You and Stella thought you were too foxy for an old man, didn't you? Well, let bygones be bygones. Stella, do you love this gnome?

STELLA (*simply*): He's the whole stage show at the Music Hall, Papa; he's Toscanini conducting Beethoven's Fifth; he's—

CLAUS (*curtly*): Enough already. Take him. From now on he's a partner in the firm. (*As all exclaim, Claus holds up his hand for silence.*) And tonight he can take my route and make the deliveries. It's the least I could do for my own flesh and blood. (*As the happy couple kiss, Claus wipes away a suspicious moisture and turns to the other gnomes.*) Boys, do you know what day tomorrow is?

GNOMES (*crowding around expectantly*): Christmas!

CLAUS: Correct. When you look in your envelopes tonight, you'll find a little present from me—a forty-percent pay cut. And the first one who opens his trap—gets this.

(*As he holds up a tear-gas bomb and beams at them, the gnomes utter cries of joy, join hands, and dance around him shouting exultantly. All except Riskin and Briskin, that is, who exchange a quick glance and go underground.*)

CURTAIN

Frou-Frou, or the Future of Vertigo

JUST IN CASE anybody here missed me at the Mermaid Tavern this afternoon when the bowl of sack was being passed, I spent most of it reclining on my chaise longue in a negligee trimmed with marabou, reading trashy bonbons and eating French yellow-backed novels. What between amnesia (inability to find my rubbers) and total recall (ability to remember all the cunning things I did last night), you might think I'd have sense enough to sit still and mind my own business. But, oh, no—not I. *I* had to start looking through *Harper's Bazaar* yet.

If a perfectly strange lady came up to you on the street and demanded, "Why don't you travel with a little raspberry-colored cashmere blanket to throw over yourself in hotels and trains?" the chances are that you would turn on your heel with dignity and hit her with a bottle. Yet that is exactly what has been happening for the past twenty months in the pages of a little raspberry-colored magazine called *Harper's Bazaar*. And don't think it does any good to pretend there *is* no magazine called *Harper's Bazaar*. I've tried that, too, and all I get is something called "circular insanity." Imagine having both circular insanity and *Harper's Bazaar*!

The first time I noticed this "Why Don't You?" department was a year ago last August while hungrily devouring news of the midsummer Paris openings. Without any preamble came the stinging query, "Why don't you rinse your blonde child's hair in dead champagne, as they do in France? Or pat her face gently with cream before she goes to bed, as they do in England?" After a quick look into the nursery, I decided to let my blonde child go to hell her own way, as they do in America, and read on. "Why don't you," continued the author, spitting on her hands, "twist her pigtails around her ears like macaroons?" I reread this several times to make sure I wasn't dreaming and then turned to the statement of ownership in the back of the magazine. Just because the Marquis de Sade wasn't mentioned didn't fool *me*; you know as well as I do who must have controlled fifty-one per cent of the stock. I slept across the foot of the crib with a loaded horse pistol until the next issue appeared.

It appeared, all right, all right, and after a quick gander at the activities of Nicky de Gunzburg, Lady Abdy, and the Vicomtesse de Noailles, which left me right back where I started, I sought out my "Why Don't You?" column. "Why don't you try the effect of diamond roses and ribbons flat on your head, as Garbo wears them when she says good-bye to Armand in their country retreat?" asked Miss Sly Boots in a low, thrilling voice. I was living in my own country retreat at the time, and as it happened to be my day to go to the post office (ordinarily the post office comes to me), I welcomed this chance to vary the monotony. Piling my head high with diamond roses and ribbons, I pulled on a pair of my stoutest *espadrilles* and set off, my cat frisking ahead of me with many a warning cry of "Here comes my master, the Marquis of Carabas!" We reached the post office without incident, except for the elderly Amish woman hoeing cabbages in her garden. As I threw her a cheery greeting, Goody Two-shoes looked up, gave a rapid exhibition of Cheyne-Stokes breathing, and immediately turned to stone. In case you ever get down that way, she is still standing there, slightly chipped but otherwise in very good condition, which is more than I can say for the postmaster. When I walked in, he was in process of spitting into the top drawer, where he keeps the money-order blanks. One look at Boxholder 14 and he went out the window without bothering to raise the sash. A second later I heard a frightened voice directing a small boy to run for the hex doctor next door to the Riegels'. I spent the night behind some willows near the Delaware and managed to work my way back to the farm without being detected, but it was a matter of months before I was able to convince the countryside that I had a twin brother, enormously wealthy but quite mad, who had eluded his guards and paid me a visit.

For a time I went on a sort of *Harper's Bazaar* wagon, tapering myself off on *Pictorial Review* and *Good Housekeeping*, but deep down I knew I was a gone goose. Whenever I got too near a newsstand bearing a current issue of the *Bazaar* and my head started to swim, I would rush home and bury myself in dress patterns. And then, one inevitable day, the dam burst. Lingering in Brentano's basement over *L'Illustration* and *Blanco y Negro*, I felt the delicious, shuddery, half-swooning sensation of being drawn into the orbit again. On a table behind me lay a huge stack of the very latest issue of *Harper's Bazaar*, smoking hot from the presses. "Ah, come on," I heard my evil genius whisper. "One little peek can't hurt you. Nobody's looking." With trembling fingers I fumbled through the advertisements for Afghan hounds, foundation garments, and bath foams to the "Why Don't You?" section. Tiny beads of perspiration stood out on my even tinier forehead as I began to read, "Why don't you build beside the sea, or in the center of your garden, a white summer dining room shaped like a tent, draped with wooden swags, with walls of screen and Venetian blinds, so you will be safe from bugs and drafts?" I recoiled, clawing the air. "No, no!" I screamed. "I won't! I can't! *Help!*" But already the column was coiling around me, its hot breath on my neck. "Why don't you concentrate on fur jackets of marvelous workmanship and cut, made of inexpensive furs with incomprehensible names? Why don't you bring back from Central Europe a huge white baroque porcelain stove to stand in your front hall, reflected in the parquet? Why don't you buy in a hardware store a plain pine knife-basket with two compartments and a handle—mount this on four legs and you will have the ideal little table to sort letters and bills on, and to carry from your bedside to the garden or wherever you happen to be?" Unfortunately I had only the two legs God gave me, but I mounted those basement stairs like a cheetah, fought off the restraining hands of voluptuous salesladies, and hurtled out into the cool, sweet air of West Forty-seventh Street. I'm sorry I snatched the paper knife out of that desk set, Mr. Brentano, but you can send around a boy for it at my expense. And by the way, do you ever have any call for back numbers of fashion magazines?

Captain Future, Block That Kick!

I GUESS I'm just an old mad scientist at bottom. Give me an underground laboratory, half a dozen atom-smashers, and a beautiful girl in a diaphanous veil waiting to be turned into a chimpanzee, and I care not who writes the nation's laws. You'll have to leave my meals on a tray outside the door because I'll be working pretty late on the secret of making myself invisible, which may take me almost until eleven o'clock. Oh, yes, and don't let's forget one more thing. I'll need a life subscription to a new quarterly journal called *Captain Future, Wizard of Science*, a bright diadem on the forehead of Better Publications, 22 West Forty-eighth Street, New York City.

As one who triggered a disintegrator with Buck Rogers and could dash off a topographical map of Mongo or Dale Arden with equal facility, I thought in my pride and arrogance I knew all there was to know about astronomical adventure. It was something of a shock, therefore, to find out several days back that I was little more than a slippered pantaloon. Beside Captain Future, Wizard of Science, Flash Gordon and the Emperor Ming pale to a couple of nursery tots chewing on Holland rusk.

The novelette in which this spectacular *caballero* makes his bow to "scientifiction" fans opens with no fumbling preamble or prosy exposition. Into the office of James Carthew, President of the Earth Government, staggers a giant ape, barely recognizable by the President as John Sperling, his most trusted secret agent. The luckless investigator had been ordered to Jupiter to look into a complaint that some merry-andrew was causing atavism among the Jovians, but apparently had got badly jobbed. Before Carthew can intervene, a frightened guard drills the ape man with a flare-pistol, and in his dying breath the latter lays the blame for his predicament squarely at the door of a mysterious being he calls the Space Emperor. As you may well imagine, Carthew is all of a tizzy. He immediately instructs his secretary to send for Captain Future in the ringing phrase, "Televise the meteorological rocket-patrol base at Spitzbergen.

Order them to flash the magnesium flare signal from the North Pole." Personally, I think Carthew might have softened this whiplike command with "And just for the hell of it, why don't you try the Princeton Club?" but perhaps I delve too deeply. In any event, the perpetual uranium clock has hardly ticked off two hours before Captain Future (or Curt Newton, to call him by his given name) appears on the escarpment with one of the most endearing speeches in my experience:

"You know my assistants," Curt Newton said shortly, "Grag the robot, Otho the android, and Simon Wright, the Living Brain. We came from the moon full speed when I saw your signal. What's wrong?"

Fiction teems with sinister escorts and everybody has his favorite, but Captain Future's three-man mob leaves the worst of them kissed off and frozen against the cushion:

> A weird shape had just leaped onto the balcony. It was a manlike figure, but one whose body was rubbery, boneless-looking, blank-white in color. He wore a metal harness, and his long, slitted green unhuman eyes peered brightly out of an alien white face. Following this rubbery android, or synthetic man, came another figure, equally as strange—a giant metal robot who strode across the balcony on padded feet. He towered seven feet high. In his bulbous metal head gleamed a pair of photoelectric eyes. The robot's left hand carried the handle of a square transparent box. Inside it a living brain was housed. In the front of the case were the Brain's two glittering glass lens-eyes. Even now they were moving on their flexible metal stalks to look at the President.

At this juncture I took time out to moisten my lips with the tip of my tongue, retrieved my own eyeballs, and plunged on. Captain Future himself was somewhat more tailored than his comrades, in fact quite swagger. "His unruly shock of red hair towered six feet four above the floor, and his wide lithe shoulders threatened to burst the jacket of his gray synthesilk zipper-suit." In pulp fiction it is a rigid convention that the hero's shoulders and the heroine's *balcon* constantly threaten to burst their bonds, a possibility which keeps the audience in a state of tense expectancy. Unfortunately for the fans, however, recent tests reveal that the wisp of chiffon which stands between the publisher and the postal laws has the tensile strength of drop-forged steel.

To acquaint the reader more fully with "that tall, cheerful, red-haired young adventurer of the ready laugh and flying fists, the implacable Nemesis of all oppressors and exploiters of the System's human and planetary races," the author interrupts his smoking narrative with a brief dossier. In the year 1990, the brilliant young Earth biologist Roger Newton, aided by the living brain of Simon Wright ("the greatest brain in scientific history"), had unravelled the secret of artificial life. Now, certain dark forces headed by one Victor Corvo were determined to appropriate Newton's secret. To confound him, Roger Newton proposed to Elaine, his wife, and the Living Brain that they conceal themselves on the moon.

"But the moon!" Elaine exclaimed, deep repulsion shadowing her eyes. "That barren, airless globe that no one ever visits!" Elaine's dainty disgust is pardonable; Far Rockaway out of season could not have been more painfully *vieux jeu*. A few weeks, nevertheless, see the little company snugly housed under the surface of Tycho crater upon the moon, where its number is swelled by the addition of the infant Curt and Grag the robot, whom Roger and the Living Brain construct in their spare time of neurons and nails and puppy dogs' tails. Eventually, still another fruit of this intellectual union—Otho, the synthetic android—is capering about the laboratory. Just as Newton is on the verge of returning to earth, up turns Public Bad Penny No. 1, Victor Corvo, and slays him and his wife. When the Brain assures him vengeance will be swift, Corvo hurls the taunt supreme at the preserved scientist: "Don't try to threaten me, you miserable bodiless brain! I'll soon silence you—" He stops throwing his weight around soon enough when Grag and Otho burst in, and, directed by the Brain, rub him out effectively if none too tidily.

Dying, Elaine Newton entrusts Curt to the care of the trio in a scene which must affect the sensibilities of the most callous:

> "Tell him to war always against those who would pervert science to sinister ambition," whispered Elaine. "I will tell him," promised the Brain, and in its toneless metallic voice was a queer catch.

The guardians justify Elaine's faith in them to a degree; by the time Curt has attained his majority, he is one lovely hunk of boy, a hybrid of Leonardo da Vinci and Dink Stover. From then on, as Captain Future, Curt ranges the solar system with his pals in an asteroidal super-ship, the *Comet*, avenging his folks and waging war on what the author is pleased to call "interplanetary crime."

But to return to our muttons, if so prosaic a term can be applied to the streamlined quartet. Speeding outward into space toward Jovopolis, chief Earthman colony on Jupiter, Captain Future plucks haunting music from his twenty-string Venusian guitar while Grag and Otho tend the controls and the Living Brain burrows into textbooks for a clue to the atavism. Their snug *Kaffeeklatsch* is blasted when a piratical black space-cruiser suddenly looms across the *Comet*'s bows and attempts to ambush the party, but Curt's proton beams force the attacker down on Callisto, outermost of Jupiter's four biggest moons. The boys warp in alongside and Grag prepares to rip open the jammed door of the pirate craft so his master may question the miscreants:

> Grag's big metal fingers were removable. The robot rapidly unscrewed two of them and replaced them with small drills which he took from a kit of scalpels, chisels, and similar tools carried in a little locker in his metal side. Then Grag touched a switch on his wrist. The two drills which had replaced two of his fingers whirled hummingly. He quickly used them to drill six holes in the edge of the ship's door. Then he replaced the drills with his fingers, hooked six fingers inside the holes he had made.

The rest is brute strength, a department in which Grag is pre-eminent. Inside are Jon Orris and Martin Skeel, whose names instantly tip them off as wrong guys. Yet it is impossible not to be moved by Orris's pathetic confession: "Skeel and I have criminal records. We fled out here after we got into a murder scrape on Mars." They admit under pressure that they are creatures of the Space Emperor, though actually they have never seen him. "He's always concealed in a big, queer black suit, and he speaks out of it in a voice that don't sound human to me," Skeel says.

Time, even on Callisto, is a-wastin', and nimbly dodging a plague of creeping crystals which bids fair to annihilate them, the space-farers resume their course. On their arrival at Jovopolis, Otho the android disguises himself as Orris and repairs to that worthy's hut to await the Space Emperor and overpower him so that Captain Future can steal up and clap the darbies on him. Arriving at the rendezvous, the Emperor promptly makes himself invisible and Curt leaps through him, only to sprawl on his finely chiselled beezer.

Recovering from this contretemps with his usual sunny equanimity, Curt hastens to the mansion of the governor, Sylvanus Quale, to reconnoitre. Here he encounters the heart interest, a plump little cabbage named Joan Randall, who is head nurse to the chief planetary physician. Lucas Brewer, a shifty radium magnate, Mark Cannig, his mine superintendent, and Eldred Kells, the vice-governor, are also at the mansion. It is apparent at once to the *cognoscenti* that any one of these worthies is the Space Emperor, and with no personal bias other than that his name had a particularly sneaky sound, I put my money on Eldred Kells. Fifty pages later I was proved right, but not before I had been locked in an atavism ward with Curt and Joan, flung into a pit by the green flipper-men, and nibbled by giant six-foot rats called "diggers" (a surprisingly mild name for a giant six-foot rat, by the way). But even such hazards, for all their jewelled prose, cannot compare with the description of the main street of Jungletown:

> Here were husky prospectors in stained zipper-suits, furtive, unshaven space-bums begging, cool-eyed interplanetary gamblers, gaunt engineers in high boots with flare-pistols at their belts, bronzed space-sailors up from Jovopolis for a carousal in the wildest new frontier-town in the System.

And so, all too soon for both Joan Randall and myself, comes the hour of parting with "the big red-head," as the author shakily describes Curt in a final burst of emotion. In the next issue, Captain Future and his creepy constabulary will doubtless be summoned forth again to combat some horror as yet to be devised. Meanwhile I like to think of his lighthearted rebuke to Otho the android, already chafing against inactivity:

"Sooner or later, there'll be another call from Earth, and then I hope there's action enough for you, you crazy coot."

There may be another call, Curt, but it won't come from Baby. Right now all he wants is a cup of hot milk and fourteen hours of shut-eye. And if it's all the same to you, he'll do his sleeping with the lights on.

Midwinter Facial Trends

A SCENARIO WRITER I know, who had been working unin-terruptedly in Hollywood for three years, finally got back to New York for a two-week vacation. He had barely unpacked his gold-backed military hairbrushes and put on a red moiré smoking jacket when a wire from his agent ordered him back to the Coast for an assignment. The young man preferred to stay, but his conscience reminded him of the two hundred and fifty thousand dollars in annuities he was carrying, and this in turn summoned up a frightening picture of a destitute old age when he might have to work on a newspaper again and ride in streetcars. After wrestling with himself for several hours, he decided to assert his independence. He sent back a spunky wire to the effect that he was working on a novel and could not return under any conditions unless his salary was raised to seventeen hundred and fifty dollars a week, instead of fifteen hundred. Then he forgot all about it, except to lie awake three nights and stay indoors waiting for the telephone to ring.

To nobody's surprise, the deal went through, and forty-eight hours later the scenario writer was sitting in a producer's office in Hollywood, a little worse for the plane trip and a box of so-dium Amytal tablets. In a few badly chosen words the producer explained his predicament. He had a terrific story; it smelled box office a mile away. But every writer on the payroll had been stumped for the last three months by one tiny detail.

"I'll tell you the meat of the story," said the producer. "It's got plenty of spontinuity when you maul it over in your mind, only just this one little thing you got to figure out."

"Give," murmured the scenario writer, closing his eyes to indicate that his faculties were purring like a Diesel engine.

"We fade in on a street in London," began the producer, fading in on a street in London. "It's about four o'clock in the morning and I see a guy dressed in rags dragging himself along through the fog, a Lon Chaney type guy. He's all twisted and crippled up. *Voom!* All of a sudden he ducks down an areaway and knocks on a door. It opens and I see a gorgeous hallway with Chinese rugs and Ming vases. We hold the camera on it and milk whatever we can from the scene. The minute the guy's inside, he straightens up, takes off this harness, and unties his leg. What I mean is, the guy's as normal as you or me. Any audience'll buy that—am I right? Then we truck with him through a door and he's in like a hospital corridor. He pulls on rubber gloves and an operating gown—"

"Wait a minute," the writer interrupted, rising. "Am I supposed to spot laughs in this?"

"Siddown," commanded the producer. "There's a million opportunities for good crazy dialogue later on. We wipe the guy into an operating room and pan around. He's got ten, fifteen beautiful dames chained to the walls with practically nothing on, and if that don't blow the audience out of the back of the houses, I don't know show business. The legal department's taking it up with the Hays office this afternoon. We follow the guy over to a bench that's full of test tubes and scientific stuff; he pours one test tube into another and hollers, 'I got it! The life secret I been hunting for years!' Mind you, this ain't dialogue—I'm just spitballing. So then he puts a little of this life secret in a hypodermic needle and rings a gong. These two assistants wheel in a table with our leading woman on it, out like a light. Our guy rubs his hands and laughs like a hyena. He picks up the hypo, bends over our girl, and that's where you got to figure out this one thing."

"What's that?" the writer inquired suspiciously. The producer bit the end off a manufacturer's-size Corona, frustration in his eyes, and shook his head.

"What kind of a business is this guy in?" he asked helplessly.

If you are inclined to brood easily, I can guarantee that this question will tease you to the brink of hysteria. It obsessed me almost constantly until I stumbled across what may very well be the answer. It is contained in a little 134-page brochure entitled *Cosmetic Surgery*, by Charles C. Miller, M.D., published by the author in 1907. Since that day several weeks ago when I first peeped into this attractive volume, bound in red sharkskin, I have been confined to my rooms in the Albany with a fairly constant attack of the rams. As if Dr. Miller's prose style were not sufficiently graphic, the text is supplemented with half a dozen photographs and a score of drawings calculated to make your scalp tingle. I am no sissy, but I will risk a sporting flutter of half a guinea that even the brothers Mayo would have flinched under *Cosmetic Surgery.*

The author starts off casually enough with instructions for correcting outstanding ears, which range all the way from tying them flat to the head to some pretty violent surgery. Personally, I have found that a short length of three-quarter-inch Manila hemp bound stoutly about the head, the knot protruding below one's felt hat, adds a rakish twist to the features and effectively prisons ears inclined to flap in the wind. A salty dash may be imparted to the ensemble by dipping the rope in tar, or even substituting oakum for hemp.

I must confess that the chapter headed "Nose with the Bulbous Tip," on page 50, fired my blood, and I read three or four pages avidly waiting for the appearance of Hercule Poirot or even Inspector Lestrade before I discovered that no crime had been committed. But on page 79, just as I finished yawning through some hints on diminishing the unduly large mouth by hemstitching it at the corners, Dr. Miller plucked the roses from my cheeks with "Marginal Tattooing as a Means of Adding to the Apparent Width of the Lips." That may not be your idea of a punchy title for the marquee of a theatre, but if Boris Karloff were in it, you'd pay your six-sixty fast enough. Living as I do on the hem of the wilderness, I was not aware that "tattooing about the margin of the lips to overcome undue thinness" had become a commonplace. The technique is as follows: "The skin is punctured or pricked open with a needle. The puncturing does not extend through the skin, but merely into the true skin. [Come, come, Doctor, let's not quibble.] After the punctures have been made, the coloring is rubbed in with the point of the needle or with a slightly flattened spud. Some reaction may be expected to follow the operation, but healing is complete in a few days." Why any reaction save boredom should follow rubbing a patient's lips with a potato is not clear to me, but I suppose that if one were allergic to potatoes, one might become restless under the massage. Speaking for myself, I have always been very partial to potatoes, especially those of the cottage-fried type.

It is on page 92, with "The Formation of the Dimple," that Dr. Miller really removes the buttons from the foils. "It is my practice in these cases," he states, "to thoroughly scrub the cheek, and then, after having the patient smile, select the point where a dimple should form under ordinary circumstances. . . . I mark this point, and insert my hypodermic needle." The operative method from now on is strikingly similar to fishing for perch through a hole in the ice. The Doctor lowers a line with a bobber and a bit of red flannel, builds a fire on the patient's forehead, and sits down to warm his hands till a dimple is hooked. The patient lies there softly whimpering, "I didn't have enough trouble, I had to have dimples like Robert Taylor yet!" And there let us leave them in the softly flickering firelight, with the thought that it will flicker much better if you pile on an occasional page out of *Cosmetic Surgery*, by Charles C. Miller.

Counter-Revolution

THE OTHER night a forty-five-year-old friend of mine, after ingesting equal portions of Greek fire and artillery punch, set out to prove that he could walk across a parquet flooring on his hands while balancing a vase on his head. As a consequence, about eleven o'clock the following morning he was being trepanned at the Harkness Pavilion and I was purchasing a bottle of Major's Cement. I had reassembled the shards and was about to uncork the cement bottle when the bold yellow leaflet in which it was wrapped caught my eye. To predict that this small circular will eventually outrank Magna Carta and the Peace of Breda in historical significance may seem audacious. Yet even the most frivolous cannot escape its implications, for in a single decisive stroke it alters the entire status of the consumer.

From its opening sentence, the document was marked by a note of brooding, reminiscent of a manifesto:

> If we could make the cement in liquid form and transparent, and at the same time as strong and as proof against moisture as it is now, we would be glad to do so. But this cannot be done.

A dozen lines further on, the manufacturer was fretting again over the possible imputation that he was holding back on his product:

> If we could make a cement transparent and in liquid form as strong as the way we make our cement, we would do it. There is no material that you could use that would make cement that way.

Obviously an *idée fixe*, I thought to myself, but aloud, I merely said quietly, "All right now, I can hear you. I use Leonard's Ear Oil as well as Major's Cement." My witty reprimand fell among thorns; a moment later the circular was behaving like a regular ogre:

> If you do not succeed the first time in mending an article, do not throw up your hands and go pulling your hair and yell out

"I have been swindled once more"; but have patience, for the Cement is all right.

By now I was thoroughly nettled. Patience, eh? Look who's telling me to have patience. Why, I've got more patience in my little fing—but my words were blotted out in a last echoing apoplectic bellow:

> If, before doing as suggested, you tell others that the Cement is no good, you are saying an untruth and injuring the reputation of Major's Cement. Remember the Golden Rule, "Do unto others as you would be done by."

Since I long ago gave instructions to strew my ashes to the four winds when the hour sounds, this precept left me with only one course open, and I took it.

It is obvious that such a *volte-face* in sales technique is fraught with the most far-reaching implications. There is every chance that Major's plaintive exasperation with the customer may yet be adopted and distorted by other firms. I take the liberty of presenting a few glamorous possibilities in a curtain-raiser, with the hope it may inspire some fellow-dramatist to attempt a more sustained flight:

(*Scene: The men's furnishing section of a large department store. As the curtain rises, a salesman, Axel Munthe, is waiting on a patron. Munthe is not related to the physician who wrote "The Story of San Michele"; it is simply an interesting coincidence. Enter Leonard DeVilbiss, a typical customer—in fact, a luggage tag reading "Mr. Average Consumer" depends from the skirt of his topcoat. He looks timidly at Munthe.*)

DeVilbiss: Do you sell Mackinaws here?

Munthe: No, we give 'em away. That's how we stay in business—giving away free Mackinaws.

DeVilbiss: I don't see any around here.

Munthe: What the devil do you think those are hanging on the rack—flounders?

(*DeVilbiss meekly takes a seat and, picking up copies of "Click," "Pic," and "Look," begins to hold the pages against the light to discover possible salacious effects.*)

PATRON (*uncertainly*): I don't know about these shorts. I had in mind something with a banjo seat.

MUNTHE: Banjo seat! Banjo seat! Why don't you wear a banjo and be done with it?

PATRON: These won't shrink, will they?

MUNTHE: Look—Boulder Dam shrank six inches last year. You want me to underwrite a pair of lousy ninety-eight-cent shorts against it?

PATRON: Hmm. Well, I think I'll look around.

MUNTHE: Not in here, you won't. If you want to browse, go to a bookstore. (*Patron exits; Munthe approaches DeVilbiss.*) All right, Buster, break it up. You're not in your club.

DEVILBISS: I'd like to try on some Mackinaws.

MUNTHE (*suspiciously*): Got any money?

DEVILBISS: Yes, sir. (*He shows Munthe some money. Latter reluctantly pulls out rack.*)

MUNTHE: Now, let me see. You want something in imported camel's hair, fleece-lined, with a lifetime guarantee, for only five dollars?

DEVILBISS (*dazzled*): Sure.

MUNTHE: That's what I thought. They all do. Well, cookie, you're in the wrong pew.

DEVILBISS (*humbly*): Haven't you any shoddy old blue plaid ones with leatheroid buttons for about fifty dollars?

MUNTHE: To fit a little shrimp like you?

DEVILBISS (*submissively*): It don't have to fit me.

MUNTHE (*bridling*): Oh, you're not going to wear it, hey? Just one of those sneaking comparison shoppers who—

DEVILBISS: No, no—I thought for carrying out the ashes —you know, around the cellar.

MUNTHE (*loftily*): You must be a pretty small-time lug to carry out your own ashes.

DEVILBISS: I am.

MUNTHE (*grudgingly*): Well, all right. Slip this on for size.

DEVILBISS (*after a struggle*): It binds me a little under the arms.

MUNTHE: You're damn right it does. If we knew how to lick that, we'd all be in clover.

DEVILBISS: Could you—I mean, maybe if a seam was let out —that is, the sleeve—

MUNTHE (*infuriated*): See here, chump, if you think I'm going to rebuild a measly fifty-dollar Mackinaw for every stumblebum who mooches in off the street—

DEVILBISS: Oh, no. I wouldn't dream of asking you! I—I was just wondering whether Alberta—that's Mrs. DeVilbiss; she's a regular whiz at things like that—and time, say, she's got all the time in the world—

MUNTHE: O.K., come on. Do you want it or don't you?

DEVILBISS: You bet your life I do! Does—er—does this model come with pockets?

MUNTHE: Yes, and we throw in two tickets to a musical and dinner at Voisin's. (*Shouting*) What the hell do you think we're running here, a raffle?

DEVILBISS: Gee, you got me wrong. I wouldn't want anything I wasn't entitled to, honest!

MUNTHE: Next thing I know you'll be chiseling me out of paper and string to carry it home.

DEVILBISS: My goodness, no! I'll put it right over my arm —it's no trouble, really!

MUNTHE (*taking money from DeVilbiss*): Say, if I'd known you had nothing but twenties—

DEVILBISS: Gosh, never mind the change—that's quite all right. Thank you very much.

MUNTHE: Well, listen, chump, watch your step. If I hear any squawk out of you about our merchandise, I'll cool you off fast enough.

(*DeVilbiss exits hurriedly. A moment later Lin Yutang, the floorwalker—also no relation to the author of "The Story of San Michele"—enters.*)

YUTANG (*glowering*): Look here, Munthe, was that a customer I just saw coming out of this section?

MUNTHE (*quickly*): Of course not, sir. It was only a shoplifter.

YUTANG: All right, then, but don't let me catch you selling anything around here. You know the policy of this store. Carry on!

(*Munthe returns his salute and, picking up a bottle of acid, begins to dump it over the goods as Yutang, arms folded, watches him approvingly.*)

CURTAIN

Beat Me, Post-Impressionist Daddy

ANY OF you kids seen Somerset Maugham? I haven't run into him lately, but I'll bet those advertisements for "The Moon and Sixpence" put the roses in his cheeks. In case you've been spending the last couple of weeks underwater, the Messrs. Loew and Lewin have just transferred to the screen Mr. Maugham's novel of the ordeal of Charles Strickland, a character closely resembling Paul Gauguin. Faced with merchandising so spiritual a problem, the producers evidently recalled that Vincent van Gogh had been popularized as a man who mailed his ear to a friend, and decided to sell their boy on a similar basis. The leitmotiv of the campaign was a busty Polynesian hussy in a pitifully shrunken sarong, lolling on her back in considerable abandon and smelling a flower. Peering out of a palm tree above, mighty lak a chimp, was George Sanders in the best beard that money could buy. "I DON'T WANT LOVE! I hate it!" he was declaring petulantly. "It interferes with my work . . . and yet . . . *I'm only human!*" A second advertisement portrayed the painter in an equally disenchanted mood, over the caption "WOMEN ARE STRANGE LITTLE BEASTS! You can treat them like dogs (*he did!*)—beat them 'til your arm aches (*he did*) . . . and still they love you (*they did*). But in the end they'll get you and you are helpless in their hands."

Although Gauguin's journal, "Avant et Après," and his correspondence with D. de Monfreid are fairly blue in spots, he is not primarily remembered as passion's plaything, and these insinuations may confound the strait-laced. Now that Hollywood has thrown the ball into play, however, the following letters I recently unearthed in my bottom bureau drawer deserve careful scrutiny. They were written by the artist to my father's barber, who lived in the bureau between 1895 and 1897. Here and there I have taken the liberty of translating the rather difficult argot into current idiom, for clarity.

48

MATAIÉA, JULY 17, 1896

DEAR MARCUS,

Well, my old, you must think I am a fine *pascudnick* indeed not to answer you before this, but man is born to trouble as the sparks fly upward and I am winging. The day after I wrote you, who should come mousing around but that little brunette, Tia, in her loose-leaf pareu, which it's enough to melt the umber on a man's palette. It so happened I was in the hut with this tall job from Papeete, dashing off a quick pastel. I told Tia to stop needling me, but she was inconsolable. Distraught, I asked what she required. "Poi," she responded. Poi is one thing I have never refused anybody yet, Marcus, so, brushing off this other head, I made with the poi. The instant we were alone, the pretty trickster revealed her design. "I'm a strange little beast!" she cried, "Beat me 'til your arm aches!" Me, a family man. *Figurez-vous*, Marcus, what could I do? I bounced her around a bit, knocked out several of her teeth, and invited her to withdraw, as I had to complete a gouache by five o'clock. *Dame!*—the next thing I knew, Miss Goody Two-shoes had sealed the door, swallowed the key [*clef*], and I was it.

As to the painting, it goes very slowly. Kindest thanks for your new calendar, which arrived in good condition. Personally, the model is somewhat skinny for my taste and there is too much drapery, but *tiens*, that is the bourgeois style. Tell me more about that youth, the son of your patron. The boy has genius, Marcus; I have an instinct for these things. Mark me well, he will yet be another Piero della Francesca.

I pinch your claws,

PAUL

MATAIÉA, NOVEMBER 12, 1896

DEAR MARCUS,

Life here becomes increasingly tiresome, my friend; the women refuse to let me alone. How I envy Vincent those days at Arles, with nothing between him and his muse but the solar spectrum. I came to this miserable hole surfeited with civilization and its trinkets. One might as well be back in the Rue Vercingétorix. Last night I attended a native fete and, like a chump, neglected to close my door. Returning home about two with a charming person who insisted on seeing my frescoes, I found the wife of the Minister of Public Works concealed under the bed. The old story—I must beat her without further ado, treat her like a dog, else she will stop loving me. *Quelle bêtise!* My arms are so tired from flailing these cows that I can hardly mix my pigments. I sit down in a workingmen's café for an infusion; immediately I am surrounded by hordes of beauties begging me to maltreat them. I arise each morning determined to spend the day seriously. A pair of dark eyes at the window, a tender glance, and *pouf* [pouf] go my resolutions. After all, I'm only human.

I have a superb conception for a canvas which would be the very antithesis of Manet's "Olympia"—a native girl stretched on the sofa, regarding the onlooker with a mixture of fear and coquetry. At this rate I shall never finish it. Every sketch I begin ends the same. I pose the model on a divan, run my hand lightly over her back to enhance the sheen—*au fond* I am a painter of highlights—and *zut*, we are off on a tangent. For the time, merely to block in the masses, I am using a rolled-up umbrella in lieu of a girl. Actually, an ironic comment on your modern woman—all ribs and cloth. Where are those big, jolly, upholstered girls one used to see?

One fault only I find with your letters: there are too many lacunae. You say your patron's son was surprised embracing his governess. *Et alors?* What ensued? You leave too much to the imagination. Describe the scene with greater fidelity. Send photographs if possible. In any event, I must have a photo of the governess, preferably in her chemise, for a composition I am engaged on. It is an airy caprice in the manner of Watteau, quite unlike my current things—the startled governess blushing profusely, repulsing yet yielding to a diminutive satyr. I call it "Tickled Pink." Don't misunderstand, *mon copain*. This is simply relaxation, a change of pace from everything else I'm doing.

As ever,

PAUL

MATAIÉA, MAY 3, 1897

DEAR MARCUS,

Epochal news! I have arrived! After years of scorn and obloquy, after a lifetime of abuse from academicians and the kept press, I have at last attained official recognition! It came in the person of Mme. Dufresnoy, wife of the new Governor General, just as I was at the lowest ebb of despair. Reconstruct the scene for yourself: I was pacing moodily before my easel, alone, forgotten, attempting to wring some inspiration from the four or five scantily clad houris grouped on the dais. Suddenly, the sound of carriage wheels, and enter a vision of loveliness, a veritable Juno. What fluid rhythm, what vibrations . . . and yet a touch of that coarseness I find so piquant—I trembled like a schoolboy! But the real surprise was still to come. Housed in this ravishing exterior is no sordid Philistine but a delicate, subtle spirit attuned to mine; in a word, a connoisseur. Tales of my work have percolated through her flunkies and plenipotentiaries, and she must see it instanter. In a trice, the details are arranged—I am to bring my best canvases to the executive mansion next Tuesday for inspection. Only one cloud mars my bliss. As the house is being plastered, the view is to be held in Madame's boudoir, a tiny room which I fear is hardly adequate to exhibit the larger oils. Perdition! . . . but we shall make the best of it. I am in a frenzy of preparation, varnishing pictures, borrowing cologne for my ear lobes, a hundred distractions—I must fly.

I embrace you, my dear fellow,
PAUL

P.S. One passage puzzled me in your last letter. How could your patron's son have penetrated to the landlady's room without climbing up the air-shaft? Curb his exuberance, I implore you, and do not fail to send me a snapshot of the landlady.

MATAIÉA, MAY 19, 1897

DEAR MARCUS,

My decision is irrevocable: I am through with painting. I have a new mission, the extermination of the official class and particularly of its wives. After that, the monastery.

The betrayal was complete, catastrophic. I waited on Mme. Dufresnoy afire with plans—a house in the Avenue Matignon, a *petite amie* purring beside me like a kitten, a villa at Chantilly. I am received by my benefactress in a filmy black peignoir, eyes sparkling with belladonna. The room is plunged in shadow;

she prefers (sweet tyrant) to examine the canvases by artificial light. I shrug at her eccentricity, swallow a *fine à l'eau* as a digestive, launch into a short preamble about my work. *Basta!* Suddenly we are in Stygian darkness and I am held in a clasp of iron. "Madame," I entreat, "let us at least sit down and talk this thing over." *Enfin*, she reluctantly disposed herself in my lap and we had just arrived at a rationale when the door flew open and the Governor General rushed in. I could have demolished the big tub of tripes with my small finger, but he was escorted by a band of *apaches*, armed to the teeth. I acquitted myself handily, nevertheless, and outside a discolored eye and a trifling compound fracture, emerged an easy victor. Thanks to Madame's intercession, I was given the most spacious room in the lockup and the assignment of whitewashing the walls. It is not painting, but working with new textures is good artistic discipline.

Your letters, as always, remain my constant solace. If I may presume on our friendship, though, please to omit all further references to that miserable little brat, your patron's son. I am not interested in his grimy amours, nor anybody else's, for that matter. I have had enough of the whole goddamned subject.

Eternally,

P. Gauguin

A Pox on You, Mine Goodly Host

A FEW NIGHTS ago I strolled into our Pompeian living room in my stocking feet, bedad, with a cigar in my mouth and a silk hat tilted back on my head, to find Maggie, with osprey plumes in her hair and a new evening cape, pulling on long white gloves. A little cluster of exclamation points and planets formed over her head as she saw me.

"Aren't you dressed yet, you bonehead?" she thundered. "Or were you sneaking down to Dinty Moore's for corned beef and cabbage with those worthless cronies of yours?" I soon assuaged the good woman's fears, and in response to my queries she drew from her reticule an advertisement clipped from the *Sun*. It displayed photographs of George S. Kaufman and Moss Hart framed in a family album over the legend "From Schrafft's Album of Distinguished Guests. The parade of luminaries who enjoy Schrafft's hearty dinners includes columnists, sportswriters, stage and radio personalities, football coaches, illustrators, producers. Adding to the glitter of this list are the distinguished names of Kaufman and Hart, who have written many a Broadway hit." Of course, nothing would do but we must dine at Schrafft's that very evening and mingle in the pageantry, so without further ado we set out.

Although it was not yet seven o'clock when our cab pulled up in front of the Forty-third Street branch, a sizable crowd of autograph-seekers had assembled and were eagerly scrutinizing each new arrival. A rapturous shout went up as I descended. "Here comes dashing Brian Aherne!" exulted a charming miss rushing forward. "Isn't it sickening?" I murmured into my wife's ear. "This happens everywhere—in stores, on buses—" "Yes, I know," she grated. "Everybody takes me for Olivia de Havilland. Get out of the way, you donkey. Don't you see the man's trying to get by?" To my surprise, I found myself brushed aside by Brian Aherne, who must have been clinging to the spare tire. As I shouldered my way after him, curious stares followed me. "That must be his bodyguard," commented a fan. "That shrimp couldn't be a cat's bodyguard," sneered his neighbor. I looked the speaker full in the eye. "That's for the cat to say," I riposted, and as the bystanders roared, I stalked through the revolving doors, conscious I had scored.

Buoyant the advertisement had been, but I was frankly dazzled by the scene which confronted me. The foyer, ablaze with lights, was peopled by personages of such distinction as few first nights attract. Diamonds of the finest water gleamed at the throats of women whose beauty put the gems to shame, and if each was not escorted by a veritable Adonis, he was at least a Greek. A hum of well-bred conversation rose from the throng, punctuated now and again by the click of expensive dentures. In one corner Nick Kenny, Jack Benny, James Rennie, Sonja Henie, and E. R. Penney, the chain-store magnate, were gaily comparing pocketbooks to see who had the most money, and in another Jim Thorpe chatted with Jay Thorpe, cheek by jowl with Walter Wanger and Percy Grainger. Here Lou Little and Elmer Layden demonstrated a new shift to a fascinated circle, while there Ann Corio demonstrated still another to an even more spellbound circle. Myron Selznick, Frank Orsatti, and Leland Hayward had just planed in from the Coast to sign everyone to agency contracts, and now, swept along by sheer momentum, were busily signing each other. As far as the eye could see, at tables in the background, gourmets were gorging themselves on chicken-giblet-and-cream-cheese sandwiches, apple pandowdy, and orange snow. One fine old epicure, who had ordered a sizzling platter without specifying what food was to be on it, was nevertheless eating the platter itself and smacking his lips noisily. Small wonder that several world-famed illustrators, among them Henry Raleigh, Norman Rockwell, and Pruett Carter, had set up easels and were limning the brilliant scene with swift strokes. I was drinking in every detail of the shifting panorama when a hostess well over nine feet tall, with ice mantling her summit, waved me toward a door marked "Credentials."

"We—we just wanted the old-fashioned nut pudding with ice-cream sauce, Ma'am," I stammered.

"That's up to the committee, Moozeer," she said briskly. "If we let in every Tom, Dick, and Harry who wanted the old-fashioned nut pudding with ice-cream sauce—ah, good evening, Contessa! Back from Hobe Sound already?"

I entered a small room exquisitely furnished in Biedermeier and took my place in a short queue of applicants. Most of them were obviously under tension, and the poor wretch in front of me was a pitiable spectacle. His eyes rolled wildly, tremors shook his frame, and it was apparent he entertained small hope of meeting the rigorous requirements.

"What have Kaufman and Hart got that I haven't got?" he demanded of me desperately. "I bought a house in Bucks County and wrote two plays, both smash hits, even if they didn't come to New York. Why, you ought to see the reviews 'Tea and Strumpets' and 'Once in a Wifetime' got in Syracuse!" I reassured him as best I could, but his premonitions were well founded, for a few moments later he was ignominiously dispatched to dine at a cafeteria. I was shuffling forward to confront the tight-lipped examiners when a scuffle broke out in the foyer and Kaufman and Hart, bundled in astrakhan greatcoats and their eyes flashing fire, were herded in unceremoniously.

"What is the meaning of this—this bestiality?" sputtered Hart. "How dare you bar us from this bourgeois *bistro*?"

"I've been thrown out of better restaurants than this!" boomed Kaufman, rapidly naming several high-class restaurants from which he had been ejected. The chairman of the board picked up a dossier and turned a cold smile on the playwrights.

"Naturally, we regret any inconvenience to you gentlemen," he said smoothly, "but our house rules are inflexible. You have a play called 'Lady in the Dark,' have you not, Mr. Hart?" Hart regarded him stonily. "With Gertrude Lawrence, I believe?"

"Yes," snapped Hart, "and she's sitting right up at the fountain this minute having a rum-and-butter-toffee sundae with chopped pecans."

"Why were we not shown the script of that play, Mr. Hart?" The chairman's voice was silky with menace. "Why was nobody in the Frank G. Shattuck organization consulted regarding casting?"

"I—I meant to," quavered Hart. "I swear I did! I told my secretary—I made a note—"

"Thought you'd smuggle it into town without us, did you?" snarled the chairman. "Let 'em read the out-of-town notices in *Variety*, eh?" A tide of crimson welled up the alabaster column of Hart's neck, and he stood downcast, staring at his toecaps. Kaufman would fain have interceded for his associate, but the chairman stopped him with a curt gesture.

"Hamburg Heaven for thirty days," he barked. "Take 'em away."

"No, no—not that, not that!" screamed the luckless duo, attempting to embrace the chairman's knees. But no vestige of pity lurked in that granite visage, and an instant later they were borne, kicking and squealing, from the chamber by two brawny attendants.

And now little else remains to be told. How I managed to elude my captors and steal the superb mocha cupcake the natives call The Star of Forty-third Street Between Sixth Avenue and Broadway must be left to another chronicle. Suffice to say that whenever your mother and I pass Schrafft's, she turns to me with a secret smile and we continue right on up to Lindy's. We can still get in there without a visa.

Bend Down, Sister

UNLESS THE *New York Times* is publishing a special edition for me alone, which would be adorable of them but rather wasteful, eyes must have popped like champagne corks the other weekend at an article in the Sunday magazine section. I rarely stray into the intimate feminine pages at the back, but I was pursuing a runover and, before I could rein in, crashed into the seraglio. I was tiptoeing out with flaming cheeks, half expecting the palace janissaries to pounce on me, when I tripped over a beauty forecast wedged in between an advertisement for Up-Rays, the V Bra, and another recounting the anguish of a matron whose slip rode up over her knees while she was reviewing troops. The author was Martha Parker, a publicist with whose work I was unfamiliar and may continue to be for some time to come. In fact, I may very well confine all future reading to clinical thermometers until the throbbing subsides.

Writing in the breathlessly waggish style dear to fashion analysts, Miss Parker treats of the readjustments women will make this autumn through curtailment of beauty aids. These range from obvious economies, like synthetic stockings, to pretty complex tinkering with the ductless glands. "The woman of the hour," advises Miss Parker, with cool disregard for natural history, "will be of slender dimensions for her pencil-slim skirts, her ankles well-turned for her low heeled walking shoes." Naturally, Miss Parker cannot reveal her sources, but this is more than a hint that the thyroid has aligned itself with the United Nations and that stylish stouts everywhere will awake to find themselves dryads. The transformation, of course, will demand a certain amount of homework:

> She will learn to take the cricks out of weary arches with gentle pressure under the metatarsals and strategic tweakings of tensed-up toes.

The scene falls readily into focus: the group of earnest, pencil-slim patriots gathered in a boudoir whose location is a military secret, gravely fondling their toes and outlining foot strategy for the morrow.

If Miss Parker set out to paint a romantic portrait of her sex preserving its glamour under duress, her hand shook in the process, for her heroine fits more neatly into a Bela Lugosi film than a salon. "The war-conscious woman will parsimoniously melt the stubby ends of lipsticks and pour them into a little paint pot for use with a brush," she predicts. "She will stow her perfume away in the darkest shadows and she will supplement it with a matching cologne to use on hair and furs, and eventually for thinning purposes." I don't know whether I care for this grubby, avaricious creature tittering over her crucibles, and I suspect Miss Parker shared my revulsion, as she adds quickly:

> Well-tubbed and well-scrubbed is the woman of the hour, with the saucy crispness of a small girl's pinafore. She lathers her face with a whipped-cream soap or a sturdy cleansing powder with soot-dispatching granules.

Frankly, I lost my footing in the swirl of imagery and, when I caught up with my guide, she was continuing her lyric tally thus:

> She has a night emollient, as soft and rich as Winter ermine, for wind-whipped cheeks, and a giant jar (made, amazingly, of polished cardboard) filled with cleansing cream of the sound and simple sort.

Why polished cardboard should evoke anyone's amazement is a trifle obscure; I personally found the following rococo item about lipsticks a good deal more surprising:

> Brilliant, sparkling reds will complement the bright, new beauty of Fall fashions and accent the subtle reserve of pale Priority beiges and greiges.

At this juncture I fell into one of my rare, unaccountable reiges and flung the *New York Times* magazine from me, demolishing a lamp but effectively breaking Miss Parker's spell.

Unfortunately, whatever nemesis had singled me out was merely allowing me a breather. Half an hour later, snatching at the first available bit of letterpress to beguile my lunch, I turned up a treatise by Natacha Rambova in the July *Harper's Bazaar*.

Under the title of "Strength . . . Serenity . . . Security," the former Mrs. Valentino listed a series of disciplines for milady's body and mind. The first was so provocative I automatically obeyed it:

> Go to your mirror. Look first at your eyes. Then your mouth. What do they tell you? Are the eyes clear and serene? The mouth relaxed and humorous?—*Humor is our most valuable asset*, indispensable in any emergency.

The eyes, I was enchanted to discover, were as clear and serene as a St. Bernard's, with the same attractive Dubonnet trim; the mouth was relaxed to the point of imbecility. Humor was there also, though somewhat obscured by a smear of oatmeal. It made me jubilant that I possessed a quality which would stop the enemy paratrooper in his tracks. I determined, at my first opportunity, to compile an assortment of Japanese quips to deflect his bayonet and render him helpless with mirth.

The physical exercises to develop these natural gifts, however, were a good deal more strenuous. "Stand up and face the window," the text advised. "Place the feet in a parallel line about eight inches apart. Empty the lungs by exhaling and coughing softly. Then inhale and *very slowly* lift the arms from the sides above the head." The unwonted effort and the strain of keeping my eyes pinned to the directions resulted in sudden vertigo, and I hastily switched to the next drill:

> Close your eyes and breathe *slowly*. Rhythmically. Listen for your heart beat and *hear it slow down* in keeping with your quiet rhythmic breathing. *Slow down your breathing.*

I slowed it down to the approximate speed of Kamongo, the lungfish of the Nile, and was pervaded by a jolly floating sensation akin to that produced by Sedormid, but cheaper. My woolly torpor was marred, nevertheless, by the suspicion that there must be some more immediate method of winning a war. Miss Rambova had anticipated that objection. "Put the hands down under the buttocks," she commanded (a fairly direct approach on such short acquaintance, I must say), "and raise both legs in the air. They should form the V for Victory as you shake them loosely." I was just becoming proficient in this gymnastic when I looked up to find the building superintendent

watching me intently from the doorway. Welcoming the emergency, I promptly brought my most valuable asset into play.
"Guess this'll jar the old Axis, eh, pal?" I commented slyly. My
pal made a significant sucking sound through his teeth and
retired to phone the landlord. Well, let them try to evict me is
all I say. I'll just flop down and give them the old V for Victory.

Beauty and the Bee

IT IS always something of a shock to approach a newsstand which handles trade publications and find the *Corset and Underwear Review* displayed next to the *American Bee Journal*. However, newsstands make strange bedfellows, as anyone who has ever slept with a newsstand can testify, and if you think about it at all (instead of sitting there in a torpor with your mouth half-open) you'd see this proximity is not only alphabetical. Both the *Corset and Underwear Review* and the *American Bee Journal* are concerned with honeys, and although I am beast enough to prefer a photograph of a succulent nymph in satin Lastex Girdleiere with Thrill Plus Bra to the most dramatic snapshot of an apiary, each has its place in my scheme.

The *Corset and Underwear Review*, which originates at the Haire Publishing Company, 1170 Broadway, New York City, is a magazine for jobbers. Whatever else a corset jobber is, he is certainly nobody's fool. The first seventy pages of the magazine comprise an album of superbly formed models posed in various attitudes of sweet surrender and sheathed in cunning artifices of whalebone, steel, and webbing. Some indication of what Milady uses to give herself a piquant front elevation may be had from the following list of goodies displayed at the Hotel McAlpin Corset Show, reported by the March, 1935, *Corset and Underwear Review*: "Flashes and Filmys, Speedies and Flexees, Sensations and Thrills, Snugfits and Even-Puls, Rite-Flex and Free-Flex, Smoothies and Silk-Skins, Imps and Teens, La Triques and Waikikis, Sis and Modern Miss, Sta-Downs and Props, Over-Tures and Reflections, Lilys and Irenes, Willo-th-wisps and Willoways, Miss Smartie and MisSimplicity, Princess Youth and Princess Chic, Miss Today and Soiree, Kordettes and Francettes, Paristyles and Rengo Belts, Vassarettes and Foundettes, Fans and Fade Aways, Beau Sveltes and Beau Formas, Madame Adrienne and Miss Typist, Stout-eze and Laceze, Symphony and Rhapsody, Naturade and Her Secret, Rollees and Twin Tops, Charma and V-Ette, La Camille and La Tec."

My neck, ordinarily an alabaster column, began to turn a dull red as I forged through the pages of the *Corset and*

Underwear Review into the section called "Buyer News." Witness the leering sensuality of a poem by Mrs. Adelle Mahone, San Francisco representative of the Hollywood-Maxwell Company, whom the magazine dubs "The Brassière Bard of the Bay District":

> Out-of-town buyers!—during your stay
> At the McAlpin, see our new display.
> There are bras for the young, support for the old,
> Up here for the shy, down to there for the bold.
> We'll have lace and nets and fabrics such as
> Sturdy broadcloths and satins luscious.
> We'll gladly help your profits transform
> If you'll come up to our room and watch us perform.
> Our new numbers are right from the Coast:
> Snappy and smart, wait!—we must not boast—
> We'll just urge you to come and solicit your smiles,
> So drop in and order your Hollywood styles.

One leaves the lacy *chinoiseries* of the *Corset and Underwear Review* with reluctance and turns to the bucolic *American Bee Journal*, published at Hamilton, Illinois, by C. P. Dadant. Here Sex is whittled down to a mere nubbin; everything is as clean as a whistle and as dull as a hoe. The bee is the bourgeois of the insect world, and his keeper is a self-sufficient stooge who needs and will get no introduction to you. The pages of the *American Bee Journal* are studded with cocky little essays like "Need of Better Methods of Controlling American Foulbrood" and "The Swarming Season in Manitoba." It is only in "The Editor's Answers," a query column conducted by Mr. Dadant, that Mr. Average Beekeeper removes his mask and permits us to peep at the warm, vibrant human beneath. The plight of the reader who signs himself "Illinois" (I've seen *that* name somewhere) is typical:

> I would like to know the easiest way to get a swarm of bees which are lodged in between the walls of a house. The walls are of brick and they are in the dead-air space. They have been there for about three years. I would like to know method to use to get the bees, not concerned about the honey.

The editor dismisses the question with some claptrap about a "bee smoker" which is too ridiculous to repeat. The best bet I see for "Illinois" is to play upon the weakness of all bees. Take a small boy smeared with honey and lower him between the walls. The bees will fasten themselves to him by the hundreds and can be scraped off when he is pulled up, after which the boy can be thrown away. If no small boy smeared with honey can be found, it may be necessary to take an ordinary small boy and smear him, which should be a pleasure.

From the Blue Grass comes an even more perplexed letter:

> I have been ordering a few queens every year and they are always sent as first-class mail and are thrown off the fast trains that pass here at a speed of 60 miles an hour. Do you think it does the queens any harm by throwing them off these fast trains? You know they get an awful jolt when they hit the ground. Some of these queens are very slow about doing anything after they are put in the hive.—KENTUCKY.

I have no desire to poach on George Cable's domain, but if that isn't the furthest North in Southern gallantry known to man, I'll eat his collected works in Macy's window at high noon. It will interest every lover of chivalry to know that since the above letter was published, queen bees in the Blue Grass have been treated with new consideration by railroad officials. A Turkey-red carpet similar to that used by the Twentieth Century is now unrolled as the train stops, and each queen, blushing to the very roots of her antennæ, is escorted to her hive by a uniformed porter. The rousing strains of the cakewalk, the comical antics of the darkies, the hiss of fried chicken sputtering in the pan, all combine to make the scene unforgettable.

But the predicaments of both "Illinois" and "Kentucky" pale into insignificance beside the problem presented by another reader:

> I have been asked to "talk on bees" at a nearby church some evening in the fall. Though I have kept bees for ten years, I am "scared stiff" because not a man in the audience knows a thing about bees and I am afraid of being too technical.
>
> I plan to take along specimens of queen, drone and worker, also a glass observatory hive with bees, smoker and tools, an extra hive, and possibly some queen cell cups, etc.

Could you suggest any manipulating that might be done for the "edification of the audience"? I've seen pictures of stunts that have been worked, like making a beard of bees; and I've heard of throwing the bees out in a ball only to have them return to the hive without bothering anyone. But, I don't know how these stunts are done, nor do I know of any that I could do with safety. (I don't mind getting a sting or two myself, but I don't want anyone in the audience to get stung, or I might lose my audience.)

I've only opened hives a few times at night, but never liked the job as the bees seem to fly up into the light and sting very readily. That makes me wonder whether any manipulating can be done in a room at night.

How long before the affair would I need to have the bees in the room to have them settle down to the hive?—NEW YORK.

The only thing wrong with "New York" is that he just doesn't like *bees*. In one of those unbuttoned moods everybody has, a little giddy with cocoa and crullers, he allowed himself to be cajoled by the vestrymen, and now, face to face with his ordeal, he is sick with loathing for bees and vestrymen alike. There is one solution, however, and that is for "New York" to wrap himself tightly in muslin the night of the lecture and stay in bed with his hat on. If the vestrymen come for him, let him throw the bees out in a ball. To hell with whether they return or not, and that goes for the vestrymen, too. It certainly goes for me. If I ever see the postman trudging toward my house with a copy of the *American Bee Journal*, I'm going to lodge myself in the dead-air space between the walls and no amount of small boys smeared with honey will ever get me out. And you be careful, *American Bee Journal*—I *bite*.

Button, Button, Who's Got the Blend?

ABOUT EIGHT o'clock last night I was lounging at the corner of Hollywood Boulevard and Vine Street, an intersection celebrated in the eclogues of Louella Parsons and Ed Sullivan, waiting for a pert baggage who had agreed to accompany me to a double feature. If I bore myself with a certain assurance, it was because I had chosen my wardrobe with some care—a shower-of-hail suit, lilac gloves, a split-sennit boater, and a light whangee cane. Altogether, I had reason for self-satisfaction; I had dined famously off a charmburger and a sky-high malt, my cigar was drawing well, and the titles of the pictures I was about to witness, "Block That Kiss" and "Khaki Buckaroo," augured gales of merriment. For a moment high spirits tempted me to invest in a box of maxixe cherries or fondant creams for my vis-à-vis, but after due reflection I fought back the impulse. How utterly cloying, how anticlimactic sweets would be after the speeches I had in store for the pretty creature!

Weary at last of studying the colorful throng eddying past me (I had already singled out Eddy Duchin, Sherwood Eddy, Eddie Cantor, Nelson Eddy, and Eddie Robinson), I fell to examining a nearby billboard. The advertisement was one of that familiar type in which an entire cross section of the population seems to be rhapsodizing about the product—in this case, a delicacy named Hostess Cup Cakes. "You should hear my bridge club rave about those Hostess Cup Cakes," an excited housewife was babbling to her friend, whose riposte was equally feverish: "I wouldn't dare pack John's lunch without putting in Hostess Cup Cakes!" Close by, a policeman smiled benignly at a baby in a carriage, addressing its mother with, "You have a lot of time for 'Precious' these afternoons, Mrs. Jones." The reason for Mrs. Jones' leisure was not unpredictable: "That's because it's easy to plan desserts with Hostess Cup Cakes." The baby itself was making no contribution to the symposium; apparently the kitten had got hold of its tongue, but you could tell from its expression that it would creep a mile for a cup cake. It was, however, with a dialogue between two small boys that the copywriter kindled my interest into flame.

"Hurry!" one of them was admonishing the other. "I've got 5¢ for Hostess Cup Cakes!" "Oh, boy!" chortled his companion. "Do I love that *secret chocolate blend*!"

Although the romantic possibilities of a secret chocolate blend and its theft by the spies of an enemy power are undeniable, I think that behind the phrase there lurks a warmer, more personal story. Naturally, the brief harlequinade which follows can indicate no more than its highlights, but if the Hostess Cup Cake people care to endow me for the next few months, I could expand it into a three-act version, suitable for annual presentation at Hollywood and Vine. I have no further use for that corner, or, may I add, for my *petite amie*, who turned up sobbing drunk with a Marine on either arm:

(*Scene: The office of Dirk van Bensdorp, president and general manager of the Hostess Cup Cake Corporation. As the curtain rises, Dirk, a forceful executive, is reading a lecture to his ne'er-do-well nephew, Jan Gluten, a minor employee of the firm. The latter, besmocked and befuddled, fidgets nervously with an icing gun. His eyes are puffy with lack of sleep and the little lines radiating from his nose attest eloquently to fondness for the grape.*)

DIRK (*warningly*): Now, look here, my boy, I'm going to talk to you like a Dutch uncle. Bakery circles are abuzz with your escapades. You had better mend your ways ere I lose patience.

JAN (*surlily*): Aw, can de sermon.

DIRK: It's a stench in the nostrils of the cup-cake trade— throwing away your guilders on fly chorus girls and driving your Stutz Bearcat in excess of sixty M.P.H.

JAN (*lighting a cigarette with nicotine-stained fingers*): I'm getting sick of dis joint. Every time I take a schnapps or two wit' de fellers, some willy boy splits on me to de front office.

DIRK (*severely*): It's your work that gives you away, my fine fellow. That last tray of fig bars you frosted was a botch!

JAN (*lamely*): Dere was a fly in de amber icing.

DIRK: Excuses, excuses! Why, the complaints I've had about your work would almost fill a book. (*He holds up a book almost filled with complaints about Jan's work, a first edition.*) And what's this about the attentions you have been paying a certain raven-haired miss in the custard division?

JAN (*fiercely*): You keep Lorene Flake's name out of dis, d'ye hear?

DIRK (*aside*): I see I have touched the lad in a vulnerable spot. This seems to be more than mere philandering.

JAN: Lorene's decent, and clean, and—and fine! She's straight as a string, I tell you!

DIRK (*who loves a good joke now and then*): That's probably why you're "knots" about her—ha-ha-ha!

JAN: Sharrap.

DIRK (*earnestly*): Why not prove yourself to the girl, Jan? Eschew your dubious associates and turn over a new chocolate leaf.

JAN: Hully gee, I ain't fit to kiss de hem of her slacks.

DIRK: Do your job and you'll win through. Make the cup cakes fly under your fingers!

JAN (*cynically*): Dat's slave psychology. Youse is attempting to fob off de speed-up system under de cloak of benevolent paternalism. (*He exits.*)

DIRK: Ah, well, there's good stuff in the boy. I was the same at his age.

(*Ten Eyck, the shop foreman, bursts in, his face ashen.*)

TEN EYCK (*panting*): The formula—

DIRK: What is it, man? What's happened?

TEN EYCK: The secret chocolate blend—gone—stolen!

DIRK (*sputtering*): Ten thousand devils! But I locked it in the safe myself last night!

TEN EYCK: I found the door wrenched off, beside it an acetylene torch and a complete set of burglar's tools.

DIRK (*instantly*): Someone must have opened the safe by force!

(*A heavy footfall is heard on the stair.*)

TEN EYCK: Why, who can that be?

DIRK: God grant that it may be Inspector Bunce, he who gave us such material assistance in that mysterious affair of the oatmeal cookies! (*His prayers are answered; Bunce enters, looks about him keenly.*) Inspector, our secret choc—

BUNCE: Yes, I know. When I find a safe prised open, a series of unfrosted cup cakes, and two middle-aged bakers in a notable state of agitation, the conclusions are fairly obvious.

DIRK: You mean that the finger of suspicion points to Loose-Wiles, the Thousand Window Bakeries, whose agents have recently been skulking about in dirty gray caps and gooseneck sweaters?

BUNCE: This is an inside job, Bensdorp. I should like a few words with your nephew.

DIRK (*paling*): Surely you don't believe Jan—

BUNCE: Please be good enough to call him. (*Dirk, bewildered, presses a button and Jan shuffles in sullenly.*) Well, Gluten, still sticking to your story?

JAN (*sneering*): I ain't got nuttin' else to add, see? I pinched de secret chocolate plans to pay for de extravagances of an actress I was infatuated wit'. It's an oft-told story, rendered none de less sordid by repetition.

BUNCE (*with deadly calm*): One moment. *Why are you shielding Vernon Flake?*

JAN (*roughly*): I never heard of de cove. Come on, clap de darbies on me wrists. I'm ready to face de music.

BUNCE: It won't wash, Jan. You found Vernon, Lorene's worthless brother, crouched before the safe and to protect the girl you love you have shouldered the blame yourself!

JAN (*modestly*): Any bloke in me shoes would have done de equivalent.

DIRK: Hooray! I was convinced of his innocence at all times!

JAN (*producing a cinnamon bun*): And here is de formula inside dis sweetmeat, where de luckless Vernon hid it for safekeeping.

BUNCE: You've a smart cub there, Bensdorp. Nephews of his stripe don't grow on trees. (*Reaching for his Persian slipper*) Well, Ten Eyck, what do you say to Sarasate at the Albert Hall tonight, eh?

TEN EYCK: Capital, my dear Bunce.

(*They exit.*)

DIRK (*embracing Jan*): Well, you young rascal, you shall have your reward for this. Henceforth our Friday specials will be known as "Cub Cakes" in your honor—and remember, there's always room for brains at the top in this organization.

JAN (*surreptitiously pocketing his uncle's stickpin*): You said a mout'ful, cul.

CURTAIN

Swing Out, Sweet Chariot

A FEW DAYS ago I happened into my newsdealer's for ten cents' worth of licorice whips and the autumn issue of *Spindrift*, a rather advanced quarterly review in which I had been following an exciting serial called "Mysticism in the Rationalist Cosmogony, or John Dewey Rides Again." In the previous number, the cattle rustlers (post-Hegelian dogma) had trapped Professor Dewey in an abandoned mine shaft (Jamesian pragmatism) and had ignited the fuse leading to a keg of dynamite (neo-Newtonian empiricism). Naturally, I was simmering with impatience to learn how the Morningside Kid would escape from this fix, and I lost no time getting back to my rooms in the Middle Temple and stuffing my crusty old brier with shag. The gesture turned out to be singularly appropriate, for I shortly discovered that my newsdealer had made a mistake in his excitement and that I would have to spend the evening with a journal called *The Jitterbug*.

The Jitterbug is a febrile paper published bimonthly by the Lex Publications, Inc., of 381 Fourth Avenue, devoted to the activities of alligators, hep-cats, and *exaltés* of swing everywhere. These activities, which consist in hurling one another violently about to popular music, riding astride one another, and generally casting out devils, are portrayed in ten or fifteen pages of photographs and cartoons that need no explanation. What will bear a little exegesis, however, is the text of the half-dozen short stories and articles. Were it not for the glossary of swing terms thoughtfully supplied by the management at the very outset, the magazine might as well be couched in Chinook. It may not concern anybody vitally that a "Scobo queen" is a girl jitterbug, that "frisking the whiskers" is warming up, that a "zeal girl" is a hot girl dancer, or that a "wheat bender" is one who plays sweet music instead of swing, but if you expect to translate such stories as "Jazz Beau," "Riffin' on the Range," and "Noodling with Love" without the aid of a pony, you are one hep-cat indeed.

The qualifications of a working jitterbug are succinctly set forth in the national organization's membership blank, which appears on page 21. It reads:

> This is to certify that —— is a jiving, hot-hosing Jitterbug, a member of the Community of Hep-Cats, and as such entitled to beat it out whenever the music swings out high, wide, and gutbucket.

The characters involved in the afore-mentioned stories are all that and more. For example, Cal Leonard, the protagonist of "Jazz Beau," is described as "a pair of Mack Truck shoulders, a grinning mouth, and wild, flame-blue eyes." I suppose there was a body linking these goodies together, but the pace is so staccato that the author neglects to mention it. Debby Waite, of "Noodling with Love," on the other hand, has body and to spare, judging from the following tender blueprint:

> Her thick, curly red-gold hair was kind of piled up on top and around her head, and it made a shining halo that framed the white oval of her face. Those sultry lips of hers were red and glistening under the lights, and her gray eyes sparkled like hot rhythm. Debby's figure was never anything to be missed, but in the two years since I'd seen her, several delectable curves I remembered had ripened. And the dress she was wearing wasn't calculated to hide that fact. Its full chiffon skirt tantalized by its seeming transparency, and it clung to the soft roundness of her hips with loving closeness. The waist was high and tight, and above that rose to shields that fitted snugly over the proud mounds of her swelling breasts.

In fine, a Schrafft's Luxuro ice-cream sundae come to life; and, as though I were not overheated enough already, the author has to pile Pelion on Ossa by telling me this glorious blob of girlhood was educated at Bennington. Look, dear, I wouldn't care if she had quit school in the sixth grade.

The plots of the short stories in my copy of *Jitterbug* are fairly basic: Scobo queen meets hep-cat, they find mutual release in barrelhouse or gut-bucket, and eventually, on the winsome revelation that one or the other is heir to half a million rugs, shag, peck, and paw their way to the altar. "Jazz Beau" may serve as a clinical example. A young lady describing herself as a Taxi-Tessie or wriggle-wren employed at the Roselane Ball-room is lured into a Broadway movie theatre by the harmonies of one Biggie Barnett and his band:

> I heard the wail of a wah-wah pump, the staccatoed stutter of skins. . . . My heart began to thump and swell with the fever of rhythm. I giggled out loud. Crazily, I slid to a stop at the aisle, in the theatre proper, scanned the seats. Full. I felt my breasts tremor angrily.

This mysterious physiological reaction, no doubt experienced by every woman at the sight of an S.R.O. sign, yields to a state bordering on epilepsy when the band really starts giving:

> I began to sway in my seat. My lashes fluttered. My head bobbed in time with the red hot ride rhythm. Jittersauce began to burn up my bloodstream.

At this point, as the *cognoscenti* begin stomping and trucking freely about in a delirium of pleasure, the surrealist owner of the Mack Truck shoulders, grinning mouth, and wild flame-blue eyes enters the proceedings:

> "Lookee," the big guy whispered, "I've *got* to get out in that aisle and whip my dogs! Do we team up? A big gazabo like me is gonna look awfully silly getting off a solo!"

Hesitating a split second lest her suppliant turn out to be a geep, or wolf, Miss Prim surrenders to his emotional plea and joins the gavotte:

> While those cats up on the stage clambaked like nobody's business, my partner and I really cut that rug. . . . All I was conscious of was the driving syncopation and lift of agony pipes, the noodling of the brass section, as barrelhouse blasts whipped my slender legs and weaving hips into a rhythmic frenzy. We did the Suzy-Q. We shagged and pecked.

His skin glowing mildly from this preliminary workout, Cal declares his intention of making a night of it. "My sox are hell-hot and I've got to hop till I wear holes in my soles to cool them off," he avers, and his escort, whose disposition is no less elastic than her frame, readily assents. "We strutted and stuffed to burning boogie-woogie, stayed in the groove un-til we were both beat right down," she whispers shyly to her diary. Thereupon, in a passage as salty as any you will find in the Kamasutra, the gymnasts take leave of each other until the following evening, when Cal "came swaggering into Roselane looking like a color-page from *Esquire*." Maybe the engraver's hand slipped, but the last color-page from *Esquire* I saw was slightly off register and showed a junior executive with a flesh-colored suit and a pale-blue herringbone face. Had Cal worn something of the sort, however, he could hardly have caused a greater sensation. In a trice the other hostesses cluster excitedly about his affinity, asking whether she knows Cal's father is a millionaire motor magnate in Detroit. The little lady loves Cal for his floy floy alone, and her disillusion and heartbreak are such that she is almost thirty seconds recovering from the shock. "You don't think of those things when you're with a guy who's slowly driving you screwball with love," she observes with icy disdain. Perhaps not, puss, but it certainly wouldn't do any harm to look the old gent up in Dun & Bradstreet—now, would it? I mean just for the heck of it.

Follows an interval of courtship in which, fanned by love and jive, Cal's passion mounts to a crescendo. He becomes a nightly visitor to Roselane, buying rolls of dance tickets and "paying out a small fortune" (probably upward of three dollars in a single evening) to keep off poachers. A drunken geep who engages our miss in the Portland fancy finds himself "bounced off two walls after Cal hit him." But Cal's importunate proposals of marriage are met with the only answer a high-grade heroine of fiction can give: "Everyone would think I was wedding you for your papa's shekels. You'd even think it yourself, after the romance wore off." The chilling presentiment of a loveless union between two graying jitterbugs retired to the bench and soaking their feet in a pail of Tiz nevertheless fails to dissuade Cal: "He begged. He pleaded. He made love with words [the last desperate throw of the dice] like Red Norvo swings 'Reverie.'" Yet all to no avail, for in a scene of renunciation worthy of Tolstoy (not Leo Tolstoy; a man I know named Charlie Tolstoy), the narrator gives the mitten to "the one and only guy who had played on my heart strings like a bass-man picks at a belly fiddle."

And now, in a Garrison finish, Cal calls forth the tenacity and cunning that have made his father a caution in the automotive

industry. He retains two geeps to enter Roselane, trip up his inamorata while dancing with her, and so humiliate her that she
is forced to resign her post. This incomprehensibly restores the
social equation between the lovers and sends them on a honeymoon wherein they "shagged and trucked and Suzy-Q-ed
and hugged and kissed." The narrative concludes, "Anyhow,
when two alligators get together and love sets in, you've got
something."

I'll say I have, sister. Did you ever hear tell of migraine?

A Couple of Quick Ones: Two Portraits

I. ARTHUR KOBER

PICTURE TO yourself a ruddy-cheeked, stocky sort of chap, dressed in loose but smelly tweeds, a stubby briar between his teeth (it has resisted the efforts of the best surgeons to extract it), with a firm yet humorous mouth, generous to a fault, ever-ready for a flagon of nut-brown ale with his cronies, possessing the courage of a lion, the tenderness of a Florence Nightingale, and the conceit of a diva, an intellectual vagabond, a connoisseur of first editions, fine vintages, and beautiful women, well above six feet in height and distinguished for his pallor, a dweller in the world of books, his keen gray eye belying the sensual lip beneath, equally at home browsing through the bookstalls along Fourth Avenue and rubbing elbows (his own elbows) in the smart literary salons of 57th Street, a rigid abstainer and non-smoker who lives entirely on dehydrated fruits, cereals, and nuts, rarely leaving his monastic cell nowadays except to dine at the Salmagundi; an intimate of Cocteau, Picasso, Joyce and Lincoln Kirstein, a dead shot, a past master of the foils and the International Woodmen of the World, dictating his novels, plays, poems, short stories, *commedias dell' arte*, aphorisms, and ripostes at lightning speed to a staff of underpaid secretaries, an expert judge of horseflesh, the owner of a model farm equipped with the most slovenly dairy devices—a man as sharp as a razor, as dull as a hoe, as clean as a whistle, as tough as nails, as white as snow, as black as the raven's wing, as poor as Job, a man up with the lark, down on your toes, and gone with the wind. A man kind and captious, sweet and sour, fat and thin, tall and short, racked with fever, plagued by the locust, beset by witches, hagridden, cross-grained, fancy-free, a funloving, addle-pated dreamer, visionary, and slippered pantaloon. Picture to yourself such a man, I say, and you won't have the faintest conception of Arthur Kober.

To begin with, the author of *Having Wonderful Time*, *My Dear Bella* and *Thunder Over the Bronx*, is only eighteen inches high. He is very sensitive about his stature and goes out only after dark, and then armed with a tiny umbrella with which he beats off cats who try to attack him. Not that he is antipathetic to cats; far from it. He loves tabbies of all kinds and has done everything to encourage a reciprocal feeling in them, even going so far as to roll in catnip nightly, but there is something about Kober that just makes cats' nerves tingle. Since he is unable to climb into his bed, which is at least two feet taller than himself, he has been forced to sleep in the lowest drawer of a bureau since childhood, and is somewhat savage as a result. He is meticulously dressed, however, and never goes abroad without his green cloth gloves and neat nankeen breeches.

His age is a matter of speculation. He claims to remember the Battle of the Boyne and on a fine night his piping may be heard in the glen, his voice lifted in the strains of *For She's My Molly-O*. Of one thing we can be sure; he was seen by unimpeachable witnesses at Austerlitz, Jena, and Wagram, where he made personal appearances through the courtesy of his agent, Milton Fink of the Fink and Biesmyer office. It is also fairly certain that he first conceived the idea of naming blucher shoes in honor of the gruff Marshal after Waterloo. That he invented the Welsbach mantle is not only improbable but downright foolish. The Welsbach mantle was invented by Teddy Welsbach, and there are plenty of the old Chalkstone Avenue gang left to prove it.

What I like most about Kober is his mouth, a jagged magenta wound etched against the unforgettable blankness of his face. It is a bright flag of surrender, a dental challenge. I love his sudden impish smile, the twinkle of his alert green eyes, and the print of his cloven foot in the shrubbery. I love the curly brown locks cascading down his receding forehead; I love the Mendelian characteristics he has inherited from his father Mendel; I love the wind in the willows, the boy in the bush, and the Seven against Thebes. I love coffee, I love tea, I love the girls, and the girls love me. And I'm going to be a civil engineer when I grow up, no matter what Mamma says.

At first blush one is inclined to wonder at the wedding of this strange talent with that of Marc Connelly, whose production and direction of *Having Wonderful Time* made his name a household word from McKeesport, Pennsylvania, to the Shanghai Bund. Connelly, the gruff, brown-faced old salt who served under Teach, Lafitte, Flint (ay, Flint, there was the flower of the flock, was Flint) and every notable buccaneer who ever careened his rakish black craft along the Caribbean; Connelly, known aboard all the pearling luggers out of Thursday Island with a cargo of shell; Connelly, the mere mention of whom would strike terror into the denizens of boozing-kens in Paramaribo and shebeens in Belfast; Connelly, with his black varnished straw hat and parrot on his shoulder, ready to swarm up the mizzen at the first shrill of the bos'n's fife; a powder-monkey under Nelson, gunners' mate under Klaw and Erlanger, and supercargo under the Shuberts. Lingering over your gin *pahit* on the porch of Shepheard's Hotel in Cairo, you will be told that if you remain there long enough Willie Maugham, Marc Connelly, and little black specks will pass before your eyes. It is no idle boast.

How, then, did Arthur Kober and Marc Connelly meet and conceive the idea of *Having Wonderful Time*? You must see in your mind's eye a tiny village in the Swiss Alps. The tinkle of bells in the distance heralds a herd of grazing cows and promises innumerable cakes of Peter's Milk Chocolate; nearby a smiling peasant who looks like the tyrant Gessler shucks almonds for the toothsome candy-bars. Across yonder snow-capped peaks Hannibal led his swaying elephants into Cisalpine Gaul. The station platform, deserted until now, suddenly becomes the scene of an altercation. At the railway bookstall, Kober, dressed in his favorite costume, a gunny sack and a pair of Thom McAn shoes, is glaring at the attendant, who has just accused him of stealing a banana. Kober's Italian is imperfect, his French is as faulty as his German, and his English is no bargain either. Haltingly he begins to explain to the attendant that he is innocent and that what is happening to him shouldn't happen to a Schnauzer. Unbeknownst to both, a dusty and middle-aged gentleman has moved a bit closer. He looks very much like the Father Brown of the immortal detective stories except that he is not dressed as a priest and he has absolutely no talent as a sleuth. This is Marc Connelly, fresh from a holiday in Paris; even now, unknown to the French *Sûreté*, the famous painting of Mona Lisa is wrapped around his body. Immediately a tensity is felt on the platform, and its sole other occupant, a St. Bernard dog, resumes scratching its fleas. A few quiet words spoken out of the side of Connelly's mouth, Kober returns the banana, and the two men fall into conversation.

Over a table in a quiet *bierstube*, Connelly learns with some surprise that Kober has written a play. Connelly, in his spare time the author of *The Wisdom Tooth*, the coauthor of *Beggar on Horseback*, *Dulcy*, *To the Ladies*, and *The Farmer Takes a Wife*, his ears still pink from the plaudits he earned from *The Green Pastures*, looks at the youth with interest. Has Kober the play with him? The words have barely escaped him before the young man whips open his satchel and is thumbing the pages of *Having Wonderful Time*, chuckling over the jokes, guffawing over the stage directions, and generally giving the waiters the horrors. Connelly, recalling the incident, winces, "Frankly, I was nonplussed. The color drained away from beneath my ordinarily healthy tan and was replaced by a greenish mixture composed of 2 gr. sodium Amytal, .005 spirits of benzoin, and a cup of farina. I realized that I would have to quiet this extraordinary individual, even at the cost of producing his play." And before he knew it, Connelly, who hates a scene, had secured a signature on a minimum basic contract from Kober, who loves a scene. The effect was more soothing than even Connelly had dreamed. At once fun and jollity reigned supreme. Kober strummed a lively air on his balalaika, cocoa and "hot wieners" were the order of the day, and Connelly, always irrepressible, found a false nose in his luggage and gave an imitation of Jimmy Durante. Not to be outdone, Jimmy Durante, who had just stepped off the Orient Express, found a false nose and gave an imitation of Marc Connelly. And late that night the deal was consummated on the exchange of five hundred Confederate dollars, which the pair jokingly pretended was real currency.

Such was their buoyancy that it was first proposed to limit admission to *Having Wonderful Time* to ten pins or whatever vegetables the patrons could muckle from their parents' kitchens; but on reconsideration Connelly decided that it would only confuse the ticket speculators, and they might as well adhere to the customary toll charges. With this point of view Kober quickly fell in; Connelly tumbled in beside him, and soon the twain, deep in their feather bed, were snoring away as pleasant as you please.

Rehearsals of the play were unique in theatrical annals in several respects. When Marc Connelly is directing, he insists that all the seats be removed from the theatre and be replaced by horsehair lounges. "The Romans," he argues, "reclined at table —Petronius will vouch for that, as well as some other pretty interesting things. Why not recline at the theater? You say the audience will not accept the idea?" Here he gives a typically Gallic shrug of the shoulders and smiles disarmingly. "There are more ways to catch a finch than by putting salt on its tail." As a result, *Having Wonderful Time* offered an additional service to playgoers. Between the acts, hundreds of finches were released in the smoking lounge and the customers were shown numerous ingenious ways of catching them. When I pointed out to Kober the fact that this bore no direct connection with his play, a picture of life in a summer camp, he gave me a typically Gallic shrug of the shoulders. "After all," he observed, trimming a goose-quill with which to tickle the leading lady, "you can't give them *everything*. We don't pretend we're 'Chu Chin Chow.'" And he accepted a pinch from my snuff-box and sprinkled it on the tail of a passing finch with a cavalier gesture.

"Pictures?" replied both Connelly and Kober, when I asked them about the future of films, a medium which both have studied at close range. "We don't think so. You'll never get people into those drafty darkened stores to look at images flickering over a sheet. You see, *mon vieux*, it's artificial. Oh yes, we've heard that a man's produced *The Great K. & A. Train Robbery*, but it'll never catch on. Passing fad and all that sort of thing, you know. Give us the theater every time. And another thing." I waited attentively, my pencil poised. "Didn't we tell you to get the hell out of this theater a half an hour ago?"

They accompanied me as far as the door, their hands resting paternally on my shoulder and collar lest I wriggle free of their grasp. I recovered my footing and dusted myself, having inadvertently tripped over a jardinière crossing the lobby. Already the lights were soft moons in the streets. I turned back to look at them as they stood framed against the ticket window, the bulbs on the marquee winking *Having Wonderful Time* as energetically as if the current had been paid for. They held up their hands, shaking their fists playfully at me in farewell. With a tug at my heart and an extra one at my trousers, I crept down Forty-fifth Street, munching an apple I had stolen from a fruit vendor, and pondering the mystery and the glamor of the theater.

2. VINCENTE MINNELLI

One sweltering summer's day a dozen years ago I had dropped into the main reading-room of the New York Public Library. I was deep in Bulfinch's *Age of Fable*, busily shading the illustrations of Greek and Roman divinities with a hard pencil and getting some truly splendid effects, when I became aware that a strange individual had entered the room. He was apparently a foreigner, for he bore in his lapel a green immigrant tag reading "Ellis Island—*Rush*." His clothes were flapping hand-me-downs greasy with travel, and altogether, he was as extraordinary an unhung horse-thief as you would encounter outside a gypsy encampment. Before him this fantastic creature propelled an ancient hurdy-gurdy, and as he ground out a wheezy catchpenny tune, made a rapid circuit of the tables, offering highest cash prices for old bones, rubber, bottles, and newspapers. Failing to stir up any interest among the few high-school boys furtively hunting for dirty words in the dictionary, this bird of ill-omen managed to secrete a set of Ridpath's *History of the World* under his rusty caftan and disappeared, obviously to rifle the coatroom. The languid librarian to whom I addressed my query contented himself with a curt "Vincente Minnelli" and resumed buffing his nails.

I had forgotten his rapacious face when one morning several weeks later he fell into step with me on Forty-fifth Street. He proposed to sell me a set of amusing postcards and a recondite pamphlet called *The Enigmatic Miss Floggy*, but when he suggested that I follow him into an alley for an inspection of these wares, I refused shortly. With no resentment, he offered me a deck of cocaine for fifty cents. I crossed the street hoping to shake him off, but he clung like a leech. Through his connections in the "milieu" he could obtain young virgins for a hundred and fifty dollars. Screaming, I fled into a cab, only to discover that he had purloined my watch-fob, a cheap German silver affair I had won in a debating contest. Outside of the sick headache I experienced, I found that I had contracted no diseases from the encounter.

I saw him occasionally in the months that followed, sometimes as a pitchman hawking mending-cement and verses of popular songs, again as a steerer for floating crap games. For a time he ran a trap-line of telephone booths, stuffing the slots and calling for the accumulated nickels each evening. Now and then he rolled a lush. His fear of risking his cowardly hide naturally kept him from participating in a really dangerous caper.

In time I began to feel a curious affection for this cheerful vagabond, possibly because he had never drawn a knife on me. After the six months he spent in the workhouse for suspected arson, I was almost glad to see him again. To my surprise I found that he had gone into a new business. Somewhere he had picked up the stub of a pencil and a square of Bristol board. The ultimate result, some years later, was a show called *Life Begins at 8:40*.

The police *dossier* on this curious starveling is limited unfortunately to the record of several shabby misdemeanors, such as his pathetic attempt to palm off a papier-mâché goose on a poultryman. This exploit would never have entangled him with the law had it not been for a remark of the poultryman. "D'ye see any green in my eye?" he demanded scornfully, flinging the goose at Minnelli's head. "Yes," replied the culprit truthfully, for it so happened that Minnelli, whose color sense even then was unerring, detected green in his eye. The ensuing fracas saw several pates broken under the quarterstaff of the churlish poultryman, and Minnelli was dragged off ingloriously to be booked. It is almost unnecessary to note that he made his escape from prison by his usual method of having a rope pie smuggled in to him.

That I should have mistaken him for a foreigner on first seeing him is hard to reconcile with the fact that he is a Middle-Westerner and had never been east of Chicago (or worn shoes, for that matter) up to his arrival in New York in 1928. His love for bizarre dress is a byword. Even today, with any number of Broadway shows behind him, he is spending next year's royalties on flowered surtouts and sword canes. It is nothing to see

Minnelli parading down Broadway of an afternoon dressed as Cameo Kirby, complete with silk tile, ruffles at his wrists, and derringer up his sleeve. That surly ruffian in black neckcloth with the craven dog at his heels who rudely elbows you aside as you enter Lindy's is less apt to be Bill Sykes than Vincente Minnelli, about to commit mayhem on a Maatjes herring.

The biographer of his early years is hard put to sift fact from legend. He was born in Delaware, Ohio, in 1906, but was implicated almost immediately in a shady episode revolving around a piece of zwieback, and had to leave town at the age of one. At sixteen Vincente, his blood fired by reports that Chicagoans were dancing the maxixe and the bunny-hug, set out to see for himself. Chicago was then a raw frontier town filled with prospectors and desperadoes like Walter Huston shooting at Gary Cooper through saloon doors. As Minnelli walked down the main street, his bandanna handkerchief tied to a peeled stick over his shoulder, munching a roll and whistling *The Lobster Is the Wise Guy, After All*, his eyes were like saucers. Little did he dream that one day he was to discover the secret of electricity and represent his country at the Court of St. James. Accosting a gamin whose dirty but humorous shoe-box marked him to be a bootblack, Vincente inquired politely where he might find lodgings for the night.

"Have yez any stamps?" inquired this personage.

"Stamps?" asked Vincente bewildered.

"Hully chee!" retorted the waif impatiently. "Kale—rhino—spondulicks—the long green! What's a matter—have yez bats in yer belfry?"

The intercession of honest old Bridget, the applewoman of Trinity, whose name was a synonym for nausea in those parts, set the confused young traveler on the right path. He had barely turned the corner when a runaway horse, dragging a surrey containing a richly dressed young lady, dashed into view. After some speculation about the probable reward, Vincente threw himself at the foaming steed and was promptly trampled down. He spent several days moodily nursing his ribs, and finally driven to want by the scanty opportunities facing an untrained second-story worker, decided to humiliate himself and take a job.

As photographer's helper in a theatrical photo studio, the young man concluded that the moth-eaten costumes in which he posed various actors and actresses were atrocious, and he promptly started sketching. His employer's eyes still twinkle at the memory of one of these drawings, a sketch of the location of the office safe, which Vincente had negligently left in his smock. Soon after, the youthful draughtsman decided on a bold stroke. He went to the offices of Balaban & Katz, whose name had always haunted him with its suggestion of a roll on the kettle-drums, and suggested the idea of allowing him to design new costumes rather than renting old ones. Balaban & Katz at that time were the largest producers of stage shows for picture houses in the region, and they were thunderstruck at his audacity.

"But—but he's a mere tyro!" wailed Balaban when Katz told him of the offer.

"Whisht," returned Katz in the County Leitrim accent he loved to affect, "let's give him a try-o." In the uproar which followed, Minnelli found himself hired, and when Balaban & Katz took over the Paramount Theatre in New York, their protégé came along to take charge of the costume department.

New York! What magic the name evoked to the gangling youth in the worn old beaver as he followed a grinning red-cap out from the train shed of Grand Central! Flinging an oath at the expectant blackamoor, Vincente hailed a passing brioche and ordered the jehu to show him the sights. His eyes fairly bulged from their sockets at Chinatown with its huddled slaves of the poppy, the Brevoort with Richard Harding Davis falling down its front steps, and all the myriad wonders of the city. But soon the beaver on his head was stirring restlessly, slapping its flat tail on the nape of Vincente's neck, and it was time to appease the inner man. The pair dined famously off several birches in Central Park, and then, curled up in a hollow tree, lay watching the sparkling lights and wondering what adventures the morrow would bring.

In a few weeks Minnelli was doing backgrounds as well as costumes, but the spicy novels of Paul de Kock and Restif de la Bretonne had begun to make him yearn for Paris. On the verge of sailing to study painting at the feet of Claude Monet

—a school had opened there a short time before—Minnelli was asked to design *The Dubarry* for Grace Moore. The opportunity of designing *The Dubarry* for Grace Moore would probably never come to him twice in his life, and he decided to accept. For the next four years, he evolved a stage show a week for the Music Hall, and then, bored with idleness, designed the settings for *Life Begins at 8:40*, *At Home Abroad*, *The Ziegfeld Follies*, and *The Show Is On*. The latter attracted the attention of a little coalition of dreamers and visionaries named Paramount Pictures, and today Minnelli is one of Hollywood's most promising young directors.

There is a saying in Hollywood that when Vincente Minnelli is working on a picture you had better hide the women and children in the cellar and stay in bed with your hat on. "The Ohio Cyclone," as he is never called, observes a rigid routine. On rising, he scrubs his face free of the India ink, Chinese white, and water color of the day before. Then he chops up a few blotters and rolls them between his fingers till they disappear. Now he is ready for his milk bath. The huge black bathtub of vitreous milk-chocolate, his most cherished possession, is filled with thirty gallons of steaming Grade A. As he lolls back in the tub, Minnelli's mind becomes a beehive of ideas. Several efficient secretaries, who work for nothing merely to be near him, take down the acid retorts, thumbnail vignettes, pithy saws, and biting sarcasms which fall from his lips. These by-products are relayed to a corps of typists who bind and ship them to a firm of publishers, who in turn bind and ship them back. Meanwhile Minnelli busies himself making toy boats of the letters he receives from feminine admirers and sends them sailing away on a puff of fragrant Turkish. If a letter from some pathetic little seamstress or love-starved housewife should happen to intrigue him, he has one of the secretaries send her a photograph of himself in a characteristic pose. However, what with the Post Office Department's complaints, the photographs have fallen off to a minimum lately. And so the days go by, and before you know it, there are the twenty-four sheets advertising a new movie directed by Vincente Minnelli.

Of his private life, I know very little. I understand that he has become immensely wealthy, inordinately sought-after, and unbelievably unaffected. I count my spoons and my sisters every time he leaves my house. He has never once offered to repay me for my German silver watch-fob. But the first time I saw the settings and costumes he did for "The Steamboat Whistle" in *At Home Abroad*, I knew that all accounts were squared between us. I owe that boy *plenty*.

Hell in the Gabardines

A N OLD subscriber of the *New Republic* am I, prudent, meditative, rigidly impartial. I am the man who reads those six-part exposés of the Southern utilities empire, savoring each dark peculation. Weekly I stroll the *couloirs* of the House and Senate with T.R.B., aghast at legislative folly. Every now and again I take issue in the correspondence pages with Kenneth Burke or Malcolm Cowley over a knotty point of aesthetics; my barbed and graceful letters counsel them to reread their Benedetto Croce. Tanned by two delightful weeks at lovely Camp Nitgedaiget, I learn twenty-nine languages by Linguaphone, sublet charming three-room apartments with gardens from May to October, send my children to the Ethical Culture School. Of an evening you can find me in a secluded corner of the White Turkey Town House, chuckling at Stark Young's review of the *Medea*. I smoke a pipe more frequently than not, sucking the match flame into the bowl with thoughtful little puffs.

Of all the specialists on that excellent journal of opinion, however, my favorite is Manny Farber, its motion-picture critic. Mr. Farber is a man zealous and incorruptible, a relentless foe of stereotypes, and an extremely subtle scholiast. If sufficiently aroused, he is likely to quote *The Cabinet of Dr. Caligari* four or five times in a single article (Mr. James Agee of the *Nation*, otherwise quite as profound, can quote it only once). It has been suggested by some that Mr. Farber's prose style is labyrinthine; they fidget as he picks up a complex sentence full of interlocking clauses and sends it rumbling down the alley. I do not share this view. With men who know rococo best, it's Farber two to one. Lulled by his Wagnerian rhythms, I snooze in my armchair, confident that the *mystique* of the talking picture is in capable hands.

It was in his most portentous vein that Mr. Farber recently sat himself down to chart the possibilities of the concealed camera. In transferring *The Lost Weekend* to the screen, you will recall, the producers sought verisimilitude by bringing Ray

Milland to Third Avenue (in the past Third Avenue had always been brought to Ray Milland) and photographing the reactions of everyday citizens to Don Birnam's torment. The necessary equipment was hidden in theatre marquees, "L" stations, and vans along the route of the historic trek, and almost nobody knew that the scenes were being registered on film. Mr. Farber heartily approved this technique and called on Hollywood to employ it more generally. To demonstrate its potentialities, he even sketched a wee scenario. "If," said he, "your plot called for some action inside of a department store, the normal activity of the store could be got by sending trained actors into it to carry on a planned business with an actor-clerk. Nobody else in the store need become conscious or self-conscious of this business, since the cameraman has been slyly concealed inside an ingeniously made store dummy and is recording everything from there."

Through a source I am not at liberty to reveal without violating medical confidence, I have come into possession of a diary which affords an interesting comment on Mr. Farber's idea. It was kept by one Leonard Flemister, formerly a clerk in the men's clothing section of Wanamaker's. I was not a customer of Flemister's, as I get my suits at a thrift shop named Sam's on the Bowery, but I had a nodding acquaintance with him; we often occupied adjoining tables at the Jumble Shop, and I remember him as a gentle, introspective man absorbed in the *New Republic* over his pecan waffle. He is at present living in seclusion (the Bonnie Brae is not a booby hatch in the old-fashioned sense) in New Jersey. I append several extracts from his diary:

JANUARY 12—Today rounds out seventeen years since I started in the men's shop at Wanamaker's, and they have been years filled with quiet satisfaction. As our great Founder constantly observed in his maxims, it is the small things that count. How truly this applies to ready-made suits! To the tyro, of course, one suit is very much like another, but to us who know, there is as much distinction between a Kuppenheimer and a Society Brand as there is between a Breughel and a Vermeer. Crusty old Thomas Carlyle knew it when he wrote *Sartor Resartus*. (Good notion, that; might pay me to have a couple of his quotations on the tip of my tongue for some of our older customers.)

Ran into Frank Portnoy yesterday at lunch; haven't seen him since he left us for Finchley's. Sound enough chap on cheviots, is Frank, but I wouldn't care to entrust him with a saxony or tweeds. He seems to have put on five or six pounds in the seat, and I thought his 22-ounce basket-weave a touch on the vulgar side. "Still working in that humdrum old place?" he asked, with a faint sneer. I kept my temper, merely remarking that he had incurred some criticism for leaving his position after only twelve years. (I did not bother to say that Mr. Witherspoon had referred to him as a grasshopper.) "Oh," he said airily, "I guess I learned enough of those lousy maxims." I said pointedly that he apparently had not learned the one about patience, and quoted it. He termed it "hogwash." "Maybe it is," I retorted, "but don't you wish you could wash a hog like that?" He turned as red as a beet and finished his meal in silence.

Read a disturbing article in the *New Republic* last night. A man named Farber advocates secreting cameramen inside clothing dummies in department stores so that the clerks may unwittingly become actors in a movie. Of course it was just a joke, but frankly, I thought it in rather poor taste.

JANUARY 14—Felt a trifle seedy today; I must find some other lunch spot besides the Green Unicorn. Their orange-and-pimento curry appears to have affected my digestion, or possibly I have had a surfeit of banana whip. In any case, during the afternoon I experienced the most extraordinary sensation, one that upset me considerably. At the rear of our sportswear section, next to the seersucker lounging robes, is a perfectly prosaic wax mannequin wearing a powder-blue ski jacket, canary-colored slacks, and synthetic elk-skin loafers. About three o'clock I was hurrying past it with an armful of corduroy windbreakers when I heard a resounding sneeze. I turned abruptly, at first supposing it had come from a customer or salesperson, but the only one in sight was Sauerwein, who was absorbed in his booklet of maxims a good thirty feet away. Ridiculous as it may sound, the noise—a very distinct "Harooch!"—seemed to have emanated from the model. A moment's reflection would have told me that my auditory nerve was rebuking me for overindulgence at table, but unfortunately, in the first access of panic, I backed into a fishing-rod display and hooked a sinker in my trousers. Mr. Witherspoon, chancing by, observed (I thought with some coarseness) that I ought to get the lead out of my pants. Sauerwein, who loves to play the toady, laughed uproariously. I shall be on my guard with Sauerwein in future; I do not think he is quite sincere.

Saw a tiptop revival of *The Cabinet of Dr. Caligari* and *Potemkin* last night at the Fifth Avenue Playhouse; they are having their annual film festival. Enjoyed them both, though most of *Caligari* was run upside down and *Potemkin* broke in three places, necessitating a short wait. Next week they are beginning their annual *Potemkin* festival, to be followed by a revival of *The Cabinet of Dr. Caligari*. Always something unusual at the Fifth Avenue.

JANUARY 17—Mr. Witherspoon is a tyrant on occasion, but as the Founder says so pungently, give the devil his due; every so often the quality that made him floorwalker shines through. This morning, for example, a customer I recall seeing at some restaurant (the Jumble Shop, I believe) created a scene. He was a peppery little gnome named, I think, Pevelman or Pedelman, with shaggy eyebrows and the tonsure of a Franciscan father. I noticed him fidgeting around the low-priced shorts for a half hour or more, trying to attract a salesman, but Sauerwein was behind on his maxims and I was busy rearranging the windbreakers. At length he strode over to Mr. Witherspoon, scarlet with rage, and demanded, in an absurd falsetto, whether he might be waited on. Mr. Witherspoon was magnificent. He surveyed Pevelman up and down and snapped, "Don't you know there's a peace on?" The customer's face turned ashen and he withdrew, clawing at his collar. Old Witherspoon was in rare good humor all morning.

Slight dizzy spell this afternoon, nothing of consequence. I wonder if anything could be amiss with my hearing. Curiously enough, it is normal except in the immediate vicinity of the mannequin, where I hear a faint, sustained clicking as though some mechanism were grinding away. Coupled with this is the inescapable conviction that my every move is somehow being observed. Several times I stole up on the dummy, hoping to prove to myself that the clicking came from within, but it ceased instanter. Could I have contracted some mysterious tropical disease from handling too many vicuña coats?

Sauerwein is watching me. He suspects all is not well.

JANUARY 20—Something is definitely wrong with me. It has nothing to do with my stomach. I have gone mad. My stomach has driven me mad.

Whatever happens, I must not lose my head and blame my stomach. A stomach blamed is a stomach spurned, as the Founder says. The only good Founder is a dead Founder. Or Flounder. Now I *know* I am mad, writing that way about the Flounder.

I must marshal my thoughts very carefully, try to remember what happened. Shortly after one, I was alone in the department, Sauerwein and Witherspoon being at lunch. I was folding boys' windbreakers at the folded boys' windbreaker counter when a customer approached me. Never having seen Fredric March in person, I cannot assert dogmatically that it was he, but the resemblance was startling. From the outset, his behavior impressed me as erratic. He first struck a pose about fifteen feet from the mannequin, taking care to keep his profile to it. As he did so, the clicking sound which had harassed me became doubly magnified. Then, in the loud, artificial tone of one who wished to be overheard, he demanded to be shown a suit with two pairs of pants.

"We haven't any," I replied. "Don't you know there's a peace on?" To my surprise, he emitted a hoarse cry of delight and slapped his thigh.

"That'll be a wow!" he chortled. "We'll leave that line in!" Seventeen years of dealing with eccentrics have taught me the wisdom of humoring them; I pretended not to have heard. He gave me an intimate wink, snatched a sharkskin suit from the rack, and vanished into a dressing room. I was on the point of summoning aid when he reappeared feverishly. The effect of the trousers, at least three sizes too large for him, was so ludicrous that I stood speechless.

"Just what I wanted," he grinned, surveying himself in the mirror. Simultaneously, almost as if by prearrangement, a young lady in flamboyant theatrical make-up appeared. To my horror, the customer forgot to hold onto his trousers and they dropped down around his ankles. "Hello, Vivian!" he cried.

"Well, I guess you caught me with my pants down!" And then —I am resolved to spare no detail—a voice from within the mannequin boomed "*Cut!*"

When I recovered consciousness in the dispensary, the nurse and Mr. Witherspoon were chafing my wrists and Sauerwein was whispering to a store detective. I seem to remember striking Sauerwein, though I also have the impression my hands were entangled in my sleeves. The rest I prefer to forget. It can be summed up in the word "nightmare." Nightmare.

FEBRUARY 5—It is very quiet here at Bonnie Brae and the food is excellent, if a little unrelieved. I could do with one of those tasty water-cress-and-palmetto salads they know so well how to prepare at the Green Unicorn. The library here is well stocked with current magazines; I keep abreast of the news via the *New Republic*, though I confess Farber does not grip me as he used to.

I have only one objection to this place. In the library is a suit of medieval armor, and very often I could swear that a pair of eyes are watching me through the casque. As soon as the weather becomes warmer, I expect to spend most of my time on the piazza.

Farewell, My Lovely Appetizer

Add Smorgasbits to your ought-to-know department, the newest of the three Betty Lee products. What in the world! Just small mouth-size pieces of herring and of pinkish tones. We crossed our heart and promised not to tell the secret of their tinting.
—*Clementine Paddleford's food column in the Herald Tribune.*

The "Hush-Hush" Blouse. We're very hush-hush about his name, but the celebrated shirtmaker who did it for us is famous on two continents for blouses with details like those deep yoke folds, the wonderful shoulder pads, the shirtband bow!
Russeks adv. in the Times.

I CAME DOWN the sixth-floor corridor of the Arbogast Building, past the World Wide Noodle Corporation, Zwinger & Rumsey, Accountants, and the Ace Secretarial Service, Mimeographing Our Specialty. The legend on the ground-glass panel next door said, "Atlas Detective Agency, Noonan & Driscoll," but Snapper Driscoll had retired two years before with a .38 slug between the shoulders, donated by a snowbird in Tacoma, and I owned what good will the firm had. I let myself into the crummy anteroom we kept to impress clients, growled good morning at Birdie Claflin.

"Well, you certainly look like something the cat dragged in," she said. She had a quick tongue. She also had eyes like dusty lapis lazuli, taffy hair, and a figure that did things to me. I kicked open the bottom drawer of her desk, let two inches of rye trickle down my craw, kissed Birdie square on her lush, red mouth, and set fire to a cigarette.

"I could go for you, sugar," I said slowly. Her face was veiled, watchful. I stared at her ears, liking the way they were joined to her head. There was something complete about them; you knew they were there for keeps. When you're a private eye, you want things to stay put.

"Any customers?"

"A woman by the name of Sigrid Bjornsterne said she'd be back. A looker."

"Swede?"

"She'd like you to think so."

I nodded toward the inner office to indicate that I was going in there, and went in there. I lay down on the davenport, took off my shoes, and bought myself a shot from the bottle I kept underneath. Four minutes later, an ash blonde with eyes the color of unset opals, in a Nettie Rosenstein basic black dress and a baum-marten stole, burst in. Her bosom was heaving and it looked even better that way. With a gasp she circled the desk, hunting for some place to hide, and then, spotting the wardrobe where I keep a change of bourbon, ran into it. I got up and wandered out into the anteroom. Birdie was deep in a crossword puzzle.

"See anyone come in here?"

"Nope." There was a thoughtful line between her brows. "Say, what's a five-letter word meaning 'trouble'?"

"Swede," I told her, and went back inside. I waited the length of time it would take a small, not very bright boy to recite *Ozymandias,* and, inching carefully along the wall, took a quick gander out the window. A thin galoot with stooping shoulders was being very busy reading a paper outside the Gristede store two blocks away. He hadn't been there an hour ago, but then, of course, neither had I. He wore a size seven dove-colored hat from Browning King, a tan Wilson Brothers shirt with pale-blue stripes, a J. Press foulard with a mixed-red-and-white figure, dark blue Interwoven socks, and an unshined pair of ox-blood London Character shoes. I let a cigarette burn down between my fingers until it made a small red mark, and then I opened the wardrobe.

"Hi," the blonde said lazily. "You Mike Noonan?" I made a noise that could have been "Yes," and waited. She yawned. I thought things over, decided to play it safe. I yawned. She yawned back, then, settling into a corner of the wardrobe, went to sleep. I let another cigarette burn down until it made a second red mark beside the first one, and then I woke her up. She sank into a chair, crossing a pair of gams that tightened my throat as I peered under the desk at them.

"Mr. Noonan," she said, "you—you've got to help me."

"My few friends call me Mike," I said pleasantly.

"Mike." She rolled the syllable on her tongue. "I don't be-lieve I've ever heard that name before. Irish?"

"Enough to know the difference between a gossoon and a bassoon."

"What *is* the difference?" she asked. I dummied up; I figured I wasn't giving anything away for free. Her eyes narrowed. I shifted my two hundred pounds slightly, lazily set fire to a finger, and watched it burn down. I could see she was admiring the interplay of muscles in my shoulders. There wasn't any extra fat on Mike Noonan, but I wasn't telling *her* that. I was playing it safe until I knew where we stood.

When she spoke again, it came with a rush. "Mr. Noonan, he thinks I'm trying to poison him. But I swear the herring was pink—I took it out of the jar myself. If I could only find out how they tinted it. I offered them money, but they wouldn't tell."

"Suppose you take it from the beginning," I suggested.

She drew a deep breath. "You've heard of the golden spintria of Hadrian?" I shook my head. "It's a tremendously valuable coin believed to have been given by the Emperor Hadrian to one of his proconsuls, Caius Vitellius. It disappeared about 150 A.D., and eventually passed into the possession of Hucbald the Fat. After the sack of Adrianople by the Turks, it was loaned by a man named Shapiro to the court physician, or hakim, of Abdul Mahmoud. Then it dropped out of sight for nearly five hundred years, until last August, when a dealer in second-hand books named Lloyd Thursday sold it to my husband."

"And now it's gone again," I finished.

"No," she said. "At least, it was lying on the dresser when I left, an hour ago." I leaned back, pretending to fumble a carbon out of the desk, and studied her legs again. This was going to be a lot more intricate than I had thought. Her voice got huskier. "Last night I brought home a jar of Smorgasbits for Walter's dinner. You know them?"

"Small mouth-size pieces of herring and of pinkish tones, aren't they?"

Her eyes darkened, lightened, got darker again. "How did you know?"

"I haven't been a private op nine years for nothing, sister. Go on."

"I—I knew right away something was wrong when Walter screamed and upset his plate. I tried to tell him the herring was supposed to be pink, but he carried on like a madman. He's been suspicious of me since—well, ever since I made him take out that life insurance."

"What was the face amount of the policy?"

"A hundred thousand. But it carried a triple-indemnity clause in case he died by sea food. Mr. Noonan—Mike"—her tone caressed me—"I've got to win back his confidence. You could find out how they tinted that herring."

"What's in it for me?"

"Anything you want." The words were a whisper. I leaned over, poked open her handbag, counted off five grand.

"This'll hold me for a while," I said. "If I need any more, I'll beat my spoon on the high chair." She got up. "Oh, while I think of it, how does this golden spintria of yours tie in with the herring?"

"It doesn't," she said calmly. "I just threw it in for glamour." She trailed past me in a cloud of scent that retailed at ninety rugs the ounce. I caught her wrist, pulled her up to me.

"I go for girls named Sigrid with opal eyes," I said.

"Where'd you learn my name?"

"I haven't been a private snoop twelve years for nothing, sister."

"It was nine last time."

"It seemed like twelve till *you* came along." I held the clinch until a faint wisp of smoke curled out of her ears, pushed her through the door. Then I slipped a pint of rye into my stomach and a heater into my kick and went looking for a book-dealer named Lloyd Thursday. I knew he had no connection with the herring caper, but in my business you don't overlook anything.

The thin galoot outside Gristede's had taken a powder when I got there; that meant we were no longer playing girls' rules. I hired a hack to Wanamaker's, cut over to Third, walked up toward Fourteenth. At Twelfth a mink-faced jasper made up as a street cleaner tailed me for a block, drifted into a dairy restaurant. At Thirteenth somebody dropped a sour tomato out of a third-story window, missing me by inches. I doubled back to Wanamaker's, hopped a bus up Fifth to Madison Square, and switched to a cab down Fourth, where the second-hand book-shops elbow each other like dirty urchins.

A flabby hombre in a Joe Carbondale rope-knit sweater, whose jowl could have used a shave, quit giggling over the Heptameron long enough to tell me he was Lloyd Thursday. His shoe-button eyes became opaque when I asked to see any first editions or incunabula relative to the *Clupea harengus*, or common herring.

"You got the wrong pitch, copper," he snarled. "That stuff is hotter than Pee Wee Russell's clarinet."

"Maybe a sawbuck'll smarten you up," I said. I folded one to the size of a postage stamp, scratched my chin with it. "There's five yards around for anyone who knows why those Smorgasbits of Sigrid Bjornsterne's happened to be pink." His eyes got crafty.

"I might talk for a grand."

"Start dealing." He motioned toward the back. I took a step forward. A second later a Roman candle exploded inside my head and I went away from there. When I came to, I was on the floor with a lump on my sconce the size of a lapwing's egg and big Terry Tremaine of Homicide was bending over me.

"Someone sapped me," I said thickly. "His name was—"

"Webster," grunted Terry. He held up a dog-eared copy of Merriam's Unabridged. "You tripped on a loose board and this fell off a shelf on your think tank."

"Yeah?" I said skeptically. "Then where's Thursday?" He pointed to the fat man lying across a pile of erotica. "He passed out cold when he saw you cave." I covered up, let Terry figure it any way he wanted. I wasn't telling him what cards I held. I was playing it safe until I knew all the angles.

In a seedy pharmacy off Astor Place, a stale Armenian whose name might have been Vulgarian but wasn't dressed my head and started asking questions. I put my knee in his groin and he lost interest. Jerking my head toward the coffee urn, I spent a nickel and the next forty minutes doing some heavy thinking. Then I holed up in a phone booth and dialled a clerk I knew called Little Farvel in a delicatessen store on Amsterdam Avenue. It took a while to get the dope I wanted because the connection was bad and Little Farvel had been dead two years, but we Noonans don't let go easily.

By the time I worked back to the Arbogast Building, via the Weehawken ferry and the George Washington Bridge to cover my tracks, all the pieces were in place. Or so I thought up to the point she came out of the wardrobe holding me between the sights of her ice-blue automatic.

"Reach for the stratosphere, gumshoe." Sigrid Bjornsterne's voice was colder than Horace Greeley and Little Farvel put together, but her clothes were plenty calorific. She wore a forest-green suit of Hockanum woollens, a Knox Wayfarer, and baby crocodile pumps. It was her blouse, though, that made tiny red hairs stand up on my knuckles. Its deep yoke folds, shoulder pads, and shirtband bow could only have been designed by some master craftsman, some Cézanne of the shears.

"Well, Nosy Parker," she sneered, "so you found out how they tinted the herring."

"Sure—grenadine," I said easily. "You knew it all along. And you planned to add a few grains of oxylbutane-cheriphosphate, which turns the same shade of pink in solution, to your husband's portion, knowing it wouldn't show in the postmortem. Then you'd collect the three hundred g's and join Harry Pestalozzi in Nogales till the heat died down. But you didn't count on me."

"You?" Mockery nicked her full-throated laugh. "What are you going to do about it?"

"This." I snaked the rug out from under her and she went down in a swirl of silken ankles. The bullet whined by me into the ceiling as I vaulted over the desk, pinioned her against the wardrobe.

"Mike." Suddenly all the hatred had drained away and her body yielded to mine. "Don't turn me in. You cared for me —once."

"It's no good, Sigrid. You'd only double-time me again."

"Try me."

"O.K. The shirtmaker who designed your blouse—what's his name?" A shudder of fear went over her; she averted her head. "He's famous on two continents. Come on Sigrid, they're your dice."

"I won't tell you. I can't. It's a secret between this—this department store and me."

"They wouldn't be loyal to *you*. They'd sell you out fast enough."

"Oh, Mike, you mustn't. You don't know what you're asking."

"For the last time."

"Oh, sweetheart, don't you see?" Her eyes were tragic pools, a cenotaph to lost illusions. "I've got so little. Don't take that away from me. I—I'd never be able to hold up my head in Russeks again."

"Well, if that's the way you want to play it . . ." There was silence in the room, broken only by Sigrid's choked sob. Then, with a strangely empty feeling, I uncradled the phone and dialled Spring 7-3100.

For an hour after they took her away, I sat alone in the taupe-colored dusk, watching lights come on and a woman in the hotel opposite adjusting a garter. Then I treated my tonsils to five fingers of firewater, jammed on my hat, and made for the anteroom. Birdie was still scowling over her crossword puzzle. She looked up crookedly at me.

"Need me any more tonight?"

"No." I dropped a grand or two in her lap. "Here, buy yourself some stardust."

"Thanks, I've got my quota." For the first time I caught a shadow of pain behind her eyes. "Mike, would—would you tell me something?"

"As long as it isn't clean," I flipped to conceal my bitterness.

"What's an eight-letter word meaning 'sentimental'?"

"Flatfoot, darling," I said, and went out into the rain.

Hit Him Again, He's Sober

HAD THE late Henry James been standing on the steps of his house at 21 Washington Place early this morning, he would have seen the deponent, his neighbor, totter out of a cab and collapse with a sob in the arms of the night elevator man. No doubt Mr. James, who oddly enough *was* standing there gassing with Mark Twain and Richard Harding Davis, imagined he was seeing just another drunk. That is Mr. James's privilege; personally, I do not give a fig for his good opinion of me. But I do most definitely want to clarify the incident before it becomes distorted. It is typical of our sick civilization that a man as temperate as myself, abstemious to the point of fanaticism, should become the butt of gossip. And yet, paradoxically, it was my very sobriety that brought down on me vilification and physical abuse worse than was ever heaped on an early Christian martyr.

The whole wretched affair began yesterday afternoon. When the late sunlight filtered through the blinds onto my Tyrian-purple couch, it revealed a very sick man. Three Lilliputians in doublet and hose, armed with nutpicks and oyster forks, were enfilading my big toe, from which the letters "O-U-C-H" zigzagged away into infinity. During the night, parties unknown had removed my corneas, varnished and replaced them, and fitted me with a curious steel helmet, several sizes too small. Lying there cradled between softest Fruit of the Loom, a deep cocoa-flavored sense of remorse welled upward from the knees and constricted my heart.

"You mucker," I said through my teeth, "if you've an ounce of manhood in your make-up, you'll get down on all fours and beg her forgiveness." This gaudy monologue continued uninterrupted through my ablutions, except when the can of tooth powder slipped from my fingers and exploded on the floor with a roar like a fragmentation bomb. A few seconds later, I entered my wife's presence with the smug exaltation of a character out of a Hall Caine novel, clothed in a white dimity frock and a blue hair ribbon, fingering the temperance badge pinned to my breast.

"I'm through," I declaimed. "Never again. Goodby, John Barleycorn, hello, Walker-Gordon. *Mens sana in corpore sano.* Look at this hand—steady as a rock." My peach blossom looked up from her buhl writing cabinet, shrugged coldly, and resumed adding up the liquor bill. Determined to prove I had undergone a moral regeneration worthy of *Pilgrim's Progress*, I conjured up a corn popper and a volume of Colley Cibber's memoirs and snuggled down before the hearth. After I had read in silence for twenty seconds, the pica type tired my eyes and I leaned my head on my hand for support. Suddenly the phone shrilled and I arose, adroitly demolishing a vase of chrysanthemums. Two members of our young married set were holding an impromptu cocktail party. Next to Mrs. George Washington Kavanaugh, they assured me, my presence would establish it as the social event of the season. I was refusing politely but firmly when I heard my wife whinny over my shoulder.

"A party! A party!" she bleated. "You never take me to a party! I want to go to the party! Party . . . party . . . party . . ." Before I could reason with her, she flung herself on the counterpane and started sobbing into the bolster. Aware of the futility of trying to combat tears with logic, I acceded wearily. On the way uptown in the taxi, however, I made it plain that my decision to abstain from alcohol was irrevocable. My wife's lip curled superciliously. "Tell it to Sweeney," she advised. I leaned over to Sweeney, who was beating an impatient tatoo on the steering wheel while waiting for the lights to change, and told him my decision to abstain was irrevocable. His contemptuous chuckle infuriated me, and I lost my head. "You wait, the two of you!" I screamed, hammering my tiny fists on the jump seat. "May I fall down dead if I so much as touch a drop!" I was still defying the lightning as we swept into the pleasure pavilion. Eighteen or twenty voluptuaries, in varying stages of repair, were holding wassail in a cosy two-room apartment. To make the proceedings more intimate, someone had introduced a Great Dane, a parakeet, and a progressive child who was busily emptying fruit rinds and cigarette ends into the men's hats. Yet amid the sickening debauch, suggesting Babylon at its most dissolute (Babylon, Long Island, that is), I stood a figure apart, a pillar unmoved by the blandishments and mockery of my fellows.

"Just one teentsy-weentsy sip," begged my hostess, a tantalizing blonde, all black georgette and open-mesh stockings. "Don't be thataway, you inflexible boy." For a moment her dear nearness maddened me, but I resolutely averted my face and called for a glass of Adam's ale. The more turbulent the carousal, the more steadfast I became; Cromwell at his flintiest was an orchid compared to me. In my foolish pride, I believed that I had found the philosopher's stone, that I was immune from disaster. And then the Moving Finger moved. The host, a broth of a boy who had once run seventy-nine yards down the Bowl with the Harvard backfield clinging to his waist, linked arms with me.

"Going get you sandwich," he proposed indistinctly. "Come on kitchen." I rashly extricated myself and stepped away. As I did, he reached down to the vicinity of his tibia and came up with a haymaker that caught me flush on the button. An interesting display of Catherine wheels, Very lights, and star shells flashed before me, and uttering a taut "Mamma," I melted into the parquet. I awoke on a pile of krimmer coats in the bedroom to discover my wife applying a cold poultice to the sub-maxillary region. In between embrocations, the Angel of the Crimea, her cheeks aflame with Martinis, informed me that I had forever alienated us from the beau monde. I had deliberately pinched the hostess, kicked two Whitneys in the shin, and smashed a priceless collection of Royal Worcester china. I protested I was innocent, a victim of some hideous conspiracy. "I'm as sober as you are!" I pleaded. "Soberer! I haven't had a dram since yesterday!" "Yes, yes," she agreed soothingly. "Help me with him, will you, Ariadne? His legs get rubbery at this stage." Before I could wrench free, kind hands thrust me into a topcoat, jammed an alien derby over my ears in the classic manner of Ben Welch, and hustled me downstairs in a freight elevator. While I kept trying to raise my head, which hung dahlia-like on its stalk, the rescuers started wrangling over my future.

"Take him home. . . . No, he'll cut himself. . . . Who is he? . . . I know a spot where we can get him some soup. . . . Yeah, soup's good." I gurgled a feeble remonstrance that passed unnoticed; when the dust blew away, I was propped up at a table in a sleazy bar off the Gay White Way, staring wanly into a bowl of buttermilk. My wife and her grouping had disappeared and a noisy Syrian, representing himself as the owner of a chain of shoe stores in Hartford, was offering to take me into partnership. Midway in his harangue, he broke off and, hailing the bartender as "Four Eyes," ordered him to serve me a highball. The gibe evidently climaxed a long, hard day for the bartender. With a hoarse bellow, he hurdled the beerpulls and uncorked a left hook that I intercepted nimbly with my ear. The Syrian thereupon lashed out handily and in a moment I was bobbing between them like a cork. The estimate is, of course, unofficial, but sports writers have since estimated that I stopped more punches than Jacob "Soldier" Bartfield in his entire career.

I came to in an alley with two handsome shiners suitable for framing and the Hall Johnson Choir singing *Stabat Mater* inside my head. My wife had mysteriously reappeared and, aided by a shrill young couple, whose dialogue had been written for them by Clyde Fitch, was sponging me off. "Now take it easy, will you?" she implored, brushing back my widow's peak. "Everything is going to be all right. Just relax." I closed my eyes with a grateful sigh. When I opened them again, I was lying on a banquette in a clip joint off Amsterdam Avenue. Dawn was peeping in at the window and a spurious gypsy violinist was rendering gems from *The Bohemian Girl*. At the next table, a gaunt trio resembling Picasso's *The Absinthe Drinker*, dimly identifiable as my wife and the Fitches, was sobbing brokenly for Alt Wien. I stumbled to my feet, flung my last bit of collateral at the management, and, herding the revellers before me, started toward the door. Right outside it stood two monumental Texans fourteen feet high, with snow on their hair, clamoring for admission. The ensuing action is somewhat hazy, but as I reconstruct it, our Mr. Fitch curtly bade Gog and Magog step aside, employing the informal phrase "you big crackers." I was scudding across the sidewalk, primly keeping my nose clean and my lips buttoned, when I abruptly felt myself seized by the collar and hoisted four feet into the air.

"What did you call me, you little measle?" one of the ogres was rumbling. "Why, I'll flatten that bugle—" He drew back a fist no larger than a peanut-fed ham; the breeze from the gesture alone dizzied me. I croaked out a pitiable denial and he let me drop. The fall nearly broke my ankles. In that instant, as

I slunk after my party, I reached the most vital decision of my life. Three times in one evening I had pursed my lips against the grape and thrice my life had hung in the balance. Come hell or high water, famine, flood, or fire, I was through with milk and large moral resolutions. From here in, it's high carnival and strange purple sins. Bring me another pair of those amber witches, waiter, and go easy on the club soda.

Physician, Steel Thyself

Do YOU happen to know how many tassels a Restoration coxcomb wore at the knee? Or the kind of chafing dish a bunch of Skidmore girls would have used in a dormitory revel in 1911? Or the exact method of quarrying peat out of a bog at the time of the Irish Corn Laws? In fact, do you know anything at all that nobody else knows or, for that matter, gives a damn about? If you do, then sit tight, because one of these days you're going to Hollywood as a technical supervisor on a million-dollar movie. You may be a bore to your own family, but you're worth your weight in piastres to the picture business.

Yes, Hollywood dearly loves a technical expert, however recondite or esoteric his field. It is a pretty picayune film that cannot afford at least one of them; sometimes they well-nigh outnumber the actors. The Sherlock Holmes series, for instance, employs three servants on a full-time basis—one who has made a lifelong study of the décor at 221-B Baker Street, a second deeply versed in the great detective's psychology and mannerisms, and a third who spots anachronisms in the script which may distress Holmesians, like penicillin and the atomic bomb. An ideal existence, you might think, and yet there have been exceptions. I knew a White Russian artillery officer at M-G-M, imported at bloodcurdling expense from Algeria as adviser on a romance of the Foreign Legion, who languished for two years in an oubliette under the Music Department. Over the noon yoghurt, his voice trembled as he spoke of his yearning to return to Russia, where they were waiting to shoot him, but the director of "Blistered Bugles" felt him indispensable. At last he departed, with close to forty thousand rutabagas in his money belt, a broken man. His sole contribution was that he had succeeded in having "*pouf*" altered to "*sacré bloo.*" Another expert I met during the same epoch was a jovial, gnarled little party named Settembrini, conceded to be the foremost wrought-iron craftsman in the country. He had been flown three thousand miles to authenticate several flambeaux shown briefly in a night shot of Versailles. We subsequently chanced to be on the same train going East, and except for the fact that he wore a gold derby and was lighting his cigar with a first-mortgage bond, he seemed untouched. "Fine place," he commented, flicking ashes into the corsage of a blonde he had brought along for the purpose. "Sunshine, pretty girls, grape-fruit ten for a quarter." I asked him whether the flambeaux had met the test. "One hundred per cent," he replied, "but they threw 'em out. In the scene where Marie Antoinette comes down the steps, a lackey holds a flashlight so she don't trip over her feet."

The latest group of specialists to be smiled upon by the cinema industry, it would appear, are the psychoanalysts. The vogue of psychological films started by *Lady in the Dark* has resulted in flush times for the profession, and anyone who can tell a frazzled id from a father fixation had better be booted and spurred for an impending summons to the Coast. The credit title of *Spellbound*, Alfred Hitchcock's recent thriller, for example, carried the acknowledgment "Psychiatric sequences supervised by Dr. May Romm," and Sidney Skolsky, reporting on a picture called *Obsessed* (formerly *One Man's Secret* and before that *One Woman's Secret*), states, "Joan Crawford is huddling with an eminent psychiatrist who will psych her forthcoming role in *The Secret* for her." A psychiatrist suddenly pitchforked into Hollywood, the ultimate nightmare, must feel rather like a small boy let loose in a toy store, but I wonder how long he can maintain a spirit of strict scientific objectivity. The ensuing vignette, a hasty attempt to adumbrate this new trend, is purely fanciful. There are, naturally, no such places as the Brown Derby, Vine Street, and Hollywood Boulevard, and if there should turn out to be, I couldn't be sorrier.

Sherman Wormser, M.D., PhD., came out of the Hollywood Plaza Hotel, somewhat lethargic after a heavy Sunday brunch, and paused indecisively on the sidewalk. The idea of taking a walk, which had seemed so inspired a moment ago in his room, now depressed him immeasurably. To the south, Vine Street stretched away interminably—unending blocks of bank-rupt night clubs, used-car lots, open-air markets, and bazaars full of unpainted furniture and garden pottery. To the north, it rose abruptly in a steep hill crowned by a cluster of funeral homes and massage parlors in tan stucco. Over all of it hung a warm miasma vaguely suggestive of a steam laundry. Sherman moved aimlessly toward the boulevard and paused for a brief self-inventory in the window of the Broadway-Hollywood department store.

Most of Dr. Wormser's patients in New York, accustomed to his neat morning coat and pencil-striped trousers, would have had some difficulty in recognizing their father confessor at the moment. He wore a pea-green play suit with deep, flaring lapels, tailored of rough, towel-like material, arbitrarily checked and striated in front but mysteriously turned to suède in back. Over a gauzy, salmon-colored polo shirt he had knotted a yellow foulard handkerchief in a bow reminiscent of George Primrose's Minstrels, and on his head was sportily perched an Alpinist's hat modelled after those worn by the tyrant Gessler. Eight weeks before, when he had arrived to check on the dream sequences of R.K.O.'s *Befuddled*, he would not have been caught dead in these vestments, but his sack suits had seemed so conspicuous that, chameleon-like, he soon developed a sense of protective coloration.

He had settled his hat at a jauntier angle and was turning away from the window when he became aware that a passer-by was staring fixedly at him. The man wore an off-white polo coat which hung open, its belt trailing on the pavement. Underneath were visible pleated lavender slacks and a monogrammed yachting jacket trimmed with brass buttons. The face under the scarlet beret was oddly familiar.

"I beg pardon," hesitated the stranger, "I think we—you're not Sherman Wormser, are you?" At the sound of his voice, Sherman's mouth opened in delight. He flung his arm about the man's shoulders.

"Why Randy Kalbfus, you old son of a gun!" he crowed. "Two years ago! The Mental Hygiene Convention in Cleveland!"

"Bull's-eye," chuckled Kalbfus. "I thought it was you, but —well, you look different, somehow."

"Why—er—I used to have a Vandyke." Wormser felt his cheeks growing pink. "I shaved it off out here. The studio, you know. Say, you had one, too, for that matter. What became of yours?"

"Same thing," Kalbfus admitted sheepishly. "My producer said it was corny. He's got a block about psychiatrists' wearing goatees."

"Yes, involuntary goatee rejection," nodded Wormser. "Stekel speaks of it. Well, well. I heard you were in town. Where you working?"

"Over at Twentieth. I'm straightening out a couple of traumas in *Delirious*."

"You don't say!" Despite himself, Sherman's tone was faintly patronizing. "I turned down that assignment, you know. Didn't feel I could justify the symbolism of the scene where Don Ameche disembowels the horse."

"Oh, that's all out now," said Kalbfus amiably. "That was the early version."

"Well," said Sherman quickly, eager to retrieve himself, "it's the early version that catches the Wormser, what?" Kalbfus laughed uproariously, less at the witticism than because this was the first time anyone had addressed him in three days.

"Look," he suggested, linking arms with Sherman, "let's hop over to the Bamboo Room and have a couple of Zombolas." On their way across to the Brown Derby, he explained the nature of the drink to Wormser, who was still a bit staid and Eastern in his choice of beverages. "It's just a tall glass of rum mixed with a jigger of gin, some camphor ice, and a twist of avocado," he said reassuringly.

"Isn't that a little potent?" asked Wormser dubiously.

"You're cooking with grass it's potent," returned his companion pertly, if inaccurately. "That's why they won't serve more than six to a customer." Seated in the cool darkness of the bar, with three Zombolas coursing through their vitals, the colleagues felt drawn to each other. No trace of professional hostility or envy lingered by the time they had finished reviewing the Cleveland convention, the rapacity of their fellow-practitioners, and their own staunch integrity.

"How do you like it out here, Randy?" Wormser inquired. "I get a slight sense of confusion. Perhaps I'm not adjusted yet."

"You're inhibited," said Kalbfus, signalling the waiter to repeat. "You won't let yourself go. Infantile denial of your environment."

"I know," said Wormser plaintively, "but a few weeks ago I saw Jack Benny in a sleigh on Sunset Boulevard—with real reindeer. And last night an old hermit in a pillowcase stopped me and claimed the world was coming to an end. When I objected, he sold me a box of figs."

"You'll get used to it," the other replied. "I've been here five months, and to me it's God country. I never eat oranges, but hell, can you imagine three dozen for a quarter?"

"I guess you're right," admitted Wormser. "Where are you staying?"

"At the Sunburst Auto Motel on Cahuenga," said Kalbfus, draining his glass. "I'm sharing a room with two extra girls from Paramount."

"Oh, I'm sorry. I—I didn't know you and Mrs. Kalbfus were separated."

"Don't be archaic. She's living there, too." Kalbfus snapped his fingers at the waiter. "Once in a while I fall into the wrong bed, but Beryl's made her emotional readjustment; she's carrying on with a Greek in Malibu. Interesting sublimation of libido under stress, isn't it? I'm doing a paper on it." Wormser raised his hand ineffectually to ward off the fifth Zombola, but Kalbfus would not be overborne.

"None of that," he said sharply. "Come on, drink up. Yes, sir, it's a great town, but I'll tell you something, Sherm. We're in the wrong end of this business. Original stories—that's the caper." He looked around and lowered his voice. "I'll let you in on a secret, if you promise not to blab. I've been collaborating with the head barber over at Fox, and we've got a ten-strike. It's about a simple, unaffected manicurist who inherits fifty million smackers."

"A fantasy, eh?" Wormser pondered. "That's a good idea."

"What the hell do you mean, fantasy?" demanded Kalbfus heatedly. "It happens every day. Wait till you hear the twist-eroo, though. This babe, who has everything—houses, yachts, cars, three men in love with her—suddenly turns around and gives back the dough."

"Why?" asked Wormser, sensing that he was expected to.

"Well, we haven't worked that out yet," said Kalbfus con-fidentially. "Probably a subconscious wealth phobia. Anyway, Zanuck's offered us a hundred and thirty G's for it, and it isn't even on paper."

"Holy cow!" breathed Wormser. "What'll you do with all that money?"

"I've got my eye on a place in Beverly," Kalbfus confessed. "It's only eighteen rooms, but a jewel box—indoor plunge, in-door rifle range, the whole place is indoors. Even the barbecue."

"That can't be," protested Wormser. "The barbecue's always outdoors."

"Not this one," beamed Kalbfus. "That's what makes it so unusual. Then, of course, I'll have to give Beryl her settlement when the divorce comes through."

"You—you just said everything was fine between you," fal-tered Wormser.

"Oh, sure, but I've really outgrown her," shrugged Kalbfus. "Listen, old man, I wouldn't want this to get into the columns. You see, I'm going to marry Ingrid Bergman."

A strange, tingling numbness, like that induced by novocain, spread downward from the tips of Wormser's ears. "I didn't know you knew her," he murmured.

"I don't," said Kalbfus, "but I saw her the other night at the Mocambo, and she gave me a look that meant only one thing." He laughed and swallowed his sixth Zombola. "It's understandable, in a way. She must have known instinctively."

"Known what?" Wormser's eyes, trained to withstand the unusual, stood out in high relief.

"Oh, just that I happen to be the strongest man in the world," said Kalbfus modestly. He rose, drew a deep breath, and picked up the table. "Watch," he ordered, and flung it crisply across the bar. Two pyramids of bottles dissolved and crashed to the floor, taking with them a Filipino bus-boy and several hundred cocktail glasses. Before the fixtures had ceased quivering, a task force of bartenders and waiters was spearing down on Kalbfus. There was an obscure interval of scuffling, during which Wormser unaccountably found himself creeping about on all fours and being kicked by a fat lady. Then the shouts and recriminations blurred, and suddenly he felt the harsh impact of the pavement. In a parking lot, eons later, the mist cleared and he was seated on the running board of a sedan, palpating a robin's egg on his jaw. Kalbfus, his face puffier than he last remembered it, was shakily imploring him to forgive and dine at his motel. Wormser slowly shook his head.

"No, thanks." Though his tongue was a bolt of flannel, Sherman strove to give his words dignity. "I like you, Kalbfuth, but you're a little unthtable." Then he got to his feet, bowed formally, and went into the Pig'n Whistle for an atomburger and a frosted mango.

Take Two Parts Sand, One Part Girl, and Stir

OUTSIDE OF the three Rs—the razor, the rope, and the revolver—I know only one sure-fire method of coping with the simmering heat we may cheerfully expect in this meridian from now to Labor Day. Whenever the mercury starts inching up the column, I take to the horizontal plane with a glass graduate trimmed with ferns, place a pinch of digitalis or any good heart stimulant at my elbow, and flip open the advertising section of *Vogue*. Fifteen minutes of that paradisaical prose, those dizzying non sequiturs, and my lips are as blue as Lake Louise. If you want a mackerel iced or a sherbet frozen, just bring it up and let me read the advertising section of *Vogue* over it. I can also take care of small picnic parties up to five. The next time you're hot and breathless, remember the name, folks: Little Labrador Chilling & Dismaying Corporation.

It would require precision instruments as yet undreamed of to decide whether *Vogue*'s advertisements contain more moonbeams per linear inch than those of its competitors, but the June issue was certainly a serious contender for the ecstasy sweepstakes. There was, for instance, the vagary which portrayed a Revolutionary heroine setting fire to a field of grain with this caption: "*The Patriotism in Her Heart Burned Wheat Fields.* It took courage that day in October, 1777 for Catherine Schuyler to apply the torch to her husband's wheat fields so that food would not fall into the hands of the enemy. The flames that consumed the wheat fields on the Schuyler estate near Saratoga burned with no greater brightness than the patriotism in Catherine Schuyler's heart." Then, with a triple forward somersault that would have done credit to Alfredo Codona, the wizard of the trapeze, the copywriter vaulted giddily into an appeal to American women to augment their loveliness with Avon Cosmetics. Somewhat breathless, I turned the page and beheld a handsome young air woman crouched on a wing of her plane. "Test Pilot—Size 10," read the text. "Nine thousand feet above the flying field, a Hellcat fighter plane screams down in the dark blur of a power dive. Holding the stick of this four-hundred-mile-an-hour ship is a small firm hand." The owner of the small firm hand, I shortly discovered in the verbal power dive that followed, is an enthusiastic patron of DuBarry Beauty Preparations. The transition in logic was so abrupt that it was only by opening my mouth and screaming briefly, a procedure I had observed in the movies, that I was able to keep my eardrums from bursting.

The most singular display of the advertiser's eternal lust for novelty, though, was a bold, full-color photograph of an olive-skinned beauty, buried up to her corsage in sand, in the interests of Marvella Simulated Pearls. A matched string of the foregoing circled her voluptuous throat, and dimly visible in the background were a conch shell and a sponge, identifying the locale as the seaside. The model's face exhibited a resentment verging on ferocity, which was eminently pardonable; anybody mired in a quicksand, with only a string of simulated pearls to show for it, has a justifiable beef. And so have I. The connection between burning wheat field and cosmetic jar, Hellcat fighter and lipstick, is tenuous enough, God knows, but somehow the copywriter managed to link them with his sophistries. Why in Tophet a scowling nude stuck bolt upright in a sand bar should influence the reader to rush to his jeweller for a particular brand of artificial pearl, however, I cannot possibly imagine.

Perhaps if we reconstruct the circumstances under which this baffling campaign was conceived, a clue might be forthcoming. Let us, therefore, don a clean collar and sidle discreetly into the offices of Meeker, Cassavant, Singleton, Doubleday & Tripler, a fairly representative advertising agency.

(*Scene: The Brain Room of the agency, a conference chamber decorated in cerebral gray, Swedish modern furniture, and the inevitable van Gogh reproductions. As the curtain rises, Duckworth, the copy chief, and four members of his staff—Farish, Munkaczi, DeGroot, and Miss Drehdel—are revealed plunged in thought.*)

DUCKWORTH (*impatiently*): Well, what do you say, Farish? Got an angle, DeGroot?

FARISH: I still keep going back to my old idea, V. J.

DUCKWORTH: What's that?

FARISH (*thirstily*): A good red-hot picture of a dame in a transparent shimmy, with plenty of thems and those (*suddenly conscious of Miss Drehdel's presence*)—oh, excuse me.

MISS DREHDEL (*wearily*): That's all right. I read Earl Wilson's column, too.

FARISH: And a balloon coming out of her mouth saying, "I've had my Vita-Ray Cheese Straws today—*have you?*"

DUCKWORTH: No-o-o, it doesn't—it doesn't *sing*, if you know what I mean. I feel there's something gay and youthful and alive about these cheese straws. That's the note I want to hear in our copy.

DEGROOT: How about a gay, newborn baby in a crib? That would include the various elements. I'd like to see a line like "No harsh abrasives to upset tender tummies."

DUCKWORTH: No it's static. To me it lacks dynamism.

MISS DREHDEL: What's wrong with a closeup of the cheese straws and "20 cents a box" underneath?

DUCKWORTH: Over-simplification. They'd never get it.

MUNKACZI (*violently*): I've got it, V. J., *I've got it!*

DUCKWORTH: What?

MUNKACZI: We'll take one of these Conover models and bury her up to her neck in sand! Maybe some driftwood or a couple of clams for drama!

FARISH: How do we tie in the cheese straws?

MUNKACZI: I haven't worked it out yet, but it smells right to me.

DUCKWORTH (*excitedly*): Wait a minute, now—you threw me into something when you said "sand." What we need is grit —punch—conflict. I see a foxhole at Anzio—shells bursting— a doughboy with shining eyes saying, "This is what I'm fighting for, Ma—freedom of purchase the American Way—the right to buy Vita-Ray Cheese Straws on every drug, grocery, and delicatessen counter from coast to coast!"

FARISH: Man, oh man, that's terrific! I'll buy that!

DEGROOT: It's poetic and yet it's timely, too! It's a block-buster, V. J.!

DUCKWORTH (*radiant*): You really mean it? You're sure you're not telling me this just because I'm the boss? (*Indignation in varying degree from all*) O.K. If there's one thing I can't abide, it's a lot of yes men around me. Now let's get on to the Hush-a-Bye Blanket account. Any hunches?

DEGROOT: We got a darb. (*Producing two photographs*) This is what the nap of a Hush-a-Bye looks like under the microscope.

FARISH: And here's the average blanket. See the difference?

DUCKWORTH: Why, yes. It has twice as many woollen fibers as the Hush-a-Bye.

DEGROOT (*happily*): Check. There's our campaign.

DUCKWORTH: Hmm. Isn't that sort of defeatist?

FARISH: A little, but it shows we don't make extravagant claims.

DEGROOT: We could always switch the photographs.

FARISH: Sure, nobody ever looks at their blanket through a microscope.

DUCKWORTH (*dubiously*): We-e-ll, I don't know. I like your approach to the challenge, but I don't think you've extracted its—its thematic milk, shall I say. Now, I for one saw a different line of attack.

FARISH (*instantly*): Me too, V. J. What I visualize is a show girl with a real nifty chassis in a peekaboo nightgown. Here, I'll draw you a sketch—

MISS DREHDEL: Don't bother. We can read your mind.

MUNKACZI: Listen, V. J., do you want a wrinkle that'll revolutionize the business? Answer yes or no.

DUCKWORTH: Does it fit in with the product?

MUNKACZI: Fit in? It grows right out of it! You're looking at a beach, see? Voom! Right in front of you is a Powers girl buried up to the bust in sand, with some horseshoe crabs or seaweed as an accent.

DUCKWORTH: Do you see a Hush-a-Bye blanket anywhere in the composition?

MUNKACZI: No, that would be hitting it on the nose. Indirection, V. J., that's the whole trend today.

DUCKWORTH: You've realized the problem, Munkaczi, but your synthesis is faulty. I miss a sense of scope. Who are we rooting for?

MUNKACZI: Well, of course I was only spitballing. I haven't had time to explore every cranny.

DUCKWORTH: Look, kids, if you don't like what I'm about to suggest, will you tell me?

FARISH (*fiercely*): I've never been a stooge for anyone yet.

DEGROOT: You said it. There's not enough money in the world to buy *my* vote.

DUCKWORTH: That's the stuff. I want guts in this organization, not a bunch of namby-pambies scared that I'll kick 'em out into the breadline. Now this is hazy, mind you, but it's all there. A beachhead in the Solomons—a plain, ordinary G. I. Joe in a slit trench, grinning at the consumer through the muck and grime on his face, and asking, "Are you backing me up with Hush-a-Bye Blankets at home? Gee, Mom, don't sabotage my birthright with sleazy, inferior brands!"

DEGROOT: Holy cow, that'll tear their hearts out!

FARISH (*with a sob*): It brings a lump to your throat. It's a portion of common everyday experience.

DUCKWORTH: Remember, men, it isn't sacred. If you think you can improve the phrasing—

DEGROOT: I wouldn't change a word of it.

FARISH: It's got balance and flow and discipline. Say it again, will you, V. J.?

DUCKWORTH: No, it's pretty near lunch and we still need a slant for the Marvella Pearl people.

MUNKACZI (*exalted*): Your troubles are over, boss. I got something that leaps from the printed page into the hearts of a million women! It's four A.M. in the Aleutians. A haggard, unshaven Marine is kneeling in a shell hole, pointing his rifle at you and whispering, "Start thinking, sister! When Johnny comes marching home are you going to be poised and serene with Marvella Pearls or just another housewife?"

FARISH: Cripes, I had the same notion, V. J. He took the words right out of my mouth!

DEGROOT: I'll go for that! It's as timely as tomorrow's newspaper!

DUCKWORTH: There's only one thing wrong with it. It's *too* timely.

DEGROOT (*eagerly*): That's what I meant. It's depressing.

FARISH: It reminds people of their troubles. Ugh!

DUCKWORTH: Precisely. Now, I've been mulling a concept which is a trifle on the exotic side but fundamentally sound.

Mark you, I'm merely talking out loud. A girl on a bathing beach, almost totally buried in the sand, with a Marvella necklace and a brooding, inscrutable expression like the Sphinx. Haunting but inviting—the eternal riddle of womankind.

DeGROOT (*emotionally*): V. J., do you want my candid opinion? I wouldn't tell this to my own mother, but you've just made advertising history!

FARISH: It's provocative, muscular, three-dimensional! It's got a *spiral* quality, the more you think of it.

DUCKWORTH: How does it hit you, Munkaczi?

MUNKACZI (*warmly*): I couldn't like it more if it was my own idea.

DUCKWORTH: I wonder if Miss Drehdel can give us the woman's reaction, in a word.

MISS DREHDEL (*rising*): You bet I can. The word I'm thinking of rhymes with Sphinx. (*Sunnily*) Well, goodbye now. If anybody wants me, I'm over at Tim's, up to here in sawdust and Cuba Libres. (*She goes; a pause.*)

FARISH: I always said there was something sneaky about her.

DeGROOT: Women and business don't mix.

MUNKACZI: You can never tell what they're really thinking.

FARISH (*cackling*): Old V. J. smoked her out though, didn't he?

DUCKWORTH (*expansively*): Yes, I may be wrong, but this is one conference she won't forget in a hurry, eh, boys? (*As the boys chuckle loyally and scuffle to light his cigar.*)

CURTAIN

Sleepy-Time Extra

WHEN IT was first noised along Publishers' Row that the John B. Pierce Foundation, a nonprofit research organization, had instituted a survey dealing with American family behavior, attitudes, and possessions, public opinion was instantly split into two camps—into the larger, and drowsier, of which I fell. There is nothing like a good, painstaking survey full of decimal points and guarded generalizations to put a glaze like a Sung vase on your eyeball. Even the fact that the results of the poll were to be printed in that most exciting of current periodicals, *Business Week*, did little to allay my fatigue. Then, one morning in early April, hell started popping at my corner stationery store. "What's good today, Clinton?" I asked, browsing over the magazine rack. "Well, I tell you," replied Clinton, thoughtfully scratching the stubble on his chin (he raised corn there last year but is letting it lie fallow this season), "we just got the new number of *Business Week* containing the John B. Pierce Foundation survey on American family behavior, attitudes, and possessions." "Well, dog my cats!" I exclaimed, struck all of a heap. "Let's have a nickel's worth of those licorice gumdrops, will you, Clinton?" "Sure," said Clinton reluctantly, "but how about this new number of *Business Week* containing the John B. Pierce Foundation—" "Listen, Clinton," I said suddenly, "did you hear a funny little click just then?" "Aha," breathed Clinton, round-eyed. "What was it?" "A customer closing his account," I snapped, closing my account and taking my custom elsewhere.

It took a stray copy of the Buffalo *Evening News*, abandoned late yesterday afternoon on my bus seat by some upstate transient, to reveal the true nature of the survey and dispel my apathy. "Married Couples Favor Double Beds," trumpeted the dispatch. "Eighty-seven per cent of husbands and wives sleep together in double beds but 5% of the wives are dissatisfied with this and 40% think maybe twin beds would be ideal, *Business Week* Magazine reported today on the basis of a survey by the John B. Pierce Foundation, nonprofit research organization.

Other conclusions of the survey . . . included: In summer, 70.3% of the wives sleep in nightgowns, 24% in pajamas, 5% in the nude, and seven-tenths of 1% in shorts. Sixteen per cent of the women reported they would like to sleep in the nude, causing the Pierce Foundation to comment: 'Here we have clear-cut evidence of an inhibition.' . . . Fifty per cent of the husbands report no activity after getting into bed, 22% read, 12% talk, 7% listen to the radio, 3% say their prayers, 4% smoke, 2% eat. Comparable percentages for wives were 40% no activity, 29% read, 11% talk, 8% listen to the radio, 5% say their prayers, 3% think, 2% smoke, 2% eat."

Though one could speculate on the foregoing until the cows came home and distill all manner of savory psychological inferences, I cannot help wondering what machinery the Foundation used to obtain its statistics. Even the most incurious student of the report, I think, must ask himself eventually whether these delicious confidences were stammered into a telephone mouthpiece, or haltingly penned in a questionnaire, or whispered to a clear-eyed, bedirndled Bennington girl at the kitchen door. Somehow there is a grim, authoritative quality about the project which convinces me that the researchers went right to the source for their data, and I venture to think that more than one must have found himself embroiled in a situation like the following:

(*Scene: The bedroom of the Stringfellows, a standard middle-aged couple. Monty Stringfellow is a large, noisy extrovert who conceals his insecurity under a boisterous good humor. He affects heavy, hobnailed Scotch brogues and leather patches at the elbows of his sports jackets, is constantly roaring out songs commanding you to quaff the nut-brown ale, and interlards his speech with salty imprecations like "Gadzooks" and "By my halidom." Tanagra, his wife, is a sultry, discontented creature on whom fifteen years of life with a jolly good fellow have left their mark. As the curtain rises, Monty, in a tweed nightgown, is seated upright in their double bed singing a rollicking tune, to which he beats time with a pewter tankard and a churchwarden pipe. Tanagra, a sleep mask over her eyes, is trying to catch a little shut-eye and getting nowhere.*)

MONTY (*con brio*):

    "Come quaff the nut-brown ale, lads,

    For youth is all too fleeting,

    We're holding high wassail, lads,

    And life's dull care unheeding,

    So quaff the nut-brown ale, lads—"

TANAGRA: Oh, shut up, for God's sake! You and your nut-brown ale.

MONTY: What's wrong?

TANAGRA: Nothing. Nothing at all. What makes you think anything's wrong?

MONTY: I don't know—you seem to be on edge lately. Every time I open my mouth, you snap my head off.

TANAGRA: Every time you open your mouth, that blasted tune comes out. Haven't you anything else in your song bag?

MONTY: Gee, Tanagra, I always looked on it as our theme song, you might say. (*Sentimentally*) Don't you remember that first night at the Union Oyster House in Boston, when you made me sing it over and over?

TANAGRA: You swept me off my feet. I was just a silly little junior at Radcliffe.

MONTY: You—you mean our moment of enchantment has passed?

TANAGRA: I'll go further. Many's the night I've lain here awake studying your fat neck and praying for a bow string to tighten around it.

MONTY (*resentfully*): That's a heck of a thing to say. You keep up that kind of talk and pretty soon we'll be sleeping in twin beds.

TANAGRA: O. K. by me, chum.

VOICE (*under bed*): Aha!

MONTY: What's that? Who said that?

TANAGRA: I'm sure I don't know.

MONTY: There's somebody under this bed!

VOICE: There's nobody here except just us researchers from the John B. Pierce Foundation.

MONTY: W-what are you doing down there?

VOICE: Conducting a survey. (*Otis "Speedball" Ismay, ace*

statistician of the Foundation, a personable young executive, crawls into view from under the Stringfellow four-poster, flips open his notebook.) Evening, friends. Close, isn't it?

TANAGRA (*archly*): I never realized how close.

ISMAY: You the lady of the house? I'd like to ask a few questions.

MONTY: Now just a minute. I don't know whether I approve—

TANAGRA: Batten down, stupid, he's not talking to you. (*Brightly*) Yes?

ISMAY: Let me see. You prefer sleeping in a nightgown rather than pajamas?

TANAGRA: Well, that depends. With this clod, a girl might as well wear a burlap bag.

ISMAY (*with a disparaging glance*): Yeah, strictly from Dixie. You know, that's a darned attractive nightie you've got on right now.

TANAGRA: What, *this* old thing?

ISMAY: It sends *me*, and I'm a tough customer. What do they call these doodads along the top?

TANAGRA: Alençon lace.

ISMAY: Cunning, aren't they?

TANAGRA (*provocatively*): Think so?

ISMAY (*tickling her*): Ootsie-kootsie!

TANAGRA: Now you stop, you bad boy.

MONTY: Hey, this is a pretty peculiar survey, if you ask me.

TANAGRA: Nobody asked you.

ISMAY: Wait a second. You *could* tell me one thing, Mister —Mister—

MONTY: Stringfellow. Monty Stringfellow.

ISMAY: Do you belong to any lodges, fraternal associations, or secret societies?

MONTY: What kind do you mean?

ISMAY (*impatiently*): It doesn't matter. Any kind that keeps you busy evenings.

MONTY: Why, yes. I'm Past Grand Chalice of the Golden Cupbearers of the World, field secretary of the Rice Institute Alumni—

ISMAY: Fine, fine. Don't bother to list them. We merely wish to know what evenings you spend away from home.

MONTY: Every Tuesday and every other Friday. Is this all part of the survey?

ISMAY: Part? It's practically the lifeblood. Well, I think you've given me all the information I need. Oh, just one more detail, Mrs. Stringfellow. You understand there's a high percentage of error in an informal cross-section of this type and naturally we like to check our findings.

TANAGRA: Naturally.

ISMAY: I'd ask you to drop in at my office, but it's being redecorated.

TANAGRA: Yes, I read something in the paper to that effect. Is it serious?

ISMAY: No, no, it'll be all right in a day or two. For the time being, I've moved my charts and figures to the Weylin Bar, third table on the left as you come in at four-fifteen tomorrow afternoon.

TANAGRA: I'll be there half an hour early.

ISMAY: Splendid. (*To Stringfellow*) Thanks, old man, don't bother to show me to the door; I'll use the fire escape. Couple more calls to make in the building. Good night, all! (*He goes.*)

MONTY (*chortling*): Ho ho, that bird certainly pulled the wool over your eyes! He's no statistician. He didn't even have a fountain pen!

TANAGRA (*placidly*): Well, I swan. He sure took me in.

MONTY: Yes siree bob, you've got to get up pretty early in the morning to fool old Monty Stringfellow! (*He slaps her thigh familiarly and Tanagra sets her alarm for six forty-five.*)

CURTAIN

Amo, Amas, Amat, Amamus, Amatis, Enough!

YESTERDAY MORNING I awoke in a pool of glorious golden sunshine laced with cracker crumbs to discover that spring had returned to Washington Square. A pair of pigeons were cooing gently directly beneath my window; two squirrels plighted their troth in a branch overhead; at the corner a handsome member of New York's finest twirled his nightstick and cast roguish glances at the saucy-eyed flower vendor. The scene could have been staged only by a Lubitsch; in fact, Lubitsch himself was seated on a bench across the street, smoking a cucumber and looking as cool as a cigar. It lacked only Nelson Eddy to appear on a penthouse terrace and loose a chorus of deep-throated song, and, as if by magic, Nelson Eddy suddenly appeared on a penthouse terrace and, with the artistry that has made his name a word, launched into an aria. A moment later, Jeanette MacDonald, in creamy negligee, joined the dashing rascal, making sixty-four teeth, and the lovers began a lilting duet. The passers-by immediately took up the refrain; windows flew up at the Brevoort, flew down again; the melody spread rapidly up Fifth Avenue, debouched into Broadway, detoured into Park, and soon the entire city was humming the infectious strain in joyous tribute to Jeanette's and Nelson's happiness.

Caught up in the mood of the moment, I donned a jaunty foulard bow, stuck a feather in my hatband and one in my throat, and set out to look over spring fashions in love. That I ultimately wound up with a slight puff under one eye and a warning from a policewoman is not germane to the discussion. Truth is a wood violet that blooms in the least likely corner, and I found it in a couple of obscure pulp magazines called *Gay Love Stories* and *Ideal Love*, which retail at a dime apiece. Twenty cents for a postgraduate course in passion—*entre nous*, kids, I think I've got the only game in town.

Biologically, it was reassuring to find that the war had wrought no intrinsic change in the characters who people cut-rate romantic fiction; the smooth and deadly function of the glands continues undisturbed by the roar of high explosives. The ladies are as cuddly and adorable as they were before Pearl Harbor, the cavaliers as manly and chivalrous as any immortalized by Nell Brinkley and Leyendecker. Consider, for instance, Linda Marshall, the colleen of "Little Ball of Catnip," in the May *Ideal Love*, as she stands lost in dreams in her garden at Santa Monica, "slender and poised in a brown and white seersucker dress, the tight bodice cunningly trimmed in rickrack braid. She had a clear skin, nicely accented by dark eyebrows, lively hazel eyes, and beautifully fashioned cherry-red lips. The general impression was that of youth on the wing." Incidentally, there seems to be a strange, almost Freudian compulsion in both magazines to describe the heroine in avian terms—*vide* Kitty Malcolm in "Barefoot Blonde" (*Gay Love*): "That evening, after finishing a careful toilette, Kitty glanced at herself in the mirror, and knew that she had never looked lovelier. The black velvet gown molded her slim figure to perfection. In the gleaming nest of curls which she had scooped atop her head, Steve's gardenias, which had arrived via messenger, provided the last, elegant touch." It seems almost picayune of Steve not to have included a clutch of cold-storage eggs, or at least a nice fat worm, for the nest atop his inamorata's head as an earnest of eventual domesticity.

An even more tempting *bonne bouche* than Kitty is Bonita Kellsinger, grooming her lovely frame for the evening in "Shadow of Her Past" (*Gay Love*, June): "The very thought of such a triumph [winning the richest boy in Barnesville] brought roses to her richly tanned cheeks, brought a fiery sparkle into her wide, greenish-blue eyes. She brushed her thick, ripe-wheat colored hair until it hung on her straight slender shoulders in rich gleaming waves. A pair of small jewelled clips held back one wave of hair on either side of the girl's high, intelligent forehead. She made an enticing red rosebud of her mouth, and wound ropes of scarlet wooden beads around her neck and arms." Small wonder indeed that her gallant fidgets impatiently off scene at the wheel of his station wagon, which the author introduces parenthetically in one of the most syncopated bits of whitewash on record: "Cary had explained that he couldn't get adequate rations of gas for any of his cars but the wagon, which he used in working hours to haul people to and from his canning factory that was so busy putting up dehydrated foods for the Army and Navy." For sheer pith, the passage deserves a niche in the Hall of Exposition beside my all-time favorite, which graced one of the early Fu Manchu films. Briefly, the artful Doctor had eluded Nayland Smith by swarming down a rope ladder into the Thames. The ensuing scene revealed a vast underground cavern, in the foreground a rough deal table piled high with crucibles, alembics, and retorts bubbling with sinister compounds. After a pause, the table swung away, a trapdoor opened, and Dr. Fu crept up, followed by a henchman (Tully Marshall). "Well, Wing Chang," remarked the Doctor with a fiendish chuckle, "these old dye works certainly make an admirable laboratory of crime, do they not?"

Since every one of the nineteen novelettes and short stories I dipped into was written by a woman, the result is a gallery of fairly glamorous males, nearly all of them named Michael. It is practically six, two, and even that at some point in the action tiny muscles are going to flicker in lean jaws, eyes crinkle up quizzically at the corners, and six feet of lanky, bronzed strength strain a reluctant miss against a rough khaki shoulder (apparently the supply of smooth khaki shoulders has been exhausted, for whatever reason). There must have been a singularly dreamy look in the eye of Betty Webb Lucas, the author of "Blue Angel," (*Gay Love*), when she hatched Dr. Michael Halliday, chief surgeon of the City Hospital: "He was more like a Greek god, in spite of the flaming hair that threatened to break into rebellious curls at any moment, and the sterile white jacket straining over broad shoulders. His eyes were incredibly blue, and his sun-bronzed skin made them seem bluer still." Much as I respect honest emotion, I am afraid Miss Lucas became a trifle too dreamy in her medical dialogue: "Judy could only stare until he said impatiently: 'Haven't you anything else to do but stand there peering at me like a—a biological specie?'" The most charitable assumption in defense of Miss Lucas must be that the dear nearness of Judy in her crisp white nurse's uniform unnerved the eminent man.

It is hardly surprising that when these golden lads and lasses finally have at one another, they produce an effect akin to the interior of a blast furnace. Observe the Wagnerian encounter between the aforementioned Bonita Kellsinger and her beau ideal: "He caught her close to him, pinned her cheek against the rough khaki shoulder of his uniform, and slowly, deliberately covered her mouth with his, in a kiss that made her forget everything for the moment in the heady rapture of it. . . . They seemed to ascend to the top of a very high mountain, where there hung a white disc of moon in a sparkling bed of stars, and a soft breeze scented with jasmine swept over them. But when his lips lifted from hers, it was as though the cables had been cut from an elevator. She hit earth with a bump that shocked her awake." While Bonita brushes the meteorites from her hair and recovers her land legs, take a hinge at Lieutenant Lex McClure flinging a bit of woo in "Glass Walls are Cold" (*Ideal*): "Sally fought against it, but she felt as though she would die of the ecstasy that poured through her body. All of her senses quickened and became alert. She smelled the piney fragrance of his tobacco [that mixture of sun-dried burley and evergreen cones so popular of late with the armed forces] and the light scent of her own perfume. Her lips softened under his pressure, then she drew away softly, drawing her cheek across his chin, feeling the roughness of his day-old beard." Luckily, as one weaned on *The Perfumed Garden* and the Mardrus translation of *The Arabian Nights*, I was able to withstand this erotic byplay. Even so, I must confess that a bestial flush invaded my cheek and I had to fight off an overmastering impulse to pinch the hired girl.

At the risk of slighting any individual author, I must say the brightest star in the galaxy is unquestionably Leonora McPheeters whose "Perfumed Slacker" (*Ideal*, May) is subheaded "How could you love a man who always smelled like a boudoir?" For timeliness, melodrama, and a good old-fashioned concupiscence like Mother used to make, I haven't met its equal since the *Decameron*. The principals in this droll tale are two: John Craig, "tall, masculine, tweedy . . . a big overgrown Newfoundland pup, with his rough tawny hair and steady brown eyes," and Judy, a *zäftick* little proposition bent on bringing him to heel. Ostensibly the pair are engaged in running a cosmetic laboratory; actually, they seem to spend the business day mousing around each other, trading molten kisses and generally overheating themselves. Occasionally Judy varies the routine by kissing Bob, a shadowy member in a soldier suit who drifts in from an unspecified reservation, but these ersatz embraces only sharpen her appetite for the brand of judo dispensed by Craig. Unfortunately, the intra-office romance withers when Judy detects her employer's lack of enthusiasm for military service, and excoriating him for a coward and a caitiff, she gives him the mitten. Then, in a whirlwind denouement, she captures two enemy agents by upsetting a carboy of wave set over their heads and learns to her stupefaction that Craig has really been evolving explosives for the government. As the curtain descends, Philemon seizes Baucis in a sizzling hammer lock, superbly indifferent to the fact that they are standing ankle-deep in thermite and TNT, and rains kisses on her upturned face.

By one of those coincidences that are positively spooky, the hired girl opened my door at this juncture and found the bossman ankle-deep in a roomful of shredded pulp fiction, baying like a timber wolf. Before she could turn to flee, five feet seven of lanky, bronzed strength reached out and strained her against a rough pajama shoulder. I'm still trying to explain things to the employment agency, but they keep hanging up on me. You don't know anybody with full-fashioned cherry-red lips and a high, intelligent forehead who could help me with the housework, do you? She needn't bother about a uniform; just tell her to meet me in the Lombardy Bar at five tomorrow. They've got the best Dutch Cleanser in town.

Send No Money, Honey

I HAVE A well-defined suspicion, bounded on the south by Fortieth Street and the north by Fifty-seventh, that anybody venturing into the Times Square area who was not already sick of phosphorescent carnations is, by now, sick of phosphorescent carnations. Exactly when the craze for these luminous hybrids captured the popular imagination is uncertain—possibly during the dimout. At any rate, since then every midtown cranny too small for a watchmaker, a popcorn machine, or a publisher's remainders boasts its own little altar of black velvet from which carnations and brooches of debatable value give off a spectral greenish glow. It is not altogether clear, incidentally, whether people buy them to wear or to worship in private. The only time I believe I ever saw one off the leash was at the Rialto Theatre, when a woman's head, radiating a distinct nimbus, rose in a grisly, disembodied fashion and floated past me up the aisle. I assume it was illuminated from below by a phosphorescent corsage, but it may merely have been an ordinary disembodied head viewing the feature at a reduced rate of admission.

The vogue could be discounted as a sheerly local phenomenon except that a short time ago a prominent jobber of glowing novelties decided to invade the mail-order field. Hiring the back cover of a breezy magazine called *Laff*, the Glow-in-the-Dark Necktie Company of Chicago exhibited a twinkling four-in-hand flashing the words "WILL YOU KISS ME IN THE DARK, BABY?," accompanied by this text:

> Girls Can't Resist this KISS ME NECKTIE as it GLOWS in the Dark! By Day a Lovely Swank Tie . . . By Night a Call to Love in Glowing Words! . . . Here's the most amazing spectacular necktie that you ever wore, a smart, wrinkleproof, tailored cravat, which at night is a thrilling sensation! It's smart, superb class by day, and just imagine in the dark it seems like a necktie of compelling allure, sheer magic! Like a miracle of light there comes a pulsing, glowing question—WILL YOU KISS ME IN THE DARK, BABY? Think of the surprise, the awe you will cause! There's no trick, no hidden batteries, no switches or

foolish horseplay, but a thing of beauty as the question emerges gradually to life, touched by the wand of darkness, and your girl will gasp with wonder as it takes form so amazingly. . . . Send no money, here's all you do . . .

However unpredictable its reception by the beau monde, there is no gainsaying the romantic appeal of the glowing necktie in terms of theatre. Before some energetic drama-tist weaves the idea into a smash operetta or Leon Leonidoff preëmpts it for one of his opulent Music Hall presentations, I hasten to stake out my claim with the following playlet. If Metro-Goldwyn-Mayer would like it as a vehicle for Greer Garson (and I'm ready to throw in a whiffle-tree and two wheels), I shall be wearing a corned-beef sandwich this eve-ning in the third booth at the Brass Rail. Just walk by rapidly and drop the three dollars on the floor.

(*Scene: The conservatory of the country club at Heublein's Fens, Ohio. Fern Replevin, an utterly lovely creature of twenty-four whose mouth wanders at will over her features in the manner of Greer Garson's, sits lost in dreams, watching a cirrus forma-tion in the moonlit sky. Offstage the usual Saturday-night dance is in progress, and as mingled laughter and music drift in to Fern, she softly hums the air the orchestra is playing, "If Love Should Call."*)

FERN:

  If love should call, and you were I,
  And I were you, and love should call,
  How happy I could be with I,
  And you with you, if love should call.
  Your shoulders broad, your instep arched,
  Without your kiss my lips are parched.
  For love comes late, and now, and soon,
  At midnight's crack and blazing noon.
  My arms are ready, the wine is heady,
  If love should call.

(*Lafcadio Replevin, Fern's father, enters. He belongs to the Vigorous and Tweedy school—is headmaster, in fact—is leader in his community and a man who knows his way around the block, if no further. He has, as the saying goes, a groats-worth of wit in a guinea-sized noddle. Maybe the saying doesn't go just this way, but it certainly describes Lafcadio.)*

LAFCADIO: Oh, there you are, daughter; I've been looking all over for you. Why aren't you inside dancing with your fiancé, Fleetwood Rumsey, that is by far the richest man in town and owner of feed mills galore throughout the vicinity? There hasn't been any tiffin' between you, has there?

FERN (*indicating some scones and tea on the table*): Only what you see on this tray.

LAFCADIO: Then why are you staring at those clouds so pensively?

FERN: Perhaps I'm more cirrus-minded than the other girls.

LAFCADIO: Well, I don't like to see you moon around. As for me, I'm going in and have a drink with that new librarian. She's as thin as a *lath* and pretty *stucco* on herself, but I guess we can get *plastered*. (*He exits chuckling. Sunk in reverie, Fern is unaware that a man has emerged from behind a rubber plant and is regarding her narrowly. Rex Beeswanger is thirty-odd, a thoroughbred from his saturnine eyebrow to the tip of his well-polished shoe. His clothes, which he wears with casual elegance, bear an unmistakable metropolitan stamp. He is shod by Thom McAn, gloved by Fownes, belted by Hickok, and cravatted by Glow-in-Dark.*)

REX (*softly*): If you don't love him, why go through with it?

FERN (*whirling*): Oh! You startled me.

REX: Did I?

FERN: Did you what?

REX: Startle you.

FERN: Yes. I mean I was sunk in a reverie, and you spoke to me suddenly, and that startled me.

REX: You see things clearly, don't you? You're a very direct person.

FERN: Am I?

REX: Are you what?

FERN: A very direct person.

REX: Yes. When I startled you out of the reverie in which you were sunk, you didn't pretend I hadn't. That would have been cheap. And you're not cheap.

FERN: What are we talking about?

REX: Does it matter? Does anything matter but silver slanting rain on the cruel lilacs and compassion in the heart's deep core?

FERN: Who are you? You haven't even told me your name.

REX: Just a bird of passage. Call me Rex Beeswanger if you like.

FERN (*savoring it*): Rex Beeswanger. I've always wanted to know someone namcd Rex Beeswanger. It's—it's instinct with springtime and the song of larks.

REX: May I kiss you?

FERN: Oh, Rex, you've got to give me time to think. We've known each other less than forty-eight hours.

REX (*fiercely*): Is that all love means to you—narrow little conventions, smug barriers holding two kinsprits apart? I thought you finer than that.

FERN: Yes, but there's so much light in here. It's like a cafeteria or something. (*For answer, Rex extinguishes the lamp. Instantly the legend "WILL YOU KISS ME IN THE DARK, BABY?" springs into relief on his tie. The music inside swells and, silhouetted against the window, Fern lifts her voice in vibrant melody.*)

FERN:
> You glowed in the dark, I saw your spark,
> You left your mark on me.
> You're wrinkleproof, and so aloof,
> You made a goof of me.
> I might have been coy with another boy,
> But not when you said "Ahoy" to me.
> I'm a pearl of a girl, so give me a whirl.
> Ah, don't be a perfect churl to me.

(*As Fern and Rex lock lips, harsh light floods the room, and Fleetwood Rumsey, his bull neck distended with rage, stands glaring balefully at the pair.*)

FLEETWOOD: So this is what gives out behind my back.

FERN (*returning his ring*): Fleetwood, I think there is something you ought to know.

FLEETWOOD: In due time. First, I mean to show this meddling upstart how we deal with kiss thieves in Heublein's Fens. (*Sidestepping nimbly, Rex pins him in a grip of steel and slowly forces him to his knees.*)

REX: *Les jeux sont faits*, "Short Weight" Rumsey!

FLEETWOOD (*paling*): You—you know me then?

REX: Your leering visage adorns every rogue's gallery in the country. (*Encircling his captive's wrists with a set of shiny handcuffs*) Thanks to you, Miss Replevin, a notorious malefactor has received his just lumps. He had been adulterating his poultry mash with sawdust and sub-specification brans, causing a serious crimp in egg production.

FERN: My woman's intuition warned me. I wouldn't wipe my feet on the best part of him.

REX: Governmental appreciation will follow in due course. We have every reason to believe him the agent of a foreign power.

FLEETWOOD (*gutturally*): I get efen wiz you for zis zome time, Mr. Rex Beeswanger!

REX: Take him away, boys. (*Fleetwood is removed by two burly operatives as a corps de ballet of forty trained dancers swirls about Fern and Rex, symbolizing the gratitude of local poultrymen and 4-H Clubs alike. As the spectacle reaches a climax, the ushers, equipped with phosphorescent truncheons, flit through the darkened theatre like myriad fireflies and awaken the audience. On second thought, I don't believe I'll be in the Brass Rail tonight after all. There's no sense sticking my chin out.*)

CURTAIN

Acres and Pains: Chapter One

I F YOU can spare the time to drive sixty miles into the back-woods of eastern Pennsylvania, crouch down in a bed of poison ivy, and peer through the sumacs, you will be rewarded by an interesting sight. What you will see is a middle-aged city dweller, as lean and bronzed as a shad's belly (I keep a shad's belly hanging up in the barn for purposes of comparison), gnawing his fingernails and wondering how to abandon a farm. Outside of burning down the buildings, I have tried every known method to dispose of it. I have raffled it off, let the taxes lapse, staked it on the turn of a card, and had it condemned by the board of health. I have cut it up into building lots which proved unsalable, turned it over to picnic parties who promptly turned it back. I have sidled up to strangers and whispered hoarsely, "Psst, brother, want to buy a hot farm?" only to have them call a policeman. One rainy day, in desperation, I even tried desertion. Lowering a dory, I shouted, "Stern all for your lives!" and began sculling away rapidly. Unfortunately, I had forgotten to remove the flowers that grew in the boat, and nightfall found me still on the lawn with a backache and a fearful head cold.

I began my career as a country squire with nothing but a high heart, a flask of citronella, and a fork for toasting marsh-mallows in case supplies ran low. In a scant fifteen years I have acquired a superb library of mortgages, mostly first editions, and the finest case of sacroiliac known to science. In that period I made several important discoveries. The first was that there are no chiggers in an air-cooled movie and that a corner delicatessen at dusk is more exciting than any rainbow. On a fine night, no matter how fragrant the scent of the nicotiana, I can smell the sharp pungency of a hot corned-beef sandwich all the way from New York. I also learned that to lock horns with Nature, the only equipment you really need is the constitution of Paul Bunyan and the basic training of a commando. Most of the handbooks on country living are written by flabby men at the Waldorf-Astoria, who lie in bed and dictate them to secretaries. The greatest naturalist I know lives in a penthouse overlooking Central Park. He hasn't raised his window shades in twenty years.

Actually I never would have found myself in the middle of eighty-three unimproved acres had I been a bit less courteous. One day back in 1932, I was riding a crosstown trolley in Manhattan when I noticed a little old lady swaying before me, arms laden with bundles. Though almost thirty, she was very well preserved; her hair was ash-blonde, her carmine lips wore a mocking pout, and there was such helpless innocence in her eyes that I sprang to her rescue. Dislodging the passenger next to me, I offered her the seat and we fell into conversation. It soon developed that we had both been reared in the country and shared a mutual love for wildflowers and jam. At the next stop, I persuaded her to accompany me to a wildflower-and-jam store where we could continue our chat. It was only after our fifth glass of jam that my new friend confided her desperate plight. Her aged parents were about to be evicted from their farm unless she could raise five hundred dollars immediately. Through sheer coincidence, I happened to have drawn that amount from the bank to buy my wife a fur coat. Knowing she would have done likewise, I pressed it on the fair stranger and signed some sort of document, the exact nature of which escaped me. After a final round of jam, she presented me with her card and left, vowing eternal gratitude. On examining it, I noticed a curious inscription in fine print. It read, "Licensed Real-Estate Agent."

I still have the card in my upper bureau drawer. Right next to it, in a holster, is a Smith & Wesson .38 I'm holding in escrow for the lady the next time we meet. And we will—don't you worry. I've got plenty of patience. That's one thing you develop in the country.

Acres and Pains: Chapter Twelve

Now that spring again weaves a nest of robins in my hair and the first installment of the income tax fades into a discolored bruise, that annual bugbear, the vegetable garden, arises to plague me. As one who achieved the symmetry of a Humphrey Bogart and the grace of a jaguar purely on pastry, I have no truck with lettuce, cabbage and similar chlorophyll. Any dietitian will tell you that a running foot of apple strudel contains four times the vitamins of a bushel of beans. In my own case, at least, greens are synonymous with poison. Every time I crunch a stalk of celery, there is a whirring crash, a shriek of tortured capillaries, and my metabolism goes to the boneyard. Yet come the middle of April, the family invariably gets an urge to see the old man beating his brains out in the garden patch. It's funny, but nobody ever gets an urge to see him snoozing on the lounge. If he isn't staggering under a wheelbarrow of manure or grubbing in the subsoil, he's a leper.

Planning the garden takes place, as all the handbooks advise, long before the frost is out of the ground, preferably on a night recalling Keats's "Eve of St. Agnes," with hail lashing the windows. The dependents reverently produce the latest seed catalogue and succumb to mass hypnosis. "Look at those radishes —two feet long!" everyone marvels. "We could have them, too, if that lazy slug didn't curl up in the hammock all day." A list of staples is speedily drawn up: Brussels sprouts the size of a rugby, eggplant like captive balloons, and yams. Granny loves corn fritters; a half acre is allotted to Golden Bantam. The children need a pumpkin for Halloween, and let's have plenty of beets, we can make our own lump sugar. Then someone discovers the hybrids—the onion crossed with a pepper or a new vanilla-flavored turnip that plays the "St. James Infirmary Blues." When the envelope is finally sealed, the savings account is a whited sepulcher and all we need is a forty-mule team to haul the order from the depot.

The moment the trees are in bud and the soil is ready to be worked, I generally come down with a crippling muscular complaint as yet unclassified by science. Suffering untold agonies, I nonetheless have myself wheeled to the side line and coach a small, gnarled man of seventy in the preparation of the seedbed. The division of labor works out perfectly; he spades, pulverizes and rakes the ground, while I call out encouragement and dock his pay whenever he straightens up to light his pipe. The relationship is an ideal one, and I know he will never leave me as long as the chain remains fastened to his leg.

Within a few weeks the plants are sturdily poking their heads through the lava and broken glass, just in time to be eaten by cutworms, scorched by drought and smothered by weeds. The weeds native to the Pennsylvania countryside surpass in luxuriance anything you would encounter in the jungles of Cochin China or French Equatorial Africa. One variety I raised last summer had the sly hangdog phiz of a bookie and whispered off-color jokes every time I passed. Another, a revolting little fat weed, possessed the power of locomotion; it used to sneak around like Pecksniff, as though butter wouldn't melt in its mouth. I was also successful in developing a curious man-eating snail; but when the news photographer arrived to get a close-up, he and the snail frightened each other off the premises.

By the end of August the residue left by the rabbits and woodchucks is ready for harvest. It is always the same—tomatoes and squash. Tomatoes and squash never fail to reach maturity. You can spray them with acid, beat them with sticks and burn them; they love it. In forty-eight hours the place is knee-deep in rotting pulp and a fearful miasma overhangs the valley. Soon the most casual acquaintances start dropping in with creaking baskets and hypocritical smiles, attempting to fob off their excess tomatoes and squash. The more desperate even abandon tiny bundles on our doorstep like infants at the House of the Good Shepherd. The kitchen becomes an inferno of steam and the wife a frenzied sorceress stirring caldrons of pink slush. Ultimately, with a fanfare comparable to launching a dreadnought, two minute jars filled with an appalling green emulsion are borne to the table. If you don't taste it, you're a cad; if you do, you're a cadaver. The only solution is to plow everything under and live on pie. Reach for the sky, partner; I'm the Crisco Kid.

Don't Bring Me Oscars
(When It's Shoesies That I Need)

Is THERE anybody hereabouts who would like to pick up, absolutely free, the exclusive American rights to one of the most thrilling documentary films ever left unfinished? I know where such a property can be acquired, together with the exclusive world-wide rights, a brand-new Bell & Howell camera, a director's whistle, a folding canvas chair (my name can always be painted out and your own substituted), a pair of white riding breeches, and a megaphone for barking orders at actors. In fact, I am even prepared to slip a deuce to anyone who removes a bundle containing the foregoing from my flat, and, what's more, I'll throw in the issue of the *Times* that inspired the whole business.

The impulse to capture on film a small but significant segment of the life around me was awakened by a feature article, in the Sunday screen section of that paper, on Roberto Rossellini. "Armed only with a movie camera and an idea," reported a Berlin correspondent, "the gifted director of *Open City* and *Paisan* has been shooting a picture called *Berlin, Year Zero*, with a nonprofessional cast headed by an eleven-year-old street urchin." It was the account of Rossellini's iconoclastic production technique that particularly riveted my attention:

> The script is literally being written as the shooting progresses in an effort to keep it as realistic as possible. When young Edmund, the star, is in a dramatic situation, Rossellini asks, "What would you say if this really happened to you?" The boy comes back with some vivid remark which probably would not get by the Eric Johnston office and if it isn't too obscene it goes into the script. Once during a street scene a truckload of bread went by. Forgetting everything, Edmund piped, "My goodness, I could eat all that bread!" "Don't cut, don't cut!" shouted Rossellini. "Leave it in!"

The unabashed, Rabelaisian coarseness of Edmund's remark understandably brought a tide of crimson to my cheeks, but when the shock had subsided, it presented a challenge.

If Edmund's exclamation was dramatic, the casual dialogue around my own household was pure Ibsen. For all I knew, the prattle I brushed aside as humdrum or picayune had a truly Shakespearean majesty and sweep; collected on celluloid, it might wring the withers of moviegoers across the nation, send them alternately sobbing and chuckling into a thousand lobbies to extol my genius. I saw myself fêted as the poet of the mundane, the man who had probed beneath the banality and commonplaceness of the American home and laid bare its essential nobility. The thought of the prestige and money about to accrue made me so giddy that I felt a need to lie down, but as I was already lying down I merely removed the *Times* from my face and consolidated my plans. Using the family as actors, and the Rossellini method of improvisation, I would make a documentary of an afternoon in the life of some average New York apartment dwellers. I summoned my kin and excitedly outlined the project. My wife's enthusiasm was immediate, though she cloaked it under a show of apathy; it was evident she was livid at not having conceived the idea herself.

"A really crackpot notion," she admitted, confusing the word with "crackerjack" with typical feminine disregard for the niceties of slang. "You've outdone yourself this time."

"I ought to be the star," whined my son, an eleven-year-old house urchin. "I was in our school play last year."

"No, me, me!" shrilled his sister. "I want to wear Mummy's mascara!"

"Get this, Mr. Burbage," I snapped, "and you too, Dame Terry. This is one picture without stars, or makeup, or any of that Hollywood muck. I want authenticity, see? Don't try to act; just be natural. Behave as if there were no camera there at all."

"If you want *complete* realism," began my wife, her face brightening hopefully, "why not do away with the cam—"

"That'll do," I interposed. "Now put on your *rebozos* and slope out of here, the lot of you. I've got a pretty heavy production schedule, and I haven't time to *schmoos* with actors. Remember, everybody on the set tomorrow at three sharp —we start grinding whether you're here or not." I spent the remainder of the day as a seasoned old showman would, gulping bicarbonate of soda, reading *Variety*, and evolving a

trademark for my stationery. The trademark offered something of a problem. After toying with the idea of combining
the emblems of J. Arthur Rank and M-G-M, to show a slave
striking a lion, I rejected it as Socialistic and devised one that
portrayed a three-toed sloth pendant from a branch, over the
motto "Multum in Parvo." The exhibitors might not understand it too well, and, frankly, I didn't either, but it had dignity
and a nice swing to it.

The first player to report at the appointed hour next day was
my son; he entered the foyer wearing an Indian war bonnet
and a bathrobe, an outfit that did not seem characteristic of
a lad fresh from school, especially in the dead of winter. He
assured me, though, that he and his mates occasionally liked to
vary their standard costume of snow jackets and arctics, and I
got a trucking shot of a small Indian in a pitch-black hallway
that I will match against anything of the sort Hollywood has
to offer. Renewing my strictures that my son was to behave
spontaneously and follow his normal routine, I dissolved to
the living room, crouched down between the andirons, and
prepared to take an arresting camera angle of his movements,
shooting through the fire screen. In a rather self-conscious,
stagy manner, the boy deposited his briefcase on a table, lit a
pipe, and, settling into an armchair, buried himself in an article
on Kierkegaard in the *Antioch Review*.
   "Hold on a second, Buster," I said, puzzled. "There's something wrong here. I don't know what it is, but an artificial
note's crept in. Somehow I get the feeling you're acting. Think
hard—is this what you actually do every afternoon?"
   "Sure." He nodded. "Sometimes I add up the checkbook
and then kick the dog, the way you do. Shall I do that?" Eventually, I managed to impress on him the difference between
reality and make-believe, a distinction philosophers have been
struggling to clarify for the last twelve hundred years, and he
consented to re-enact his habitual procedure, warning me, in
all fairness, that it might entail a certain amount of damage.
   "Smash anything you like," I ordered impatiently. "Let's have
the truth, the more gusto the better. The rest is mere bookkeeping." He shrugged and, retrieving his briefcase, scaled it
across the room to indicate how he generally discarded it. An

exquisite porcelain Buddha that had cost me thirty dollars and
two days of haggling in Hong Kong crashed to the floor. It
made such a superb closeup that I could not repress a cry of
elation.

"Bravo! Tiptop!" I encouraged. "Whatever you do, keep
rolling—don't break the rhythm! I'm getting it all!" Humming
a gay little air, the actor turned into the kitchen and helped
himself to a bowl of rice pudding, half a cream cheese, an orange, a stalk of celery, and a glass of charged water, leaving the
cap off the bottle and the door of the refrigerator open. I then
panned with him to the breadbox, where he surreptitiously
trailed his finger through the icing on a chocolate cake and
nibbled the corner of a napoleon. In the ensuing shot, another
transition, we milked the hall closet for some surefire footage.
He made a routine check of my overcoat, observing that he
frequently found change in the pockets and that it tended to
gather rust if left there indefinitely. On the threshold of his
room, a strange hesitancy overcame him. He paused, obviously
loath to reveal the next phase for fear of parental censure.

"I—I just turn on Jack Armstrong and do my homework till
it's time to black Sister's eye," he said evasively.

"Come, come," I prodded. "We're not in the cutting room
yet. You left something out."

"Well-l-l," he said, "once in a while I blow up the toilet."

"What for?" I demanded, aghast.

"Nothing," he replied. "It makes a nice sound." All the fel-
las, it appeared on cross-examination, diverted themselves with
this scholarly pastime, and since I realized that my canvas must
stand or fall on its fidelity to nature, I set myself to film it.
Preparations were soon complete; with smooth efficiency, the
boy emptied a can of lye into the bowl, attached a long cord to
the handle, and, flinging a lighted match into the lye, yanked
the cord. There was a moment's ominous silence. Then a roar
like the bombardment of Port Arthur shook the plumbing, and
a nine-foot geyser of water reared skyward, subsiding in a curtain of mist. The effect, photographically speaking, was similar
to what one sees when standing under Niagara Falls (except for
the towels and the toothbrushes in the background, of course);
actuarially speaking, it shortened my life ten years. The end
result, nevertheless, was worth while, for in his exultation the

child uttered a line immeasurably more graphic than that of Rossellini's young hero.

"My goodness!" he exclaimed. "I'd certainly hate to have to mop up all that water!"

"Don't cut, don't cut!" I shouted. "Leave it in!" The fact that we had no sound equipment and that Junior's *mot* had not been recorded in the first place weakened my position somewhat, but then, you can't have everything.

With the poor sense of timing you might expect of amateurs, my wife and daughter chose this, of all moments, to arrange their entrance, arms heaped with groceries, and in the restricted area of the foyer I was unable to jockey the camera to obtain a first-rate composition. The good woman instantly raised a hue and cry over the state of the bathroom, forgetful of the fundamental movie axiom that omelets are never made without breaking eggs. My brief statement that we had simply blown up the toilet reassured her, however, and, pointing out how the overhead was piling up, I urged her to go about her customary activities. A sequence chock-full of human interest resulted, in which she deliberately mislaid or hid all my important papers and shirt studs, sent out the wrong ties to the cleaners, and made a series of dinner dates on the telephone with people she knew I could not abide. To quicken the tempo and ensure flexibility of mood, I intercut several shots of my daughter daubing water colors on the rug and writhing in a tantrum before her music stand.

"Capital," I applauded my troupe. (Performers, and very young ones in particular, are like children—you have to play upon their vanity.) "Now, son," I said, "you'll have to handle the camera, because here's where I usually come home." To a man, they all cringed involuntarily, but my directorial eye was quick to detect and rectify the fallacy. "Get those two shakers of Martinis ready, and remember, everyone, shouts of glee when Daddy walks in." In a trice, I had slipped into the part —merely a matter of sagging a shoulder or two and assuming a murderous scowl. Just as I was shuffling toward the outside door to build up suspense for my arrival, it burst open violently, and three characters I had not foreseen in my budget catapulted in. In the order of their ascending hysteria, they were the furnaceman, the elevator boy, and the superintendent. The last carried what we theatrical folk call a prop—a fire ax—and, in the parlance of the greenroom, he was winging.

The scene that followed, though noisy and fraught with tension, was of little cinematic consequence. It dealt with some argle-bargle about a flood in the apartment below, and its audience appeal, except to plumbers and, possibly, a lawyer or two, would be slight. I understand that additional scenes, or "retakes," are to be made on it very shortly in Essex Market Court. I may drop down there just out of sheer curiosity. My schedule isn't nearly as heavy as it was, now that I've shut down active production at the studio.

Rancors Aweigh

SEVEN HUNDRED TONS of icy green water curled off the crest of the California ground swell and struck with malignant fury at the starboard plates of the S. S. *President Cleveland*, westbound out of San Francisco for Honolulu, Manila, and Hong Kong. Midway along its deserted promenade, huddled in a blanket, a solitary passenger sprawled in his deck-chair, pondering between spasmodic intakes of breath the tangled web of circumstance that had enmeshed him. To even the most cursory eye—and there was no shortage of cursory eyes among the stewards hurrying past—it was instantly apparent that the man was exceptional, a *rara avis*. Under a brow purer than that of Michelangelo's David, capped by a handful of sparse and greasy hairs, brooded a pair of fiery orbs, glittering like zircons behind ten-cent-store spectacles. His superbly chiseled lips, ordinarily compressed in a grim line that bespoke indomitable will, at the moment hung open flaccidly, revealing row on row of pearly white teeth and a slim, patrician tongue. In the angle of the obdurate outthrust jaw, buckwheat-flecked from the morning meal, one read quenchless resolve, a nature scornful of compromise and dedicated to squeezing the last nickel out of any enterprise. The body of a Greek god, each powerful muscle the servant of his veriest whim, rippled beneath the blanket, stubbornly disputing every roll of the ship. And yet this man, who by sheer poise and magnetism had surmounted the handicap of almost ethereal beauty and whose name, whispered in any chancellery in Europe, was a talisman from Threadneedle Street to the Shanghai Bund, was prey to acute misery. What grotesque tale lurked behind that penetrable mask? What dark forces had moved to speed him on his desperate journey, what scarlet thread in Destiny's twisted skein?

It was a story of betrayal, of a woman's perfidy beside which the recidivism of Guy Fawkes, Major André, and the infamous Murrel paled to child's play. That the woman should have been my own wife was harrowing enough. More bitter than aloes, however, was the knowledge that as I lay supine in my

deck-chair, gasping out my life, the traitress herself sat complacently fifty feet below in the dining saloon, bolting the table
d'hôte luncheon and lampooning me to my own children. Her
brazen effrontery, her heartless rejection of one who for twenty
years had worshiped her this side of idolatry and consecrated
himself to indulging her merest caprice, sent a shudder through
my frame. Coarse peasant whom I had rescued from a Ukrainian
wheat-field, equipped with shoes, and ennobled with my name,
she had rewarded me with the Judas kiss. Reviewing for the
hundredth time the horrid events leading up to my imbroglio,
I scourged myself with her duplicity and groaned aloud.

The actual sell-out had taken place one autumn evening
three months before in New York. Weary of pub-crawling and
eager to recapture the zest of courtship, we had stayed home
to leaf over our library of bills, many of them first editions. As
always, it was chock-full of delicious surprises: overdrafts, mo-
distes' and milliners statements my cosset had concealed from
me, charge accounts unpaid since the Crusades. If I felt any
vexation, however, I was far too cunning to admit it. Instead,
I turned my pockets inside out to feign insolvency, smote my
forehead distractedly in the tradition of the Yiddish theater,
and quoted terse abstracts from the bankruptcy laws. But
fiendish feminine intuition was not slow to divine my true feelings. Just as I had uncovered a bill from Hattie Carnegie for
a brocaded bungalow apron and was brandishing it under her
nose, my wife suddenly turned pettish.

"Sixteen dollars!" I was screaming. "Gold lamé you need
yet! Who do you think you are, Catherine of Aragon? Why
don't you rip up the foyer and pave it in malachite?" With a
single dramatic gesture, I rent open my shirt. "Go ahead!" I
shouted. "Milk me—drain me dry! Marshalsea prison! A pau-
per's grave!"

"Ease off before you perforate your ulcer," she enjoined.
"You're waking up the children."

"You think sixteen dollars grows on trees?" I pleaded, seeking to arouse in her some elementary sense of shame. "*Corpo
di Bacco*, for sixteen dollars a family like ours could live in Siam
a whole year! With nine servants to boot!"

"And you're the boy who could boot 'em," my wife agreed.
"Listen, ever since you and that other pool-room loafer
Hirschfeld got back from your trip around the world last year,

all I've heard is Siam, morning, noon, and night. Lover, let us not dissemble longer. *Je m'en fiche de Siam.*"

"Oh, is that so?" I roared. "Well, I wish I were back there this minute! Those gentle, courteous people, those age-old temples, those placid winding canals overhung with acacia——" Overhung with nostalgia and a little cordial I had taken to ward off a chill, I gave way to racking sobs. And then, when my defenses were down and I was at my most vulnerable, the woman threw off the veneer of civilization and struck like a puff adder.

"O.K.," she said briskly. "Let's go."

"Go?" I repeated stupidly. "Go where?"

"To Siam, of course," she returned. "Where'd you think I meant—Norumbega Park?" For a full fifteen seconds I stared at her, unable to encompass such treachery.

"Are you crazy?" I demanded, trembling. "How would I make a living there? What would we eat?"

"Those mangosteens and papayas you're always prating about," she replied. "If the breadfruit gives out, you're still spry enough to chop cotton."

"B-but the kiddies!" I whimpered, seeking to arouse her maternal sense. "What about their schooling—their clay and rhythms? Who'll teach them to blow glass and stain those repugnant tie-racks, all the basic techniques they need to grow up into decent, useful citizens?"

"I'll buy a book on it," she said carelessly.

"Yes, do," I urged, "and while you're at it, buy one on the snakes and lizards of Southeast Asia. Geckos under your pillow, cobras in the bathtub—not that there *are* any bathtubs —termites, ants, scorpions——"

"You'll cope with them," she asserted. "You did all right with that viper on Martha's Vineyard last summer. The one in the electric-blue swim-suit and the pancake make-up."

"I see no reason to drag personalities into this," I thundered. Deftly changing the subject, I explained as patiently as I could that Siam was a vast malarial marsh, oppressively hot and crowded with underprivileged folk scratching out a submarginal existence. "You and I would stifle there, darling," I went on. "It's a cultural Sahara. No theaters, no art shows, no symphony concerts——"

"By the way," she observed irrelevantly (women can never

absorb generalities), "how was that symphony you attended Tuesday at the Copa? You were seen with another music-lover, a lynx-eyed mannequin in black sequins featuring a Lillian Russell balcony."

"I brand that as a lie," I said quietly, turning my back to remove a baseball constricting my larynx. "A dastardly, barefaced lie."

"Possibly," she shrugged. "We'll know better when the Wideawake Agency develops the negative. In any case, Buster, your next mail address is Bangkok." In vain to instance the strife and rebellion sweeping Asia, the plagues and political upheaval; with the literal-mindedness of her sex, the stubborn creature kept casting up some overwrought declaration I had made to the effect that there was not a subway or a psychoanalyst north of Singapore.

"No," I said savagely, "nor a pediatrician, an orthodontist, or a can of puréed spinach in a thousand miles."

"That's what I've been dreaming of," she murmured. "Keep talking. The more you say, the lovelier it sounds." At last, spars shot away and my guns silenced, I prepared to dip my ensign, but not without one final rapier thrust.

"Well, you've made your bed," I said cruelly. "I wash my hands. Bye-bye Martinis." The blow told; I saw her blanch and lunged home. "There's not a drop of French vermouth between San Francisco and Saint Tropez." For an instant, as she strove with the animal in her, my fate hung in the balance. Then, squaring her shoulders, her magnificent eyes blazing defiance, she flung the shaker into the grate, smashing it to smithereens.

"Anything you can do, I can do better," she said in a voice that rang like metal. "Fetch up the seven-league boots. Thailand, here I come."

Had the ex-Vicereine of India attended the Durbar in a G-string, it would have occasioned less tittle-tattle than the casual revelation to our circle that we were breaking camp to migrate to the Land of the White Elephant. "She dassen't show her face at the Colony," the tongues clacked. "They say he smokes two catties of yen shee gow before breakfast. *In Reno veritas.*" Rumors flew thick and fast. They ranged from sniggered allusions to the bar sinister to reports that we were actually bound for the leper colony at Molokai, the majority opinion holding that we were lammisters from the FBI. The more charitable among our friends took it upon themselves to scotch these old wives' tales. "He's merely had a nervous breakdown," they said loyally. "You can tell by the way he drums his fingers when she's talking." Our children, they added, were not real albinos, nor was it true I had been made contact man for a white slave ring in Saigon. I was much too yellow.

The reaction of the bairns was equally heart-warming. When the flash came that they were shortly transplanting to the Orient, they received it impassively. Adam, a sturdy lad of twelve, retired to his den, barricaded the door with a bureau, and hid under the bed with Flents in his ears in readiness for headhunters. His sister Abby, whose geography at ten was still fairly embryonic, remained tractable until she discovered that Siam was not an annex of Macy's. She thereupon spread-eagled herself on the parquet and howled like a muezzin, her face tinted a terrifying blue. Toward evening the keening subsided and both were cajoled into taking a little nourishment through a tube. On discussing the matter tranquilly, I was gratified to find they had been laboring under a misapprehension. They had supposed we were going to discontinue their arithmetic and spelling, a situation they regarded as worse than death. When I convinced them that, on the contrary, they might do five hours of homework daily even en route, their jubilation was unbounded. They promptly contrived wax effigies of their parents and, puncturing them with pins, intoned a rubric in which the phrase "hole in the head" recurred from time to time.

Ignoring the tradesmen who, under the curious delusion that we were about to shoot the moon, crowded in to collect their accounts, we fell to work assembling the gear necessary for an extended stay out East. Perhaps my most difficult task was to dissuade the memsahib from taking along her eighty-six-piece Royal Doulton dinner service. I tried to explain that we would probably crouch on our hams in the dust and gnaw dried fish wrapped in a pandanus leaf, but you can sooner tame the typhoon than sway the bourgeois mentality. Within a week, our flat was waist-high in potato graters, pressure cookers, pop-up toasters, and poultry shears; to the whine of saws and clang of hammers, crews of carpenters boxed everything in sight, including the toilet, for shipment overseas. My wife's cronies, lured by the excitement like bears to wild honey, clustered about loading her with dress patterns, recipes for chowchow, and commissions for Shantung and rubies, while children scrambled about underfoot flourishing marlinspikes and igniting shipwreck flares. Through the press circulated my insurance broker, who had taken the bit in his teeth and was excitedly underwriting everyone against barratry and heartburn. Doctors bearing Martinis in one hand and hypodermics in the other immunized people at will; a cauldron of noodles steamed in a corner and an enterprising Chinese barber worked apace shaving heads. The confusion was unnerving. You would have sworn some nomad tribe like the Torguts was on the move.

A lifelong gift of retaining my aplomb under stress, nevertheless, aided me to function smoothly and efficiently. Cucumber-cool and rocket-swift, canny as Sir Basil Zaharoff, I set about leasing our farm in the Delaware Valley and our New York apartment. The problem of securing responsible tenants was a thorny one, but I met it brilliantly. The farm, naturally, was the easier to dispose of, there being a perennial demand for dank stone houses, well screened by poison sumac, moldering on an outcropping of red shale. Various inducements were forthcoming; ultimately, by paying a friend six hundred dollars and threatening to expose his extramarital capers, I gained his grudging consent to visit it occasionally. Disposing of our scatter in town, though, was rather more complex. The renting agents I consulted were blunt. The rooms were too large and sunny, they warned me; sublessees were not minded to run the risk of snow blindness. Washington Square, moreover, was deficient in traffic noise and monoxide, and in any event, the housing shortage had evaporated twelve minutes before. Of course, they would try, but it was a pity our place wasn't a warehouse. Everybody wanted warehouses.

The first prospects to appear were two rigidly corseted and excessively genteel beldames in caracul who tiptoed through the stash as gingerly as though it were a Raines Law hotel. It developed that they were scouts for a celebrated Hungarian pianist named Larczny, and their annoyance on learning that we owned no concert grand was marked. I observed amiably that inasmuch as Larczny had begun his career playing for throw money at Madame Rosebud's on Bienville Street, he might feel at home with the beer rings on our Minipiano. The door had hardly slammed shut before it was reopened by a quartet of behemoths from Georgia Tech. Wiping the residue of pot-likker from his chin with his sleeve, their spokesman offered to engage the premises as a bachelor apartment. The deal bogged down when I refused to furnish iron spiders for their fatback and worm gears for their still.

Interest the next couple of days was sporadic. A furtive gentleman, who kept the collar of his Chesterfield turned up during the interview, was definitely beguiled, but did not feel our floor would sustain the weight of a flat-bed press. He evidently ran some sort of small engraving business, cigar-store coupons as I understood it. Our hopes rose when Sir Hamish Sphincter, chief of the British delegation to United Nations, cabled from the *Queen Elizabeth* earmarking the rooms for his stay. Unfortunately, on arriving to inspect our digs, the baronet and his lady found them in a somewhat disordered state. Our janitor, in a hailstorm of plaster, was just demolishing the bathroom wall to get at a plumbing stoppage. By the time he dredged up the multiplication tables the children had cached there, Sir Hamish was bowling toward the Waldorf. We never actually met the person who rented the flat after our departure, but his manners were described as exquisite and his faro bank, until the law knocked it over, was said to be unrivaled in downtown Manhattan. I still wear on my watch-chain a .38 slug which creased the mantelpiece and one of his patrons, though not in the order named.

Dusk was settling down on Washington Square that early January afternoon and a chill wind soughed through the leafless trees as I marshaled our brave little band for the take-off. Trench-coated and Burberryed, festooned with binoculars, Rolleiflexes, sextants, hygrometers, and instruments for sounding the ocean floor, we were a formidable sight. The adults, their nerves honed to razor sharpness by weeks of barbital and bourbon, were as volatile as nitroglycerine; the slightest opposition flung them into apocalyptic rages followed by floods of tears. Without having covered a single parasang, the children had already accumulated more verdigris and grime than if they had traversed Cambodia on foot. The bandage on Adam's hand acquired in a last-minute chemistry experiment had unwound, but he was dexterously managing to engorge popcorn, read a comic, and maneuver an eel-spear at the same time. Abby, bent double under her three-quarter-size 'cello, snuffled as her current beau, a hatchet-faced sneak of eleven, pledged eternal fealty. Heaped by the curb were fourteen pieces of baggage exclusive of trunks; in the background, like figures in an antique frieze, stood the janitor, the handyman, and the elevator operators, their palms mutely extended. I could see that they were too choked with emotion to speak, these men who I know not at what cost to themselves had labored to withhold steam from us and jam our dumbwaiters with refuse. Finally one grizzled veteran, bolder than his fellows, stepped forward with an obsequious tug at his forelock.

"We won't forget this day, sir," the honest chap said, twisting his cap in his gnarled hands. "Will we, mates?" A low growl of assent ran round the circle. "Many's the time we've carried you through that lobby and a reek of juniper off you a man could smell five miles down wind. We've seen some strange sights in this house and we've handled some spectacular creeps; it's a kind of a microcosm like, you might say. But we want you to know that never, not even in the nitrate fields of Chile, the smelters of Nevada, or the sweatshops of the teeming East Side, has there been a man——" His voice broke and I stopped him gently.

"Friends," I said huskily, "I'm not rich in worldly goods, but let me say this—what little I have is mine. If you ever need anything, whether jewels, money, or negotiable securities, remember these words: you're barking up the wrong tree. Geronimo."

Their cheers were still ringing in my ears twenty minutes later as our cab swerved down the ramp into Pennsylvania Station. Against the hushed cacophony of the Map Room, I began to hear another and more exotic theme, the tinkle of gamelans and the mounting whine of the anopheles mosquito. The overture was ending. The first movement, *molto con citronella*, had begun.

Mama Don't Want No Rice

O N A DANK winter's day shortly after the Chinese New Year, the population of Upper Lascar Row in Hong Kong was enjoying its midmorning snack of bêche-de-mer and jasmine tea when the street was galvanized by the advent of a quartet of foreign devils so manifestly aching to be plundered that a mighty hosanna welled up the length of Queen's Road Central. Abacuses began clicking furiously, catchpenny ivories of the goddess Kwan Yin bloomed on every curio dealer's shelf, factory-fresh Ming horses were hastily baptized with dust to simulate age and tempting whiffs of Lapsang Soochong wafted about to decoy the Outer Barbarians. While the latter bore no placard proclaiming their nationality, certain obscure indications tended to establish them as an American family. In typically Yankee matriarchal style, the party was headed by a well-preserved woman of thirty-odd, her features distorted by an insensate craving for bargains and an iron resolve to paper the Thieves' Market with her husband's money. Trotting at her heels, as obedient as a coach-dog, came the present deponent, bearing in his arms the gallimaufry of opium lamps, snuff-bottles, door-knockers, sandalwood fans, and ceremonial scrolls she had bartered for his heart's blood. A man of rare gentleness, possessed of almost Socratic wisdom and a patience outrivaling Job's, he recognized no law but his wife's airy caprice; at her bidding (provided, of course, that he was not otherwise occupied), he was prepared to scale the snows of Everest or plumb deepest Lake Titicaca. Straggling behind and alternately whining, sassing their parents, and cudgeling each other, there followed two wiry hooligans in levis and polychromatic flannel jumpers. It was a sight for sore eyes, this close-knit, harmonious little company sprinkling valuta indiscriminately over the crown colony, and many miraculous cures were subsequently reported by local opticians. The day dawns, nevertheless, when even the Comstock Lode yields up nothing but gravel, and finally, on the very brink of insolvency, I brought the juggernaut to a halt. Straining at a gnat and swallowing the smoke of a

Camel, I slapped from my wife's hand the Sung pipkin she had purchased with our last greenback.

"That's enough rubbish for one day, sweetheart," I hinted. "Back to the carbarn before I touch a whip to your flanks." My sally, as I anticipated, awoke no response from the stolid creature, whose sense of humor seldom rose above the Punch and Judy level. Flushed with resentment, eyes akimbo, she planted herself squarely in my path and declined to move. Fortunately, I happened to recall an apothegm of the T'ang dynasty to the effect that more flies may be captured with honey than with vinegar. I adroitly introduced the subject of food and suggested that we have a spot of tiffin in a tiny Szechuanese restaurant near by, where the sweet-and-sour squid and *gedämpfte* kelp boasted an international reputation.

"I refuse to taste another spoonful of that excelsior!" announced the margravine in a ringing voice. "We've been on this blasted reef four days and all we've eaten is barnacles and boiled string! I want something that sticks to the ribs."

"Hamburgers!" the children caught up her refrain. "We want flapjacks with maple syrup—chicken enchiladas—apple pandowdy!" By now a crowd of several hundred Chinese was pressing in on us, eager to miss none of the fireworks; so, distributing to them a rough translation of the proceedings in the Fukien dialect, concluding with an impassioned appeal never to marry, never to have children, and never to travel abroad with their wives and children, I made our adieux. We dined sumptuously on triple-decker sandwiches and quadruple malteds at a busy soda fountain off Chater Road, whose neon lighting and ulcerous tempo afforded a reasonably repugnant facsimile of our neighborhood drugstore. Over the postprandial Bisodol tablet, I bade my bride close her eyes and placed in her outstretched palm a bulky envelope. Her wee brow wrinkled in perplexity as she spelt out the destination of the steamer tickets within.

"What's this?" she asked suspiciously. "Why does it stand 'Macassar' on these?"

"Because that's where the steamer goes, honey," I smiled. "It's the principal port on the island of Celebes."

"Is that anywhere near Bangkok?" she demanded. "Come on, answer me—none of that Eric Ambler stuff!"

"Well—er—vaguely," I hedged. "About twenty-seven hundred miles as the crow flies, more or less. Naturally, we won't——"

"Just a second, Jocko," she interrupted, quivering with anger. "Do I interpret this to mean that you inveigled me all the way to Siam and then switched the deck on us?"

"Of course not," I said placatingly. "It's a little extra dividend —kind of a warm-up for Siam, so to speak. By the time you get back from the Moluccas—if you ever *do* come back—Siam will look like Rockefeller Plaza." Exactly as instinct had warned me, the poor thing kicked up the most preposterous fuss. She drew a ghoulish picture of a remote and unexplored archipelago swarming with vampire bats, anthropophagi, and virulent diseases; cited some absurd fiddle-faddle about the war in Java (a grotesque designation for the minor police action in which the Dutch, to preserve order, had unavoidably bombed Djokjakarta and were being forced to kill a few thousand extremists); and having pilloried me as irresponsible, a delayed juvenile, and an erotic dreamer nourished on *Terry and the Pirates*, flung her arms around the children and defied Lucifer himself to drag her to the East Indies. To overcome such a hash of obscurantism and prejudice was a task calculated to intimidate a lesser man, but I flatter myself I brought it off rather well. Tapping a monogrammed Zira on the wafer-thin, solid gold cigarette case conferred on me by the Sublime Porte in connection with certain trifling services in the matter of the Missing Halvah, I pointed out with a silky smile that through a freak of bookkeeping, I alone was privileged to endorse our express cheques, which gave me what is known in sporting circles as an edge. "Do you not think, *cara mia*," I pursued, "that, though undeniably colorful and renowned for its hospitality, Hong Kong would not be the most ideal place for an attractive matron—who, parenthetically, is not getting any younger—and two helpless minors to go on the beach? I ask this, mind you, in an altogether objective spirit, knowing that your opinion will be couched likewise."

"You rat," replied my wife, employing a pet name she had found useful in domestic crises when logic failed. It being self-evident that she should never have crossed foils with so superior an adversary, I gallantly forgave her temerity and proceeded to outline our itinerary: two weeks' voyage aboard the M/s *Kochleffel* along the periphery of Java via the South China Sea, calling at Batavia, Semarang, and Surabaya, and thence northward to Macassar. "What happens there?" she asked wearily, a look of dumb resignation investing her face. "I suppose we all remove our drawers and plunge into the canebrake."

"In the hands of Disraeli, irony can be a formidable weapon," I rejoined. "In a lout it becomes merely offensive. At Macassar we transfer to the *Cinnabar*, a snug little coaster in the interisland copra trade, which will convey us to Pare-Pare, Donggala, Menado, Ternate, Morotai, Sorong (the westernmost tip of New Guinea), Batjan, and Amboina—in short, a sketchy circumnavigation of Celebes and the historic Spice Islands. I also plan, if the changing monsoon permits, to pay a visit to Banda Neira, that celebrated outpost of the Dutch nutmeg trade."

"There must be a gimmick in all this," she observed, moodily gnawing a piece of stem ginger. "In twenty years I have yet to detect you in a disinterested act."

"There is," I acknowledged. "The terminal point for our soiled laundry will be that jewel of the Lesser Sundas, the island of Bali."

"Aha!" she exclaimed triumphantly. "Everything falls into place. I was puzzled by the goatish gleam in your eye, but now I'm tuned in."

"Are you implying by any chance, madam," I asked scathingly, "that I would deliberately haul three persons on a five-thousand-mile journey through swamp and mangrove just to catch a glimpse of a bunch of superbly formed, mocha-colored young women in their nether garments? Because if you are," I said, rising haughtily, "I have nothing more to say."

"That," she said succinctly, "will be a relief all around—eh, kids?" The children's reply was inaudible, mainly because they had taken a powder during our tête-à-tête and made a beeline for Pedder Street, the informal bourse of Hong Kong. On being corralled outside the Swatow Lace Store, they disclosed a flimflam worthy of Ponzi, having thimblerigged the moneychangers with a dizzying parlay of soap wrappers into Portuguese escudos into Singapore dollars. I could not bring myself to reprove them, particularly since they had cleared a tidy profit, but as a lesson to cut me into their grift in future, I made them finance a tour of the Tiger Balm Gardens at Causeway Bay.

This curious nonesuch, a conceit of Aw Boon Haw, the noted patent-medicine taipan and philanthropist, beggars description; it is at once a potpourri of Madame Tussaud's waxworks, the castle of Otranto, and a theatrical prop shop, the whole tinctured with fumes of the Mexican drug called mescal. Just what its eighteen acres of nightmare statuary, turrets, grottoes, mazes, and cloud-borne pagodas signify, nobody on earth knows—not even its proud parent, upon whom I called for a fast exegesis next morning at his headquarters in Wanchai Road. Prior to our interview, Mr. Haw's interpreter, a Celestial version of Russell Birdwell, coated me with the customary schmaltz about his employer's humble origins, business genius, and benevolence. He then expanded with equal tedium on the virtues of Tiger Balm itself, which he unhesitatingly hailed as a specific for everything from St. Anthony's fire to milk leg. Apparently this was the universal belief, for I afterward observed Chinese air passengers rubbing it on their foreheads to forestall airsickness, at the same time smearing it furtively on the fuselage to insure the plane's staying aloft. For a preparation consisting largely of menthol and balsam, it undoubtedly has extraordinary powers. They may derive from Mr. Haw himself, a mettlesome old party in carpet slippers, who gripped my hand with such extraordinary vigor that I was forced whimpering to my knees.

"Now exactly what do you wish to know?" the interpreter began. Feeling that some preamble was required, I teed off with salutations from several American mandarins of comparable importance—Eugene S. Grace, Lee Shubert, and the chairman of the New York State Boxing Commission.

"In a few badly chosen words, how would you sum up the theme of the Tiger Balm Gardens?" I inquired.

"Mr. Haw has presented to various hospitals and deserving charities an amount in excess of eighteen million Hong Kong dollars," replied the spokesman. "He is a beloved figure, asking nothing for himself but the right to serve his fellow man."

"He exudes an aura of goodness," I agreed courteously, cracking a sunflower seed between my mandibles, "but to return to the meaning of the Gardens. I sensed a definite surrealist influence, as though Max Ernst and the St. Louis Cardinals had collaborated on their design."

"The purely material is no longer of any consequence to Mr. Haw," the interpreter explained. "Spiritual salvation alone can save mankind from the abyss, as he points out in today's editorial in his three Chinese-language newspapers."

"I am hastening home to read it," I assured him. "But before I do, may I be allowed to put one more query?"

"What is that?"

"Has Mr. Haw given any inkling yet as to who will inherit his moola? If not, I should like to include my name among the legatees."

"I am afraid there is a fundamental cleavage between the East and the West," apologized the subordinate. "This way to your rickshaw, please." Nevertheless, as I bowled back to the Repulse Bay Hotel, gently flicking the coolie with a switch to ward off the flies, the audience did not seem wholly without benefit. It had given me an insight into the complexities of the Oriental mind such as one never gets from the sixty-five-cent luncheon at Chin Lee's and it had enabled the family in my absence to dream up a brand-new batch of complaints.

The most grievous, predictably, came from the missy, who was loud in her accusations that I had withheld her from the night life of Hong Kong. "What did I pack my evening dresses for, to wear in a Malay prahu?" she blubbered. "If I were Alexis Smith you'd be in a cummerbund fast enough." She contemptuously brushed aside my protest that Catteraugus, New York, was more diverting by far; she knew all about the evil waterfront haunts, the swarthy lascars, and the Eurasian adventuresses from the novels of Achmed Abdullah. The upshot was that at midnight we found ourselves in a titanic, murky cabaret almost devoid of heat and customers, watching the only untalented Negro in the world execute a cakewalk to the music of a Filipino fife and drum corps. At its conclusion, as though my hair was not sufficiently streaked with silver, he broke into "Mammy's Little Coal Black Rose." I pushed away the plate of stone-cold spaghetti and signaled to the waiter.

"Bring me a check and a steel-blue automatic," I directed. My wife plucked at my sleeve, but I ignored her. "Also, please ask that minstrel to wait for me in his dressing room."

"Listen," she said insistently, "some people in that corner are waving at you." The arrivals proved to be an old college classmate now in the consular service and two extremely decorative chickadees, from Canton and Outer Mongolia respectively. A coalition was quickly arranged, half a dozen bottles of Polish vodka burgeoned from the tablecloth, and in a trice we were yoked in close harmony, warbling "Brunonia, Mother of Men" in pidgin. Before long a pair of laughing almond eyes cajoled me to the dance floor, where my 1922-vintage toddle excited wide admiration, especially from those who had never seen a man dancing with a pair of laughing almond eyes. I had just consented after considerable suasion to call on the fair Tartar some afternoon and inspect a rare old sheepskin which had been in her family since the reign of Kublai Khan when my wife was stricken with one of her infrequent migraine headaches. There was no possible remedy but to frog-march me into a cab, drive to the hotel, and bind my hands to the bedpost with a sheet. This relieved her suffering somewhat, and soon the only sound in the corridor was her uneven breathing, interspersed with maledictions I had not dreamt she possessed.

Three days later, in a freezing wind that turned our noses blue with cold, we swayed up the accommodation ladder of the *Kochleffel*, buffeted by coolies groaning under our trunks. The harbor traffic flowed on briskly around the ship, oblivious of the importance of the occasion; toplofty little steamers bound for Macao rocked up-river, Kowloon-side ferries scraped past the bows, and quaint junks wallowed by, laden with Parker pens, self-winding Rolexes, and other imports vital to China's existence. Free of her buoy at last, the vessel moved at half speed past the bare brown hills; the last cluster of government buildings dropped astern, and we were at sea. Already the bar had begun to echo with guttural commands of "*Jonges!* Bring me here a Bols!" and toasts to Wilhelmina. Knocking the embers from my pipe into a lifeboat to prevent their scattering, I descended to our cabins. My three companions sat in the quickening gloom amid jumbled suitcases. It was obvious that their moral barometer was falling fast.

"Chin up, friends!" I adjured them jovially. "Before you know it, you'll be in Java."

"And that's practically home," added my wife in a lifeless voice. She rose and stared thoughtfully out the porthole. "Did I ever tell you," she went on, "that in order to marry you, I jilted an explorer?"

"Honestly?" I asked. "What did you tell him?"

"I wish I could remember," she murmured. "It sure would come in handy."

Columbia, the Crumb of the Ocean

O F ALL the sorry places on earth one might have elected to be caught in that February forenoon, it seemed to me that mine was easily the most wretched. To recline at full length in a wicker chair three miles off the coast of Borneo, shielded from the tropical sun by a snowy ship's awning and caressed by the vagrant airs of the west monsoon, and, between cooling draughts of lime squash tempered with a little gin, to contemplate the plight of my friends in New York, was as painful an experience as any I had ever endured. I pictured them drearily slogging through the blackened midwinter slush on sleeveless errands, hunched over their desks falsifying Hooper ratings and evolving new catch-phrases to sell merchandise nobody wanted, writing music that would never be hummed and novels that would be remaindered on publication day. I saw them, faces taut with nervous tension, bolting their food in the rough and tumble of crowded restaurants, having their pants pressed by dollar cleaners, teeth drilled by painless dentists, psyches purged by cut-rate analysts. My heart bled for them. With every fiber of my being I longed to be at their side, making their burden a little heavier and lending a deaf ear to their troubles, but unfortunately I was ten thousand miles away and getting farther every minute. Was there not some way I could pay tribute from this distant clime to their bulldog fortitude? I racked my brain without success, and then, of a sudden, it came to me. Touching the bell at my elbow I had had installed by a cunning artificer in Hong Kong, I instructed the Chinese bar steward to replenish my drink with three more. I was not actually drinking them for my own sake, I explained, but rather for my friends *in absentia*. He understood immediately (the Chinese have a quick awareness of the obligations of friendship), and sped away like the wind. I sighed contentedly and lay back, watching the milky jade wake of the vessel bubble astern as her mighty engines churned on toward the Indies.

Though scarcely seventy-two hours had elapsed since I had embarked my troupe on the *Kochleffel* for Batavia, I already felt a not inconsiderable affection for the ship. A stubby, comfortable packet built in the early Twenties for the Java-China-Japan service, her mahogany panels and brass fittings somehow reminded me of the old Fall River Line; I had the same exhilarating sense of sin and derring-do I had known in youth making a first overnight excursion from Providence to New York. What was sadly lacking, to be sure, was a couple of those raucous, scarlet-faced drummers smoking Hoffman Fancy Tales and bragging about their amorous triumphs, but at least we had an exotic equivalent in the two dozen Chinese émigrés from Amoy sharing first class with us. A number of these were dispersed about the deck at the moment, lapping up the ubiquitous orange soda of the East and dandling those extraordinary fat and cheerful infants characteristic of Chinese families on every economic level. Thirty feet off, my own lar-vae, puffy with sunburn, were absorbed in a cutthroat game of deck golf with Mynheer Vogt-Bensdorp, an elephantine Dutch lawyer from Java, and his equally massive vrouw. It was a gay and heart-warming scene, especially viewed through the hazy perspective of several toddies, and I was just falling into a di-vine snooze when my wife, with a woman's unfailing flair for disrupting her husband's well-being, erupted from a gangway. She leaned coquettishly on the arm of the captain, a Teutonic, bottle-nosed Hollander who had clearly just finished paying her some heavy gallantry, and the simper on their faces as they bore down on me was alarmingly like that of Kay Francis and Paul Henreid in a short-budget domestic comedy.

"Why, *there* you are, darling," she drawled with the same aristocratic hauteur Maggie was wont to assume toward Jiggs when she discovered his stockinged feet on the Chippendale. "Whatever are you doing with all those glasses?"

"Draining 'em," I replied tersely. "The same thing you were doing up in the chartroom when I peeked in a while ago."

"Oh, that," she smiled carelessly. "Captain van Popinjay was explaining the sextant to me, weren't you, captain?"

"I bet he was," I said. "With his arm around you to steady you against the roll of the ship. I don't know what we need a gyroscope for, the way this salt-water mink goes around steady-ing passengers against the roll of the ship."

"Please?" said the captain blandly. "I do not believe I understand very well."

"You're doing all right, Casanova," I growled. "Just keep those flippers of yours in the wheelhouse where they belong, *compisco?*" My spouse intervened nervously, knowing that if my ire were sufficiently aroused, I could demolish a grape with a single blow of my fist, and we adjourned to the veranda for the customary pre-luncheon ritual.

This institution, a sacrament aboard every Dutch cockleshell since the reign of William of Orange, was religiously attended by the entire Occidental contingent of nine, including the chief mate and the engineer, a young missionary of some obscure order bound for Flores, and a stolid housewife, heavily *enceinte*, who rarely lifted her eyes from her embroidery hoop. The routine was unvarying; we all sat rigidly upright in a circle gulping down countless ponies of Bols while our shipmates dredged up as many insults to America as they could think of. To describe in a paragraph the scope and malignity of their hatred would be impossible; suffice to say it took every form from mere boorishness to almost psychotic malevolence. Faced with the realization that their colonial empire was coming apart at the seams like a wet paper box, that after three centuries of befriending the Asiatic brother, their noses were being plucked out of the feedbag, and that their homeland within a few years must again shrink to an insignificant pimple on the North Sea, our Dutch cousins were in a truly fearful wax. By some nightmarish process of logic, they had succeeded in convincing themselves that the UNO was responsible for their debacle in Indonesia, and hence that we, as American nationals, were legitimate targets for their barbs. As we joined the *Kaffeeklatsch*, Father de Groot, the young missionary, favored us with a dazzling smile.

"I was just telling my countrymen," he said, "that if it were not for Hendrick Hudson, you Yankees would still be eating dried buffalo meat and scalping each other."

"Yes, and don't forget Peter Stuyvesant, and Cornelius Vanderbilt," chimed in the chief engineer. "They civilized the barbarians and now the dirty money-grubbers are telling us how to rule our own subjects."

"Well, of course the Americans are not really civilized," observed Mynheer Vogt-Bensdorp, drawing comfortably on his perfecto. "Gangsters—assassins. Do you know that it is not safe for a girl to go out on the streets of Chicago?"

"Personally, I cannot warm up to the American girls," interpolated the first mate. "They remind me of dried herrings —skinny, half-dead creatures. All they want is money, money, money."

"Ugh, how can anybody live in such a country?" Mevrouw Vogt-Bensdorp shuddered. "No culture, no traditions, just the almighty dollar and jazzing around the whole time with the cocktails."

"You know, I had an experience," Captain van Popinjay mused. "I was during the war in the same prison camp with some Yank soldiers and you can't even understand what language the *Dummkopfs* are talking."

"No, it's easy," the chief engineer corrected him. He turned to me with a mischievous twinkle. "Coca-Cola hot dog stick 'em up!" The group dissolved in helpless laughter. I disengaged my fingers from the arm of my chair, which I had squeezed to matchwood, loosened my collar to afford more clearance for my Adam's apple, and stood up.

"If you muzzlers have finished sprinkling Paris green on my appetite," I said courteously, "we should like to be excused to disinfect ourselves before dining. Don't bother to get up, gentlemen; my wife isn't used to these little niceties." Descending the companionway, I overheard them agreeing that all Americans were roughnecks and that our social graces were on a par with those of the African wart-hog.

The meal that followed these didoes was no less enchanting. Prepared with a shrewd eye to the ninety-degree temperatures, it led off with a large basin of boiling pea soup dotted with sausage and booby-trapped with a pig's knuckle sprinkled with fried onions. On the heels of this dainty *Vorspeise* came *paupiettes de veau*, a highly lethal meatball garnished with soggy boiled potatoes and hillocks of that most diuretic of all vegetables, purslane. I cannot honestly say I wolfed the *paupiettes* down greedily, principally because, back in 1932, I fed one of them to a champion schnauzer I was bringing back from Europe on the old S. S. *Columbus* and the poor beast dropped dead off the Hen and Chickens lightship. In the sweetmeat division of the *Kochleffel*'s menu, the choice of dessert generally lay between semolina pudding, a tasteless batter that paralyzed the craw on contact, and the epicurean nonesuch called Gouda, whose esoteric flavor I could never distinguish from mouse cheese. To add a final fillip, our dismal groceries were served at breakneck tempo by seven Chinese waiters and enlivened with further running commentary from the Lowlanders on our children's table manners, slovenly dress, and general swinishness.

Once, however, we managed to anesthetize ourselves to a few minor details like the food and the unrelenting xenophobia, shipboard life fell into a fairly pleasant pattern. There were always enough fresh excitements—flying fish, squalls, prahus, sea birds, and innumerable islands—to punctuate our indolent routine, and it was difficult to believe, the morning we anchored at Tandjong Priok, the harbor of Batavia, that the South China Sea lay behind us. Since the steamer was due to sail the next morning for Surabaya, our glimpse of Batavia was hardly more than fleeting. Through the good offices of a friend of Hirschfeld's—who, incidentally, had traversed this territory fifteen years before and left a trail of worthless chits —we were privileged to drive around the city, glut ourselves with dream-boat Chinese food, and visit the museum. Batavia, apart from the old fort and a sprinkling of seventeenth-century houses, offers approximately as much appeal to the senses as Poughkeepsie, except that it is hotter and devoid of Vassar girls; but the museum is a fit subject for dithyrambs, and were it not for the fact that a dithyrambectomy in childhood inhibits me from using them freely, I could unlimber some pretty lush superlatives. The Hindu-Brahmin sculptures from the Borobudur, the batiks, and the jewelry in the Gold Room certainly dwarf any similar collections in the West; and among other charming relics on view, if the sightseer's arches can stand the gaff, is the very room Captain Bligh occupied after his epochal longboat voyage from the South Pacific to Timor, containing some exceptional memorabilia. There were in the capital, it should be noted, no visible signs of the blood-letting that was rife in the interior of Java, the daily ambush of Dutch convoys and the extinction of whole kampongs in reprisal. The Dutch, apparently impervious to world-wide censure of their invasion of the Republic of Indonesia, were currently pretending that their *coup de main* was successful and that everyone would be playing patty-cakes shortly. The truth was, nevertheless, that they controlled only a few isolated areas and those only by overwhelming weight of arms. You had merely to witness the sullen contempt with which the Javanese treated their white protectors to realize that the imperial goose was cooked forever—a dismaying fact from which Britain in Malaya and France in Indo-China were still girlishly hiding their eyes.

Soon after the *Kochleffel* cleared Tandjong Priok for Semarang, three new passengers made their appearance: Mr. Chen, a young Chinese businessman en route, like ourselves, to the Moluccas, and a Mr. and Mrs. Hoogmeister. Mr. Chen was one of those fantastic Celestials who, at twenty-four, have acquired the poise and commercial acumen of a merchant prince. He knew to a decimal what the zloty and the pengö were being quoted at in the free markets of Tangier and Bangkok, he had dealt in every outlandish commodity from gum copal to rhinoceros horn, and there was hardly a port from Tsingtao to Thursday Island he had not set foot in at one time or another. His shy and self-deprecatory manner concealed a host of accomplishments; he played the electric guitar like Charlie Christian and the violin passably, was an adept sleight-of-hand performer and a formidable opponent at chess, and had an absolutely hypnotic touch with cards. The impact of so versatile a talent upon our children, who by now had had a surfeit of flying fish, was as pronounced as though Houdini himself had come on board. Within half an hour, the three were holed up in our cabin with cigars clenched in their teeth (my daughter handled hers surprisingly for a girl of eleven), playing canasta for three guilders a point. Perhaps our most grisly moment, though, occurred when we stumbled on Abby and Mr. Chen in the smoking saloon, sawing out a 'cello-and-violin duet of "Slow Boat to China." The possibility that I had whelped a future member of Phil Spitalny's all-girl orchestra so completely unnerved me that I collapsed in my wife's arms and had to be revived with intravenous injections of Courvoisier.

Mr. and Mrs. Hoogmeister, the other new arrivals, constituted no such social addition but were quite as remarkable. The former was a wizen-faced, Ichabod Cranelike exporter from Celebes, married a fortnight to a Frenchwoman thirty years his junior and uxorious to the point of folly. Though the lady was not downright misshapen, she was certainly nothing to heat the blood, and the surveillance he kept her under, his elaborate concern lest she stray out of his sight, brought to mind a Palais Royal farce. Madame Hoogmeister was seeing the Orient for the first time, her husband confided to me; he had fixed up what he described as a lavish home for her in Macassar, complete with a new Studebaker and a Frigidaire—had, in fact, gone to the devil's own expense to gratify her caprice, but it was pathetically plain that the bride was already fairly cheesed off on her surroundings. She kept complaining about the heat, the helicopter cockroaches which disrupted her sleep, the coarse and uninspired food. Hoogmeister was in a swivet; one's heart went out to him since he was, by his own admission, such a humane and lovable figure. When he talked about the Indonesians, whom he called "my children," the hackles were assured plenty of exercise. He was fond of observing that in the good old times, the natives always crouched on the floor in his presence to show their subservience, but nowadays, emboldened by our American rubbish about democracy, they invariably stood up, as if they were his equals.

"Mind you, I'm a decent chap," he protested. "If a coolie asked me for a light for his cigarette, in a proper tone, I'd gladly give him one." His wife cocked her head and regarded him affectionately.

"You really like these people, don't you, dear?" she inquired.

"Like them?" he repeated oracularly. "I don't like them— I *love* them!"

Any expectation we entertained of visiting Semarang, we learned on reaching it, was fatuous; the Dutch military had proscribed the port as too dangerous for civilians to land. Consequently, the ship lay well out in the bay while its cargo was being lightered ashore through swarms of sharks and angelfish ceaselessly circling about for food. As landlubbers might, we were understandably impressed by sharks fourteen feet in length, but Captain van Popinjay pooh-poohed them as small fry. In 1928, he informed us, he had captured a thirty-foot specimen off Billiton whose stomach contained an amazing variety of objects. I cannot remember them all, but among them were a complete set of the Waverley novels in half Morocco, a bicycle pump, an ocarina, a roll of sprigged muslin, a miter box, and an early portrait of the Duchess of Richmond by Lely.

It was somewhere between Semarang and Surabaya that I began to get an inkling of the friendly interest being taken in our party by the Dutch. Father de Groot had repeatedly tried to inveigle me into a political discussion, hoping I would reveal myself as a secret agent, but to no avail. One afternoon, the children bounced in with tidings that he had been grilling them about my opinions. Was it not true that their daddy held a Communist party card and deeply admired Russia? Did he seem distressed or jubilant at the news that Dewey had lost the election? For whom had he voted—Wallace? Had they noticed any bearded individuals, redolent of vodka and caraway seeds, frequenting our home? The tots conducted themselves with textbook sang-froid. They replied that on the few occasions I came home, I was too befuddled with malt to talk intelligibly about anything, let alone politics. Having spent most of my life in jail, they continued, I was ineligible to vote. The only bearded visitor they recollected was a man named Hirschfeld, who drew amusing doodles on cardboard but otherwise appeared to have no grasp on reality. Father de Groot retired snarling to his breviary and thereafter made only one reference to any of us. He told Mr. Chen that our children were much too precocious.

On Sunday noon, in a white-hot glare that made the pavements dance and shriveled the brain to a raisin, the four of us teetered down the main street of Surabaya toward its principal oasis, the Oranje Hotel. More leisurely and countrified than Batavia, and perceptibly cleaner, Java's second largest city also seemed far more colorful. The people strolling past represented every conceivable racial strain: pert Javanese youths in immaculate whites and Moslem caps, tall melancholy Hindus, Buginese boatmen, delectable Madurese ladies in bajus and sarongs, and prosperous Chinese compradores, twirling cotton umbrellas, in striped pajamas and sola topi. The particular sound that struck the ear and set the rhythm of Surabaya was the measured, musical clack of teklets, the wooden clogs worn everywhere in the archipelago, but by nobody with as much élan as the Madurese charmers I refer to. Stooping to retrieve one that had fallen squarely in my path (a teklet, that is), I suddenly found myself swept full-tilt into the Oranje lobby by my wife.

"I know that gambit, Jack," she said coldly. "You're stalemated before you start. Now you freeze right there while I scare up some *rijsttafel*." Two hours later, distended with rice, we picked our way heavily to a stifling movie theater where we sat like overfed pythons until sundown. The feature was some hoary masterpiece with Esther Ralston and Monte Blue, but it made no evident difference to the Javanese consumers or the thirty-odd Dutch troopers scattered about the house with carbines on their backs. I was told on returning to the ship that we had seriously imperiled our lives entering the cinema, as some dissident had tossed a grenade into it the previous week. My wife, with her eyes fixed on Father de Groot, commented in offhand fashion that explosives were second nature to me, since I had for years been personal bodyguard to Joseph Stalin. The padre gave her a sour grimace and buried his nose in his semolina.

The night before the *Kochleffel* was due in Macassar was a busy one. In our sweltering stateroom, tripping over each other's feet as we worked, the signora and I laboriously packed our anarchical baggage—unknowing that for the next four days, owing to the shortage of hotel space in Macassar, we would be forced to remain *in situ*. Then, weak with exhaustion, we crawled out on the forward boat-deck to drink in the cool midnight breeze blowing up from the Arafura Sea. A heavy footfall sounded near us; dimly in the glow of his cigar stump, I discerned the features of Captain van Popinjay.

"Well," he remarked, indicating the East Indies with a proprietary wave, "you don't have anything like this in America, do you? Go on—take a good look, it belongs to everybody."

"Check," I agreed, "and when he finally realizes it, sugar, you'd better stay in bed with your hat on."

Whenas in Sulks My Julia Goes

"HAVE YOU ever been lonely/ Have you ever been blue?" The lachrymose, velveteen voice of Perry Como, released from wax by the dubious magic of a gramophone needle, soared upward on the tropical night, floated across the courtyard of the Princess Hotel in Bali, and wove like a dental drill into the room where I sat sunk in a bamboo armchair. For the fifteenth time in as many minutes, I beat a clenched fist against my skull to relieve the pressure slowly forcing it asunder and strove to focus on the page before me. Lytton Strachey had never been more lucid; his sonorous, balanced sentences, almost Biblical in their majesty, rolled on relentlessly detailing the final tragedy of Chinese Gordon, but concentrate as I might, nothing emerged but the plaintive bleat of unrequited love. Without raising her head from the dressing-table where she was seated lacquering her nails, my wife addressed me.

"Well, Bright Eyes," she remarked in the detached, over-casual manner with which wives introduce a topic they have been brooding over for hours, "if you've finished your imitation of Cozy Cole, I'd like to file a few words. We've been on this island paradise exactly two weeks. When, if I may borrow a phrase from that twilit world of the St. Nicholas Arena and the Hotel Alamac in which you love to skulk, do you propose to throw in the towel?"

Ordinarily, so bumptious a statement would have stung me to a quick retort; I would have annihilated the woman with a single glance, excoriated her for a virago and a Philistine insensitive to the beauty about us, and made her grovel for her presumption. Yet, as I proceeded to take rapid inventory of the past fortnight, there was no denying our sojourn on Bali had been a notably dismal one. Aside from several extraordinary Legong and monkey dances and some really bewitching scenery, the balance definitely stood on the debit side. For nearly the entire period, our young had been hors de combat with dysentery, jungle boils, and ulcers of the leg—none of them especially fatal complaints, to be sure, but frustrating when one's medical kit consisted of phenobarbital and bobbie pins.

Through five days of fever and delirium, I myself had wrestled with an unclassified bacillus, now bivouacked in my Eustachian tubes as snugly as a bear in a hollow tree. As for our quarters, which had stirred me to madrigals after the rigors of Banda, they too seemed a little less overwhelming; the arcades lined with machine-made carvings, the fruit salad and dinner music both drawn from cans, and the excessively genteel management, one rapacious eye riveted on the guest's pocketbook, somehow brought to mind a high-class Southern California motel. Granted that the Balinese were engaging, handsome folk and that despite the inroads of tourism, they still retained some of the artistic talent and exotic innocence of their forefathers. The chilling truth, however, was that when you had seen one cremation, one tooth-filing ceremony, and one cockfight, you had seen them all. Lodged in our trunks were the tiger masks, the wayang dolls, the batiks, the krisses, and all the authentic kickshaws that would prove to our detractors that we had actually passed through Bali. There was no point in fighting our custard, in blinking the unblinkable. It was time to vamoose.

Every family has its moments of disrepair, when the collective nose tends to run and the corporate eye to blear, but on the evening mine straggled off the plane in Batavia after eight weeks in the hinterlands of Indonesia, we were a fearsome sight. Fricasseed by the sun, yellowed by quinine, dehydrated to shadows, bellies bloated with the heavy Dutch provender we had been subsisting on, we looked like a provincial company of *Tobacco Road*. Our togs were even more eccentric; the sultana had long since struck her colors and was garbed in palmetto fronds, and the moppets and I were as bankrupt of oomph as Bozo Snyder. All that was lacking to bring us up to concert pitch was six hours of insomnia in a stifling bed and a washbowl stuffed with banana skins, and Destiny had already prepared them. For good measure, she also threw in a wild-animal dealer in the adjoining room, who, as nearly as we could gauge, kept chasing and beating a cassowary all night long. By the time the four of us swayed out of the waiting room of the airport next morning to continue the trip to Singapore and Bangkok, we were so snowbound with seconal that we had to be hoisted into the aircraft. It was just as well I had cushioned my nervous system with the handy white shock absorbers, in view of the cable awaiting us at Singapore. It had been sent by my pettifogging lawyer in New York (collect, of course), and its message was stark and unadorned: "Tenant of your apartment evicted today after gun battle stop Sashes and doors still intact but oh boy stop Have fun cousin you'll need it."

"The spoons!" screamed my wife in a tone that must have penetrated to the headwaters of the Irrawaddy. "I told you not to leave that momzer our silver when we sublet the flat!"

"I didn't leave it!" I shouted. "I locked it in the guest closet!"

"Yes, and gave him a duplicate key," she wailed. "Well, that concludes twenty years of light housekeeping. Easy come, easy go!" The children, not quite comprehending what was afoot but intuitively sensing disaster, burst into convulsive sobs; the other occupants of the plane sprang to the conclusion that I was a wife-beater and began to mutter menacingly; the lingering pain in my throat suddenly redoubled; and altogether, the proceedings took on the nightmare aspect of a surrealist film. Happily, two decades of domesticity had taught me how to cope with such family crises. Immuring myself in the powder room of the flying machine, I permitted myself just enough hysterics to calm and refresh me, painted my trachea with brandy, and reappeared a confident, well-organized personality. Within the six-hour flight to Bangkok, I managed, by a judicious mixture of sophistry and Hennessy, to convince my helpmate that life without flat silver was not insupportable, and recklessly vowing that if we ever struck another thrift shop I would replace her service ten times over, passed out cold.

Only a distaste for unnecessary sadism prevents me from recounting the ordeal in which, during the days that ensued, I found shelter in Bangkok for four bodies and twenty-one pieces of luggage. To anyone inclined to scoff at our plight, I can merely echo the trenchant words of the Beard of Avon, viz., that he jests at scars that never felt a wound. Because of the war in China and Siam's relative prosperity, the capital had been evolving since 1947 into a crossroads of commerce and was completely chock-a-block. Every available bed had been pre-empted by legation staffs and business panjandrums evacuated from Shanghai, fantastic premiums were being offered for the veriest lean-to, and the one vacancy in town, the snake pit at the Pasteur Institute untenanted after the death of their hamadryad, was too cramped for my quartet. Under the circumstances, the stash I finally ferreted out was a windfall. It was a modest, ramshackle pension in the Thung Mahamek district, operated by a Frenchwoman popularly credited with having been the plaything of Ivar Kreuger. Madame Sauvage may indeed have tiptoed through the Wamsutta with the Swedish match king, but I rather suspect she fostered the myth to give her premises glamour. A slightly overblown peony in a bush-jacket that unsuccessfully struggled to conceal her charms, she had the lazy, mascaraed come-hither of the whole generation of vamps typified by Valeska Suratt and Clara Kimball Young. Our fellow boarders were out of a later, post-Biograph epoch, but they were equally calculated to warm the cockles of Alfred Hitchcock's heart. To mention but four who came and went, there was an introspective French archaeologist who sold shoe-polish and vitamin capsules on the side; an ebullient Jugoslav acting as agent for a Swiss bicycle firm; a disputatious Dutch accountant with a roomful of bar-bells and punching-bags, and a woebegone Portuguese vice-consul who had fallen out of favor at Lisbon, and like a policeman banished to Staten Island, was pounding the diplomatic beat in Southeast Asia.

The first item on the agenda, naturally, was orienting the family to its new surroundings. This entailed a program of sightseeing, afternoon calls, and dinner parties I could have cheerfully dispensed with, but the fat was in the fire and I bared my throat to the knife with as much grace as I could muster. The kindest thing that can be said for the social life of the American colony in Bangkok is that nobody has ever died of ennui, though there were times when I felt like a very poor insurance risk. To be trapped helplessly at a dinner table between two Gorgon-faced matrons discussing revers and fag-goting, while your collar wilts in the overpowering heat and mosquitoes batten on your legs, is a form of martyrdom that no early Christian father was ever called on to endure. Many of my compatriots, particularly the newer embassy crowd, were living on an extremely dickty scale; they had grandiose establishments, whole corps of servants, outriders and lackeys innumerable, and similar juicy perquisites, a circumstance which occasionally tempted them to behave like demigods and hand down magisterial judgments. Over the walnuts and wine, they were given to teetering on their heels and spouting pompous rubbish that made the toes curl with embarrassment. Most of it was a warmed-over hash of what they had read in *Time* or *Reader's Digest*, salted with the Princetonian self-esteem that flourishes in the foreign service. I decided I had met my Waterloo the night a twenty-two-year-old graduate of the Pentagon raised his glass and proposed a toast to the greatest American since Lincoln, Henry Luce. From then on, I dined in Chinese cook-shops, snatching a bowl of bean sprouts or a filet of squid on the wing. The food was far less plushy, but the dialogue was also considerably less fraught with heartburn.

Generally speaking, Bangkok was pretty much as I remembered it from two years before, a pleasant hodgepodge of metropolis and village, interlarded with temples, waterways swarming with sampans, and an agreeable polyglot population. Nevertheless, a pronounced change had taken place in the interval; the shaky dictatorship of Pibul Songgram, tightening its grip after two unsuccessful coups d'état, and the Nationalist collapse in the South China provinces, had produced a bumper harvest of tensions and anxieties in everyday life. Roadblocks, civilian search, and military surveillance of automobiles were now accepted as normal, and it was more and more apparent that behind its bucolic façade, Siam was fast flowering into a fairly nasty little police state. I am not altogether certain when the first faint canker of disillusion began gnawing at me, but I awoke one morning some weeks after our arrival with a small Rhode Island millstone, approximately twelve feet across, resting squarely on my chest. The air inside the mosquito netting was as heavy as flannel and through the room swirled the pervasive stench of canal mud which is one of the minor blessings of Bangkok. To my surprise, the queen bee was propped upright in bed, immersed in a travel folder. The instant she felt my gaze, she attempted to bury the leaflet under her pillow, but not before I saw that it dealt with the French Riviera.

"So that's what's been going on behind my back," I breathed. "Where'd you get that?"

"Out of your top bureau drawer, where you hid it under those pornographic postcards," she returned. "Listen, I'm sick of this cat-and-mouse game. Why don't we both come clean?"

"You—you mean you're tired of Bangkok?" I asked evasively.

"Of course not, silly boy," she said, disentangling a lizard from her hair and tossing it into the commode. "I think it's the prettiest place I've ever seen—next to Woodlawn Cemetery, that is. I love the long, steamy afternoons of lounging in this teakwood stall with the sweat cascading down my frame, the voluptuous nights of swapping cake recipes with army wives and fly-specked gallantries with their husbands, the whole vibrant pattern of colonial suburbia. It's like life in an antiquated fireless cooker."

"The kids are happy here, though," I said feebly. "I mean, they haven't tried to drown themselves or anything, have they?"

"They're too bushed," she said. "They're so done up with the heat they've stopped kicking each other, and Snookums, that's a bad sign."

"You know, dear," I observed, clearing my throat tentatively, "I didn't want to upset you heretofore, but I've been over to the Hindu soothsayers in Suriwong Road, and—well, I'm afraid they gave me some pretty momentous news."

"You're going to take a long trip," she hazarded, with that peculiar feminine clairvoyance science is at such a loss to explain. "Did they say anything about a tall, dark-tempered brunette and two children?"

"Why, no," I confessed. "Of course, I only got the two-bit horoscope."

"Next time buy the economy family size," she recommended, "or better still, give me the quarter. I can read you like a book." Significantly enough, from the moment the cat was out of the bag and the yoke of self-imposed exile lifted from our necks, our spirits rocketed. Bangkok, once we had ruthlessly exorcised the obligation to linger in it, immediately became picturesque again; the quaint, teeming thoroughfares had never seemed so romantic, and our friends, enraptured by the knowledge that we were only a temporary nuisance, smothered us with conviviality. Infused with fresh vitality, we dedicated ourselves to oiling the machinery of departure. My share of the labor was soon accomplished; I escorted my letter of credit to the air booking office, paced the anteroom feverishly while it was given a spinal and delivered of four inky tickets to Istanbul, Rome, and Nice, and left it in a local pawnshop for fresh plasma to ease the postoperative shock. The mem and children, meanwhile, systematically winnowed every novelty shop and curio bazaar in the five-mile length of the New Road, disinterring undreamt-of treasures—cravats woven of snakeskin, model junks that glowed in the dark, porcelain umbrella jars, and a collection of walking sticks, parasols, and riding crops that would make our attic the peer of any in Pennsylvania. Preparations were going forward apace and our acquisitions overflowed two hangars at the airport when a chance remark of Madame Sauvage over the dinner table wrought new complications.

"Why don't you take back a pet for the little ones?" she suggested. "A Korat cat or a gibbon to remind them of the exciting days they passed in Thailand."

"His check stubs'll do that," commented my wife affectionately. "With nowhere as many fleas."

"What you need is a mynah bird," broke in Mr. Krosig, the Balkan roomer. "It never stays still from morning to night. All the time chattering and whistling and imitating the various sounds."

"Ah, the old crab would shut it off the way he does my radio," grumbled my son. The old crab gave him a look that singed three buttons off his jumper and switched the conversation to the large number of boys annually eaten by werewolves. Mr. Krosig, who had been in Transylvania and had some pertinent data on the subject, took it up avidly, and I thought I had effectively disposed of the matter until my daughter commenced needling me. She would forgo her allowance for the next eight years if I only bought a mynah; she would go to second-rate boarding schools, bleach her own hair, live on scraps, weave her own clothing. Ultimately, badgered into submission, I capitulated. A circuit of the bird market revealed plenty of mynahs, but none sufficiently glossy and articulate. At last, outside a Chinese firecracker store, we discovered a specimen endowed with purple plumage, a primrose-yellow comb, a spirited eye, and a reasonably fluent vocabulary of Siamese invective. The asking price of fifty ticals, approximately two and a half dollars, was pure formality; before the dicker was sealed, I had been conned into buying five bags of Roman candles and pinwheels, a mandarin coat, and two tins of preserved lychee nuts. Whatever Tong Cha's shortcomings as a roommate—he rose with the sun and exercised his repertory until the last eardrum cried uncle—, he was a matchless antidote for tedium poisoning. I spent the two days prior to our take-off gyrating about Bangkok for health certificates to transport him to Europe, subordinated comfort and sanity to outfitting him with a proper cage, securing a special bird's-size ticket and visas, and assembling his food, a balanced regimen of rice, chili peppers, bananas, and hard-boiled eggs. He demonstrated his worth beyond cavil, however, and in a fashion that left no doubt about his intelligence. When the Siamese exit customs closed in and started to burrow through our effects in the usual search for cocaine and Annamite girls, he sprayed them with a shower of Sanskrit cuss-words that reduced them to jelly. He never told me what he said, but if I could learn the English equivalent, my name would rank with that of Rabelais.

Inside the dimly lit cabin of the Constellation droning toward Calcutta, I lay wrapped in a blissful, air-conditioned Nirvana, somnolently intent on one of the truly enduring contributions to Western technology, the smoothly undulating haunches of the hostess as she moved up the aisle administering to the needy. Perhaps, I thought drowsily, I had been the victim of a major error the past five months; perhaps the air-foam seat I sat in, the aromatic coffee I sipped, and that brave vibration each way free, as Herrick had so succinctly put it, were worth all the tea in China. Was I an epicene old goat that I should be content to nibble among the ivory, apes, and peacocks of a moribund continent, or, after all, a mettlesome middle-aged goat whose hoofs Nature had designed to twinkle from as yet unexplored crags? I thought of asking my wife, sleeping peacefully beside me, but I could pretty well envision her answer. Let the morrow bring what it would, I decided, as our motorized kite slid across the Bay of Bengal and I cuddled closer to the Sandman. Buddha might get me in the last great round-up, but for the moment, Baby was still on the range.

Cloudland Revisited: Why, Doctor, What Big Green Eyes You Have!

Halfway through the summer of 1916, I was living on the rim of Narragansett Bay, a fur-bearing adolescent with cheeks as yet unscarred by my first Durham Duplex razor, when I read a book that exerted a considerable influence on my bedtime habits. Up to then, I had slept in normal twelve-year-old fashion, with the lights full on, a blanket muffling my head from succubi and afreets, a chair wedged under the doorknob, and a complex network of strings festooned across the room in a way scientifically designed to entrap any tres-passer, corporeal or not. On finishing the romance in question, however, I realized that the protection I had been relying on was woefully inadequate and that I had merely been crowd-ing my luck. Every night thereafter, before retiring, I spent an extra half hour barricading the door with a chest of drawers, sprinkling tacks along the window sills, and strewing crum-pled newspapers about the floor to warn me of approaching footsteps. As a minor added precaution, I slept under the bed, a ruse that did not make for refreshing slumber but at least threw my enemies off the scent. Whether it was constant vigi-lance or natural stamina, I somehow survived, and, indeed, re-ceived a surprising number of compliments on my appearance when I returned to grammar school that fall. I guess nobody in those parts had ever seen a boy with snow-white hair and a green skin.

Perhaps the hobgoblins who plagued me in that Rhode Is-land beach cottage were no more virulent than the reader's own childhood favorites, but the particular one I was intro-duced to in the book I've mentioned could hold up his head in any concourse of fiends. Even after thirty-five years, the lines that ushered him onstage still cause an involuntary shudder:

"Imagine, a person, tall, lean and feline, high-shouldered, with a brow like Shakespeare and a face like Satan, a close-shaven skull, and long, magnetic eyes of the true cat-green. Invest him with all the cruel cunning of an entire Eastern race, accumulated in one giant intellect, with all the resources of science, past and present, with all the resources, if you will, of a wealthy government—which, however, already has denied all knowledge of his existence. . . . This man, whether a fanatic or a duly appointed agent, is, unquestionably, the most malign and formidable personality existing in the world today. He is a linguist who speaks with almost equal facility in any of the civilized languages, and in most of the barbaric. He is an adept in all the arts and sciences which a great university could teach him. He also is an adept in certain obscure arts and sciences which *no* university of today can teach. He has the brains of any three men of genius. . . . Imagine that awful being, and you have a mental picture of Dr. Fu-Manchu, the yellow peril incarnate in one man."

Yes, it is the reptilian Doctor himself, one of the most sinister figures ever to slither out of a novelist's inkwell, and many a present-day comic book, if the truth were told, is indebted to his machinations, his underground laboratories, carnivorous orchids, rare Oriental poisons, dacoits, and stranglers. An authentic vampire in the great tradition, Fu-Manchu horrified the popular imagination in a long series of best-sellers by Sax Rohmer, passed through several profitable reincarnations in Hollywood, and (I thought) retired to the limbo of the second-hand bookshop, remembered only by a few slippered pantaloons like me. Some while ago, though, a casual reference by my daughter to Thuggee over her morning oatmeal made me prick up my ears. On close questioning, I found she had been bedevilling herself with "The Mystery of Dr. Fu-Manchu," the very volume that had induced my youthful fantods. I delivered a hypocritical little lecture, worthy of Pecksniff, in which I pointed out that Laurence Hope's "Indian Love" was far more suitable for her age level, and, confiscating the book, holed up for a retrospective look at it. I see now how phlegmatic I have become with advancing age. Apart from causing me to cry out occasionally in my sleep and populating my pillow with a swarm of nonexistent spiders, Rohmer's thriller was as abrasive to the nerves as a cup of Ovaltine.

The plot of "The Mystery of Dr. Fu-Manchu" is at once engagingly simple and monstrously confused. In essence, it is a duel of wits between the malevolent Celestial, who dreams of a world dominated by his countrymen, and Commissioner Nayland Smith, a purportedly brilliant sleuth, whose confidant, Dr. Petrie, serves as narrator. Fu-Manchu comes to England bent on the extermination of half a dozen distinguished Foreign Office servants, Orientalists, and other buttinskies privy to his scheme; Smith and Petrie constantly scud about in a web-footed attempt to warn the prey, who are usually defunct by the time they arrive, or busy themselves with being waylaid, sandbagged, drugged, kidnapped, poisoned, or garrotted by Fu-Manchu's deputies. These assaults, however, are never downright lethal, for regularly, at the eleventh hour, a beautiful slave of Fu-Manchu named Kâramanèh betrays her master and delivers the pair from jeopardy. The story, consequently, has somewhat the same porous texture as a Pearl White serial. An episode may end with Smith and Petrie plummeting through a trapdoor to nameless horrors below; the next opens on them comfortably sipping whiskey-and-soda in their chambers, analyzing their hairbreadth escape and speculating about the adversary's next move. To synopsize this kind of ectoplasmic yarn with any degree of fidelity would be to connive at criminal boredom, and I have no intention of doing so, but it might be fruitful to dip a spoon into the curry at random to gain some notion of its flavor.

Lest doubt prevail at the outset as to the utter malignancy of Fu-Manchu, the author catapults Nayland Smith into Petrie's rooms in the dead of night with the following portentous declaration of his purpose: "Petrie, I have travelled from Burma not in the interests of the British government merely, but in the interest of the entire white race, and I honestly believe —though I pray I may be wrong—that its survival depends largely on the success of my mission." Can Petrie, demands Smith, spare a few days from his medical duties for "the strangest business, I promise you, that ever was recorded in fact or fiction"? He gets the expected answer: "I agreed readily enough, for, unfortunately, my professional duties were not onerous." The alacrity with which doctors of that epoch deserted their practice has never ceased to impress me. Holmes had only to crook his finger and Watson went bowling away in a four-wheeler, leaving his patients to fend for themselves. If the foregoing is at all indicative, the mortality rate of London in the nineteen-hundreds must have been appalling; the average physician seems to have spent much less time in diagnosis than in mousing around Wapping Old Stairs with a dark lantern. The white race, apparently, was a lot tougher than one would suspect.

At any rate, the duo hasten forthwith to caution a worthy named Sir Crichton Davey that his life is in peril, and, predictably, discover him already cheesed off. His death, it develops, stemmed from a giant red centipede, lowered down the chimney of his study by Fu-Manchu's dacoits, regarding whom Smith makes the charmingly offhand statement "Oh, dacoity, though quiescent, is by no means extinct." Smith also seizes the opportunity to expatiate on the archcriminal in some fairly delicious double-talk: "As to his mission among men. Why did M. Jules Furneaux fall dead in a Paris operahouse? Because of heart failure? No! Because his last speech had shown that he held the key to the secret of Tongking. What became of the Grand Duke Stanislaus? Elopement? Suicide? Nothing of the kind. He alone was fully alive to Russia's growing peril. He alone knew the truth about Mongolia. Why was Sir Crichton Davey murdered? Because, had the work he was engaged upon ever seen the light, it would have shown him to be the only living Englishman who understood the importance of the Tibetan frontiers." In between these rhetorical flourishes, Petrie is accosted by Kâramanèh, Fu-Manchu's houri, who is bearing a deadly perfumed letter intended to destroy Smith. The device fails, but the encounter begets a romantic interest that saves Petrie's neck on his next excursion. Disguised as rough seafaring men, he and Smith have tracked down Fu-Manchu at Singapore Charlie's, an opium shop on the Thames dockside. Here, for the first time, Petrie gets a good hinge at the monster's eyes: ". . . their unique horror lay in a certain filminess (it made me think of the *membrana nictitans* in a bird) which, obscuring them as I threw wide the door, seemed to lift as I actually passed the threshold, revealing the eyes in all their brilliant viridescence." Before he can polish his ornithological metaphor, however, Petrie is plunged through a trapdoor into the river, the den goes up in flames, and it looks like curtains for the adventurous physician. But Providence, in the form of a hideous old Chinese, intervenes. Stripping off his ugly, grinning mask, he discloses himself as Kâramanèh; she extends her false pigtail to Petrie and, after pulling him to safety, melts into the night. It is at approximately this juncture that one begins to appreciate how lightly the laws of probability weighed on Sax Rohmer. Once you step with him into Never-Never Land, the grave's the limit, and no character is deemed extinct until you can use his skull as a paper-weight.

Impatient at the snail's pace with which his conspiracy is maturing, Fu-Manchu now takes the buttons off the foils. He tries to abduct a missionary who has flummoxed his plans in China, but succeeds only in slaying the latter's collie and destroying his manservant's memory—on the whole, a pretty footling morning's work. He then pumps chlorine gas into a sarcophagus belonging to Sir Lionel Barton, a bothersome explorer, with correspondingly disappointing results; this time the bag is another collie—sorry, a coolie—and a no-account ginzo secretary.

The villain's next foray is more heartening. He manages to overpower Smith and Petrie by some unspecified means (undoubtedly the "rather rare essential oil" that Smith says he has met with before, "though never in Europe") and chains them up in his noisome cellars. The scene wherein he twits his captives has a nice poetic lilt: "A marmoset landed on the shoulder of Dr. Fu-Manchu and peered grotesquely into the dreadful yellow face. The Doctor raised his bony hand and fondled the little creature, crooning to it. 'One of my pets, Mr. Smith,' he said, suddenly opening his eyes fully so that they blazed like green lamps. 'I have others, equally useful. My scorpions —have you met my scorpions? No? My pythons and hamadryads? Then there are my fungi and my tiny allies, the bacilli. I have a collection in my laboratory quite unique. Have you ever visited Molokai, the leper island, Doctor? No? But Mr. Nayland Smith will be familiar with the asylum at Rangoon! And we must not forget my black spiders, with their diamond eyes —my spiders, that sit in the dark and watch—then leap!'" Yet, having labored to create so auspicious a buildup, the author inexplicably cheats his suspense and lets it go for naught. No sooner has Fu-Manchu turned his back to attend to a poisoned soufflé in the oven than Kâramanèh pops up and strikes off the prisoners' gyves, and the whole grisly quadrille starts all over again. Smith and Petrie, without so much as a change of deer-stalker hats, nip away to warn another prospective victim, and run full tilt into a covey of *phansigars*, the religious stranglers familiar to devotees of the *American Weekly* as Thugs. They outwit them, to be sure, but the pace is beginning to tell on Petrie, who observes ruefully, "In retrospect, that restless time offers a chaotic prospect, with few peaceful spots amid its tur-moils." Frankly, I don't know what Petrie is beefing about. My compassion goes out, rather, to his patients, whom I envision by now as driven by default to extracting their own tonsils and quarrying each other's gallstones. *They're* the ones who need sympathy, Petrie, old boy.

With puff adders, tarantulas, and highbinders blooming in every hedge-row, the hole-and-corner pursuit of Fu-Manchu drums along through the next hundred pages at about the same tempo, resolutely shying away from climaxes like Hin-dus from meat. Even the episode in which Smith and Petrie, through the good offices of Kâramanèh, eventually hold the Doctor at gun point aboard his floating laboratory in the Thames proves just a pretext for further bombination about those filmy greenish eyes; a shower of adjectives explodes in the reader's face, and he is whisked off on a hunt for certain stolen plans of an aero-torpedo, an interlude that veers dan-gerously close to the exploits of the indomitable Tom Swift. The sequence that follows, as rich in voodoo as it is innocent of logic, is heavily fraught with hypnosis, Fu-Manchu having unaccountably imprisoned a peer named Lord Southery and Kâramanèh's brother Aziz in a cataleptic trance. They are fi-nally revived by injections of a specific called the Golden Elixir —a few drops of which I myself could have used to advantage at this point—and the story sashays fuzzily into its penultimate phase. Accompanied by a sizable police detail, Smith, Petrie, and a Scotland Yard inspector surprise Fu-Manchu in an opium sleep at his hideout. A dénouement seems unavoidable, but if there was one branch of literary hopscotch Rohmer excelled in, it was avoiding dénouements. When the three leaders of the party recover consciousness (yes, the indispensable trapdoor again, now on a wholesale basis), they lie bound and gagged in a subterranean vault, watching their captor sacrifice their subordinates by pelting them with poisonous toadstools. The prose rises to an almost lyrical pitch: "Like powdered snow the white spores fell from the roof, frosting the writhing shapes of the already poisoned men. Before my horrified gaze, *the fungus grew*; it spread from the head to the feet of those it touched; it enveloped them as in glittering shrouds. 'They die like flies!' screamed Fu-Manchu, with a sudden febrile excitement; and I felt assured of something I had long suspected: that that magnificent, perverted brain was the brain of a homicidal maniac —though Smith would never accept the theory." Since no hint is given of what theory Smith preferred, we have to fall back on conjecture. More than likely, he smiled indulgently under his gag and dismissed the whole escapade as the prankishness of a spoiled, self-indulgent child.

The ensuing events, while gaudy, are altogether too labyrinthine to unravel. As a matter of fact they puzzled Rohmer, too. He says helplessly, "Any curiosity with which this narrative may leave the reader burdened is shared by the writer." After reading that, my curiosity shrank to the vanishing point; I certainly wasn't going to beat my brains out over a riddle the author himself did not pretend to understand. With a superhuman effort, I rallied just enough inquisitiveness to turn to the last page for some clue to Fu-Manchu's end. It takes place, as nearly as I could gather, in a blazing cottage outside London, and the note he addresses to his antagonists clears the way for plenty of sequels: "To Mr. Commissioner Nayland Smith and Dr. Petrie—Greeting! I am recalled home by One who may not be denied. In much that I came to do I have failed. Much that I have done I would undo; some little I have undone. Out of fire I came—the smoldering fire of a thing one day to be a consuming flame; in fire I go. Seek not my ashes. I am the lord of the fires! Farewell. Fu-Manchu."

I daresay it was the combination of this passage, the cheery hearth in front of which I reread it, and my underwrought condition, but I thought I detected in the Doctor's valedictory an unmistakable mandate. Rising stealthily, I tiptoed up to my daughter's bedchamber and peered in. A shaft of moonlight picked out her ankles protruding from beneath the bed, where she lay peacefully sleeping, secure from dacoity and Thuggee. Obviously, it would take more than a little crackle of the flames below to arouse her. I slipped downstairs and, loosening the binding of "The Mystery of Dr. Fu-Manchu" to insure a good supply of oxygen, consigned the lord of the fires to his native element. As he crumbled into ash, I could have sworn I smelled a rather rare essential oil and felt a pair of baleful green eyes fixed on me from the staircase. It was probably the cat, though I really didn't take the trouble to check. I just strolled into the kitchen, made sure there was no trapdoor under the icebox, and curled up for the night. That's how phlegmatic a chap gets in later life.

Chewies the Goat but Flicks Need Hypo

IT APPEARS to be more than a rumor that *Variety*, that reliable and colorful barometer of show business, may shortly change its name. According to my source (a papaya-juice vender on West Forty-sixth Street, whose identity I cannot disclose for fear of reprisals), the editors plan, by the simple expedient of altering three letters, to rechristen their paper *Anxiety*, a title more suited to its contents these days. This decision, between ourselves, comes as no surprise to me. Every Wednesday of late, skimming through *Variety*'s picture grosses and film chatter, I have run into palpitations and anguish not normally aired outside the *American Journal of Orthopsychiatry*. To judge from these bedside reports, the movie business is clearly *in extremis*; bats and mice are daily replacing audiences in theatres across the land, cobwebs are forming on the ushers, and exhibitors, hysterically accusing television, politics, substandard product, and even sunspots, have succumbed to panic. The most Talmudic reasons have been adduced to explain the decline in the box office, and it was inevitable that before long some Hawkshaw would try to pin the rap on that old whipping boy, the human stomach.

By the human stomach, of course, I refer in a broad, generic sense to the goodies—the caramel popcorn, molasses chews, coconut bars, and similar delicacies—sold in cinema lobbies. The suspicion has been gaining ground among showmen, says *Variety*, that "the annoyance of other customers' munch-crunch and the emphasis some houses are putting on selling of sweets" underlie the crisis. It quotes in support a conversation overheard by a member of the Allied Theatre Owners of Indiana. Four women sitting at the table next to him in a restaurant, he reported, "all agreed with one of the ladies, who said very emphatically that her family never attended the ———— theatre any more because they were tired of all the efforts made there to sell concessions, all the people in the audience munching during the show, and, most of all, having to sit through advertising trailers telling about how delicious were the concession-stand wares. Is it possible that theatre-lobby merchandising can be a factor why people are staying away from the movies, and is it worth a little restudy?"

Restudy, if I may make so bold, is not only indicated here; it is downright mandatory. The plain truth is that the Allied Theatre Owners of Indiana, and exhibitors generally, are staggering under a tremendous burden of mistaken, self-imposed guilt. As their patrons dwindle, keening about the pressures exerted on them to purchase sweets, the poor simps neurotically look inward for the reason instead of westward. The real culprit, I submit, is Hollywood itself. The industry has been locked too long in its ivory tower, too long preoccupied with artistic considerations better left to highbrows like Johnny Ruskin or Walt Pater. What the situation cries out for is pictures that will tell a gripping story and at the same time subtly sell the eatables in the lounge. With the aid of a small hand loom, I have woven a few necessary elements into an action-packed, down-to-earth yarn that may serve as a model, appealing to the gustatory as well as the visual instinct. It may not wheedle customers into the show shop, but at least it will act as a tourniquet.

We fade in on the porte-cochère of a mansion ablaze with lights, and, as sleek motors laden with impeccably groomed men of aristocratic visage and women garbed in the *dernier cri* from Paris disgorge their human freight, establish that this is the home of Monica, Lady Beltravers, arbiter of Bombay society. Monica, an Irene Dunne–type chatelaine that is the very essence of the chicly poised British gentlewoman, loiters on the stoop greeting her guests. "Sir Cyprian Chetwynd—what a surprise!" she exclaims cordially to one imperious, hawk-nosed oldster as he alights from his equipage. "I certainly never expected the Home Secretary himself at my ball, crowning event of the social season albeit it is!" To another arrival, a swarthy potentate in whose turban glows a single magnificent ruby, she observes laughingly, "Well, Hara Singh, I guess we will not be having to press our crystal chandelier into service, now that the Star of Assam is shedding its beam on the courtly throng!" From hints like the foregoing, it is blueprinted that her Ladyship's annual rout is the smartest affair in the Punjab, and that even the Viceroy would count himself lucky to get the nod from her. Monica, the cynosure of all eyes, wears on her queenly head the famous Beltravers tiara, and as we truck indoors with her through the assemblage, we garner numerous startled reactions. (The reactions are startled not because she is wearing the tiara on her head, where it should be, but because of its splendor.) Everybody thinks she is goofy to display so costly a bauble, for is it not an open secret that Tony Pickering, the most elusive international-society jewel thief in the Empire, is somewhere in the area, pledged to steal it from under the fair owner's nose? Monica, notwithstanding, snaps her pretty fingers at the ravens who croak disaster, graciously urging them to sample the lavish feed arrayed on the sideboard —turkey, tongue in aspic, slaw, and suchlike viands. And right here, without slackening pace, is an ideal spot to slip in an offbeat allusion to the comestibles available to moviegoers in the lobby.

"Bless me, Monica, what a toothsome collation," remarks one of the dowagers, enviously scanning it through her lorgnette.

"Thanks, Baroness," Lady Beltravers replies. "And, speaking of matters edible, the fans watching this need not fall prey to the green-eyed monster, for adjacent to their chairs they will lamp a pleasing selection of mint drops, chocolate creams, and candied apples to beguile themselves stomach-wise." Needless to say, I am not writing dialogue, just spitballing to indicate how smoothly the pitch blends in with the action.

To pick up our story thread: Unsuspected by the merrymakers, Tony Pickering, a debonair figure in flawless tails (Randolph Scott), saunters nonchalantly amid the waltzing couples. The Beltravers tiara is almost within his grasp. Suddenly, he comes face to face with Sandra Thrale (Greer Garson), the second-most-elusive society jewel thief in the Empire. A sardonic situation, fraught with boffs—two devil-may-care tricksters bent on the same perilous mission. Who will emerge victor? The lovers (for so they soon prove to be, despite their mutual antagonism) strike a bargain, snatch the prize in some ingenious fashion as yet to be devised, and show their pursuers a clean pair of heels. Sprinkled through the chase I see a couple of knockabout Hindu comics, on the order of Karl Dane and George K. Arthur, whose uproarious antics constantly land them in hot water and reap a rich harvest of laffs. This concludes the first sequence, a high-octane mixture of suspense, comedy, and romance guaranteed to keep people on the edge of their seats but still not allow them full mobility.

Sidi-bel-abbès, headquarters of the French Foreign Legion. Sand . . . heat . . . primitive passions fanned into flame by a word, a look. Into this port of nameless men drifts the flotsam of many races, asking only one thing—to forget. And with it, seeking salvation under the remorseless African sun, has come Tony Pickering. He and Sandra, after a senseless quarrel in Rome, during which she cast the tiara into the Tiber in a fit of pique, have broken. We iris down on him idling through the bazaars shortly before his regiment leaves for El Kébir, a remote desert outpost. A vivid background and a perfect opportunity to insinuate a timely message to the savages out front.

"Look, *mon capitaine*," a merchant whines, plucking at Tony's sleeve. "Splendid fresh figs, succulent as a Bedouin maid."

"Yes, and just as tricky," comments Pickering acidly. "That's where folks buying peanuts in their neighborhood flicks have the jump on us creatures of the silver screen. Those tasty goobers, warranted bacteria-free, speed directly from the roaster into sanitized glassine bags and thence to grateful palates. Boy, I could eat a slew of them." In other words, rather than hit the patrons over the head with a crass commercial, we actually use it to further the narrative. From now on, every man, woman, and child in the building is psychologically primed to rush out and give his taste buds a treat, except that the action is moving so fast he dassn't tear himself away.

We now deliver a surprise twist, a terrific sock that nobody but a clairvoyant could anticipate. In the ordinary scenario, the next scene would portray El Kébir beleaguered by tribesmen; Tony and brutal Sergeant Lepic (Brod Crawford), the only survivors in the fort, have posted their dead comrades on the parapet with rifles in their hands to hoodwink the attackers when a relief column led by Sandra (who has followed her swain unbeknownst to Algeria) raises the siege. Instead of this tepid dénouement, which would merely generate yawns, we dissolve to a hunting lodge in the Canadian Rockies, where Sandra's wealthy father (Charles Coburn) has taken her to cure her infatuation for Tony. Since their spat in Rome, the girl has paid her debt to society and become a brilliant woman psychiatrist, a leader in her profession. Yet—irony of ironies—she, who brings happiness to others, is denied it herself, for Cupid has laid waste her heart. She cannot decide between Tony, now a world-famed construction engineer, and Jim Stafford (John Wayne), New York's most outstanding criminal lawyer. As father and daughter breakfast in their mountain retreat, unaware that a consuming forest fire rages toward them, the kindly old millionaire is concerned anent her birdlike appetite.

"You haven't eaten a crumb, sweet," Thrale chides her. "Try one of these speckled beauties which I captured it with rod and reel outside our door this morning."

"They *are* scrumptious, Daddy," she makes wistful reply, "but you'll never know bliss till you tackle Frosticles, the jet-powered ice-cream sensation." Thrale's curiosity is piqued, as anyone's would be, and he inquires where the confection may be obtained, whereupon Sandra enlightens him. The scene can be made doubly effective by dispatching candy-butchers down the aisle on cue, shouting "Frosticles!" They should, however, be cautioned against shouting so loud that the audience loses the thread. Once that happens, the jig is up.

The framework of the story being elastic, we now have two possibilities to milk for a climax. In one, Tony and Jim, who have renounced their careers to be near Sandra and are loggers in a lumber camp close by, fight a sensational watery duel for her hand with peaveys. The flames soon bring them to their senses and, good-naturedly laying aside their rivalry, they race to save the trapped pair, but they arrive too late. Since this line is a little on the defeatist side, it might be better to develop the other, a device that gives the plot a neat switch. We lap-dissolve to a primitive raft becalmed in the South Pacific and plant that Tony, Jim, and four Norwegian buddies have all but given up hope for the success of their expedition. Tony has staked his reputation as a world-famous anthologist to prove that certain old-time Peruvians migrated to Tahiti on a raft made of balsam logs. The gallant sextet's provisions have run short, and in his delirium each man dreams longingly of his favorite dish on terra firma. If only he could feel the icy trickle of a cola drink between his parched lips, muses Tony, or nibble the delectable taffy that even the humblest filmgoer has at his beck and call. The various dainties pass in review in balloons over his head, to hammer the point home to the most obtuse. And then we belt into a sizzling washup. A typhoon strikes the frail craft, the seafarers are drenched to the bone, and one of the Norwegians is revealed to be Sandra, who has renounced her psychiatric career to be near Tony. As they joyfully nestle in each other's arms, the cry of "Polynesia ho!" echoes from the yardarm. Tony's scientific thesis is vindicated, Jim sportingly acknowledges him the better man, and we squeeze on a tag wherein the couple sails homeward to the strains of "Aloha Oe." By then, the projectionist can breeze right into "Coming Attractions," for the patrons will be streaking toward the lobby to gorge themselves or apply for refunds, as the case may be.

Well, there it is—no "Intolerance" or "Gone with the Wind," I grant you, but a nice, sound program film that'll hold up its end on any double bill and yield a good many mandolin picks after the run is finished. I've even written a score for it, containing half a dozen songs of "Hit Parade" calibre, and if Hammerstein's fee is excessive, I'll throw in a hatful of lyrics for good measure. The main thing is to release it pronto and get rid of all that glucose in the lobby before the mice get at it. You don't want sagebrush growing in your bathtub, do you, Mr. Selznick?

Salesman, Spare that Psyche

L ET'S HAVE a show of hands—how many people here know what they'd like to be in their next incarnation? I mean if you had your choice, would you want to be, say, the curator of the British Museum or a crackerjack circus aerialist or the best of breed at the Empire Cat Show or what? Every thoughtful person interested in which way his soul is going to jump, whether he subscribes to the Buddhist system of musical chairs or not, must have asked himself this question at one time or another, and inasmuch as I happen to have just stumbled on an ideal future identity, with about as much omnipotence as anyone could ever hope to attain, I'd like to register it before it's snapped up. Comes the transmigration, I want to be vice-president in charge of sales of a twenty-million-dollar cosmetics corporation. Not any old vice-president but one in particular—a chap named Martin Revson. Martin Revson can be me if he likes, or if he wishes to sublet to some other tenant, we can work that out, too. He'll find me perfectly flexible.

My admiration for Mr. Revson, I hasten to say, is in no way vitiated by the fact that up till yesterday I didn't know him from Adam's off ox. It was an interview in a recent issue of *Business Week*, entitled "Smart Words, Quality, and Freud," that introduced me to the man and, specifically, to his technique for salvaging sterile personnel, possibly the most singular in American industry. Using a portable microphone to capture the full, idiomatic flavor of Revson's words, *Business Week* cornered the executive to ascertain how the Revlon Products Corporation launches and sells new makeup aids. The beautycoon, as I flinch at calling him, opened his heart. "The reason women buy cosmetics," he said, laying his nose slyly alongside his finger, "is because they buy hope. In other words," he added, glomming a phrase from an impractical *schlemiel* named Henry David Thoreau, who gets himself quoted in the damnedest contexts, "most women lead lives of dullness, quiet desperation, and I think cosmetics are a wonderful escape from it." He then cited a liquid foundation called Touch and Glow that apparently confers powers of escape analogous to those enjoyed by Harry Houdini, and recounted how this product was born, packaged, publicized, and merchandised. By and large, his revelations were a shade less than epochal, but one minor disclosure about the mechanics of radio publicity deserves mention: "Well, those things are done sort of inadvertently—what you do is go to see Hope or Skelton or somebody of that nature and tell them about your new product coming out with, oh, a couple of million dollars in advertising, and then the script writer writes it in. We try to plan it with the writer and say—here, this script you are using two weeks hence, if you have a chance to use it—if you've got a girl in there that is known to be funny on the program for eight or ten weeks, and he says she has the Touch and Glow look, that would bring an ordinary yak from the people listening in. So that's the way we get it in—sort of inadvertently." The easy negligence of the whole thing is truly captivating. For sheer insouciance, nothing could surpass the spectacle of an incipient Mark Twain grinding out cosmetic yaks with a two-million-dollar pitchfork lightly pinking his bottom. No wonder the corridors of Radio City are gritty with Benzedrine.

The crux of the interview, however, was Revson's exposition of his company's policy toward its unproductive salesmen. "Incidentally, what about these sales meetings I hear about called Psycho-Revlons?" his inquisitor demanded. "What exactly are they? Why are they called 'psycho'?" Pared down to essentials, the answers run as follows: "Well, we feel that the salesman may not be as good as he appears to be outwardly. And he has to be analyzed when his sales are not good. He doesn't recognize, unless he is analyzed, what the hell is the matter with him. Now, instead of firing men, we have salvaged them—men with brains and intelligence—merely by using the Psycho-Revlon method. Sitting a man down and reviewing with him all the things that are wrong with him. Even though the man may be in his forties . . . Further than that, we show scenes—action scenes and motion pictures of live actors—depicting the mental blocks that arise in a salesman's mind, and we try to remove those mental blocks."

Perhaps we can best evaluate Revlon's sales clinic by visiting a similar rehabilitation center at the Sassoon Tweezer Corporation, world's largest manufacturers of styptic pencils. It is one of the contradictions of our highly complex society that the Sassoon Tweezer Corporation should market nothing but styptic pencils, whereas the Sassoon Pencil Corporation controls the entire tweezer output. Ah, well, far better leave such anomalies to wiser heads and raise the curtain.

(*Scene: A Psycho-Sassoon, about eleven o'clock in the morning. The setting is a small, trapezoid-shaped chamber draped with yards of filmy gray cheesecloth, calculated to convey an atmosphere of intense cerebration. Since this décor, in addition to being hideously inflammable, tends to engulf the dramatis personae, they may have to spend most of the action in a crouching position, with fire extinguishers playing over them, but a good actor can project anywhere. Three men are discovered on-stage: Loudermilk, vice-president in charge of sales; Bultitude, a district supervisor; and Folger, a salesman.*)

BULTITUDE (*angrily*): What's the use of coddling the little skunk, Mr. Loudermilk? I say kick him out on his tail and be done with it.

LOUDERMILK: Tut, tut, no point in bullying the fellow. We'll never straighten him out if you take that line.

BULTITUDE: Well, I give up. I wash my hands. *You* deal with him. (*He flings away in a pet, promptly entangles himself in the draperies, and spends the rest of the production struggling to work free.*)

LOUDERMILK (*frowning over a report*): This sales chart of yours, Folger—it's a mite baffling.

FOLGER: In what way, sir?

LOUDERMILK: Well, according to your breakdown, you've just made a three-week swing through the Middle Atlantic States and sold over six million dollars' worth of styptic pencils.

FOLGER: You said it. I guess that's pretty near an all-time record.

LOUDERMILK: It is. The only trouble is we've checked with

ten or fifteen of the retailers and they disclaimed ever ordering the goods.

FOLGER: No kidding.

LOUDERMILK: Furthermore, none of them remembered ever seeing you. Didn't know your name, in fact.

FOLGER: I couldn't have made a very deep impression, could I?

LOUDERMILK: No, not if you didn't go into the stores.

FOLGER: You've got a point there, Mr. Loudermilk.

LOUDERMILK: Man to man, Folger—have you ever been in the Middle Atlantic States?

FOLGER: To the best of my recollection, no, sir.

LOUDERMILK: Under the circumstances, then, these orders can hardly be construed as binding, can they?

FOLGER: Well-l-l, if you want to be technical . . .

LOUDERMILK: What do you suggest we do now?

FOLGER: Of course, I can always resign—if you feel you can dispense with a man who brings in six million dollars' worth of business.

LOUDERMILK: I think you incline to be a faulty logician at times. I mean to say those orders are more or less mythical, aren't they?

FOLGER: That's so. I keep forgetting.

LOUDERMILK: Your expense account, on the other hand, is, regrettably, all too real. Do you recall any details of that?

FOLGER: Er—no. Would you mind refreshing me?

LOUDERMILK: Not in the least. It comes to about forty-five hundred, including the champagne.

FOLGER: Well, I certainly loved every moment of it. And I'm confident Gloria would agree. (*As Loudermilk's eyebrows elevate*) My sweetie. *Petite amie*, as the French say.

LOUDERMILK: Oh? I—er—I had always understood you were a respectable married man.

FOLGER: I'd like to see anyone better qualified. I've got wives in three different cities.

LOUDERMILK: Look here, Folger, I'm going to talk to you straight from the shoulder. A man's private life is his own—

FOLGER: Check. Everybody's entitled to a little fun on the side.

LOUDERMILK: Sure he is. For instance, I have a babe tucked away in a nest on Seventy-third Street, and I tell you she's been an inspiration to me. By the way, you won't say anything to Mrs. Loudermilk about this?

FOLGER: Not unless I need a quick century note or the equivalent. You know how it is when you get caught in a squeeze.

LOUDERMILK: You bet I do. Just come around any time and I'll help you out. No, what I'm driving at is your work.

FOLGER (*peevishly*): Oh, shoot, do we have to go into that now? I promised to meet Gloria at Jaeckel's and look at a broadtail coat.

LOUDERMILK: This shouldn't take more than a few minutes. You see, I have a hunch your whole sales approach is wrong. There's some sort of mental block or kink that prevents you from functioning properly, and I'm going to iron it out. Press that switch on the desk, will you? (*As Folger complies, the room darkens and a screen lights up at rear.*)

FOLGER (*enchanted*): Oh, boy! Movies!

LOUDERMILK: You like them, eh?

FOLGER: I eat 'em up. I go to two, three every afternoon.

LOUDERMILK: Well, this one's kind of special, because you appear in it. (*Folger starts.*) Now, don't get panicky; it's all in the family and I'm only showing it to help you. We made it with a concealed camera in a Syracuse drugstore. Remember that trip?

FOLGER: Not very well, sir. I was plastered a good deal of the time.

LOUDERMILK: It'll come back to you. (*A white-coated figure, backed by shelves of pharmaceuticals, settles into focus.*) There, that's the prospect—old man Hornaday, isn't it?

FOLGER: In person, and, brother, what a crab.

LOUDERMILK: No, just a misfit. Doesn't know how to get along with salesmen. O.K., here's a shot from the reverse angle as you come in.

FOLGER: Oops, look at that display of yoghurt. I really knocked that for a loop.

LOUDERMILK: Hornaday should have fastened it down, he'll have a lawsuit one of these days. This next part's a trifle blurred. You seem to be tangling with a customer.

FOLGER: Ah, some wacky dame. She tried to inveigle me into the phone booth.

LOUDERMILK: Oh, that's why she's slapping you; I couldn't figure out. Anyway, here you've finished wiping off the lipstick and you start your pitch to Hornaday.

FOLGER: Wait a minute. Something's been omitted. What's he grappling me by the seat of the pants for?

LOUDERMILK: We're really lost without a sound track. If you could reconstruct your dialogue, maybe we could analyze your failure to clinch the sale.

FOLGER: Search me. I gave him the standard buildup. "Ever nick yourself shaving?" I said. When he said yes, I sprang the convincer I've been using. "Try an electric razor," I said, "and you can laugh at styptic pencils." I can't imagine why—Holy mackerel!

LOUDERMILK (*encouragingly*): Go ahead, lad. I think I know what you're going to say.

FOLGER: It just dawned on me. I was touting him off styptic pencils without realizing it!

LOUDERMILK: Exactly. Instead of *selling* the product, you were *undermining* it. What we call the will to stop eating.

FOLGER (*snuffling*): Oh, my God, how could anybody be so blind?

LOUDERMILK: Don't reproach yourself, old man. In the dark, subterranean river of the unconscious we all have these lurks quirking.

FOLGER: Quirks lurking, you mean. Take the mush out of your mouth.

LOUDERMILK (*apologetically*): I'm sorry. After you get into your forties, you—well, you slip a cog now and then. Like poor Bultitude, there, for instance—look at him floundering around in that cheesecloth.

FOLGER: Poor Bultitude nothing. There's no room in a high-pressure business organization for weaklings. If you can't fish, cut bait. If you can't cut bait, get out.

LOUDERMILK: Folger, you're dead right. Listen, we need a district supervisor with energy and imagination. Anybody who can think in terms of six-million-dollar orders is good enough for me. How soon can you step into Bultitude's shoes?

FOLGER: Well, I'd sort of like to talk it over with my wives.

LOUDERMILK: Do that, and, what's more, take a couple of weeks in White Sulphur Springs at our expense. We want you back on the job in fighting trim.

FOLGER: Thanks, Chief, I feel like a new man. Who knows? One of these days you might even have a vacancy here for a vice-president in charge of sales.

LOUDERMILK (*tolerantly*): Now, now, boy, you've just found your pin-feathers. You haven't yet begun to fly.

FOLGER: No, but to punch home your avian simile, I'll never lack for worms as long as you hold onto that little nest in Seventy-third Street. So long, Doc, and love to Mrs. Loudermilk. (*He exits whistling. His superior stares after him, plunged in a brown study. Then, reaching for the telephone directory, he begins scrabbling through it for the number of "Business Week.*")

CURTAIN

The Song Is Endless,
but the Malady Lingers On

HEAVEN KNOWS, nobody wants to bring the whole medical profession down around his ears like a swarm of B_1, and yet, judging from a couple of indications that have filtered through to me recently, I may have to tie up the old family physician and fall back on herbs and simples. I realize that in saying so I am deliberately courting a scalpel between the ribs in a dark alley; nevertheless, it looks as if the layman might well brace himself against some sizzling surprises that the boys in the crisp white tunics are preparing. It might be a very good idea not to swallow any chicken bones until the emergency passes, and if a cinder lodges in your eye, get your neighborhood jeweller to extract it. Personally, I intend to ask my insurance counsellor whether he can't rig up a temporary floater to protect me against Dr. Kildare during the next few months. Nothing elaborate, just some sort of medical collision-and-proximity damage to keep the healers away.

The first inkling of what lies in store for the unwary patient comes from a report, in the New York *Times*, of a recent meeting of the New Jersey Medical Society. At the close of the session, the members were presented with three-minute hourglass egg timers as ammunition in an all-out fight against socialized medicine. Directions for their use ran as follows:

> Place the timer on your desk in the consulting room. When the patient enters, up-end the glass without offering an explanation for your actions. After approximately three minutes, the sand has run through the glass and the consultation usually will have just begun. At this point explain to the patient that had he or she been in England or had we socialized medicine here, the consultation would be over. Another application of the plan is by way of showing that socialized medicine in the United States, based on an estimate of $15,000,000,000 per year, would cost $90,000 for the period it takes the sand to run through the timer.

An admirable propaganda scheme, especially with the patient paying admission to the lecture; all it lacks is the added refinement, overlooked by its sponsors, that he supply free sand as well. A further intimation that tempests may lurk in the path of the laity henceforward is contained in an article by Brian P. Flanagan, M.C., in the *Current Medical Digest* for March. Making a plea for more interesting case histories, the author urges doctors to couch their medical narratives in a vigorous literary style, to combine drama with clarity and conciseness. He furnishes three samples, the second of which demands quotation at some length to do it justice:

Name of Patient: John Everyman.
Age: 39.
Operation: Appendectomy.
Operative Note: Nervous and distraught, Emily paced up and down the sterile, comfortless hospital waiting room. Would John love her after the operation as much as he had before? She had been a good and faithful wife. What about Cecelia Bronson—that calculating, scheming scrub nurse? Emily knew that Cecelia was after John's money and would stop at nothing to get John away from her. In her distraught mind Emily could picture Cecelia up there in the operating room—her smooth cold face half-hidden by a surgical mask, her soft but cold eyes watching the operation as the white robed surgeon made the usual McBurney's incision, separated the muscles transversely in layers and exposed the peritoneum. She could hear his slow regular breathing as John lay unconscious while the anesthetist watched the pentothal oxygen and curare. She could see the flashing Kelly clamps as the appendiceal blood vessels were clamped and sutured, as the appendix was clamped, ligated, touched with phenol and inverted with a purse-string suture. She could see Cecelia handing the surgeon the sutures as the peritoneum and muscles were closed in layers with double o chromic catgut and the skin closed with B.S.S. What would it mean to John that Cecelia was there in this moment of suffering, while she—his own wife—was forced to wait, nervous and distraught in the waiting room? "Patient returned to room in good condition," the chart would read—yes, his body in good condition, but what about his heart? Would it still belong to her—post-op?

It is hard to foretell what impact the suggestions put forward by the New Jersey Medical Society and Dr. Flanagan will have on the average practitioner; the impact on the average patient—specifically, me—is numbing. Under the rosiest conditions, a visit to the doctor's office is no picnic, and I suspect that these Gothic touches, if they meet with professional favor, may transform it into a tolerably bloodcurdling experience. In the absence of formal laboratory equipment, I have been steeping the potentialities in an old earthenware crock sutured to the top of my spinal column and have distilled a vignette that outlines the dimensions of the problem:

Crystal Laidlaw snapped the elastic over the cover of her stenographer's notebook, tucked back a ribbon on her starched nurse's cap, and, smothering a yawn, peered furtively at her wristwatch. Inured as she was to the eccentricities of Dr. Fergus Culpepper, his growing tendency to interrupt dictation and hash over his literary output with colleagues on the phone was fast undermining her. The morning before, ignoring an anteroom full of patients, he had wasted a full half hour recapitulating to Trefflich, the orthopedist, the stirring disposition he had made of a fractured tibia. Trefflich, not to be outdone, had countered with an effort of his own provisionally dubbed "The Adventures of a Clavicle," in which a collarbone detailed the sensations attendant upon its owner's being flung off a motorcycle. To Crystal, fidgeting restlessly in her chair, the two sounded like a pair of journalism majors in Schrafft's recalling their themes and exulting over purple passages. Now her employer was off again, she noted with despair, this time on the saga he had composed about Mrs. Wainwright's dyspepsia.

"Of course, I knew it was only heartburn from the start, Ned," he was explaining volubly into the mouthpiece. "Cripes, you'd have to be a Zola to get any conflict or characterization out of a puny subject like that. Well, just as I was at my wit's end, the patient laid the plot right in my lap—got up in the middle of the night for bicarbonate, missed her footing, and rolled down a flight of stairs. . . . No, merely a few contusions, worse luck. . . . Well, anyway, it gave me the story line I was desperate for, and everything fell into place. Want to hear a dynamite opening? Get this: 'Writhing with pain whose origin was clearly psychosomatic, Emma Wainwright tossed about in her disordered bed. In her equally disordered mind, there was no vestige of pity for the luckless husband tossing beside her, or for the long-suffering physician she was about to awaken and plague with her symptoms.' Pretty suspenseful stuff, what? . . . Well, I haven't decided yet, but *Argosy*'s clamoring for it and I promised to let them have first crack. How's that pancreas serial coming along? . . . Splendid. See you soon." He hung up, and his face, as he swivelled back toward Crystal, was creased by a frown. "Jealous old dodo," he said testily. "He knows I can write rings around him. Oh, well . . . Where'd we leave off?"

"You were just comparing Mr. Folwell's liver to the Rose Window at Chartres," replied his nurse. "But don't you think you'd better see Mr. Duveneck? He's been waiting outside almost an hour."

"Blast," growled Culpepper. "The minute I get really creative, these damn patients begin milling around here in droves. O.K., send him in." Reaching into a drawer, he brought forth an hourglass egg timer, an electric toaster, and a coffee percolator, which he ranged on the blotter before him. He was hacking off a slice of bread from a stale loaf when Duveneck, a pale, haggard man of forty with a day-old beard, sidled into the room nervously twisting his panama.

"Hello, Doc," he said, with a wan, conciliatory smile. "Gee, I didn't mean to interrupt your breakfast."

"You're not," Culpepper replied, upending the hourglass. "I ate it four hours ago."

"Then why are you setting up all those things? It looks as if—"

"Don't pry, Duveneck," the Doctor said severely. "Remember, curiosity killed a cat, and he was a lot nimbler than you, brother. Hmm, that's rather neat; may as well jot it down. I can use a nifty or two in that Folwell yarn to lighten it up. All right, now, what's ailing you?"

"Well, I'm not exactly sure," faltered Duveneck. "It started last night at my summer place up in Mahopac. You see, a fuse blew out and I went down cellar to fix it."

"Hold your horses," commanded Culpepper. "Stop right there. Do you realize," he asked impressively, holding up the egg timer between his thumb and forefinger, "that if you and I were in England now, this interview would be over?"

"Why, yes," said his caller uncertainly. "It's five hours later over there than it is here."

"So it is," said the Doctor, thunderstruck. "Blow me down. The Society didn't think of that when they dreamed up this hourglass to illustrate the wastefulness of socialized medicine."

"Is—is that what the toaster and percolator are for, too?" inquired Duveneck.

"Search me," admitted the other. "I figured the idea needed some kind of production—window dressing, you might say. Well," he said, rising and extending his hand, "so long, and remind me to try out the patter on you the next time you come in. I'll have the right answers by then."

"But listen," protested Duveneck, "you haven't even heard my story."

"Something about a fuse, wasn't it?" observed the Doctor perfunctorily. "Here, take two of these capsules before each meal; the tingling ought to subside in about three days. How's Mrs. Duveneck?"

"Look, Doc," pleaded Duveneck, piteously indicating the crown of his head. "A whole carton of Mason jars fell off the shelf on me. I've got a lump the size of a walnut—it might be a concussion—"

"Nonsense," said Culpepper brusquely. "It's only a little tertiary swelling, nothing to speak of. You don't expect me to base a readable case history on that, do you?"

"No, but couldn't you just feel it and give me an opinion or something?" Duveneck implored. "I wouldn't tell anybody, I promise."

"I'm afraid not, old man." The Doctor's lips compressed into a thin line. "There *is* such a thing as medical ethics, you know. Now, if it was a colorful injury, a gunshot wound or whatnot, I'd be delighted to help—always provided it had a good exciting background, naturally."

"Honest, our cellar'd make a peach of a setting, Dr. Culpepper," insisted Duveneck. "You could do a great job on all those cobwebs and dark corners. No kidding, it's the spookiest place you ever saw. They—they say it used to be a station on the Underground Railroad."

"Kind of an Edgar Allan Poe slant, eh?" pondered the Doctor, chewing thoughtfully on his pencil. "We-e-ll, it might be the basis for a short short, though hardly the way it stands. I'd have to rearrange most of the action and dialogue."

"Oh, sure, sure, whatever you say," said Duveneck quickly.

"I mean if you'd rather lay it in the attic, where I knock my head against a rafter—"

"One moment, Duveneck," Culpepper interrupted, with hauteur. "I wasn't aware we were collaborating on this. I'm perfectly capable of handling it without any outside assistance."

"Of course you are," agreed the suppliant, cringing. "Gosh, I hate people who tell professionals how to write, don't you? Oh—er—to get back to this bump again—"

"There's no necessity to," said Culpepper crisply. "I'll probably use an entirely different motivation; I might decide to have you stumble over a shovel or wrench your back colliding with the furnace. The device is unimportant. What I've got to capture and convey to the reader is a man's panic and isolation at an instant of crisis." He sprang up and described a wide, sweeping gesture. "By George, I might even climax with you lying there slowly gasping out your life while scarcely fifteen feet away your wife rocks placidly over her knitting, unaware of your predicament. Think of that for irony!"

"I am—I mean I will," Duveneck assured him, "but in the meantime isn't there anything I could put on my head? It throbs something awful."

"Yes, try a cold poultice or a knife blade," said the Doctor indifferently. "And take my card. In case you fall down senseless in the street, I can be reached either here or at the Authors League." Picking up his patient's hat, he escorted him to the door. "Ta-ta, now," he said with an abstracted smile. "Drop in any old time." For a minute after Duveneck had gone, he stood absorbed in thought. Then he darted to his desk and dialled a number.

"Lucas?" he asked. "Fergus Culpepper. . . . First-rate, how are you? . . . Say, you once treated Hammerstein or Rodgers, I forgot which. . . . Yes, I *knew* I was right. . . . Well, could you arrange to introduce us? I've got a melodramatic musical comedy all worked out, and, if I do say so, it's a humdinger. . . . I know that, but do me a favor and listen to the first scene. It's the cellar of a Long Island mansion, see, and the owner, a chap on the order of Rex Harrison, has just left a very gay dinner party to replace a fuse. . . ."

A Girl and a Boy Anthropoid Were Dancing

THERE IS MANY a justly celebrated name in the pantheon of show business, but last Saturday, looking over a small pantheon I keep handy so I can get at it in a hurry, I was struck by one omission. In the subsection enshrining stripteasers, I found no mention of Rozina Carlomusto. All the others were there: dazzling Lili St. Cyr, who electrified Las Vegas a while back by peeling down to the ultimate rosette, jettisoning that, and landing in quod, an exploit that boosted her salary to five thousand dollars a week; Sherry Britten of the flamboyant torso, sometimes likened to a human acetylene torch; the immortal Gypsy Rose, Georgia Sothern, Hinda Wasau, Margie Hart, Ann Corio, and others too numerous to list. But of Rozina not a whisper, not even a footnote to remind posterity of her sensational performance with a stuffed gorilla which made theatrical history two short months ago.

The exact nature of the lady's specialty is not altogether clear; it seems to have been a cross between jujitsu and a gavotte, from which her partner invariably emerged victor. The ensuing chaotic account of the act and its repercussions appeared in the New York *Daily News*:

> CALUMET CITY, ILL., Oct. 9 (UP)—Justice of the Peace Ted Styka today tossed out the case against dancer Rozina Carlomusto, accused of staging a lewd wrestling match with a stuffed gorilla in a night club. "Insufficient evidence," Styka ruled, even though authorities had claimed that Miss Carlomusto always lost the fall to the gorilla. The police said it appeared that the gorilla completed a seduction of the dancer during the act . . . It (the gorilla) is still in the hands of the State's Attorney's office as evidence. Last month the dancer gave a command performance in court so that Styka could judge for himself whether the act was "lewd and lascivious" as charged. She stripped to the bare essentials in chambers and went into an animated tussle with the stuffed beast. Sure enough, the gorilla won, pinning Rozina in 10 minutes flat. "This is a work of art," she said. "I've performed the same show hundreds of times in Panama and before soldiers in U.S.O. shows. This is the first time anybody questioned the dance."

What the poor, bewildered kid doesn't realize, of course, is that she is a victim of the same quidnuncs and busybodies who have plagued every artist from Zola and D. H. Lawrence to Joyce Hawley. Here is a girl quietly wrestling away with a gorilla in a spotlight, enriching the cultural life of her community and impinging on nobody's livelihood. You can depend on some salvation-happy bluenose, with a paid-up annuity in Paradise, to begin reading things into it. I don't want to borrow trouble, but once such folk get the upper hand, we are finished —*ausgespielt*. It will no longer be possible for your daughter and mine to disrobe on a night-club floor and juggle a pair of doves or plastic bubbles, and before you know it, all the calendars will be featuring depressing snow scenes and collies instead of voluptuous maidens in black net curled around a telephone. If we aren't heading into the most repressive era since Cromwell, I'm a Chinaman.

The thing that really riles me, though, is the aura of secrecy surrounding Rozina's demonstration in court. We are told that "she stripped to the bare essentials in chambers and went into an animated tussle with the stuffed beast." Does Mr. Styka suppose for a moment that he can dismiss an enormously complex legal process in so bald a fashion? No matter how incurious the reader may be, his mind is flooded with a host of questions. Who else witnessed these star-chamber proceedings? Any disinterested zoophile or art connoisseur qualified to advise the justice? Any other gorillas? What assurance have we, indeed, that the exhibition took place in an atmosphere free of prejudice toward the lower order of primates? Lacking a court record or similar certified testimony, one is forced to reconstruct the circumstances as a paleontologist does a brontosaurus, from a single, ossified splinter. In my own restoration, which follows, none of the characters represent real persons, mid-Western or otherwise. The ape, however, is modelled after Ngonga, a young Lowlands gorilla with whom I conducted a half-hearted love affair last summer at the San Diego Zoo. And to her, in memory of what might have been, I dedicate it.

(*Scene: The private chambers of Milo Usufruct, a justice of the peace. A cheerless room dominated by a rolltop desk overflowing*

*with writs, torts, and estoppels. A Globe-Wernicke sectional book-
case at left contains half a dozen moldy law books and a greenish pair of arctics. On the walls, two steel engravings, one of
Blackstone and the other of a stag beleaguered by wolves. At rise,
Usufruct is bent over a venerable, table-type Victor talking machine, fiddling at it with a screwdriver. He is a thin, bald rad-
ish of a man with watery, protuberant eyes. Miss Ripperger, his
secretary and a woman polarized to attract every catastrophe, is
unwrapping several phonograph records.)*

USUFRUCT (*peevishly*): Something's scraping inside. There
was nothing wrong with it when I put it away thirty years ago.

MISS RIPPERGER: It's probably all corroded. Or else somebody dropped it and smashed the mechanism.

USUFRUCT: If the mechanism was smashed, the turntable
wouldn't revolve.

MISS RIPPERGER: You better not fool with that thing. You're
liable to cut your finger and get blood poisoning. A nephew
of mine—

USUFRUCT: Yes, yes. How about the records I wanted?

MISS RIPPERGER: They don't have any African tom-tom
numbers.

USUFRUCT: Well, then, did you ask for wrestling music, like
I told you?

MISS RIPPERGER: He said he never heard of any special songs
a person could wrestle to. He gave me some Sousa marches—
here's "Under the Double Eagle"—

USUFRUCT: Never mind, they'll do. That's all for now.

MISS RIPPERGER: If you'd give me more of an idea what it
was for, I could try one of the big record stores downtown.

USUFRUCT (*evasively*): Just a hearing I've called—doesn't
matter. Now look, you go to lunch, and take an extra hour.
I'm expecting a party, a Miss LaFlange.

MISS RIPPERGER: Is she the one in the Ziegler assault case?

USUFRUCT: Er—no, no, some theatrical mixup. Go on, run
along. (*She exits. Her employer burrows into a desk drawer, produces a pocket mirror and comb, and trains a few filaments of
hair across his scalp. He has seated himself and joined his fin-
gertips judicially when a light knock sounds at the door. Opal
LaFlange enters, carrying a fibre sample-case. She is a statuesque*

blonde clad in tomato-colored satin. A trifle steatopygous and endowed with what the poet Herrick has felicitously described as "that brave vibration each way free." Her flaxen hair, worn long over her shoulders, and milk-white skin recall to mind the pneumatic nudes who used to be portrayed on jackknives.)

OPAL (*in a childish treble*): Hill-oo-oo! How are yoo-oo?

USUFRUCT: Ah, good morning! And how is our—ahem—little transgressor today?

OPAL: Just finely, judge. My, what a darling office! Is this where you do all your studying and stuff?

USUFRUCT: Yes, I—er—I'm a bug on privacy. You see, in my type work I have to get off by my lonesome and ponder over the—uh—briefs, so to speak. Do you like it?

OPAL: Oh, it's adorable! So snug and well—sort of anteem, if you know what I mean.

USUFRUCT: Precisely. No buttinskis around to distract— (*He starts as Opal zips open her dress and begins pulling it over her head.*) Hey, what are you doing there?

OPAL: Why, getting ready for my routine with Bombo. I thought you wanted to see the way we work in the clubs.

USUFRUCT (*scuttling to the door and shooting the bolt*): Sure, but after all, people might misunderstand. A man in my position can't be too careful.

OPAL: You can say that again, brother. (*She discards her slip.*) If anyone broke down that door right now, you'd have a hell of a time explaining.

USUFRUCT: L-listen, maybe we ought to skip it for the time being. I—I've got to run over to the Board of Estimate. I'll see your act at the Tropics tonight.

OPAL: Not unless you're a mind reader you won't. The coppers padlocked the joint three days ago.

USUFRUCT: Then we'll put it on in a field somewhere—at the Elks Club-house—

OPAL: Gorgeous, when I strip down to dance, I dance. Here, help me blow up Bombo. (*She draws an inert bundle of fur and a bicycle pump from the sample case, hands him the pump.*) This lousy valve in his belly button, it never did work right. . . . There. Now come on, lover, put your back into it.

USUFRUCT (*panting*): I . . . I'm doing the best I can . . . phew . . .

OPAL: Keep at it—the chest has to come out a whole foot yet. (*She spots the phonograph.*) Say, don't tell me! Got any fast tempo tunes—"Cow-Cow Boogie" or anything like that?

USUFRUCT (*the veins in his forehead bulging*): Uh . . . just those there. . . . Look, I'm getting winded. . . .

OPAL: "The Stars and Stripes Forever." "Semper Fidelis." "Washington Post March." Jeez, what cornball picked these out? (*The gorilla, a remarkable simulacrum with bared fangs, towers menacingly over Usufruct, who instinctively cowers away from it. A resounding blare of brass issues from the phonograph.*)

USUFRUCT: Good grief, are you crazy? Turn that noise down —we'll have the whole building in here!

OPAL: O.K., O.K., keep your girdle on. (*She mutes the music, detaches the pump, and twines the gorilla's arms about her.*) Well, here we go. Opening announcement, green dimmers on the lights, and we're on. (*She and Bombo rock across the floor, pantomiming a struggle to capsize each other. Suddenly, as Usufruct stares open-mouthed, a sharp knocking at the door is heard.*)

USUFRUCT (*aghast*): Oh, my God. . . . Turn it off—*stop!*

OPAL: I can't—he's crushing me in his mighty arms—spare me, Bombo—

USUFRUCT (*babbling to himself*): I'm locked in here with a mental case. (*He snaps off the phonograph, and with a strength born of desperation, wrenches apart Opal and Bombo.*)

OPAL: Take your hands off me, you popeyed little shrimp!

USUFRUCT: Sh-h-h! Get in the closet there, quick—your petticoat—no, no, don't put it on—wait a minute, the satchel too— (*As he thrusts her through the door and slams it, the knocking grows more insistent. In an agony of apprehension, he steals to the door and opens it. Flitcraft, the town's leading banker, and Zeugma, a retired merchant and pillar of the church, appear on the threshold. They exhibit obvious concern.*)

FLITCRAFT: Are you all right, Milo? We heard some sort of struggle—a crash—

ZEUGMA: We were afraid you had a seizure—apoplexy or something—

USUFRUCT (*with a ghastly attempt at jauntiness*): Who, me? Ah ha ha ha. . . .

ZEUGMA: Well, you do look kind of shaky, doesn't he, Simeon? Look at the cold sweat on his forehead.

USUFRUCT: I—I was trying to repair the ape—I mean, the apparatus—that is, the Victrola there. (*Sponging his brow*) Gentlemen, if you could come back in an hour—

FLITCRAFT (*entering*): Tell the truth, Milo, this is rather important; we'd like to have a little chin with you right now.

ZEUGMA: Yes, indeed. (*Grimly*) There are some very, very peculiar things going on in Tigris County, my friend. The sooner we put them right, the better. (*Usufruct twitches uncontrollably as his callers dispose themselves in chairs.*)

FLITCRAFT: Let's not beat around the bush, Milo. The political administration in this town is rotten to the core. You know who runs it? A lot of crooked gamblers, racketeers, and gorillas. (*Usufruct reacts, dislodges a phonograph record which shatters on the floor.*) My word, man, you're nervous today. What's wrong?

ZEUGMA: Shouldn't wonder he's coming down with the grippe.

FLITCRAFT: Yes, plenty of it around. Well, anyway, speaking for the law-abiding element in the community, Zeugma and I say they've made a monkey of us long enough.

USUFRUCT (*faintly*): Fellows, I feel a bit feverish. I—I believe I'll go on home and lie down for a spell.

FLITCRAFT: A very good idea, but first, tell me—have you ever thought of running for public office?

ZEUGMA: We need a decent, upright citizen to clean house. Throw the rascals out, that's my motto.

FLITCRAFT: Just so. Now, Milo, we've been over your record and your life is an open book. (*He breaks off, his eyes pinned on the closet door.*) Say, that's funny. What's that hanging out of there?

USUFRUCT (*teeth chattering*): A fur rug—a lap robe. You know, to cover up when you're driving in a sleigh. It b-belonged to my grandfather.

FLITCRAFT: Hmm. (*Rising*) If you don't mind, I'd like to see the rest of that robe. (*As he starts toward it, Usufruct frantically interposes himself.*)

USUFRUCT: Simeon, you've known me thirty years! I swear on everything holy that I never—

MISS RIPPERGER (*entering*): Mr. Flitcraft! Mr. Flitcraft!

FLITCRAFT: What is it?

MISS RIPPERGER: They just held up the bank—three men in

a Buick coop! The police are chasing them down Wentworth Avenue!

FLITCRAFT: Great Scott! (*He runs out, followed by Zeugma. As they exit, Usufruct's knees buckle and he goes horizontal. Miss Ripperger hurries to him, and kneeling, begins to chafe his wrists.*)

MISS RIPPERGER: Oh . . . Oh . . . I just knew something was going to happen when I got up this morning! (*She raises her eyes inquiringly as the closet door opens.*)

CURTAIN

Cloudland Revisited:
Rock-a-Bye, Viscount, in the Treetop

A COUPLE OF MONTHS BACK, the firm of Bramhall & Rixey, Ltd., a shipping concern on lower Broadway operating a string of freighters to West African ports, received an unusual communication. It was inscribed in pencil on both sides of a sheet of lined yellow paper of the sort commonly employed in secondary schools, and its numerous erasures and interlineations attested to the care that had gone into its composition. The correspondent identified himself as a prominent New York sportsman and big-game hunter who was contemplating a safari into the heart of the Dark Continent (Africa, he explained in a helpful aside). Without going into wearisome detail, he was in a position to assure Bramhall & Rixey that the expedition would eclipse anything of the kind on record. Not only was he planning to bring back a number of gorillas, man-eating lions, and comparably gaudy fauna but, if time allowed, he proposed to search out King Solomon's mines and corroborate the existence of a mysterious white goddess ruling a vast empire of blacks in the Cameroons. Obviously, any wide-awake shipping company could appreciate what enormous publicity must accrue to it if chosen to transport such an enterprise. Should Bramhall & Rixey agree to carry the party —without charge, of course—the sportsman thought he might prevail on his associates to assent, though he warned that they rather favored a rival fleet. Stressing the need for an immediate decision, due to the impending monsoon rains (whether in Manhattan or Africa he did not specify), the writer enclosed a self-addressed postal for a speedy reply.

My first reaction when I came across a postal in my morning mail several days ago with the terse admonition "Wipe your nose, bub," signed by Bramhall & Rixey, was one of spontaneous irritation. I caught up the phone, forgetting for the moment that my fourteen-year-old son had been enthralled this past summer by a book called "Tarzan of the Apes" and that he had been treating the family to a sustained panegyric on Africa.

"I'll teach you whose nose to wipe!" I shouted into it. "I've half a mind to come down and cane you people publicly in Beaver Street!" Fortunately, they were spared the humiliation, as, in my wrath, I forgot to dial their number, and by the time I tumbled to the probable culprit and documented his guilt, I was able to take a much more lenient view of the incident. The fact of the matter is that back in 1918, the year I myself first encountered Edgar Rice Burroughs' electrifying fable, it exercised a similarly hypnotic effect on me. Insofar as the topography of Rhode Island and my physique permitted, I modelled myself so closely on Tarzan that I drove the community to the brink of collapse. I flung spears at the neighbors' laundry, exacerbated their watchdogs, swung around their piazzas gibbering and thumping my chest, made reply only in half-human grunts interspersed with unearthly howls, and took great pains generally to qualify as a stench in the civic nostril. The hallucination passed as abruptly as it had set in; one morning I awoke with an overwhelming ennui for everything related to Africa, weak but lucid. My kinsfolk were distrustful for a while, but as soon as they saw me constructing a catamaran in which to explore the Everglades, they knew I was rational again.

Curious as to why Tarzan had enraptured two generations and begotten so many sequels, movie serials, and comics, I commandeered my son's copy of the novel and my wife's chaise longue and staged a reunion. Like most sentimental excursions into the past, it was faintly tinged with disillusion. Across the decades, Burroughs' erstwhile jaunty narrative had developed countless crow's-feet and wrinkles; passages that I remembered outracing Barney Oldfield now seemed to puff and wheeze like a donkey engine. The comparison was aided by a donkey engine puffing directly outside my window, and frequently, in all honesty, its rhythmic snoring was amplified by my own. Nevertheless, I got the gist of the story, and for gist-lovers who prefer to sniff the candy at long range, that little may suffice.

Strictly speaking, the saga begins in the African forest with the adoption by a female anthropoid ape of an English baby of lofty lineage, but to render this association feasible, if not palatable, some valiant exposition is required. Lord and Lady Greystoke, outward bound on the barkentine *Fuwalda* from

Freetown in the summer of 1888, are en route "to make a peculiarly delicate investigation of conditions" in a British West
Coast colony when mutiny breaks out among the crew. Considering that the captain and his mates are forever emptying
revolvers into the men and felling them with belaying pins,
Burroughs' appraisal of the situation is dazzlingly understated:
"There was in the whole atmosphere of the craft that unde-
finable something which presages disaster." The lid ultimately
blows off, and a lamentable scene ensues: "Both sides were
cursing and swearing in a frightful manner, which, together
with the reports of the firearms and the screams and groans
of the wounded, turned the deck of the *Fuwalda* to the likeness of a madhouse." Lord Greystoke, however, behaves with
the sang-froid one expects of a British peer; through it all, he
"stood leaning carelessly beside the companionway puffing
meditatively upon his pipe as though he had been but watching an indifferent cricket match." After the mutineers have disposed of authority, the fate of the couple trembles briefly in
the balance. Then Black Michael, the ringleader, intercedes for
them and persuades his colleagues to maroon the Greystokes
in a secluded spot. The speech transmitting this decision somehow recalls the rhetoric of Gilbert and Sullivan's magnanimous
scalawags. "You may be all right," he explains kindly, "but it
would be a hard matter to land you in civilization without a
lot o' questions being asked, and none o' us here has any very
convincin' answers up our sleeves."

To skim over the rest of the prologue, the blue bloods
survive the immediate rigors of life in the bush; Greystoke,
exhibiting a virtuosity rarely met with in castaways and almost never in the House of Lords, builds a stuccoed log
cabin furnished with cozy appurtenances like bamboo curtains and bookcases, and his wife, materially aiding the story
line, presents him with a male child. But all unbeknownst to
the patrician pair, their hourglass is already running out. Her
Ladyship, badly frightened by a marauding ape, expires on
the boy's first birthday, and as her husband sits stricken at the
deathbed, a band of apes bent on stealing his rifle invade the
cabin and kill him. Among them is Kala, a female whose own
babe has just been destroyed by the king of the tribe. Obey-
ing what Burroughs reverently terms "the call of universal

motherhood within her wild breast," and the even greater urgency for a gimmick to set the narrative rolling, she snatches up the English tot, deposits her lifeless one in its cradle, and streaks into the greenery. The blueprint is now technically complete, but the author, ever a man to pile Pelion upon Ossa, contrives an extra, masterly touch. Since the cabin contains the schoolbooks from which the lad will learn to read eventually, as well as his father's diary—capriciously written in French—proving his identity, it must be preserved intact. The king ape, therefore, accidentally discharges Greystoke's gun and, fleeing in terror, slams the door shut. Burroughs may foozle his prose on occasion, but when it comes to mortising a plot, he is Foxy Grandpa himself.

It would serve no useful purpose to retrace the arduous youthhood and adolescence of Tarzan (whose name, incidentally, means "White-Skin," there being no equivalent for Greystoke in ape language), his sanguinary triumphs over a long roster of enemies like leopards, pythons, and boars, and his easy emergence as undisputed boss of the jungle. Superior heredity, of course, gives "the aristocratic scion of an old English house" a vast edge over his primitive associates. Thanks to the invaluable schoolbooks in the cabin, he instinctively learns to read and write—not without hardship, for, says Burroughs, "of the meaning and use of the articles and conjunctions, verbs and adverbs and pronouns, he had but the faintest and haziest conception." But he perseveres, and along with literacy come further civilized attributes. He bathes assiduously, covers his nakedness with pelts, and, out of some dim recess of his consciousness, produces a really definitive method of distinguishing himself from brute creation: "Almost daily, he whetted his keen knife and scraped and whittled at his young beard to eradicate this degrading emblem of apehood. And so he learned to shave—rudely and painfully, it is true—but, nevertheless, effectively." No reasonably astute reader needs to be told twice that when the hero of a popular novel, whether he is Willie Baxter or an ape man, starts shaving, a pair of mischievous blue eyes are right around the corner. However astute, though, no reader could possibly anticipate a simp of the proportions of Jane Porter, or the quartet of frowzy vaudeville stereotypes that now bumbles into the picture.

The newcomers, it appears, are a party of treasure-seekers hailing from Baltimore, headed by an absent-minded peda-gogue called Professor Archimedes Q. Porter, complete with frock coat and shiny plug hat. In his retinue are Samuel T. Philander, an elderly fusspot secretary straight from the pages of *Puck*; Esmeralda, a corpulent Negro maid aquiver with fear and malapropisms; his daughter Jane, whose beauty rav-ishes the senses; and, finally, Charley-horsing the long arm of coincidence, Tarzan's own cousin and the incumbent Lord Greystoke, William Cecil Clayton. They, too, have just been embroiled in a ship's mutiny—Burroughs' favorite literary calamity, evidently—and are now marooned in Tarzan's very parish. Using these piquant ingredients for all they are worth, the author hereupon proceeds to stir up the most delirious chowder of larceny, homicide, aboriginal passion, and haphaz-ard skulduggery ever assembled outside the Newgate calendar. In all this, Tarzan plays the role of the Admirable Crichton, snatching each of the characters, in turn, from the jaws of death and, inevitably, turning Jane Porter's head. The section in which she betrays her partiality for him is a sockdolager. Tar-zan is putting the kayo on Terkoz, a bull ape who has abducted Jane: "As the great muscles of the man's back and shoulders knotted beneath the tension of his efforts, and the huge biceps and forearm held at bay those mighty tusks, the veil of cen-turies of civilization and culture was swept from the blurred vision of the Baltimore girl. When the long knife drank deep a dozen times of Terkoz' heart's blood, and the great carcass rolled lifeless upon the ground, it was a primeval woman who sprang forward with outstretched arms toward the primeval man who had fought for her and won her. And Tarzan? He did what no red-blooded man needs lessons in doing. He took his woman in his arms and smothered her upturned, panting lips with kisses. For a moment Jane Porter lay there with half-closed eyes. . . . But as suddenly as the veil had been withdrawn it dropped again, and an outraged conscience suffused her face with its scarlet mantle, and a mortified woman thrust Tarzan of the Apes from her and buried her face in her hands. . . . She turned upon him like a tigress, striking his great breast with her tiny hands. Tarzan could not understand it." If Tarzan, who was so intimately involved, was baffled, you can imagine

my own bewilderment, especially with a donkey engine puffing in my ear. Had the yarn not been so compelling and the
chaise longue so comfortable, I would have abandoned both,
bearded the Baltimore Chamber of Commerce, and given
them my opinion of such a heartless flirt.

While one properly expects major characters as vital as Tarzan and Jane to dominate the canvas, it would be grossly unfair
to ignore the figures in the background. Professor Archimedes
Q. Porter and his secretary carry the burden of the comic relief,
and their sidesplitting misadventures evoke chuckles galore.
Herewith, for example, is the Professor's tart rejoinder when
Philander nervously informs him they are being stalked by a
lion: "'Tut, tut, Mr. Philander,' he chided. 'How often must
I ask you to seek that absolute concentration of your mental
faculties which alone may permit you to bring to bear the highest powers of intellectuality upon the momentous problems
which naturally fall to the lot of great minds? And now I find
you guilty of a most flagrant breach of courtesy in interrupting
my learned discourse to call attention to a mere quadruped
of the genus *Felis*. . . . Never, Mr. Philander, never before
have I known one of these animals to be permitted to roam at
large from its cage. I shall most certainly report this outrageous
breach of ethics to the directors of the adjacent zoological garden.'" Can you tie that? The poor boob's so absent-minded he
doesn't even realize he's in *Africa*. An equally rich humorous
conceit is Esmeralda, the maid, who is constantly "disgranu-
lated" by all the "gorilephants" and "hipponocerouses" about
her. I doubt if Amos 'n' Andy at their most inventive have ever
surpassed her attempt to soothe Jane at a moment of crisis:
"Yas'm, honey, now you-all go right to sleep. Yo' nerves am
all on aidge. What wif all dese ripotamuses and man eaten geniuses dat Marse Philander been a-tellin' about—laws, it ain't
no wonder we all get nervous prosecution."

Indeed it ain't, and while the subject of nerves is on the tapis,
I suspect that at this point in the action Burroughs himself
became a trifle discombobulated. With two-thirds of the piece
behind him, he still had to unravel Tarzan's complex genealogy, resolve the love story, account for the Professor's treasure
(lost and found half a dozen times throughout), and return
his puppets intact to everyday life. Accordingly, he introduces

a French cruiser to rescue the Baltimoreans and Clayton, and, once they are safely over the horizon, begins untangling the labyrinthine threads that remain. An officer of the vessel, one D'Arnot, has fallen into the clutches of some local cannibals; Tarzan saves the captive and, in return, is taught French, an accomplishment that enables him to translate his father's diary and legally prove himself the real Lord Greystoke. Armed with the proofs, he hurries to America to claim his mate, but Burroughs is just ahead of him, piling up barriers faster than Tarzan can surmount them. Before he can clasp Jane in his arms, he is compelled to rescue her from a Wisconsin forest fire and eliminate her current fiancé, a Scrooge who financed her father's expedition. The minor matter of the treasure is washed up with a check for two hundred and forty-one thousand dollars, which, the ape man fluently explains to Professor Porter, is its market value. And then, as the lovers' last obstacle vanishes, the author, consummate magician that he is, yanks a final bunny from his hat. Jane jilts Tarzan for his cousin, William Cecil Clayton, and Tarzan, placing her happiness above all, deliberately conceals his true identity. There may be scenes of self-renunciation in Tolstoy that lacerate the heart, but none, I contend, as devastatingly bittersweet as the closing one between the two Greystoke cousins: "'I say, old man,' cried Clayton. 'I haven't had a chance to thank you for all you've done for us. It seems as though you had your hands full saving our lives in Africa and here. . . . We must get better acquainted. . . . If it's any of my business, how the devil did you ever get into that bally jungle?' 'I was born there,' said Tarzan quietly. 'My mother was an Ape, and of course, she couldn't tell me much about it. I never knew who my father was.'"

Ordinarily, my fleeting sojourn in such an equatorial mishmash might have had no worse consequences than myopia and a pronounced revulsion from all noble savages thereafter. As luck would have it, though, the Venetian blind above me slipped its moorings as I finished the romance, and, doubtless overstimulated by Tarzan's gymnastics, I climbed up to restore it. Halfway through the process, the cornice gave way and I was left hanging by my fingernails from the picture molding that encircles the room. At this juncture, a certain fourteen-year-old busybody, who has no better means of employing his time than sending postals to shipowners, came snooping into the room. His pitiless gaze travelled slowly from my pendent form to his copy of "Tarzan of the Apes." "Watch out, Buster, you'll strain your milk!" he cautioned. "Better leave that stuff to Weissmuller." Yes, sir, it's pretty disheartening. You lie on your back all day worrying about the junk your children read, you hang from moldings, and that's the thanks you get. It's regusting.

Cloudland Revisited: When to the Sessions of Sweet Silent Films . . .

ON A slumberous afternoon in the autumn of 1919, the shopkeepers along Weybosset Street in Providence, Rhode Island, were nonplused by a mysterious blinding flash. Simultaneously, they heard a sound like a gigantic champagne cork being sucked out of a bottle, and their windows bulged inward as though Dario Resta's Peugeot had passed, traveling at incalculable speed. Erupting from their bazaars, they saw a puny figure streaking in the direction of the Victory, the town's leading cinema. The first report, that anarchists had blown the cupola off the state capitol, swiftly yielded to a second, that a gopher mob had knocked over the vault of the Mercers' & Pursers' Trust Co. Before either rumor could be checked, a bystander appeared with a green baize bag dropped by the fugitive, establishing him as a sophomore at the Classical High School. Among its contents were a copy of Caesar's Gallic commentaries, a half-eaten jelly sandwich, and a newspaper advertisement announcing the première that afternoon at the Victory of Cecil B. DeMille's newest epic, *Male and Female*, starring Thomas Meighan, Gloria Swanson, and Lila Lee.

By the time the foregoing had been pieced together, of course, the sophomore in question—whose measurements coincided exactly with my own—was hanging out of a balcony seat at the Victory in a catatonic state, impervious to everything but the photoplay dancing on the screen. My absorption was fortunate, for at regular intervals the ushers circulated through the aisles, spraying the audience with an orange scent that practically ate away the mucous membrane. Whether this was intended to stimulate the libido or inhibit it, I never found out, but twenty years later, when I met Mr. DeMille in Hollywood, I could have sworn he exuded the same fragrance. The fact that we met in an orange grove, while relevant, did not materially alter my conviction.

Male and Female, as moviegoers of that epoch will recall, was based on James M. Barrie's *The Admirable Crichton*, a play

that derided caste and sought to demonstrate how a family of
hochgeboren snobs, marooned on a desert island, was salvaged
physically and spiritually by its butler. That so special a problem could enthrall a youth living on a New England chicken
farm might seem unlikely, but it did, and to such a degree that
I saw the picture twice over again on the spot. The silken luxury of its settings, the worldliness and bon ton of the characters, and their harrowing privations held me spellbound. I was
bewitched in particular by the butler as portrayed by Thomas
Meighan. His devastating aplomb, the cool, quiet authority
with which he administered his island kingdom and subdued
the spitfire Lady Mary Lasenby, played by Miss Swanson, dis-
placed every previous matinée idol from my heart. For weeks
afterward, while toting mash to the hens or fumigating their
perches, I would fall into noble attitudes and apostrophize the
flock with lines like "One cannot tell what may be in a man,
Milady. If all were to return to Nature tomorrow, the same
man might not be master, nor the same man servant. Shall I
serve the ices in the conservatory?" The consequences of this
sort of lallygagging soon made themselves felt. There was a
sharp decline in egg production, followed almost immediately
by word from the Classical High School that I had achieved
the lowest grade ever recorded in second-year Latin.

Quite recently, through the good offices of the Museum of
Modern Art, I was enabled to re-examine the masterwork that
gave me so profound a catharsis. It was a reassuring experience;
I discovered that although the world is topsy-turvy, DeMille
still remains the same. His latest pictures display the same baroque pomp, the same good old five-cent philosophy, and the
same lofty disregard for sense. *Male and Female* could be re-
made today with equal success at the box office. All I ask in
return for the suggestion is that prior to its release I be given
twenty-four hours' head start.

The film begins with a pious explanation that its title is derived from the passage in Genesis "Male and female created
He them," and first introduces a scullery maid named Tweeny,
in the person of Lila Lee. Tweeny is employed at fashionable
Loam House, in London, where she nurses a violent, unrecip-
rocated passion for its major-domo, Crichton. We now meet,

in a series of keyhole shots, the various members of the Loam family as they appear to an impudent pageboy delivering their boots. They are, respectively, the Earl (Theodore Roberts), his silly-ass cousin Ernest (Raymond Hatton), and his daughters, Lady Mary and Lady Agatha. Miss Swanson, the former, reclines on a couch worthy of the Serpent of the Nile, having her nails and hair done by a pair of maids. This lovely sybarite is to learn, says an acid subtitle, that "hands are not only to be manicured but to work with, heads not only to dress but to think with, hearts not only to beat but to love with." Her sister, a languid wraith engaged in scrutinizing her cosmetic mask, fares no more kindly: "Lady Agatha, who is to find like most beauties that the condition of her face is less important than to learn to face conditions." There follows a piquant scene wherein Miss Swanson dons a peekaboo negligee, sinuously peels to enter a sunken marble tub, and sluices down in a shower containing a spigot marked "Toilet Water." Emerging, she finds a box of long-stemmed roses sent by an admirer named Lord Brocklehurst. The accompanying card read (as I thought), "My Lady of the Roses: I am coming over to show you something interesting for the slim white finger of your slim third hand," but this seemed so Surrealist in mood that I had the projectionist run it again. The actual phrase, "slim third finger of your slim white hand," is pretty humdrum by comparison.

Depicted next is the ritual of Lady Mary's breakfast, served by three underlings and presided over by Crichton. "The toast is spoiled," declares his mistress capriciously. "It's entirely too soft." Ever the flower of courtesy, Crichton pinks her neatly in the ego with a deadpan riposte: "Are you sure, Milady, that the toast is the only thing that is spoiled?" Leaving her to gnash her teeth on the soggy toast, he descends to the library, where Tweeny is dusting, and proceeds to read aloud, for no cogent reason, a dollop of poesy by William Ernest Henley beginning, "I was a King in Babylon and you were a Christian slave." The scullery maid, eyes swimming with adoration, furtively strokes his instep. "I wouldn't be nobody's slave, I wouldn't," she murmurs. "Unless maybe your slave." Lady Mary, who by a spooky coincidence has been reading the very same book earlier, now enters just in time to hear Crichton declaiming, "I saw, I took,

I cast you by, I gently broke your pride." The delicious spectacle of varlets pretending to understand poetry evokes her patrician mirth, and, imperiously requisitioning the book, she goes to greet Lord Brocklehurst, her suitor.

Brocklehurst, by and large, is an inconsequential character in the drama—merely a lay figure dragged in to spice the budding romance between Lady Mary and Crichton. The plot, which has been betraying definite symptoms of rigor mortis, comes alive about teatime, when the Loams, frantic with ennui, determine to cruise to the South Seas in their yacht. As they animatedly begin studying maps, a confidante of Lady Mary's, Lady Eileen Duncraigie, drops in to consult her about a glandular dilemma. She is infatuated with her chauffeur—one of those typical crushes that followed in the wake of the internal-combustion engine—and wonders whether she stands any chance of happiness. Lady Mary smiles commiseratingly. Indicating a bird cage nearby, she poses a searching zoological parallel: "Would you put a jackdaw and a bird of paradise in the same cage? It's *kind to kind*, Eileen, and you and I can never change it." Well, sir, you know what happens to people who run off at the mouth like that. It's even money La Belle Swanson will be eating crow before the turn of the monsoon, and the cinematic bobbin shuttles madly back and forth as it starts weaving her comeuppance.

Dissolving to the Loam yacht at sea, we observe our principals leading the same unregenerate existence—squabbling endlessly and being coddled by Crichton, whose insteps, in turn, are being dogged by Tweeny. In a newspaper presumably flown to her by albatross, Lady Mary reads of her friend's marriage to her chauffeur. "I suppose," waggishly remarks Ernest, "that if one married a chauffeur, one would soon *tire* of him —get it?" Lady Mary haughtily rejoins that the whole affair is ridiculous—exactly as if she were to marry Crichton. The latter's face freezes as he overhears the slur, and when Thomas Meighan's face, already icy to begin with, froze, it looked like Christmas at Crawford Notch. "And there," explains a crunchy caption, "it might have ended had they not been blown by the Winds of Chance into uncharted Tropic Seas with Destiny smiling at the wheel." Which, draining away the schmaltz, is to say that the yacht runs aground, the crew obligingly perishes, and the Loams, plus their retinue, are washed up intact. The shot that gave one the old *frisson* in 1919, of course, was Meighan carrying Miss Swanson, more dead than alive and more naked than not, out of the surf. It is still gripping, and for those who are curious about its effect on Meighan—inasmuch as there is no clue to be found in his features—the succeeding title is helpful: "Suddenly, like mist melting before the sun, she was no longer a great lady to him, but just a woman, a very helpless and beautiful woman." Brother, they don't write subtitles like that any more. The fellows who dream up the scenarios nowadays are daffy enough, to be sure, but there's no *poetry* in them.

It takes approximately a reel and a half of celluloid and some of the most cumbersome foolery since the retirement of Louise Fazenda to reunite the shipwrecked party. The Earl, who has landed in a dressing gown and yachting cap, chewing the celebrated Theodore Roberts cigar, becomes embroiled in various comic misadventures, such as nestling against a turtle he mistakes for a boulder and disputing possession of a coconut with some chimpanzees. The mishmash of fauna on the island, by the way, would confound any naturalist past the age of twelve; I doubt whether Alfred Russel Wallace, either in the depths of the Malay Archipelago or malarial fever, ever saw apes and mountain goats, wild boars and leopards, sharing a Pacific atoll. When noses are finally counted, the survivors number seven—the four Loams, Crichton and Tweeny, and an unidentified young minister whose presence is never quite explained but whom DeMille was doubtless limbering up for one of his later Biblical productions. Crichton borrows the padre's watch crystal to light a fire, allots various chores to the group, and in short order manages to arouse Lady Mary's anger. When he proposes to use her gold lace stole as a fish net, she rebels openly and talks the others into seceding, but the revolt soon collapses. One by one, the insurgents sneak back to Crichton's fire and his kettle of seaweed broth, leaving her impenitent and alone. Then she too weakens, for, as the subtitle puts it, "You may resist hunger, you may resist cold, but the fear of the unseen can break the strongest will." The unseen in this case takes the form of a moth-eaten cheetah rented from Charlie Gay's lion farm in El Monte. As he noses through the undergrowth, Lady Mary's nerve cracks and she scurries to Crichton for protection. Ultimately, after much digging of her toe awkwardly in the hot sand, or what used to be known as the Charlie Ray school of acting, she knocks under and ponies up the gold lace stole. The sequence, or the round, or whatever it is, ends with both breathing hard but not the least bit winded—considerably more, goodness knows, than can be said for the spectator.

"Under the whiplash of necessity," the narrative continues sonorously, "they come to find that the wilderness is cruel only to the drone, that her grassy slopes may clothe the ragged, her wild boar feed the hungry, her wild goats slake their thirst." Two years, we discover, have wrought substantial changes in the castaways. They have fashioned themselves a nobby compound, domesticated everything in sight but the chiggers, and dwell contentedly under a benevolent despotism set up by Crichton. Lady Mary and Lady Agatha, in play suits of woven bark and in Robinson Crusoe hats, skip over the savannas hunting wild fowl with bow and arrow; the Earl, still chewing the same cigar stump, hauls lobster pots on the lagoon; Ernest and the anonymous divine milk goats in a corral; Tweeny, whose status nothing apparently can alter, stirs a caldron of poi in the kitchen; and Crichton, garbed in a tunic resembling a Roman centurion's made of palm fronds, labors in his study on a Boob McNutt contraption designed to ignite a rescue flare on the cliffs. His new eminence is illustrated at mealtime that evening, when he is revealed dining in splendid isolation, fanned by a punkah that is operated by Lady Mary. Henley's poems, providentially saved from the wreck, are propped up before him, and he is rereading "I was a King in Babylon," the eternal references to which were beginning to give me a dull pain in the base of my scullery. It presently develops that the greedy old Earl has eaten some figs earmarked for Crichton's dessert, and Lady Mary hurries to pick more. Learning she has gone to "the drinking place of the leopards," Crichton hastens after her and transfixes one of the beasts as it attacks. She gratefully flings herself into his arms, and confesses her belief that he is the reincarnation of a king in Babylon. "Then you were a Christian slave," he says with sudden understanding, turning her face up to his. The action thereupon pauses for what is unquestionably the snazziest flashback that has ever emerged from silver nitrate. Meighan, duked out as a Semitic tyrant on the order of Ashurbanipal, receives from a vassal a tigerish, scantily clad slave girl—i.e., Miss Swanson—who repays his tentative caresses by biting him in the wrist. With a cruel sneer, he promises to tame her, and she is borne off snarling defiance in the classic tradition. In due time, she re-enters on a palanquin powered by Nubians, clothed in sequins and wearing on her head a triumph of the taxidermist's art, a stuffed white peacock. "Bring forth the sacred lions of Ishtar," Meighan commands, gesturing toward an arena installed meanwhile by the studio carpenters. "Choose thine own fate. Yield to me willingly or thou shalt know the fitting cage built for thee, O Tiger Woman." Secure in her long-term contract, Miss Swanson proudly elevates her chin. "Through lives and lives you shall pay, O King," she predicts, and advances into the pit. As the episode concludes, we are back on the island, with Crichton telling Lady Mary, in mettlesome spondees, "I know I've paid through lives and lives, but I loved you then as I love you now." A Zbyszko hammer lock, and at long last their lips, parched with rhetoric, meet in a lingering kiss.

The note of implied finality, however, is only a ruse; if the fable is to come full circle, its characters must show the effect of their sojourn away from civilization. Just as the pair are being united by the preacher, a ship appears on the horizon. Lady Mary tries to dissuade her chieftain from signaling for help, but he knows the code and gallantly bows to it. "Babylon has fallen and Crichton must play the game," he announces, gently unyoking her arms and yoking the metaphors.

Transported back to England in an agile dissolve, master and servant promptly revert to type. Lady Mary agrees to wed Lord Brocklehurst, though she reveals her heartbreak to Lady Eileen, whose marriage to her chauffeur has spelled social obloquy. Crichton retaliates by proposing to Tweeny, and, in a penultimate scene, we see them, between kisses, operating an Australian sheep farm. For the tag, or washup, DeMille chose a bittersweet dying fall. On the lawn of a vast country house, amid drifting petals, Lady Mary toys with her parasol and dreams of what might have been. The title reads, "You may break, you may shatter, the vase if you will, but the scent of the roses will hang around her still. Thus does the great sacrifice shed its fragrance over a lifetime." Enter a beflanneled Brocklehurst, who stands regarding her with doglike devotion. "I understand, my dear, why you postponed our marriage," he declares, manfully sweeping up the loose exposition. "You loved Crichton, the admirable Crichton. I'll be waiting for you at the judgment day." He raises her hand to his lips, Lady Mary's eyes under her picture hat fill with tears, and, to use a very apt technical term, we squeeze.

I suspect that a lot of people in my generation, the kind of romantics who blubber at the sight of a Maxfield Parrish print or a Jordan roadster, would not have withstood my sentimental excursion as gracefully as I did, and would have wound up fractured at the Jumble Shop, harmonizing "The Japanese Sandman." Matter of fact, I ran into a couple of these romantics *at* the Jumble Shop, strangely enough, right after seeing *Male and Female*. We got to talking, and darned if they hadn't seen it too as kids. Well, we had a bite of supper, took in the ice show at the Hotel New Yorker, and then, armed with plenty of ratchets, started back to the Museum about midnight so I could screen the picture for them. Luckily, their car hit a hydrant en route and I managed to slip away unnoticed. If I hadn't kept my wits about me, though, the whole day might have ended with much worse than eyestrain. As a middle-aged movie fan, I've learned one lesson: Lay off that nostalgia, cousin. It's lethal.

No Starch in the Dhoti, S'il Vous Plaît

U P UNTIL RECENTLY, I had always believed that nobody on earth could deliver a throwaway line with quite the sang-froid of a certain comedian I worked for in Hollywood during the thirties. You probably don't recall the chap, but his hallmark was a big black mustache, a cigar, and a loping gait, and his three brothers, also in the act, impersonated with varying degrees of success a mute, an Italian, and a clean-cut boy. My respect for Julio (to cloak his identity partially) stemmed from a number of pearls that fell from his lips during our association, notably one inspired by an argument over dietary customs. We were having dinner at an off-Broadway hotel, in the noisiest locale imaginable outside the annual fair at Nizhnii Novgorod. There were at least a dozen people in the party— lawyers, producers, agents, brokers, astrologers, tipsters, and various assorted sycophants—for, like all celebrated theatrical personages, my man liked to travel with a retinue. The dining room was jammed, some paid-up ghoul from Local 802 was interpreting the "Habanera" on an electric organ over the uproar, and, just to insure dyspepsia, a pair of adagio dancers were flinging themselves with abandon in and out of our food. I was seated next to Julio, who was discoursing learnedly to me on his favorite subject, anatomical deviations among showgirls. Halfway through the meal, we abruptly became aware of a dispute across the table between several of our companions.

"It is *not* just religious!" one was declaring hotly. "They knew a damn sight more about hygiene than you think in those Biblical days!"

"That still don't answer my question!" shouted the man he had addressed. "If they allow veal and mutton and beef, why do they forbid pork?"

"Because it's unclean, you dummy," the other rasped. "I'm trying to tell you—the pig is an unclean animal!"

"What's that?" demanded Julio, his voice slicing through the altercation. "The pig an unclean animal?" He rose from his chair and repeated the charge to be certain everyone within fifty feet was listening. "The pig an unclean animal? Why, the

pig is the cleanest animal there is—except my father, of course."
And dropped like a falcon back into his chow mein.

As I say, I'd gone along for years considering Julio pre-
eminent in tossing off this kind of grenade, and then one Sunday a few weeks ago, in the *Times* Magazine, I stumbled across
an item that leaves no doubt he has been deposed. The new
champ is Robert Trumbull, the former Indian correspondent
of the paper and a most affable bird with whom I once spent
an afternoon crawling around the Qutb Minar, outside New
Delhi. In the course of an article called "Portrait of a Symbol Named Nehru," Mr. Trumbull had the following to say:
"Nehru is accused of having a congenital distaste for Americans because of their all too frequent habit of bragging and
of being patronizing when in unfamiliar surroundings. It is
said that in the luxurious and gracious house of his father, the
late Pandit Motilal Nehru—who sent his laundry to Paris—the
young Jawaharlal's British nurse used to make caustic remarks
to the impressionable boy about the table manners of his father's American guests."

It was, of course, the utter nonchalance of the phrase "who
sent his laundry to Paris" that knocked me galley-west. Obviously, Trumbull wasn't referring to one isolated occasion;
he meant that the Pandit made a practice of consigning his
laundry to the post, the way one used to under the academic
elms. But this was no callow sophomore shipping his wash
home to save money. A man willful and wealthy enough to
have it shuttled from one hemisphere to another could hardly
have been prompted by considerations of thrift. He must have
been a consummate perfectionist, a fussbudget who wanted
every last pleat in order, and, remembering my own Homeric
wrangles with laundrymen just around the corner, I blenched
at the complications his overseas dispatch must have entailed.
Conducted long before there was any air service between India
and Europe, it would have involved posting the stuff by sea—
a minimum of three weeks in each direction, in addition to the
time it took for processing. Each trip would have created problems of customs examination, valuation, duty (unless Nehru
senior got friends to take it through for him, which was improbable; most people detest transporting laundry across the
world, even their own). The old gentleman had evidently had

a limitless wardrobe, to be able to dispense with portions of it for three months at a time.

The major headache, as I saw it, though, would have been coping with the *blanchisseur* himself. How did Pandit Motilal get any service or redress out of him at such long range? There were the countless vexations that always arise: the missing sock, the half-pulverized button, the insistence on petrifying everything with starch despite the most detailed instructions. The more I thought about it, the clearer it became that he must have been enmeshed in an unending correspondence with the laundry owner. I suggest, accordingly, that while the exact nature of his letters can only be guessed at, it might be useful—or, by the same token, useless—to reconstruct a few, together with the replies they evoked. Even if they accomplish nothing else, they should help widen the breach between East and West.

ALLAHABAD,
UNITED PROVINCES,
JUNE 7, 1903

Pleurniche et Cie.,
124, Avenue de la Grande Armée, Paris.
MY DEAR M. PLEURNICHE:

You may be interested to learn—though I doubt that anything would stir you out of your vegetable torpor—that your pompous, florid, and illiterate scrawl of the 27th arrived here with insufficient postage, forcing me to disgorge one rupee three annas to the mailman. How symbolic of your character, how magnificently consistent! Not content with impugning the quality of the cambric in my drawers, you contrive to make me *pay* for the insult. That transcends mere nastiness, you know. If an international award for odium is ever projected, have no fear of the outcome as far as India is concerned. You can rely on my support.

And à propos of symbols, there is something approaching genius in the one that graces your letterhead, the golden fleece. Could any trademark be more apt for a type who charges six francs to wash a cummerbund? I realize that appealing to your sense of logic is like whistling an aria to the deaf, but I paid half that for it originally, and the Muslim who sold it to me was the worst thief in the bazaar. Enlighten me, my dear fellow, since I have never been a tradesman myself—what passes through your head when you mulct a customer in this outrageous fashion? Is it glee? Triumph? Self-approbation at the cunning with which you have swindled your betters? I ask altogether without malice, solely from a desire to fathom the dark intricacies of the human mind.

To revert now to the subject of the drawers. It will do you no good to bombinate endlessly about sleazy material, deterioration from pounding on stones, etc. That they were immersed in an acid bath powerful enough to corrode a zinc plate, that they were wrenched through a mangle with utmost ferocity, that they were deliberately spattered with grease and kicked about the floor of your establishment, and, finally, that a white-hot iron was appliquéd on their seat—the whole sordid tale of maltreatment is writ there for anybody to see. The motive, however, is far less apparent, and I have speculated for hours on why I should be the target of vandalism. Only one explanation fits the facts. Quite clearly, for all your extortionate rates, you underpay your workmen, and one of them, seeking to revenge himself, wreaked his spite on my undergarment. While I sympathize with the poor rascal's plight, I wish it understood that I hold you responsible to the very last sou. I therefore deduct from the enclosed draft nine francs fifty, which will hardly compensate me for the damage to my raiment and my nerves, and remain, with the most transitory assurances of my regard,

Sincerely yours,
PANDIT MOTILAL NEHRU

PARIS,
JULY 18, 1903

Pandit Motilal Nehru,
Allahabad, U.P., India.
DEAR PANDIT MOTILAL:

I am desolated beyond words at the pique I sense between the lines in your recent letter, and I affirm to you on my wife's honor that in the six generations the family has conducted this business, yours is the first complaint we have ever received. Were I to list the illustrious clients we have satisfied

—Robespierre, the Duc d'Enghien, Saint-Saëns, Coquelin, Mérimée, Bouguereau, and Dr. Pasteur, to name but a handful —it would read like a roll call of the immortals. Only yesterday, Marcel Proust, an author you will hear more of one of these days, called at our *établissement* (establishment) to felicitate us in person. The work we do for him is peculiarly exacting; due to his penchant for making notes on his cuffs, we must observe the greatest discretion in selecting which to launder. In fine, our function is as much editorial as sanitary, and he stated unreservedly that he holds our literary judgment in the highest esteem. I ask you, could a firm with traditions like these stoop to the pettifoggery you imply?

You can be sure, however, that if our staff has been guilty of any oversight, it will not be repeated. Between ourselves, we have been zealously weeding out a Socialist element among the employees, malcontents who seek to inflame them with vicious nonsense about an eleven-hour day and compulsory ventilation. Our firm refusal to compromise one iota has borne fruit; we now have a hard core of loyal and spiritless drudges, many of them so lackluster that they do not even pause for lunch, which means a substantial time saving and consequently much speedier service for the customer. As you see, my dear Pandit Motilal, efficiency and devotion to our clientele dominate every waking thought at Pleurniche.

As regards your last consignment, all seems to be in order; I ask leave, though, to beg one trifling favor that will help us execute your work more rapidly in future. Would you request whoever mails the laundry to make certain it contains no living organisms? When the current order was unpacked, a small yellow-black serpent, scarcely larger than a pencil but quite dynamic, wriggled out of one of your *dhotis* and spread terror in the workroom. We succeeded in decapitating it after a modicum of trouble and bore it to the Jardin d'Acclimatation, where the curator identified it as a krait, the most lethal of your indigenous snakes. Mind you, I personally thought M. Ratisbon an alarmist—the little émigré impressed me as a rather cunning fellow, vivacious, intelligent, and capable of transformation into a household pet if one had leisure. Unfortunately, we have none, so fervent is our desire to accelerate your shipments, and you will aid us materially by a hint in the right quarter, if you will. Accept, I implore of you, my salutations the most distinguished.

Yours cordially,
OCTAVE-HIPPOLYTE PLEURNICHE

ALLAHABAD, U.P.,
SEPTEMBER 11, 1903

DEAR M. PLEURNICHE:

If I were a hothead, I might be tempted to horsewhip a Yahoo who has the effrontery to set himself up as a patron of letters; if a humanitarian, to garrote him and earn the gratitude of the miserable wretches under his heel. As I am neither, but simply an idealist fatuous enough to believe he is entitled to what he pays for, I have a favor to ask of you, in turn. Spare me, I pray, your turgid rhetoric and bootlicking protestations, and be equally sparing of the bleach you use on my shirts. After a single baptism in your vats, my sky-blue *jibbahs* faded to a ghastly greenish-white and the fabric evaporates under one's touch. Merciful God, whence springs this compulsion to eliminate every trace of color from my dress? Have you now become arbiters of fashion as well as littérateurs?

In your anxiety to ingratiate yourselves, incidentally, you have exposed me to as repugnant an experience as I can remember. Five or six days ago, a verminous individual named Champignon arrived here from Pondichéry, asserting that he was your nephew, delegated by you to expedite my household laundry problems. The blend of unction and cheek he displayed, reminiscent of a process server, should have warned me to beware, but, tenderhearted ninny that I am, I obeyed our Brahmin laws of hospitality and permitted him to remain the night. Needless to say, he distinguished himself. After a show of gluttony to dismay Falstaff, he proceeded to regale the dinner table with a disquisition on the art of love, bolstering it with quotations from the Kamasutra so coarse that one of the ladies present fainted dead away. Somewhat later, I surprised him in the kitchen tickling a female servant, and when I demurred, he rudely advised me to stick to my rope trick and stay out of matters that did not concern me. He was gone before daylight, accompanied by a Jaipur enamel necklace of incalculable value and all our spoons. I felt it was a trivial price to be rid of him. Nevertheless, I question your wisdom, from a commercial standpoint, in employing such emissaries. Is it not safer to rob the customer in the old humdrum fashion, a franc here and a franc there, than to stake everything on a youth's judgment and risk possible disaster? I subscribe myself, as always,

Your well-wisher,
PANDIT MOTILAL NEHRU

PARIS,
OCTOBER 25, 1903

DEAR PANDIT MOTILAL:

We trust that you have received the bundle shipped five weeks since and that our work continues to gratify. It is also pleasing to learn that our relative M. Champignon called on you and managed to be of assistance. If there is any further way he can serve you, do not hesitate to notify him.

I enclose herewith a cutting which possibly needs a brief explanation. As you see, it is a newspaper advertisement embodying your photograph and a text woven out of laudatory remarks culled from your letters to us. Knowing you would gladly concur, I took the liberty of altering a word or two in places to clarify the meaning and underline the regard you hold us in. This dramatic license, so to speak, in no way vitiates the sense of what you wrote; it is quite usual in theatrical advertising to touch up critical opinion, and to judge from comment I have already heard, you will enjoy publicity throughout the continent of Europe for years to come. Believe us, dear Pandit, your eternal debtor, and allow me to remain

Yours fraternally,
OCTAVE-HIPPOLYTE PLEURNICHE

ALLAHABAD,
NOVEMBER 14, 1903

DEAR M. PLEURNICHE:

The barristers I retained immediately on perusing your letter —Messrs. Bulstrode & Hawfinch, of Covent Garden, a firm you will hear more of one of these days—have cautioned me not to communicate with you henceforth, but the urge to speak one final word is irresistible. After all, when their suit for a million francs breaks over you like a thunderclap, when the bailiffs seize your business and you are reduced to sleeping along the *quais* and subsisting on the carrot greens you pick up around Les Halles, you may mistakenly attribute your predicament to my malignity, to voodoo, djinns, etc. Nothing of the sort, my dear chap. Using me to publicize your filthy little concern is only a secondary factor in your downfall. What doomed you from the start was the bumbling incompetence, the ingrained slovenliness, that characterizes everyone in your calling. A man too indolent to replace the snaps he tears from a waistcoat or expunge the rust he sprinkles on a brand-new Kashmiri shawl is obviously capable of any infamy, and it ill becomes him to snivel when retribution overtakes him in the end.

Adieu then, *mon brave*, and try to exhibit in the dock at least the dignity you have failed to heretofore. With every good wish and the certainty that nothing I have said has made the slightest possible impression on a brain addled by steam, I am,

Compassionately,
PANDIT MOTILAL NEHRU

Cloudland Revisited: The Wickedest Woman in Larchmont

IF YOU were born anywhere near the beginning of the century and had access at any time during the winter of 1914–15 to thirty-five cents in cash, the chances are that after a legitimate deduction for nonpareils you blew in the balance on a movie called *A Fool There Was.* What gave the picture significance, assuming that it had any, was neither its story, which was paltry, nor its acting, which was aboriginal, but a pyrogenic half pint by the name of Theda Bara, who immortalized the vamp just as Little Egypt, at the World's Fair in 1893, had the hoochie-coochie. My own discovery of Miss Bara dates back to the sixth grade at grammar school and was due to a boy named Raymond Bugbee, a detestable bully who sat at the desk behind mine. Bugbee was a fiend incarnate, a hulking, evil-faced youth related on both sides of his family to Torquemada and dedicated to making my life insupportable. He had perfected a technique of catapulting BB shot through his teeth with such force that some of them are still imbedded in my poll, causing a sensation like *tic douloureux* when it rains. Day after day, under threat of the most ghastly reprisals if I squealed, I was pinched, gouged, and nicked with paper clips, spitballs, and rubber bands. Too wispy to stand up to my oppressor, I took refuge in a subdued blubbering, which soon abraded the teacher's nerves and earned me the reputation of being refractory. One day, Bugbee finally overreached himself. Attaching a steel pen point to the welt of his shoe, he jabbed it upward into my posterior. I rose into the air caterwauling and, in the attendant ruckus, was condemned to stay after school and clap erasers. Late that afternoon, as I was numbly toiling away in a cloud of chalk dust, I accidentally got my first intimation of Miss Bara from a couple of teachers excitedly discussing her.

"If you rearrange the letters in her name, they spell 'Arab Death,'" one of them was saying, with a delicious shudder. "I've never seen an actress kiss the way she does. She just sort of glues herself onto a man and drains the strength out of him."

"I know—isn't it revolting?" sighed the other rapturously. "Let's go see her again tonight!" Needless to add, I was in the theater before either of them, and my reaction was no less fervent. For a full month afterward, I gave myself up to fantasies in which I lay with my head pillowed in the seductress's lap, intoxicated by coal-black eyes smoldering with belladonna. At her bidding, I eschewed family, social position, my brilliant career—a rather hazy combination of African explorer and private sleuth—to follow her to the ends of the earth. I saw myself, oblivious of everything but the nectar of her lips, being cashiered for cheating at cards (I was also a major in the Horse Dragoons), descending to drugs, and ultimately winding up as a beachcomber in the South Seas, with a saintly, ascetic face like H. B. Warner's. Between Bugbee's persecutions that winter and the moral quicksands I floundered into as a result of *A Fool There Was*, it's a wonder I ever lived through to Arbor Day.

A week or so ago, seeking to ascertain whether my inflammability to Miss Bara had lessened over the years, I had a retrospective look at her early triumph. Unfortunately, I could not duplicate the original conditions under which I had seen her, since the Museum of Modern Art projection room is roach-free and lacks those powerful candy-vending machines on the chairs that kicked like a Colt .45. Nonetheless, I managed to glean a fairly comprehensive idea of what used to accelerate the juices in 1915, and anyone who'd like a taste is welcome to step up to the tureen and skim off a cupful.

Produced by William Fox and based on the play by Porter Emerson Browne, *A Fool There Was* maunders through a good sixth of its footage establishing a whole spiral nebula of minor characters before it centers down on its two luminaries, the Vampire and the Fool. As succinctly as I can put it, the supporting players are the latter's wife Kate, an ambulatory laundry bag played by Mabel Frenyear; their daughter, an implacably arch young hoyden of nine, unidentified; Kate's sister (May Allison); her beau, a corpulent slob, also anonymous; and a headlong butler seemingly afflicted with locomotor ataxia. All these inhabit a depressing chalet in Larchmont, where, as far as I could discover, they do nothing but shake hands effusively. A tremendous amount of handshaking, by the way, distinguished the flicks in their infancy; no director worth his whipcord breeches would have dreamed of beginning a plot before everybody had exchanged greetings like a French wedding party entering a café. In any case, the orgy of salutation has just begun to die down when John Schuyler, the Fool, arrives by yacht to join his kin, and the handshaking starts all over again. Schuyler (Edward José), a florid, beefy lawyer in a high Belmont collar, is hardly what you would envision as passion's plaything, but I imagine it took stamina to be a leading man for Theda Bara—someone she could get her teeth into, so to speak. We now ricochet to the Vampire and her current victim, Parmalee (Victor Benoit), strolling on a grassy sward nearby. The siren, in billowing draperies and a period hat, carries almost as much sail as the Golden Hind, making it a bit difficult to assess her charms; however, they seem to have unmanned the young ne'er-do-well with her to the point where he is unable to light the Zira he is fumbling with. Their affair, it appears, has burned itself out, and Parmalee, wallowing in self-pity, is being given the mitten. Midway through his reproaches, a chauffeur-driven Simplex, sparkling with brass, pulls alongside, Miss Bara shoves him impatiently into it, and the pair whisk offscreen. These turgid formalities completed, the picture settles down to business, and high time. In another moment, I myself would have been shaking hands and manumitting the projectionist to the ball game I was keeping him from.

In a telegram from the President (Woodrow Wilson presumably chose his envoys in an extremely haphazard manner), Schuyler is ordered to England on some delicate mission, such as fixing the impost on crumpets, and makes ready to leave. He expects to be accompanied by Kate and his daughter, but just prior to sailing, his sister-in-law clumsily falls out of the tonneau of her speedster, and Kate remains behind to nurse her. The Vampire reads of Schuyler's appointment, and decides to cross on the same vessel and enmesh him in her toils. As she enters the pier, an aged derelict accosts her, observing mournfully, "See what you have made of me—and still you prosper, you hellcat." Meanwhile, Parmalee, learning of her desertion from a Japanese servant whose eyelids are taped back with two pieces of court plaster, smashes all the bric-a-brac and ferns in their love nest, tears down the portieres, and hastens to intercept her. The derelict waylays him at the gangplank. "I might have known you'd follow her, Parmalee," he croaks. "Our predecessor, Van Diemen, rots in prison for her." The plea to desist from his folly falls on deaf ears; Parmalee sequesters his Circe on the promenade deck and, clapping a pistol to his temple, declares his intention of destroying himself if she abandons him. She smilingly flicks it aside with a rose and a line of dialogue that is unquestionably one of the most hallowed in dramaturgy: "Kiss me, my fool." Willful boy that he is, however, Parmalee must have his own way and shoots himself dead. The gesture, sad to say, is wasted, exciting only desultory interest. The body is hustled off the ship, a steward briskly mops up the deck, and by the time the *Gigantic* has cleared Sandy Hook, Theda and her new conquest are making googly eyes and preparing to fracture the Seventh Commandment by sending their laundry to the same *blanchisseuse* in Paris.

A time lapse of two months, and in a hideaway on the Italian Riviera choked with rubber plants and jardinieres, the lovers play amorous tag like Dido and Aeneas, and nibble languidly on each other's ears. Although everything seems to be leeches and cream, a distinct undercurrent of tension is discernible between them; Schuyler dreams betimes of Suburbia, his dusky cook who used to make such good flapjacks, and when Theda jealously tears up a letter from his wife, acrimony ensues. Soon after, while registering at a hotel, Schuyler is recognized by acquaintances, who, much to his anguish, recoil as from an adder. Back in Westchester, Kate has learned of his peccadilloes through a gossip sheet. She confronts Schuyler's law partner and, with typical feminine chauvinism, lambastes the innocent fellow: "You men shield each other's sins, but if the woman were at fault, how quick you'd be to condemn her!" Mrs. Schuyler's behavior, in fact, does little to ingratiate her. Not content with barging into a busy law office and disrupting its routine, she then runs home and poisons a child's mind against its father. "Mama," inquires her daughter, looking up from one of Schuyler's letters, "is a cross a sign for love?" "Yes," Kate retorts spitefully, "and love often means a cross." The fair sex (God bless them) can be really extraordinary at times.

In our next glimpse of the lotus-eaters, in London, Schuyler has already begun paying the piper; his eyes are berimmed with kohl, his step is palsied, and his hair is covered with flour.

Theda, contrariwise, is thriving like the green bay tree, still tearing up his correspondence and wrestling him into embraces that char the woodwork. Their idyl is abruptly cut short by a waspish cable from the Secretary of State, which reads, in a code easily decipherable to the audience, "ON ACCOUNT OF YOUR DISGRACEFUL CONDUCT, YOU ARE HEREBY DISMISSED." Remorse and *Heimweh*, those twin powerful antibiotics, temporarily dispel the kissing bug that has laid Schuyler low. He returns to the States determined to rid himself of his incubus, but she clings and forces him to install her in a Fifth Avenue mansion. Humiliations multiply as she insists on attending the opera with him in a blaze of aigrettes, and there is an affecting scene when their phaeton is overtaken by his wife's auto near the Public Library and his daughter entreats him, "Papa, dear, I want you." But the call of the wild is too potent, and despite pressure from in-laws and colleagues alike, Schuyler sinks deeper into debauchery. Kate, meanwhile, is keening away amid a houseful of relatives, all of them shaking hands as dementedly as ever and proffering unsound advice. There is such a hollering and a rending of garments and a tohubohu in the joint that you can't really blame Schuyler for staying away. When a man has worn himself down to the rubber struggling in a vampire's toils, he wants to come home to a place where he can read his paper in peace, not a loony bin.

Six months of revelry and an overzealous makeup man have left their stamp on the Fool when we again see him; the poor chap is shipping water fast. He reels around the mansion squirting seltzer at the help and boxing with double-exposure phantoms, and Theda, whose interest in her admirers wanes at the drop of a security, is already stalking a new meatball. Apprised of the situation, Kate goes to her husband bearing an olive branch, but their reunion is thwarted by his mistress, who unexpectedly checks in and kisses him back into submission. The action now grows staccato; Schuyler stages a monumental jamboree, at which his guests drink carboys of champagne and dance the bunny hug very fast, and then, overcome by delirium tremens, he violently expels them into the night. Kate, in the meantime, has decided to take his daughter to him as a last appeal. Preceded by her sister's beau (the Slob), the pair arrive at the mansion to find Schuyler in parlous shape. The child throws herself on him—a dubious service to anyone suffering from the horrors—and the adults beseech the wastrel to come home and, one infers, be committed to a nice, quiet milieu where his expenditures can be regulated. His dilemma is resolved by the reappearance of Theda; Schuyler grovels before her, eradicating any doubt as to his fealty, and the folks exit checkmated. The last few seconds of the picture, in a somber key unmatched outside the tragedies of D'Annunzio, depict the Fool, obsessed by a montage of his sins, squirming on his belly through an openwork balustrade and collapsing in a vestibule. "So some of him lived," comments a final sepulchral title, "but the soul of him died." And over what remains, there appears a grinning presentment of Miss Bara, impenitent and sleek in black velvet and pearls, strewing rose petals as we fade out.

For all its bathos and musty histrionics, *A Fool There Was*, I am convinced, still retains some mysterious moral sachet, if the experience I had after seeing it is at all indicative. As I was quietly recuperating in a West Side snug over a thimble of sherry and the poems of St. John Perse, a young woman who was manifestly no better than she should be slid into the banquette adjoining mine. So absorbed was I in the poet's meter that it was almost two minutes before I detected her wanton gaze straying toward me in unmistakable invitation. I removed my spectacles and carefully placed them in their shagreen case. "Mademoiselle," I said, "the flirtation you propose, while ostensibly harmless, could develop unless checked into a dangerous liaison. I am a full-blooded man, and one who does not do things by halves. Were I to set foot on the primrose path, scenes of carnival and license to shame Petronius might well ensue. No, my dear young lady," I said, draining my glass and rising, "succulent morsel though you are, I have no desire to end my days like John Schuyler, crawling through balustrades and being sprinkled with blooms." As luck would have it, her escort, whose existence I had somehow neglected to allow for, materialized behind me at this juncture and, pinioning me, questioned my motives. I gave him a brief résumé of *A Fool There Was* to amplify my position, but he acted as though I had invented the whole thing. Maybe I have. Still, who could have made up Theda Bara?

Swindle Sheet with Blueblood
Engrailed, Arrant Fibs Rampant

I PROMISE YOU I hadn't a clue, when I unfolded my *Times* one recent morning at the bootblack's, that it would contain the most electrifying news to come out of England in a generation—the biggest, indeed, since the relief of Lucknow. As invariably happens after one passes forty, the paper sagged open to the obituary page; I skimmed it quickly to make sure I wasn't listed, and then, having winnowed the theatrical, movie, and book gossip, began reading the paper as every enlightened coward does nowadays, back to front. There, prominently boxed in the second section, was the particular dispatch—terse and devoid of bravura, yet charged with a kind of ragged dignity. "BRITAIN'S INDIGENT LORDS ASK EXPENSE ACCOUNTS," it announced over a London dateline, and went on, "Some peers are too impoverished in the highly taxed present-day welfare state to travel to London and do their duty without pay, the House of Lords was told today. The Upper House, shorn by the last Labor Government of much of its power, was debating its own possible reform. One of its proposals was for giving expense money to those members who do trouble to come to Westminster. At present the Lords get no salaries and nothing but bare traveling expenses. On an average day no more than one peer in ten is present."

"Well, well!" I exclaimed involuntarily. "It's high time, if you ask me."

"What'd you say?" inquired the bootblack with a start, almost spilling the jonquil-colored dye with which he was defacing my shoes.

"This story about the British peers," I replied. "Poor chaps are practically on the dole—beggars-on-horseback sort of thing. Pretty ironical situation, what?"

He threw me a sidelong glance, plainly uncertain whether it was safe to commit himself. "You a peer?" he asked cautiously.

"No," I said, "but I do think England's in a hell of a state when your Gloucesters and your Somersets have to get down on their knees and scrounge expense money."

"Yeah, the whole world's falling apart," he said, scratching his ear reflectively with his dauber. "A couple of shmos like you and me, we can't even get up our rent, whereas them dukes and earls and all those other highbinders over there are rolling in dough."

"But they're not," I objected. "Judging from this, they've hardly enough carfare to get from their ancestral seats to London."

"That's what I said—it's all topsy-turvy," he returned. His inflection made it abundantly clear that he was humoring an imbecile. "Look, should I put some new laces in here? These are full of knots."

"I prefer them that way," I said icily, and retired behind the paper. The snub, though momentarily soothing to my ego, cost me dear; in retaliation, he gave me such a flamboyant shine that an old gorgon on the sidewalk mistook me for a minstrel and demanded to know where I was hiding my tambourine.

Fletcherizing the news item subsequently in a more tranquil setting, it occurred to me that while the projected expense accounts might seem a godsend at first glance, they could also be a potential source of embarrassment to the noble lords. No matter how august their lineage, they will eventually have to undergo the scrutiny of, and explain every last deduction to, a corps of income-tax ferrets rated among the keenest in the world. I have been speculating about just how, in these circumstances, one applies the thumbscrews to a man whose title dates back four or five centuries—how, in other words, the British tax inquisitor manages to grovel and browbeat at the same time. Obviously, the best way to find out is to secrete ourselves behind the arras at such an examination. Softly, then, and remember, everything you see or hear henceforth is in strictest confidence.

(*Scene: The office of Simon Auger, an inspector in the review division of the Board of Inland Revenue. A small, cheerless room equipped with the standard instruments of torture—a desk, two chairs, a filing cabinet. As a decorative touch rather than for its psychological effect, someone has hung on the wall a kiboko, or rhinoceros-hide whip. When the curtain rises, Auger, a dyspeptic of forty-odd, is finishing a frugal lunch of Holland Rusk, wheat germ, and parsnips, a copy of* Burke's Peerage *propped up before him. For the most part, his face is expressionless, but occasionally it betrays a wintry smile of the kind observable in barracudas. At length, he sighs deeply, stashes the book in the desk, and, withdrawing a bottle of Lucknow's Instant Relief, downs a spoonful. The phone rings.)*

AUGER: Auger here . . . Who? . . . Ah, yes. Please ask His Lordship to come in, won't you? (*The door opens to admit Llewellyn Fitzpoultice, ninth Viscount Zeugma. He is in his mid-sixties, ramrod-straight, affects a white cavalry mustache and a buttonhole, and is well dressed to the point of dandyism. Having fortified himself with four brandy-and-sodas at lunch, his complexion—already bronzed by twenty-five years on the Northwest Frontier—glows like an old mahogany sideboard.*)

ZEUGMA (*jauntily*): Afternoon. Hope I'm not terribly late.

AUGER: Not at all. No more than three-quarters of an hour or so.

ZEUGMA: Frightfully sorry. This filthy traffic, you know. I defy anyone to find a cab in Greek Street.

AUGER: Your Lordship was lunching in Soho?

ZEUGMA: Yes, I found a rather decent little place there—Stiletto's. They do you quite well for five guineas—*coquilles St. Jacques*, snails, a tart, and a passable *rosé*. You must try it sometime.

AUGER: I could hardly afford to, at my salary.

ZEUGMA: Between ourselves, I can't either, but the Crown pays for it—ha ha ha. (*Blandly*) Necessary business expense in connection with my duties in the Upper House.

AUGER: Indeed. (*He jots down a note.*) By the way, I believe I had the pleasure of meeting a relative of yours about a fortnight ago—the Right Honourable Anthony de Profundis.

ZEUGMA: Wild young cub—Tony. What's the boy been up to?

AUGER: Little matter of evasion and fraud. He was sly, but we specialize in those sly ones—ha ha ha. (*Opening a dossier*)

Well, let's get on with it, shall we? Your address remains the same, I take it—The Grange, Regurgingham-supra-Mare, Dotards, Broome Abbas, Warwickshire.

ZEUGMA: That's right. But why do you ask?

AUGER: Because your nephew changed his unexpectedly last week, if you follow me.

ZEUGMA: I—I say, it seems dreadfully warm in here. Could we open a window?

AUGER: I'm afraid not. Whoever designed this stage set forgot to include one. However, to resume. According to your return, you made thirty-one trips here from Warwickshire during the last Parliamentary session.

ZEUGMA (*muffled*): Whole avalanche of measures directly affecting my constituency. Crucial decisions. No time for shilly-shallying.

AUGER: I have no doubt. Still, in glancing over the minutes of the Upper House I notice Your Lordship didn't speak once in all that period.

ZEUGMA: Blasted committees chained me down. Paperwork from dawn to dark. Closeted with Winnie weeks on end. Barely able to snatch a sandwich.

AUGER: Yes, few of us realize how unselfishly England's public men give of their energy. Notwithstanding, you did find time to squeeze in sixty-three meals, excluding breakfasts, for a total of four hundred fifty-seven pounds thirteen shillings. These were all concerned with legislative matters?

ZEUGMA: Every blessed one. (*Spluttering*) Confound it, are you questioning my word?

AUGER: I wouldn't dream of it. I was merely giving you what we call a surface probe—to make certain there was no aura of peculation, as it were. Now suppose we cast an eye at your hotel appropriation. These five-room suites you habitually took at the Dorchester—weren't they a bit grandiose for an overnight stay?

ZEUGMA: By Gad, sir, if you expect me to crawl into some greasy boarding house in Kensington and fry my own kippers—

AUGER: Certainly not, certainly not. One can't conceivably imagine Lady Zeugma in such an atmosphere.

ZEUGMA (*unwarily*): She wasn't with me—er, that is, I was batching it most of the term—

AUGER (*smoothly*): I see. And the rest of the time you shared the accommodations with another legislator?

ZEUGMA: Well—uh—in a way. My staff secretary—or, rather, my secretarial adviser. Mrs. Thistle Fotheringay, of Stoke Poges.

AUGER: Ah, that explains these miscellaneous charges—one hundred eighteen quid for champagne, forty-two pounds ten for caviar, and so on. Naturally, neither you nor Mrs. Fotheringay ever partook of these delicacies paid for by the state?

ZEUGMA (*struggling to dislodge an emery board from his trachea*): N-no, of course not. I just kept 'em on hand for colleagues—for other viscounts, you understand. Haven't touched a drop of bubbly in years. It's death to my liver.

AUGER: Really. Then perhaps you'd care to examine this cutting from a recent issue of the *Tatler*. It shows you and your —ahem—secretarial adviser with upraised champagne glasses, dining at the Bagatelle.

ZEUGMA: Demnition . . . I say, old man, mind if I pass it along to Mrs. Fotheringay? Women like to preserve sentimental slop like this.

AUGER: I know. That's why I thought of sending it to Lady Zeugma.

ZEUGMA (*agitatedly*): Wait a bit, let's not— We mustn't go off half— By Jove, I've just had an absolutely wizard idea!

AUGER: Amazing how they pop out of nowhere, isn't it?

ZEUGMA: You revenue blokes have some kind of fraternal organization, don't you? I mean where you take the missus to Blackpool, toffee for the kiddies, all that drill?

AUGER: Quite. And if I may anticipate Your Lordship, you'd like to make a small donation to our outing fund.

ZEUGMA: Why, how did you guess?

AUGER: One becomes surprisingly clairvoyant in this line of work.

ZEUGMA: Fancy that. Well, suppose you put me down for about five hundred pounds. Needn't use my name, necessarily. Call it "Compliments of a Friend."

AUGER: Very magnanimous of you, I'm sure.

ZEUGMA: Nonsense—live and let live's my motto. Let sleeping dogs lie, I always say.

AUGER: Yes, and whilst you're raking up proverbs, don't forget there's no fool like an old fool. (*He replaces the dossier in the desk, extends a packaged handkerchief to his illustrious caller.*) Would you care for one of these? Your own seems to be wringing wet.

ZEUGMA (*undone*): Ah, yes, many tax—that is, you're most welcome. Pip-pip. Cheerio. (*He exits, tripping over his stick and ricocheting off the filing cabinet. Auger's eyes crinkle up at the corners and he hums two or three bars of a tuneless little melody. Then, reopening* Burke's Peerage, *he begins nibbling a carrot reflectively as the curtain falls.*)

Cloudland Revisited: I'm
Sorry I Made Me Cry

THE CONSULTING room I sat in that dun December afternoon in 1920 was a perfect setting for a senior Rhode Island eye specialist, and Dr. Adrian Budlong was perfectly cast
in the role of the specialist. A septuagenarian with a sunken,
emaciated face, and as angular as a praying mantis, Dr. Budlong
bore a chilling resemblance to the mummified Rameses II, and
it would not have surprised me to learn that he kept his entrails
in an alabaster canopic jar under his desk. The room itself was
rather like a crypt, dark and redolent of musty bindings and
iodoform; behind the Doctor's head, in the shadows, a bust
of Galen just large enough for a raven to perch on scowled
down at me balefully. For forty-five minutes, Dr. Budlong, in
an effort to discover why my eyelids were swollen like Smyrna
figs, had submitted me to every test known to ophthalmology.
He had checked my vision with all manner of graduated charts
and images, made me swivel my eyeballs until they bellied
from their sockets, peered endlessly into my irises with sinister flashlights. The examination, clearly, had been fruitless, for
he was now bombarding me with questions that struck me as
irrelevant, if not fatuous. Had I eaten any toadstools recently,
been stung by any wasps or hornets? Had I wittingly stepped
on a rattlesnake or serpent of any description?

"I—I swim under water a lot at the Y.M.C.A.," I faltered.
"Maybe the disinfectant—"

"Chlorine never hurt anybody," he snapped. "Clears the
brain." With a palsied clawlike hand, he plucked the optical
mirror from his death's-head and dropped it on the blotter.
"Humph—no reason a boy of your age should suddenly start
looking like a bullfrog. Have you been under any mental strain
lately? What kind of stuff d'ye read?"

"Er—mostly history," I said evasively. "Balzac's *Droll Stories*, the *Decameron*, Brantôme's *Lives of Fair and Gallant
Ladies*—"

"Nothing there that would affect the lids especially," he said, with what I considered unnecessary coarseness. "Now let's stop paltering around, young man. What have you been crying about?" Somewhere deep in my consciousness, a louver flew open and I saw the façade of the Providence Opera House, the temple where every moviegoer in town had been snuffling uncontrollably over D. W. Griffith's great tear-jerker *Way Down East*. Choking back a sob, I confessed shamefacedly that I had seen the picture three times. Dr. Budlong regarded me for a full twenty minutes in silence, patently undecided whether to have me certified or bastinadoed. Then, making no effort to conceal his spleen, he prescribed cold poultices and a moratorium on cinematic pathos, and flung me out. By an evil circumstance, the trolley car that bore me homeward passed the Opera House. Hours later, streaked with tears, and blubbering from my fourth exposure to the masterpiece, I informed my folks that Budlong had pronounced me a victim of winter hay fever. The diagnosis aroused no visible furor. By then the family was impervious to shock.

Not long ago, examining the network of laughter lines around my eyes in the mirror, it occurred to me that I was in peril of becoming a slippered popinjay. Life since forty had been so rollicking and mirthful that I had allowed my sentimental, nobler instincts to retrogress; what I needed, and pronto, was a profound emotional *nettoyage*. Accordingly, I downed twenty pages of Thomas Merton, the spiritual equivalent of sulphur and molasses, listened to Jan Peerce's superbly emetic recording of "What Is a Boy?" and topped it off with a matinée of *Way Down East* at the Museum of Modern Art. I can get around the house passably by holding on to the furniture, but I still feel a mite queasy.

The leitmotiv of *Way Down East*, like that of so many early film melodramas, was innocence betrayed, virtue—doggedly sullied through ten reels—rising triumphant and kneeing its traducer in the groin. The sweet resignation with which Lillian Gish, the heroine, underwent every vicissitude of fortune from bastardy to frostbite, and the lacquered, mandarin composure of Richard Barthelmess in the face of ostracism and blizzard, have rarely been surpassed on celluloid. It was, however, Lowell Sherman, that peerless actor, who, in his delineation of the villain, copped the honors. Exquisitely groomed, a trifle flaccid, the epitome of the jaded roué, he moved catlike through the action, stalking his prey, his face a mask of smiling insincerity that occasionally let slip a barbered sneer. When he tapped a cigarette deliberately on his silver case and cast a cool, speculative glance into a woman's bodice, you knew she would never survive the rabbit test. Sidney Blackmer, Henry Daniell, Robert Morley—there have been many able varmints since, but none quite as silky or loathsome as Lowell Sherman. They had to spray him with fungicide between takes to keep the mushrooms from forming on him.

Way Down East, billed in its opening title as "a simple story for plain people" (the adjectives would seem to be interchangeable), starts off with a windy hundred-and-twenty-two-word essay containing far less juice than pulp and seeds. Its general content is that while polygamy is on the wane, monogamy is not yet worldwide—an assertion calculated to lacerate nobody's feelings, whether Bedouin or Baptist. The locale of the drama, continues the preamble, is "in the story world of make-believe; characters nowhere, yet everywhere." Having slaked the passion for universality that constantly assailed him, Griffith yielded the stage to his puppets. Anna Moore (Miss Gish) and her widowed mother, destitute in a New England village, decide to put the sleeve on the Tremonts, their rich Boston relatives. Clad in gingham and a black wide-awake straw, Anna sets off for their mansion, bumbling into a stylish musicale they are giving and discomfiting her snobbish female cousins. In order to make character with a rich, eccentric aunt, however, the Tremonts swallow their resentment and take Anna in. Simultaneously, the girl has a fleeting encounter with her seducer-to-be, dashing Lennox Sanderson (Lowell Sherman), who smirks into her cleavage and earmarks her for future spoliation. We now whisk to the countervailing influence in Anna's life, David Bartlett (Richard Barthelmess), as he scratches a pigeon's neck on his father's farm, adjacent to Sanderson's country estate. "Though of plain stock," the subtitle explains, "he has been tutored by poets and vision wide as the world." He has also had access, it might be noted, to a remarkable pomade, which keeps his hair snugly plastered to his scalp no matter how turbulent the action becomes. The secret of Barthelmess's hair has never ceased to fascinate me. In every picture I recall him in, from *Broken Blossoms* and *Tol'able David* to *The Idol Dancer* and *The Love Flower*, nothing ever disturbed that sleek coiffure. Cockney bruisers beat the daylights out of Barthelmess, bullying mates kicked him down hatchways and flailed him with marlinspikes, and Papuans boiled him in kettles, but he always looked as though he had just emerged from the Dawn Patrol Barbershop. Of course, there is no external evidence that his hair was real; it may merely have been Duco, sprayed on him between takes, like Sherman's fungicide, but how they ever prevented it from cracking is beyond me.

Anna's downfall, the next item on the agenda, is one of the most precipitous and brutal since the sack of Constantinople by the Turks. Sanderson spies her at a society rout, almost unbearably ethereal in soft focus and a cloud of tulle, and, closing in, murmurs thickly, "In your beauty lives again Elaine, the Lily Maid, love-dreaming at Astolat." Enchanted by this verbal zircon, Anna dimples from head to toe and implores, "Tell me more." He obliges, with such notable effect that she ultimately agrees to a secret marriage ceremony, unaware that the parson is bogus and the witnesses fixed. From then on, the poor creature is fed through the dramatic wringer with relentless ferocity. After her return home, she finds she is gravid, appeals to Sanderson—who, meanwhile, has gone on to other amorous diversions—and discovers that she has been euchred. Sanderson callously deserts her, on the pretext that he will be disinherited if their liaison comes to light, and Anna's mother, with typical maternal spitefulness, dies off just when she is most needed. The baby languishes from birth; when it succumbs, giving Anna endless golden opportunities for histrionics, she is expelled from her lodgings by a righteous landlady, and the first portion of her Gethsemane concludes. The least sophisticated movie fan senses, though, that his tear ducts are being permitted only the briefest respite. Better than any director before or since, Griffith understood the use of the bean ball, and he now prepares to pitch it square at his leading lady and reduce everyone to jelly.

Drawn by the peculiar magnetism that polarizes movie characters, Anna wanders to the Bartlett farm, meets David, and so generally excites pity that Squire Bartlett, his gruff, bigoted father, gives her a minor post agitating a churn. The farm hums with all sorts of romantic activity. There is, for instance, a visiting niece named Kate who is alternately being courted by Hi Holler, the hired man, and the Professor, an absent-minded pedagogue with a butterfly net. Gusty bucolic comedy ensues when the former, daubing his shoes and hair with axle grease to enhance his charm, is struck on the head by a new-laid egg and backs into a pitchfork. Also on hand to provoke chuckles is a rustic twosome made up of Martha Perkins, the village gossip, and her perennial admirer, a hayseed in a linen duster who quaffs Long Life Bitters. The story meanders sluggishly along for a spell, washing up tender symbols like cooing buds and bursting doves to blueprint David's bias for Anna, and then Lennox Sanderson pops in again, this time mousing around after Kate. He berates Anna for remaining in his bailiwick and, in truly heartless fashion, orders her to clear off. As she is about to, though, David shyly confesses his *béguin* for her (and nobody could confess a *béguin* more shyly than Barthelmess, without moving so much as a muscle in his face). At length, sorely troubled, she decides to stay—a difficult decision and similar to one that I myself, by a coincidence, was having to make. Confidentially, it was touch and go.

Except for love's gradual ripening, the next thousand feet of the film are as devoid of incident as a Fitzpatrick travel talk on Costa Rica, Land of the Coffee Bean. There is a plethora of fields choked with daisies, misty-eyed colloquies, and orotund subtitles like "One heart for one heart, one soul for one soul, one love, even through eternity. At last the great overwhelming love, only to be halted by the stark ghost of her past." With the onset of winter, the plot registers a sudden galvanic twitch. Just as Anna is stalemated between David's proposal, which she cannot bring herself to accept, and Sanderson's renewed persecutions, her onetime landlady happens into the village, recognizes her, and recounts her shame to the sewing circle. Martha Perkins, of course, instantly hurries to the Squire to apprise him that he is harboring a Jezebel, and the fat is in the fire. Anna is excoriated in front of the entire household and driven forth despite David's protestations, but not before she castigates Sanderson as her betrayer. A blizzard, which has been picking its teeth in the wings, now comes in on cue, and enfolding the outcast, whirls her toward the icebound river. David, who meanwhile has been locked in mortal combat with Sanderson (without having his hair mussed, naturally), flattens his adversary and runs to intercept Anna; the ice goes out, she is swept to the brink of the falls, and her lover, exhibiting the nimblest footwork since Packey McFarland, saves her from annihilation. The rest of the spool portrays Sanderson, surprisingly natty after his drubbing, offering his dupe legitimate wedlock and sighing with relief when she disdains him, and a multiple marriage in which Anna and David, Kate and the Professor, and Martha and her apple-knocker are united. So ends the morality, with no hard feelings except in the gluteus, and with that unique sense of degradation that attends a trip to the movies during daylight.

As it happens, the only known antidote for the foregoing is a double banana split with oodles of fudge sauce, and immediately on quitting *Way Down East* I sought one out at a neighboring drugstore. As I was burrowing into it like a snowplow, I became conscious of the soda jerker's intent scrutiny. "Say, din I use to see you around the old Opera House in Providence?" he inquired narrowly. "I took tickets there when I was a kid." Judging from the man's decrepitude, I would have had to dandle Bronson Alcott on my knee to be his contemporary, but I waived the point and held still for a spate of theatrical reminiscence. At last, as a sort of tourniquet, I mentioned *Way Down East* and suggested he might enjoy seeing it again. He drew himself up, offended. "Listen, wise guy," he retorted. "I may handle slop for a living, but I don't have to look at it." I slunk out with flaming cheeks, made even pinker by the cashier's recalling me to settle the check. Altogether, it was a shattering afternoon. The next time my nobler nature gets the upper hand, I aim for the nearest Turkish bath.

Sorry—No Phone or Mail Orders

WHEN A perfume called Chaqueneau-K was launched a couple of seasons ago with a campaign designed to prevent women from buying it, there was a lot of headshaking around the Advertising Club of New York, and more than one scarlet-faced old member gloomily prophesied, over his gin-and-French, the death of retailing. "Damn it all, sir, it won't go down," the Tories sputtered. "Bullyrag the consumer, deride him if you will, but you can't dispense with the beggar altogether. Someone's got to move the bloody stuff off the shelves." The forebodings were, as it turned out, groundless; ladies bent on achieving the unattainable cozened their menfolk into procuring it for them, and today any *femme soignée* would consider herself *vieux jeu* without a flacon of Chaqueneau-K in her *parfumoir*. (Well, almost any *femme soignée*.) Quite recently, the technique has been gaining ground among other storekeepers, notably Macy's and a men's-apparel firm in Baltimore named Lebow Brothers. The former's announcement of a fur sale, while not out-and-out preventive advertising, narrowed down the market to a mere handful of the élite: "Just 10 very precious natural ranch mink cape stoles go on sale tomorrow—$377. Hard to believe a lustrous, deeply piled natural ranch mink cape stole could cost so little? It's true true true at Macy's tomorrow! Just 10 very lucky women will get ten very precious mink buys," etc., etc. Lebow Brothers, apostrophizing a men's cashmere jacket in the pages of *Vogue*, was even more dickty: "Cashmiracle . . . so rare each coat is registered. Woven by the famous Worumbo Mill. This miracle in cashmere makes a truly proud possession. The finest underdown of 20 goats makes one jacket. In Oyster White, Moonlight Blue, Mulberry, Bamboo." The text opens a whole host of nerve-tingling possibilities, such as the hijacking by goniffs of an armored car laden with Cashmiracles, or the crisis at Worumbo when, in the course of looming a jacket for some noted coxcomb like Danton Walker, one of his twenty sacrificial goats is found to possess no underdown. The temptation to substitute the hair of a Bedlington terrier or a yak might understandably arise, though I imagine Worumbo's blenders are incorruptible—and heavily bonded, to boot. In which case, of course, the suspense would stem from some rival columnist, say Ed Sullivan or Barry Gray, attempting to suborn a blender into using the ersatz to discredit Walker. In short, the dramatic complications could be hilarious, especially if you added a Shakespearean holocaust and killed off all the protagonists in the end.

The upshot of this constricted merchandising, foreseeably, is that the average shopper may soon be frozen out of the picture, and, unless he has a controlling interest in the United States Gypsum Corporation, a listing in Debrett, and a membership in the Jockey Club of France, will be unable to purchase the ordinary necessities of life. The easiest way to appreciate his plight, perhaps, is to follow an exemplar named Leo Champollion, whose garter has snapped while crossing against a light, into a haberdashery in the East Fifties. The establishment, deeply carpeted and indirectly lit, has no vulgar fixtures like showcases or spittoons to identify it as an outfitter's; given another urn or two, it could be a mortuary or a gastroenterologist's waiting room. As Champollion enters in a crouching position, tugging at his socks, Elphinstone, a lard-faced salesman, finishes pinning a camellia in his lapel and approaches languidly.

ELPHINSTONE (*from across a gulf*): You wished—?

CHAMPOLLION: I busted a garter just now—the elastic's all shot.

ELPHINSTONE: Soddy, we don't vulcanize old rubber. There's a garage over on Second Avenue that may conceivably aid you.

CHAMPOLLION: Aw heck, she's not worth fixing. I'll take a new pair.

ELPHINSTONE (*suavely*): Indeed? May I have your name, please?

CHAMPOLLION: Why—er—Champollion. But what difference does it make? I just want an inexpensive—

ELPHINSTONE: Champollion, eh? Any relative of the distinguished Egyptologist?

CHAMPOLLION: No-o-o, not as I know it. I'm with the Cattaraugus Yeast Company, in the enzyme division.

ELPHINSTONE: I see. And who recommended you to us?

CHAMPOLLION: Nobody. I happened to look up and see your sign "Cravatoor."

ELPHINSTONE: You mean you haven't been previously introduced or filed application to enroll as a customer?

CHAMPOLLION: I—I didn't know you had to.

ELPHINSTONE: My dear fellow, the clientele of this shop comprises some of the biggest gazebos in the country. If we were to bother with every whippersnapper who blunders in off the street, how long do you think we'd stay in business?

CHAMPOLLION (*piteously*): But I can't walk around this way, like a college boy! How can I call on the prospects with my sock hanging down?

ELPHINSTONE: That's your headache. Mine is to safeguard the stock so that pikers won't sneak in and buy it out from under our nose. Good day.

CHAMPOLLION: Look, I'll pay double the usual price! (*His voice becomes incoherent.*) I'm a family man, with two little chiggers—I mean two little nippers—

ELPHINSTONE (*relenting*): Well, I'll make an exception this time, but if it ever leaks out, it'll cost me my job.

CHAMPOLLION: I won't tell anybody—honest I won't. I'll say I stole them.

ELPHINSTONE: All right, then, sit down and I'll take your measurements. (*Pulls on surgical gloves.*) Now, hoist up your trousers; I don't want to get these septic. . . . Hmm, that's a pretty scrawny-looking calf you've got there.

CHAMPOLLION: It's wiry, though. I used to beat everybody at stickball.

ELPHINSTONE: Well, you could have done with a bit of polo. Let's see, we might anchor a catch here—

CHAMPOLLION (*diffidently*): Look, wouldn't a regular-sized garter fit me? You know, just ordinary ones—maroon or navy blue. There don't have to be those naked girls on the webbing.

ELPHINSTONE: It isn't a question of size, and anyway, when the time comes *we'll* decide what pattern is best on you. What I'm concerned with now is the contour of your leg so I can fill out my sculptor's report.

CHAMPOLLION: Hanh? What's that for?

ELPHINSTONE: To aid him in modeling the garter, man. (*Impatiently*) Don't you understand? Each pair is sculptured to the wearer's individual requirements by an artist specially commissioned for the task. In your case, it could be one of the academicians, like Paul Manship or Wheeler Williams, if your knees aren't too knobby.

CHAMPOLLION: Wh-what if they are?

ELPHINSTONE: Ah, then we'd have to call in an abstractionist —Henry Moore or Calder. Naturally, their fees are higher and you'd have to sustain the cable charges should we send your specifications abroad.

CHAMPOLLION (*uneasily*): I wasn't figuring on too much expense, to tell you the truth.

ELPHINSTONE: Possibly not, but you don't realize the trouble involved. First, we have to make a plaster-of-Paris form of your shinbone, then a mockup in laminated wood, which is baked under pressure, sanitized, and aged. This guides the sculptor so he can rough out his cast.

CHAMPOLLION: But I can't wear stone garters! I have to be on my feet all day.

ELPHINSTONE: We wouldn't allow you to. They're simply the matrix from which we execute your personalized accessory in a variety of materials. Here's a swatch to give you an idea. This one, as you see, simulates pickled pine.

CHAMPOLLION: What's that one—plastic?

ELPHINSTONE: No, it only simulates plastic; it's infinitely more costly. Here's one in a fabric so nearly resembling human flesh that customers frequently can't find their garters once they're on.

CHAMPOLLION: Is that good?

ELPHINSTONE (*stiffly*): We're not here to answer metaphysical questions, Mr. Champollion. We're here to not sell merchandise.

CHAMPOLLION: I was only asking. I didn't mean to sound fresh. (*Peering at another sample*) Say, isn't this what I've got on?

ELPHINSTONE: Hardly. That's what we call *trompe-l'œil*. It may look like worn-out elastic, but it's not elastic at all. It's grypton, the sleaziest plastic known.

CHAMPOLLION: Jeekers, you can't keep up with science nowadays, can you?

ELPHINSTONE (*with Olympian amusement*): No. I suppose it must be rather confusing for a layman. Well, let's start with the mold—

CHAMPOLLION: Uh—I was wondering—couldn't you advance me a pair of garters just for the time being, till I get back to Yonkers?

ELPHINSTONE: Quite impossible. Our vaults close at three.

CHAMPOLLION (*supplicatory*): Or even a piece of twine, so's I could finish my calls. I'd send it back by messenger.

ELPHINSTONE: No, but in view of the circumstances, I'll stretch a point and expedite the psychological quiz. (*Flicks the switch of a Dictograph concealed in an urn.*) Elphinstone to Glintenkamp. Will you be good enough to come in here, Doctor? (*Before Champollion's motor apparatus can function, a dynamic young man enters from rear. He wears a speculum and a physician's smock improvised from an old flour sack, on the back of which is visible, in faded blue letters, the legend "Ceresota —Best by Test."*)

GLINTENKAMP: Eligibility prognosis?

ELPHINSTONE: If you please. Solvency dubious, physique zero minus four.

CHAMPOLLION (*eyes rolling affrightedly*): I can't stay any longer. My boss'll have a connip—

GLINTENKAMP: Now, now, nobody's going to hurt you. Just look at these cards and tell us what the various shapes suggest to you. Come on.

CHAMPOLLION: S-someone spilled gravy on it. Juice of some kind.

GLINTENKAMP: No, no, they're blots of ink. Try to concentrate, now—don't they remind you of anything?

CHAMPOLLION: Well, the top part there . . . um . . . that could be a face, a man's profile.

GLINTENKAMP: Anyone you know?

CHAMPOLLION: Uh-uh. Wait a minute, though. It's a little like Mr. Bastinado.

GLINTENKAMP: Your boss?

CHAMPOLLION: No, a credit manager up our way. He works for the Procrustes Finance people.

GLINTENKAMP (*significantly*): I see. Go ahead, keep trying.

CHAMPOLLION: This one on the side looks like—well, like pencils in a cup.

GLINTENKAMP: That'll do. (*To Elphinstone*) Impoverishment fixation. Strictly a vag. Boost him.

CHAMPOLLION (*anxiously*): Did I pass? Am I going to get the garters?

ELPHINSTONE: Just close your flap and pretend to be a special-delivery letter. You're practically in Yonkers. (*As one man, he and Glintenkamp sweep up Champollion, propel him to the door, and toss him into oblivion.*)

GLINTENKAMP (*consulting his watch*): Well, five o'clock. The end of a perfect day.

ELPHINSTONE: Yep, all the goods intact and not a cent in the register. I tell you, Doc, this business is going places. Another year like this and we'll be moving over onto the Avenue. (*Radiant, the two of them exit to prepare a banner advertisement for* Vogue *celebrating their collapse.*)

CURTAIN

Next Week at the Prado: Frankie Goya Plus Monster Cast

IT MUST HAVE been about a quarter to four when I entered Rumpelmayer's the other afternoon, and except for a pair of spurious Hungarians crouched over their *Gugelhupfe*, hissing objurgations at Sir Alexander Korda, the place was empty of customers. A headwaitress, all whalebone and basic black, undulated in my direction, executed a crisp sergeant major's flourish toward a table reserved for pariahs, and dismissed me with a venomous glare as I chose another, at dead center. My request for cinnamon toast and tea engendered such dismay that I ordered a *Dobos Torte* I needed like a hole in the duodenum, but I figured that perhaps my friend Federbush might eat it when he arrived. He had always been an incurable pastry addict; I recalled how years before, while we were collaborating on *Mother Carey's Chiclets*, an abortive musical comedy based on a book by Kate Douglas Wiggin, he used to consume éclairs, napoleons, *petits fours*, and strudel by the trayful, and the fact he had proposed Rumpelmayer's for our reunion intimated that he was still on the starch.

Even so, I was unprepared for the moonfaced dumpling who presently spun out of the revolving door enveloped in a billowing balmacaan, a green velours dicer cocked on his head, and bore down on me with outspread arms. The duckbill nose and shoe-button eyes were still Federbush's, but fifteen years of lotus-eating in Hollywood had not made him any more ascetic. To put it conservatively, he had ballooned.

"Lover!" he sang out, enfolding me. "You look younger than springtime—exactly like the day we died in Wilmington! How the hell do you do it?"

"Well—er—you see, my face never changes," I replied evasively, "but there's this portrait of me that ages instead."

"And eventually we build to a dénouement where you stab the picture and are found dead beside it, a loathsome old man," he finished, tossing his coat at the waitress. "It's threadbare, kid. Oscar Wilde lifted it from Goethe, who copped it from

Marlowe, who probably got it from the *Upanishads*. Anyway, you certainly don't look your age. If it wasn't for the bald spot, you could pass for a man of fifty-one."

"Gee, thanks," I said, with the sort of boyish twinkle Lon Chaney used to excel at. "You haven't changed either. Listen, what'll you have? I got you some pastry—you always liked it in the old days."

"Ancient history, my boy," he said tragically. "Shades of young men among the *mille-feuilles*. It's strictly fronds and hot water now—no more carbohydrates for me. One French cruller and I'm liable to drop in my tracks." He waved aside the menu the waitress was presenting and ordered two soda crackers and a cup of Ovaltine. Then, his lower lip atremble with nostalgia, he fell to musing over the past. Did I remember Dave's Blue Room, a delicatessen at the corner of Sixth Avenue and Washington Place along about 1926? "Boy, what groceries," he sighed. "That Dave was the Michelangelo of the sandwich world. I'll never forget the one he called the Dr. Flandina Reducing Special—goose liver, raisins, Swiss cheese, mangoes, poppyseed, and almond paste. Many's the night I'd stop in there on my way home to dinner and eat two of 'em. I was an iron man."

"You still are," I comforted him. "Anyone who's lasted as long as you in Hollywood must have the constitution of a yak."

"No more," he said. "I'm all shot—a bundle of nerves. Sometimes, after a day at the studio, I'm so hypertensed I can barely find my own Mercedes in the parking lot." Then he added thoughtfully, crumbling a saltine, "Yep, everything's different, here and out on the Coast, too. How long since you been in Hollywood?"

"Pretty near three years."

"You wouldn't know the place," said Federbush. "All those torpedoes who used to run the industry are gone; everybody's an aesthete. Nowadays, they only make two kinds of pictures there—encyclopedic Russian novels and biographies of famous artists. Take this *War and Peace* hassle, for instance. It's eighty-six years since Tolstoy published it and nobody once thought of turning it into a flicker. All of a sudden, four different impresarios are rushing it into production—Mike Todd, David Selznick, Metro-Goldwyn-Mayer, and an Italian team, Ponti–De

Laurentiis, in association with Paramount. Both Todd and the ginzos claim that Marshal Tito promised them the Yugoslavian Army for their battle sequences, and they'll probably go to court about it. The other day, Stravinsky indignantly denies a statement by the Italians that he's doing their score. The word around Chasen's, however, is that Julie Styne has already written it on the q.t. That'll give you a dim inkling of what's going on."

"But why is everyone filming the same story?" I demanded.

"My argument precisely," said Federbush. "I said to one of those donkeys last week, 'Branch out, for Crisakes,' I said. 'Why don't you make some other Russian masterpiece for a change? A good lively musical of *Dead Souls*, let's say, with Piper Laurie and Tony Curtis.' Well, I was just hollering down a rain barrel. He never even heard of the property."

"The famous painters are my dish of tea, though," I said. "First Rembrandt, then Gauguin, then Toulouse-Lautrec. Now I read in the paper that M-G-M's busy on a life of van Gogh. You know, it isn't going to be easy persuading José Ferrer to slice off an ear."

"Personally, I doubt whether Ferrer's available for the role," said Federbush. "As soon as he's through being Mahatma Gandhi, he's scheduled to play Goya. Don't tell me you haven't heard about *that*." I confessed ignorance and sued for details. "It all started a few weeks back with Joseph L. Mankiewicz," he disclosed. "Right after he announced he was producing a life of Goya in Spain for United Artists. Within twenty-four hours, an Italian outfit named Titanus Films began squawking. According to them, they had planned the same thing for two years and were lining up Ferrer as Goya and Gina Lollobrigida as the Duchess of Alba. The payoff, though, is that neither Mankiewicz or these jokers know about the third version."

"Which is what?" I asked, confused.

"The one *I've* been working on under cover," he replied, removing a cigar from a small aluminum dirigible. "Keep it dark, but I'm readying a sensational Goya script using these same two mummers. The only difference is in mine Lollobrigida plays Goya and José Ferrer is the Duchess."

"Rather revolutionary casting, isn't that?" I ventured.

"Not necessarily," said Federbush. "Ferrer has impersonated

women before. Don't you remember him in *Charley's Aunt?* That was how I got the idea. . . . Why, don't you like it?"

"Oh, sure, sure," I said quickly. "I was merely wondering whether you wouldn't lose—ah—certain romantic overtones by transposing the sex of the characters."

"Don't be obtuse," he returned. "Basically it's still the same story—two people overwhelmed by a reckless tidal wave of passion which it snaps its fingers at the petty-bourgeois standards of the time."

"Only the girl happens to be a Spanish court painter and the boy's a duchess," I said reflectively.

"Correct," said Federbush. "After all, how many people in your audience know whether Goya was a man or a woman in the first place?" His face became animated. "The beauty of my setup is that one sizzling situation piles on top of the next. Like when Goya—that is, Lollobrigida—is painting the Duke of Wellington. All of a sudden, the bluff old war dog digs the fact that his limner is a woman—a beautiful, desirable woman —and he makes a pass. As she's struggling and pleading for mercy—"

"Wait a minute," I broke in. "Why does she struggle?"

"For conflict, goddam it," snapped Federbush. "If she didn't, you wouldn't have any picture. Don't interrupt me . . . So while she's pushing over taborets and refectory tables to stem his advances, we cut to Ferrer in a lavish suite of the ducal palace, all dittied out in a black lace mantilla and surrounded by these scantily clad duennas that they're ministering to his wants. Naturally, they never dream the Duchess is a man, which of course opens up a myriad opportunities for good hoke comedy and maybe even a tug at the heartstrings. Anyway, some powerful empathy between the lovers warns Ferrer that his sweetheart Goya is in jeopardy. He hastens to her studio, arriving just as Wellington is rending apart her smock, and we climax with a battle royal wherein José kayoes the Iron Duke."

"Sounds plausible," I said. "How are you handling the business of the two portraits? I mean the study of her in the nude and the one Goya painted to show her husband."

"That incident, candidly, I had to drop," he admitted candidly. "It didn't fit in with my approach. Between you and me and the Breen office, I don't think the world is thirsting for a shot of José Ferrer naked on a bearskin rug. When he was six months old, yes, but not now."

"Well," I said. "To be honest, I can't quite visualize Lollobrigida as an Old Master, but I suppose all those wars and bullfights and court intrigues Goya was mixed up in offer lots of scope for drama."

"Brother, you can embroider that on a sampler," said Federbush warmly. "One of my most gripping scenes is where she defies the command of Charles IV to use egg tempera on the famous portrait of the royal family. 'Sire,' she says, flinging aside her maulstick and drawing herself up proudly. 'You may swing me from yon gibbet, break me on the wheel, suffer crows to peck out mine eyes, but by my maidenhead, I shall never use egg tempera.' That sequence is pure TNT, if I say so myself. By the way, what *is* egg tempera?"

"Search me," I replied. "But before it gets to celluloid, you'd better do some fast research at the Art Students League."

"Ach, it don't matter," he said carelessly. "It's the sense of the thing I'm after—the clash of wills. What really bothers me is how to end the story. I wanted to have the two of them going away to Tahiti to begin a new life together, but I'm not so sure it's believable."

"No, it seems out of key with the rest of it," I agreed. "Have you hit on a title yet? You mentioned the Iron Duke a second ago. How about *The Tinfoil Duchess*?"

Federbush shook his head. "Uh-uh," he said. "It has to evoke Goya's work somehow—you know what I mean? For the time being, I'm calling it *The Disasters of the Heart*."

"I'll buy that," I said. "Yes sirree, I'll underwrite that." I arose and extended my hand. "Well, Jacques," I said. "I hate to run, but I promised to pick up my wife at a *vernissage* at five, and she ought to be nearly dry by now."

"It's been a treat," said Federbush simply. "I needn't tell you that if you ever come out to the Coast—"

"And I needn't tell you that if you ever come East again—" I echoed.

We left it like that, neither of us predicting what might happen. With people like Federbush and me, almost everything is tacit. Or will be from now on. You can lay money on that.

You're My Everything, Plus City Sales Tax

D O I TAKE it everybody's familiar with a magazine called *Town & Country*? (If I know my luck, it'll turn out that there *is* no magazine called *Town & Country*, or else that there are five with nearly identical titles—*Town & Poultry, Hound & Gentry, Grouse & Peltry*, etc.) Anyhow, the one I mean is a fashionable paper costing six bits that chronicles the activities of the quality, and hence doesn't circulate around the Luxor steam baths or most of the other places I do. Several weeks ago, though, while waiting for the lacquer to dry on a new toupee at my wigmaker's, I noticed a copy of the September issue on his credenza and began thumbing through it. Before I could determine what cotillions were upcoming or which supper clubs the Braganzas favored, my attention was impaled on a singular advertisement for Dayton Koolfoam Pillows. In case you're a square like me, who never heard of it, the Dayton Koolfoam isn't just a conventional bolster; in the eyes of its sponsors it's a whole *mystique*, almost a philosophical system. "Yes, Dayton Koolfoam is *more* than a pillow . . . it's a *way* of life," the text announced with marked exaltation, "for its relaxing sleep-ability rejuvenates you for another day. And it's *more* than *foam*, for its patented process gives a unique, velvety 'open-pore' surface that assures ever-changing fresh air." What corralled me specifically, however, was the superimposed color photograph of a patrician young person musing over a note from some impassioned gallant that contained the following bit of meringue: "Betty dear . . . being away from you makes every day seem like a week, every week like a month. But here's a kiss . . . tuck it under your Koolfoam and dream of me."

This inveterate disposition of the advertiser to cuddle, to yoke his product to the consumer's emotional life and stability, is, of course, nothing new. Brand Names Foundation, Inc., a fellowship dedicated to making the public label-conscious, has been piping away on the same theme for quite a while now. Its most touching effort, perhaps, was the advertisement a year or so back that showed a family moving into a new home in a strange city, friendless and utterly without roots. Everybody was thoroughly woebegone, but, said the copy, there was no occasion for despair. Close at hand were nationally advertised wares to restore a sense of kinship and continuity—old cronies, I gathered, like the O-Cedar Mop for Mom, the cheerful red tin of Prince Albert for Dad, Kiwi Shoe Polish for Junior, and Mogen David Wines for Sister. And, it might have added, a full selection of dependable roscoes, like the Smith & Wesson, if things got really unendurable.

Granting the fact that Koolfoam has pioneered in cross-pollinating love and commerce, my sole objection to its romantic correspondence is that it tantalizes instead of enlightening; no sooner does it start a provocative hare than it inexplicably abandons the chase. Just what, I wonder, is the status of the lady's pen pal that he speaks so jauntily of her pillow? Most men in the early stages of courtship, at least, haven't the faintest idea whether their sweethearts sleep in Utica or in burlap, and, even after a *modus amandi* is established, rarely quiz them about their preference in pillows. To be sure, she may have thrown hers at him in a hoydenish moment while larking around her *garçonnière*, but nobody with red blood in his veins studies labels at a time like that . . . I beg pardon? . . . Oh, I thought you said something. If, on the other hand, the charmer is intended to be a young matron, are we to assume that she and her husband routinely exchange love letters freighted with advertising? The whole thing becomes more cryptic the longer you speculate on it, and since everyone knows that intense speculation can easily unhinge the reason, I'd like to make a proposal. I have here, by a coincidence that those prone to stagger may regard as staggering, a series of letters very similar in content to Koolfoam's, and I think their perusal might reward the peruser. They came out of a desk I acquired at a country auction last weekend, whose previous owner, a bachelor friend of ours, emplaned quite precipitately before the sale for an extended stay in Europe. Ordinarily, I would hesitate to publish the letters because of their intimate flavor, but as he left no forwarding address and has undoubtedly changed his name by now, I consider I'm not violating any confidence. The lady concerned can fend for herself. She seems to have done ably thus far.

SEPTEMBER 8

GUY DARLING,

I suppose you'll think I'm a silly little goose to write this, but I felt I simply *had* to apologize for Eliot's behavior the other evening at dinner. Also, I can't resist any opportunity to use my new Parker 51, which, as you know, takes the drudgery out of correspondence. Did you realize, by the way, that its patented Vacuum-Flo suction barrel, embodying a revolutionary concept in pen styling, guards against seepage? Yes, it's goodbye to ink-stained fingers and annoying blots. The stationery, of course, is Eaton's Wedgwood, obtainable in eleven inviting colors. It's sort of a hallmark with fastidious people like myself, those who appreciate the finer things. Guy, you'd adore their fascinating free booklet, "The Romance of Paper." Why not send for it today?

I'm afraid Eliot made a perfectly horrid impression on you when you arrived, but the poor dear caught cold on his way home from the office and, instead of employing Vicks Inhaler, your doctor's recommendation at the first sign of sniffles, drank practically a fifth of Haig & Haig. That's his very own favorite, and I guess it's the choice of the discriminating everywhere, because it's light without being heavy and just smoky enough so it isn't clear. Well, the old green-eyed monster always comes out in Eliot whenever he's had one too many, and he started grilling me in this relentless fashion about where I'd met you, etc. Fortunately, I know those moods of his; had I spilled the fact that we'd sort of picked each other up in the lobby of the Bellevue-Stratford, he'd have brained you the moment you walked in. So I acted real vague—classmate-of-my-brother double-talk—and he quieted down pronto. All that glowering of his, and the playful pass he made at you with the carving knife, was just his way of showing off. Speaking of the knife, did you notice our dinner service? It's Gorham's Damascene pattern, and the apogee of elegance from a hostess's point of view. Master craftsmen have lavished years of experience on this loveliest of all cutlery.

Are you by any chance free this Thursday? Eliot has to fly out to Cincinnati overnight for some tiresome insurance symposium, and I thought you might like to buzz over and take potluck. Of course, it won't be very exciting, just the two of us, but I'll get one of those divine Hormel hams—and they *are* scrumptious, with their mouth-watering goodness sealed into each tin in gigantic pressure ovens—and afterward we can laze around the fire and talk if we have to. I've been dying for a chance to flaunt my new negligee from Bergdorf Goodman's. It's so sheer that Eliot won't let me wear it when we have company. Still, I don't think it's fair for anyone way out in Cincinnati to impose his whim on people, do you? Let's teach him a lesson.

Affectionately,
BRENDA

SEPTEMBER 17

DEAREST GUY,

I'm sure you'll never forgive me for popping into your secluded bachelor retreat yesterday afternoon without warning, and I do hope you won't think me terribly forward. Needless to say, I wouldn't have dreamed of acting that impulsively except it seemed the only way out of my dilemma. I was so wet and spent after getting lost on those twisty back roads that when I saw your mailbox, I almost sobbed with relief. And when you insisted on bundling me out of my damp things and sharing that hot brandy punch, I could have hugged you. Or did I? It's all a bit fuzzy, but definitely on the enchanted side. Is that your impression?

Incidentally, I love the upstairs part of your lair, the imaginative way you've treated the walls and ceilings—Kem-Tone, isn't it? It gives such a satisfying patina, and contractors no less than homeowners swear by its durability. So washable, too; cobwebs and lint scamper at the flick of a dustcloth. Everything you've done, in fact, is calculated to extract "oh"s and "ah"s, with a single exception. Will you disown me if I make one teeny-weeny criticism, lover? In poking around the kitchen, I noticed your refrigerator needs defrosting. Now, Guy, we both know that false icebox economy spells whopping electric bills, as unbiased surveys conclusively reveal. Don't put off that visit to your Westinghouse dealer's to see his dazzling new line of 1957 models. The most generous trade-in allowance in years now makes it possible in some instances to get not only a factory-fresh unit but a cash dividend of several hundred dollars as well. My, can't you just hear everyone's budget purr?

I'll tell you a secret if you swear not to repeat it: I'm becoming the least bit concerned about Eliot. He flies into the most jealous rages over positively nothing. Last night, for instance, he suddenly rounded on me and demanded where I'd found the Madras sports shirt from Brooks that you loaned me. Darned if he didn't catch me off balance and I almost told him, but some instinct saved me. I said the laundry'd sent it back with his by mistake. He kept staring at it all evening, trying to place it, because of course you'd worn it the night he met you. Isn't that hilarious? I knew it'd amuse you.

A clairvoyant little birdie just whispered something in my ear. He said that next Monday, about two-thirty, I'd be in the bar of the Carverstown Hotel, at one of those rear tables in the dark, looking for mischief. If you happen to be driving through Carverstown around then, it might be fun to see whether he's right. Aren't you dying of curiosity? I am.

Expectantly,
BRENDA

OCTOBER I
SWEETIE,

I've never known anything so uncanny as our running into each other in Bloomingdale's upholstery section yesterday morning. Of course, I knew you often ran up to New York for the day, but of all the unlikely places to encounter one's neighbors! We didn't get very much shopping accomplished, though, did we? And I saw ever so many tempting things as we were leaving—those stunning nine-by-twelve Gulistans whose rich, glowing designs complement your furniture whatever its period, the new Waring blender that whips up foamy puddings and sauces when unexpected guests drop in, a whole cornucopia of sturdy gadgets to gladden the housewife's heart. Promise me to browse through their kitchenwares the *very* first chance you get.

The *escargots* in your little French restaurant on Fifty-third Street were delectable, and as for their stingers, I don't even recall leaving the place. Where on earth did we progress to afterward? I have a hazy recollection of an automatic elevator and your fussing with a shoelace, and the next I knew, the conductor was shaking me and calling out Flemington Junction. Eliot was fit to be tied when I rolled up in the taxi. Seems he'd left the car for me at the station as we'd agreed at breakfast, but I could barely focus, let alone remember a trivial detail like that. To make matters worse, some busybody—Ailsa Spurgeon, I'll bet, she's always hated me—had called up and reported that she'd spotted us reeling out of the Carverstown Hotel last week. Well, you should have seen the fireworks. All kinds of wild threats about breaking every bone in your body and hiring a private eye and Lord knows what—sheer bluff, naturally, since he hasn't a blessed shred of evidence except the monogrammed belt buckle you left behind the night he was in Cincinnati. I thought of mentioning it to you afterward, but I hate postmortems, don't you? So dampening.

I may be attending an alumnae luncheon in Philadelphia Wednesday—at least, Eliot's convinced I am, and it seems pointless to disillusion him. Shall we say the theology section of Leary's Bookstore at one? I'll look properly demure to fit the surroundings, but I could turn into a bacchante in the right environment. Here's a kiss . . . tuck it under your Chemex and heat your coffee on it.

Consumingly,
BRENDA

OCTOBER 6

MY POOR LAMBIE,

No words can convey how *pulverized* I was at the news. I'm absolutely shattered, but obviously I can't rush over to nurse and otherwise console you, because Eliot hasn't stirred out of the house for two whole days and keeps watching me like a lynx. However, I'm slipping this to the handyman, and with luck you'll get it tomorrow.

You must have been petrified when Eliot barged into Leary's out of the blue and began punching you, but you can't say I didn't warn you; he's a fiend when aroused, and tricky as he can be. I'm convinced after putting two and two together that he must have steamed open my last letter—which I see now I should never have given him to mail—and then sent me a phony wire from Mother luring me up to New York. I wouldn't believe he could be so base; it shows you can't trust *anybody*. Did he really blacken both your eyes, as he keeps cackling to me? When the swelling goes down, try brushing the discolored areas with Max Factor's Pan-Cake. You'll be amazed how this smoother, *balmier* makeup irons out crow's-feet and restores tissue tone. Small cuts and nicks, too, yield to its snowflake touch. At better drugstores and beauticians everywhere.

As soon as you're presentable, why don't you drop over here early some afternoon for a cozy little drinkie? Or, if you'd rather, I could wander by your chalet. Don't be apprehensive about Eliot. He has these tantrums from time to time, but they usually blow over. Oceans of love, and, whatever you do, don't forget to claim

> Your baggage,
> BRENDA

Eine Kleine Mothmusik

WAR ON MOTHS BEGINS

The moths are beginning to eat. Even if the weather seems cool, this is their season for gluttony. Miss Rose Finkel, manager of Keystone Cleaners at 313 West Fifty-seventh Street, urges that these precautions be taken:

All winter clothes should be dry-cleaned, even if no stains are apparent. Moths feast on soiled clothes, and if a garment has been worn several times in the last few months, it should be cleaned.

Clean clothes may be kept in the closet in a plastic bag. It is safer, however, to send all woolens to a dry cleaner to put in cold storage.

Customers should check to make sure that their clothes are really sent to a cold storage and not hung in the back of the store.—*The Times.*

GAY HEAD,
MARTHA'S VINEYARD, MASS.,
JULY 14

Mr. Stanley Merlin,
Busy Bee Cleaners,
161 Macdougal Street,
New York City

DEAR MR. MERLIN:

I heard on the radio this morning before I went for my swim that the heat in New York is catastrophic, but you wouldn't guess it up here. There is a dandy breeze at all times, and the salt-water bathing, as you can imagine, is superlative. Miles of glorious white beach, marvelous breakers, rainbow-colored cliffs—in short, paradise. One feels so rested, so completely purified, that it seems profane to mention anything as sordid as dry cleaning. Still, that's not exactly your problem, is it? I have one that is.

Do you, by chance, remember a tan gabardine suit I sent in to be pressed three or four years ago? It's a very expensive garment, made of that changeable, shimmering material they call solari cloth. The reverse side is a reddish color, like cayenne pepper; during the British occupation of India, as you doubt-less know, it was widely used for officers' dress uniforms. Any-way, I'm a trifle concerned lest moths get into the closet where I left it in our apartment. The suit isn't really stained, mind you; there's just a faint smudge of lychee syrup on the right sleeve, about the size of your pinkie, that I got in a Chinese restaurant last winter. (I identify it only to help you expunge it without too much friction. I mean, it's a pretty costly garment, and the nap could be damaged if some boob started rubbing it with pumice or whatever.)

Will you, hence, arrange to have your delivery boy pick up the suit at my flat any time next Thursday morning after nine-fifteen? He'll have to show before ten-twenty, since the maid leaves on the dot and would certainly split a gusset if she had to sit around a hot apartment waiting for a delivery boy. (You know how they are, Mr. Merlin.) Tell the boy to be sure and take the right suit; it's hanging next to one made of covert cloth with diagonal flap pockets, and as the Venetian blinds are drawn, he could easily make a mistake in the dark. Flotilla, the maid, is new, so I think I'd better explain which closet to look in. It's in the hall, on his right when he stands facing the bedroom windows. If he stands facing the other way, naturally it's on his left. The main thing, tell him, is not to get rattled and look in the closet *opposite*, because there may be a gabar-dine suit in there, without pockets, but that isn't the one I have reference to.

Should Flotilla have gone, the visiting super will admit your boy to the flat if he arrives before eleven; otherwise, he is to press our landlord's bell (Coopersmith), in the next building, and ask them for the key. They can't very well give it to him, as they're in Amalfi, but they have a Yugoslav woman dusting for them, a highly intelligent person, to whom he can explain the situation. This woman speaks English.

After the suit is dry-cleaned—which, I repeat, is not essential if you'll only brush the stain with a little moist flannel—make certain that it goes into cold storage at once. I read a piece in the newspaper recently that upset me. It quoted a prominent lady in your profession, a Miss Rose Finkel, to the effect that some dry cleaners have been known to hang such orders in the back of their store. You and I have had such a long, cordial relationship, Mr. Merlin, that I realize you'd never do anything so unethical, but I just thought I'd underscore it.

Incidentally, and since I know what the temperature in your shop must be these days, let me pass on a couple of hot-weather tips. Eat lots of curries—the spicier the better—and try to take at least a three-hour siesta in the middle of the day. I learned this trick in India, where Old Sol can be a cruel taskmaster indeed. That's also the place, you'll recall, where solari cloth used to get a big play in officers' dress uniforms. Wears like iron, if you don't abuse it. With every good wish,

Yours sincerely,
S. J. PERELMAN

NEW YORK CITY,
JULY 22

DEAR MR. PEARLMAN:

I got your letter of instructions spelling everything out, and was happy to hear what a glorious vacation you are enjoying in that paradise. I only hope you will be careful to not run any fishhooks in your hand, or step in the undertow, or sunburn your body so badly you lay in the hospital. These troubles I personally don't have. I am a poor man with a wife and family to support, not like some people with stocks and bonds that they can sit in a resort all summer and look down their nose on the rest of humanity. Also my pressing machine was out of commission two days and we are shorthanded. Except for this, everything is peaches and cream.

I sent the boy over like you told me on Thursday. There was no sign of the maid, but for your information he found a note under the door saying she has quit. She says you need a bulldozer, not a servant, and the pay is so small she can do better on relief. Your landlady, by the way, is back from Amalfi, because some of the tenants, she didn't name names, are slow with the rent. She let the boy in the apartment, and while he was finding your red suit she checked over the icebox and the stove, which she claims are very greasy. (I am not criticizing your housekeeping, only reporting what she said.) She also examined the mail in the bureau drawers to see if the post office was forwarding your bills, urgent telegrams, etc.

I don't believe in telling a man his own business. Mine is

dry cleaning, yours I don't know what, but you're deceiving yourself about this Indian outfit you gave us. It was one big stain from top to bottom. Maybe you leaned up against the stove or the icebox? (Just kidding.) The plant used every kind of solvent they had on it—benzine, naphtha, turpentine, even lighter fluid—and knocked out the spots, all right, but I warn you beforehand, there are a few brownish rings. The lining was shot to begin with, so that will be no surprise to you; according to the label, you had the suit since 1944. If you want us to replace same, I can supply a first-class, all-satin quarter lining for $91.50, workmanship included. Finally, buttons. Some of my beatnik customers wear the jacket open and don't need them. For a conservative man like yourself, I would advise spending another eight dollars.

As regards your worry about hiding cold-storage articles in the back of my store, I am not now nor have I ever been a chiseler, and I defy you to prove different. Every season like clockwork, I get one crackpot who expects me to be Santa Claus and haul his clothing up to the North Pole or someplace. My motto is live and let live, which it certainly is not this Rose Finkel's to go around destroying people's confidence in their dry cleaner. Who is she, anyway? I had one of these experts working for me already, in 1951, that nearly put me in the hands of the receivers. She told a good customer of ours, an artist who brought in some hand-painted ties to be rainproofed, to save his money and throw them in the Harlem River. To a client that showed her a dinner dress with a smear on the waist, she recommends the woman should go buy a bib. I am surprised that you, a high-school graduate, a man that pretends to be intelligent, would listen to such poison. But in this business you meet all kinds. Regards to the Mrs.

Yours truly,
S. MERLIN

GAY HEAD, MASS.,
JULY 25

DEAR MR. MERLIN:

While I'm altogether sympathetic to your plight and fully aware that your shop's an inferno at the moment—I myself am wearing an imported cashmere sweater as I write—I must say you misinterpreted my letter. My only motive in relaying Miss Stricture's finkels (excuse me, the strictures of Miss Finkel) on the subject of proper cold storage was concern for a favorite garment. I was not accusing you of duplicity, and I refuse to share the opinion, widespread among persons who deal with them frequently, that most dry cleaners are crooks. It is understandably somewhat off-putting to hear that my suit arrived at your establishment in ruinous condition, and, to be devastatingly candid, I wonder whether your boy may not have collided with a soup kitchen in transit. But each of us must answer to his own conscience, Merlin, and I am ready, if less than overjoyed, to regard yours as immaculate.

Answering your question about Miss Finkel's identity, I have never laid eyes on her, needless to say, though reason dictates that if a distinguished newspaper like the *Times* publishes her counsel, she must be an authority. Furthermore, if the practice of withholding clothes from cold storage were uncommon, why would she have broached the subject at all? No, my friend, it is both useless and ungenerous of you to attempt to undermine Miss Finkel. From the way you lashed out at her, I deduce that she touched you on the raw, in a most vulnerable area of our relationship, and that brings me to the core of this communication.

Nowhere in your letter is there any direct assertion that you *did* send my valuable solari suit to storage, or, correlatively, that you are *not* hiding it in the back of the store. I treasure my peace of mind too much to sit up here gnawed by anxiety. I must therefore demand from you a categorical statement by return airmail special delivery. Is this garment in your possession or not? Unless a definite answer is forthcoming within forty-eight hours, I shall be forced to take action.

Yours truly,
S. J. PERELMAN

NEW YORK CITY,
JULY 27

DEAR MR. PERLEMAN:

If all you can do with yourself in a summer place is hang indoors and write me love letters about Rose Finkel, I must say I have pity on you. Rose Finkel, Rose Finkel—why don't you marry this woman that you are so crazy about her. Then she could clean your suits at home and stick them in the icebox—after she cleans that, too. What do you want from me? Sometimes I think I am walking around in a dream.

Look, I will do anything you say. Should I parcel-post the suit to you so you can examine it under a microscope for holes? Should I board up my store, give the help a week free vacation in the mountains, and bring it to you personally in my Cadillac? I tell you once, twice, a million times—it went to cold storage. I didn't send it myself; I gave orders to my assistant, which she has been in my employ eleven years. From her I have no secrets, and you neither. She told me about some of the mail she found in your pants.

It is quite warm here today, but we are keeping busy and don't notice. My tailor collapsed last night with heat prostration, so I am handling alterations, pressing, ticketing, and hiding customers' property in the back of the store. Also looking up psychiatrists in the Yellow Pages.

Yours truly,
S. MERLIN

GAY HEAD, MASS.,
JULY 29

DEAR MR. MERLIN:

My gravest doubts are at last confirmed: You are unable to say unequivocally, without tergiversating, that you *saw* my suit put into cold storage. Knowing full well that the apparel was irreplaceable, now that the British Raj has been supplanted—knowing that it was the keystone of my entire wardrobe, the *sine qua non* of sartorial taste—you deliberately entrusted it to your creature, a cat's-paw who you admit rifles my pockets as a matter of routine. Your airy disavowal of your responsibility, therefore, leaves me with but one alternative. By this same post, I am delegating a close friend of mine, Irving Wiesel, to visit your place of business and ferret out the truth. You can lay your cards on the table with Wiesel or not, as you see fit. When he finishes with you, you will have neither cards nor table.

It would be plainly superfluous, at this crucial stage in our association, to hark back to such petty and characteristic vandalism as your penchant for jabbing pins into my rainwear, pressing buttons halfway through lapels, and the like. If I pass over these details now, however, do not yield to exultation. I shall expatiate at length in the proper surroundings; viz., in court. Wishing you every success in your next vocation,

Yours truly,
S. J. PERELMAN

NEW YORK CITY,
AUGUST 5

DEAR MR. PERLMAN:

I hope you received by now from my radiologist the two X-rays; he printed your name with white ink on the ulcer so you should be satisfied that you, and you alone, murdered me. I wanted him to print also "Here lies an honest man that he slaved for years like a dog, schlepped through rain and snow to put bread in his children's mouths, and see what gratitude a customer gave him," but he said there wasn't room. Are you satisfied now, you Cossack you? Even my *radiologist* is on your side.

You didn't need to tell me in advance that Wiesel was a friend of yours; it was stamped all over him the minute he walked in the store. Walked? He was staggering from the highballs you and your bohemian cronies bathe in. No how-do-you-do, explanations, nothing. Ran like a hooligan to the back and turned the whole stock upside down, pulled everything off the racks. I wouldn't mind he wrecked a filing system it cost me hundreds of dollars to install. Before I could grab the man, he makes a beeline for the dressing room. So put yourself for a second in someone else's shoes. A young, refined matron from Boston, first time in the Village, is waiting for her dress to be spot-cleaned, quietly loafing through *Harper's Bazaar*. Suddenly a roughneck, for all she knows a plainclothesman, a junkie, tears aside the curtain. Your delegate Wiesel.

I am not going to soil myself by calling you names, you are a sick man and besides on vacation, so will make you a proposition. You owe me for cleaning the suit, the destruction you caused in my racks, medical advice, and general aggravation. I owe you for the suit, which you might as well know is kaput. The cold-storage people called me this morning. It seems like all the brownish rings in the material fell out and they will not assume responsibility for a sieve. This evens up everything between us, and I trust that on your return I will have the privilege of serving you and family as in years past. All work guaranteed, invisible weaving our specialty. Please remember me to your lovely wife.

Sincerely yours,
STANLEY MERLIN

Where Do You Work-a, John?

Sᴀʏ, ɢᴀɴɢ, pardon me if my voice gets a trifle reedy with excitement, but something really big's just taken place. Remember those bull sessions at your frat when the brothers used to start discussing Schopenhauer and Omar Khayyám and the true meaning of life? I mean one of those nights that fairly crackled with good talk, everybody puffing on corncobs and interrupting the other man, and—gee, I don't know, you had the feeling you'd stripped away all the pretense and sham and come somewhere near the core of things. And before you could say Oscar Fingal O'Flahertie Wills Wilde, the room was blue with smoke, the whole bunch of you were logy with near beer, and the first flush of dawn had appeared over the trees on the campus. Then someone, probably a senior or some cuss with more perspective than the rest, suddenly said "Applesauce" and threw open a window, and in came a cool, refreshing current of air that dispersed all the palaver and fakery. Remember the relief of it? Well, that's precisely what has happened. A man named George W. Reinoehl, executive vice-president of the Executive Furniture Executives' Guild—I may have one too many "executive"s in there—has flung open a casement and introduced a new, revolutionary concept of artistic creation, or perhaps I should say re-creation. It's a bit early as yet to foresee its implications, but there's no doubt Reinoehl is a man who is going places, though it's a bit early likewise to foresee what places.

Under the trig and forceful exterior that Reinoehl presented in a double-spread advertisement in *The New Yorker* not long ago, it was clear to the most negligent reader that there dwelt a visionary. Crew-topped, bespectacled, and natty, flanked by a violin and a metronome, he stood encircling a bust of Beethoven with a familiar arm, his pose a mixture of camaraderie and ownership. The accompanying text, ratified by his signature, set forth his credo. "What I did for Beethoven, I can do for you!" he proclaimed ebulliently. "One afternoon as I sat all alone listening to Beethoven's Ninth, I got to thinking what sheer genius the man must have had to accomplish so

276

much under such primitive working conditions—handicapped by clutter, poor workspace, drafts, noise and bad lighting. So . . . I picked up my sketch pad—just for fun—and designed the poor fellow an office *worthy* of his greatness, with every detail as personal as his scrawl on a manuscript. Ludwig, I think, would have been happy here. But—let's talk about *you*. Why not let me develop for you, through your Executive Furniture Guild member dealer and his staff, an office worthy of your position," etc., etc.

So enraptured was I by Mr. Reinoehl's smuggling himself into Parnassus aboard the composer's coattails, his blissful intimation that he had helped to accouche the Ninth Symphony even *post factum*, that I was forced to lie down. Unluckily, the office in which I read his *affiche* contained nothing but a desk and chair, a rather grubby bookcase, and several hundredweight of yellowing newspapers, and I had to recline on the floor until equilibrium returned. As I lay there, it struck me that, in a curious way, the very things that had hampered Beethoven—the litter, the drafts, the medieval lighting—also shackled me. While admittedly less sheer, my own genius might conceivably flower in more congenial surroundings. The sensible course, manifestly, was to pose my situation to Reinoehl, or, better yet, to someone of his ilk I could afford. The Yellow Pages of the directory, ever a beacon to the perplexed, turned up a firm of experts on office décor who responded vibrantly to my quandary. Their consultant, a Mr. Morninghoff, had instilled harmony into the lives of innumerable folk, from scientists to sonneteers, whose names were available on request. He would drop by the next morning to make a survey; the only payment he asked was a chance to aid me in realizing my creative potential. It sounded like a bonanza offer.

At eleven the following day, my doorbell rang peremptorily and a hatless young man with a globular head and a portfolio under his arm—only the portfolio under his arm, to be exact—ascended the stairs. He wore a dark-blue trench coat of the type affected by Italian black-marketeers, and his manner was rather more cavalier than I had expected of a friendly diagnostician. It was, in fact, tinged with unmistakable peevishness.

"Is this supposed to be an office building?" he demanded as he reached my landing. "I smelled cooking in the lower hall."

"That's the Moroccan who runs the travel bureau," I said. "He's probably making a pilaf or couscous down there—you know, with pine nuts and rice."

"You needn't explain," he rejoined haughtily. "I've been in all those places. Fez . . . Marrakech . . . Do you know Ouedi-bel-Youfni?" I shook my head, and a scornful smile creased his lips. "Well, if you don't know Ouedi-bel-Youfni, you don't know North Africa," he said. "It's the place everyone who's anyone raves about. Just a tiny, sun-drenched oasis with a few Berbers, but the only view of the dunes that makes any sense. Cocteau discovered it."

"Is that so?" I murmured. "Must be pretty special if he lives there."

"Oh, he pulled out long ago," my caller said, with disdain. "The whole area's overrun with Philistines. By the way," he went on, turning in the doorway, "Toby Morninghoff, who was scheduled to do you over, is laid up with an impacted hip. I'm Eveninghoff, his second in command."

I courteously assured him that my problem was unworthy of his stature (an opinion he showed no inclination to contradict), and disembarrassed him of his coat. He threw a disparaging glance at the contents of the small antechamber—the tableful of discarded books, the spavined coat tree, and the miscellany of photographs helter-skelter on the wall. "That's my high-school class," I volunteered as he paused to inspect one of them. "I'm the sensitive-faced kid, third from the end, in the Mackinaw."

"Hmm," he said, cocking his head critically. "You should have gone on wearing those bangs. They softened your features."

I withheld a riposte that would have seared him if I had been able to think of it, and followed him into the office. Candidly, it had never looked less prepossessing. A half-empty coffee container awash with cigarette ends topped an accumulation of mail on the desk; crumpled newspapers overflowed the wastebasket; and grime impenetrable obscured the windows. Mr. Eveninghoff made a slow, deadly inventory of the premises that finally included me.

"Unspeakable," he said, at length. "I don't mind a challenge, but this— It's frightening."

"Isn't there some way to liven it up a little?" I appealed. "I thought maybe we could stipple the walls—hang up some bead curtains . . ."

"You mean like those gypsy stores on Sixth Avenue where they read your palm?" I noticed that he habitually lifted one eyebrow in an ironic, quizzical fashion—a trick clearly gleaned from looking at old stills of Rod La Rocque. "I understood from my call sheet that you wrote something or other here— TV commercials, or advertising jingles."

"Er—not exactly," I said. "Puppet plays for colleges, inspirational verse for trade papers—that type of thing. I haven't hit the jackpot yet—"

"You will, you will," he said encouragingly. "But you'd better get one thing straight, my friend. You're defeating yourself. Nothing worth while ever came out of a hole like this." He raised his hand before I could answer. "I know," he said. "You're going to bring up Edgar Allan Poe, or John Keats in his garret. Very well, then, have a look at this." He reached into his portfolio and handed me a color sketch. It portrayed a spacious book-lined library some eighty feet long, with a massive fireplace and a variegated-marble floor. The teak-paneled walls were hung with abstract paintings, the deep club chairs upholstered in pastel tints of glove leather, the avant-garde desk flanked by a unit containing a dictaphone, playback, and television screen. "That's where Keats would have written 'The Eve of St. Agnes' if I'd had anything to say about it," he informed me. "And furthermore, the air-filtration system would have doubled his life span. Think how long Edgar Guest survived under modern conditions."

"I often think of it," I confessed.

"Here's another one," said Eveninghoff, reopening his portfolio. "Ever heard of Thoreau? He was an eccentric who wrote nature stories up in New England. A brilliant talent, but he, too, stymied himself working in a distasteful environment. This is how I redesigned his shack at Walden Pond." The interior he presented could have housed the entire community of Yaddo, all its members functioning harmoniously. Indoors and out had been blended in an airy decorative scheme broken up by banquettes and rattan screens; end tables served as storage space for electric typewriters and encyclopedias; and the sun deck beyond displayed every diversion from Crokinole to hi-fi.

I swallowed. "Old Henry would have flipped, and that's for sure," I said, employing the only idiom that seemed to fit the circumstances.

"He did anyway, but he would have flipped in comfort," Eveninghoff returned complacently. "We décor engineers are like Houdini—we remove the handcuffs from the creative mind. Now, take this place of yours, for instance. The first thing I'd do is rip out the windows and substitute glass brick."

"But I *like* to look at the clotheslines," I objected. "The wash is so snowy and crisp, and those gingham frocks dance in the wind—"

"Then as regards floor space," he went on, unheeding. "We could pick up a good twenty feet if we broke through that side wall. Don't interrupt," he snapped as I tried to mime the pants factory that lay behind. "You and your landlord can work it out—I'm not a real-estate broker. What I'm questing for is a furniture mood to express your personality. . . . Let's see, puppet plays. It ought to smack of the theater, the world of tinsel and make-believe . . . shadows, contrasts. . . . Wait —yes, I've got it!"

"What?" I asked, checking myself lest I be swept away by his fervor.

"Try to visualize it as I block in the tones," he commanded, forefinger extended and eyes narrowed in concentration. "Turkey-red carpeting and ebony walls—not coal black, charcoal relieved by tiny gold accents—with, of course, candelabra sidelights to match. At the far end there, an Empire sofa, covered in lime-and-silver stripes, between a pair of broken columns." I thought of my Latvian handmaid flicking her feather duster, and cringed. "In this area, a Renaissance coffee table —or, rather, the memory of a coffee table—surrounded by Swedish-modern chairs."

"Not Latvian?" I interposed. "I say that because—"

"You're right," said Eveninghoff graciously. "Chairwise, the Latvians have done some very arresting things lately. And now your work sector—for, after all, we mustn't forget that this is where you create, must we?" He gave me a flash of teeth—or, rather, the memory of teeth—that failed to captivate. "I see a gigantic refectory table here—modified Jacobean, in cherry wood simulating walnut—with a desk set of tooled Florentine leather. You dictate your things, I suppose."

"Not as a rule," I said. "I—ah—generally write in longhand with a quill pen, and shake pumice over the manuscript to dry it."

"Good—then you won't need recording equipment," he approved. "I loathe the mechanized feeling it imparts to one's *ambiance*. However, for illumination I don't think we should cleave to period. Do you insist on wax tapers? . . . I'm glad. Fluorescence it'll be, and much more contemporary. Well, now," he concluded, wheeling toward me, "how does it strike you?"

"Between the eyes," I admitted. "There's just one thing, though. You don't feel the black walls are a little—well, Aubrey Beardsley?"

"Is he using them this season?" Eveninghoff queried. "I never look at other decorators' work—I don't want to be influenced. Still, if black stifles anything in you they can always be changed to rust, or a subdued plum."

"No, sir, they cannot," I said emphatically. "They're the keystone, the very essence, of your whole design. Without them it's meaningless. I'm sorry, Mr. Eveninghoff," I added, trying to palliate my words, "but I guess it's not for me."

"But look here," he said, plainly chopfallen. "I'm not inflexible. We want the client to fulfill himself. If you'd prefer monk's cloth . . ."

"No, no," I said, herding him toward the door. "I'd sooner ask Pan to abandon his pipes or Krupa his drums than have you give up black. I won't compromise, and it would degrade me to force you to."

Eveninghoff's lips puckered as though tears were imminent. "Well, if you feel that strongly . . ."

"I'm afraid I do," I said regretfully. "Goodbye, old man. Watch out for rice on the stairs."

As the door closed behind him, I re-entered the office, got out the directory, and thumbed through the Yellow Pages. Then I dialed the number of a place on Third Avenue. "Mr. Pandora?" I said. "Could you have a look around your box? I need a pair of bead curtains."

Portrait of the Artist as a Young Mime

"Song Without End" features the highlights of Franz Liszt's life. . . . The music was recorded by Jorge Bolet, one of America's foremost pianists. . . . Most dramatic story behind the scenes of the making of "Song Without End" was the coaching of Dirk Bogarde by Victor Aller to enable the actor to give a flawless visual performance at the keyboard to match Bolet's already recorded score. Mr. Aller, a master pianist, also is Hollywood's best known piano coach for stars. Dirk Bogarde had never played a note in his life! Not only did he have to learn how to play the piano—he had to learn to play like genius Franz Liszt.
— *The Journal-American*.

THE DAY started off, as all mine do, at a snail's pace. I got to my studio on Carmine Street about a quarter of ten, closed the skylight and lit the kerosene stove—oxygen, however essential to aeronautics and snorkeling, is death to the creative process —and settled down with the coffee and Danish I pick up every morning en route from the subway. Then I emptied the ashtrays into the hall and washed out a few brushes, meanwhile listening to WQXR and studying the canvas I had on the easel. Shortly before eleven, I ran out of excuses for cerebration and began mixing my colors. That's inevitably the moment some nuisance takes it into his head to phone, and in this case it was the bloodiest of them all—Vetlugin, my dealer. His voice trembled with excitement.

"Did he call you? What did he say?" he asked feverishly. Good old Vetlugin, the Tower of Babble. He opens his mouth and out comes confusion; the man has an absolute genius for muddle. By valiant effort, I finally extracted a modicum of sense from his bumbling. Some Hollywood nabob named Harry Hubris, reputedly a top producer at Twentieth Century-Fox, was clamoring to discuss a matter of utmost urgency. Ever quick to sniff out a kopeck, Vetlugin, in direct violation of orders, had promptly spilled my whereabouts. "I figured it'd save time if he came down to see you personally," he cooed. "The precise nature of what he wants he wouldn't reveal, but I smelled there must be dough in it."

"Listen, you Bessarabian Judas," I groaned. "How many times have I told you never, under any circumstances, to divulge—" Like all arguments with leeches, this one was futile; muttering some claptrap about ingratitude, he hung up and left me biting my own tail. It was a half hour before I calmed down sufficiently to resume work, but I knew the jig was up when the doorbell rang, and one look at the character bounding upstairs confirmed my fears. From his perky velvet dicer to the tips of his English brogues, he was as brash a highbinder as ever scurried out of Sardi's. The saffron polo coat draped impresario-fashion over his shoulders must have cost twelve hundred dollars.

"Say, are you kidding?" he exclaimed, fastidiously dusting a bit of plaster from his sleeve. "Those terrific abstractions of yours—you don't actually *paint* them here?"

"I do when I'm not interrupted," I said pointedly.

"Well, you're risking your life," he declared. "I've seen firetraps in my time, boychick, but this ain't for real. If I showed it in a picture, they'd say it was overdone." He stuck out a paw. "Harry Hubris," he said. "I guess you've heard of me."

Other than feigning an attack of scrofula, there was no escape now that Vetlugin had crossed me up, so I motioned him in.

He made a quick, beady inventory of the décor. "Go figure it," he said, with a shrug. "It always kills me an artist should hole up in a fleabag to conceive a masterpiece. Still, everybody to their own ulcer. Zuckmayer, I want you to know I consider you one of the nine foremost painters of our time."

"Indeed," I said. "Who are the other eight?"

"Look, pal, don't get me started or I'm liable to talk all night," he said. "I've got maybe the most important collection in the Los Angeles area—five Jackson Pollocks, three Abe Rattners, two of yours—"

"Which ones?"

"I can't remember offhand," he said irritably. "A houseful of paintings, you wouldn't expect me to recall every title. But let's get down to basics. What would you say if I offered you two thousand bucks for an hour's work?"

"I'd be even more suspicious than I am now, which is plenty."

"A blunt answer," he approved. "Well, here's the dodge, and you needn't worry, it's strictly legit. Did you perchance read

Irving Stonehenge's biography of John Singer Sargent, *The Tortured Bostonian?*"

I shook my head, and he frowned.

"You're the one guy in America that didn't," he said. "In my humble opinion, it's going to make the greatest documentary-type motion picture since *Lust for Life*. Just visualize Rob Roy Fruitwell in the leading role and tell me how it could miss."

I visualized as best I could, but, never having heard of the man, got nowhere. "Who is he?" I asked.

"Rob Roy?" Hubris's scorn for my ignorance was Olympian. "Only the biggest potential draw in pictures today, that's all," he affirmed. "Properly handled, Fruitwell can be another Kirk Douglas, *and*," he went on, lowering his voice, "I'll breathe you something in strictest confidence. After he has his dimple deepened next spring, you won't be able to tell them apart. My immediate headache, though, and the reason I contacted you, is this. The kid's a born actor and he'll play the hell out of Sargent, but thus far he's appeared exclusively in horse operas—Westerns. What he requires is a little coaching from an expert —a professional artist like you."

"My dear Mr. Hubris," I said. "If you think I can transform a numskull into a master in one lesson—"

"For crisakes, smarten up, will you?" he implored. "All you got to furnish is the pantomime. Show him how to hold a brush, what a palette's for, which end of the tube the color comes out. Remember, this lug don't know from beauty or the Muse. Two years ago he was a busboy in Fort Wayne."

"But I've never dealt with actors," I objected. "I haven't the faintest clue to their mentality."

"Mentality's one problem you won't have with Rob Roy Fruitwell, brother," Hubris guaranteed. "He's got none. He's just a matzo ball, a sensitized sponge that'll soak up the info you give him and delineate it on the screen."

"Well, I'd have to think it over," I said. "I'm assembling a show at the moment—"

"So your dealer mentioned," he said. "And believe me, Mr. Zuckmayer, I feel like a rat pressuring you, but the point is, we're in a bind. You see, in view of the fact that we start shooting Friday, I had Rob Roy sky in from the Coast last night solely on purpose to huddle with you."

"Then you can jolly well sky him back," I began, and stopped short. After all, if this gasbag was aching to shell out a fat fee for an hour of *expertise*, it'd be downright loony to stand on dignity; my anemic budget could certainly use a transfusion. Obviously sensing I was tempted, Hubris threw in the clincher. Not only would he raise the ante another five hundred, but he was prepared to hand over a check on the spot provided I saw Fruitwell that afternoon. "Well-l-l, all right," I said, overborne. "Have him down here at four o'clock and I'll see what I can do."

"Attaboy!" chortled my caller, whipping out a pen. "You mark my words, Zuckmayer—this may be a turning point in your career. Once the critics dig your name up there in the credits—'Artistic Consultant to the Producer, Harry Hubris' —the whole industry'll be knocking on your door!"

"Don't bother to freeze my blood, please," I said. "Just write out the check."

Hubris made no pretense of concealing his umbrage. "You're a strange apple," he said. "What makes all you artists so antisocial?"

I knew why, but it would have been too expensive to reply. I needed the money.

I was tied up at the framer's after lunch, discussing a new molding of kelp on tinfoil for my show, and didn't get back to the studio until four-fifteen. There was a big rented Cadillac parked outside, the driver of which, a harassed plug-ugly in uniform, was standing off a mob of teen-agers screeching and waving autograph books. We had a dandy hassle proving I was kosher, but he finally let me upstairs to the unholy trinity awaiting me. Fruitwell was a standard prize bullock with a Brando tonsure and capped teeth, in a gooseneck sweater under his Italian silk suit which kept riding up to expose his thorax. His agent, a fat little party indistinguishable from a tapir, had apparently been summoned from the hunt, for he wore a Tattersall vest and a deep-skirted hacking coat. The third member of the group, a bearded aesthete dressed entirely in suède, flaunted a whistle on a silver chain encircling his throat. "I'm Dory Gallwise, the assistant director," he introduced himself. "We had to force the lock to get in here. Hope you don't mind."

"Not at all," I said. "Sorry the place is such a pigsty, but—well, you know how bohemians are."

"Oh, it's not so bad," he said graciously. "Of course, as I was just explaining to Rob Roy here, the studio he'll occupy as Sargent will be a lot more imposing. The size of Carnegie Hall, in fact."

"*Natürlich*," I said. "Now, before we commence, Mr. Fruitwell, do you have any questions about art? Anything you'd like me to clarify?"

Immersed in contemplation of a torso on the wall, the young man did not respond at once. Then he lifted his head sleepily. "Yeah, this thing here," he said. "What's it supposed to be—a woman?"

I admitted I had embodied certain female elements, and he snickered.

"You really see that when you look at a dame?" he asked, with a quizzical smile. "Bud, you need therapy. Don't he, Monroe?"

His agent shot me a placatory wink. "Well, I wouldn't go *that* far, Rob Roy," he temporized. "Mr. Zuckmayer reacts to the world around him in a particular way—through the intellect, shall we say? He embodies certain elements—"

"Don't give me that bushwa," the other retorted. "I've dated Mamie van Doren, Marilyn Maxwell, and Diana Dors, and take it from me, pappy, they don't have any corners like that. This moke's in trouble."

"Ha, ha—who isn't?" Gallwise put in with wild gaiety. He cleared his throat nervously. "Listen, boys, let's not hold up Mr. Zuckmayer—he's a busy person." Snapping open his dispatch case, he drew forth a smock and a beret. "Here, Rob Roy, slip these on so you'll get used to the feel of 'em."

"Wait a second," said Fruitwell, clouding over, and wheeled on Monroe. "What the hell are we making, a costume picture? You said I wear a sweat shirt and dungarees."

"In the love scenes, baby," Monroe specified, "but when you're sketching, and like dreaming up your different masterpieces, why, they got to blueprint you're an artist. It establishes your identity."

"Sure, the way a sheriff puts on a tin star," said Gallwise.

"Or a busboy his white coat," I added helpfully.

Fruitwell turned and gave me a long, penetrating look. Then, evidently concluding his ears had deceived him, he surlily donned the habit, and for the next quarter of an hour submitted himself to our charade. I soon perceived that Hubris's depiction of him as a chowderhead was rank flattery. Totally devoid of either co-ordination or the ability to retain, he lumbered about upsetting jars of pigment, gashed himself disastrously with my palette knife, and in a burst of almost inspired clumsiness sprayed fixative into Monroe's eyeball, temporarily blinding the poor wretch. While the latter lay prostrate, whimpering under the poultices with which Gallwise and I rushed to allay his torment, Rob Roy leaned out of the skylight to mollify his fans. Since, however, they had dispersed meanwhile, his largess was wasted, and he was in a distinct pet by the time Monroe was ambulatory.

"You guys through playing beatnik?" he fretted. "Come on, let's blow. If the dauber's got any more dope, he can phone it in to Hubris, or I'll get it from research, on the Coast."

"Rob Roy—honey," pleaded Gallwise. "We'll spring you in two shakes, but just co-operate ten minutes more. I want Mr. Zuckmayer to check on a couple of scenes—you know, to make sure you don't pull a booboo. Here," he said, forcibly planting his charge in a chair. "Run through the situation where Vincent Youmans tries to win you back to your wife."

"Hold on," I protested. "How does *he* come into this?"

"A dramatic license we took to justify the score," he said hurriedly. "He's a young music student at Harvard that Sargent befriends. Can you remember the lines, Rob Roy?"

Fruitwell contorted his forehead in a simulation of deep thought.

"Never mind—spitball some dialogue to give the general idea," said Gallwise. "Go ahead, I'll cue you. I'll be Youmans."

"Hello, Youmans," complied Fruitwell, in a monotone. "Where you been, man?"

"Oh, just studying my counterpoint over in Cambridge," said Gallwise. "But you certainly are a storm center these days, John Singer. All Beacon Hill is agog the way you threw up your job as stockbroker and abandoned your family. Can a pair of saucy blue orbs underlie this move, as wagging tongues imply?"

Fruitwell uttered a cynical hoot reminiscent of a puppy yelping for a biscuit. "Women!" he scoffed. "I'm tired of those silly little creatures casting their spell on me. I want to paint—to paint, do you hear? I've got to express what I feel deep down inside me! The agony, the heartbreak!"

His agent, who was following the recital from behind a crumpled handkerchief, sprang forward and embraced him. "Lover, don't change a word, a syllable," he begged. "Do that on camera and I personally—Monroe Sweetmeat—promise you an Academy Award. What about it, Mr. Zuckmayer?" he inquired anxiously. "Does it ring true from the artist's point of view?"

"Frighteningly," I agreed. "You've caught the very essence of the creative urge. I have only one criticism." Gallwise stiffened expectantly. "Mr. Fruitwell's got his smock on backwards. The audience might conceivably mistake him for a hairdresser."

"How could they, with that dialogue?" he demanded.

"That's what I mean," I said.

"Well, it's a point to watch," ruminated the director. "Remember that, Rob Roy. Now the key scene, where you get your big break from the hotel manager. The plot point here, Mr. Z., is that Sargent's down and out in New York. It's Christmas Day, the landlord's shut off the gas, and he's starving."

"Tell him about the onion," Monroe giggled.

"A bit of comedy relief," Gallwise explained. "He's so hungry that he finally has to eat this still-life of an onion and a herring."

"What, the canvas itself?" I asked.

"No, no—the objects he's painting," he said impatiently. "Anyway, just at his darkest hour, in comes Tuesday Weld, the coatroom girl at the St. Regis that's been secretly in love with him. She's persuaded the manager to let Sargent paint a mural of King Cole for the men's bar."

"Using the pseudonym of Maxfield Parrish," I supplemented.

"God damn it," burst out Fruitwell, "I've got an eight-man team of writers from the New York *Post* waiting to interview me! Let's do the *scene!*"

Gallwise recoiled as if from a blast furnace. "Uh—on second thought, maybe we don't have to," he stammered, a muscle twitching in his cheek. "I only wanted to corroborate one small detail. Halfway through the action, Mr. Zuckmayer, as Sargent holds Tuesday in his arms, he suddenly stumbles on the idea for his greatest composition, 'The Kiss.' How would a painter react in those circumstances? What exact phraseology would he employ?"

"To herald an inspiration, you mean?" I pondered. "Well, I always smite my forehead and use a simple Greek word —eureka."

Fruitwell ripped off his smock and flung it at his agent. "And for this you fly me from the Coast, you muzzler," he snarled. "Any coffeepot could of told you that!" Suffused with outrage, he stalked to the door, pulverized me and my artifacts with a glance, and was gone. Monroe scampered after him, his face stricken.

Gallwise stood immobilized an instant. Then, swallowing painfully, he folded the smock into the dispatch case like a somnambulist and crossed to the threshold. The crucified smile he turned on me was purest Fra Angelico. "Temperament," he apologized. "But don't be afraid, Mr. Zuckmayer—there won't be a trace of it on the screen. The kid's a great trouper."

It was such nirvana, standing there tranquilly in the dusk after he had left, that I let the phone ring for a full minute. I knew who it was, and my parfait was complete without a Bessarabian cherry, but I also knew Vetlugin's tenacity. I picked up the receiver.

"It's me, Tovarisch." He spoke in such a conspiratorial whisper that for a moment I had trouble distinguishing him. "Look, which painting should I give Mr. Hubris?" he asked breathlessly. "He says he deserves a big one, on account of the publicity you'll get from the film. I claim—"

"I'll settle it." I cut him short. "Call him to the phone."

"But I said you were working—I had orders not to disturb—"

"I've finished," I said. "It's catharsis time."

And it was.

This Is the Forest Primeval?

O NE SATURDAY AFTERNOON early in January of this year, an individual who was neither sportsman nor scholar, poet nor peasant, but, in fact, a remarkable combination of all four arrived in Nairobi, capital of the East African colony of Kenya. As he descended from an airways bus before the New Stanley Hotel, the handful of loungers basking on the sidewalk stiffened to inattention. The stranger, patently, was a man accustomed to giving orders and having them disobeyed. His profile, oddly akin to that of the youthful D'Annunzio, bespoke a spirit as wild and free as the vultures circling above him in welcome. He wore a reach-me-down trench coat, three buttons of which had disappeared and been replaced with safety pins. Slung over his shoulder was a complex of cameras, binoculars, and first-aid kits bulging with every sort of nostrum—antimalarial compounds like paludrine, daraprim, and atabrin, tube on tube of molds and yeasts designed to combat blackwater fever, bilharzia, and tsetse fly, antivenins without number, embrocations, febrifuges, heat lotions, and sedatives— a pharmacopoeia, in short, to dazzle a Schweitzer. Perceiving that there was, however, no Schweitzer present to dazzle, the traveler picked up his satchels, entered the hotel, and fractured the laws of coincidence by affixing my name to the register.

"Your room's just being made up, sir," apologized the receptionist, a sparrowlike person resembling Mildred Natwick. "The painters just finished within the hour."

"Ah?" I returned pleasantly. "Redecorating it, are they?"

"Well, rather," she said, pursing her lips. "When those blighters got through with the last occupant, the place *was* a shambles. Goodness!"

I cleared the rust out of my voice and kept it as buoyant as I could. "I say, I'm just in from overshoes—I mean overseas," I said. "You weren't by any chance referring to the—er—Mau Mau?"

"Why, of course not," she said, her face suddenly wooden. "Whatever gave you that idea? Here, boy, take this gentleman's things up to three-seventeen."

"I—I believe I'll have a tup of kee in the lounge," I interposed quickly. "I feel a trifle giddy—the altitude, no doubt."

"Yes, it bothers everyone at first," she agreed. "Better not run up any stairs for a day or two—that is, unless you have to."

I promised to heed her advice and, disengaging my sleeve from the inkwell, headed toward the lounge. Halfway across the lobby, I heard my name called out. Turning, I beheld a gaunt young Englishman with a Mephistophelean beard and a falcon's eye, followed by a vision of loveliness in yellow Tootal.

"I'm Eric Mothersill of the tourist association," he introduced himself affably. "This is Xanthia, my wife."

"Enchanted," I said as our hands met. "From the luminous eyes and name, I gather that Madame is Greek?"

"Yes, but reared in Egypt," she replied, enslaving me with her smile. "Monsieur is very observant."

"O-oh, I've knocked about a bit," I admitted modestly.

"Good," said Mothersill. "Then you'll certainly enjoy the outing we've planned for this weekend. It's different." In the following few minutes, and with only gin-and-lime as anesthetic, I got a portent of what my East African sojourn might be like. This afternoon, it appeared, there was merely time for an hors d'oeuvre—a quick circuit of the suburbs, the Ngong Hills, the Rift Valley Escarpment, a sisal farm or two, and the Kikuyu Reserve—followed by an informal dinner party *chez* Mothersill. Early next morning, though, we were leaving by motor for Treetops, the lodge in the Aberdare Range where one eavesdropped on rhino, elephant, and similar big game. "By the way," went on Mothersill, obviously a master of the *arrière pensée*, "I forgot to mention that it's in the heart of the Mau Mau country."

"It's *where*?" I asked, recoiling.

"Now, there's no reason whatever for apprehension," he soothed me. "Xanthia and I'll both be armed, and, moreover, the hotel's promised us a convoy for our walk in."

There was a brief silence while I fought to free my tongue, which had somehow become lodged in my epiglottis. "Look here," I said, oozing more nobility than one of Landseer's dogs, "you two have gone to a lot of trouble planning this holiday, and the last thing you want is an extra man along. I'm a married man and I know how married couples are." I maundered off into a long, woolly discourse on matrimony, reminiscent of a women's magazine, that brought tears to my eyes but failed to stir anyone else. Before I could rally, the two of them had pinioned my arms and propelled me through the door to the curb. With a sinking heart, I crawled into the rear of their convertible and prepared to sell my life as cheaply as possible.

Some eight hours later, I entered my hotel room and collapsed on the bed. My skin was intact enough, but I retained only a blurred, kaleidoscopic memory of the interval—the herds of wildebeest and zebra in the Nairobi National Park, the omnipresent roadblocks manned by the King's African Rifles, a coffee plantation near Limuru with a stable yard lifted straight out of Devonshire, the groups of philoprogenitive Hindus picnic-bound in consumptive jalopies, the detention camps placarded with the winning understatement "Protected Area," and the cryptic chitchat around the Mothersills' dinner table. A fatigue pervaded my bones as profound as if I had gone without sleep for three nights, which, indeed, I had. And just to compound matters, I recalled with sudden heartburn, tomorrow I was being thrown to the lions in the middle of a holocaust—I, a peaceable, flabby burgess who had never even shot a chipmunk. The full anguish of my plight was more than I could bear. Burying my face in the bolster, I burst into long, racking sobs.

Toward noon the following day, a Humber saloon covered with red dust slued into the driveway of the Outspan Hotel at Nyeri, a hamlet about seventy miles north of Nairobi. Its khaki-clad chauffeur, a Kipsigis with ears nattily twisted into rosettes in the characteristic fashion of his tribe, reined in under the porte-cochère and, whipping open the door with a flourish, handed down our threesome. To the Mothersills, inured to East African roads, the four-hour trip had been trivial, but it had reduced me to library paste. Mile on mile, we had jounced over a corduroy highway devoid of traffic but full of hairpin bends ideally suited to ambush. Every now and again, the driver would point out some inglenook where the Mau Mau had butchered a party of Europeans or been surprised in turn, and once, when the car stalled momentarily in a wooded divide, I closed my eyes and sat mutely intoning the serial number of my insurance policy. My hosts, contrariwise, never lost their sang-froid. Except for pronounced facial tics and a tendency to reach for their heaters every time the engine missed, they betrayed not the slightest awareness of danger.

"Well, you must admit it was worth the trip," observed Xanthia later, as we dawdled over tea on the veranda. "Isn't this a heavenly place? I haven't felt so relaxed in years."

"Yes, it's certainly a bit of all right," Eric assented. "Look at the weaverbirds in that golden acacia tree." We both followed his eyes, bewitched by the jeweled flash of wings. It was, indeed, a superb vista—flowering quince against a background of mango, jacaranda, and flamboyant trees, and, beyond, the sun glinting on the masses of barbed wire surrounding the hotel. At intervals all too infrequent, a pair of gaily plumaged sentries, with carbines on their backs, supplied a vivid accent to the scene.

"When do we make this—ah—excursion to Treetops?" I inquired, with a bright musical-comedy smile that would have sickened my intimates.

"Right after lunch tomorrow," said Eric. "I understand there'll be eight in the party. A safari car takes us to the forest edge, where we'll rendezvous with our guards. Actually, it's a very short trek to the lodge—only a third of a mile—but it's fairly thick cover and it *could* be sticky if we ran into the odd rhino or a terrorist patrol."

I casually extinguished my cigarette in the wild-currant jam. "That place you spoke of, up in the tree," I said. "I presume we stay there only an hour or two?"

"Quite the opposite, old boy," he replied. "We stay the night. At night is when you see the really wizard stuff milling around the salt lick. Imagine—elephant and buffalo right under one's feet! Fantastic, what?"

"Now, darling, don't spoil it for him; he'll expect too much," Xanthia chided. "Anyway, it's time we were dressing for dinner. See you in the bar *tout à l'heure?*"

The shadows were lengthening as I went meditatively to my room to change, but it was still light enough to make an interesting discovery. The French windows at one end, which opened into the garden, were secured by an absurdly flimsy catch that could be unfastened from outside. The room also seemed to have a plethora of closets, all of them just large enough to hold a man nursing a grievance. I took a shower and dressed hastily, though trying to get into my pants with one foot braced against the bathroom door impeded me somewhat. By the time the Mothersills rejoined me, I had managed to fortify myself for the evening, and it passed off agreeably. Around one-thirty, when nobody appeared willing to stay up any longer, I turned in and, having made a rapid tally of the closets, dossed down with the poems of Anais Nin.

Just as I was dropping off, a bloodcurdling crash, unmistakably caused by someone hammering on the door with a *panga*, or African machete, echoed through the room. I jackknifed upward in bed and, completely forgetting where I was, called out "Come in!" Simultaneously, I realized the folly of my words; if it was the visitors I suspected, there was no need for fulsome hospitality. I awaited developments, but none came. After a bit, the anvil blows in my pulse subsided, and I worked out a hypothesis. Somebody in the room overhead must have dropped his pipe on the tile floor—rather a large pipe, as I visualized it. In fact, it might even be one of those Turkish pipes—a hubble-bubble or a chibouk or whatever they called it. I fell asleep with a smile, musing over the odd crotchets one encounters in foreign lands. The next morning, of course, I discovered there *was* no room overhead, but by then the sun was shining and birds were clamorous.

It was an assorted lot that piled into the safari car after lunch —an elderly British noblewoman, a Canadian couple, a pair of young matrons from Rhodesia, the Mothersills, and myself. The mood of the party was definitely one of nervous bravado; as each of us signed waivers absolving the hotel of responsibility for breakage, it was greeted with hollow giggles and japes of a mortuary turn. The route into the Aberdare National Park led through precipitous terrain overgrown with scrub evocative of New Jersey at its most dismal. Less than a mile inside was the staging point for our hike. The quartet waiting there to escort us was as lethal as anything ever assembled outside a comic book. Mr. Oakeshott, the manager of the hotel, and

Colonel Bagby, a retired white hunter, displayed side arms and express rifles, and two chunky subalterns, on leave from the Royal Devons, were fondling Sten guns. While our African bearers finished packing linen, blankets, and food into sacks, Mr. Oakeshott outlined the plan of march.

"We'll go up the path in single file," he said. "Please keep your voices low so that we don't—ahem—attract unnecessary attention. Here and there, you'll notice ladders on the trees. We probably shan't encounter game of any size, but if we do raise a stray buff or rhino, just nip up a ladder until he clears off. Are there any questions? . . . What? . . . Oh, I thought the gentleman there with the green face said something. Righto, then, let's get started."

To survive the hazardous next ten minutes, I fell back on an expedient that has pulled me out of many a tight corner. Emptying the air from my lungs, as one would from an old pair of water wings, I not only kept pace with the others but several times almost outstripped them. The twelve of us snaked through the bush at a gait midway between a shuffle and a squirm that would have taxed the powers even of Eleanora Sears. Once, I cautiously turned to appraise the scenery, but my neck gave off a creak like a New Year's ratchet and I hastily withdrew it into my shell. When we finally gained the giant fig tree containing the lodge, most of my companions were pink with exertion, whereas I, curiously enough, was hardly breathing. Indeed, as we toiled up the gangway that led to our leafy aerie, I was in a state of such tranquillity that I could barely count the spots before my eyes.

The lodge, on investigation, proved to be a two-story structure about thirty feet square, partitioned off into screened porches, bedrooms, and a dining alcove. Twelve or fifteen yards below its far side was the salt lick and water hole where the game congregated nightly. At the moment, only a family of baboons was visible, but with the onset of dusk, Mr. Oakeshott explained, various quadrupeds large and small would be arriving.

"By the bye," I observed offhandedly to Mothersill, "d'ye suppose those Mau Mau chaps know we're up here?" I thought he might have overlooked the possibility, and it would be churlish not to bring it to his attention.

"Of course they do," he said. "They've an incredible communications system. Probably watched us every foot of the way in."

"But listen," I said in an urgent undertone, trying not to alarm the rest of the group. "What prevents them from, say, setting fire to this tree and smoking us out like a nest of bees?"

"Quite, quite," he agreed. "A very feasible idea. I certainly hope it doesn't occur to them. However, no use borrowing trouble. Here, do try one of these rock buns—they're frightfully good."

I declined, my appetite having been under par all day, and, borrowing his field glasses, beguiled the afternoon watching the forest for any suspicious movement. Outside the racket of the baboons and an occasional squadron of planes roaring overhead to bomb the terrorist hideouts nearby on Mount Kenya, the landscape was as peaceful as a country vicarage. Shortly after sunset, however, half a dozen wart hogs materialized below, rooted about noisily in the salt, and departed. They were succeeded by several gazelles and waterbuck, who yielded the stage, just before dark, to a herd of fifteen giant forest hogs. The adults of the troupe, fearsome swine well over four feet high and exhibiting wicked tusks, held a brief conference, evidently trying to decide whether to gnaw down our perch, but cooler heads must have prevailed, for they soon retired. By now, it was pitch black outside and impossible to distinguish anything on the salt lick, though we ourselves had plenty of light within. In fact, as I felt constrained to point out to Colonel Bagby, we were brightly silhouetted against the windows for any snipers who happened to be mousing about.

"You're dead right, old man," he said warmly. "Some night those wretched sods'll pick one of us off and there'll be a proper dustup. Still, it does lend a certain zest to the occasion, what?"

It was roughly half an hour after dinner—a capital tureen of chicken pie warmed up on a Primus stove—that the rhino began moving in. An amber spotlight simulating the full moon had been turned on, and it made the beasts seem even more antediluvian than normally. One by one, seven bulls and cows, a couple of them suckling calves, detached themselves soundlessly from the darkness and circulated about underneath us. They were plainly in a bilious humor—engendered,

I was told, by their favorite diet of thorns—and they kept chivying each other and rumbling like Frenchmen in a street altercation. Once in a while, a jackal or bushbuck would drift into their orbit to browse, but the rhino ignored it and, with a tact worthy of Emily Post, confined their spleen to their kinsfolk. Absorbing spectacle though it was, I found after a couple of hours that an element of tedium was creeping in. A headache induced by eyestrain clove my skull, I was *hors de combat* with laryngitis from conversing in whispers, and my teeth chattered with cold. Waiting until the Mothersills relaxed their guard, I stole off to a rear bedroom, gulped down some nirvana powder, and curled up in a blanket. All around me an awesome nocturnal symphony was tuning up— leopards coughing, hyenas and monkeys howling, the whole jungle awakening to life. As the Demerol slowly took hold, the realization smote me that I was missing one of the experiences of my life. I rolled over and slept like a baby.

I awoke with a horrid start; someone was shaking me violently, but it was too dark to see his face and I was too addled to make out what he was whispering. Luckily, before I could scream—which I had every intention of doing—he identified himself by clapping his hand over my mouth.

"Sh-h-h!" he hissed. "It's Eric! Come quick—elephant!" I rose groggily and, clutching his arm, blundered out to the porch. Below it to the right stood a gigantic hulk, its ears fanned out and its trunk lifted, facing an animal with tremendous, heavily bossed horns less than forty feet away. Though it bore no more resemblance to our bison than a barracuda does to a smelt, I knew instinctively that it was a buffalo. Mothersill was palpitant with joy. "Great Scott, man, this is the rarest sight in Africa!" he babbled into my ear. "They're deadly enemies—it'll be a massacre!" As he spoke, the elephant let forth a shriek that loosened the bark on every tree within a nine-mile radius, and charged. The buffalo stood his ground, saving face until the last possible moment. There were scarcely five yards between them when he wheeled with incredible speed and vamoosed, his adversary hot on his heels. In the distance, we heard apocalyptic sounds of branches being rent and the elephant trumpeting in fury. Several minutes passed, during which a sizable dew condensed on everyone's forehead, and then the elephant reappeared. In the manner of a British constable assuring himself that all was tickety-boo, he made a slow, majestic circuit of the salt lick, and melted into the night.

A couple of weeks later, in Nairobi, I was having a glass of sherry with an Iowa chick named Ruby Querschnitt, a member of an American all-girl safari that had recently arrived in a blaze of flash bulbs. She had asked me, as an old Kenya hand, to vet her itinerary, and since she was friendless and a rather appealing little thing, I consented. It was an ambitious program—a fortnight's shooting in Tanganyika, a tour of the coast, a motor trip through the eastern Congo, and a journey by launch to Murchison Falls.

"What I really wanted to see was Treetops," she said disconsolately, "but they've closed it till the emergency's over. It's supposed to be awfully dangerous."

"Balderdash," I said, smoothing my mustache. "A bit tiresome, if you must know. It gets a chap down, rather—nothing but Mau Mau and elephant mucking about."

"Gee, some people are certainly blasé," she said. "Tell me, is it true that out of the party you went with, only twelve came back?"

I allowed myself a fatalistic shrug. "That's Africa, lassie," I said. "One gets used to it in time."

"Well," she said pensively, "just the same, you must be pretty brave."

"Think so?" I said. "Say, let's have another one of these. . . . Wait, I've got an idea. Have you ever tried a gin-and-lime?"

Impresario on the Lam

THE VOICE that came over the wire last Thursday was full of gravel and Hollywood subjunctives. It was a voice trained to cut through the din of night clubs and theater rehearsals, a flexible instrument that could shift from adulation to abuse in a syllable, ingratiating yet peremptory, a rich syrup of unction and specious authority. "Listen, Clyde, you don't know me from a hole in the ground," it began with deadly accuracy, "but I'm the agent for a friend of yours, Morris Flesh." Before I could disavow ever having heard of Flesh, his representative had washed his hands of him and was scuttling down the fairway. "I've got a client deeply interested in putting on a revue," he confided. "A smart, intimate show that kids the passing scene, the various fads and foibles like television and mahjongg and psychoanalysis—dig me? Morris recommends you to pen the sketches, and while I personally would rather have a name, I'm willing to gamble on his opinion. Now, here's the score, Pops. My backer is strictly from Dixie, a peasant from the tall rhubarbs. I'm running the creative side and this is what I have in mind." I laid the receiver gently on the desk and went out to lunch. When I returned two hours later, the monologue was purling on as inexorably as the Blue Nile. "This girl composer has got Vassar in an uproar, baby," the voice was affirming. "She's the hottest thing that ever hit Poughkeepsie —another Cole Porter, only younger. Sophisticated but simple at the same time." I hung up, and dialing the business office, vanished into the limbo of unlisted telephone subscribers.

Though not constitutionally averse to the crackle of greenbacks, I learned many years ago—twenty-eight, in fact—that of all the roads to insolvency open to my profession, entanglement in a revue is the shortest. Every revue since *The Garrick Gaieties* has been hatched from the same larva, an impassioned declaration by some seer flushed with Martinis that what Broadway needs this season is a smart, intimate show like *The Garrick Gaieties*. In 1932, Poultney Kerr, a onetime yacht broker riding out the depression on a cask of brandy, said it with such persistence that a group of idealists gave him a hundred thousand dollars to demonstrate, and he did so with a *cauche-mar* called *Sherry Flip*. Kerr's qualifications as a producer, apart from a honeyed tongue, were minimal. His executive ability was pitiful, his judgment paltry, and his equilibrium unstable in crisis. He did, nevertheless, look the big wheel—a corpulent, natty man given to Homburg hats and carnations in the buttonhole, with the classic empurpled nose of the *bon vivant* and a talent for imbibing oceans of Courvoisier without crumpling. I met him at a low ebb in my fortunes and left him at a lower. In between, I got so concentrated a dose of hysteria and wormwood that I still quail at the mention of sherry.

At a moment when my wallet was at its flabbiest, the project started in the classic tradition with an urgent phone call from Lytton Swazey, a lyric writer I had known casually around the doughnut shop in Times Square we both frequented. Could I, he asked, confer with him and his composer that afternoon at Kerr's apartment about an upcoming revue patterned after *The Garrick Gaieties*? I blacked my shoes in a flash and pelted over. The portents seemed dazzling. Swazey, after years of grinding out special material for willowy chanteuses in cocktail bars, had recently teamed up with a Russian composer named Herman Earl. Together they had confected a valiseful of show tunes, and it was on these, plus the half-dozen sketches I would supply, that *Sherry Flip* was to be based.

It may have been wishful thinking that warped my perspective, or a greenhorn's superstitious awe of song writers as demigods, but Swazey had hardly bawled out a couple of ballads before I put down my glass and emotionally announced, "Gentlemen, count me in." Needless to say, our sponsor was not outraged by my quick assent. He plied me with flattery and cognac, hailed me as a theatrical sibyl rivaling Daniel Frohman. The few tentative ideas for sketches I broached evoked paroxysms of laughter. "I don't want to put a jinx on it, boys," exulted Kerr, wrenching the cork from a fresh bottle of Hennessy, "but I think we've got a hit." What with all the self-congratulation and the mirage of fat royalties he conjured up, I agreed to terms that even a Mexican migrant worker would have flouted, and bowled off straightaway to Bachrach to be photographed. I figured I might not have the leisure to sit for him later when I became the toast of Broadway.

Lodged in an airless cubicle in Kerr's offices, I spent the next five weeks chewing licorice fortified with Benzedrine and evolving skits, emerging only to replenish myself with corned-beef sandwiches. *Sherry Flip*, meanwhile, was subtly changing from a collection of grandiose phrases into a living organism. A director, scenic designer, and choreographer materialized; the anteroom boiled with singers and dancers, tumblers and ventriloquists, sister acts and precocious children. Kerr himself preserved a state of Olympian detachment for the most part, huddling with lawyers in his sanctum. There were disquieting whispers that our finances were shaky, but as rehearsal day neared, he secured additional pledges, sounds of wassail again rang through the corridors, and we began work on a note of the most buoyant optimism.

Rehearsals went swimmingly the first fortnight. Not a speck of artistic temperament marked the cast; everyone was bewitched by the vivacity of the score and the brilliance of the sketches. Manners were impeccable, the atmosphere as sunny as a Monet picnic. Then, abruptly, the lid blew off. Halfway through her big solo one afternoon, our prima donna developed an acute attack of paranoia. Derogating the number as an inept Russian plagiarism of "Rio Rita," she declared that she would never sully her reputation by singing it in public. The composer, justifiably stung to fury, flew into a storm of picturesque Muscovite cuss-words. He offered to punch her nose —which, he added parenthetically, was bobbed—and threatened to bring her up before Equity on charges. The director patched up a shaky truce, but the incident had abraded the company's nerves and opened the door to further insubordination. Mysterious excrescences began to appear on the material I had furnished the actors. A diplomatic travesty of mine suddenly blossomed out with a routine in which, using a wallet stuffed with toilet paper, our top banana flimflammed a Polish butcher from Scranton. When I complained, I was told that it had scored a triumph on every burlesque wheel in America. If it offended Percy Bysshe Shelley—as he jocosely referred to me—I could return to writing for the little magazines. The barometer, in short, was falling, there were mutterings in the fo'c'sl, and one didn't have to be Ziegfeld to prophesy that *Sherry Flip* was in for many a squall before it reached port.

By the week prior to the Boston tryout, stilettos were flashing in earnest and the company buzzed like a hive of bees. The comedians, made overweening by victory, had woven a crazy quilt of drolleries and *double-entendres* that made the brain reel. They impersonated androgynes and humorous tramps, thwacked the showgirls' bottoms with rolled-up newspapers, and squirted water from their boutonnieres. Their improvisations totally unnerved Wigmore, the director, an able man around an Ibsen revival but a newcomer to the musical theater. The poor man fluttered about in a continual wax, wringing his hands like ZaSu Pitts and trying to assert his authority. In the dance department, there was a similar lack of co-ordination. The production numbers, two portentous ballets in the style colloquially known as "Fire in a Whorehouse," were being revised from day to day. Muscle-bound youths stamped about bearing dryads who whinnied in ecstasy; shoals of coryphees fled helter-skelter across the stage; and out on the apron, chin cupped in his hand, the choreographer brooded, dreaming up new flights of symbolism. To aggravate matters, a protegée of the composer's, a $55-dollar-a-week soprano with whom he had dallied in good faith, was loudly demanding a featured spot in the show, on pain of divulging the escapade to her husband. Whatever *Sherry Flip* lacked in smartness, its intimacy was unquestionable.

The *estocada*, however, was yet to come. Six o'clock of the evening before our departure for Boston, Murray Zweifel, the company manager, called me aside to retail alarming news—our producer had disappeared. Murray, a Broadway veteran, was on the verge of prostration. "He's quit the show," he said brokenly. "Walked out cold. We're done for." The particulars were simple enough, readily comprehensible to any student of alcohol. Kerr, unmanned by dissension with his backers and loath to open the show on what he contemptuously termed a shoestring, had taken refuge in the grape and abdicated. "The goddam fool is winging," Murray snuffled, grasping my lapels. "You've got to find him and get him on that train, baby. You're the only one who can do it—he won't listen to common sense."

The compliment was equivocal at best, and nine weeks of nightmare tension had taken their toll of me, but I realized that the welfare of sixty-odd folk was at stake, my own among theirs, and I knocked under. Pulling on a pair of waders, I set out to comb the bars that Kerr frequented. About ten-thirty, after a fruitless search of the West Side that extended to the clipjoints of Columbus Avenue, I flushed my man in a blind pig on East 54th Street. He was arm in arm with a prosperous Greek restaurateur from Bellows Falls; they had just consummated a deal to open a chain of diners in Thessaly and were toasting the venture in boilermakers. For all his carousing, Kerr was clear-eyed and crisp as muslin. He embraced me affectionately and insisted we pour a libation on the altar of friendship. The moment I disclosed my purpose, however, he grew violent. He was done with tinsel and sawdust, he declaimed; he wanted no more of the theater and its cutthroat machinations. I tried guile, supplication, and saccharine, but to no avail. Toward midnight, I phoned Zweifel for counsel.

"For crisake don't lose him!" he pleaded. "Feed him a Mickey—anything! If he's not on the nine o'clock to Boston, we're dead!"

"He's an iron man, Murray," I wailed. "He's mixing Scotch, vodka, bourbon—"

"Listen," he broke in. "Dr. Proctor's his physician—he'll cool him out with a sleeping powder! I'll phone him to expect you."

The process of extricating Kerr from the Greek took a full hour and the cunning of serpents. Eventually, though, I prevailed and, a trifle jingled from the soda I had taken in the line of duty, got him to the doctor's flat. A party was in progress, celebrating, I believe, Jenner's epochal discovery of the principle of vaccine, but not all the guests were medical. Out of the haze, I recall a tête-à-tête on a davenport with a blonde in salmon-pink satin, who read my palm and forecast business reverses. The augury cast a chill on our friendship, and moving off, I fell into a long, senseless wrangle about George Antheil with a musician resembling a carp. At intervals, Dr. Proctor's bibulous face swam into my field of vision, giving me conspiratorial winks and assuring me, in tones from outer space, that Kerr was under control. "Chloral hydrate," I heard him intone. "Just a few drops in his glass. He'll cave any time now." Hours later, I remember clinging to some portieres to steady myself while the doctor thickly conceded defeat. "Can't understand it," he said, laboring to focus his eyes. "Enough there to foal an ox. Average person go down like a felled ax. Got to hand it to old Poultney. Hard as nails." I groped past him to a book-lined alcove where Kerr was waltzing cheek to cheek with a ca-daverous, sloe-eyed beauty on the order of Jetta Goudal. Now that drugs and entreaty had failed, my only recourse was insult. Castigating him for a yellow-belly and a welsher, I challenged him to redeem himself.

"I dare you to fly up to Boston!" I cried. "I've never been on a plane, but I'll do it if you will. That is," I said witheringly, "if you've got the moxie."

His brow darkened and he discarded the bush-league Eur-asian with an oath. "We'll see who's got more moxie," he snarled. "Come along, you little four-eyed shrimp!"

I had won the first round; speeding through deserted streets toward the Newark Airport, my impresario's choler abated and he sank into a light coma. Instinct told me that if I could only lure him aboard the milk plane, his egotism would make him stick till the curtain rose. But Fate was dealing from the bot-tom of the deck. A dense, pea-soup fog blanketed the field, and the solitary clerk at the terminal held out little promise of improvement. The entire coast was closed in from Hatteras to the Bay of Fundy, he reported, savoring the despair on my face; even the mails were grounded. Kerr, meanwhile, had seized the opportunity to vanish into the washroom, where I found him draining a fifth of gin he had somehow managed to se-crete in his clothes. There was only one hope now, to shanghai him back to the morning train; but with no taxi in sight and a bankroll of forty cents, it would obviously take some fancy logistics. Day was breaking when I finally wheedled the driver of a towel-supply truck into dropping us at the nearest sub-way stop. The ensuing ride into Manhattan unraveled what remained of my ganglia. In his sheltered life, Kerr, it appeared, had never ridden on a subway. He was seized with repugnance for the overalled workmen about him, their unshaven faces and their surly glances, and promptly went pukka sahib.

"Look at these swine!" he barked into my ear. "That's who we beat our brains out to amuse! Do they appreciate what I've gone through, the aggravation, the sleepless nights I've spent over that show? Give 'em bread and circuses, hey? If I had my way, I'd give 'em something else!"

Heads turned the length of the car, and over the din I detected a subdued muttering like the sans-culottes in a Metro costume film. But Kerr, caught up in a crusading mood in which he identified himself with the Scarlet Pimpernel, was not to be diverted. He launched into a tirade on unions and the New Deal, concluding with a few generalizations that would have abashed even a Republican steering committee. I still marvel that we emerged intact from the Hudson Tubes. Up to the moment we did, I fully expected to expire in a blitzkrieg of lunch-pails.

Thanks to the headwaiter of the Biltmore, a paragon who refused to be intimidated by Kerr's hiccups and our crapulous exteriors, I got some breakfast into my charge, and at eight o'clock, Murray Zweifel appeared. His arrival was the signal for repeated fireworks. We were bracketed with Benedict Arnold and consigned to the devil, roundly notified by Kerr that hell would freeze over before he accompanied us to Boston. We argued and pleaded; at one point, under pretense of visiting the lav, Kerr slipped into a phone booth and was confiding all to Winchell when we extricated him by main force. In the quarter hour before train-time, the fracas degenerated into delirium. Just as the gates were closing, Murray and I bucked our way across Grand Central through a sea of astonished commuters, using Kerr as a battering ram. He was yelling vilification at us, a cataclysmic headache throbbed in my skull, and my reason hung by a thread, but nothing else mattered—the production was saved. From now on, I could relax, for the pathway ahead was strewn with roses. I was fated to learn something about botany, to say nothing of show business.

In the entertainment game, as Sir Arthur Wing Pinero was wont to observe in far loftier language, it don't pay to count your turkeys. At the Hub City premiere of *Sherry Flip*, the traveler curtain failed to open in the conventional fashion. Instead, it billowed out and sank down over the orchestra pit, perceptibly muffling the overture. The musicians fiddled manfully underneath, but Herman Earl's score was too fragile and lilting to overcome the handicap. The comedy, contrariwise, was all too robust—so much so that the police stepped in next day and excised four sketches. The reviews were unanimous. The show, it was agreed, was lavish enough to preclude spending another nickel on it; it should be closed as it stood. And then, on the very threshold of disaster, Kerr decided to rally. He fired the director and restaged the show himself, cut salaries to the bone, and sent a case of cognac to every critic in New York. His acumen bore fruit; we ran five nights there, and those who saw it grow garrulous even today at the memory of *Sherry Flip*. The last time I saw Poultney Kerr, he was a television nabob and beyond mortal ken, but he could not conceal his nostalgia for Broadway. He told me he was mulling an idea for a revue—a smart, intimate romp on the order of *The Garrick Gaieties*.

Revulsion in the Desert

THE DOORS of the D train slid shut, and as I dropped into a seat and, exhaling, looked up across the aisle, the whole aviary in my head burst into song. She was a living doll and no mistake—the blue-black bang, the wide cheekbones, olive-flushed, that betrayed the Cherokee strain in her Midwestern lineage, and the mouth whose only fault, in the novelist's carping phrase, was that the lower lip was a trifle too voluptuous. From what I was able to gauge in a swift, greedy glance, the figure inside the coral-colored bouclé dress was stupefying. All the accessories, obviously, had come from Hermès or Gucci, and you knew that some latter-day Cellini, some wizard of the pliers like Mario Buccellati, must have fashioned the gold accents at her throat and wrists. She was absorbed in a paperback, the nature of which I guessed instinctively; it was either Rilke or Baudelaire, or even, to judge by the withdrawn and meditative expression on her lovely face, Pascal. Suddenly a pair of lynx eyes, gray and exquisitely slanting, lifted from the page and fixed on me a long, intent scrutiny that set my knees trembling like jellied consommé. Could she have divined my adoration in her telepathic feminine way? Ought I spring forward, commandeer the book, and read out to her the one passage that would make us kinsprits forever? Before I could act, the issue had decided itself. The train ground to a stop at the Thirty-fourth Street station, and as she arose and stowed the book in her handbag, I saw that it was Ovid's *Art of Love*.

A lump of anguish welled up in my throat at the opportunity I had let slip, the encounter that might have altered my whole destiny; I sought surcease in the advertising placards overhead, but they were as bitter aloes. How could a craven like me dare aspire to Miss Subways, whose measurements were 37-24-33, whose hair was auburn, and who was an enthusiastic kegler? Vic Tanny, urging me to discard adipose tissue at his health club, was at best a cruel reminder that I was no longer the arrowy Don Juan I supposed, and Breakstone's injunction to diet on its cottage cheese merely compounded the affront. I was preparing to debark at Forty-second Street, lacerated by self-pity, when I beheld a poster that mercifully set me off on quite another tangent. "Win a fantabulous week for two at the Cloudburst in Las Vegas plus $3500 in cash!" it trumpeted. "Play Falcon Pencil Company's Super-Duper Guessing Game!" I never ascertained whether I was to watch for some magic serial number or to hawk the pencils from door to door. In the next breath, I was ejected to the platform, and there superimposed itself on my mind a memory of this selfsame Cloudburst, fantabulous indeed, as I saw it during a brief enforced visit to Las Vegas just a year ago.

My trip to the gambling mecca was no casual stopover between planes; I flew there from Rome, a matter of seven thousand–odd miles, to honeyfogle an actor, and I undertook the journey with the direst misgivings. The circumstances were somewhat as follows. Several months before, an Italian film producer had engaged me to devise a vehicle for a meteoric American tenor, whom it might be prudent to call Larry Fauntleroy. The latter, through his records and personal appearances, had scored a phenomenal success in the United States and Europe; his presence in a picture, it was universally felt, would make it a bonanza; and Signor Bombasti, from the moment I began work in Rome, announced himself ready to go to any lengths to win Fauntleroy's approval of our story. I soon found out what he meant. Shortly after completing the treatment, which is to say the narrative outline of the scenario, I was summoned to my employer, hailed as a composite of Congreve, Pirandello, and Norman Krasna, and urged to convey the manuscript in person to Fauntleroy. Nobody else, affirmed Bombasti, could adequately interpret its gusto and sparkle, its rippling mirth and delicious nuances. (And nobody else in the organization, he might well have added, spoke even rudimentary English.) My expostulations, my protests that I was anathema to performers, went for naught; in a supplication that would have reduced even Louis B. Mayer to tears, Bombasti entreated me, for the sake of the team, if not my own future, to comply. Seven hours later, I weighed in at Ciampino West airdrome.

The Milky Way, the hotel where I was scheduled to stay in Las Vegas and whose floor show Fauntleroy was currently headlining, was the town's newest—a vast, foolish beehive of

plate glass rearing fifteen stories above the sagebrush, so ruthlessly air-conditioned that I was wheezing like an accordion by
the time I unpacked. My quarters could only be described as
a harlot's dream. The dominant colors of the sleeping chamber, a thirty-five-foot-long parallelogram, were jonquil and
azure. A bed large enough to accommodate a *ménage à trois*,
flanked by modernique gooseneck lamps with purple shades,
occupied one wall; along the other, three abstract chairs in yellow plastic confronted a lacquer-red television set. To facilitate
any makeup I might require, there was a theatrical vanity bor-
dered with hundred-watt bulbs in the adjacent dressing room.
Beyond it lay a ghastly black-tiled bathroom from which one
momentarily expected Lionel Atwill to emerge in the guise of
a mad surgeon, flourishing a cleaver.

Within a few minutes, my reason was sufficiently unsettled
to regard the décor as normal, and, having erased the ravages
of travel, I went in search of Fauntleroy. He was breakfasting at
a table near the pool, encircled by the usual retinue of the popular entertainer—agents, managers, song pluggers, masseurs,
and touts—all of them vying with each other to inflate his
ego. I was introduced boisterously, if inaccurately, to the rest
of the levée; Bombasti's cable heralding my arrival, it seemed,
had miscarried, and for a while the troubadour was under the
impression that I was a disc jockey from Cleveland. Rather
than launch into tedious explanations, I accepted the role and
ordered a steak and a cigar to render myself inconspicuous.
Sprinkled around us on the greensward, half a hundred of the
Milky Way's guests dozed in the fierce sunlight, leaching away
their cares to the strains of Nelson Riddle. When the voice of
Frankie Stentorian started booming forth "Ciaou Ciaou Bam-
bina," I chose the auspicious moment to properly identify myself as the emissary from Italy.

"Man, that story you wrote for me is a gasser!" Fauntleroy
chortled, wringing my hand. "I haven't had a chance to read it
yet, on account of I just opened here, but I'll get to it tonight
between shows. Then you and I can spend the whole day tomorrow tearing it apart, analyzing and tightening so the plot
practically writes itself. How does that suit you?"

I assured him I could hardly wait to eviscerate my handiwork, and, amid ecstatic predictions from his claque that the

picture would outgross *The King of Kings*, withdrew. Inside the Milky Way casino, though it was only noon, several dozen patrons were already gathered at the faro and crap tables. They all moved with the languor of somnambulists—woebegone creatures condemned to spend eternity hopelessly defying the laws of chance. I watched a couple of blue-haired clubwomen pump silver dollars into the slot machines until their *cafard* communicated itself to me, and then progressed into a coffee shop that might have been lifted, along with its clientele, from a Southern bus terminal. Just as I was struggling to master a sandwich composed largely of lettuce and toothpicks, a music arranger out of my Hollywood past, named Dave Jessup, accosted me. Our salutations could not have been more joyful had we met on a sheep station in Queensland.

"Listen," said Jessup, after we had exhumed the age of fable and interred it again. "Everybody here flips about this new spectacle at the Cloudburst—the French revue called 'Oo La La!' What say we catch it tonight?"

To be candid, I was planning to retire early with the copy of Ruskin's *Stones of Venice* I had begun on the plane, as I wanted to see how it came out, but, sensing Jessup's desperate need of companionship, I good-naturedly yielded. Shortly before six, the fashionable dinner hour in Las Vegas, a cab deposited the pair of us under the neon volcano that skyrocketed from the block-long façade of the Cloudburst. In a ballroom the size of the Cirque Médrano, five hundred hysteroids in play togs were gorging themselves to a medley of jump tunes, magnified tenfold by microphones, issuing from a boxful of musicians on one wall. The din was catastrophic; we were shoved pell-mell into a booth, barricaded behind a cheval-de-frise of celery, and supplied with vases of whiskey that drenched our shirt fronts. A distracted waiter, hovering on the verge of collapse, unhesitatingly recommended snails as our main course, only to reappear in the blink of an eye with two filets that drooped over the sides of the plate. What with the uproar and the kaleidoscope flickering upon us, it was not easy to find my dish in the murk, and but for a sudden agonizing stab as Jessup tried to sever my knuckles, I never would have known I had eaten half his steak. Then our dinner vanished altogether, and as the orchestra sounded a fanfare, a deafening Gallic voice ushered in the pageant.

Whoever the creators of "Oo La La!" were, they were admirers of the undraped female form, for after establishing the locale as Montmartre with an apache dance and a chorus of gendarmes, they got down to brass tacks. A procession of sinuous long-stemmed beauties wound its way to the footlights attired in peasant costumes, large sections of which evidently had been lost in shipment from France. The mishap seemed to occasion the ladies small concern, however; they bore themselves proudly and endured the gaze of the audience without flinching. Their fortitude was rewarded by hearty applause intermingled with whistles, and as the last of them undulated offstage the scene inexplicably shifted to Naples. A *festa* was in progress, and a number of masked revelers of all sexes were holding carnival, dancing the tarantella and beating tambourines fit to wake the dead. Suddenly the clamor subsided, and another procession of coryphées, whose clothes had arrived piecemeal from Italy, wove downstage. They exhibited as much aplomb in the face of adversity as their French cousins had, and the audience paid them equal tribute. In both Turkey and Polynesia, to which we were then whisked in quick succession, the same regrettable shortages prevailed, but the houris and wahines were similarly undaunted. Having demonstrated to everyone's satisfaction that human nature under duress is constant the world over, the production soared to a climax. Four embossed trapdoors in the ceiling, hitherto masquerading as ventilators, vibrated shakily downward in time to the "Skaters' Waltz," disclosing a quartet of robust and untrammeled vestals clad in wisps of stockinet. They were lit from below, an angle calculated to maximize their charms, and the effect was hauntingly reminiscent of that greatest of all equine masterpieces Rosa Bonheur's "The Horse Fair."

I had become so preoccupied with the entertainment that I was ready to watch it a second, or even a third, time to familiarize myself with its catchy tunes and stage business, but Jessup demurred. He had arranged with two shapely girl violinists at the Golden Drugget, which from his description appeared to be a branch of the Juilliard School, to help them with their solfeggio, and invited me to accompany him. Mindful of the commitment I had made to disembowel my script the next day, however, I begged off and turned in at eight-thirty. About four, a phone call from Fauntleroy aroused me. He apologized for the intrusion, but he was terribly upset by the few pages of the treatment he had read. The background, the characters, the entire orientation were wrong. Nevertheless, he added quickly, I was not to agitate myself; I must get a good sound sleep, and in due course he would assess all the shortcomings. I rolled over and slept like a log.

It was midafternoon before I finally managed to awaken Fauntleroy, and another hour before he tottered into the coffee shop, unshaven and numb with seconal. When dexamyl had loosened his tongue, his whole mood changed. All the apprehensions he had voiced earlier on the phone, he told me, were groundless. Somewhere between sleep and waking he had evolved an idea for a series of production numbers that would make ours the most talked-of film of the century. "This is a whole fresh approach to the story, mind you," he began. "So for crisake be flexible in your thinking. Instead of a happy-go-lucky archeologist, the way you wrote me, I figure I'm a happy-go-lucky talent scout or an agent—sort of a singing Irving Lazar. I'm always going around to various exotic places, like France, Naples, Turkey, and Tahiti, rounding up these gorgeous contest winners for a floor show at the Copa or the Rainbow Room. So far so good. Now, here comes your drama. These girls arrive in plenty of time for the opening, all right, but the different parts of their native wardrobes are always confiscated at the last minute by the customs or lost in a typhoon or something. Do you get it? It's a race against overwhelming odds—a suspenseful strip tease that grows out of a real human situation. . . ."

Seventy-two hours afterward, in the Eternal City, Signor Bombasti beamed at me across the managerial mahogany and rubbed his hands in satisfaction. Not only was I the wiliest diplomat since Prince Metternich, he declared, but, as Fauntleroy's cable in front of him attested, I was a grand human being. "And let us remember something else in our hour of triumph, my dear fellow," he reminded me. "It was I, Ettore

Bombasti, who had the vision and the genius to marry your two outstanding talents."

"I'll remember it till the day I die," I said fervently. "I thought of it every minute I was in Las Vegas."

"Good," he said. "So long as you and our Larry saw eye to eye, so long as there was a meeting of minds, I ask for nothing more. This will be the biggest box-office attraction since *The King of Kings*. Now go back to your study and write as you have never written before."

I did. In fact, I wrote as *nobody* had ever written before.

Are You Decent, Memsahib?

A young Malayan belly dancer became a peeress today with the death of Lord Moynihan, a former chairman of Britain's Liberal party.

The new Lady Moynihan is the former Shirin Berry, known professionally as Princess Amina, who was married in 1958 to Anthony P. A. Moynihan, the Baron's son, at a secret Moslem ceremony in Tangier, Morocco.

A year later they were married again in England. Mr. Moynihan, a devotee of rock 'n' roll, resigned his reserve commission in the Brigade of Guards and played the bongo drums at his wife's worldwide cabaret appearances.—*The Times.*

HAVE YOU ever gazed into your mirror, girls, and longed to be dazzlingly lovely, breathtakingly so, no matter how stiff a price you had to pay for pulchritude? Of course you have; nor do you reck that beauty can ofttimes lead to woe. And yours truly has good reason to know, for when the gods lavished their gifts on me, an obscure little cipher from Scranton, Pa., and grafted an angelic countenance onto a physique divine, I sure as hell thought the world was my personal oyster. Which I don't mean that my success was handed to me on a platter—far from it. I had to hustle aplenty to climb that pinnacle. Still and all, I doubt whether anybody who saw Shirley Mazchstyck in pigtails could predict that out of this drab cocoon there would one day emerge a gorgeous butterfly yclept Sherry Muscatel, America's No. 1 stripteuse. Or that the latter would ever blossom forth into an Indian begum with the power of life and death over her subjects. Let's face it—the whole thing was just too fab.

The story of how I climbed the show-biz ladder to its topmost rung has been told so often in *Sizzle, Roister, Smolder,* and the other picture magazines that I don't have to burden your brain with it. Suffice it to say that, thanks to the smartest talent booker any star ever had, Solly Positano, I zoomed into the ace spot five years ago and stayed there. Why do I command top money and pick my engagements, you ask? Pure and simply because, unlike your average strip act, mine has no taint of vulgarity. As Solly analyzed, I give them something artistic that is lacking in their lives, a spectacle they wouldn't be ashamed to take their mother or sister to. The framework that my specialty is built on is the four seasons; i.e., winter, summer, fall, and spring. I make my entrance in winter garb, bundled up in mink, and after gliding around to the "Skaters' Waltz" peel down to fur briefies and matching bra. For the summer bit, I wear like a milkmaid frock of gingham, very demure, with batiste underthings and a parasol. I love working with a parasol; it makes everything you do seem so much more sexy. Anyhow, such is the basic routine, and even family-style resorts like Grossinger's and the Concord consider me so clean and educational that they outbid each other for repeats. From Thanksgiving on, I usually play the Fontainebleau or Eden Roc in Miami Beach, alternating with the Sands or the Desert Inn at Vegas. Even if Uncle Sam and Solly take out a big chunk between them, it is still a very nice dollar.

Well, one fine day last spring, I was laying off for a week at the Americana in New York when Solly phones me—a *megillah* about this inspiration that he and some other bookers had that morning in the steam room. They're going to put on an evening of old-fashioned burlesque in Boston. There used to be a house up there called the Old Howard that was very big in the days of the Columbia Wheel, the Gus Sun circuit, and the Izzy Herk time, but nobody remembers it now except a few elderly gaffers.

"Like you and your cronies," I said fliply. "It'll bomb, Solly. I predict you'll lose your shirt."

"Listen, Shirley girlie," he said. "You've got the best chassis in the business and you can shimmy like my sister Kate, but a predictor you're not. I tell you the public will eat it up. Look at the way they go for the old cars, ragtime tunes, et cetera. Anyway, I penciled you in, so make a note—the fourteenth of next month in Beantown."

I'm a straightforward person, and if I'm wrong I'm the first to admit it. The show was a sensation; we killed the people, we fractured them. God only knows where they dug up the performers from—the baggy-pants Dutch and Hebe comics, the soubrettes, and the crummy tenors with their lantern slides —but they didn't miss a one. And the material! Hokey old sketches like "Irish Justice," routines like "Flugel Street"—the audience was rolling in the aisles. But you should have heard them whistle and stomp when I came on, and the reason why was plain. Most of them were collegians from Harvard and Tufts which, while they bought the corn, secretly hungered for my more sophisticated approach. Well, I don't have to tell you. By halfway through, I had them howling like wolves, and those final bumps and grinds on my exit did the trick. The stage manager had to ring down the house curtain so the show could go on. A very clever team of acrobats, Anaxagoras Bros. & Delphine, followed me, but they didn't get a thing. The kids were too wrought up.

There was such a crush in my dressing room afterwards that when Solly barged in with this Oriental-type fellow and introduced him as Lam Chowdri, a Harvard boy, I thought it was a rib on account of it sounded like clam chowder. But he was legit, all right—a real dyed-in-the-wool Hindu, kind of good-looking in an offbeat way, and, from what Solly said, one of the wealthiest kids in India. He kept raving away about my act and said I reminded him of the native dancers back home on the temple friezes.

"You bet," said Solly, who can't resist a gag. "She freezes our temples over here too, don't you, Sherry? She turns strong men to like stone."

I could see from Lam Chowdri's face that he didn't dig but he was too polite to say. Instead, he invites me to have supper with him, and while I don't as a rule go with civilians, I made an exception. As soon as I heard him ask the maître d' at Locke-Ober's for a private room, I got the message. Oho, I thought, here it comes. Lobsters and champagne, and for dessert a wild chase around the table. Well, I didn't need to worry; he never stepped out of line, not once. It surprised me how Americanized he was. I thought Hindus spent all their time crouching on a bed of nails or worshipping a cow, but not he. He knew the name of every pop singer on TV, he was posted on any current events you could mention, and he was a fluent conversationalist. I also found out something those graybeards up at Harvard didn't know. He was a maharajah, the head of a section in India called Cawnpone, where his uncle, a regent, was minding the store while Lam finished his education.

Well, talk about your whirlwind courtships—this one was a tornado. For the next three weeks, not a day went by without caviar, orchids, little fantasies from Cartier's to keep your wrists cool, and special-delivery letters that got more excited on every page. I was his meadowlark, his bulbul, his fleet-footed gazelle, everything but his water buffalo. At the time, I was working a string of clubs in the Midwest, one-night stands, and each airport I got to, why, I was met by a chauffeur-driven Rolls that Lam had laid on. (Somebody gave the item to Lennie Lyons, but they had the wrong Indian, and it came out "Cherokee" instead of "Chowdri.") Anyway, the minute my tour wound up in New York, there was Lam waiting to pop the question, and, of course, he has to pick a real kookie locale like the Mayflower Donut Shop at 2:30 in the morning. Love among the crullers. But he was so sweetly sincere that it brought a lump to my throat, and I decided to lay my cards on the table too. I told him about my ex-husbands, the jockey and the druggist—I skipped the brassière manufacturer because we split out after two weeks—and how my search for happiness had failed.

"Oh, moon of my delight," he says, grabbing my hands. "Life has bruised your wings, my little shama thrush. All I ask is a simple boon. Let me spend the rest of my life catering to your smallest whim."

No woman can resist that kind of a pitch, especially if it's a maharajah talking, and twelve hours later a j.p. in Virginia tied the knot. I wanted to call Solly right away so as to give Earl Wilson an exclusive, but Lam talked me out of it. He said we had to keep it dark for a month, till he finished Harvard, and then he would stage a big ceremony in Cawnpone, with painted elephants and sword swallowers and the whole *tzimmas*. Well, that was a bringdown for me, natch, because I had visions of sweeping into Sardi's East, everyone kowtowing and murmuring, "Good evening, Highness. My, what a gorgeous gold sari." Still, rather than launch our honeymoon with a spat, I made like I was ecstatic over the idea, and Lam slipped the judge a deuce to button up to the press. Everything was peachy keen—so I thought.

It was like two days after he went back to Cambridge that I got my first jolt. I walk in the flat one night from Jersey, where

I'm headlining the show at the Migraine Room of the Hotel Winograd, in Newark, and there's my royal master, lock, stock, and baggage. He's quit college because he can't stand being separated, but that's only for openers. The real wallop—are you ready?—is that he's gone and renounced his throne because it would always stand between us. From here in, he's devoting himself full time to my career, and, in fact, he's dreamed up a way to weave himself into my act. I was so flabbergasted I could hardly talk.

"Wait a minute, Buster," I said. "A maharajah can't quit like a short-order cook. Don't you have to go back to India to renounce your title?"

"No, I renounced it on the phone," he said. "But that's only a detail. Listen to my idea for our new act."

In my turmoil, I didn't follow too closely, but the *drehdel* was that he would be costumed like an Indian snake charmer, in a turban and a diaper, kneeling on the floor in front of this large basket and playing a flute. And pretty soon, after the applause for his solo dies down, out of the basket would come you-know-who and go into her number. Except that it wouldn't be a strip exactly, more of a slow cooch.

Well, I knew I couldn't handle the situation alone, so I ran to a guy whose business was trouble—viz. and to wit, Solly—and spilled the whole story. I must say he was a doll. Never a word of criticism; only trying to be helpful. He came up with a solution pronto.

"I got the perfect identity for him," he says. "A candy butcher. In between your changes, he circulates around the floor with an old-fashioned spiel: 'Ladies and gents, if I may have your kind attention. Introducing America's biggest-selling candy, Greenfield's Confections, a prize in each and every package.' It's a great comedy touch, Shirl, and we can get a million tieups with Loft's, Whitman, whoever. And think of the publicity! 'Sweets for the Sweetie. Ex-Maharajah Vends Bonbons for Love.'"

It sounded like a natural, but when I sprang it on Lam he blew his stack. Nineteen generations of royalty would revolve in their grave if he became a hawker. Solly was a cheap vulgarian, he stormed, and then, like *that*, he suddenly has another brain wave. Why not let him represent me instead of

Solly and save all that commission? I almost told him that those nineteen generations would spin like a Waring mixer if he went into the agency racket, but I was afraid he might slap me across the chops. When those Hindus get angry, man, it's Amoksville. So I pretended his notion was marvy but I needed a few days to mull it over. And that very evening Mr. Nuroddin checks in from Cawnpone.

Mr. Nuroddin is what they call a Parsee, this very high-toned sect of fire worshippers that almost every one of them is a rich, influential banker or merchant. He's the family lawyer and he's been sent over by Lam's uncle, the regent, to rescue the boy from my coils. Well, the scene he put on was right out of *East Lynne*. Within two minutes, he's using words like "adventuress," and when he brought out his checkbook and asked "How much?" I really let him have it. I called him every name I could think of, I threw a jar of Albolene at his head, and I made such an uproar that he ran out quaking like an aspirin. But if you think that was the end of him, you don't know Mr. Nuroddin. He starts showing up at a ringside table every performance, sending me mangoes and skirt lengths of madras and mooning around till after my late show. At first I thought it was like a ruse to break up Lam and I. Then I realized the old *nudnik* is serious, for God's sake. He's carrying a torch, but he's not worshipping *it*—he's idolizing *me*. I chewed him out good and proper.

"Why don't you act your age, Nuroddin?" I said. "You ought to be ashamed, a man of your standing in the legal profession behaving like a stage-door John."

"I can't help it, O beauteous one," he snuffles, wringing his hands. "To me you're the sun in the morning and the moon at night. I adore you, my little nightingale."

My life isn't complicated enough already; now I have an old Parsee mouthpiece to contend with. "Listen, Clyde," I said to him. "You better watch out or you'll be wearing a silk thread around your larnix. Lam's getting suspicious—he asked me when you were going back home."

Then the stove explodes. "I'm not. Never again," he says. "I just sent off a cable to Cawnpone resigning from my law firm. From now on, every ounce of my being is devoted to serving you."

"Are you out of your *mind*?" I said. "What about your family? Don't you have any wives?"

"None to compare with you, my ringdove," he says. I was beginning to feel like a zoo. "Let me do your bidding, my lovely tigress. Walk on me, tread on me."

Well, what could I do? I told Lam I needed a secretary and I took on the old buzzard—not that a stripper has that much paperwork, but like Solly said, it was good publicity. I guess he was right; Louis Sobol wrote that I was the only ecdysiast on record with a Zoroastrian amanuensis. That didn't sit so well with Hubby, Nuroddin crowding him out of the spotlight, and the two of them started catfooting around, exchanging these vicious little digs—in Hindi yet. If it was in Scrantonese, which I'm fluent, I could have coped, but they drove me right up the wall. So that's how matters stood when Uncle Nooj, the regent, blows in.

You'd have to see this joker to believe him—he's right out of *The Arabian Nights* or some pageant Sol Hurok imported. A skinny little man with a big bugle, which one flange has a diamond the size of your pinkie welded into it. He has on a shift embroidered with rubies, and around his neck five strands of pearls like Mary Garden or Schumann-Heink in the *Victor Book of the Opera*. But there the resemblance ends; he's got a high, squeaky voice like a peanut whistle and he beams it straight at me. Well, brother, you could write the dialogue. I'm Valerie Vampire, and what kind of a hex did I put on his nephew and his legal eagle? They must have drunk a love filter I prepared, whatever the hell that is. He's going to annul the marriage if it takes Louis Nizer's weight in platinum, and in the meantime he's got a table next to the band that night to watch me work my voodoo.

Well, do I have to spell it out? It was love's old sweet song, and I'm the gal who put the sex in sexagenarians. As I ran off in my birthday suit with the peasants yelling, I look back and there's Nooj standing on the table, squealing for an encore, but in my dodge you have nowhere to go, as they say. The flowers and the trinkets started arriving on schedule, and if you never saw an emerald the size of an Idaho baked potato, neither had I. I don't know who was ruling over Cawnpone while Nooj was absent, but whoever it was, they kept the supply lines open. Solly used to come by nights in an armored car to haul the stuff to the bank. You can imagine how Lam and Nuroddin reacted to Nooj. It's a wonder they didn't drop a krait down his peplum or something. And the topper, of course, was the matinée that he shows up in a business suit too large for him and a tweed cap cocked over one eye. He looked like a pinboy I used to go around with in Scranton. "I have a very startling piece of news for you, my eaglet," he says, undressing me with those goo-goo eyes.

"Don't tell me—let me guess," I said. "You went and renounced your title. You're over here permanent from now on."

His jaw dropped with such a clang you could almost hear it. "How did you guess?"

"Well," I said. "It's becoming pretty common around here. Do you know anything about how to use Carbona?"

"I never heard of it," he says. "What is it?"

"Well, you better find out," I said, "because from now on you're in charge of all my cleaning and pressing. Here's a key, and you can use the locker right next to Lam and Nuroddin. Good luck."

That's what I told *him*. But I was the one who needed it.

Tell Me Clear, Parachutist Dear,
Are You Man or Mouse?

W EE, SLEEKIT, cow-rin', tim'rous beastie," sang Robert
Burns, dipping his pen into triple-distilled schmaltz to
apostrophize a mouse, "O what a panic's in thy breastie!" That
the little creatures are capable of inducing similar and immoderate panic in someone else's breastie is, of course, a commonplace, but until quite recently nobody seems to have had the
imagination to use them as deliberate instruments of terror.
The first inkling I had of their conversion was in a dispatch
to the *Times* from Britain about a year ago. "Rita Houlton, a
clerk, was alone in a small shop in the London suburbs," it said.
"Two young men entered, one carrying a paper bag. Without
a word, the youth placed the bag on the counter and opened
it. Out scampered four white mice. Out of the store scampered Rita, in shrieking flight from the mice. The youths then
stepped out a side door, got into the shop's delivery truck, and
drove away." Soon afterward, another blitz involving rodents,
this time political, occurred in the Iberian peninsula. During
a concert in Madrid by a group of singers and dancers from
Havana, according to the *Times* of London, a group of Cuban
exiles created an uproar by shouting abuse at the performers,
hurling stink bombs, and showering the audience with leaflets. "The release in the stalls of mice—and some claim there
were a few rats," the correspondent noted with relish, "added
to the confusion as women screamed and shrieked." It took
an equally volatile but more enterprising race, the Italians,
however, to perfect the weapon. *This Week in Rome*, a bulletin of convenient information for tourists, reported that Luigi
Squarzina, author of a play called *Romagnola*, had filed suit
against a clutch of Neo-Fascist hoodlums for attempting to
sabotage its première. Two other disturbances from the same
source made news, continued the item, "one particularly on
account of the fact that mice were let down on parachutes
from the balcony into the stalls."

The selection of mice staunch enough to become paratroopers, their indoctrination, and the Commando training requisite for such warfare are too complex for anyone less than Hanson W. Baldwin to explicate. Nevertheless, one aspect of the subject cries out—all right, whimpers—for clarification. The artisan who confects these minuscule parachutes—what manner of chap is he? What specialized problems and stresses confront him? Rather than indulge in windy hypotheses, let's slip into something brief and gossamer-sheer, like a playlet, and see if we can't gain an insight into his temperament and associates. Settle down, please—curtain's up.

(*Scene: A workroom in a fifth-floor tenement in the Trastevere quarter of Rome. In the weak light filtering through the windows at rear, nearly opaque with dust and accumulated spiderwebs, two small figures are dimly visible, seated cross-legged on a bench. They are apparently occupied in some form of invisible weaving, for each squints through a magnifying lens as he plies a needle, threaded with filaments imperceptible to the naked eye, through minute scallops of nylon. Baldassare Volante, the elder of the pair and boss of the firm, is a wizened Tom Thumb who, poised on tiptoe, would measure a scant forty-eight inches. Scarcely a head taller is Beppo, his apprentice, a robust cockerel in his twenties with unruly blond curls and a dimple sufficiently like Kirk Douglas's to flutter any feminine heart.*)

VOLANTE (*tossing a finished parachute onto a pile*): *Basta!* There—that's thirty-five, and with your fifteen, the Twentieth Century-Fox order is complete. Yes siree, Beppo— a few more commissions from minority stockholders bent on disrupting their annual meeting and we'll be on Via Agiata (Easy Street).

BEPPO: With respect to that, Signor Volante, and with all due respect to yourself, may I respectfully speak what is in my heart?

VOLANTE: Respect, respect—take the polenta out of your mouth! What are you trying to say, man?

BEPPO: Just that my conscience impels me to warn you, *padrone*. Our business is in mortal peril.

VOLANTE (*agitatedly*): You've overheard some rumors . . . some gossip . . .

BEPPO: No, no—

VOLANTE (*seizing him by the throat*): Somebody's betrayed us to the police, to the Ministry of Sanitation! Who was it? Spit it out, you dog!

BEPPO: Sir, I entreat you on my sainted mother's virtue— your fears are groundless—

VOLANTE: It's Serafina, that old hag of a *portiera* downstairs. She offered me her body eighteen years ago, and I recoiled in contempt. Now she's brought an information against me.

BEPPO: But you forget, *commendatore*—there's nothing illegal about our product. We furnish little parachutes to anyone who needs them.

VOLANTE: Why, that's right, come to think of it. We're a service organization, aren't we?

BEPPO: Nothing more. And are we responsible if they're used to create disorder? When some elderly virgin, unhinged by jealousy, hurls a phial of acid at a voluptuous nude by Titian, is the apothecary who sold it to blame?

VOLANTE: Of course not. A brilliant analogy, Beppo. I never realized you had a poetic gift.

BEPPO: Coming from one in whose veins there flows the blood of Dante Alighieri, that is praise indeed, *eminenza*. I thank you humbly.

VOLANTE: Yes, you'll go far in this business, my boy. But tell me—what, then, is the danger you speak of?

BEPPO: Overspecialization, sir. We must branch out, I beseech you. In the hurly-burly of modern combat (*nel chiasso del combattimento moderno*), the airborne warrior requires a modicum of equipment to survive, be he man or quadruped.

VOLANTE: Now, don't start that stuff again. We're not tooled up to produce little jump suits and shockproof watches.

BEPPO (*pleading*): But a pair of boots at the very least, sir, if only for the psychological effect. It vitiates all the menace to drop from the sky with four naked feet.

VOLANTE (*shortly*): If naked feet were good enough for Icarus, they're good enough for a mouse. Let's have no more schmoos.

BEPPO: I defer to your vastly superior judgment, Excellency. I spoke as youth is wont to, in a freshet of impetuosity.

VOLANTE: I sensed that, *figliuolo*. In any case, I have other matters to occupy me. This is a red-letter day, Beppo. As all the world knows, my beautiful daughter Ippolita, who has just graduated from Perugia U., is due home momentarily, and I must hie me on down to the *drogheria* to buy some cakes and wine for a celebration.

BEPPO: Maestro, I shall defend the premises with my very life till you return.

VOLANTE: Never mind the rodomontade—just keep your paws out of the cash drawer. (*He exits.*)

BEPPO (*chuckling*): *Che riso sardonico!* Little does the old pantaloon suspect that Ippolita and I have been secretly affianced for months, that we daily exchange burning epistles, and that I would enclasp her hair in a snood of stars, so enslaved am I by her charms. (*He stiffens at the sound of a soft, repeated knock on the window at rear. As he hastens to it and raises the sash, Ippolita, a toothsome blend of Claudia Cardinale and Anouk Aimée, whose eyes bespeak intelligence on a par with Amy Lowell's, is disclosed on the fire escape, suitcase and diploma in hand.*) Ippolita *carissima*! What are you doing there?

IPPOLITA: This is no time for chin music (*stridore di denti*). Lift me down. (*Beppo complies—not without visible effort, since she towers above him.*) Listen, I must have a word with you before my father comes back. A serious crisis is imminent.

BEPPO: What's wrong?

IPPOLITA: Have you ever heard of a publishing firm in America named Barber & Farber? Concentrate—rack your brain.

BEPPO: Let me think. I seem to recall . . . why, of course —that big package there on the shelf! I was just shipping them a consignment by air express.

IPPOLITA: Of two hundred chutes. Am I correct?

BEPPO (*bewildered*): Yes, but how on earth did you know?

IPPOLITA: Because Barbara Sparber, my roommate at Perugia, is the daughter of Marboro Sparber, the distinguished New York publisher who is their deadliest rival. Do you follow?

BEPPO: I . . . I think so.

IPPOLITA: Good. Well, late last night, Marboro Sparber telephoned Barbara that his firm's best-selling novel, *Scarborough Harbor*, by Sahbra Garber, was a certainty to win the National Book Award next week. . . . Why do you look so puzzled?

BEPPO (*faintly*): Er— Nothing, nothing. Go on.

IPPOLITA: Now, attend me closely, for here comes the wienie. Marboro Sparber has been tipped off that a moment before the award is announced in the grand ballroom of the Hotel Astor, hirelings of Barber & Farber are going to strafe the assemblage from the mezzanine. At a given signal, the lights will be extinguished, and two hundred mice, dipped in phosphorus to glow in the dark, will flutter down on the guests, ninety per cent of whom are female. The veriest donkey could divine the consequences.

BEPPO (*duly divining them*): It will be a catastrophe—*un panico universale!*

IPPOLITA: That's for sure. The resultant melee will discredit the National Book Award, make my Barbara's father a laughing stock in Publishers' Row, and wash up her engagement to Tabori Czabo, a Hungarian boy at Harvard she's mad about. Beppo, this rotten stratagem must be thwarted at all costs.

BEPPO: Shucks, honey, what can *I* do? I'm only an obscure apprentice—

IPPOLITA: Simpleton. Idiot boy. Don't you see? You and you alone have the power to knock the whole scheme into a cocked hat.

BEPPO (*cunningly*): You mean, by not sending the chutes to Barber & Farber?

IPPOLITA: Nothing of the sort, stupid. Ship them, by all means—but first, prick each and every one with a needle so they'll collapse in midair!

BEPPO: But how does that help matters? The mice would plummet down with even greater force on the target.

IPPOLITA (*carelessly*): Oh, once the element of showmanship is removed, the audience, already narcotized by the speeches, will hardly notice. Well, how's about it?

BEPPO: Ippolita—do you realize what you're saying? You're asking me to sacrifice your father's reputation. He's built up a clientele by years of hard work—

IPPOLITA: *Ach*, can the sentimental slop. I'm offering you a choice.

BEPPO: I . . . I don't understand.

IPPOLITA: Between love and duty, you clod. Either do as I ask or it's all over between us—*capisci*?

BEPPO (*with a nobility Sydney Carton would have envied*): Very well, then. Bastinado my feet, reduce me to mincemeat, boil me in Vesuvius—I shall never betray Baldassare Volante. Goodbye.

VOLANTE (*flinging open the door*): Bravo! What did I tell you, Ippolita!

IPPOLITA: Beppo, *angelo mio*—come into my arms! (*She stoops, sweeps him up in an embrace.*) Oh, darling, how happy you've made me!

BEPPO (*flummoxed*): Is this all a dream? Am I in Paradise? What's happened?

VOLANTE: Merely that you've passed our test with flying colors. I wanted to be sure of my future son-in-law.

BEPPO: Then—the whole thing about the publishers was a confection?

IPPOLITA: Totally. Papa and I made it up between us, every bit.

BEPPO: But I *know* the Hotel Astor exists. I once smoked a cigar by that name.

IPPOLITA: A coincidence. I can assure you that there's no such thing as the National Book Award—and even if there were, a few mice here and there wouldn't make a scrap of difference.

BEPPO (*emotionally*): Signor Volante, I'd like you to know one thing. You haven't lost a daughter, you've gained a son.

VOLANTE: I withdraw what I said earlier about your poetic gift. (*Resignedly.*) *Allora*, take her, my boy, and one of these days, no doubt, there'll be another little warrior descending from Heaven—but this time a biped with no strings attached. (*Maidenly blushes from Ippolita and suitably hymeneal music.*)

CURTAIN

Sex and the Single Boy

L ET'S SEE NOW—exactly what do we know about Phil? He's twenty-five years old, he's an investment broker, and he went to Yale. We know he likes girls, because, by his own candid admission, he's got a little black book carefully dividing them into four categories—"pretty," "great to go to bed with," "nice to take to parties," and "nice to talk to." Any chap with that many categories, it follows, must be darned attractive, and Phil doesn't bother to deny it: "I average a couple or three calls a night from girls. . . . They're all the same old girls. But they call. Sure, they'll come over and cook your dinner, and sure, they'll stay all night, and sure, they'll move in if you want." Yes, indeed, he's quite a tiger, is Phil, as he emerges from that tape recording. Ah, but I'm getting ahead of myself. You haven't a glimmer as to what tape I mean, or how it evolved—right? Permit me to sketch in the background.

Well, sir, it all originated in some fertile editorial brain over at *Mademoiselle*, which was celebrating its thirtieth anniversary with a number roguishly designated "Man Talk Issue." The notion, in brief, was that five young men-about-New York should freely discuss the strategy and techniques they use to artfully entangle unattached women. In the resulting twenty-one-column symposium, "How Do Bachelors Get Away with It?," the quintet of participants, shepherded by a moderator, included Spencer, an advertising man; Tom, an airline employee; Max, a magazine editor; Larry, a municipal-bond trader; and the aforesaid Phil, the fiddler with feminine virtue. On the face of it, the juxtaposition of such divergent stags might be expected to produce at least several novel methods of conquest. What actually eventuated, however, was a vast quantity of flatulent chin music, studded with words like "communication," "relationship," and "chemistry." Spencer, for example, advanced a master plan of enticement based on three dates with his quarry, as follows: "The first evening you have quite a good dinner somewhere, where the opportunity essentially exists to talk a great deal and get to know the person. . . . The second date is usually a very offbeat sort of thing. It may be a hamburger or a Forty-second Street movie. . . . The third date is: I cook dinner in my apartment. . . . I happen to be a very good cook." This culinary approach, presumably, creates such ardor that on the fourth date the two reach fulfillment in *her* pad, sleeves rolled up and exchanging recipes like mad.

Phil's reaction to so premeditated a campaign, it appeared, was contemptuous in the extreme. "My life is such that I take it as it comes," he said, doubtless fingering a hairline mustache in the manner of the late Lew Cody. To illustrate, he evidenced the case of a recent amour that flowered from a haphazard encounter with a lady whose party he chanced to attend: "She was a very honest and shy little girl, so the next week I called her up for a date. It was a week night. I wanted to have a football pumped up. [A not unreasonable yearning in one recently graduated from Yale.] I had a friend who had a football pump, and we went over and pumped up the football and then went out and had a drink." Whether Phil's *petite amie* was subsequently classified under his "great to go to bed with" heading he was too gallant to divulge. Perhaps he had a secret fifth category—"nice to pump up a football with."

While *Mademoiselle*'s *conversazione*, by and large, added nothing of significance to the technique of seduction, it did produce one blockbuster—a generalization about womankind that struck me as revolutionary. It was expounded by Phil, never a man to mince words: "I find that they hop into bed with you a lot faster if they really think you are interested in them as human beings, even if you are not. . . . Unless you really try to be nice to them and treat them as human beings, you won't get anywhere."

The magnitude of Phil's discovery, the sheer audacity of his postulate that women belong to the same species men do and must perforce be regarded as hominoids, transfixed me in my chair. I daresay that although the transcript gives no hint of it, there was an instant of stunned silence among his confreres. The question that immediately springs to mind, of course, is how Phil came to arrive at this conclusion. Was it the end product of painful trial and error or a sudden blinding revelation? I suggest that we might possibly derive some clue from portions of what I imagine to be his diary. It's worth a few moments' study.

FEBRUARY 25

Another rough day at the office. The minute I walked in this morning and the new girl at the switchboard saw me, I knew I was in for trouble. Her first response, I could tell, was one of incredulity—I mean, she'd probably seen fellows like Robert Goulet or Marcello Mastroianni on the screen, but to have their actual flesh-and-blood counterpart materialize before her was to her magical. I stood there, cool and amused, while she fought to regain control, and then asked her if she had any messages for me.

"Oh, golly," she said faintly. "Your voice is just what I expected it to be—sort of husky yet caressing. What are you doing for lunch?"

"Easy does it, sister," I said, stopping her. "Take your place in line. I'll let you know when there's a vacancy."

"I'm available day or night, on very short notice," she said. "My, I wish somebody'd pinch me to see if I'm dreaming. Would you mind?"

I was strongly tempted, but my life is complicated enough already, God knows. "Sorry, little one, you're not my type," I said. "Now, then, who phoned?"

"A party named Vivian Reifsnyder," she said. "She wants to come over this evening and cook your dinner. Oh, yes, and another—a Miss Foltis, or Poultice. She offered to stay all night."

I told her not to put through any further social calls today, no matter how urgent, and went along to my desk. Less than an hour later, she buzzed me.

"Phil, darling?" she said. "This is Sondra, on the switchboard. I hope you don't mind my calling you that."

"You're a pretty fast worker, I'd say."

"Pappy, I've only started," she said. "Look, I've been thinking—you're a Yale man, and you must have a lot of dusty pennants at your flat that need washing. I have a friend who's got a washing machine. Why don't we take them around there tonight, and afterwards go out for some drinks?"

Well, if I do say so myself, I'm a fairly sophisticated guy, and plenty of girls have tried to pull the wool over my eyes, but this was such an unusual pitch that I nearly fell for it. I sat there trying to figure out what the catch was, and all of a sudden it dawned on me. I didn't have any pennants in my flat; therefore, how could they be dusty? The whole thing was a ruse Sondra had dreamed up, a pretext to get me sufficiently stoned to be easy prey for her wiles. Rather than humiliate the kid by accusing her, though, I played it cagey. I advised her to quit acting ape and said she was a no-good little tramp who didn't fit into any of my categories. That slowed her up, by jingo. She gave a strange little whimper like an animal, except that it sounded —well, almost human, though, of course, that couldn't be. I guess I've been working too hard.

MARCH 1

I wonder if people ever stop to think what a drag it is to be criminally handsome, to have every damned salesgirl and waitress and receptionist slavering over you, trying to date you up and get your phone number. It really drives me up the wall to hear those females whinnying and whistling when I walk down a subway platform. And they're even worse on a bus, where they swarm around you like flies, mooning over your profile and ignoring the driver's pleas to move to the rear. I often ask myself, Are these birdbrains members of my own species?

Take this Sondra effect, for instance. I thought I'd squelched her for good that first go-around, but after a day or two she was on the make again—not openly but in a sneaky, underhanded fashion I didn't dig right off. One afternoon, on returning from lunch, I found her crying her heart out at the switchboard. She had a hankie crumpled against her lips and she looked so woebegone that, against my better judgment, I asked what was wrong. Boiled down to essentials, her problem was that the Miss Subways contest, in which she was a finalist, required a set of her measurements, and, living alone as she did, she didn't have anyone to help her take them accurately. The poor creature was desperate, I could see; she had all the necessary equipment—the tape measure, the pad and pencil—and yet, without somebody to assist her, she was likely to be disqualified. Suddenly, as we were mulling over her predicament, an inspiration seized her.

"Why didn't I think of it before?" she burst out. "Oh, Phil, couldn't *you* do it—just as a favor to me? I realize you hate me . . ."

"I don't hate you," I corrected her. "You merely don't exist, as far as I'm concerned."

"I know," she said humbly, "but the contest means so much to me. *Please*. I'll never ask another thing of you." She unclasped her pocketbook and plucked out the tape measure. "Now, wind it here."

I was complying with her instructions when, without any warning, she wriggled around with the agility of an eel and, gluing her mouth to mine, imprisoned me in a kiss. It took all my strength to uncoil her arms from my neck and thrust her away. I guess the shock of my rejection and her disappointment were more than she could stand, because she keeled over in a dead faint. Now, fundamentally, I'm a decent guy; the sight of anybody in distress bothers me, and I'll go out of my way not to step on a worm if I can avoid it. I thought of getting someone to throw a pail of water over Sondra or chafe her wrists, but the truth was she didn't deserve it. After all, she'd put me in a hell of a spot, deliberately tying up the switchboard to block any incoming calls from girls who wanted to cook my dinner and spend the night. So I just let her lie there and work it out as best she could. It's a funny thing, though— my Puritan conscience, or whatever they instill in you at Yale, kept gnawing away at me the rest of the day. Maybe my whole scale of values was gaga and this kook was a real person—not altogether human but struggling to be. . . . No, it was too fantastic. I wish I knew more about biology.

MARCH 3

Well, I suppose I had it coming to me and I should have been prepared. I notice that every time I'm riding high and start to congratulate myself Fate throws me a curve. And boy, what a lulu this one was! I've lost my little black book. Why a tiny mishap like that should throw me is beyond my ken, but the minute I discovered it was gone I got panicky. Not that I needed the twenty or thirty phone numbers of those various dolls; I was fairly confident they'd check in soon enough, for the simple reason that they couldn't get along without me.

My headache was how the devil to remember their categories —which I just talked to, which I allowed to shack up with me, etc. A fine investment banker I must be, investing years of effort in tabulating those chicks and ending up with a bunch of ninepins nobody could tell apart.

Then a very odd thing happened. My entire stable began phoning me, all right, but the calls were short and each had the same refrain—"Goodbye forever." You never heard such fury. "So I'm pretty, but not the kind you take to a party, eh?" they hollered. "O.K. to climb into the sack with, but not to talk to—is that the idea?" One after the other, they crucified me, ordered me to get lost, or, still better, drop dead. I could almost swear they knew how I'd rated them in my book. It was uncanny.

Anyhow, for the time being, my life's much less strenuous. Now I can relax at home and watch TV without some silly dame tousling my hair or messing around in the kitchenette. I get sort of restless once in a while, and I walk up and down the room a lot, but that'll wear off. I may even get a cat or a dog for companionship.

MARCH 5

There comes a point when a man has to face up to himself, and thank God I'm big enough to admit it—I was wrong. Sondra is a human being, just like me. Perhaps her brain isn't as well developed as mine. Perhaps it never can be. Nevertheless, in the light of what happened last night, my whole concept of her has undergone a change.

I was pretty bushed when I got home after work, and, to tell the truth, I was still brooding about the loss of my address book. As I closed the door and pressed the light switch, this peculiar feeling hit me that there was someone else in the room. I whirled around, and my hunch was right—it was Sondra. She was holding a big bag of groceries in one arm and had a nightie folded over the other.

"What are you doing here?" I started to say, and then, Lord only knows why, the riddle that was bugging me was solved in a flash. "It was you!" I cried out. "*You* stole my little black book, didn't you? You called those girls!"

Her eyes filled with tears. "Yes," she said. "Oh, Phil, it was a rotten, a contemptible thing to do, but I had to convince you I was a woman. I had to prove there were no lengths I wouldn't go to in order to win you."

To my surprise, tears sprang to my own eyes, hardened cynic though I am. In her blind, fumbling way, Sondra had risked everything to express her devotion. Was I worthy of it? Or was I only a heartless Don Juan who rode roughshod over his casual loves? It was up to me to show her my true stature, and I did. I took the groceries from her very gently and cooked dinner for us both. Then I put my bed at her disposal, tucked her in, and contrived a shakedown for myself on the floor. Tonight we're going to have a meal out, at some place where we can communicate and discuss our relationship and chemistry. . . . Can this be love? I don't know. Given two human beings, anything can happen.

A Soft Answer Turneth Away Royalties

"PLEASE DON'T give it another thought!" I shouted at my vis-à-vis over the uproar of the cocktail party. "It's perfectly all right!"

"I can't hear you!" she shouted back, her nose wrinkling in frustration. "What did you say?" She was an angular hyperthyroid in green herringbone, with a fur piece slung across her jib, and we stood glued to each other amid the crush like lovers in an Indian erotic sculpture, but without intimacy. My left sleeve, down which she had just emptied two-thirds of her highball, was waterlogged, and a fearful premonition gripped me that I might spend eternity bonded to this afreet unless some miracle intervened. Providentially, it did; somewhere in the hurly-burly a drunk sank to the floor, the axis of the party shifted, and I found myself confronting Stanley Prang.

Though we had caromed into one another intermittently around New York over the past couple of decades, all I really knew of Prang was that he did editorial work for some major publishing firm and, I distantly recalled, kept his finger on the British literary pulse. Since he, in turn, always exhibited equal incuriosity about me, our encounters had been lubricated with an exchange of grins or platitudes on the weather. Today, however, I seemed to produce an effect like adrenalin on the chap. His pupils distended to the size of agates, and, seizing my arm, he wrenched me into an adjacent hallway. "I want you to read something," he said, feverishly extracting an envelope. "In twenty-three years of working with authors, nothing like this has ever happened to me." I reached for it, but he struck aside my hand, determined to finish his preamble. "Of all the ingrates on earth," he declaimed, "of all the crabs, malcontents, and faultfinders, writers are the worst. You coddle them, correct their grammar, soothe their wretched little egos, turn yourself inside out to please them—and what do you get? A kick in the head. Not one speck of gratitude, appreciation—just more bellyaches. Well, anyhow," he broke off, obviously conscious of his failure to ignite a pile of wet leaves, "that's why I'm going to frame this document. It's historic!"

The letter, a barely decipherable scrawl on pale violet note-paper, was the handiwork of an English lady novelist too eminent, asserted Prang, to have her identity noised about. Its tone was emotional, almost elegiac. Acknowledging the receipt of a romance of hers he had just issued, she hailed it as a masterpiece of the bookmaker's art, a milestone in publishing. Everything about it—type, format, binding—bespoke the most refined taste; indeed, she declared, the setting was so exquisite that she feared it shamed her poor bauble. The beauty of the end papers was only rivalled by the ingenuity of the chapter headings, and, as for the dust jacket, she planned to have its breathtaking design duplicated on a negligee. True, the publisher's blurb was a bit fulsome; she could not truly regard herself as the peer of Dostoevski, Dickens, Balzac, Flaubert, and Zola, but perhaps such encomiums were necessary to stimulate sales.

"And that isn't all!" Prang added vehemently. "On publication day, she cabled flowers to the entire editorial staff, and begged us to cut her royalties in half because she felt our advertising appropriation was overgenerous."

"Jiminetty!" I said. "Well, I hope you send me a copy. Good book, is it?"

"Unreadable," he snapped. "A bomb. That's not the point, though. This dame's behavior throws a brand-new sidelight on authors." He shook his head perplexedly. "Maybe the bastards *are* human, after all."

For a moment, I thought of vindicating my profession dramatically with a right cross to the man's jaw, but it occurred to me that he might vindicate his with a right cross to mine, and I forbore. Reviewing the episode later, however, I wondered if the lady's testimonial, while magnanimous in the extreme, may not be fraught with perilous implications. Across the years, publishing has come to expect—in fact, to predicate its very existence on—the author's mistrust, his rancor and perversity. If suddenly he were to start fawning on his sponsors like a coach dog and rhapsodizing all over the place, his *amour-propre* would vanish overnight, a generation of executives trained to grovel and demean themselves would become obsolete, and the whole structure of the business might disintegrate. As a corrective to any such trend, as well as an illustration of how one creative artist combatted it, I submit a brief correspondence between Marshall Crump, a prominent New York publisher, and Cyprian Wynkoop, a fledgling poet:

FEBRUARY 13

MY DEAR MR. WYNKOOP,

I guess each one of us gets tongue-tied when writing to his idol, be he Joe Blow scratching out a fan missive to Sinatra or a prominent New York publisher lauding a genius like yourself. This is the third stab I have made at expressing my homage to you; I tore up the other two stabs, because, frankly, I was afraid you would deem them a bit overboard. Nevertheless, and at the risk of earning your ill will, I must speak my piece. In my humble opinion, Cyprian Wynkoop is destined to rank among the literary greats of all time. He stands like a colossus among his contemporaries, already enshrined on Olympus albeit he is very much alive and at the pinnacle of his powers. To his detractors (not that you have any, Mr. Wynkoop—a mere figure of speech) I say, show me one scrivener fit to tie Wynkoop's shoe. They cannot, by George, and I will tell you why. Because he is a giant among pygmies.

I can just picture a sardonic smile wreathing your physiognomy as, meerschaum in hand, you peruse these lines in your study. I can just hear you speculating, how does a roach like him have the crust, the presumption, to approach an immortal! The answer, sir, is that I refuse to be muzzled any longer. There is a conspiracy of silence aimed at keeping you in the dark, and I will not be a party to it. Your present publishers, Winograd & Totentanz, are crucifying you. All unbeknownst to you, they have dumped your latest brilliant compendium of poems, *Arabesque for a Gay Hetaera*, in a cut-rate drugstore off Nassau Street. A fine comment on our time—the American Keats remaindered for thirty-nine cents by a couple of pitchmen that I happen to know began their career demonstrating silver polish on the Atlantic City boardwalk. To such lengths will hoodlums go to clear their inventory.

Well, just wanted to pass along this tip in return for the profound sock you hand me whenever I run across your work, which will be quite often now that it is retailing for thirty-nine cents. Incidentally, if you feel restless for any reason in your current publishing setup, we certainly would mortgage the old homestead to have your clever pen in our stable. How are you fixed for lunch Tuesday? If agreeable to you, let's meet at the Puritan Doughnut Shop, at Ninth Avenue and Twenty-eighth Street. I usually eat at the Plaza or "21," but if some columnist spied us in a huddle, Winograd & Totentanz might do a burn, and the way things are breaking for you, you need all the friends you can get.

Cordially yours,
MARSHALL CRUMP

FEBRUARY 22

DEAR MR. CRUMP,

The noise in the cruller shop the other day was so deafening that I did not understand your proposition too clearly, and the cigar stump you chewed throughout lunch did nothing to clarify your diction. Hence, I am rather confused as to whether you offered me a twenty-five-thousand-dollar advance to show you the first twenty-five pages of a novel or twenty-five dollars for the first twenty-five thousand words. In either case, I carried away the impression of a glib trickster who would bear watching, and your frantic insistence that I pony up eighty-five cents for my share of the check further disturbed me. Please note that whereas you consumed a London broil with mashed turnips and beets, cabinet pudding, and coffee, I ate only two jelly doughnuts and a cup custard. If your firm has published all the best-sellers you claim, why should our initial meeting leave me forty cents the loser? It seems a poor augury for business relations.

On the other hand, Mr. Crump, despite the revulsion you filled me with, I have decided on mature reflection to flout every dictate of common sense and let you issue my next book. The financial details are inconsequential; my basic motive is altruism, the *réclame* your paltry imprint would acquire by publishing me. What consternation this has evoked in my circle I need not describe. To a man, my friends predict disaster, excoriating you as sneak thieves, pushcart peddlers, and worse. I, too, sense my utter folly but, quixotic simpleton that

I am, rush headlong into the abattoir. With best wishes and no illusions whatever,

> Yours,
> CYPRIAN WYNKOOP

FEBRUARY 27

DEAR WYNKOOP,

Sorry to have been out of the office when you visited us yesterday. The mixup about our twenty-five-dollar check bouncing was a stupid clerical error, and I assume complete responsibility. Miss Overbite, our bookkeeper, had drops put in her eyes for new glasses and on the way home from the specialist took a bus to White Plains by mistake. When she didn't come back after lunch, I naturally thought she had absconded, and stopped payment on several items. If you will deposit the check again in two weeks—three weeks, to be on the safe side —it should breeze right through.

And now for the big news, my boy. I stayed up till after two this morning reading the eleven pages you brought in of the new novel. I'm a pretty tough audience, Wynkoop, but this is perfection—this is the jackpot. There isn't an extra word, or comma. Except for the hero, the girl, and her parents, none of whom really come off, it's the merriest, most tragic, searching, and yet least depressing thing I have glimpsed in many a moon. Even if you never added another line, it would stand as a complete work of art—and right here is where my keen publisher's instinct bids me speak up. Let us not tamper with it, I say; let us bring out this sterling prose fragment as a novella that will sell like hot chickpeas now and whet the public's appetite for the finished product next fall. The idea had such a sensational impact around the office that a couple of the staff could hardly speak for a few minutes. Anyway, the book is already at the linotypers and you will have proofs inside two weeks. The only hitch I foresee is getting a classy enough portrait of you for the jacket. Could you possibly fly up to Canada this weekend and be photographed by Karsh? If the old writing schedule is too tight, of course, just holler and will get Karsh flown down to you. Meanwhile, best personal regards from

> Your devoted fan,
> MARSHALL CRUMP

MARCH 15

DEAR MR. CRUMP,

It took me the better part of an hour yesterday to decode the hysterical phone message you left here with my Lithuanian cleaning woman. I finally gathered that Hollywood was offering three hundred and fifty thousand dollars for the screen rights of my novella, that it had been chosen by both the Book-of-the-Month and the Literary Guild, and that William Inge and Gore Vidal were vying with each other to dramatize it. Whether the foregoing had actually happened or was imminent, I was unable to tell, owing to my handmaiden's tendency to scramble past and future tenses. One conclusion, nevertheless, was inescapable—that by bandying my work around the market place you have cheapened and degraded it beyond repair. All your vaunted reverence for my talent, your sycophantic flattery, is nothing but camouflage for your real purpose —to emblazon my name on the best-seller list, hamstring me with adulation and pelf, and convert me into a hack.

The attorneys I have retained to collect damages for the humiliation and loss of ego arising from your indignities are confident that any jury would instantly indemnify me to the tune of half a million dollars. Rather than expose your villainy in open court, though, I herewith offer you a proposal. Withdraw the novella from general sale and issue instead a limited edition, for collectors only, of one hundred copies on Japanese vellum. While you have permanently blasted whatever hope I cherished of attaining the status of a cult, I may yet regain the integrity I once had.

Yours truly,
CYPRIAN WYNKOOP

MARCH 28

DEAR CYPRIAN,

I apologize for not answering before; I have been laid up with a small stroke that hit me the day I got your letter. (Please do not feel you are responsible in any way—just overwork, aggravation caused by other writers, etc.) Owing to my absence, there was a little slipup in the office. My assistant, Miss

Overbite, forgot to notify the printer of your wishes, so the original trade edition of thirty-five hundred copies was shipped to the bookstores. Of course, I fired her, also stopped payment on the printer's check, but, after all, nobody is superhuman. In my condition, I did the best I could.

Fortunately, I have good news, too. The critics must have guessed our predicament and decided to let you down easy, because not one of them reviewed the book. How is that for professional courtesy? Only a man of your stature gets a break like that, and maybe the ball-point pens I distribute annually to the press don't hurt, either.

On the sales front, we anticipate plenty of action, as there is a terrific word-of-mouth across the country. To nudge it along, we are remaindering the book for thirty-nine cents in a few key spots like bus terminals, drugstores around Nassau Street where the brokerage crowd lunches, etc. Well, baby, so long for the present, and any time you're near the office, drop in and chew the fat with us. It should be Old Home Week for you now that we have decided to merge with Winograd & Totentanz.

Yours ever,
MARSHALL CRUMP

MARCH 30

DEAR MR. CRUMP,

To say that you have hoodwinked me and undermined my self-respect, forever destroyed any claim I may have had to artistic purity, would be the palest simulacrum of the truth. I have just come from Brentano's, where with my own eyes I saw half a dozen copies of my novella sold in as many minutes. The sight of those brutish, dishevelled customers pawing my work as if it were dress goods so revolted me that I groaned aloud. "Stop!" I wanted to cry. "Don't you realize you're stealing my birthright, you Philistines—that every book you buy diminishes me that much more?" That is what I wanted to cry, but somehow I could not.

Perhaps this nightmare in which you have embroiled me was a necessary ordeal; perhaps I shall emerge the nobler artist for it. In any event, this letter formally dissolves our association.

I have just signed a contract with an altogether obscure publisher of chess books and almanacs in Philadelphia. He may not have a fancy office, a scapegoat like Miss Overbite, and a pair of unprincipled yahoos as partners, but at least he has facilities for keeping his author's books out of the hands of the public. Wishing you every conceivable tribulation, I am,

As always,
CYPRIAN WYNKOOP

Hello, Central, Give Me That Jolly Old Pelf

I WAS TEETERING on my heels the other evening before our fireplace, quaffing a tankard of mulled ale, puffing on a churchwarden, and waving both in unison to a rousing stave—altogether a frightfully good simulacrum of one of Surtees' English sporting squires—when a wayward spark from the hearth suddenly ignited the skirts of my shooting coat. My whipcords stood out like veins, and in consequence I was obliged to remain *hors de combat* the next couple of days, propped up on my elbows and reading the most mealy prose. The situation might have proved less irksome had I been permitted some real intellectual exercise—I was halfway through Newman's *Apologia pro Vita Sua* and frantic to know how it came out—but my physician, in an effort to immobilize me, had decreed a strict invalid's diet of newspapers and predigested periodicals. The only redeeming feature of the entire affair, in retrospect, was that it enabled me to catch up with a few late developments in the advertising world as seen through the high-powered lens of Mr. Peter Bart, of the *Times*.

Inasmuch as Mr. Bart's column is buried deep in the financial section of the paper, and deals in large part with shifts of advertising appropriations and personnel, the casual reader may easily miss his more delectable tidbits. Typical of these was a report in mid-July of the aggressive strategy agency officals employ to secure new accounts. A couple of them, for example, "arranged to have two athletes in gymnastic attire break into the presentation. One carried a huge steel spike and the other an immense hammer. After one athlete hammered the spike into the floor with a resounding blow, the agency president called out dramatically: 'We can give your advertising greater impact.'" Whether the recipient of these attentions crowed in delight, ground his canines in rage, or merely sank deeper into apathy is not crystal-clear; what does emerge with certainty from Mr. Bart's chronicles is that advertising men stick at nothing in their creative frenzy: "One ad man who had proposed an unorthodox campaign to a prospect . . . rented a horse, painted it blue, and deposited it in the front yard of his prospect's Greenwich, Conn. home. Around the neck of the blue horse was a sign urging: 'Don't be afraid of being a horse of a different color.'" This tactic must have evoked many a chuckle from the owner of the horse and the A.S.P.C.A., to say nothing of anybody conversant with Swift's pungent chapters on the Houyhnhnms and the Yahoos in *Gulliver's Travels*.

Another, and rather more disturbing, anecdote of Mr. Bart's dealt with a new wrinkle for tapping the feminine market— a sort of sinister conversational chain reaction. An agency called Inform Associates, founded by a former schoolteacher named George Levine, has set up a network of housewives in four Eastern cities, each member of the sodality pledged to deliver a hundred one-minute commercials to her friends and acquaintances. "To keep track of their output," the story explained, "the women carry around a pocket-sized meter on which they register their commercials, delivered either in person or by telephone. The women consist mostly of active club members who circulate a great deal in their communities, says Mr. Levine. . . . Some women may be irritated when they find out that their friends are firing commercials at them, but Mr. Levine does not believe this problem to be serious. 'Consumers are so conditioned to constant commercial interruptions on radio and television that, like the Pavlovian dog, they miss them when they are not forthcoming,' he states." Intent on his target, Mr. Levine appears to be blissfully unmindful (or do I mean mindless?) of the hullabaloo, the sheer bedlam, the scheme may result in. However torpid one's imagination, it cannot help but reel at the thought of thousands of scarlet-faced club ladies, their glottises distended and their meters clicking as they bombard each other with panegyrics to their favorite detergent, laxative, or anti-perspirant. Goodbye Walden; hello Donnybrook Fair.

The most provocative item in Mr. Bart's bag of goodies, however, concerned the holiday season looming ahead. "A new service will be offered this Christmas to children who are bored with writing their requests to Santa Claus," he reported. "This year they can talk to Santa directly via something called the Santa Phone. Santa Phones will be set up at banks and department stores. . . . The service works like this: Stores having Santa Phones will invite children to pick up the receiver and talk directly to Santa in the North Pole. Santa, to be sure, turns out to be an employee in the back room who asks the child what he wants for Christmas. He also asks his name and address. This information is duly recorded, and a few days later the child's parents receive an envelope containing direct mail advertising for the products requested by the children. In the end, the children may get their presents, but the parents, not Santa, foot the bill."

That Madison Avenue has at last managed to strip Christmas of all the sentimental argel-bargel that has veiled it and transform the holiday into a pure, unbridled orgy of merchandising is epochal news. Henceforth, children will get the gifts they hunger for, no matter how fanciful, and their parents will be held liable for the cost, however crippling. The simplest way to demonstrate the fiendish beauty of the Santa Phone, I suggest, is to drop in on the household of Roy and Murine Isnook, a representative suburban couple engulfed by the Yuletide and desperately treading water.

(*Scene: The Isnook living room the night before Christmas. As the curtain rises, Roy Isnook, panting with exertion, has just finished gift-wrapping a sizable doll house and a Flexible Flyer in gossamer-thin, billowing pliofilm. His wife is perched on a kitchen ladder, trying to suspend a freshly baked gingerbread man, which keeps crumbling to bits under her fingers, from the topmost branch of their Christmas tree.*)

ROY (*with satisfaction*): Well, honey, this is one holiday that won't put a crimp in the family exchequer, by the Lord Harry. Thanks to our native resourcefulness, these presents for our little nippers—Cosette, aged eleven, and Robin, nine—add up to a piffling sum.

MURINE: You mean that you actually fabricated that doll house, indistinguishable from those that F.A.O. Schwarz retails at five hundred berries, out of an old crate you wheedled from our local supermart? And that the sled was a factory second, discarded by the inspectors, which you quick-wittedly glommed from the company ash heap?

ROY: Yes, that is precisely what I mean. Can you blame me for preening myself on my sagacity?

MURINE: No, but I fear lest we may have carried economy too far, as witness this gingerbread man flaking into limbo. Maybe I should have used more cornstarch to bind the various elements together.

ROY: Ah, well, no need to pummel our brains over bygones now that the exposition is complete. Tell me, hon—just for curiosity's sake—did the little shavers happen to mention what they wanted for Christmas?

MURINE: Not directly, but when we were in the bank last week I overheard them speaking over the Santa Phone. Albeit she is still wet behind the ears, Cosette asked for a sable wrap and a baguette-diamond bracelet. Her brother said he was figuring on a sleek convertible—a Rolls, if memory serves.

ROY (*derisively*): Boy, what a couple of boobs. I suppose they think Kriss Kringle or somebody's going to drive up here and bring 'em that stuff. (*The purr of a sleek convertible, scarcely audible to anybody but a dog or a reader of David Ogilvy, and therefore more likely than not a Rolls, is heard offscene.*) Who in the world can that be?

MURINE (*peering through the Venetian blind*): Search me. A corpulent individual of executive mien, under whose arm I descry a cardboard box bearing the legend "Revillon Frères," seems to be striding forcefully up to the front door.

ROY: Mr. Follansbee, our bank manager, answers closely to that description, but why should he pay us a midnight call? (*Follansbee, a portly Mr. Gotrox in a befrogged astrakhan greatcoat, his smile reminiscent of a cheese blintz freshly fried in butter, enters briskly.*)

FOLLANSBEE: Evening, all. This the Isnook residence?

ROY: That's right. I'm Roy Isnook, and this is my wife, Murine.

FOLLANSBEE: Glad to make the pleasure of your acquaintance, friends. I'm Hollis P. Follansbee, of the Counterfeiters' and Kiters' National.

ROY: You don't have to tell me. I'm a depositor there.

FOLLANSBEE (*his banker's caution suddenly aroused*): You are, eh? How do I know that?

ROY: Why—er—lemme see. (*Producing his wallet*) Here's a blank check.

FOLLANSBEE: That doesn't make you a depositor, Mac. Anybody can carry around a blank check.

ROY: Are you calling me a liar?

FOLLANSBEE (*His smile reveals four rows of teeth, like a basking shark.*): Not at all. I'm merely asking you to identify yourself.

ROY: O.K.! O.K.! Don't take *my* word for it. Ask her who I am!

FOLLANSBEE: Why should I?

ROY: Because she's been living under the same roof with me for twelve years. She's my missus!

FOLLANSBEE: She is, eh? How do I know that?

ROY (*heatedly*): Would she be standing there holding a gingerbread man if she wasn't?

FOLLANSBEE: Listen, Pappy, when you're in the banking business as long as I am, you get used to some pretty weird sights.

MURINE (*indignantly*): What's wrong with my flannel housecoat?

FOLLANSBEE: The fleur-de-lis device is upside down.

MURINE: That's the way it was in the pattern, wise guy. You think you know more than the Butterick people?

FOLLANSBEE: You bet I do. I hold a second mortgage on their plant.

MURINE: Well, go ahead and foreclose! I hope you drop dead, you rummy!

FOLLANSBEE (*stung*): Look here, madam, I went out of my way this Christmas Eve to bring your children their presents! I drove over icy roads without any chains—

ROY: He's right, dear. The least we could do is show our hospitality—ask him to sit down or something.

MURINE: Well, I don't like his attitude. The man from United Parcel always has a nice smile, even when they're on strike.

ROY (*wigwagging*): But Mr. Follansbee's from the *bank*—you know, the monthly payments on our pool, the refrigerator—

MURINE: Oh, *that* Mr. Follansbee? (*Hastily*) Here, do sit down and have a drop of this leekoor, Mr. Follansbee! They call it Fiore d'Alpi, on account of that little tree inside the bottle.

FOLLANSBEE: No, thanks muchly. I just stopped off to deliver the youngsters' presents so they won't be disappointed in the morning. Here is Cosette's wrap, nestling inside the sleeve of which reposes her diamond bauble. The auto her baby brother specified, needless to say, is purring in the driveway.

MURINE (*sobbing*): To think that practically yesterday my little boy was riding up and down there on his scooter.

FOLLANSBEE: No use hiding your heads in the sand, folks. You can't turn back the clock. (*Extending a delivery slip*) Here, sign on the bottom.

ROY: Gorry, Mr. Follansbee, you'll never know how happy . . . (*Gulps*) I got such a lump in my throat I can't even say it.

FOLLANSBEE: What?

ROY: Those kids'll never believe there ain't a Santa Claus. Of course, you and I know it's only an employee in the back room.

FOLLANSBEE: We do, eh?

MURINE (*anxiously*): Of course. Isn't—isn't that what Mr. Bart had in his column in the New York *Times*?

FOLLANSBEE (*his eyes twin gimlets set rather close together*): *Times*? What's that—some tomfool newspaper or other down there?

ROY: We—we got a fat envelope from you people last Thursday with—uh—some leaflets, like, inside, but I thought—that is, *she* thought—it was only an ad. (*Whimpering*) It came third class. . . .

FOLLANSBEE: Yup. (*Extracting a document from his greatcoat*) Well, just sign this form in triplicate, both of you, and I'll fill in the details from your installment card at the bank. The gifts total thirty-three nine hundred—let's say thirty-five grand for convenience. Added to what you already owe on the house, your car, the TV, the children's tuition, the washer, the cruiser, the freezer— Have I overlooked anything? (*Roy and Murine shake their heads mutely.*) Wait a minute. Didn't you buy a dog on time? An Irish wolfhound, from the Bosthoon Kennels?

MURINE (*snuffling*): He was run over by the milkman two months after.

FOLLANSBEE: Tough luck, but you still owe a two-hundred-and-twelve balance on him. O.K. Let's say that all comes to another thirty-five Gs. Add another twenty for interest. Mmmm. Ninety thousand. Over a twelve-month period, that works out at seventy-five hundred a month—exclusive of carrying charges, natch.

ROY: Mr. Follansbee, I make a hundred and twenty-four dollars and fifty cents a week—one hundred and five and eighty-nine cents after deductions—

FOLLANSBEE (*brightly*): Then why not consolidate all your debts? We'll loan you a hundred thousand at twenty per cent —that's a hundred and twenty thousand at forty per cent, or a hundred and sixty-eight at eighty per cent, if we handle the paper. Or you can go to Handelsman Associates, the creative-management group, borrow the money from them, pay us, borrow the money from us, pay them, and amortize the children. (*He sponges the foam from his lips.*) What was the dog's name?

MURINE: Garryowen. His—his great-grandfather belonged to a gombeen man in Dublican. I mean a publican in Dub, a Mr. Kieran.

FOLLANSBEE (*shortly*): I've met the man. We served in the Easter Rebellion together—him and I and Patrick Ahearn, or, as he now likes to style himself, Myles Na gCopaleen.

ROY: Mr. Follansbee, we're giving the presents back! You can't hold us to what a couple of dopey kids asked for on the phone!

MURINE: That's right, Roy—they're minors! We're not legally responsible!

FOLLANSBEE (*silkily*): For a tape recording in which Mrs. Isnook approves the order?

MURINE: I didn't any such thing!

FOLLANSBEE: Let me read you the relevant portion of the transcript. (*Affixes pince-nez to his cheeseparing nose*) As Cosette finishes, ROBIN'S VOICE: "If she gets all that, I'm figuring on a Rolls-Royce convertible!" An adult voice cuts in. WOMAN'S VOICE: "O.K.! O.K.! Come on along!" (*To Murine, pleasantly*) I don't think twelve jurors good and true should have any difficulty in distinguishing that voice, do you, Mrs. Isnook?

MURINE: I was only trying to get those little idiots away from the phone!

FOLLANSBEE (*At his smile, icicles form on the tree.*): That's what the jury'll be called on to decide, Mrs. Isnook! (*Refrogging the shawl collar of his astrakhan*) Well, friends, a Merry Christmas to the four of you, and don't bother to walk me to the bus. I'm as warm as toast. (*He opens the door, admitting a gust of snowflakes and a gaunt, stoop-shouldered individual resembling Eamon de Valera bundled in a worn trench coat and a long green muffler. As the two jockey and sidestep each other,*

Follansbee starts in recognition, then hurtles out the doorway into the darkness. The visitor blinks at the Isnooks through steam-veiled pebble spectacles.)

VISITOR: Good evenin' to yez all. Ahearn's my name, Myles Na gCopaleen to my friends, and it's good news I have for someone named Isnook holdin' ticket BNX6556 in the Irish Hospitals' Sweeps. Would annyone here offer a thravel-stained wayfarer a cup of tay?

CURTAIN

The Sweet Chick Gone

[*Another Plum from the Anthropomorphic Pie Containing* Born Free, Ring of Bright Water, *etc.*]

THE FIRST faint flush of dawn silvered the bedroom windows of my Sherry-Netherland suite this morning as I awoke, stretched voluptuously, and, slipping into a peignoir, perched on the vanity. While not given to excessive conceit —we White Leghorns, if less flamboyant than your Orpingtons and Wyandottes, take pride in our classic tailored lines— I was pleased by the reflection the mirror gave back to me. My opulent comb and wattles, the snowy plumage on my bosom, and the aristocratic elegance of each yellow leg adorned by its manicured claws all bespoke generations of breeding. In this great metropolis that slumbered around me, was there, I asked myself, one pullet half so celebrated and successful, a single fowl who could contest my supremacy? I had beauty, wealth, the adoration of the multitude—and yet, on either side of my aching beak, I saw tiny telltale grooves of discontent, and I knew that, despite its outward glitter, mine was a hollow triumph. I had reached a pinnacle undreamed of in poultrydom, but at what fearful cost.

With an impatient cluck, I shrugged off my introspective mood and hopped into the living room. The reek of cigars, the overflowing ashtrays, and the highball glasses mutely attested to the parasites—the agents and lawyers, tax experts and business managers—who battened off me. Here they revelled away their evenings, sipping my liqueur Scotch and (I ofttimes suspected) jeering at my artlessness. "She's only a silly little White Leghorn," I could hear them commenting cynically to each other. "Better get yours while the getting's good." Well, I reflected, at least I didn't suffer from the illusion that money purchased loyalty and affection; S. G. Prebleman had seen to *that*. At the thought of my first and greatest benefactor, a wave of such intense anguish enveloped me, such acute yearning to nestle in his arms, that I was forced to cling to a drape until equilibrium returned. Then, fluttering to the window sill, I stared down over the greenery of Central Park and surrendered to a train of bittersweet memories.

A yellow ball of fluff cheeping in a New Jersey incubator —why had Fate capriciously singled me out for greatness from that swarming brood? I remembered how anonymous I had felt on my emergence from egghood, deafened by the clamor of my hatchmates, buffeted in the melee around the feeding troughs. Scarcely were my pinfeathers dry when I was swept into a carton with a score of others, whirled through the maelstrom of the postal system, and deposited outside a hardware store in Perkasie, Pennsylvania. Those were halcyon days for us fledglings; basking in the adulation of passersby, simpered at and fawned over, we strutted about like harem favorites, imagining ourselves the hub of the universe. As time wore on, though, I grew increasingly restive at the inane cackle of my companions. Most of them were brainless females, interested only in the narrow, circumscribed world of the barnyard. Their one ambition was to mate with some supercilious rooster, bear his progeny, and lapse into stultified cold storage. A strong dash of nonconformism, inherited from who can say what remote gamecock ancestor, prompted me to cavil with them, and when—to my surprise as much as theirs—I found I could put my rebelliousness into words, I earned their universal enmity. A glib chick indeed—by what right had I acquired the power of speech? The pain of social ostracism was more than I could endure, and, dimly sensing that verbalization was taboo, I then and there took a vow of silence. If a fluent tongue condemned me to be a pariah, never again, I swore, would I open my mouth.

It was at this crucial point that the catalyst appeared, the person who was to change my life—S. G. Prebleman. As he later confessed to me, he had no more prescience than I of the fateful meeting that impended; he and his wife had driven into Perkasie that forenoon for a new hammock and some onion sets, and the impulse to buy a few baby chicks was wholly spontaneous. The sound of his voice, before I even saw him, struck a deep, responsive chord in my being. "Fourteen cents apiece?" I overheard it exclaim incredulously. "Honey, they're a steal! We could stick a bunch of these in the barn, feed 'em table scraps—it'd cut our grocery bills in half!"

"Good grief, haven't we trouble enough already?" a weary contralto voice protested. "Next thing I know, you'll be raising chinchillas."

"Which it's a daffy idea, I suppose," the male voice rejoined. "Well, Bright Eyes, just for your information, there happens to be big money in chinchillas. I read an article the other day in the *American Boy*—"

"Senility, here we come," she interjected. "The *American Boy* collapsed ages ago. But don't mind me—you go on reading it if it gives you pleasure. Listen, I'll meet you at the parking lot."

As her footsteps receded, a florid face bisected by a piebald mustache loomed into view overhead. The eyes behind the tiny steel-rimmed lenses devoured us greedily for a moment; then our whole world went topsy-turvy again. Huddled in a basket on the floor of a station wagon, a dozen of us jounced into another and far more precarious phase of adolescence. Prebleman, whose bucolic knowledge derived in the main from *Walden*, knew nothing whatever about rearing domestic fowls. He constructed a sleazy coop out of several fly screens, and, in lieu of the traditional diet of mash and cracked corn, fed us potato chips, olives and soggy cashews, stale hors d'oeuvres, soufflés that had failed to rise, and similar leftovers. Odd as it may seem, I thrived on this regimen— the only one who did, I must admit, for my eleven comrades croaked almost at once—and developed into a fine, meaty bird. As sole survivor of the flock, I naturally attained a special niche in Prebleman's affections. Whenever he trundled a barrowful of empty bottles to the dump (a daily ritual, it seemed), he would stop by to gloat over my progress. I had no inkling of the future until, one spring day, he leaned over my run and blurted it out.

"Hi ya, gorgeous," he cooed, smacking his lips. "Mm-hmm, I can just see you in a platter of gravy next week, with those juicy dumplings swimming around you. Hot ziggety!"

Horrified at the doom in store, snatching at the only means I had to avert it, I groped for and recovered my faculty of speech. "You—you vampire!" I spat at him. "So this is why you coddled me—fattened me—"

"What did you say?" he quavered, turning deathly pale.

"Not half of what I'm going to!" I said distractedly. "Wait till I spill my story to *Confidential* and the tabloids. Wife beater! Lothario! Wineskin! I'll blow you higher than a kite!"

He stuffed his fingers into his ears and backed away. "Help! Help!" he screamed. "It spoke—I heard it! A talking chicken!" He stumbled off down the slope, and seconds later the household was rent by agitated babble. From what little I could glean, his recital was dismissed as just another attack of the fantods, but when he reappeared toward dusk with a peace offering of kasha steeped in milk, I instantly sensed a profound change. His manner was conciliatory, almost servile.

"Look, Miss, we're not cannibals," he began awkwardly. "That stuff about eating you was only bantam—I mean . . ."

One cannot but display magnanimity toward genuine contrition; I besought him to ignore the whole incident, and we soon established a healthy rapport. After satisfying himself with a few questions as to my verbal ability, he put forward a most arresting proposal—in essence, that we collaborate on the story of my life. Flattering though the offer sounded, I felt obliged to point out that I had never written anything. "*Ach,* you won't have to," he assured me. "I'll put it into prose. All you do is talk into a tape recorder, off the top of your head—er, excuse me, at random."

"But isn't a chicken's career rather stodgy?" I demurred. "I'm afraid people wouldn't find it very exciting."

"Honey, I'll make you a prediction," said Prebleman, producing a contract and a fountain pen. "Three days after this book of ours appears, it'll lead the best-seller list. You'll have guest shots on Paar, Sullivan, Como—you pick 'em. The magazine rights alone'll net us three hundred Gs. Add to that the movie sale, the dramatization, and, of course, the diary you keep meanwhile, which George Abbott turns into a musical so the whole shooting match starts all over again. No more whitewashed roosts for you, girlie. You'll be sleeping between percale sheets!"

What with visions of myself sporting diamonds the size of hen's eggs, and his honeyed assurance that our agreement surpassed Zsa Zsa Gabor's with Gerold Frank, I was too dazzled to mull it carefully, and while I thought Prebleman's ninety-per-cent cut excessive, I signed. The project, we found,

demanded readjustment of both our schedules. To avoid rousing his wife's suspicions, my collaborator proposed we work at
night. I countered that, unlike him, I was generically unfitted
for slumbering in the daytime. At last, we compromised by
foregathering at 3 A.M., spurring ourselves on with black coffee and NoDoz. On occasion, our creative ardors did in fact
awaken Mrs. Prebleman, but her spouse quick-wittedly clapped
me under his dressing gown and feigned somnambulism.

To recount the tribulations we underwent once our task was
finished would serve no useful purpose. Suffice it to say that
my story everywhere met reactions ranging from skepticism to
open hostility. Time and again, Prebleman offered in vain to
transport me to Publishers' Row to prove the manuscript's le-
gitimacy. Unfortunately, at the one audition he contrived—an
address to the partners of Charnel House—I was stricken with
laryngitis, and the meeting broke up amid catcalls. Finally, Arthur Pelf, a weasel who ordinarily published spurious sex counsel and curiosa on birching, consented to sponsor the book.
The rest is literary history; overnight, *Vocal Yolkel* became a
sensation, a veritable prairie fire. Five editions were exhausted
in a fortnight, Sol Hurok pacted me to a speaking tour of fifty
principal cities, and David Susskind announced a four-way
telecast between the two of him, myself, and Julian Huxley
on the topic "Which Came First?" The critical reception we
evoked was quite as overwhelming. John Barkham and Virgilia
Peterson coined enough superlatives to fill a book, which was
immediately published by Bernard Geis Associates, converted
into a musical by George Abbott, and closed in New Haven
after one performance.

But my gratification was destined to be short-lived. Although astronomical revenue poured in from these and other
sources as well, like records and mechanical toys, I saw none
of it. Prebleman had tucked me away in a shabby theatrical
hotel on New York's West Side, under the watchful eye of an
ex-pugilist friend, the while he lolled in luxury at the Waldorf
collecting the lion's share of our income. At my merest allusion
to money or an accounting, he either clammed up or shrilly
accused me of ingratitude and venality. Heartsick that success
had disrupted us, but powerless to act, I prayed for any release from my intolerable plight. It came from an unexpected

quarter. One afternoon, while my custodian was absent in the barbershop, a floor waiter entered stealthily, carrying a pillowcase. "Sh-h-h!" he warned. "Listen, fools rush in where Wiseman fears to tread."

"Wha—what do you mean?" I asked.

"That I adopted this guise to spring you," he whispered. "I'm Phil Wiseman of the Amalgamated Talent office, and we can break your contract with that muzzler."

"That's what all you agents say," I said distrustfully. "Supposing Prebleman drags me to court."

"He wouldn't dare," Wiseman asserted. "We could blackmail him for transporting a chicken across a state line. Here —slip into this bag."

While the idea of such Machiavellian tactics was abhorrent, it was the only way out of my dilemma, and I reluctantly acceded. Wiseman sped me to a prepared hideout in Fordham Road, a kosher butcher shop where I remained incognito in a flock of other Leghorns until the litigation subsided. As I had prophesied, Prebleman did his utmost to discredit me, but was ultimately persuaded to accept a cash settlement. We never saw each other again; many months afterward, I heard he was haunting various obscure Pennsylvania hatcheries, pathetically mumbling to the crates of chicks as they emerged and hoping to duplicate his coup.

And here was I, I reflected as I gazed at the pigeons wheeling over Bergdorf Goodman, at once the luckiest and loneliest creature on earth. I had everything—my own television program, a syndicated newspaper column, reserved seats at every preem, jewels, cars, furs—but it was so much tinsel. I would gladly yield it all to nuzzle the man's dressing gown again, to caress that prognathous jaw and see those pinpoint eyes twinkle in the lamplight. For I realized ineluctably that, despite his avarice, treachery, and general swinishness, S. G. Prebleman was the most lovable galoot I had ever known.

Nobody Knows the Rubble I've Seen/
Nobody Knows but Croesus

YOU MEET them wherever you roam, in Helsinki or Hong Kong, Patchogue or Perugia, Moscow or Martha's Vineyard—those aromatic, imperious, gravel-voiced characters with unlit Coronas embedded in mahogany faces, clad in Italian silk suits tailored by Sy Devore. Their fashionably haggard wives flaunt Buccellati's latest brooch or Gucci's shiniest handbag and sprinkle their speech with melting allusion to Billy (Wilder), Irving (Lazar), Harry (Kurnitz), Irwin (Shaw), and all the other gods of Leonard Lyons' daily pantheon. They drive Aston-Martins as a matter of status but secretly prefer Cadillacs, maintain a *dacha* in Palm Springs but yearn for one at Klosters, and frenziedly collect the more abstract Expressionists, disdaining any upstart who owns less than two Rothkos and a Rauschenberg or, in exceptional cases, two Rauschenbergs and a Rothko. Whether in Nyack or Nairobi, Bessarabia or Bonwit Teller, "21" or Timbuktu, they are as unique, unmistakable and easily identified as the water moccasin, and just as lovable. Though they migrate widely and mate wildly, they always return in due course to their native habitat, six square miles of reclaimed desert in southern California called Beverly Hills.

For economic reasons too painful to enlarge on here—my father was euchred out of his share of the Iraq oil fields by Calouste Gulbenkian, and, lacking the adroitness to pick pockets, I was forced to become a screenwriter—I dwelt among these high rollers for more than a decade, from 1931 to 1942. But for the sunny benevolence that was my sole heritage from Dad, I might well have been scarred for life. So awesome was the display of ostentation around Beverly in the thirties, so reminiscent of Maggie and Jiggs the lordly swagger and mincing condescension, that it made one's toes curl. In the words of a friend of mine characterizing a movie mogul, a member of the community, it was a case of "from Poland to polo in one generation." Like that fabled satrap, most of the residents were

picture folk—producers, actors and directors—and they strove
to outdo each other socially, sartorially, and, above all, archi-
tecturally. The broad, palm-fringed streets of the compound
were lined with *estancias* worthy of Porfirio Díaz, ante-bellum
Southern mansions that put Natchez to shame, Renaissance
palazzos, Japanese pagodas, and turreted Norman châteaux
with catapults designed to hurl boiling schmaltz onto the in-
vader. Over the immaculately barbered lawns and the exotic
shrubbery lay a vast cathedral hush like that of an expensive insane asylum. No bee droned in the greenery unless his credentials were checked; the whole district, from Coldwater Canyon
to the La Brea tar pits, was off limits to the commoner, and
anybody chancing into it on foot was promptly lagged on suspicion of vagrancy. The late Mr. William Faulkner, taking a
quiet constitutional along Alta Placenta of a Sunday morning,
was whisked off to the jug to languish five hours, plaintively
protesting, in his hominy-grits accent, that he was a harmless
scribbler. The desk sergeant finally sprung him, though not
without an admonition that Faulkner looked like a cat burglar
and had better hire himself a Thunderbird PDQ if he wanted
to stay out of the pokey.

If a Nobel Prize winner could stub his toe so unwittingly, it
was no wonder that my wife and I were wide-eyed greenhorns
at our first sight of the Promised Land. Never had we beheld
anything as paradisiacal as Hollywood: the benign sunshine,
the vast open-air markets bursting with produce, the friendly
passersby lithe and tanned in their sportswear, the cunning
boutiques full of bronze baby shoes, miniature turtles, Mexican saddles worked in silver, and photos of real-life movie stars.
Oranges six dozen for a quarter! Hillocks of succulent figs and
dates for a dime! Totally forgetting our hatred of citrus in any
form save lime rickeys and old-fashioneds, we raced around
amassing bushels of tangelos, grapefruits, lemons and nectar-
ines. Inside three days, our hotel swarmed with flies and we had
generated enough acid to charge every storage battery at River
Rouge. Meanwhile, the scales had begun to fall from our eyes
and we were acquiring some perspective on the inhabitants of
this Arcadia. Every mother's son was on the muscle, trying to
sell us an authentic Vermeer exhumed from a Pasadena hock
shop, to trace our genealogy, to get a studio audition for a

gifted ten-year-old who played the musical saw like Heifetz or to bury us in an exclusive cemetery guaranteed free of seepage. Their buoyant health, needless to say, was pure illusion; hypochondriacs all, they subsisted on cracked sawdust and parsnip juice, and daily shrank their brains on the analytic couch to purge themselves of devils. In between obeisances to Freud, they banded into a hundred weird sects; the town boiled with Swedenborgians, fire worshippers, Gnostics, Anabaptists, students of Bahaism, Penitentes, Vedantists, Puseyites. When I returned from the studio one afternoon and found my wife, two joss sticks protruding from her ears, recumbent before a statue of Ishtar, I knew it was Curtainsville. What we needed was a little white cottage as far away from Hollywood as possible, where my angel could bake salt-rising bread and I could potter around with a pair of shears, snipping *Mammalia ponderosa* from the girlie magazines. I sprang to the Yellow Pages and began combing them for a reliable real-estate agent.

Mrs. Pandora was an angular harpy in a set of cashmere sweaters and three strands of pearls, with alabaster choppers gleaming in a face clearly inherited from a praying mantis. In purest Santa Barbara labials, she apprised us instanter that she was a blue blood reared at Snedens Landing and that she dealt only in Beverly Hills rentals. To shoehorn a couple of plebeians into the preserve would demand all her guile, but she regarded it as a challenge. Cringing and knuckling our forelocks, we besought Mrs. Pandora to open her box. The first place she showed us was a Louis XVI *gentilhommière* of thirty-six rooms and nine baths on a bluff overlooking Sunset Boulevard. It had a boxwood maze in which the original owner, an Osage Indian lush, had lost his way and perished of thirst. Prior to his demise —or perhaps afterward, Mrs. Pandora was not quite sure—he had shot the bulbs out of all the candelabra, which made the house a difficult one to entertain in.

"What's that clanking sound I hear?" my wife inquired of the caretaker, peering into the murk.

"Oh, that's just the oil rig, ma'am," he replied. "Mr. Wildgoose had it installed in the basement to pump his bourbon upstairs. I leave it run to remind me of him like."

A steal though the house was at twelve hundred a month, the noise revived memories of my lost patrimony, and we mushed on. In rapid succession, Mrs. Pandora unveiled a Moorish mosque which, to provide adequate muezzins for its minarets, would have bankrupted us; an all-glass dwelling, whose rooms were demarcated by curtains of toilet chains; and a swank bootery opposite the Beverly-Wilshire that she felt would convert into a home at trifling cost. The profusion of footstools made it an ideal setting for bingo parties or a minstrel show, but Madame, with typical feminine capriciousness, insisted on a more conventional abode. At last we hit on the perfect solution, a modest Cape Cod Colonial of primrose stucco flanked by a pool. Depositing fifteen hundred dollars and three gills of blood as security, we moved in, hired a maladroit Estonian cook, and prepared to live graciously. At seven the next morning, I was aroused by a deafening tattoo at the front door. I stumbled downstairs and found a woolly mammoth on the order of Andy Devine, garbed in a seersucker robe and swim trunks.

"Whassamatter, stupid, you got sleeping sickness?" he bawled. "I been half an hour here waiting for my dip!"

Before I could marshal my wits, he elbowed me aside and, bursting open the French doors with a crash that showered the patio with glass, flung himself into the pool. As he wallowed about, spitting and snorting through his blowholes, I rushed to inspect the terms of our lease under an infrared lamp. Sure enough, there it was—a sneaky codicil entitling any chum of the landlord to use the premises whenever the whim overtook him. The ensuing two months were purgatory. Hordes of loafers trooped through the house filching cold chicken from the icebox, phoning friends in Marrakesh and Tasmania and scrawling graffiti on the bathroom walls. The coup de grâce was a wienie roast staged in the garage by a couple of the *vitelloni* employing an armful of first editions and a jerrican of gas. When the insurance adjuster finished assaying the remnants of our Auburn coupé and handed me a settlement of $3.17, I threw in the towel and sent out an SOS for Mrs. Pandora.

A rigid diet of dandelions and spaghetti over the next two years, plus the pittance my wife earned demonstrating potato graters at the Farmers' Market, enabled us to meet the rent on a cavernous bungalow of California redwood off Benedict

Canyon. Its Stygian interior was full of black widows, but since we could afford only wood alcohol and were blinded much of the time, the darkness scarcely mattered. To redeem matters somewhat, I was doing well at the studios; a movie I had written, in which two people find love after their sexes are transposed by a mad scientist, was being hailed by the critics and my salary had tripled. This determined us to move into a residence befitting our new prestige in the community. Mrs. Pandora was radiant at the news.

"I've got just the spot for you!" she exulted. "A teensy jewel box over on Salpiglossis Drive, authentic Queen Anne and furnished with the most adorable antiques. Of course Mrs. Pinchpfennig would never accept your social references—her people practically founded Altoona, you know—but let's offer her an extra hundred a month to overlook your background."

The bribe was effective and the stash everything she had claimed—a decorator's dream, all Chippendale and rare Chinese wallpaper, carpeted in Aubusson and upholstered in *toile de Jouy*. My wife's bliss as she fussed over the tea service was touching, but I felt unfulfilled; the house lacked warmth—ideally a majestic, wrinkled bloodhound snoozing on the hearth. From earliest youth, I ululated, all through my bachelorhood, I had craved one of these noble creatures. I conjugated my longing so persistently that at length the poor woman gave way. Within minutes, I was onto a kennel in Sherman Oaks, where a litter of outstanding pups was visible. An hour later, eleven velvety little rascals with soulful eyes were tumbling over me in their pen, gnawing my ears and kissing me. From their number I chose, after long deliberation, a ravishing female, a Barbara La Marr of the dog world, and christened her Liza. Since we paused frequently on the homeward journey to neck, the trip was a long one and Liza ravenous on arrival. As my wife watched her gulp down three pounds of hamburger, a box of charcoal biscuits, half a dozen raw eggs, and a slab of jack cheese, her face paled in apprehension.

"Listen," she said nervously. "This cannibal queen you came up with—do you think we can support her?"

Conscious of what an impulsive ass I had been, I took refuge in bluster. "O.K., that tears it!" I shouted. "Begrudge me the one thing I've ever wanted—a homeless little puppy! What if she does eat a few scraps? Why, the dough you squander on shoes alone—"

"In heaven's name, stop screaming," she broke in. "No wonder your birthstone's the amethyst—your face is the very same color. I'm sure the dog'll find something to eat."

Her words were prophetic; during the night, Liza managed to extricate a crown rib roast and a pecan pie from the kitchen, and for good measure ate the legs off a fiddleback chair. Chained to a jardiniere the following night, she freed herself with a mere headshake and consumed several petit point cushions and a George III shaving stand. Toward dawn, she was stricken by the memory of our necking party and began baying, a doleful, unending howl that echoed from Laurel Canyon to the shores of Malibu. Word that a manhunt was in progress spread like wildfire, and pandemonium reigned supreme. Lying abed with my teeth clenched, I reached the only possible conclusion. I threw on a coat over my pajamas, slung Liza into the car, and broke every speed limit back to the kennel. Nobody stirred to witness the prodigal's return; I deftly inserted her into the cage among her kinsmen and vamoosed, leaving the owner a puzzle that probably triggered a nervous breakdown. As for Mrs. Pinchpfennig, she magnanimously agreed to a compromise of $2,200 in court, which, added to my legal fees of $1,750, got us neatly off the hook, and we moved into a motel.

When the swallows returning to Capistrano deposited a small pink-and-white bundle on our doorstep, a gypsy existence was no longer feasible, and Mrs. Pandora reappeared with her Aladdin's lamp. This time, she produced a Spanish hacienda the size of the Alcázar, its massive walls embossed with bulls' heads squirting water into fountains. The property was particularly favored by writers, she confided as she led us on a tour of inspection; in fact it was currently occupied by some novelist named Aldous Hochspiel or the like, said to be terribly famous, who was writing a musical for George Raft at M-G-M. I had never met Huxley, toward whom I was idolatrous, and my disappointment grew as we traversed the rooms without even a glimpse of him. Just as we were leaving, Mrs. Pandora smote her forehead.

"Gracious, what a ninny I am!" she squealed. "I forgot to show you the upstairs powder room!" Useless our protest that we could imagine it; she refused to listen. "No, no, you've got to," she insisted, herding us back. "It's simply delightful, an absolute dream!"

Up we trudged through an endless circuit of corridors, and eventually, with a triumphant bleat, she threw open a door. There, in the middle of a hexagonal room lined with mirrors, crouched my hero, myopically pecking at a Hermes portable. As he caught sight of us, he sprang upright, defensively clutching the machine to his breast in a flutter of yellow second sheets that swirled about him like leaves. For an aeon, the three of us hung there confronting genius at bay reflected from every known angle. Then Mrs. Pandora broke the spell.

"Thank you, Mr. Hochspiel," she chirruped. "Well, that's the upstairs powder room."

Why we ever rented the place, except that I fatuously hoped to absorb Huxley's gift by osmosis, I cannot remember; but two months afterward, we had cause to regret it. One evening, as the maladroit Estonian was serving dinner, she idly informed us that a man had called that morning about the rats in the trees.

"The wh-which in the trees?" my wife stammered, dropping her fork.

"The rats," said Narishka impatiently. "You know, that palm tree in the patio where the baby naps. He stuck on some kind of a collar to keep 'em from jumping down."

I chuckled at the improbable tale and, overturning a plate of soup to reassure the child's mother, strolled out to investigate. To my consternation, there was indeed a baffle on the tree trunk, of the sort used on ship's hawsers in port. With the smoothness of a well-oiled mechanism (which I was at the moment), I leaped into action. I flew back into the house, dabbed ammonia on my spouse to revive her, and phoned the police that an outbreak of cholera was imminent. Then, wrapping our infant in an Andalusian shawl, I fled with it to Schwab's drugstore and instructed Sidney Skolsky to put the story on the A.P. wire.

Back at the *ranchería*, meanwhile, my wife had hastily thrown together a few necessities like her Buccellati brooch

and Gucci handbag, and in less than an eyeblink we caught
the midnight choochoo back to Alabam'. Months later, in the
Swiss Alps, I received a note from the authorities explaining
the mystery. Our next-door neighbor, an elderly Gorgon afflicted with insomnia, had neurotically convinced herself that
the dry clashing of the palm fronds was caused by rodents and
had so complained to the Board of Health. Hailing my vigilant
public spirit, the note extended a warm invitation to revisit
Beverly Hills and the promise of a lively welcome on our return. I may very well, if nothing better turns up, but frankly,
I've always considered tar and feathers so unbecoming to a
chap. Don't you?

Three Loves Had I, in Assorted Flavors

THERE IT LAY in a dusty recess of our Pennsylvania attic, atop a pile of other discarded records—Cole Porter's "Experiment," played by Ray Noble and his orchestra—and there I crouched that winter's day, heart-stricken, simianlike, to avoid concussing myself against the rafters. To think that a quarter of a century had elapsed since I used to play it over and over, marveling at the smooth precision of the brass, the buoyant lines in the refrain so characteristic of Porter: "The apple on the top of the tree/ Is never too high to achieve./ So take an example from Eve./ Experiment!" Heavy with nostalgia, I bore it downstairs, and when our laundryman peered through the window ten minutes later, he saw his customer, eyeballs capsized, gliding about with a broom in his arms, an unreasonable facsimile of Fred Astaire. Why I was thus engaged, or what associations the song held for me, I could never explain to such a hayseed, but I can do so here. "Experiment" was the outstanding tune in *Nymph Errant*, an English musical I labored to convert into a Hollywood film back in the thirties, and now that TV's jackals roam where once I fought and bled, the sorry tale may finally be told.

The architect of my misfortunes was, in actuality, a very decent bird—a producer named Sonny LoPresto, who himself was a successful songwriter and Broadway celebrity. From the outset his attitude was refreshingly candid and succinct; he made no effort to minimize the problems ahead. "Kid, I'll be honest with you," he said through his knees. (The armchairs in his office were so deep that we could hardly discern each other's face.) "This property was wished on me by Wingfoot Shaughnessy, the head of the studio. He saw it in London, with Gertie Lawrence in the lead, and he flipped—bought it on the spot. Now, it's a great Cole Porter score, a crackerjack, but the book— Well, it's going to need lots of elbow grease to get a picture out of it. Which is why I'm teaming you with Cy Horniman on the screenplay."

"Cy Horniman?" I repeated incredulously. "But his specialty is hoods. He wrote all that underworld stuff for Cagney over at Warner's."

"Damn right he did," said LoPresto, beaming. "He's got a terrific plot sense—he'll give you enough situations to make a hundred musicals. So what if the guy only thinks in terms of blood and guts? Use him—milk his brain!"

It baffled me that, of the twelve hundred and fifty members of the Screen Writers' Guild, LoPresto couldn't have picked a pen with a daintier nib to complement mine. However, professional ethics enjoined silence, and I acquiesced—not without foreboding.

Horniman was hours late for our initial conference the next morning, and when he did totter in, unshaven and half asleep, he looked pretty shopworn. His face, which bore remnants of the starry-eyed beauty typified by Nell Brinkley's Adonises in the Hearst press, was puffy with dissipation, and a resentful scowl, as of one persecuted beyond endurance, corroded his forehead. As he fell back on the davenport in my office, racked by yawns, I noticed he was wearing a suede tie spattered with food stains. It was an unimportant detail, but I had a premonition our union was going to be shortlived.

"Christ, what a hangover," he murmured, combing his hair with his fingers. "We must have killed two quarts of tequila last night in Olvera Street, this Mexican cooz and I. My head is so hot you could fry an egg on it." He paused—I suspected, waiting for me to produce a skillet—but I registered polite concern and said nothing. "Well, anyhow," he resumed, "I wish I'd met Conchita ten years ago. I wouldn't be paying alimony to those two vampire bats I married. They stripped me of everything but what I've got on."

I could understand why they had left him his tie; nevertheless, I pretended commiseration, and delicately inched around to our project. Horniman confessed he had not yet read the basic material, but he said he would digest it that evening.

Two days passed by without any word, during which I built up a substantial head of steam. On the third he phoned to propose that we work at his home to escape the distractions of the studio. His lair, when I ultimately found it, thirteen miles below the Signal Hill oil fields, turned out to be a bungalow in a heavily wooded canyon—a refuge, he explained, from leeches like process servers and federal tax agents.

"Hell, it's too late in the day to talk script," he said, and cracked his knuckles. "I had Conchita prepare us lunch before she left for the cannery, so we'll just have a little snort and relax. Do you drink Moscow mules?"

I never had; nor, judging from the effects, will I ever be induced to again. After a purely nominal intake I experienced a feeling of exaltation, in the course of which I gobbled quantities of cold frijoles washed down with muscatel. There ensued a sudden thunderclap, as though I had been hit with a broadaxe, and then I was face down on the patio listening to my collaborator, garbed in a sarape and sombrero, pick out "Las Cuatro Milpas" on a guitar. The subject of *Nymph Errant* did not arise, needless to say, and our two subsequent meetings at the studio were similarly fruitless. Horniman was in a strange comatose state on both occasions; his conversation rambled, and I detected a sickly-sweet odor, unfamiliar to me at that time, emanating from his cigarettes.

A day or two afterward LoPresto summoned me to his office. "Don't bother to tell me how the yarn is going," he said. "I'll tell you. Your partner's on Cloud Nine and I've decided to replace him. From now on, you work with Byron Burrows, the author of *Dead on Arrival*."

"Sonny, this is a *musical*," I protested. "What kind of casting is that? Burrows is Horniman all over again—another gangland expert!"

"Yep, and a first-rate story mind," he said. "He's just the man to supply the skeleton for your brittle, sparkling japes. So get over there pronto and huddle with him—he's in that adobe villa across from Wardrobe."

Whereas most scenarists were housed in buildings like the Irving J. Thalberg Memorial, at Metro—whose façade doubled as an apartment dwelling or a high-grade mortuary on occasion—Burrows was permitted his own bower, and it was a lulu. To paraphrase Dashiell Hammett's dictum "The cheaper the crook the gaudier the patter," it was a case of the cheaper the scribe the gaudier the pad. The décor was a mixture of schools—the pecky-cypress walls adorned with pewter, fusing La Cienega Boulevard with Louisburg Square;

an English kneehole desk; *toile-de-Jouy* curtains; and even a ceramic fox of the sort found in Madison Avenue antique shops. Burrows, a pallid, bespectacled chap, arose to greet me from a swollen red-leather lounge chair. In a community where facial tics were a commonplace, his were exceptional; they literally pursued each other across his features like snipe. The source of his turbulence soon became apparent—he was the most fearful hypochondriac I had ever met. We had barely started to discuss an approach to *Nymph Errant* when Burrows chanced to emit a slight cough. Instantly he was on his feet, groping toward a shelf crammed with medical books. He thumbed through one of them, hurriedly consulted an illustration, and collapsed into his chair.

"Finished," he croaked. "I've had it—I'm done for. Oh, my God."

I took the volume—Koch's standard work on tuberculosis —and looked at the plate, a detail drawing of lymph nodes in technicolor warranted to freeze the marrow. In my naïveté I sought to persuade the man that his alarm was unfounded, but he was impervious to reason. Throughout our association he was forever swallowing lozenges, spraying his throat, scanning his fingers for nonexistent pustules, and palpating his abdomen, and much of the time he was so busy taking his temperature that he was speechless. Like all imaginary invalids, he felt he had evolved a regimen that catered to his special needs. At II A.M. our secretary brought him a tall glass of buttermilk and half a glass of bourbon. At four the dosage was reversed —a large bourbon followed by a small buttermilk. During our fortnight together there was no visible change in his condition, but we managed to eviscerate *Nymph Errant* and construct a species of framework. Though we had minor disagreements— like his insistence that Dion O'Banion and Bugs Moran would quicken the action—our relationship was amicable. One Monday, though, the secretary greeted me with chilling news. Burrows had suffered an attack of the rams over the Sabbath and had been removed to a rest home in Tucson to dehydrate.

"Buck up, my boy," Sonny LoPresto counseled as I sat in his quarters, profoundly discouraged. He quoted numberless ordeals out of his Broadway past that had ended in triumph. "I know how rough it's been, but we're out of the woods at last. I've been combing the agents' lists and I've got you the perfect teammate—Lothar Perfidiasch, the noted Hungarian playwright."

"And plagiarist," I supplemented. "He's been sued for every play and movie he ever wrote—or, rather, didn't."

"Granted, but a great constructionist," he emphasized. "After all, there's only six basic plots in the world, and it's up to you, with your shrewd nose for the unusual, to winnow out his ideas and select the least obvious. He's waiting for you in the commissary."

As indeed he was, over a third *Schlagobers*, his crafty eyes atwinkle above the white carnation he always sported; he was well aware of the disarming influence of flowers. The usual anecdotes about Ferenc Molnár and Budapest tricksters consumed our first afternoon. Subsequently Perfidiasch started bunting plots at me one after another, all too familiar to steal —*Fifty Million Frenchmen*, *Lady, Be Good*, *Roberta*, *A Connecticut Yankee*, along with everything Maugham and Sherwood and Coward had written. In the end I consented to one I couldn't identify—a farce of Georges Feydeau's, I discovered years later—and we fell to work.

Some seven weeks thence, just as we were nearing the final sequence of the screenplay, LoPresto called us in. He was pink with embarrassment. "Men, it kills me to break the news to you, but there's been a terrible mistake," he said. "Wingfoot Shaughnessy is convinced that the *Nymph Errant* he saw in London was about some dames who open a charm school for sourdoughs in the Klondike. Maybe it was, or maybe he ate too many liqueur candies that night. Anyway, he's the boss, and when I told him our version he blew his stack and canceled the picture. Turn in your kimonos."

I was eastward bound aboard the Chief the following noon, and it was many months before I heard the coda to our *Phantasiestück*. On the day I left, a young novelist, freshly arrived from New York to adapt his book, checked into the studio and was assigned my office. In rummaging through the desk, he came upon our script and, eager to absorb the technique of screenwriting, lay down on the davenport to peruse it. Uninured to the damp chill of southern California, he switched on the petcock of the gas radiator, nobody having warned him that it must be lit manually. He was slowly drifting toward the Final Fadeout when, by the happiest of coincidences, salvation appeared in the form of my collaborator. Perfidiasch, in search of his cigar case, threw open the door and beheld the recumbent azure-faced stranger. His behavior, if indefensible by medical standards, at least saved the young man's bacon. He pummeled and shook him violently back to consciousness, and, before the other could rally his thoughts, began excoriating him. "What are you doing, you idiot?" he shouted. "Are you crazy? They find you here, a stiff with these dialogue pages on your chest, and the next thing you know, my friend is dragged off the train at Needles on a murder rap! . . . *Say*—could this be an idea for a picture? Excuse me, I must call up Sol Wurtzel at Fox right away. . . ."

Be a Cat's-Paw! Lose Big Money!

A NYBODY CAN BE a wiseacre after the fact, so let's get one thing straight at the outset. In chronicling the complications that arose from a note I found this spring in a bottle on Martha's Vineyard, I am not whining for sympathy or seeking to condone my behavior. If a totally unselfish gesture to a stranger—a benefaction, really—is wrong, then I was culpable and richly deserving of what I got. Impulsive, overly sentimental I may have been, but never throughout the ensuing imbroglio, I contend, was I prompted by base or ignoble motives. On the contrary, I like to think that, though an innocent dupe, I acquitted myself at all times with a dignity, a gentility, few other dupes in my position would have displayed. That is what I like to think.

The circumstances under which I discovered the note couldn't have been less dramatic. I was strolling along South Beach on the Vineyard one morning midway between Gay Head and Zack's Cliffs, and there, squarely in my path, lay a flask of the sort that usually contains stuffed olives. On the scrap of paper inside, in a clearly juvenile hand, was the following: "My name is Donald Cropsey. I am twelve years old. I live at 1322 Catalpa Way, Reliance, Ohio. I have been visiting on Nantucket for a week. I threw this bottle off the ferryboat between Nantucket and Woods Hole, Mass., on Saturday. Please write me a note telling me when and where you found it."

Now, twelve-year-old boys, and especially those who litter the shoreline with glass, invariably raise my hackles, but somehow this message disarmed me. Its style was direct and unaffected, there was nothing cringing or subservient about it, and it exuded a manly independence characteristic of the wide-awake youngsters that Horatio Alger and Oliver Optic used to portray. I therefore pocketed the note—figuratively, that is, since I wore only bathing trunks—and later in the day complied with Donald's request. After recounting how it had reached me, I felicitated him on his vigorous, clean-cut rhetoric and his astuteness in modeling himself on such masters of English prose as Hazlitt and Defoe. Lest his ego become inflated, however, I hastened to point out that his handwriting was sorely deficient. "You will forgive me if I speak quite bluntly, my boy," I wrote, "but this progressive-school script of yours demeans you. I cannot stress too strongly the importance of good calligraphy in molding your future. A firm business hand with well-shaped capitals is a prerequisite in every field, be it the counting house, a mercantile establishment, or a profession like law or medicine. I suggest, accordingly, that you proceed with all dispatch to perfect yourself in the exercise known as Hammond arm movement, keeping the wrist flexible at all times and practicing the letter 'l' lying on its side."

As I weighed the foregoing prior to sealing the letter, it struck me that a few words of counsel to the lad on his reading would not be amiss. I recommended, hence, that he familiarize himself with all the works of Henty, with the stories of Harry Castlemon (*Frank Before Vicksburg*, *Frank on a Gunboat*, etc.), with Ralph Henry Barbour's *Around the End*, and with anything by Altsheler he could find. He might also browse through the files of Hearst's *American Weekly* with profit, I added, quoting examples of the curious lore to be found there—the *S.S. Vaterland* posed vertically against the Singer Building to contrast their size, the eye of the common housefly magnified a hundredfold, the milk baths and other beauty secrets of Lina Cavalieri and Gaby Deslys, the advice on physical fitness from Jess Willard, and the disclosures about high society's Four Hundred by Count Boni de Castellane. In closing, I extended warm wishes and urged him to put his best foot forward, his shoulder to the wheel, and his nose to the grindstone—a pose guaranteed to excite the compassion of influential folk who might help him in his career.

I had quite forgotten the episode when, a month later in New York, I received a letter from a Mrs. Rhonda Cropsey. Writing on the stationery of a midtown hotel, she identified herself as Donald's mother and thanked me effusively for my epistle. She had taken the liberty of opening it, inasmuch as her son was in El Moribundo, California, visiting his father, from whom she was estranged. So brilliant, so truly inspired was my letter that before forwarding it she had made a copy, which she reread daily until every syllable was engraved on her heart.

"What a wonderful person you must be," she went on. "A kind of saint, I imagine. Who else would trouble to reply to a child they didn't know, or bother to outline a program of studies to enlarge the little fellow's horizon? Never in all my twenty-eight years—yes, I am that young, even if I sound like an old fuddy-duddy—have I felt such gratitude to an individual. I really would do anything to reward them. . . . But here I am wasting your valuable time with my silly-billy compliments; I guess I just can't help 'fessing up to hero worship if I feel same. Anyway, the reason for my contacting you at present is that I am in your bailiwick a day or two shopping for some feminine 'frillies' and wonder could we meet for five minutes to discuss little Don's next educational step. Won't you ring me very soon, pretty please?"

Well, that put me on the spot for fair. Here was a doting mama, undoubtedly a frump from backwoods Ohio, thirsting to talk me deaf, dumb, and blind about her precious darling, and yet to ignore her appeal would be tantamount to a slap in the face. I stewed over the problem for a good ten minutes and finally had an inspiration. I'd humor the woman and phone, but avoid any confrontation, wheedle or coax me though she might.

"Hello? . . . Yes, this is Rhonda Cropsey." The voice wasn't at all what I'd expected. It was low-pitched and cool, and there was a delicious tremor in it that made one's spine tingle. "O-oh, can it really be *you*?"

"Who else?" I stammered. "I mean—hello. Yes, it's me. Look—er—I've just had a cancellation. I'm terribly busy as a rule, but I could be at some central point like the Plaza bar in half an hour, if that's not inconvenient for you."

Not in the least, she quickly assured me—that would be ideal. I then gave her painstaking, explicit instructions as to which bar I meant, in case she blundered into the Palm Court or the Edwardian Room. Actually, my fears were groundless; far from a flibbertigibbet, Mrs. Cropsey proved to be not only alert but a demure and strikingly attractive young matron. If her figure was a shade too sensual for true beauty, it was compensated for by features that some Pre-Raphaelite painter—Burne-Jones or Dante Gabriel Rossetti—might have limned. Under a wealth of corn-colored hair worn in a snood, a pair of

blue eyes looked out at the world with such trustful innocence
that it wrung your heart. Her lack of sophistication became
further evident when I asked what beverage she fancied.

"I-I've never tasted anything stronger than fruit juice,"
she confessed shamefacedly. "That cocktail you're having—
a sidecar—what is it?"

I explained it was a mild digestive, compounded of the mer-
est trace of brandy and a drop of Cointreau, and, reassured,
she ordered one also. In a few moments our initial constraint
had vanished and we were chatting away like old friends. It
seemed hardly possible, I remarked, that one so girlish could
have a twelve-year-old son, and she was equally incredulous at
my laughing admission that I was past thirty. From the wisdom, the magnanimity implicit in my letter to Donald, she was
prepared for a man twice, if not thrice, my years.

"Gracious, what a difference between you and that husband
of mine!" she murmured, a shadow of pain contorting her
lovely forehead. "Do you know that that swine used to beat
me black and blue?"

Since I had never laid eyes on the swine in question, I felt ill-
equipped to pass judgment, so, limiting my reaction to a pity-
ing headshake, I ordered another round of drinks and deftly
steered the conversation to her son. Precisely what advice did
she seek from me about his schooling? A guilty blush suffused
Mrs. Cropsey's cheek, and she hung her head penitently. Concerned as she was for the boy's welfare, she admitted to an
ulterior motive in approaching me. She had tentatively selected
a number of frocks, suits, and coats at a Fifth Avenue store and
wanted me, her sole friend in New York and a man of faultless
discrimination and taste, to choose the most becoming from
among them. She realized it was a dreadful imposition, she
was already indebted to me beyond measure, but this one final boon would forever enshrine me in her affections, elevate
me to Olympus. . . . In vain I protested my inadequacy to
judge feminine fashions; the more vehement I grew, the more
insistent she became, and at last, succumbing to a mixture of
cajolery and sidecars, I broke down and assented.

In actual fact, the decisions Mrs. Cropsey exacted of me
turned out to be trifling enough. I ran my eye expertly over
the garments she was considering, compared various details of

design and workmanship, and unerringly chose the best. The salesladies were frankly awed at my acumen, doubtless supposing that I was some biggie from the garment center. So harmonious was the atmosphere and so obliging the staff that my companion bought a few other articles—an expensive negligee, a couple of imported handbags, six pairs of shoes, and some diamond clips suitable for sportswear. At her request, and for a bumper fee, all the purchases were dispatched by messenger to her hotel, and a floorwalker, rubbing his hands and bowing obsequiously, escorted us to the credit office, where she was to make payment. Suddenly, as she was rummaging in her bag, she emitted a startled exclamation. "My traveler's checks!" she gasped. "They're gone—they've been stolen! No—no—wait! I remember now—I left them behind at the hotel."

Drumming his fingers on the desk top, Seamus Mandamus, my lawyer, regarded me fixedly for several seconds over his glasses. "I see," he said with infinite sympathy. "So you helped her out, I take it. You wrote a check for the amount and then returned to her hotel so she could reimburse you."

I stared at him nonplussed. "How did you know?"

"Oh, just instinct." His smile radiated sheer benevolence. "Now, let me guess. When you got there, Mrs. Cropsey remembered something else. She *hadn't* left her checks in the hotel safe, as she thought at first, but in her room. So you accompanied her upstairs—right?"

"It wasn't a room—it was a suite," I corrected. "She had a living room with a pantry, a bedroom—"

"Yes, yes, I know what a suite is," he said impatiently. "Anyhow, there was a fifth of Scotch and some ice in the pantry, so she invited you to fix a drink while she went into the bedroom to fetch the checks."

"This is uncanny!" I exclaimed. "I swear, you sound as though you'd been there the whole time."

"If I had, Buster, you wouldn't be sitting here now with an ashen face," he rejoined. "One minor point, though. How did you reconcile the bottle of hooch with the lady's earlier statement that she never drank anything stronger than fruit juice?"

"Why—uh—it didn't occur to me," I said. "I may have been a little fuzzy from the sidecars."

"And the strain of shopping and all." He nodded benignly. "But I imagine the fuzziness evaporated pronto when Mrs. Cropsey reappeared, eh? Weren't you startled that she had slipped into something more comfortable—something clinging and filmy?"

"Great, Scott, man, you must be clairvoyant!" I marveled. "Matter of fact, I *was* bowled over. But then, on top of everything, before I could catch my breath, those two hooligans with the camera burst in. There was this blinding flash—"

"You needn't go on," he interrupted. "It's cut and dried, a standard procedure. Did the fair one break into hysterical sobs after they left and lock herself in the bedroom?"

"You took the words out of my mouth," I said. "I hammered on the door for over half an hour, but not a tumble did I get. That was the last of Rhonda Cropsey."

"Not quite," replied Mandamus gently. "In case you still don't know the score, it becomes my painful duty to enlighten you. You are currently a co-respondent in the divorce action of Cropsey *v.* Cropsey, and a large, angry department store whose check you stopped is suing you for eleven hundred and eighty-five dollars in merchandise. I wonder whether you've learned anything from this experience."

I certainly had, though I wouldn't admit it to *that* shyster. The next time I see a bottle on a beach—or anywhere else—I intend to compress my lips in a thin line and kick it out of my path. And that goes for all twelve-year-old brats on the Nantucket boat and their blasted mothers.

Moonstruck at Sunset

I BELIEVE IT was Hippolyte Taine, the historian—or possibly Monroe Taine, the tailor, a philosophical chap who used to press my pants forty years ago in the Village—who once observed that immortality is a chancy matter, subject to the caprice of the unborn. Not every notable wins his niche in the hall of fame on precisely the terms he would have chosen, and for every marbled dignitary in the Borghese Gardens or the Bois de Boulogne there is another who survives only as the trademark of a cigar, an italicized entry on a menu. Could Dickens have visualized himself as the patron saint of a tap-room on West Tenth Street, or Van Gogh as the tutelary god of an Eighth Avenue cleaning establishment? Neither Dame Nellie Melba nor Lily Langtry, certainly, would have been content to face posterity as they have, one as a dessert and the other as a foundation garment. Perhaps the most eccentric parlay of this kind I know of, though, was unwittingly generated in the brain of a British novelist named Robert Hichens. When he spun his famous tale of Domini Enfilden's desert love and entitled it *The Garden of Allah*, he never could have foreseen the landmark by that name—or, worse yet, a punning version of it—that would rise one day in Hollywood to perpetuate the glory of a Russian actress.

The actress, of course, was Alla Nazimova, and in naming a cluster of hotel bungalows on Sunset Boulevard the Garden of Allah the builder paid impressive tribute to her talent. (Since the builder happened to be Nazimova herself, there was never any question of her sincerity. With the passage of time, unfortunately, Nazimova's reputation waned and the Islamic cognomen prevailed.) As Hollywood architecture went, the place was fairly restrained—a sprinkle of tile-roofed, Neo-Spanish villas centered about a free-form pool—and its clientele equally so. Most of the hotel's guests were migratory actors, playwrights, and similar gypsies with tenuous links to the picture business, and if they reveled, they did so discreetly and in whispers. This was a source of perplexity to the press, notably a Manhattan columnist I once encountered on the grounds. It was his conviction that debauchery was mother's milk to screen folk, and he had selected the Garden of Allah as a vantage point to study it. Unable to find any orgies, he became morose, drank an immoderate amount of whiskey one night, and dove headlong into the pool in his dinner clothes. After his return to the East, he wrote a description of a couple of saturnalias he had attended in the Garden which would have shocked Petronius out of his toga.

The time was 1931, and my wife and I were recent arrivals in Hollywood, unfamiliar with its mores and domiciled in a sleazy bungalow court near the studio where I was undergoing my novitiate as a screenwriter. Our flat was less a home than a bivouac. The walls were plasterboard, the pastel-tinted furniture the flimsy type found in nurseries, the rugs and draperies tawdry, and the kitchenware minimal. As for the conversation of our fellow residents that filtered through the walls, that also promoted no feeling of stability. They seemed to be constantly staving off bill collectors and betting on horses that never finished, exchanging symptoms of incurable diseases and rehearsing roles inevitably excised from films in the cutting room. But the rent was nominal and our discomfort somewhat allayed by the usual will-o'-the-wisp delusion that we were saving money hand over fist.

One evening I came home to find my wife dissolved in tears. After crystallizing her over a Bunsen burner, I managed to elicit the reason. A matron in Beverly Hills whom she knew had visited the premises that afternoon and pronounced them sordid. Ostracism, swift and pitiless, loomed in Filmdom unless we moved at once, her friend declared; the only possible locale that might restore the face we had lost was the Garden of Allah. I spurned the idea with such vehemence that the neighbors beat on the walls to quiet me, but their protests went for naught. In rhetoric that must have reminded them of Edmund Burke denouncing Warren Hastings, I poured vials of wrath on suburban snobbery; I blasted the colony's *nouveaux riches* until the welkin rang. When its strains died away, I realized the futility of argument and meekly started packing.

Since all the villas at the Garden were chockablock at the moment, we were lodged for an interval in a two-story annex overlooking the pool. The prospect from our windows was a soothing one—barbered lawns and shrubbery, emerald water rippling in the balmy California sunshine, and over all a genteel hush that bespoke affluence and contempt for vulgar display. Guests were rarely visible on the walks; occasionally a seamed old plutocrat in canary-yellow slacks doddered forth to exercise a Pekingese, or a European movie director in overtight satin shorts, mistakenly believing himself on the Riviera, would dog-paddle cumbrously about the pool, but otherwise the drowsy, peaceful scene was seldom marred. The first intimation of anything unusual came the second night after our arrival. Fire broke out in an apartment house nearby whose name immortalized still another celebrity—the Voltaire Arms —and some two dozen occupants of the Garden converged excitedly on the grass to watch. Among them were several screen personalities of both sexes whom we had no trouble identifying, as well as a number of prominent playwrights, executives, and agents. They were all officially married, but not to their present roommates. While startling, there was nothing indecorous about the assemblage; its members looked like sleepy children as they stood knuckling their eyes and gaping at the fire engines. One wondered if their faces would reflect the same dewy innocence in the divorce court.

Once ensconced in a villa of our own, it soon became evident that our neighbors, if more solvent than those in the bungalow court, were as peculiar. The man next door, for example, was a wizened homunculus who had edited one of the New York tabloids during the Peaches Browning era. Behind the smoked glasses that hid his saffron-colored face his eyes were on continual alert for some unseen enemy. I thought that perhaps he feared reprisals from gangland chiefs he had exposed, for he never ventured out except in a polo coat with upturned collar, and then only a few steps from his burrow. The explanation given my wife by our maid was more mundane: he was beset by process servers trying to collect the alimony he owed five women. His misogyny one day bore fruit. He wrote a book chronicling his vicissitudes, a best seller that became a hit play and eventually a musical smash—but his wives triumphed. They garnisheed his royalties, and he ended his days a bankrupt on a New Jersey goat farm.

In the cottage adjoining his was another enigma, a celebrated character actor whose behavior also occasioned intense
speculation. A suave, courtly leading man popular on Broadway and in films, he was married to a society beauty no less
distinguished than himself. Always arm in arm and solicitous
of each other, they seemed a devoted couple, except that she
often appeared in public with a black eye. He and I developed
a nodding acquaintance, and one afternoon, quite without
prompting, he confided to me that his wife had fallen the night
before and struck her eye on a birdbath. A few days later she
exhibited another shiner, contracted, he told me, in the same
manner. The third time it happened I was tactless enough to
ask if there was a birdbath in their villa, as I had seen none on
the grounds. Our friendship curdled abruptly, which may have
been providential. There were probably more black eyes where
his wife's had come from.

Gradually, as time wore on, other transients whose actions
defied analysis passed through the Garden—a gray-haired poetess who strummed a lyre outside her door for inspiration
while composing her verses, a nautical couple who hung out a
mess flag whenever they dined, and an Englishman who owned
what appeared to be a haunted Rolls-Royce. The car, a vintage
model, persisted in rolling out of the garage with nobody at
the wheel—a habit he vainly sought to curb by keeping chocks
under it and tying the gearshift with clothesline. It was obviously no easy task to minister to the whims of such diverse
folk, and how Virgil, the hotel's one-man staff, accomplished
it I could never understand. A stoop-shouldered, overworked
wraith with an air of patient resignation like that of ZaSu Pitts,
he doubled as clerk, bellhop, and Florence Nightingale, forever in transit to Schwab's drugstore to fetch midnight sandwiches for the tenants, searching out bootleggers to allay their
thirst, and nursing them through their subsequent hangovers.
Whatever the commodity or service one demanded, whether it
was caviar, a seamstress, bookends, or a massage, Virgil was the
genie who supplied it, and after repeated demonstrations of
his resourcefulness we began to regard him as superhuman. I
found out otherwise when, yielding to his incessant entreaties, I
bought two tickets to a spectacle called *The Love Life of Dorian
Gray*, an amateur production then current at a neighborhood

theater. The play was a fearful hash of epigrams torn out of context from the novel and refurbished with homemade apothegms such as "Love is like a lobster trap; those who are in wish to be out, and those who are out wish to be in." It was acted with unbearable elegance by a cast of heavily peroxided young men and one ill-favored girl, who clearly had backed the venture. Such was the lethargy it induced that by the final curtain all five of us in the audience—two drunken sailors, a nine-year-old boy, and ourselves—were petrified in our seats, unable to move. In the light of what ensued, though, I have to admit that the evening was not entirely wasted. The leading man, ranging the rest of the company before the footlights, requested our attention. "Ladies and gentlemen," he said earnestly, "exactly fifty-three years, six weeks, and four days ago, a traveler arrived at customs in New York who, when asked what he had to declare, responded, 'I have nothing to declare except my genius.' May I therefore ask you, my friends, to bow your heads along with ours in one minute of homage to a great playwright and a gallant gentleman—Oscar Wilde."

Though my horoscope failed to reveal that we were destined to revisit the Garden of Allah often in the following decade, one episode in that first tenancy remains forever etched on my memory. The film script I was crocheting at Paramount was a vehicle for a quartet of buffoons whose private lives were as bourgeois as their behavior on the screen was unbridled. Their actual identity is unimportant, but for those who insist on solving puzzles the ringleader of the group affected a sizable painted mustache and a cigar, and his three henchmen impersonated, respectively, a mute harpist afflicted with satyriasis, a larcenous Italian, and a jaunty young coxcomb who carried the love interest. Having supped repeatedly at the homes of all four, my spouse felt obliged to reply in kind, and, in an ill-considered burst of generosity, invited them and their wives to dinner at the Garden. "We'll have drinks and canapés in our place beforehand," she informed me, "and then take them over to the dining room." Overriding my protest that it was a catacomb, she said, "Yes, yes, I know how depressing it is, but Virgil's promised to put in two more forty-watt bulbs, and, anyway, they'll have such a skinful by then that they won't know what they're eating."

"OK, but that's only half the problem," I said. "How about the dog?" We had a fairly unruly pet at the time, a standard schnauzer who ate everything he could get his paws on. "He's never seen people like these—I better keep him locked up in the bedroom so he doesn't bite one of them. After all, they're my livelihood."

Deriding me as a Cassandra and a calamity howler, she went ahead with her preparations, ordering flowers and liquor as lavishly as if for a wedding and mailing elaborate reminder notes to the members of the troupe. On the appointed evening they appeared with their wives, the latter exhibiting noticeably sullen faces. I was not aware then of something I learned much later—that these kinswomen were at daggers drawn and never saw each other socially. While the men stood around glumly draining their cocktails, the ladies began exchanging barbs so venomous that I was afraid homicide might follow.

"I *love* your hat, darling," one complimented another who was wearing a cloche composed entirely of feathers. "You know something? It makes you look exactly like a little brown hen."

"You don't say," her sister-in-law replied sweetly. "Well, it's a long time since anyone called *you* a chicken."

As the tension mounted and the atmosphere became charged, I grew panic-stricken, and I may have mixed stronger drinks for the company than was prudent. At any rate, I, for one, was sufficiently expansive by the time we were midway through dinner to nourish the illusion that the party was a roaring success. In my relief at having averted mayhem, it mattered not that the food was inedible, the service appalling; I skipped about in the murk lightheartedly refilling everyone's wineglass, joshing the men and charming the ladies—I was, in a word, the perfect host. Indeed, my gaiety was so infectious that the assemblage sat there openmouthed, whether in wonder or overcome by yawns it was too dark to determine. Finally, however, my cornucopia of badinage and jollification was emptied, and the guests trooped back to our villa to retrieve their wraps. I strode ahead of them, giving my version of Richard Tauber interpreting the "Song of the Volga Boatmen" and, as I threw open the door, was confronted by a startling tableau: Cradled in the mink coat that belonged to Mustachio's wife lay our schnauzer, with an object I dimly recognized as her cloche bonnet between his forefeet. He had just stripped the very last feather from its surface and was smirking at us with the pride of an artisan whose work is well done.

Gone is the Garden today, and on its site there stands a curious structure that is either a bank housing an art gallery or an art gallery housing a bank—in Hollywood one never knows. Nowhere inside, though, will the cinema buff find a plaque or any clue to commemorate the shrine a Russian tragedienne erected to herself, and yet none is really necessary. Whenever I traverse Sunset Boulevard nowadays (which, praise God, is hardly ever), I always stop and bow my head in one minute of homage to a great actress and a gallant real-estatenik—Alla Nazimova.

THE BEAUTY PART

A COMEDY IN TWO ACTS

CHARACTERS

(*In Order of Appearance*)

OCTAVIA WEATHERWAX
MIKE MULROY
MILO LEOTARD ALLARDYCE
  DUPLESSIS WEATHERWAX
LANCE WEATHERWAX
SAM FUSSFELD
APRIL MONKHOOD
BUNCE
VAN LENNEP
HAGEDORN
VISHNU
HYACINTH BEDDOES
  LAFFOON
GODDARD QUAGMEYER
GLORIA KRUMGOLD
SEYMOUR KRUMGOLD
HARRY HUBRIS
ROB ROY FRUITWELL
MAURICE BLOUNT
BORIS PICKWICK
CHENILLE SCHREIBER
KITTY ENTRAIL
VERNON EQUINOX
MRS. YOUNGHUSBAND

GRACE FINGERHEAD
CURTIS FINGERHEAD
FISH-MARKET BOY
EMMETT STAGG
WORMSER
NELSON SMEDLEY
ROWENA INCHCAPE
RUKEYSER
WAGNERIAN
SHERRY QUICKLIME
ELMO
HENNEPIN
POTEAT
CAMERA MAN
HANRATTY
COURT STENOGRAPHER
POLICEMAN
JUDGE HERMAN J.
  RINDERBRUST
BAILIFF
ROXANA DEVILBISS
JOE GOURIELLI
MRS. LAFCADIO MIFFLIN

ACT ONE

ACT TWO

The Beauty Part

ACT ONE
Scene i

SCENE: *The library of the luxurious Park Avenue triplex of Mr. and Mrs. Milo Weatherwax. The decor is posh Madison Avenue Oriental crossed with Ginsberg and Levy early American. Constance Spry flower arrangements, a Buddha head, a vase, and two abstract paintings on walls.*

TIME: *Late afternoon.*

AT RISE: *As the STAGE LIGHTS up,* OCTAVIA WEATHERWAX, *a chic, poised woman in her late thirties, paces nervously* D.S.L. *and* R., *a crumpled handkerchief pressed against her lips.* MIKE MULROY, *a private eye in the classic Raymond Chandler tradition, stands nearby consulting a pocket notebook.*

MULROY: (*As* OCTAVIA *crosses* D.L.) No use being huffy, Mrs. Weatherwax. A private eye like I—like me, that is—I've got to know which skeleton's in what closet.

OCTAVIA: (*Crosses* D.S. *by* L. *end of couch.*) Your line of work makes a man pretty nosey, I daresay.

MULROY: (*Crosses* U.S., *puts hat on* C. *table.*) Look, Mrs. Weatherwax. I've got a dusty office in the Arbogast Building. My clients pay me a hundred dollars down as a retainer and ten cents a mile, but that doesn't entitle them to poke into my psyche.

OCTAVIA: Then we understand each other. Suppose you give me your report. (*Sits couch,* R. *end.*)

MULROY: (*Sits armchair. Nods.*) Mr. Weatherwax left the house at 11:14, took a hack to a dairy restaurant on Second Avenue, and had a plate of soup containing kreplach. I checked that out with the manager. He lives in the Bath Beach section of Brooklyn. Mr. Weatherwax then made a seven-minute call from a pay phone to a party on the Regent exchange.

OCTAVIA: A woman?

MULROY: (*Evasively.*) Well, I really don't like to say—

OCTAVIA: (*Rises and crosses L. of* MULROY.) See here, Mulroy
—I hired you to investigate my husband's extramarital didoes.
Let's not be *coy.* (*Crosses L., sits on couch.*)

MULROY: Yes, ma'am.

OCTAVIA: Now, who was she? Who is this person?

MULROY: A television actress, Mrs. Weatherwax.

OCTAVIA: A what?

MULROY: (*Rises, crosses L.*) Well, not really an actress. She
poses for commercials.

OCTAVIA: What kind?

MULROY: (*Crosses L. of chair.*) Er—ladies' underthings, I
believe.

OCTAVIA: What kind?

MULROY: (*Crosses R. of chair.*) Gee, Mrs. Weatherwax, does
that make any difference?

OCTAVIA: *What kind?*

MULROY: All right. Brassieres.

OCTAVIA: I deserve it for asking. How old is she?

MULROY: She's no chicken—at least twenty-three. A very ordinary girl—long legs—tiny waist. Her lips are too lush—kind
of ripples when she walks— (*Crosses R. to front of chair.*)

OCTAVIA: What does?

MULROY: (*Pantomimes.*) Her hair. It's chestnut and she
wears it loose— (*Sits chair C.S.*) cascading down her shoulders
—and when she laughs—

OCTAVIA: (*Rises, crosses R.* MULROY *rises. Sharply.*) That'll
do, Mulroy. You needn't launch into a rhapsody.

MULROY: Yes, ma'am.

OCTAVIA: This apartment you spoke of is where?

MULROY: East 73rd, between Park and Lex. Modified French
Provincial furniture with mirror accents and white wall-to-wall
carpeting. Foam chairs in fake zebra and a coffee table made
out of an old set of bellows. (*Refers to notes.*) The bedroom is
done in pink, with ruffles—

OCTAVIA: (*Crosses L., front of* MULROY *to front of couch.*)
Never mind. I can visualize it.

MULROY: (*Steps L.*) I'm sorry, I realize what a shock it always
is. I haven't been a private snoop nine years for nothing—

OCTAVIA: Thank you. Nice of you to empathize.

MULROY: (*Steps* L.) Mrs. Weatherwax, I'm not very good at putting my thoughts into words.

OCTAVIA: Say it in your own way.

MULROY: May I kiss you?

OCTAVIA: (*Crosses* L. *of* MULROY.) If you like. (*They embrace. She turns* D.S., *his arms around her.*) Oh, Mulroy, what's to become of us?

MULROY: I don't know. I don't care. All I know is that you've spoiled me for other girls.

OCTAVIA: I felt that in my heart's deep core.

MULROY: Octavia—

OCTAVIA: (*Back* L.) How dare you call me by my first name!

MULROY: (*Sheepishly.*) Maybe I overstepped.

OCTAVIA: (*Sits* R. *end of couch.*) You have. I'm one of the richest women in America, Mulroy. A mere nod from me creates a convulsion in Wall Street. My son, Lance, is Skull and Bones at Yale. It's time for you to leave the room.

MULROY: Yes, ma'am. (*Crosses* U.C. *table, picks up vase. Taking it from stand.*) My, that's lovely. Genuine Sèvres, isn't it?

OCTAVIA: Yes. How did you know?

MULROY: Oh, I dabble in porcelain a bit.

OCTAVIA: Isn't that strange? I rather sensed you had a flair.

MULROY: (*Puts vase back; picks up hat.*) I haven't been a private snoop twelve years for nothing.

OCTAVIA: It was nine last time.

MULROY: It seemed like twelve till you came along. (*Kneels* R. *of* OCTAVIA.)

OCTAVIA: That will be sufficient, Mr. Mulroy.

MULROY: (*Rises, crosses front of couch to* L. *of couch. Chagrined.*) Yes, I'd better get back and relieve my partner, Costello. He's on the fire escape outside her flat.

OCTAVIA: Yes, you'd better.

MULROY: (*Sits,* L. *end of couch.*) You ought to meet that Costello. He's the talented one. He's been exhibited at the Guggenheim.

OCTAVIA: Oh?

MULROY: He does these collages out of seawood and graham crackers.

(*Offstage SQUEAL and "Oh, Mr. Weatherwax!"*)

OCTAVIA: It's Milo. He's home.

MULROY: Hasta luego. (*Exits* L.)

(*SCREAMS from Off* R.)

OCTAVIA: Milo!

(MILO *enters.*)

MILO: (*Crosses back of chair.*) Now, look here, Octavia, I just had to give our French maid a severe dressing down.

OCTAVIA: So I heard.

MILO: (*Crossing* U.R.) There's loose rubies all over the foyer. A person could break their ankle! What are we living in, a pig pen? (*Opens painting to reveal bar.*)

OCTAVIA: How was your board meeting, dear?

MILO: (*At bar, pouring drink.*) Meeting? Why—er— (*Busies himself with glasses, then crosses* D.S.) I didn't attend. I had other fish to fry.

OCTAVIA: Yes, and they crackled, didn't they? (*Crosses* U.S. *of chair.*) Milo, this is the handwriting on the wall. Our marriage is washed up—napoo—*ausgespielt.*

MILO: (*Turns to her.*) You're trying to tell me something.

OCTAVIA: I mean that I'm restless, unhappy, bored, and you are, too. (*Sits in chair.*)

MILO: Maybe you're right. I'll admit I've been chafing at the bit a bit. (*Crosses* L. *of* OCTAVIA.)

OCTAVIA: Ah, well, the fat's in the fire. How are we to break the news to Lance?

MILO: (*Crosses* D.S.) What Lance is that?

OCTAVIA: Why, our twenty-year-old son, which he's home from Yale on his midyears and don't suspicion his folks are rifting.

MILO: Of course, of course. (*Crosses* L.) Reached man's estate already, has he? (*Front of couch, he sits. Shakes his head.*) Where is our cub at the present writing?

OCTAVIA: In the tack room, furbishing up the accoutrements of his polo ponies.

MILO: (*Acidly.*) Far better to be furbishing up on his Euclid, lest he drag the name of Weatherwax through the scholastic mire.

LANCE: (*Off* R.) Dads! Mums!

OCTAVIA: Shush! Here he comes now. (*Crosses* L.) You had best handle this. I'm laying down on my chaise lounge with a vinegar compress. (*Exits.*)

(LANCE *enters.*)

LANCE: (*Crosses* R. *of* C. *chair.*) Hi, Dads! Where's Mums?

MILO: (*Rises, crosses* L. *of* C. *chair.*) Son, we are facing a family crisis. The Weatherwax union has blown a gasket.

LANCE: I don't dig you, Guv.

MILO: To employ the vulgate, your mother and I have split out!

LANCE: (*Sobered, a hand on* MILO'S *shoulder.*) Rum go, Dads.

MILO: (*Crosses front of couch.*) Yes, it's hard on us oldsters, but it isn't going to be easy for you, either.

LANCE: (*Frightened.*) You mean I've got to go to work?

MILO: Don't be asinine! Not as long as there's a penny of your mother's money left. (*Sits couch.*)

LANCE: (*Crosses* R. *end of couch.*) Look, Pater, I—that is, me —aw, jeepers, can I ask you something man to man?

MILO: Lance, a chap with a sympathetic sire don't have to beat about the bush.

LANCE: (*Crosses back of couch.*) Thanks, Pop. Well, I've been running with a pretty serious crowd up at New Haven—lots of bull sessions about "Lolita" and Oscar Wilde.

MILO: That's the stuff to cut your eye-teeth on, son. A fellow has to learn to crawl before he can walk.

LANCE: Reet. (*Crosses* L. *to* L. *end of front of couch.*) And I've been wondering more and more of late. Where does our money come from?

MILO: (*Evasively; rises.*) Why—er—uh—the doctor brings it. In a little black bag. (*Crosses* C.)

LANCE: (*Sits* L. *end of couch.*) Aw, gee, Dad, I'm old enough to know. *Please.*

MILO: (*Pacing* L. *and* R.) My, you children grow up quick nowadays. (*Crosses* R.) Very well, have you ever heard of the Weatherwax All-Weather Garbage Disposal Plan?

LANCE: You—you mean whereby garbage is disposed of in all weathers by having neatly uniformed attendants call for and remove it?

MILO: Yes. That is the genesis of our scratch.

LANCE: (*Clenches his fists to control himself.*) Oh, sir, I want to die!

MILO: (*Crosses, puts hand on* LANCE'S *shoulder.*) Steady on, lad. After all, think of the millions which, were it not for our kindly ministrations, their homes would be a welter of chicken bones, fruit peels, and rancid yogurt.

LANCE: (*Voice breaks.*) I'll never be able to hold up my head in Bulldog circles again.

MILO: (*Crosses* R. *and* L.) Nonsense, lad. Why, you wear the keenest threads on the campus and you're persona grata to myriad Eli frats.

LANCE: (*A pause. Rises.*) No, Father. (*Crosses* R.) This is the end of halcyon days in the groves of Academe. I'm going away. (*Crosses front of chair.*)

MILO: Going away? Where? Why?

LANCE: No, Dad—it isn't only your revelation that turned my world topsy-turvy. There's another reason I've got to prove myself. I've fallen in love with a wonderful person.

MILO: (*Steps* L.) Hm-m-m, I thought there was a colored gentleman in the woodpile.

LANCE: No, Dad, this is a girl—I met her last Christmas in Greenwich Village.

MILO: (*Crosses to bar, puts down glass.*) Well, you mustn't fling your cap over the moon. (*Turns* L.) Remember, an apple knocker like you could easily fall into the hands of an adventuress.

LANCE: (*Hotly; Upstage side of chair.*) Adventuress? April Monkhood's the most sincere human being who ever lived!

MILO: (*Crosses* R. *of chair.*) April Monkhood! (*Turns to* LANCE.) I didn't quite catch that name.

LANCE: She's a designer.

MILO: It figures.

LANCE: (*Sits chair.*) You'd love her, sir, honest you would. She's spiritual—vibrant—artistic to the nth degree. April awoke something in me I never knew existed. A thirst for beauty, and I've got to express it somehow—in words or paint or music.

MILO: (*Crosses* L.) I know, my boy, I know. I had the same creative urge when I was your age.

LANCE: What became of it?

MILO: (*Front of couch.*) I sublimated it. Nowadays I sponsor a few gifted individuals on the side—sopranos—drum majorettes . . .

LANCE: Each of us has to work out their own salvation, Dad. What was yours?

MILO: Sex, and plenty of it.

LANCE: (*Rises, puts chair on* C. *platform. Crosses* D.C.) Mine's in the arts somewhere, in what branch I can't say until I try them all. But I'm not going to compromise. April's never compromised, and if I'm going to be worthy of her, I've got to hew to my resolve.

MILO: (*Rises, crosses* L. *of* LANCE. *Shrugs, extracts envelope.*) Very well, then. Before you start, I want you to have this keepsake.

LANCE: Gee, Dads.

MILO: It won't buy much except dreams, but it's been in the family for generations.

LANCE: What is it?

MILO: A letter of credit.

LANCE: (*Crosses* L., *squaring his chin.*) I can't take it, sir. To me it's like—tainted.

MILO: (*Crosses* R. *of* LANCE.) Great Scott, lad, you can't leave here empty-handed. You'll need money, introductions, shelter—

LANCE: No, Dad.

MILO: But I won't let you sleep in the street! There's our old railroad car underneath the Waldorf Astoria. Take it—it's only using up steam.

LANCE: (*Simply.*) I'm sorry, Dad. From now on, I walk alone. (*He exits.*)

(OCTAVIA *enters, looking nonplussed after the exiting* LANCE.)

OCTAVIA: Why, goodness, whatever ails the child? Milo, my woman's intuition tells me you've just had a stormy colloquy with LANCE.

MILO: What Lance is that?

OCTAVIA: Why, our twenty-two-year-old son, which he's home from Yale on his midyears and don't suspicion his folks are rifting.

MILO: Of course. If you need me I'm laying down on my chaise lounge with a vinegar compress. (*Exits* R.)

OCTAVIA: (*Throws up hands despairingly.*) Incorrigible boy! I wonder where it will all end.

(*She exits* L. *MUSIC starts. And we revolve to:*)

ACT ONE
SCENE 2

SCENE: *April Monkhood's apartment. A standard village lo-cale such as is occupied by any young career woman, but recently redecorated to express the personality of the occupant. Fishnet looped around walls, interspersed with glass spheres. Two or three score notary seals, both gold and red, pasted indiscriminately on window-shades, drapes, and in box on sofa. A profusion of fake leopard-skin upholstery, fake Negro sculpture and any of the clap-trap extant along East 8th St. judged suitable.*

TIME: *Two days after Scene 1.*

AT RISE: APRIL, *sitting* C. *platform. As unit stops, crosses up, mounts a small aluminum stepladder hanging a small fern. Downstage, at end-table,* FUSSFELD, *a telephone repairman, has been working on the instrument, his tin kit on the settee.*

FUSSFELD: (*Upstage of couch, on phone.*) Checking ALgon-quin 4-1014 . . . (*PHONE rings.*) Loud and clear. (*Hangs up, addresses* APRIL *as he reassembles kit.*) Well, you're O.K. now, Miss Monkhood. (*Crosses* D.S., R. *of phone.*)

APRIL: (*On ladder putting fern in holder.*) Thank heavens—I was on the brink of suicide. Absolutely bereft! I get so many calls in my business I couldn't exist without a second phone.

FUSSFELD: (*At tools,* R. *end of couch.*) Oh? What line you in, may I ask?

APRIL: Well, several, but chiefly jewelry design. Abstract things—you know, conversation pieces.

FUSSFELD: You don't say.

APRIL: (*Crosses, pulls pouf* D.S., *crosses* L. *of couch, picks up box.*) I handle just a few connoisseurs. If someone comes to me—say, a cynic with an appetite for subtle blasphemies—or a woman in a black gown with a sense of what's stark and dramatic—or a man whose id cries out for a massive and tortured ring—I distil their personality. (*Crosses* U.S., *back of couch.*)

FUSSFELD: (*Crosses* C.) I pegged you for some artistic field when I walked in your place.

APRIL: Yes, I've been redecorating. Of course, it's incomplete as yet. (*Looks about worriedly.*)

FUSSFELD: I'd sprinkle a couple of magazines around, or maybe a dish of cashews. They're tasty and they help soak up the humidity.

APRIL: No, no, what it really yearns for is a great splendid tree right over there—I've ordered a Bechtel's flowering crab.

FUSSFELD: A tree? Wouldn't the landlord raise the roof?

APRIL: (*Sunnily.*) Oh, yes, he promised he would. (*Sound of DOOR BUZZER off.*) Would you just let in whoever that is on your way? (*Rises, puts box on window sill.*)

FUSSFELD: Sure. G'bye. (*To himself, as he exits* S.L.) Raise the roof!

LANCE: (*Off.*) April! April!

APRIL: (*Crosses* R. *of* LANCE *as he enters.*) Lance Weatherwax! Whatever in the world are you doing here?

LANCE: (*Crosses* C., *tensely.*) April—I've got to talk to you. Right away.

APRIL: (*Crosses* L. *of* LANCE.) Of course, dear. Come in—(*With concern.*) You look so distrait. Has something happened? (*Takes off his coat.*)

LANCE: Well, yes—kind of. I bet I've walked fifty miles the past couple of days, trying to think things through.

APRIL: You must have been in real travail.

LANCE: I was.

APRIL: (*Crosses* U.L., *hangs up his coat.*) You poor boy.

LANCE: (*Crosses front of couch. Reacts to decor for the first time.*) What—what's going on here?

APRIL: I've had it done over. Isn't it delectable?

LANCE: Oh, it's great. I mean, it like hits you right in the eye.

APRIL: (*Crosses* L. *of* LANCE.) Does it say anything to you? You don't feel it's overdone?

LANCE: *Over*done? It's underdone! You couldn't omit a single detail without damaging the—the entire concept.

APRIL: (*Hugs him.*) You old sorcerer. You know just the words to thaw a woman's heart. (*She kisses him and crosses back of couch.*) Let's have a drink to celebrate. Set ye doon— (*Pushes him gently onto couch.*) and I'll open a bottle of Old Rabbinical. (*Crosses* U.S. *of couch, and whisks bottle from window sill. The PHONE rings; she answers hurriedly.*) Yes? . . . Who? . . . Oh, hi! . . . No, I can't. I have people here. . . . What? No, I have to wash my hair. . . . Yes, silly. . . . Why don't you do that? I'm always here. . . . 'Bye. (*Hangs up.*) Honestly, some men are just impossible. They think all they have to do is whistle. (*She picks up glasses, crosses* D.S., L. *of couch.*)

LANCE: Who was that?

APRIL: My ex-fiancé, of all people.

LANCE: Hanh? You never told me you'd been engaged.

APRIL: (*Gives* LANCE *glass.*) Oh, Sensualdo and I haven't seen each other in ages. He's a monster—an absolute fiend. (*Pours* LANCE *drink.*)

LANCE: Sensualdo? His name sounds Mexican.

APRIL: Uh-uh—Peruvian. (*Pours own drink.*) One of those insanely jealous types. Tried to stab a man I was having a Coke with. That's what broke up our engagement. (*Crosses* U.S., *puts down bottle.*)

LANCE: Is he—er—back there now?

APRIL: In Peruvia? Well, he shuttles between there and Staten Island. Something to do with vicunas or emeralds, I believe—I really don't know. . . . I haven't been in touch with him in ages! (*Crosses to pouf.*)

LANCE: (*Urgently.*) April, there is something very important I—

APRIL: As a matter of fact, he was a prince compared to my first fiancé. Did you ever hear of Benno Vontz, the sculptor?

LANCE: No, I can't say that I have, but—

APRIL: Benno designed that abstract saddle on top of Neiman-Marcus's in Dallas. A brilliant boy, but terribly neurotic. (*Sits pouf.*) He used to wake me up in the middle of the day, claiming I'd had affairs with all kinds of people— osteopaths, car-hops, bakers. It was a nightmare, my dear—an absolute *cauchemar*. I was practically on the verge of a neurasthenia when I met Ricky. (*Rises.*)

LANCE: Ricky?

APRIL: (*Crosses L. of couch.*) He was an auctioneer that I met in Atlantic City. Naturally, one thing led to another. (*Crosses L. of* LANCE.)

LANCE: And you got engaged.

APRIL: (*Crosses back of couch, takes glasses to bar.*) No! Benno found out! One night Ricky and I were driving home in a downpour and his brakes overheated near Asbury Park and we had to take refuge in a motel. (*Sits back of couch.*) Next thing we knew, Benno was all over us with flash bulbs. (*A tragic Mrs. Malaprop.*) My *dear*, it was too sorbid.

LANCE: (*Takes her hand.*) You poor kid. It's a wonder to me you could live through so much and still remain gay and joie de vivre.

APRIL: (*Crosses R., sits end of couch.*) That's because I sublimate myself in my work, LANCE. Whenever life gets frantic, why I rush to my bench and fashion a brooch or earrings that crystallize a dewdrop of ecstasy. Your great craftsmen have always done that, right back to Cellini.

LANCE: April, if you only knew how your eyes light up when you talk about art.

APRIL: (*Leaning nearer.*) Do they?

LANCE: There's a kind of a glow in them. They're like mysterious violet pools, full of wisdom and understanding . . . and—oh, terrific tolerance. Not like those empty-headed little debs I used to date before I met you.

APRIL: Why, Lance, I've never heard you so articulate before. It's as if you'd been freed, somehow.

LANCE: (*Vehemently.*) I have. I've come to a very important decision about my future, April. I have to know right away how you feel.

APRIL: (*Placing finger on his lips.*) Please, Lance, for both our sakes—don't say anything you might regret.

LANCE: (*Rises.*) No, no—I've got to. You see, this door suddenly opened in my mind and I realized what truly matters to me.

APRIL: (*Tempest-tossed.*) Oh, Lance, do you know what you're saying?

LANCE: (*Kneels L. of* APRIL.) Yes, yes, I do. April, I've decided to become a writer.

APRIL: You *what*?

LANCE: Or maybe a painter.

APRIL: (*Barely-suppressed irritation.*) Oh, Lance, don't be an Airedale.

LANCE: (*Rises, wounded.*) What's the matter? Don't you think I have the ability?

APRIL: (*Rises, crosses* L. *of pouf.*) Er—of course, but—well, I was just a little overwhelmed. I mean, it's such a tremendous challenge.

LANCE: (*Crosses* R. *of pouf.*) I want to accept that challenge —I want to unleash whatever creative powers there are inside me. But my problem is—how do I become a writer?

APRIL: Buy a magazine—or maybe a chain of them. I understand the Saturday Evening Post is up for grabs—

LANCE: (*Rises, crosses* R.) No, siree, I won't be a lousy dilettante. I'm going to start humbly, get the smell of printer's ink . . .

APRIL: (*Rises,* R. *of pouf. Lighting up.*) Wait—wait! Eureka!

LANCE: I beg your pardon?

APRIL: What a blind little fool I've been! The perfect way to express yourself—it's right in front of you!

LANCE: I don't follow.

APRIL: (*Sits* LANCE R. *of her on couch.*) Let's plunge into the depths together. Scale the heights together.

LANCE: How?

APRIL: Well, you know what a disorganized scatterbrain I am away from my workbench—I haven't a clue to facts or figures. I need someone with divine good taste to counsel me —someone whose judgment I respect.

LANCE: But where would I contribute my creative talent?

APRIL: Why, in a hundred ways. . . . Right here, for example— (*Extracts crumpled paper from under phone.*) this came in the morning mail. What does it mean?

LANCE: It's from the bank. It says they're returning your check for $471 due to insufficient funds.

APRIL: (*Rises, crosses* D.S.) It must be that consignment of turquoise nut-picks I ordered from Santa Fe. Those Navajos are so grasping. What should I do about it? (*Crosses* L. *of couch.*)

LANCE: You must put the money in the bank to cover the overdraft.

APRIL: (*Triumphantly.*) There—you see how much more practical you are than I? Very well—you handle it, love.

LANCE: How do you mean?

APRIL: Why, when you leave here, just drop by the Centerboard National and deposit that amount—until I get straightened out.

LANCE: But I haven't any money.

APRIL: Of course—how dense of me. Nobody carries that much around. Well, here's a thought—ring up your father's accountant and tell him to deposit it.

LANCE: I don't think you understand, April—I've cut myself off. I've broken with my family.

APRIL: But you haven't broken with your accountant, surely.

LANCE: With everybody.

APRIL: You're teasing.

LANCE: (*Exhibiting a few coins.*) This is all the money I have.

APRIL: (*Instantly.*) Lance, I don't think we're quite ready to work together. Obey your original impulse—go and get the smell of printer's ink. Go see Hyacinth Beddoes Laffoon, right away.

LANCE: Who is she?

APRIL: The woman who publishes all those magazines— "Gory Story"—"Sanguinary Love"—"Spicy Mortician."

LANCE: But they're just pulp fiction, full of blood and thunder. . . .

APRIL: My dear Lance, wake *up*. Some of our most enduring American authors come out of that milieu.

LANCE: (*Fired.*) Maybe you're right, April. Maybe I ought to contact her.

APRIL: Without further ado! Now you buzz right over to Laffoon House and storm the redoubts. I'd help you storm except I have to rush out to an appointment.

LANCE: (*As she turns away.*) When am I going to see you again?

APRIL: *Quien sabe corazon?* (*A sudden inspiration.*) I'll tell you what—why don't you drop in at my house-warming next Tuesday? And dig up an itty-bitty case of Scotch on the way, will you? There's a dear. (*Pushes him out, turns back into room. PHONE rings; she answers brusquely.*) Yes? . . . Who? . . .

Oh, it's you again. Now listen, Sensualdo, I told you, no monkey business—what? What new emeralds? (*Second PHONE rings.*) Look—hold on just one minute— (*Snatches up other receiver.*) Hello?—Who? . . . Well, stranger! . . . Of course I have, Benno darling—absolutely heartsick. . . . No—no, I couldn't. . . . Anselmo who? . . . Olivetti? Not the *typewriter* Olivettis? . . . Honey, wait one second, my other phone . . . (*Clasps phone to her, jabbers into the other.*) Look, Sensualdo, I just stepped out of my shower and I'm holding a big bag of groceries. Why don't we meet at the Drake about midnight and you bring along the adding machine . . . I mean the emeralds. . . .

(*The SCENERY has been moving during end of speech, and now segues into:*)

ACT ONE
SCENE 3

SCENE: *Office of Hyacinth Beddoes Laffoon. A chamber devoid of furniture and of uncompromising severity with only enough indications to stamp it as a publisher's sanctum. The walls may display a couple of lurid pulp magazine covers with violent themes and broad mammary exposure.*

TIME: *A week later.*

AT RISE: BUNCE, VAN LENNEP, HAGEDORN *and* VISHNU— *four typical crew-haired and brain-washed editorial assistants, Christmas tigers all—are grouped* R. *They wear identical blazers with breast patches exhibiting the letter "L" (cf. employees of Prentice-Hall), and buzz between themselves as they look over at* LANCE *isolated at* L.

VAN LENNEP: (*From* R.) When did you hear about it?
HAGEDORN: (*From* R.) I didn't—when I arrived this morning, there was a strange polo coat in my locker.
BUNCE: (*Worriedly.*) I was told not one word by Mrs. Hyacinth Beddoes Laffoon about a new editorial assistant.
VAN LENNEP: Nor me. She usually gives me an intimation —if only a wink—

HAGEDORN: (*Crosses* L. *of* VAN LENNEP.) She kind of winked at me at yesterday's meeting.

VAN LENNEP: (*Superior.*) No, I saw that. It was a belch.

VISHNU: (*Crosses* L. *of* VAN LENNEP.) That's right. She took a spoon of bicarb right after.

BUNCE: (*Crosses* L. *of* VAN LENNEP.) Besides, which magazine's got a vacancy? We're full up.

VAN LENNEP: He might be taking over that gland column —"You and Your Gonads."

VISHNU: (*Crosses* L. *of* VAN LENNEP. *Aghast.*) Say—you don't suppose it's the doctor she spoke of?

HAGEDORN: What one?

VISHNU: She said we all needed a good proctologist.

VAN LENNEP: Cheese it! Here she comes now!

(*With the silken smoothness of a Cadillac, an executive desk glides in, behind it* HYACINTH BEDDOES LAFFOON. *She is the epitome of female editors (cf. Mesdames Luce and Cowles)—chic, sleek, and murderous. Desktop holds a neat stack of magazines, dictagraph.*)

HYACINTH: Good morning, good morning, good morning! (*Cordially.*) How are you, Weatherwax?

LANCE: Fine, Mrs. Laffoon.

HYACINTH: Men, I want you to welcome a new member to our editorial family—Mr. Lance Weatherwax.

(*Ad lib greetings; the staff bestow saccharine smiles as they scan* LANCE.)

BUNCE: (*Delicately.*) Er—how would you describe Mr. Weatherwax, Chief? Is he a writer?

HYACINTH: (*Coldly.*) I don't believe in labels, Bunce. When I smell a fresh, original talent in the marketplace, I buy it. This young man is going to be a dynamic addition to our team. All right, now, drain the sludge out of your think-tanks. (*Sits.*) We're going to brainstorm. (MEN *step* D.S. *Chattering sound.*) What's that chattering sound?

BUNCE: (*Leans in to* HYACINTH. *Eagerly.*) It's Hagedorn's teeth, Mrs. Laffoon. I've been meaning to squeal on him. Gosh, you ought to hear the noise he makes over the partition! A man can hardly concentrate.

HYACINTH: Oh, you have trouble concentrating, do you?

BUNCE: (*Back up.*) No, no—it'd take a lot more than that to upset *me*! I could work in a boiler factory!

HYACINTH: You may yet. Meanwhile, Hagedorn, let's have those choppers out before our next conference.

HAGEDORN: I'll see my extractionist in the lunch hour, Chief.

HYACINTH: Well, see that you do. Now, then, I've had my ear to the ground lately and I get a very—strange—impression. Some of you disagree with the policy of my new magazine —"Shroud."

VAN LENNEP: Hell's bells, Hyacinth! Where'd you ever pick up a crazy idea like that?

HYACINTH: From the dictaphone I had installed in the water cooler. Does this sound familiar, Van Lennep? (*Reads from flimsy.*) "Just give the old windbag enough rope. You'll see, the public'll pin her ears back."

VAN LENNEP: (*Squirming.*) I—I was referring to Miss Lovibond, who solicits those ads for lost manhood. You said yourself the magazine needed more chic.

HYACINTH: Well, you squirmed out of that one all right, but watch your step. I'm sentimental enough to think this organization can't function without one-hundred-percent loyalty.

VISHNU: And you've got it, Mrs. Laffoon.

BUNCE: Why, we venerate the ground you walk on!

VAN LENNEP: Right down the line.

HAGEDORN: I'll say, Chief.

HYACINTH: At the same time—no ass-kissing! I want honest, sturdy, independent reactions—is that clear?

BUNCE: Like crystal!

HAGEDORN: Boy, I wish I could express myself so forcefully!

VAN LENNEP: She really cuts it, doesn't she?

VISHNU: What an editor!

HYACINTH: O.K. Well, I've just had a couple of skull-busters that I'd like to try out on you. (*Rises, crosses to* L. *of* BUNCE, *crosses* D.S., *front of desk.*) First, these covers we've been running. Look at this one—who's responsible for this? (*Taps pile of them on desk.*) A naked girl tied to a bed-post and a chimpanzee brandishing a whip. No more punch than a seed catalogue. (*Throws magazine on desk.*)

VAN LENNEP: I see the structural weakness.

BUNCE: Demands too much of the reader.

HYACINTH: Correct. We've got to drill him right between the eyes. Now, I visualize a cover with a real revolver barrel pointing at you.

OMNES: (MEN *close in—kneel—eyes lighting up.*) Hey . . .

HYACINTH: And a wisp of smoke curling out. The smoke would be engendered in a mechanism hinged to the back cover.

OMNES: Hey!

LANCE: But, Mrs. Laffoon, wouldn't it be kind of bulky?

HYACINTH: Yes, and we could run afoul of the Sullivan Law.

VAN LENNEP: (*Rises.*) Nah, that can all be worked out.

HAGEDORN: (*Rises, crosses* R.) Baby, what an inspiration.

VISHNU: (*Rises, crosses* L. *of* HAGEDORN.) It'll knock Publishers' Row right back on their heels!

BUNCE: (*Rises, crosses* L. *of* VISHNU.) Hyacinth, I don't say these things lightly. This idea's got undertow.

VAN LENNEP: I can hear those dimes and nickels showering down!

HYACINTH: You bet you can. It's the cashier counting your severance pay. So long, Van Lennep! (VAN LENNEP *crosses.*) Sayonara! (*As he exits chopfallen.*) There's no room at the top for a yes-man. Good thinking, Weatherwax. (*Crosses* R. *of* VISHNU.) As of today, you take over Van Lennep's duties. (*Crosses, sits* L. *of desk.*) You can wear his blazer till yours comes through.

LANCE: Gee, thanks, Mrs. Laffoon.

HYACINTH: (*Sits,* L. *end of desk.*) Now, let's see how my next idea appeals. What about a country-wide golem contest?

VISHNU: (*Crosses to* R. *of desk.*) Could you clarify that a bit for us, Chief?

HYACINTH: (*Crosses to* VISHNU.) A competition among our teen-age readers for the best Frankenstein monster built in a home workshop. (*Crosses* R. *to* L. *of* BUNCE.) How does that lay on the stomach, Bunce?

BUNCE: It stirs me and yet it leaves me cold.

HAGEDORN: I want to throw my arms around it, but something holds me back.

VISHNU: It's as broad as it is long.

BUNCE: How do you—

VISHNU: —feel about it—

HAGEDORN: —yourself?

HYACINTH: (*Crosses* L. *of* VISHNU; *simpers.*) Well, of course, it's my idea.

VISHNU: And you can afford to crow. . . . I know I'd be proud of it.

HYACINTH: Well, I'm not—it's a *bomb*. (*Crosses* R., *significantly.*) Vishnu, I wish you'd reconsider leaving us. We need you here.

VISHNU: And I feel there's a place for me.

HYACINTH: (*Crosses* L. *front of desk.*) Not right here, but in the stockroom. Scout around, find an opening, (VISHNU *exits.*) and clean it. Arrivaducci! (*As* VISHNU *exits* R., HYACINTH *crosses* R. *of* LANCE.) By the by, Weatherwax, I didn't catch your reaction to my idea just now.

LANCE: What idea?

HYACINTH: Ho-ho, that's foxy of you—very good! Pretended you didn't hear it! You've got real executive stature, lad. (*Crosses behind desk.*)

LANCE: Gee, thanks, ma'am!

HYACINTH: Nothing at all. Now, leave me, all of you—run along. You stay, Weatherwax.

BUNCE: (*Back* R. *with* HAGEDORN.) But you might need us, boss.

HYACINTH: Go—go—go!

HAGEDORN: Oh, he's the palace favorite now, is he?

(BUNCE *and* HAGEDORN *withdraw, exit* R., *casting black glances at him.* HYACINTH *has withdrawn lacy handkerchief which she presses to her lips with anguished expression.*)

HYACINTH: Oh, the jealousies, the intrigues— (*Sits, shoulders heaving.*) Oh, it's too much. It's insupportable.

LANCE: (L. *of desk.*) What is?

HYACINTH: I feel so alone—so inadequate. I'm only a woman in a man's world, trying to cope.

LANCE: But you're on top—I mean, you're in charge. What you say goes.

HYACINTH: (*Emotionally.*) Do you think that way lies true happiness, Weatherwax? Under this artificial exterior there's a helpless creature that wants to be dominated—to be adored. . . .

LANCE: (L. *of* HYACINTH.) Everybody loves you, Mrs. Laffoon. Honest they do.

HYACINTH: (*Rises, crosses* R.) No, no—you're all toadies, parasites. There's not a single living thing I can rely on. Not even a dog.

LANCE: (*Fervently.*) You could depend on me. Just try.

HYACINTH: (*Blinking at him through unshed tears.*) You mean it?

LANCE: Oh, I do! Really I do!

HYACINTH: Oh, how wonderful to hear those words! (*Sits desk.*) Weatherwax, as I sit here, I suddenly have a vision. I see a vast publishing enterprise, with two of us at the helm. Not one of those cockamamy affairs that Henry Luce runs, but a farflung empire embracing every printed word. (*BUZZER sounds. She flips switch: a raucous, unidentifiable BARK.*) Hello! The who? . . . The Weatherwax Trust & Loan Co. Good—put them on. . . . (*Grabs phone, sugar and spice.*) Well, are we getting that little half-a-million loan for "Shroud" Magazine? (*Her face clouds over.*) Oh, we're not! (*Cradles phone, outraged.*)

LANCE: You were saying . . .

HYACINTH: That you're clean and straight and fine, and I say to you—get out before it's too late.

LANCE: But I only started this morn—

HYACINTH: (*Rising.*) Are you getting out, or do I have to have you thrown out?

LANCE: (*Crosses* L., *stops, turns* R.) Er—yes, ma'am—I only thought—

HYACINTH: (*With a snort.*) Hit the road! (*He exits confused.* HYACINTH *resumes seat, picks up documents and glares after him.*) He only thought. That's the trouble with the world nowadays . . . too much thinking. (*She flips dictagraph switch.*) Lorna? Get me Barry Goldwater. (*The DESK begins moving as she utters the foregoing, and segue into:*)

ACT ONE
SCENE 4

SCENE: *Goddard Quagmeyer's studio, Greenwich Village. The studio of a professional painter, devoid of any hint of dilettantism. Skylight at rear facing into street. At* C. *an easel with a partially-complete abstract painting, beside it a taboret laden with pigment, fixative bomb, etc. At rear also, an antique Greek plaster cast of a head, tableful of sketch pads, jars of brushes, pencils, dividers, maul-stick. A disordered cot dimly in evidence in background. A small radio on a table near easel; phone.*

TIME: *A spring morning, several days later.*

AT RISE: *The studio is empty of human life. Then a key is heard in the lock and* GODDARD QUAGMEYER *enters carrying a paper bag. Switching on RADIO, he picks up ash-tray heaped with butts, crosses to door, and empties them into hallway. He now snaps door-bolt shut and proceeds to sip coffee from a container he extracts from bag, nibbling on a Danish butterhorn and intently considering the painting on easel. He has picked up palette and begun work on canvas when a KNOCK sounds at door.* QUAGMEYER *reacts with irritation, attempts to continue. Another couple of knocks, more insistent.*

QUAGMEYER: (*Calls Off, attention glued to canvas.*) Go 'way —nobody's home! (*Another KNOCK; he half-turns.*) Quiet— we're recording! (*Repeated KNOCK; he shouts.*) Stop that, will you? Someone's dead here!

(*Still another KNOCK.* QUAGMEYER *starts convulsively, crosses to door, unbolts it.* LANCE *enters tentatively.*)

LANCE: Mr. Quagmeyer.

QUAGMEYER: Yes—what is it?

LANCE: (*Steps* R.) You probably don't recall me.

QUAGMEYER: Your intuition is faultless.

LANCE: (*Steps* R.) I'd Iike to talk to you if I could.

QUAGMEYER: Well, you can't. I've got a gouache to finish and it's drying on me.

LANCE: My name is Weatherwax. I'm not trying to sell anything.

QUAGMEYER: But *I* am.

LANCE: (*Steps* R.) Lance Weatherwax. My mother owns two of your paintings.

QUAGMEYER: (*Reacting.*) Oh? . . . Yes, that's right—she does. (*Takes container of coffee.*) And as I remember, she paid a tidy little sum for them.

LANCE: (L. *of chair* C.) Mr. Quagmeyer, how can a person like me tell whether they really have the creative spark?

QUAGMEYER: If it sets fire to your pants.

LANCE: Oh, I know how naive it sounds—me, Lance Weatherwax, aspiring to the arts.

QUAGMEYER: You've got plenty of company. Every housewife in the country's got a novel under her apron.

LANCE: (*Turns chair around, sits.*) No, I'm more interested in the visual—

QUAGMEYER: (*Crosses* L. *to* R. *of* LANCE.) And the dentists are even worse. Do you realize there are twice as many dentists painting in their spare time as there are painters practicing dentistry? (*Crosses to easel.*)

LANCE: I have to fulfill myself, Mr. Quagmeyer—

QUAGMEYER: All over this tremendous country, millions of poor worn-out bastards are schlepping home to frozen casseroles because their wives are out studying psycho-ceramics.

LANCE: If I could like write the perfect sonnet or paint one masterpiece, I'd die happy.

QUAGMEYER: (*Sits chair on No. 3 unit.*) Well, you'll never die of starvation, that's one comfort. Your folks have more bread than the Sheikh of Kuwait.

LANCE: (*Rises, with spirit.*) They can keep it. The whole six hundred million.

QUAGMEYER: (*Rises.*) Look, headstrong boy . . . (*Crosses* L. *of* LANCE.) Even Lorenzo de' Medici and Huntington Hartford didn't go that far. . . . But, tell me, what do you want from me?

LANCE: Mr. Quagmeyer. From the little you've seen of me, do I have the raw material to be a painter?

QUAGMEYER: Sonny—I'm pressed for time, so you'll excuse me for being blunt. Lay off the Muses—it's a very tough dollar.

LANCE: It's not the financial rewards I'm striving for, sir— it's self-realization! Like Gauguin was searching for when he went to the South Seas.

QUAGMEYER: (*Crosses easel.*) Oh. Well, in that case, you might have to do the same thing.

LANCE: (*Crosses* R. *of easel.*) Do you mean it? Do you think maybe I ought to lose myself in some place like Tahiti—live like the natives do?

QUAGMEYER: Yes, but easy on the poontang.

MRS. KRUMGOLD: (*Offstage.*) Do me one favor, Seymour, and shut up!

(MR. *and* MRS. KRUMGOLD *enter.*)

MR. KRUMGOLD: Last stop! Last stop! You said that an hour ago at the place we bought the Siamese fighting fish.

MRS. KRUMGOLD: (D.S. *of No. 3.*) Oblige me once in your life and button your lip!

MR. KRUMGOLD: (*Crosses* R.) Now you drag me down to Greenwich Village and make me climb five flights of stairs. Me with my duodenal. (*Sits chair.* MRS. KRUMGOLD *sneers.*) You can laugh. Laugh! I was so tensed up last night, I could hardly hold my pinochle hand.

MRS. KRUMGOLD: That'd be a tragedy, all right!

QUAGMEYER: (*Crosses* L. *to* L. *of* MRS. KRUMGOLD.) Excuse me.

MRS. KRUMGOLD: Don't interrupt, please! (*Crosses* L. *of* MR. KRUMGOLD.)

MR. KRUMGOLD: You'd like to see me keel over, wouldn't you? (*Crosses* R. *of* C. *chair.*) Any woman that sits around the house studying her husband's insurance policy.

MRS. KRUMGOLD: I resent that deeply!

QUAGMEYER: I beg your pardon.

MRS. KRUMGOLD: (*Crosses* L. *of* MR. KRUMGOLD.) You keep out of this!

MR. KRUMGOLD: (*Rises.*) I wouldn't put it past you to hire assassins.

MRS. KRUMGOLD: You're paranoid!

MR. KRUMGOLD: What about those two truck drivers that stopped me for a light just now? The one wearing mascara looked like a pretty tough customer.

MRS. KRUMGOLD: Those were Bennington girls.

MR. KRUMGOLD: I'm glad I don't have your dirty mind. (*Crosses* U.S.)

MRS. KRUMGOLD: Oh, shut up! (*Crosses* R. *of* QUAGMEYER.) I'm terribly sorry we're late. Seymour was trapped with his tax consultant.

MR. KRUMGOLD: That lousy crook!

QUAGMEYER: I think you've made a mistake, lady.

MRS. KRUMGOLD: Aren't you Goddard Quagmeyer? I'm Zimmy Vetlugin's cousin. He's your art dealer, isn't he?

QUAGMEYER: Yes.

MRS. KRUMGOLD: Well, I'm Gloria Krumgold. We're here about the painting.

QUAGMEYER: Oh—oh—of course. Now—which canvas was it? It's slipped my mind.

MRS. KRUMGOLD: That Zimmy—I can see he didn't tell you anything.

MR. KRUMGOLD: Gloria, for God's sake— (*Crosses* R. *of* MRS. KRUMGOLD.)

MRS. KRUMGOLD: Seymour!

(MR. KRUMGOLD *crosses* U.S.L. *on No. 3.*)

QUAGMEYER: Perfectly all right, Mrs. Krumgold. What sort of thing are you looking for?

(MR. KRUMGOLD *holds chair*, MRS. KRUMGOLD *sits* C. *chair.*)

MRS. KRUMGOLD: We have a special problem—I better describe it. You see, Seymour and I have just built this very lovely home in Passaic Hills. The last word in modrun, except for the stables.

QUAGMEYER: (*Steps* R.) Sounds very attractive.

MRS. KRUMGOLD: We need something for the living room. The idea is, in the center there's a sunken conversation pit.

QUAGMEYER: Sounds dangerous.

MRS. KRUMGOLD: But that's not our problem. It's the free-standing fireplace in the middle. We need a picture that would be suitable.

QUAGMEYER: (L. *of* MRS. KRUMGOLD.) To do what?

MRS. KRUMGOLD: (*Gestures.*) To go around it.

QUAGMEYER: (*Crosses slightly away.*) I don't paint round pictures.

MRS. KRUMGOLD: (*Patiently.*) Canvas wouldn't work naturally on a fireplace, so we thought maybe you would do it on formica. Not only would it be heat-resistant, but it would be easy to wash.

QUAGMEYER: Well—I've never done anything quite like it before, but I suppose we all have to move with the times.

MRS. KRUMGOLD: Marvelous. Seymour, I told you.

MR. KRUMGOLD: (*Crosses* R. *of* QUAGMEYER.) Let's not start celebrating. We haven't talked price.

QUAGMEYER: I'm sure we can come to some agreement. But look here—there's one thing we've overlooked—the subject matter.

MRS. KRUMGOLD: Oh, who cares? So long as it doesn't clash with the drapes. They're silver blue.

MR. KRUMGOLD: (*Crossing to* QUAGMEYER.) And my mother comes to dinner every Friday night. It shouldn't be smutty.

MRS. KRUMGOLD: (*Brightly.*) Well, now that it's all settled, when can we expect it?

QUAGMEYER: Never.

MRS. KRUMGOLD: I beg your pardon.

MR. KRUMGOLD: What kind of a way is this to do business?

QUAGMEYER: My way.

MRS. KRUMGOLD: (*Lightly.*) Well—if that's how you feel about it. Could you recommend a good restaurant around here?

QUAGMEYER: (*Crosses* R.—*inhales deeply.*) Lady, I'm a quiet, middle-aged man with a receding hairline and most of my own teeth—by profession a painter.

MRS. KRUMGOLD: So?

QUAGMEYER: So every morning, while nine million people are rushing to Wall Street and the Garment Center and Radio City, I come here to my little nook and ply my craft. By no stretch of the imagination would you confuse me with Giotto or El Greco or Picasso, but I don't bother anyone.

MRS. KRUMGOLD: Look, there are plenty of other painters—

QUAGMEYER: (*Holds up his hand as she starts to speak.*) Please —I'm not finished. Now, don't think I'm complaining. I make a mediocre living, but my career suits me. I'm adjusted to it, the way a maple tree manages to grow in a cement sidewalk. The only drawback to my existence, though, is the hyenas.

MRS. KRUMGOLD: The what?

QUAGMEYER: Every so often, the door opens and a couple of hyenas walk in. You can't tell they're hyenas because they walk like people, dress like people, and they have bank accounts, (MRS. KRUMGOLD *rises.*) but you know 'em the minute they open their mouths. Well, I'll tell you how I protect myself.

Over here behind the curtain, I keep a heavy club. First I warn them, and if they don't heed my warning, I count to ten and go for the *club*. (*Crosses* L.) One . . . two . . . three . . . four . . . (*Crosses* R. *of* MRS. KRUMGOLD. *The* KRUMGOLDS *exit precipitately.*) five . . . six . . . seven, eight, (*Crosses* R.) nine, ten!

LANCE: (*Crosses* L.) That was an experience, Mr. Quagmeyer.

QUAGMEYER: Nothing unusual.

LANCE: (U.S. *to* R. *of* QUAGMEYER.) Integrity in action. It was a privilege to see it.

QUAGMEYER: (*Grimly.*) Yes, no doubt. (*Crosses easel.*)

LANCE: (*By* C. *chair.*) I'm just beginning to realize what discipline an artist has to have.

QUAGMEYER: Well, then, your time hasn't been wasted.

LANCE: If you had a secretary or an assistant, like, to protect you, you'd be free to concentrate.

QUAGMEYER: Are you proposing yourself for the post?

LANCE: I could be real helpful, Mr. Quagmeyer. I'll run errands, take messages, and in between, you could give me various pointers on your craft.

QUAGMEYER: (*Crosses* L., *nodding.*) Like those apprentices the Old Masters used to have. (*Sits chair.*)

LANCE: (*Crosses* L. *of* QUAGMEYER.) That's it, sir—exactly!

QUAGMEYER: I see. Well, forget it. The last thing I need here is a nudnick asking a lot of damn fool questions.

LANCE: I wouldn't get in your way.

QUAGMEYER: I refuse to consider it, I tell you.

LANCE: (L. *of* QUAGMEYER.) Couldn't we give it a trial— please? If it didn't work out . . . (QUAGMEYER, *indomitable, shakes head.*) Mr. Quagmeyer, when you were just beginning, didn't anyone ever lend you a hand?

QUAGMEYER: (*A pause.*) Well—O.K. (*Rises. As* LANCE *brightens.*) But remember, you're on probation. If I bounce you into the street, no spaniel eyes or bawling—do you hear?

LANCE: Don't you worry.

QUAGMEYER: Right. (*Glances at wrist watch.*) Now, look— the morning's shot. I've got to get some stretchers. While I'm gone, you can begin your first lesson. (*Gets coat.*)

LANCE: Yes, sir.

QUAGMEYER: In oil painting, the brushwork is everything. (*Produces long-handled floor brush from behind stove* L.) Get into those corners. And if you shape up, I may let you wash the skylight.

(*He exits.* LANCE *stands holding brush, exhales slow sigh of delirious happiness. He moves about for a moment, inspecting studio. Then puts broom on No. 3, crosses to easel; he timidly picks up palette and brush, poses himself in his conception of painter at work. A pause, then, heralded by a perfunctory KNOCK at door,* HARRY HUBRIS *enters* L.)

HUBRIS: (*Stops short, fastidiously dusts sleeves.*) Hi, there, Maestro. Harry Hubris—Hubbub Productions.

LANCE: Harry Hubris?—the movie producer?

HUBRIS: (L. *of* C. *chair. Surveys studio with distaste.*) Roger! Say, are you kidding? Those terrific abstractions of yours—you don't actually *paint* them here?

LANCE: (*Puts palette down.*) No, I'm only the apprentice— Mr. Quagmeyer's not here—

HUBRIS: (*Crosses easel; amused scorn.*) Listen, I know that dodge. Your dealer told me about your publicity phobia. (*Crosses* L. *to below No. 3, gazes around studio, shakes head.*) Go figure it. It always kills me an artist should hole up in a flea-bag to conceive a masterpiece. Still, everybody to their own ulcer. (*Crosses* U.L., *sets attaché case down.*)

LANCE: (*Urgently.*) Mr. Hubris, I'm trying to tell you. I'm not Goddard Quagmeyer.

HUBRIS: (*Turns* L. *of* LANCE; *overtaxed.*) Pops, will you drop dead on that Salinger kick? I recognized you the minute I walked in. And I want you to know that I consider you one of the nine foremost painters of our time. (*Crosses* L.)

LANCE: Who are the other eight?

HUBRIS: (*Turns, crosses* L.) Don't get me started, pal. I've got maybe the most important collection in the L. A. area. Four Jackson Pollocks, three Ben Shahns, five Lipchitzes, one of yours— (*Crosses* L.)

LANCE: Which one?

HUBRIS: (*Impatiently.*) Ask my wife, that's her department. (*Crosses* U.S.) All I know is she bought it in 1956, right after I had my thyroid out. . . . (*Sits* L. *armchair.*) But look here

—let's get down to basics. Did you perchance read "The Tortured Bostonian"?

LANCE: What is it?

HUBRIS: The biography of John Singer Sargent—by Irving Stonehenge.

LANCE: (*Crosses R. of* HUBRIS.) Oh—oh, yes—I think I read the plot in Time Magazine. It was very intriguing.

HUBRIS: I paid two hundred and seventy big ones for the picture rights—that's how intriguing. (*Extends index finger at* LANCE.) Just imagine Rob Roy Fruitwell in the lead!

LANCE: Who is he?

HUBRIS: (*Rises.*) Rob Roy? Only the biggest potential draw in pictures today. Properly handled, Fruitwell could be another Kirk Douglas, *and*— (*Crosses D.S., taking* LANCE *with him, lowers voice.*) I'll exhale you something in the strictest confidence. Next season you won't be able to tell them apart— after Fruitwell has his dimple deepened! (*Starts L., knits brow purposefully.*) But my immediate headache is this. Rob Roy's a born actor, and he'll play the hell out of Sargent, but what he requires is— (*Crosses L.*) a little coaching from a professional artist like you.

LANCE: How could anybody teach a man to paint in one lesson?

HUBRIS: (*Crosses R. of* LANCE.) For God's sake, smarten up, will you? This lug don't know from the muse. All you got to do is show him how to hold a brush . . . (*Indicates palette.*) what that board is for . . . which end of the tube the paint comes out. Two years ago he was a bus-boy in Fort Wayne. (*Crosses L.*)

LANCE: I've never dealt with actors. I haven't any clue to their mentality.

HUBRIS: Mentality's one problem you won't have with Rob Roy Fruitwell. Strictly a matzo ball.

LANCE: But John Singer Sargent was a genius.

HUBRIS: (*Triumphantly.*) That's the beauty part. (*Sits* LANCE *in* C. *chair, paces* L. *of him.*) This cluck is a sensitized sponge that he'll soak up the info you give him and project it. So, in view of the fact that we start shooting Friday, I had Rob Roy sky in from the Coast last night solely on purpose to huddle with you.

LANCE: (*Rises, crosses easel.*) Well, you're wasting your time, Mr. Hubris. There's one thing you'd better understand. Money won't buy everything.

HUBRIS: (*Crosses* L. *of* LANCE.) I consider that a highly un-American attitude. What are you, a Red or something?

LANCE: This is the studio of a dedicated painter—a person with ideals. You're asking a man to betray his birthright.

HUBRIS: You know, fellow, I'm deeply disenchanted with you. You talk like a mouth-breather.

ROB ROY FRUITWELL: (*From doorway.*) Hey, Harry!

(ROB ROY FRUITWELL *slouches in from* L. *He is a standard prize bullock with Brando tonsure and capped teeth, in Sy Devore silks and gooseneck sweater exposing thorax.* HUBRIS'S *irritation instantly turns to saccharine.* ROB ROY *crosses* D.S. *of No. 3 chair.*)

HUBRIS: Hiya, Rob Roy, sweetheart? (*Crosses* L.)

ROB ROY: (L. *of* HUBRIS; *looks around with distaste.*) Man, where's the Board of Health? It's like Roachville here.

HUBRIS: (*Crosses* L. *of* ROB ROY.) Don't mind this rat trap, baby. In the picture, you're going to have a studio the size of Carnegie Hall.

ROB ROY: Big deal. O.K., come on—what's the action? I left a broad in the kip.

HUBRIS: (*To* LANCE.) It's a technical term. Rob Roy, this is the artist I told you about.

(ROB ROY *crosses* L. *of easel.*)

LANCE: (*Crosses* L.) But, Mr. Hubris—I'm trying to tell you—

ROB ROY: (*Facing easel.*) Hey, Jack, this doodle here. What's it supposed to be—a woman?

LANCE: Of course. Don't you see the various female elements?

ROB ROY: Man, you need therapy.

HUBRIS: (*Crosses* L. *to* ROB ROY.) Well, I wouldn't go *that* far, Rob Roy. You know, a artist reacts to the world around him cranium-wise—through the old noggin.

ROB ROY: Don't give me that bushwa. I've dated Mamie Van Doren, Jayne Mansfield and Diana Dors, and take it from me, Clyde, they don't have any corners. This moke's in trouble.

HUBRIS: (*Crosses bag at No. 3, with wild gaiety.*) Ha-ha—who isn't? . . . Now, Rob Roy, doll, I just want to check on a couple of scenes to insure we don't make a booboo. (*Whips open attaché case, produces smock and beret, crosses L. of* ROB ROY.) Here, slip these on so you'll get used to the feel of 'em.

ROB ROY: What the hell are we making, a costume picture? You said I wear a sweatshirt and jeans.

HUBRIS: (*Dripping with sucrose.*) In the love scenes, pussycat. But when you're like sketching and dreaming up your different masterpieces, we got to blue-print you're an artist. It establishes your identity.

ROB ROY: The way a sheriff puts on a tin star?

HUBRIS: Or a bus-boy his white coat. (*Crosses L.*)

ROB ROY: (*Reacts, wheels towards* HUBRIS.) What did you say?

HUBRIS: (*Gets script from No. 3, turns to* ROB ROY.) Me? Not a thing, honey—nothing. (*Muttering,* ROB ROY *dons smock in reverse.* HUBRIS *gropes a script from attaché case. Crosses* R. *of* LANCE, *behind* LANCE.) Now, first of all, Rob Roy, run through the situation where Vincent Youmans tries to win you back to your wife.

LANCE: Vincent Youmans, the composer? How does he come into this?

HUBRIS: (*Crosses, pushes* LANCE L.) A dramatic license we took to justify the score. You see, Youmans is a young music student at Harvard that Sargent befriends. (*Crosses L. of* ROB ROY.) Can you remember the lines, Rob Roy?

ROB ROY: (*Contorting forehead.*) I don't know. There's a coupla hard words.

HUBRIS: Never mind. Spitball some dialogue to give the sense. Go ahead, I'll cue you. I'll be Youmans. (*Crosses C.*) "Good morrow, Sargent!"

ROB ROY: (*Crosses L. to* HUBRIS. *Tonelessly.*) Hello, Youmans. Where you been, man?

HUBRIS: And he don't even know Lee Strasberg. (*Reads dialogue from script.*) "Oh, just studying my counterpoint over in Cambridge. But you certainly are a storm center these days, John Singer. All Beacon Hill is agog the way you threw up your job as stockbroker and abandoned your family. Can a pair of saucy blue eyes underlie this move, as waggling tongues imply?"

ROB ROY: (*Crosses* R., *with a purportedly cynical hoot.*) Women! I'm tired of those silly little creatures casting their spell on me. I want to paint—to paint, do you hear? (*Crosses* L.) I've got to express what I feel deep down inside me! The agony, the heartbreak!

HUBRIS: Beautiful—beautiful! Sweetheart, don't change a word, a syllable! Do that on camera, and I'll guarantee you an Oscar! (*Wheeling toward* LANCE.) How did it sound? Does it ring true from the artist's point of view?

LANCE: Well, yes, on the whole, but I noticed one thing wrong. Mr. Fruitwell's got his smock on backwards.

HUBRIS: You're dead right—the audience might mistake him for a barber. Watch that, Rob Roy.

ROB ROY: (*Crosses* L., *as one crucified.*) Damn it, Harry, you gonna hang around this mother-grabbin' place all night? I got an eight-man team of writers from the New York *Post* waiting to interview me!

HUBRIS: (*Crosses* L. *of* LANCE.) Be patient another ten seconds, baby—I got to corroborate one more detail. The key scene where you get your big break from the hotel manager. (ROB ROY *crosses* U.S., *sits chair on No. 3.* HUBRIS *takes* LANCE R. HUBRIS L. *of* LANCE.) The plot point here, Maestro, is that Sargent's down and out in New York. It's Christmas Day, the landlord's shut off the gas, and he's starving.

LANCE: The landlord?

HUBRIS: No, no—*Sargent.* (*Sorely impatient.*) Anyway, just at his darkest hour, in comes Tuesday Weld, the hat check girl at the St. Regis Hotel, which she's been secretly in love with him. She's persuaded the Hotel Manager to let Sargent paint a mural of Old King Cole . . . in the men's room. (LANCE *nods.*) How would a painter react in those circumstances? What exact phraseology would he employ?

LANCE: (*Ponders.*) Well, let me see. (*Crosses* R. *of* C.) Sometimes they smite their forehead— (*Demonstrates.*) and use a simple Greek word, like "Eureka!"

ROB ROY: (*Rises, crosses* D.S., *taking off beret,* L. *of* HUBRIS.) And for this you fly me from the Coast, you *schlep*!

HUBRIS: (*Crossing to him.*) I only did it for your good, baby—

ROB ROY: (*Raging.*) Don't try to con me, you muzzler! I'm walking off your stinking picture!

HUBRIS: Now calm down, you're tired—

ROB ROY: You bet I am! Tired of being pushed around by you and that turpentine peddler. (*Taking off smock.*) I'm calling my agent, Monroe Sweetmeat, right now to break my contract! (*Crosses to chair No. 3.*)

HUBRIS: (*Crosses R. of* ROB ROY, *takes him* D.C., HUBRIS R. *of* ROB ROY. *Panicky.*) Rob Roy, I sensed you were unhappy in this role—I had a premonition. I've decided to buy you the property you begged me for—"Laughing Stevedore." Tomorrow I ink a new pact with Monroe doubling your salary to five-fifty a week!

ROB ROY: (*Crosses* L.) Ink your head off! You're a loser, Hubris. I'm planing to Rome tonight to see Carlo Ponti! (*Crosses* L.)

HUBRIS: (*Crosses* L. *to* R. *of* ROB ROY.) Ponti?

ROB ROY: You heard me!

HUBRIS: That pizza peddler! What can he give you?

ROB ROY: Top billing and some of the greatest zook in Europe!

HUBRIS: Yeah? (*Scrabbles in pockets, extracts a fragment of paper and leads* ROB ROY D.S. *out of earshot of* LANCE. *Then the ensuing four speeches are read* sotto voce.) Can Carlo Ponti give you that? . . . Answer me!

ROB ROY: "April Monkhood, 33 Perry Street." (*His eyes narrow lustfully.*) Is she built? Is she stacked?

HUBRIS: Who cares? She's alive and she's there!

ROB ROY: (*Starting toward door.*) Come on!

HUBRIS: Go ahead—I'll folly you. . . . (*Turning back to* LANCE, *with intense conviction—crosses to chair* L.) A household word in two years! That's what I predict for that young man!

LANCE: (*Dubiously.*) Yes, he seems to be very gifted. . . .

HUBRIS: He's a lot more than that, Buster—he's going to be an annuity for my old age. Well, thanks for the dope you gave me. (*His voice sweetens.*) Say, Rembrandt—in view of all the publicity you're getting, you ought to present me with a little token of your esteem. This sketch here, for instance . . .

(*As he crosses to easel and removes painting,* QUAGMEYER *enters carrying a couple of stretchers.*)

QUAGMEYER: What are you doing there? Leave that alone!

HUBRIS: (*Crosses* R. *of chair. Belligerently.*) Yeah? Why should I?

QUAGMEYER: Because it's mine—that's why. Drop it, I said! (*Takes painting from* HUBRIS, *sets it on easel.*)

HUBRIS: (*Puzzled, to* LANCE.) Who is this bird?

LANCE: He's Mr. Quagmeyer—the one you came here to see! (*To* QUAGMEYER.) I tried to tell him I wasn't you, but he was too bullheaded to listen!

HUBRIS: (*Crosses* L. *of* QUAGMEYER; *sunnily.*) Oh, well, what's the diff, so long as we finally connected? Quagmeyer, I'm Harry Hubris of Hubbub Productions in Hollywood— and I badly need a technical advisor for my new picture—based on the life of John Singer Sargent.

QUAGMEYER: (*Turning away.*) Save your breath, Mr. Hubris —you just want to use my name to merchandise your junk—

HUBRIS: Yeah? Well, you listen to me, pal: What if I gave you complete control over the whole artistic end?

QUAGMEYER: You mean absolute authority?

HUBRIS: (*Crosses* L. *with* QUAGMEYER *on his* R. *Transported.*) I'll tell you how absolute. You need a certain statue from the Louvre? I'll glom it for you. You want a particular type beret for Sargent's head? I'll steam it for you. You'll be the chief shamus of the whole God-damned production!

QUAGMEYER: Well . . . that's different.

HUBRIS: You bet your rosy pratt it is. (*Crosses* R., QUAGMEYER R. *of* HUBRIS.) Now, as to the fee, we don't expect anything free gratis. I'm buying a reputation, and I'm prepared to lay it on the line.

QUAGMEYER: What did you have in mind?

HUBRIS: One-fifty a week, a four-week guarantee, and half your bus fare.

QUAGMEYER: That doesn't seem like very much. . . .

HUBRIS: Fifteen hundred a week!

QUAGMEYER: We're in business.

LANCE: (*Outraged.*) Mr. Quagmeyer—how can you lend yourself to such practices? I thought you had some integrity

—that you stood for something clean and straight and fine. But there's nothing people won't do for the almighty dollar, is there? . . . O.K., go ahead and sell your soul to the Devil. I for one won't watch it! (*He exits violently.*)

HUBRIS: (*Blandly.*) Typical. A rebel without a cause. (*He dismisses it with a wave.*) But getting back to our deal, Quag. Instead of fifteen hundred in a lump sum, what about thirty-five dollars down, fifty at the preview, and the balance the minute the negative cost is paid off? (*Energetically.*) Or maybe you'd prefer ten bucks now and a percentage deal, like a half share of the Antarctica rights? As a matter of fact, you stand to make twice as much dough that way. . . .

(*As he closes in on* QUAGMEYER, *fraternally clasping his shoulders, we SEGUE into:*)

ACT ONE
SCENE 5

SCENE: *April Monkhood's apartment.*

TIME: *Half an hour later.*

AT RISE: *April's housewarming, a cocktail party, is in progress.* MAURICE BLOUNT, *a fly-by-night publisher,* BORIS PICKWICK, *a flautist, the* KRUMGOLDS, *and* CHENILLE SCHREIBER, *a beatnik, grouped Downstage chattering ad lib.* APRIL *hurries in from kitchen bearing tray of drinks. Subdued Muzak if needed.*

APRIL: (*Crosses* C., *distractedly.*) Now who hasn't met who? Oh, Gloria! Maurice, do you know the Krumgolds? They're earth people. Gloria! Seymour! (*To latter.*) Maurice Blount's one of our most distinguished publishers of erotica. . . .

(BLOUNT *rises, puts drink on table.*)

MR. KRUMGOLD: I'm in the textile shrinking game.

MRS. KRUMGOLD: A publisher . . . how fascinating. (*Crosses* L. *of* BLOUNT.)

APRIL: And, Seymour, this is Boris Pickwick, first flautist of the Utica Symphony . . . (*Crosses* U.R.)

PICKWICK: Where's Vernon? (*Crosses* U.R.)

APRIL: Oh, he'll be along in a wink. (*To* MR. KRUMGOLD.) Vernon Equinox, that is. He writes non-prose for magazines like "Angst," and he also paints under the influence of mescaline. (*Crosses* U.S., *gets two drinks from table.*)

MR. KRUMGOLD: I once smoked a reefer with a couple of girls from Bayonne, and boy, was I sick.

MRS. KRUMGOLD: Nobody wants to hear about your orgies.

(*They exchange glances of hatred, separate.* MR. KRUMGOLD *sits pouf.* APRIL *crosses* R. *and gives* MRS. KRUMGOLD *drink and moves* U.S. MRS. KRUMGOLD *and* BLOUNT *sit couch.* KITTY EN-TRAIL, *an intense minor poetess in paisley and hoop earrings enters with* VERNON EQUINOX *from* L.)

APRIL: (*Crosses* L. *of* C.) Kitty, how divine to see you. But where's Rolf?

KITTY: (*Crosses* L. *of* APRIL.) He couldn't come, he's laid up with an impacted hip.

APRIL: I'll send him two pounds of caviar tomorrow. Vernon!

VERNON: Who are all these people? My dear, it's the copulation explosion!

APRIL: (*Crosses* L. *of* KITTY.) Vernon, when did you get back from Haiti? (*Takes his hand, leads him* R.)

VERNON: (L. *of* KITTY.) Oaxaca. Nobody goes to Haiti any more.

APRIL: Of course—I forgot.

VERNON: (*Crosses* L. APRIL *follows.*) Not Oaxaca proper, mind you. A tiny village sixty miles south—San Juan Doloroso. Sabu and I lived there for three pesos a day.

APRIL: Incredible. But I suppose it's already spoiled.

VERNON: Not inside the volcano. Only on the rim.

KITTY: Darling, I adore your new ambiente. It's too Aubrey Beardsley, isn't it, Vernon?

VERNON: (*Critically.*) Hm-m-m, I'm not sure about that area over there. I'd like to see a Renaissance credenza— (*Crosses* L.)

KITTY: Or rather, the memory of a credenza.

(*Talk from* COMPANY.)

APRIL: (*Takes* KITTY L.; VERNON *crosses* U.S., APRIL R. *to* MR. KRUMGOLD.) Seymour, this is Kitty Entrail.

KITTY: *Enchanté.*

MR. KRUMGOLD: I'm in the textile shrinking game.

APRIL: Kitty is a minor poetess.

MR. KRUMGOLD: A poetess, eh! I always wanted to know —what do you get for a poem?

KITTY: Heartbreak, Mr. Krumgold, heartbreak.

MR. KRUMGOLD: Same in the textile game.

(KITTY *crosses* U.L., *then* D.S. *of* APRIL. APRIL *crosses* L. KRUMGOLD *sits pouf. LOUD TALK.*)

BLOUNT: (*Crosses* D.C. *to front of couch.* MRS. KRUMGOLD L. *of him.*) I can't believe it! (*To* MRS. KRUMGOLD.) Did I understand you never read the memoirs of Polly Adler? You missed one of the great experiences!

MRS. KRUMGOLD: What is it—some kind of a historical work?

BLOUNT: (*Crosses* L.) No, more of a true-confessions type thing. I'll mail you a copy tomorrow in a plain wrapper.

MRS. KRUMGOLD: (*Archly.*) Do I have to read it in a plain wrapper?

BLOUNT: (*Crosses* R.) I got a closetful of fancy ones. Come up to my place and we'll read it together.

MRS. KRUMGOLD: (*Slaps his hand away.*) Don't get fresh with me, you measle.

BLOUNT: (*With dignity, crosses* L.) Excuse me, I got to correct some proofs. (*Crosses* U.L.)

(*LOUD TALK.*)

MRS. KRUMGOLD: Oh, my goodness. (*Laughs. Sits couch.*)

CHENILLE: (*Crosses* D.S.) But, Boris, MacDougal Alley's the very reason I left Bridgeport. (*Crosses front to* R. *end of couch.*)

(VERNON *crosses* R. *of* APRIL. BLOUNT *crosses* L. *of* VERNON.)

PICKWICK: (*Crosses* L. *above couch.*) The trouble with MacDougal Alley is, it has only two dimensions. The people over there is strictly a lot of cheap crumbs. Now in my winter home, in Cortina d'Ampezzo—

KITTY: (*Crosses* L.) Cortina d'Ampezzo! The echolalia of that name! It's so—so steeped in the bright black creosote of authenticity.

PICKWICK: You see what I mean?

KITTY: (*Ecstatically.*) Oh, I do, I do!

PICKWICK: Then explain it to me.

KITTY: Get that woman away from me!

APRIL: (*Crosses* D.S. *with* VERNON.) Vernon, I'm furious with you. Everyone's avid to see those puppets you twist out of pipe-cleaners.

VERNON: (*Crosses table* R., *gets tray.*) I'm through with that dilettante stuff. I've been designing some non-objective marionettes—a combination of dance and mime. Aaron Copland's wild to do the music.

APRIL: Oh, do let him.

(VERNON *crosses* L. *of* APRIL.)

MR. KRUMGOLD: (*Rises, crossing* D.R. *of* MRS. KRUMGOLD.) Gloria, for God's sake! . . . I . . .

GLORIA: (*Shouts.*) Seymour! (*Turns back smiling.*)

APRIL: By the way, how do you like the Krumgolds?

VERNON: (*Sincerely—eating canape.*) They're the most delicious things I've ever eaten. (*Crosses* D.S. *of couch.*)

(LANCE *enters* R.)

LANCE: (*Crosses* L. *of* C.) April! April!

APRIL: Lance Weatherwax! Whatever in the world are you doing here?

LANCE: You invited me!

APRIL: (*Crosses* R. *of* LANCE.) Then where have you been, for God's sake? I've had to do everything myself.

LANCE: I'm sorry, April. I had a terrible experience. I went over to see Goddard Quagmeyer about my problem.

APRIL: You can tell me all about it tomorrow. (*Pushes him across to her* R.) Run and get a muscatel for Kitty.

LANCE: I will, but when you hear what that man did—

APRIL: (*Impatiently.*) Now, really, Lance—is this the time or place to air your petty personal concerns? (*Turning toward guests; raises voice.*) Out in the hall, everybody! Dinner's ready on the stairs!

(GUESTS *drift off, but* LANCE *delays* APRIL.)

LANCE: You told me to go see him—

APRIL: Who?

LANCE: Quagmeyer. You were wrong—he's as corrupt as anybody else. (*Crosses* L.)

APRIL: (*Crosses telephone table.*) Are you still harping on him?

LANCE: (*Crosses R.*) Anybody that sells out his principles for fifteen hundred dollars. It was disgusting! (*Crosses L.*) You wouldn't believe it. There was this movie actor there—Rob Roy Fruitwell— (*Crosses C.*)

APRIL: (D.S. *of couch.*) Rob Roy Fruitwell! That hoodlum! I've seen those movies of his—he's an animal. (*Crosses R. of* LANCE.)

LANCE: I'll admit he's very masculine, but Mr. Quagmeyer—

APRIL: Masculine? He's like something out of the primordial ooze. Is that what you admire in people?

LANCE: (*Crosses L. of* APRIL.) No—no—no—

APRIL: Lance, I'm surprised at you, I detest everything he stands for.

(ROB ROY *enters from* D.L., *crosses R.*)

LANCE: Yes, yes—but Mr. Quagmeyer—

APRIL: I know his type, believe me. He thinks all he has to do is look at a girl, nod in her direction— (ROB ROY *looks at* APRIL *as he passes her and exits* R.) and she'll go lusting after him. (APRIL *follows* ROB ROY *out* R.)

LANCE: April! (D.S. *of couch.*)

(HARRY HUBRIS *enters jovially from* L.)

HUBRIS: (*Crosses L. of* LANCE.) Say, have you seen Rob Roy Fruitwell?

LANCE: She's gone!

HUBRIS: (*Recognizing* LANCE.) It's the mouth-breather. (*Chuckles.*) I got to hand it to you, Clyde, I really mistook you for an artist before.

LANCE: (*Brokenly.*) I knew it couldn't last. I was only deceiving myself.

HUBRIS: Well, you fooled me, and I'm a pretty tough customer.

LANCE: She's left me—abandoned me. Oh, what am I going to do?

HUBRIS: For openers you could clean up these olive pits. (*Crosses L.*)

LANCE: She was my guiding star—my beacon, (*Crosses L. of* C.) but there's no point in life any more.

HUBRIS: Hey, Willie, you need some fresh air. (*Looks at initial on* LANCE'S *sweater.*) Back to the "Y" and take a cold shower.

LANCE: (*Bitterly.*) I've been on the wrong track all along. What good is art if it only leads to heartbreak? (*Crosses, sits pouf.*)

HUBRIS: (*Crosses* U.S., L. *of* LANCE.) Say, this is a soul in torment.

LANCE: I'm through with the ivory tower. I'm going to work in the mass media. I'll show her what beauty I can create—

HUBRIS: (*Patronizingly.*) Listen, bub, what are you—a chicken-flicker? An elevator operator in a one-story building? (*Crosses* R.)

LANCE: One day when I'm immortal, she'll know the sacrifices I made.

HUBRIS: Sacrifices? A rabbi—is that what you are?

LANCE: (*Rises.*) She'll remember me to her dying day, you wait. She'll remember the name of Lance Weatherwax.

HUBRIS: (*Crosses* R. *of* LANCE. *Electrified.*) Lance Weatherwax? Not the Weatherwax All-Weather Garbage Disposal Plan?

LANCE: Yes.

HUBRIS: (*Crossing.*) Then I'll tell you what you are—you're a movie director! (*Takes* LANCE D.S.) You're going to direct my new picture, "The Guns of Appomattox," the biggest grosser in the next ten years! The Music Hall's got it pencilled in for Easter Week, and it's not even written yet! (*Hitting* LANCE *hard on shoulder to emphasize remarks.*) And you're the bozo that's going to direct it!

LANCE: I never directed before—

HUBRIS: A fresh mind, a primitive! Willie Wyler wants to do it but he's too shallow. John Huston wants it—he's too deep. You're the logical man! (*Arm business again.*)

LANCE: Golly, sir—are you really serious?

HUBRIS: (*Encircling* LANCE'S *shoulders.*) I'll tell you how serious. To show my faith in you, I'm going to let your folks put up the money for an independent production! (*As he steers* LANCE *out.*) Hollywood—here you come! (*Crosses* L.)

CURTAIN

END OF ACT ONE

ACT TWO
SCENE I

SCENE: *Mrs. Younghusband's Agency, an employment office for select domestics in Santa Barbara, California. A fairly shallow set, approximately one-and-a-half. The furnishings are simple: a desk at R.C., matching chair and filing cabinet, wall calendar, a large photo of Del Monte coastline with twisted cypresses. Facing desk, two wicker chairs for clients. Door to exterior at L.*

TIME: *Morning, two weeks later.*

AT RISE: MRS. YOUNGHUSBAND, *a desiccated gentlewoman in her forties, professionally* hochgeboren *and attired in a cardigan sweater set and pearls, sits at desk, speaks animatedly into phone.*

MRS. YOUNGHUSBAND: (*Into phone.*) Now, Chang Fat, I have a simply marvelous situation for you—a yachtsman down at Balboa. He's got a 63-foot yawl with a balloon jib, and he needs a wideawake Chinese boy to do for him. . . . What? . . . No—only the summer. In the winter, he lives at Pancreas Hall, that sanitarium in Glendale. . . . No, poor man, he thinks a weevil is eating his liver. . . . All right then, three o'clock— Good-bye.

HUBRIS: (*Entering from L. Crosses L. of desk.*) Dolores, Dolores, Dolores.

MRS. YOUNGHUSBAND: (*Rises. Gummy.*) So generous of you to come up to Santa Barbara, Mr. Hubris. I know how valuable your time is.

HUBRIS: (*Sits L. of desk.*) Dolores, Tom Younghusband—your husband—may he rest in peace—was the greatest stunt man that ever worked for me. The day that Egyptian temple fell on him, I made a resolve his widow would never want for a thing.

MRS. YOUNGHUSBAND: (*Sits R. of desk.*) There should be more people like you, Mr. Hubris. This world would be a better place.

HUBRIS: (*Rises, crosses L.*) Of course! Now you said you got a problem. You said you got a client needs a first-rate houseboy.

MRS. YOUNGHUSBAND: The Rising Sun Domestic Employment Agency handles only top quality Oriental personnel.

HUBRIS: (*Crosses* L. *of desk.*) I got him. I got him . . . a
Cambodian.

MRS. YOUNGHUSBAND: These people, Mr. and Mrs. Fingerhead, are terribly particular. One thing they won't tolerate is a
jazz baby. You know the type gook I mean.

HUBRIS: They can rest easy, dear lady. Wing Loo studied
three years at U.C.L.A. He was on the dean's list morning,
noon, and night. (*Sits* L. *of desk.*)

MRS. YOUNGHUSBAND: (*Makes note.*) And you can vouch for
his cooking, can you?

HUBRIS: Don't ask me—ask a gourmet like Darryl Zanuck
—Hedda Hopper—Duke Wayne—people which they make a
shrine of their stomach. Every time I throw a luau, they're in
the kitchen trying to hire Wing Loo away from me.

MRS. YOUNGHUSBAND: An authentic Cambodian, you said?

HUBRIS: (*Rising.*) Right off the boat—a greenhorn. Look,
you'll see for yourself. (*Rises. Calls through door.*) Oh, Wing
Loo, Wing Loo! (*Crosses* L. DOLORES *crosses* R. *of* C. LANCE
enters L., *his appearance perceptibly altered. He wears Chinese
garb, pigtail. His eyes have a strikingly Oriental slant and his
skin color is distinct yellow. Carries a cheap cardboard suitcase.*)
Did I exaggerate?

MRS. YOUNGHUSBAND: (LANCE *bows.* MRS. YOUNGHUS-
BAND *nods approvingly.*) Yes, he's the real thing, all right. (MRS.
YOUNGHUSBAND *crosses* R. *of* HUBRIS.)

HUBRIS: Like night and day from a false Cambodian.

MRS. YOUNGHUSBAND: You've just had the most glowing
reference, Wing Loo. I hope you create a good impression on
the Fingerheads, now.

LANCE: It sounds like a golden opportunity.

MRS. YOUNGHUSBAND: It is!

HUBRIS: (*Moves* R. *Elaborate nonchalance.*) Now—correct
me if I'm wrong but did I hear you say the lady of the house
was a writer, no?

MRS. YOUNGHUSBAND: Her husband, too. They're both experts on the Civil War. Written scads of books about it. Well,
it's all set. (*Crosses* R.) If you'll excuse me, I have to run next
door to the vegetarian bar. (*Crosses to door.*) I have a very

serious iron deficiency. The doctors gave me only nine hours to live. I have to go get my parsnip juice.

HUBRIS: (*As she exits.*) A parsnip condition, she should wear a metal tag. (*Energetically.*) Now, look—we can't waste any time. You remember my instructions?

LANCE: To find out the plot of Mrs. Fingerhead's new Civil War novel. The one I'm going to direct.

HUBRIS: Right.

LANCE: Golly, Mr. Hubris, it was a great day when I met you. And now I'm going to express myself in film. Directing movies— (*Gratefully.*) You sure have been swell, Mr. Hubris.

HUBRIS: (*Crosses* R.) Nothing at all—nothing at all!

LANCE: The only thing . . . (*Indicates makeup.*) What does all this have to do with making movies?

HUBRIS: (*Crosses* R. *of* LANCE.) It's the most important part —stealing the property! Everybody in the trade'll be shooting a Civil War spectacular on account of it's the Centennial. We got to be there fustest with the mostest—*vershsteh*?

LANCE: (*Dubiously.*) I guess so . . .

HUBRIS: You're the undercover man, the camera eye recording every little detail. And if you can heist the manuscript, so much the better.

LANCE: The whole thing?

HUBRIS: As much as you can carry. How's the makeup?

LANCE: The adhesive tape hurts my eyes.

HUBRIS: Take it off at night. But don't forget—keep that Jap-a-lac on your face, and lots of Scuff-Koat on the hair. (*Crosses* L. *of* LANCE.)

LANCE: What about the meals?

HUBRIS: Don't worry! They're Southerners. Just look mysterious and give 'em grits.

LANCE: Suppose they order something fancy.

HUBRIS: (*Crosses* L. *to* L. *of* C.) I'll send you a couple of books. "The Joy of Cooking" and "Love and Knishes," by Sara Kasdan.

LANCE: Mr. Hubris—what I'm doing—are you sure it's legal? . . . Couldn't I get arrested?

HUBRIS: For what? Impersonating a Cambodian?

LANCE: It just doesn't seem right.

HUBRIS: (*Crosses* L. *of* LANCE.) Of course it ain't! It's sneaky

—lowdown—beneath contempt! But you listen to me. Suppose Harry Lime refused to water down that black-market penicillin in "The Third Man"? (*Crosses* R.) Suppose Janet Leigh didn't take that shower in "Psycho"? (*Crosses* LANCE.) Suppose Simone Signoret didn't shack up with that guy in "Room At The Top"? Where would this great industry be today?

LANCE: Gosh, I never thought of it that way.

HUBRIS: Of course!

(*Steps* D.S. *of* LANCE. *They start to exit* L. HUBRIS *looks out front, registering satisfaction at the logic that has convinced* LANCE. *As they exit, we SEGUE to:*)

ACT TWO
SCENE 2

SCENE: *Kitchen of the Fingerhead residence. Window rear over a sink unit flanked by work counters and cupboards. Wall phone. At* C., *a table bearing a silver pitcher, creamer, spoons and forks, candlesticks, silver polish, rags. Door to living room* L., *door to garden* R.

TIME: *Noon, five days later.*

AT RISE: LANCE, *in houseman's striped apron, is polishing silver. After a moment,* GRACE FINGERHEAD *enters from living room wearing a floppy garden hat, carries flower basket containing shears over arm.* LANCE *on chair* R. *He rises.*

GRACE: (*Crosses to counter.*) Good morning, Wing Loo.

LANCE: Good morning, Mrs. Fingerhead.

GRACE: The lobelias look so lovely this morning I can't resist them. I'm going down to the lower garden and snip off their little pods.

LANCE: (*Sits.*) Yes, ma'am.

GRACE: (*At counter, turns* R.) Whose motorcycle was that I heard in the driveway just now?

LANCE: The fish-market with our order.

GRACE: (*Crosses back of* L. *chair.*) Oh, your halibut squares . . . Wing Loo, I know you're making every effort, but I wish you'd stick to the menu I give you. Now that noodle ring you made for dinner last night!

LANCE: I'm sorry, Mrs. Fingerhead. I guess I put in too many raisins.

GRACE: (*Crosses* L. *of* L. *chair.*) And just because your last employer loved frozen blintzes, I see no reason to get them three nights running.

LANCE: Yes, ma'am.

GRACE: (*Crosses to behind counter.*) Is Mr. Fingerhead up yet?

LANCE: No, ma'am. He worked all night again. I heard him dictating into his machine.

GRACE: A lot of good it'll do him. My book'll be out long before his. Congratulate me. Wing Loo, I've just completed the final chapter—the burning of Natchez. (*Crosses* R.)

LANCE: (*Reacting.*) Oh? You're all finished?

GRACE: Four years' work! Why, I've *discarded* more than a million and a half words. (*Crosses behind table.*) Even so, the manuscript runs to eleven hundred pages. (*Crosses* R.)

LANCE: I hope Madam has a great success.

GRACE: (R. *of* LANCE.) Well, thank you, dear, I feel I deserve it. Nobody before ever looked at the Confederacy through the eyes of a Creole call girl. (*Picks up clipping from desk. Crosses desk.*) Call me visionary, Wing Loo, but some day the character of Stephanie Lavabeau will stand with Madame Bovary and Becky Sharpe. (*Crosses desk.*) What's this?

LANCE: Mr. Fingerhead left it here for you. He cut it out of the New York Times *Book Review.*

GRACE: (*Crosses* R. *of* LANCE. *Hands it to him.*) What does it say?

LANCE: "Curtis Fingerhead, one of our most constant observers of the Southern literary scene—"

GRACE: (*Angrily.*) What are they talking about, the idiots? I've observed it twice as much as he has! (*Crosses behind table.*)

LANCE: "—is promising a new novel for the fall season based on the loves of Stonewall Jackson."

GRACE: (*Grabs clipping, tears it up; spitefully.*) Promising is right! He wrote two chapters of the wretched thing and bogged down. And even if he got it done, I doubt whether he'd sell more than twelve copies. (*Throws scraps on* C. *table, crosses* L., *sits stool.*)

(CURTIS FINGERHEAD *enters, attired in bathrobe.*)

CURTIS: (*Coldly; steps to* D.S. *end of counter.*) I heard that. And may I observe that anyone whose conception of the Union breastworks at Vicksburg is so Freudian—

GRACE: Thank you, my dear. I didn't realize you'd ever read my best seller "Spoon Bread and Powderhorns."

CURTIS: I haven't, but I occasionally do run across your reviews. (*Producing clipping from bathrobe pocket.*) This one, for instance, from the Nashville "Scimitar": "Author Grace Fingerhead betrays her usual ineptitude—"

GRACE: (*Crumples it and puts it in pocket.*) Mr. Fingerhead! Must you vent your spleen in front of the help? Not that I think Wing Loo is indiscreet.

CURTIS: (*Crosses* L. *of* L. *chair.*) Oh, I've met a couple of gabby Chinks in my time. Boy, did they run off at the mouth! (*Chuckles.*) Or maybe it was two other Chinamen, they all look alike to me.

GRACE: I doubt whether Wing Loo is very interested in your past.

CURTIS: (*Crosses behind table.*) Well, I'm interested in his. Bet you saw plenty of orgies down there in Hollywood, eh? (LANCE *lowers eyes modestly.*) Lots of naked little starlets chasing around in—what do they call 'em—teddies?

GRACE: Curtis, what a thing to say.

CURTIS: (*Back of table.*) Ah, everybody knows what goes on. Swimming pools full of champagne, mixed bathing— (*Crosses* R.)

GRACE: Well, Wing Loo won't encounter that sort of thing at our house.

CURTIS: No, he sure won't. (*Exits swinging door.*)

GRACE: (*Crosses swinging door, crosses back to chair* L., *sits.*) Do you want to know how downright evil some people can be? (*Looks around quickly.*) I've a notion he's trying to steal the manuscript of my book!

LANCE: (*Petrified.*) Ma'am?

GRACE: Well, you've noticed that old-fashioned safe upstairs in my closet?—behind my dresses?

LANCE: Uh—I'm not sure. . . .

GRACE: Oh, naturally, you'd have no reason to go poking about up there, but anyway, that's where I keep it, the manuscript, that is, and someone's been fooling with the combination recently. I put some axle grease on the knob a day or two ago, and sure enough, it's all smudged!

LANCE: Why—why would Mr. Fingerhead do a thing like that?

GRACE: Because he's consumed with jealousy, don't you see? It's killing him that Emmett Stagg, the head of Charnel House, wants to publish my novel. (*Sharp bark of laughter. Crosses to counter, gets basket.*) Well, Curtis won't get away with it. (*Crosses U.S. of table.*) I bought a fingerprint kit! (*Crosses R. of* LANCE *behind him.*)

LANCE: Holy Moses.

GRACE: (*Shrugs.*) Oh, well, I suppose one should be more compassionate. His last urinalysis came out 94 per cent cognac. (*Exits swinging doors.*)

(*She exits.* LANCE *crosses swiftly to phone, dials.*)

LANCE: (*Crosses desk, sits and dials. On phone. Rises.*) Hello? Hubbub Productions? Give me extension 354—Yes, yes, it's urgent! . . . (*Sits.*) Listen, Miriam, this is Lance again— I have to speak to Mr. Hubris right away. . . . (*Rises.*) What do you mean, you can't find him? You *have* to find him— get a message to him. . . . He *knows* that. I told him all about Stephanie Lavabeau—I told him it was in the safe but I couldn't—what? Look—tell him I'm in danger, they suspect something—

GRACE: (*Offstage.*) Wing Loo!

LANCE: I got to hang up, someone's coming— (*Crosses L. of table.*)

GRACE: (*Crosses above R. chair. Excitedly re-enters.*) Wing Loo—Wing Loo! I have the most thrilling surprise for you! Guess who just walked into the laundry area! (*Crosses L. of swinging door. He gapes.*) Your father! From Cambodia!

(*As* LANCE *emits a startled exclamation,* HARRY HUBRIS *enters past her. He is also garbed as a Chinese.*)

HUBRIS: (*Crosses front of R. chair, drops bag. Emotionally, as he beholds* LANCE.) My little tiger-cub. Come to me, pride of your ancestors.

LANCE: (*Frozen with fright, advances to him, bobs jerkily.*) Honored sire.

(*Bowing to each other.* LANCE *keeps bowing.* HUBRIS *stops him.*)

HUBRIS: Enough already!

GRACE: (*Crosses* D.S., R. *of* HUBRIS. *Eyes protrude in awe.*) Filial respect . . . it's a tradition . . .

HUBRIS: (*Turns to her, speaks in stilted English.*) Five thousand years ago, the great sage, Matzo Tongue, he say, "If pepper seed take wing, it will turn into a dragon-fly. But if dragon-fly lose wing, it will not turn into pepper seed." That is what the sage he say, five thousand year ago.

GRACE: The inscrutable wisdom of the East. (*Sighs.*) But I mustn't intrude—you two have so much to say to each other. (*Exits swinging door.*)

HUBRIS: (*Crosses* L. *to* D.S. *of stool.*) O.K., enough with the laundryman bit. Where's the safe?

LANCE: (*Follows* R. *of* HUBRIS.) Mr. Hubris, I just called you —we're in trouble!

HUBRIS: (*Reassuringly, indicates portmanteau.*) Relax. The tools I got there can open anything.

(LANCE *starts to pick up bag.*)

GRACE: (*Offstage.*) Wing Loo-oo!

(LANCE *drops bag—bows to* HUBRIS—*speaks Chinese.* LANCE *lapses into Chinese.*)

HUBRIS: *Vuss?*

GRACE: (*Enters.*) Wing Loo, do offer your father a cup of oolong. He looks exhausted. (*Exits.*)

LANCE: The safe's upstairs.

HUBRIS: (*Crosses* L. *of* LANCE.) Well, go and get it!

LANCE: (*Horrified.*) You mean, carry the whole safe out?

HUBRIS: Certainly. You're a big strong boy, you could lift a house. I can't lift on account of my thyroid, but I'll supervise. (*Energetically.*) Here's the dope. First—you're positive the whole script is inside, no loose fragments laying around?

LANCE: No, it's all there— She told me the plot—it's mostly sex.

HUBRIS: That's the two most important drives. Sex and what I got—hunger. . . . Okay. You beat it upstairs and carry down the box while I stand guard. Capisco?

LANCE: But we're going to need a truck, or a car—

HUBRIS: I made a deal with a motorcycle kid from a fish market. The safe goes into the side-car. And the two of us can hang onto the kid. Go on, now, upstairs and work fast.

(LANCE *gets bag and exits* L. HUBRIS *runs to swinging door* R., *hears someone coming and runs* L. *and hides behind the counter* L. CURTIS *enters swinging door and goes stealthily across Stage and out* L. FISH MARKET BOY *enters immediately* U.R., *looks around, and goes out swinging door.* GRACE *enters* U.R., *looks around, sees* HUBRIS, *screams, and exits through swinging door.* EMMETT STAGG—*owl-faced, bouncy—bespectacled, a pipe stuck jauntily in teeth—enters. Surveys kitchen cursorily, exits* U.R. HUBRIS *reappears from behind counter, crosses to swinging door, listens, and then runs to table. He picks up silverware and starts to stuff it into his coat.* GRACE *enters swinging door humming to herself.* HUBRIS *drops silver and crosses* D.L. GRACE *picks up microfilm package from desk and walks* D.R. *and addresses audience.*)

GRACE: Well, well. So—my envious husband reckons to steal my manuscript. Well, I'll fix his wagon. Here it is, transferred to microfilm and all that remains is to smuggle it out of the house. Hello—this guileless Oriental is meet for my purpose. He should yield readily to my blandishments. (*Crosses* R. *of* HUBRIS. *To* HUBRIS.) Well, Mr. Loo, how did you find your son?

HUBRIS: I rook around—I see him.

GRACE: Ha ha—very nicely phrased. Mr. Loo, would you do me a favor?

HUBRIS: Me do anysing fo' plitty lady.

GRACE: Would you just drop this in the nearest mailbox? It's a wedding present for my niece.

HUBRIS: (*Takes package, puts in pocket.*) Me keepum light here, next to ticker.

GRACE: Why, how gallant of you, Mr. Loo. I'm much obriged.

HUBRIS: Obliged.

GRACE: Of course. Thank you so much. (*Starts* R.)

HUBRIS: (*Bowing her off* R.) My preasure. My preasure.

GRACE: Charming. You're too kind.

(*She exits.* HUBRIS *assures himself she is safely out of the way, re-crosses to living room door and looks off anxiously. He then returns to the table at* C., *picks up silverware again.* CURTIS *enters furtively, steals Downstage.* HUBRIS *sits* R. *chair—starts to polish silver.*)

CURTIS: (*Aside.*) Well, my devious stratagems are coming to fruition at last. (*Exhibits duplicate of Grace's brown package.*) Thanks to technological advance, I now possess a duplicate microfilm copy of Grace's novel. To fob it off as my own, I shall need a cat's-paw. (*Descries* HUBRIS *Upstage.*) Oh, by jove, the very man. This wily Oriental, skilled in intrigue, is meet for my purpose. . . . I say there, Wing Loo! (*Crosses* U.S. *back of* L. *chair.*)

HUBRIS: Yassuh— Yassuh, Bwana?

CURTIS: (*Stares at him.*) Humph. I don't know what it is about Santa Barbara, but it sure ages people. Look, boy, can you run an errand for me chop-chop? (*Sits* L. *chair.*)

HUBRIS: Solly, no can do. Missy tell me stay here, shine silber.

CURTIS: Oh, banana oil! I'm the one that pays your salary, do you hear? (HUBRIS *bobs assent.* CURTIS *addresses package.*) Now run out and mail this manuscript for me.

HUBRIS: (*Pricking up ears.*) Manusclipt?

CURTIS: Yes, you wouldn't understand, but it's my novel of the Confederacy as seen through the eyes of a Creole call girl.

HUBRIS: (*Reaches eagerly for it.*) Yes siree. Me complihend! (*Takes package.*)

CURTIS: (*Takes package, rises, breaks* L.) On second thought, maybe I shouldn't entrust it to the mails—

HUBRIS: (*Rises, crosses* R. *of* CURTIS.) Me velly careful—me insure it! (*Takes package.*)

CURTIS: No, wait a minute. (*Takes package.*) Film's got to be packed in a fire-proof container— (*Crosses* L.)

HUBRIS: Me packee! Me packee! Me *packee*!! (*Crosses* L., *grabs package.*)

CURTIS: (*Holds on to the package. They wrestle for it. Suspiciously, thrusting it behind him.*) Oh, no, you won't, you cunning heathen. Nobody's handling this but yours truly— (*Gets package.*) not after the pains it's cost me. (*Exits* L. *door.* HUBRIS *crosses* L. *door and crosses behind counter.*)

(EMMETT STAGG *re-enters from* U.R.)

STAGG: (*Crosses front of counter. Entering* U.R.) Grace!! Grace!! Anybody home? (*Breezily.*) Hi there, John. I'm Emmett Stagg, Mrs. Fingerhead's publisher. I'm on my semi-annual lecture tour of the West Coast, playing to packed houses everywhere, and thought I'd stop in.

HUBRIS: I bereave I see you on terevision.

STAGG: Every Sunday night, unless you're blind. (*Crosses front of table to* R. *Crosses* U.S.) Well, I can't wait. Lenny Bruce and eighteen of America's foremost sick comics are throwing me a—ha-ha—Stagg dinner at Hillcrest. (*Fumbles out calling card and pencil. Crosses counter.*) Here's my number—I'm staying with Tony Curtis in Bel Air. . . .

HUBRIS: Tory Curis in Berair.

STAGG: You're dead right—Tony wouldn't want his phone bruited about. Tell you what, I'll leave Burt Lancaster's—

(*As he bends down to write,* CURTIS *re-enters.*)

CURTIS: (*Crosses* L. *of* L. *chair, looks about vaguely.*) Where's that almond-eyed son-of-a-bitch was in here a minute ago?

STAGG: Hello—ha-ha—Fingerhead—

CURTIS: Emmett! What are you doing in this neck of the woods?

STAGG: Well, I'm on my semi-annual lecture tour of the West Coast—playing to packed houses everywhere—thought I'd drop in.

CURTIS: (*Crosses* R.) Fine. But what am I being so cordial to you for? You're only here to see Grace.

STAGG: Curtis, that was unfair. Bring me a piece of work you've got faith in, and by tarnation, I'll paint your name across the sky!

CURTIS: (*Sneering.*) Do you think that pipsqueak firm of yours is big enough to handle a runaway best seller? (*Sits* R. *chair.*)

STAGG: (*Crosses* L. *around table, sits* L. *chair.*) Who copped the National Book Award last year? Charnel House—with our number one smash hit, "A Child's Life of Liberace."

(HUBRIS *crosses* R. *of* CURTIS, *tries to pick package out of his pocket.*)

CURTIS: (*Querulously.*) I've got a taste in my mouth like a motorman's shoe. Where's that slippery Mongolian? (*He catches sight of* HUBRIS.) Hey, you! Fix me a highball—and heavy on the brandy.

HUBRIS: Me bling whole bottle. (*Crosses* R. *through swinging door. He moves off slowly, straining to catch the drift of the others' conversation.*)

STAGG: Curtis, I see a sly little look in your eye. (*Wheedling.*) Have you got a book in the oven?

CURTIS: A book, for God's sake? A cataclysm—a Vesuvius!

STAGG: You think there's a movie in it?

CURTIS: Ho ho—and how! Why, there are scenes in it that'll make Grace Metalious look like Mother Goose! (HUBRIS *enters, crosses above table, pours drink.*) Wait till you read about the orgies at Rebel headquarters, the mixed bathing! No one before has ever looked at the Confederacy through the eyes of a Creole call girl.

STAGG: Man, we'll have to print that on asbestos—

CURTIS: All honeysuckle and spitfire—that's Stephanie Lavabeau!

(HUBRIS *reacts.*)

STAGG: Who?

HUBRIS: Stephanie Lavabeau. . . .

CURTIS: (*Gleefully.*) See that, Emmett? That heathen ignites at the name and he doesn't even speak the language.

(HUBRIS *crosses front of counter.*)

STAGG: (*Excitedly.*) Now listen to me, pal, because I mean business. You let me have that book and I'll print a hundred and fifty thousand copies before publication.

CURTIS: Peanuts. Simon & Schuster offered me that for the outline. All I have to do is pick up a phone.

STAGG: *I'll* pick up a phone. (*Rises, crosses to phone* R., *dials.*)

CURTIS: Who are you calling?

STAGG: What does the phrase "movie sale" mean to you?

CURTIS: Now you're cooking!

STAGG: (*Sits phone chair; into phone.*) Goldie? Mr. Stagg—I'm up in Santa Barbara. Give me a tie line. Hollywood— Hubbub

Productions. . . . That's right. I want to speak to Harry Hubris personally.

CURTIS: Harry Hubris, the movie mogul? You know *him*?

STAGG: (*Sits chair.*) We've never met vis-a-vis, Curtis, but in the aristocracy of success, there are no strangers.

(HUBRIS, *his astonishment at* STAGG'S *effrontery mingled with admiration, moves Downstage and addresses audience.*)

HUBRIS: (*With relish.*) Why, the four eyed weasel—there goes my plan to steal the manuscript. Oh, well, I'll just have to buy it.

STAGG: (*Into phone.* CURTIS *rises, crosses* L. *of* STAGG.) Yes, I'm on . . . Hubbub Productions? This is Emmett Stagg. Put me through to Harry Hubris. . . . Harry? Emmett Stagg. How are you, Harry?

HUBRIS: I'm fine—how are you?

STAGG: (*Into phone, unctuously.*) Harry, I've got a book. No, I'm not going to let you read it. I'm just going to tell you one thing. (*Chuckles.*) It'll be a tidal wave, and I'm letting you on my surfboard. You've got first crack at the movie rights for three hundred G's!

HUBRIS: (*Crosses back of table.*) Three hundred?

STAGG: (*Into phone.*) Correct, dear heart, but you better talk fast—I've got Otto Preminger on the other phone!

HUBRIS: Two-fifty.

STAGG: (*Into phone.*) Why, you cheap scavenger, you presume to haggle over a symphony?

HUBRIS: (*Steps* R.) Two-seventy-five.

STAGG: (*Into phone.*) Make it two-eighty and we call it *schluss*.

HUBRIS: You got a deal.

STAGG: O.K., Harry—the rest is bookkeeping. (*Slams up phone, revolves around.*)

LANCE: (*Enters* L. *door. The* THREE *turn.* STAGG *rises.* LANCE *is doubled over, the safe in a sling on his back.*) I've got it! Mr. Hubris, I've got the manuscript, Mr. Hubris!

HUBRIS: Shhh!— Shut up—shut up!!

STAGG: Who the hell is that?

HUBRIS: Could be Atlas. (*Virtuously.*) I never saw him before in my life!

STAGG: (*Crosses* R. *of* HUBRIS.) Hubris—? (*He stares at him dumbfounded.*) Why, you low-down crook! Beating me down while all the time you were stealing it!

CURTIS: (*Wheeling on* STAGG.) Emmett Stagg, you phony bastard!

HUBRIS: (*Crosses* L. *of* CURTIS. *To* CURTIS, *indignantly.*) You should talk, you pickpocket! You copped the whole thing from your wife! (*Turning on* STAGG.) And you sold it to me! That makes you a receiver of stolen goods—a fence!

STAGG: I acted in all good faith! He told me he had a novel—

CURTIS: (*Producing his brown paper package.*) And so I have, right here!

HUBRIS: Then what are we all foompheting about? That's the property I bought—we've got a deal!

STAGG: (*Turning to* CURTIS.) By God, we have, haven't we?

LANCE: (*Puffing, eyes on floor.*) Is everything all right, Mr. Hubris?

HUBRIS: (*Crosses* R. *of* LANCE. *Outraged.*) What do you mean, all right? We caught you stealing a safe, young man! (*Righteous.*) Now, take that box upstairs and clear out while I still have pity on you. Go on. (*He gives* LANCE *a push toward door* L. *and latter totters out.* HUBRIS *turns, crosses* R.) Where's the story?

CURTIS: (*Hands him brown package.*) Here.

HUBRIS: We're going to make a bundle with this, boys.

GRACE: (*Emerging from behind portal.*) Oh, no, you won't, gentlemen. All you've got there is a hodge-podge of recipes from "Love and Knishes."

HUBRIS: (*Crosses* L. *of* GRACE.) Then where *is* the novel?

GRACE: Right next to your ticker, where it's been reposing all along. Do you want to hand it over, or would you prefer the police to search you?

HUBRIS: Dear lady, we're all friends here. Why should we wash our dirty linen in public? (*Crosses* R. *of* STAGG. *Points to* STAGG.) He's got a contract to publish your book, Mrs. Fingerhead. I got a deal to make a blockbuster out of it. All we need is a top-flight screen writer. (*Points to* CURTIS.)

CURTIS: Gee, thanks, Harry.

GRACE: (*Crosses* L.) Well, this has been a most profitable encounter. Shall we adjourn to the rumpus room for a libation on the altar of friendship? (*She exits* L.)

CURTIS: (*Crosses* L.) I'll mix you my special long-life gimlet
—Somerset Maugham's recipe. (*Exits* L.)

STAGG: Nothing like a drink when the day's work is done.
Join me, Harry?

HUBRIS: (*Crosses* L.) Emmett, it's a pleasure to do business
with a momzer like you. (*As he takes the latter's arm to go.*) You
know, regarding the picture—instead of two-eighty big ones,
how about an escalator deal?

STAGG: How do you mean?

HUBRIS: A hundred bucks down and fifty percent of the
Transylvania rights . . .

(*They start to exit* U.L. *as:*)

CURTAIN CLOSES

ACT TWO
SCENE 3

SCENE: *Conservatory of the Pasadena estate of Nelson Smedley, millionaire founder of the Smedley Snacketerias, a coast-to-
coast restaurant chain. The set, a two-dimensional tracery of
metal in the Art Nouveau style, is so constructed as to suggest
glass behind it. Several exotic plants (philodendron and century
plants intertwined with liana) ranged at front. At Stage L., an
ornamental high-backed Hong Kong rattan chair; at Stage R.,
a stone bench.*

TIME: *Three days later.*

AT RISE: *Stage deserted. After a moment,* WORMSER, *Smedley's
private secretary, enters, beckoning to* LANCE, *who bears manila
envelope under his arm.*

WORMSER: (*Crosses* C. *with oily deference.*) Right this way,
Mr. Weatherwax, and welcome to Pasadena. Mr. Smedley was
so delighted to get your telegram. (*Indicating bench.*) Do sit
down, won't you?

LANCE: (*Sits* R.) Thank you.

WORMSER: (*Winningly.*) I don't know *how* our restaurants
could function without the Weatherwax All-Weather Garbage
Disposal Plan.

LANCE: I'm not here representing the company, Mr. Wormser. It's about a television program I'm planning—

WORMSER: Oh, doesn't matter in the least—just having you drop in will be such a treat for the Commander. He'll be down as soon as he has his paraffin injection.

LANCE: Golly, is it ever hot in this conservatory here. It must be close to 95.

WORMSER: 112, actually, but one gets used to it in time. (*Extracting paper.*) Ah—just one trifle—this questionnaire you completed at the lower gate. Now, among your various clubs, you've listed something called the Y.C.L. (*Sudden harsh note.*) Now, what does that signify—the Young Communist League?

LANCE: Oh, no, sir—the Yale Camera Lovers. It was my extra-curricular activity.

WORMSER: Of course, of course. But you do understand, we can't be too careful with all this subversion around. I'll fetch Mr. Smedley.

(*He exits* L. *As* LANCE *proceeds to examine plants,* APRIL *enters garbed in nurse's World War I uniform à la Edith Cavell, pushing wheeled medicine tray.*)

LANCE: (*Rises.*) April!

APRIL: (*Crosses* L. *of* LANCE.) Lance Weatherwax! Whatever in the world are you doing here? (*Before he can recover.*) The last time I saw you, you were standing in the middle of my living room creating a scene. I've a good mind not even to speak to you. (*Puts tray down.*)

LANCE: I wasn't to blame for that, April. I tried to explain but you got me all rattled.

APRIL: And I can see you're still just as confused, dear boy. Why are you staring at me in that extraordinary fashion?

LANCE: Well—uh—you look different somehow—

APRIL: (*On the seventh astral plane.*) I *am* different, Lance —as utterly and totally different as can be from the person you used to know.

LANCE: I don't understand—

APRIL: (*Infinitely patient, infinitely sweet.*) Ah, there's so much you'll never understand, my dear. If I could only bring you to comprehend the change I've undergone. (*Sits* L. *chair.*) Lance, do you know what it's like to come under the influence of a truly dynamic individual?

LANCE: (*Still smarting.*) You mean that Rob Roy Fruitwell? (*Sits bench.*)

APRIL: (*With contempt.*) That hoodlum—of course not. I mean Nelson Smedley—the founder of Smedley Snacketerias.

LANCE: Well, I know he's a genius in the restaurant game —but what else does he do?

APRIL: He lives life to the fullest. He's vital—uncompromising. He rises above the drab, petty things of life. He inspires every single person around him to serve, to give unstintingly. But of course, you haven't any conception of what I'm talking about, poor boy. You're still the same sweet naive creature.

LANCE: (*Rises, crosses* R. *of* APRIL. *With warmth.*) Oh, no, I'm not. I had some very rough experiences after I struck out for myself, April. I was pushed around and abused by all kinds of sharpers, like that Harry Hubris . . . but I've learned my lesson.

APRIL: (*Patronizingly.*) Which is what?

LANCE: To create my own opportunities, (*Kneels* R. *of* APRIL.) to make myself worthy of you, April. I want to earn your respect—to prove myself, so that one day I can claim you.

APRIL: Oh, Lance, Lance, you have so far to go.

LANCE: No, no. (*Taps envelope.*) Wait till Mr. Smedley hears the idea I've got in this folder . . . about the Chocolate Soda Rhapsody! He'll flip, I guarantee you!

APRIL: Now I hope you're not going to upset him. (*Rises.*) Mr. Smedley is a very delicately balanced man.

(NELSON SMEDLEY, *supported by* WORMSER, *totters on. He wears a smoking jacket and skull-cap, is swathed in muffler, shawl and afghan.*)

WORMSER: (*Enters* L., U.S. *of* SMEDLEY, *helping him.*) Be careful, Mr. Smedley.

SMEDLEY: (*Pulling his arm away.*) Keep your paws off me! I can walk as good as the next man— (WORMSER *removes his arm, and* SMEDLEY *falls to the floor.* APRIL *crosses* U.S. *of* SMEDLEY. *They help him up.*) Pushed me again, didn't you? Always pushing—push, push, push, push— (*They cross to big chair*, WORMSER L. *and* APRIL R. WORMSER *helps him into his chair.*) Who turned off the heat? It's an icebox in here!

WORMSER: It's 118, Mr. Smedley. The putty's melting in the windows.

SMEDLEY: The hell with it. Tell the janitor to put on another coal.

WORMSER: But the boilers are red-hot.

SMEDLEY: (*Agitated.*) What? What's that about red? Who's red? There's reds in the house! Reds in the house!

WORMSER: No—no—it's all right. Don't get alarmed. . . . April, help me—

SMEDLEY *and* WORMSER: No—no! No—no! (APRIL *and* WORMSER *soothe* SMEDLEY, *lower him back into rattan chair.* SMEDLEY *meanwhile utters peevish whines and grunts like a baby teething. He suddenly catches sight of* LANCE.) Who's he? What's he after?

WORMSER: It's the young man who wired you, sir.

SMEDLEY: Did you screen him? (WORMSER *nods.*) There's a bulge in his pocket? It's round—it's a hand-grenade—it's a hand-grenade!

LANCE: (*Producing orange.*) No, sir, it's an orange. I found it on the lawn.

SMEDLEY: (*Shrilly.*) He tried to steal my orange! Stop, thief! Stop, thief!

WORMSER: (*To* LANCE, *affrightedly.*) Look, give it back —quick—

(*Ad libs*—APRIL, LANCE, WORMSER. LANCE *extends it to* SMEDLEY, *who burrows it into his coverings like a chipmunk, chattering his teeth.*)

APRIL: (*Resentfully, to* LANCE.) Now you got him all worked up. Aren't you ashamed?

LANCE: I'm sorry . . .

APRIL: (*She removes pill from bottle, pours water from carafe, extends both to* SMEDLEY.) All right, Commander dear. Down goes the liver spansule.

SMEDLEY: (*Gritting his teeth.*) No, no! Won't take it! Won't take it!

APRIL: There's a brave little boy.

SMEDLEY: Can't make me. Can't make me!

APRIL: All right, Mr. Stubborn—we won't have our five o'clock romp.

SMEDLEY: I'll take it.

WORMSER: (SMEDLEY *spits out pill.*) Now, Commander! (*Maneuvering* LANCE *up to* SMEDLEY.) This is Lance Weatherwax, Commander—you know, the party you consented to see.

SMEDLEY: (*Suspiciously.*) He looks like the other one—the one that stole my orange. Stop, thief! Stop, thief!

WORMSER: No, that one went away. This is Milo Weatherwax's son.

SMEDLEY: Milo Weatherwax! Knew him well. We were the same class at Groton. Dirtiest feeder in the school—always covered with farina!

WORMSER: This is Milo Weatherwax's son.

LANCE: (*Seeking to ingratiate.*) My dad often mentions you, Mr. Smedley.

SMEDLEY: Yeah? Well, tell him to give me back that elastic supporter he borrowed. What do you want?

LANCE: (*Withdraws place-mat from envelope.*) Well, I tell you, sir. I've got a sensational idea. I happened to drop into one of your Snacketerias between here and Santa Barbara, and this place-mat caught my eye—

SMEDLEY: Hold on there! Stole that from one of my restaurants? Stop, thief!

WORMSER: No—no! That thief went away.

SMEDLEY: Oh? He went away?

LANCE: I bought it at the souvenir counter.

SMEDLEY: Check on that, Wormser.

LANCE: The thing is, sir—are you familiar with what it says? The text about the chocolate soda? Let me read it to you—

SMEDLEY: (*Snatching it.*) I can read, you young squirt. I went to Groton. (*As he starts to read his hands shake.* APRIL *and* WORMSER *steady him. Clears his throat volcanically.*) "Hymn to a Chocolate Soda." (*Hands shake again.* APRIL *and* WORMSER *steady him.*) Stop shaking! (*Returns to place-mat.*) "Arise, ye troubadours, and sing a song of nectar. See the great satin ball of mouth-watering mocha, the luscious bubbles whose every secret cell is pledged to arouse—" (*Breaks off abruptly.*) Secret cell? Wormser! *Wormser*, where are you?

WORMSER: Right here, Commander.

SMEDLEY: Who wrote this Commie propaganda? What's all this about cells?

WORMSER: I'll have that deleted pronto, sir. Don't you worry.

SMEDLEY: (*Growling.*) Musta been written by one of those wetbacks. Goddam aliens come in and use up all our paper towels. . . . Goddam foreigners—hang 'em all—hang 'em! Kill 'em—kill 'em all—goddam foreigners!

APRIL: (*Indignantly, to* LANCE.) Really, Lance, you deserve to be locked up, raising Mr. Smedley's blood-pressure with such nonsense! }(*Ad libs.*)

LANCE: I wasn't trying to excite him—

SMEDLEY: Shut up—a man can hardly hear himself read. Where's all the printing? It went away! Now, where was I? You made me lose my place! Oh, here we are! (*Hands shake again.* WORMSER *and* APRIL *steady him. Returning to placemat.*) "Now gird yourself for the climax supreme. Discard the straw, tilt back your head, and treat your tonsils to the celestial ambrosia of flavor, action and chill." (*He looks up.*) Who the hell wrote this?

WORMSER: You did, sir.

SMEDLEY: Fire 'em! Fire 'em!

WORMSER: No, you don't understand. You wrote it yourself.

SMEDLEY: Pretty good!

LANCE: (*Eagerly.*) Do you see it, sir? Do you get it?

SMEDLEY: What?

LANCE: It's a natural—the germ for a sensational TV documentary—a spectacular! "Rhapsody in Bubbles"—an hour TV program showing the importance of the ice-cream soda in our culture!

SMEDLEY: M-m-m, I don't know.

LANCE: Now, wait till you hear my production plans, sir! Step one—I send a crew to the high Andes to film the life cycle of the cocoa bean. (*Kneels* R. *of him.*) Step two—we move a unit into Hershey, Pennsylvania, and live with the syrup as it evolves. (SMEDLEY *falls asleep.*) Step three—the marriage of the siphon and the scoop. And mind you—that's only the background for the titles!

WORMSER: (*Shakes* SMEDLEY.) Commander!

SMEDLEY: Get away from me! I want to hear this. Might have possibilities. . . .

LANCE: (R. *of* SMEDLEY. *Encouraged.*) I haven't even touched the story, sir! We plant candid cameras in a drugstore—reproduce an actual *soda fountain* and for the music I see a really great score—Virgil Thomson—

SMEDLEY: No—no—no—no! That wouldn't sell a lemon phosphate! You haven't thought it through. (*Gives* LANCE *place-mat.*)

LANCE: In what way, Mr. Smedley?

SMEDLEY: (*Pontifically.*) Now let me tell you something, young man—the story of the ice-cream soda—is the story of Nelson Smedley. You gotta combine the two!

LANCE: By Jiminy, sir, that's a genuinely creative idea! You're dead right!

SMEDLEY: I'm always right! I'll tell you how it should be done. You open the program with me sitting on a big banana split, with a large chocolate float on each side. (*To* WORMSER.) What d'ye think of that, Wormser?

WORMSER: Commander, you want my honest opinion? The night they televise that, Khrushchev better barricade himself in the Kremlin!

(ALL *laugh.* SMEDLEY *goes suddenly to sleep.*)

LANCE: (*Exultantly.*) Boy oh boy, we'll knock 'em cold with that opening—won't we, April?

APRIL: (*Crosses* R., *sits bench.*) I really wouldn't know, Mr. Weatherwax.

LANCE: (*Wakes up* SMEDLEY.) Well, Mr. Smedley, what do you think? Would you sponsor a program like that?

SMEDLEY: I don't know. I'd have to see a budget first! The scenery alone could cost a fortune.

LANCE: That's right, Mr. Smedley. We've got to be practical about this. (SMEDLEY *back to sleep.*) What we want is an estimate for the entire production. I better get going. (*Turns to* APRIL.) April, I may have something pretty definite to say to you the next time we meet. . . . (*Turns back to* SMEDLEY, *taps his shoulder.*) I'll be reporting back to you shortly, Commander. (*He exits quickly.*)

SMEDLEY: (*He wakes.*) Who's that? What'd he steal?

WORMSER: (*Calms him.*) No, no, sir—that was the young man about the television show, Lance Weatherwax.

SMEDLEY: (*Awakening.*) Oh, yes—yes. Milo's boy. Seems a pretty bright fella. . . .

APRIL: Yes, you always bring out the best in people, Commander. It's fabulous the way you handle them. You instinctively sense what they want.

SMEDLEY: Damn tootin'. That's why I drew up that document this morning.

APRIL: What document?

SMEDLEY: Tell her, Wormser.

WORMSER: (*Crosses* R. *of* SMEDLEY.) Well, Mr. Smedley felt that inasmuch as you've behaved with such devotion and selflessness, he ought to take cognizance of it.

APRIL: Oh, Nelson, you shouldn't have. Your gratitude is enough reward.

WORMSER: So he's left you his old watch-fob—and the rest of his money goes to the fight against Social Security.

APRIL: He WHAT?

SMEDLEY: That's right, honeybun.

APRIL: You're . . . you're joking.

SMEDLEY: Never joke about money, dumpling.

APRIL: (*Rises.*) Why, you—you— That's the last straw! I gave up everything for you. My emotional life, my career, my friends. And for what? (*Crosses* L.) I won't remain in this house a moment longer! (*Turns* R.) I wouldn't demean myself! (*She exits outraged.*)

SMEDLEY: He he he! A clever little minx, but they have to get up early in the morning to pull the wool over Nelson Smedley.

WORMSER: They sure do. (*Glancing at watch.*) Well, Commander, it's almost three.

SMEDLEY: Yup—time to watch television. Help me up, Wormser, (*He helps him up*, R. *of him.*) and we'll go see who we can blacklist. (SMEDLEY *pulls his arm away.*) Get your paws off me! I can walk as good as the next man!

(WORMSER *removes his arm and* SMEDLEY *crashes to the floor once again.*)

BLACKOUT
(*And CURTAIN opens into:*)

ACT TWO
SCENE 4

SCENE: *A corner of the workshop, the Whirlaway Scenic Studios in Los Angeles. The deeper end of the set,* L., *contains a litter of flats, lumber, and scenery paint pots. At* R., *a sculptor's workstand displaying the head of a collie carved from soap; beside it a taboret with chisel, mallet, etc. Exit to shop far* R.

TIME: *Noon, two days later.*

AT RISE: ROWENA INCHCAPE, *a matron in her advanced thirties, is engaged in work on the collie's head. She is garbed in a green smock, has an uncompromising henna-colored Dutch bob, wears heavy horn-rimmed spectacles. A short pause, and* LANCE *enters uncertainly.*

LANCE: (*In door.*) Pardon me, would this be the Whirlaway Scenic Studios?

ROWENA: (*Without looking up.*) It would.

LANCE: They said you build displays for parades and department stores—all kinds of floats—

ROWENA: They hit the bulls-eye.

LANCE: Then this is the place. I'm Lance Weatherwax.

ROWENA: Hallelujah. I'm Rowena Inchcape. (*She resumes work with her spatula.* LANCE *draws nearer, his interest in her sculpture plainly aroused.*)

LANCE: Excuse me. Is that an actual portrait, or more of an idealized conception, like?

ROWENA: Half and half. I based it on our Timmy. He passed over several weeks ago.

LANCE: Oh—I'm sorry.

ROWENA: It was about time, if you ask me. He was twenty-three.

LANCE: You don't say. (*Crosses* L. *Sympathetically.*) Did he die of natural causes?

ROWENA: (*On step.*) No, he fell down a well. Nobody's been able to drink out of it since. (*She regards* LANCE *steadily for a moment, nods toward sculpture.*) Do you like it?

LANCE: Well, you certainly got a good likeness. Of course, I never knew Timmy. . . .

ROWENA: You bet you didn't. If he were alive, you'd never be standing there. He'd have torn you limb from limb.

LANCE: They're great pets, collies. I guess his death was a real loss.

ROWENA: I can't imagine to whom. He bit everybody, right up to the man who chloroformed him.

LANCE: I . . . I understood you to say he fell down a well.

ROWENA: After they chloroformed him. That's how ornery he was. (*Appraising him coolly over her shoulder.*) But I suppose you're one of those sentimentalists who get mushy about animals.

LANCE: Yes, ma'am—I mean, no, ma'am. . . . May I ask what medium you're using there?

ROWENA: Soap—castile soap. I'm doing it on a Procter & Gamble Fellowship. (*Crosses* U.S. *behind dog.*)

LANCE: A head like that must take quite a few bars.

ROWENA: There's enough here to wash a family of fifteen.

LANCE: I always wonder how creative people get started. Were you interested in sculpture from a child?

ROWENA: No, it was an afterthought. I had a joint on Hollywood Boulevard where I eternalized baby shoes.

LANCE: I beg pardon?

ROWENA: Dipped 'em in bronze for ashtrays and souvenirs.

LANCE: But that didn't fulfill you, I guess. The artist is a special case.

ROWENA: The artist is a leech. (*Starts down to second step.*) Scratch any one of 'em and you'll find there's money from home.

LANCE: Ah, that's most interesting. Tell me, which way from here is the float department?

ROWENA: I don't read you, stranger. (*Crosses down steps to front of platform.*)

LANCE: I'm interested in placing a quite sizable order. I have in mind a banana split approximately eighteen feet long and twelve feet high.

ROWENA: How deep?

LANCE: (*Crosses* D.S.) Oh, only about six or eight inches. . . .

ROWENA: I see. Do you want nuts on it . . . or just the usual whipped cream?

LANCE: I don't think I've made myself clear. That's only part of it. I also need a chocolate float on each side, maybe—oh, thirty feet high.

ROWENA: Listen, Tom, you're a nice upstanding kid. Why don't you kick that nose candy? There's no future in it.

LANCE: Oh, no—you don't understand. You see, I'm doing this TV spectacular—"Rhapsody in Bubbles"—for Mr. Smedley—you know—of Smedley's Snacketerias.

ROWENA: (*Crosses L.*) Look, you're telling me more than I want to know.

LANCE: We have this great opening shot of Mr. Smedley posed against this banana split.

ROWENA: Yeah, yeah. What did you say your name was? Weather what?

LANCE: Wax.

ROWENA: Look, Wax. I only rent studio space here for my work. The party you want is Rukeyser, the foreman of this drop. Hey, Virgil! Well, Tom, nice to talk to you. Good luck with the spec.

(RUKEYSER *enters.*)

RUKEYSER: What's up, Rowena?

ROWENA: (*Crosses L. of* RUKEYSER.) This civilian's got problems. Get out your slide rule. Abbadabba. (*She exits L.*)

RUKEYSER: O.K., sonny. What's bugging you?

LANCE: (D.S. *of steps.*) Well, I've got a two-float order, Mr. Rukeyser, and I need an estimate for it—I had some rough drawings made to show you. Here— (*He spreads them on the floor.*)

(*As* RUKEYSER, *with a long-suffering sigh, bends to examine the drawings,* WAGNERIAN *bursts on from* L.)

WAGNERIAN: (*Crosses D.S.*) Now look here, Mr. Rukeyser, I am calling my union.

RUKEYSER: (*Rises, crosses R. of* WAGNERIAN.) Just a minute, sonny. What's the matter now, Wagnerian? Isn't the pie finished?

WAGNERIAN: How can I spray on the white of egg until I know if the mechanism works?

RUKEYSER: We're waiting for the broad they ordered for the stag banquet. The clients are coming over for a demo.

WAGNERIAN: She's here! (*Crosses* L.) She's been cooling her heels for thirty minutes. . . .

RUKEYSER: Then tell her to get undressed.

WAGNERIAN: (*Turns* R.) I can't do that! I'm engaged!

RUKEYSER: Do I have to do everything around here? Handle the clients—run after strippers—?

WAGNERIAN: Very well! . . . But I'm calling my union! (*Exits* L.)

(*As* RUKEYSER, *with a long-suffering sigh, bends to examine the drawings,* GODDARD QUAGMEYER, *followed by a* GIRL, *enters* R. *He is a changed man; his manner is brash and assertive, and sartorially he has become a Hollywood peacock. The* GIRL *is a standard film-colony bimbo.*)

QUAGMEYER: (*Crosses* R. *of* C. GIRL *stays* R.) Listen, Rukeyser, what's with those blueprints I sent over for the waterfall set?

RUKEYSER: (*To* QUAGMEYER.) Hiya, Quagmeyer! Didn't you get my message?

(QUAGMEYER *crosses* L.)

LANCE: (*Rises. Reacting.*) Mr. Quagmeyer!

QUAGMEYER: (*Waving him aside.*) Please, no autographs! . . . We've lost two days' shooting already!

RUKEYSER: I told you—we ran into complications—

QUAGMEYER: For God's sake! An ordinary fifty-foot waterfall with some iridescent rocks!

RUKEYSER: Where the hell do I get the mother-of-pearl for the rainbow?

QUAGMEYER: Call up a button factory—a jewelry-supply house—how do I know? I've got enough aggravation.

RUKEYSER: (*Aggrievedly.*) And my life is a peach Melba, I suppose!

LANCE: Mr. Quagmeyer—

QUAGMEYER: I told you I was busy, didn't I?

LANCE: Don't you remember me, sir? Lance Weatherwax?

QUAGMEYER: (*Turns. Crosses* L. *of* LANCE, *pats his shoulders.*) Bubby! What are you doing out here?

LANCE: I'm a producer.

QUAGMEYER: It figures. Anything can happen in Tomorrowland. Look at me. (*Crosses* L. *of* GIRL. *To* GIRL.) The last time this joker saw me, I was schmeering my heart out in a New York tenement—I was so hung up on art and all that fakery, I'd have been there yet if it wasn't for him.

LANCE: For me?

QUAGMEYER: That's right! Remember the day you bawled me out—said I had integrity poisoning?

LANCE: Did I say that?

QUAGMEYER: Yeah. That sank home, Weatherwax. I brooded over it all night and finally realized what a fool I was. Yes, siree, you gave me a whole fresh set of values.

LANCE: But I didn't mean—

QUAGMEYER: (*Boisterously.*) Who cares what you meant? (*Crosses* R. *to* L. *of* GIRL.) All I know is I've got a five-year contract at Fox, a white Jag, and the sweetest little head since Helen Twelvetrees.

GIRL: (*Slaps his hand away.*) Is this your idea of a fun time, shooting the breeze in a junk shop?

QUAGMEYER: All right, gorgeous, we go toot sweet. (*Smirks at* LANCE. QUAGMEYER *crosses* R.) You see? I'm her slave. . . . Well, thanks again, fella, be seeing you. If you ever feel like a hot meal, just contact me through my flesh peddler, Monroe Sweetmeat, which he handles Rob Roy Fruitwell and all the biggies.

(*He waves, exits with* GIRL. RUKEYSER *turns back to* LANCE.)

RUKEYSER: (L. *of* LANCE.) All right, bud, what's your pleasure? I haven't got all day.

LANCE: (*Kneeling by the drawings again.*) We need an exact replica of a chocolate float in duplicate, Mr. Rukeyser.

(WAGNERIAN *and* ELMO *appear, wheeling a large papier-mâché pie, roughly five feet in diameter by twenty inches deep, on a dolly.* ELMO R. *of pie.*)

WAGNERIAN: (L. *of pie.*) Sure, it's heavy. You put a zoftick dame in a deep dish pie and you've got engineering problems.

RUKEYSER: (*Crosses* R. *of pie. Pushing* ELMO *aside.*) O.K., Elmo, I'll handle this. (*To* WAGNERIAN, *as* ELMO *exits.*) I hope she can breathe in there.

WAGNERIAN: She's in clover. I put in plenty of air holes.

RUKEYSER: Well, as long as the mechanism works. If it don't we got a nice little lawsuit on our hands.

(HENNEPIN *and* POTEAT, *two gentlemen of distinct executive bearing, in Homburgs, enter.*)

HENNEPIN: Mr. Rukeyser?

RUKEYSER: (*Turns, steps* R.) Speaking.

HENNEPIN: I'm Hennepin of the banquet committee.

POTEAT: (*Crosses* R. *of* RUKEYSER.) And I'm Poteat. You know—the send-off we're giving Floyd Geduldig, our associate in the utilities field?

(WAGNERIAN *crosses* D.L. *of pie.*)

RUKEYSER: Yep. Well, there's your prop, but let me tell you, brother, it's the last pie I build without specifications.

WAGNERIAN: The whole thing was guesswork.

HENNEPIN: No doubt, no doubt. (*Crosses* L. *Major Hoople cough.*) However, in such a delicate matter, you can't very well expect us to put anything on paper.

POTEAT: The slightest breath of a scandal . . .

RUKEYSER: What's scandalous? You're throwing a feed where a bimbo comes out of a pie and dances with a gorilla. Whose business is that?

HENNEPIN: Ha ha—quite—of course. (*Inspects pie critically.*) Frankly, Mr. Rukeyser, I envisioned something a good deal smaller, with a real biscuit crust.

POTEAT: We were planning to distribute a wedge to everybody after the lady pops out.

RUKEYSER: Biscuit crust? Are you nuts? How would she pop out if she's laying under ninety pounds of dough reinforced with chicken wire?

HENNEPIN: He's got a point, Poteat—it does sound a bit unwieldy. Will this cover of yours lift off readily?

RUKEYSER: Watch. (*Calling Offstage.*) Start the music!

(*He presses a button on exterior of pie; the crust jackknifes skyward, and* APRIL MONKHOOD, *clad in the world's scantiest bikini, springs forth.* RUKEYSER, WAGNERIAN *help* APRIL *out of pie.*)

APRIL: Whee! (*She does a few sinuous steps, climaxing in a bump as* LANCE *gapes at her open-mouthed. Then she turns Upstage as a figure clad in super-realistic* GORILLA *costume emerges from behind flat. The latter seizes her in his arms and they exe-cute short tango routine Downstage, at climax of which* GORILLA *bends* APRIL *backward.* APRIL, *carried away, moans in ecstasy.*) Bombo—you're crushing me in your mighty arms! Release me, Bombo!

RUKEYSER: She's a mental case! Stop the music, stop the music!

LANCE: April!

APRIL: (*Blinking as she regains perspective.*) Lance Weather-wax! Whatever in the world are you doing here?

HENNEPIN: (*Crosses* L. *of* APRIL; POTEAT R. *of* LANCE.) O.K.— That's jim-dandy. (*Producing card-case briskly.*) Los Angeles Vice Squad. Young lady, you're under arrest for con-spiracy to come out of a pie and dance with a gorilla.

(RUKEYSER, WAGNERIAN *and* GORILLA *push pie off* L.)

APRIL: Why, you rotten, contemptible slobs—

(APRIL *crosses* R. POTEAT *stops her* R. *of* LANCE. *She turns to flee;* POTEAT *grabs her wrist,* LANCE *springs forward to unhand* APRIL.)

LANCE: (L. *of* APRIL.) Let go of her, you!

HENNEPIN: (*Crosses* R. *of* APRIL. *Thrusts him aside.*) Lay off, punk, or we'll take you along, too!

LANCE: You're going to regret this, you wait! That lady's innocent!

POTEAT: Yeah, it's another Dreyfus case. (*Yanks* APRIL'S *wrist.*) Come on. You can explain it all to Judge Rinderbrust. (*Starts off* R.)

LANCE: Oh, April, how could you ever get involved in such a sordid awful mess?

APRIL: (*Crosses* R. *of* LANCE. HENNEPIN, POTEAT *follow.*) Don't you criticize me, you mealy-mouth! I'd never have been here if it wasn't for you!

LANCE: For me?

APRIL: That's right! You rejected me at my darkest hour— I offered you love and understanding—

HENNEPIN: (*They pull her* R. *Impatiently.*) Get going— you're breaking my heart.

APRIL: (*Crosses* R. *of* LANCE. HENNEPIN *and* POTEAT *follow her. Hysterically, to* LANCE.) Go back to your polo ponies, you rotten little poseur! You're nothing but a dilettante—a play-boy! And you can marry the whole Social Register for all I care—I hate you!

(HENNEPIN *and* POTEAT *drag her off.* LANCE *stands overwhelmed a moment.*)

LANCE: (*Crosses* L. *With a groan.*) Oh, my god—what kind of a selfish, spoiled brat have I been? Nelson Smedley and his chocolate soda be damned! I've got to save the woman I love!

(*Squaring his jaw, he rushes off, and we SEGUE to:*)

ACT TWO
SCENE 5

SCENE: *A courtroom in the Los Angeles Hall of Justice.*

TIME: *Three days later.*

AT RISE: *A* TELEVISION MAN *pushes on a camera.* SECRETARY *and* HANRATTY *enter* L.

CAMERA MAN: (*Crosses* R. *of* HANRATTY.) Bring it in—push the dimmer up, Voltage. Where the hell's Judge Rinderbrust? We go on the air at one o'clock sharp.

HANRATTY: (*Crosses* R. *of* CAMERA MAN.) He's officiating at a baby derby in Cucamonga. Probably got caught in traffic. Don't worry about Herman J. Rinderbrust. In addition to being the foremost jurist in Southern California, he's all show biz. Kefauver and McClellan pointed the way, but Rinderbrust put the cherry on the parfait. (*Crosses up to desk.*) Real-life court cases—living offenders tried before your very eyes. (*Crosses* R. *of* CAMERA MAN.)

CAMERA MAN: (*Crosses to camera.*) We go on network at ten A.M., East Coast Time. If we got to throw in "The Mark of Zorro" once more, the agency'll have our heads.

HANRATTY: Rinderbrust'll be here. He's a real trouper.

(JUDGE RINDERBRUST *hurries on clad in his judicial robes.*)

JUDGE: (*Crosses* R. *Angrily.*) See here, Hanratty, I get a new makeup man by air-time tomorrow, or I don't go on!

HANRATTY: (*Crosses* R.) I'll call the account exec right after the session, Your Honor.

JUDGE: That flunkey! Don't deal with ribbon clerks. Call the sponsor direct!

HANRATTY: Yes, sir.

JUDGE: (*Crosses* R. *of* HANRATTY.) And burn his keyster about that feature story in "TV Guide." It's cheapening. (*Patting toupee girlishly.*) By the way, Hanratty, how do you like the new rug? Mrs. Rinderbrust says it makes me look like David Susskind.

HANRATTY: The women viewers'll eat it up.

JUDGE: (*Thoughtfully.*) We won't know till the mail starts coming in . . . O.K., what's on the docket?

HANRATTY: (*Reads from pad.*) Just routine stuff, except for a murder charge and a conspiracy to come out of a pie and dance with a gorilla.

JUDGE: Um—gorilla dancer—not bad. I'll throw the book at her. Should goose the rating. (*Crosses* R.) What's the commercial for today!

HANRATTY: (*Producing cue-cards.*) The usual for Respighi's Bubble Gum—and a new spot for Glo-in-the-Dark Falsies.

JUDGE: Glo-in-the-Dark Falsies? Out, out—I don't plug any product I don't believe in.

(BAILIFF *enters, sits in his chair.*)

CAMERA MAN: Thirty seconds to air and we've got a new advertiser, the Elysian Fields Cemetery Guild in the 1100 block on Lankershim Boulevard.

JUDGE: (*Crosses* R. *to* L. *of* CAMERA MAN.) Cemetery? What are you talking about? I own a row of stores on that block.

HANRATTY: It's the property out back.

JUDGE: Out back is a bog, ten feet under water. A stiff wouldn't last a day in there.

HANRATTY: They're piping the water into fountains, with colored lights. It's a great effect—like Mardi Gras.

JUDGE: Well, that's different. I'll buy that, so long as it's dignified.

CAMERA MAN: Judge Rinderbrust! Ten seconds to air! (JUDGE *crosses to bench—looking at mirror held by* HANRATTY.) Five, four . . . three . . . two . . . whoof!

JUDGE: (*Into camera.*) Good morning, fellow-citizens, and

welcome to "The Scales of Justice"—the only program that brings you real law-breakers, malefactors and hoodlums—people like yourselves in a peck of trouble. Yours, truly, Judge Herman J. Rinderbrust starring! (*Raps gavel.*) All right—bring on the first culprit.

(POLICEMAN *enters from* L., *crosses* L. *of bench.* ROXANA, *in skimpy nurse's uniform, follows to front of witness chair.*)

BAILIFF: The people of the State of California, the County of Los Angeles, versus Miss Roxana DeVilbiss.

JUDGE: (*Licking his lips.*) And what's the charge against this little transgressor?

BAILIFF: (*Sitting.*) Operating an unlicensed massage parlor.

JUDGE: (*Regards Roxana's garb intently.*) So you're a masoose, are you? My, what a lovely turtle-neck sweater.

ROXANA: (*Indignant hauteur.*) Your Honor, (*Sits.*) this is a miscarriage of justice! I'm a respectable college grad—the Slenderola Body Institute in San Berdoo. (*Leans forward.*)

JUDGE: This court has a very warm feeling towards San Berdoo. They raise the largest casabas in the West.

ROXANA: Thank you, Judge. Now, me and my colleagues at the Idle Hour Massage Parlour— (*Skirt over knee.*) —perform a very important role in the community.

JUDGE: You restore men's souls as well as their bodies—right?

ROXANA: Exactly! By what we call psycho-massage.

JUDGE: (*Emotionally.*) You nurse your fellow man back to health, you bring roses to his cheeks.

ROXANA: Oh, definitely, Judge!

JUDGE: In short, you rediscovered the Fountain of Youth.

ROXANA: Yes!

JUDGE: (*Angrily.*) And for this those lousy Puritans—those keyhole peepers—seek to penalize you! (*Turns majestically into camera.*) Ladies and gentlemen of the TV audience, I want you to look upon this tiny defendant, and I want you to remember another frail little person without a license—Florence Nightingale. (*Rising.*) As long as I wear these judicial robes, the sovereign state of California will remain a haven and a refuge for all healers of the feminine gender, with or without certificates! Case dismissed.

ROXANA: Gee, Herman, you've been a peach.

JUDGE: I'll drop in at your store to see that my orders are carried out.

ROXANA: I'll tell the girls!

BAILIFF: (*As* ROXANA *exits.*) The People of the State of California, the County of Los Angeles, versus Joe Gourielli, alias the Truth Swami, Haroun Azeez.

(GOURIELLI *enters, clad in turban and business suit.*)

JUDGE: (*With papers.*) Swami, you're charged with creating a public disturbance. On the night of the 24th, at the intersection of La Paloma and Alta Yenta, you did willfully stage a human sacrifice. Think fast, Gourielli.

SWAMI: The sacrifice, yes—the disturbance, no. The Apostles got over-heated and started to grab souvenirs from the funeral pyre.

JUDGE: (*Outraged.*) Who do you think you are, knocking off citizens like they are clay pigeons!

SWAMI: They're followers!

JUDGE: Makes no difference! This is America, Gourielli, and everybody's entitled to four square meals, a second car, and the right to croak when he sees fit—not when some wog sets fire to him. This is an extremely grave offense.

HANRATTY: (*Anxiously, with papers.*) Judge, just a minute. (*Faces camera.*) Ladies and gentlemen, while the Judge is pondering the facts of the case, we pause briefly for station identification. (*To* JUDGE.) Don't be too tough on him, Judge. Remember, our new sponsor, the Elysian Fields Cemetery Guild.

JUDGE: By Jove, you're right! We mustn't discourage business. This zombie is good for forty plots a week. Give me a close-up. (BAILIFF *holds up mirror.* JUDGE *looks, slaps his hand away.* HANRATTY *gets cue card from* R. *Holds it high over camera from rear.* JUDGE *climbs on stool to read it.* HANRATTY *then stoops down in front of camera.* JUDGE *tries to read.*) Ladies and gentlemen—on due— (*To* HANRATTY.) I'm reading your thumb. (HANRATTY *crosses to* U.S. *of camera.* JUDGE *reads; into camera.*) Ladies and gentlemen—on due consideration, everybody's entitled to religious freedom and to a fine, decent funeral at reasonable prices. If you have a loved one who has recently given up the ghost, insure their future through the Elysian Fields Cemetery Guild. Make their journey to the Happy Hunting Grounds a memorable experience for relatives and cadaver alike. (*Carried away, he starts to sing "Dear Old Girl," stops himself. To* SWAMI.) All right, Gourielli, back to your devotions but keep your nose clean.

(GOURIELLI *exits* L.)

BAILIFF: Miss April Monkhood. Charged with conspiracy to come out of a pie and dance with a gorilla. (APRIL *has entered, clad in virginal coat.*)

JUDGE: Ah, the Gorilla Dancer! (*Into camera.*) Television viewers . . . once in every jurist's career, he is confronted by a case so shocking that the mind reels. The one you are about to witness surpasses anything in my vast experience. The culprit did knowingly plot and agree with accomplices unknown to emerge from a pastry and engage in a lascivious dance with an anthropoid. Behavior like this would have the most dubious effect on your American womanhood, and I, as its legal guardian, intend to squelch it root, branch, lock, stock and barrel. (*Turns to* APRIL.) Now, then, young woman, what do you have to say for yourself?

APRIL: (*Crosses, sits witness chair.*) I was tricked, Your Honor. They claimed it was an experiment.

JUDGE: None of your shilly-shally. How do you plead—guilty or not?

(*A hubbub at* L. *from which emerge voices of* BAILIFF *and* LANCE *as latter struggles to enter.*)

BAILIFF: Stand back there, you!
LANCE: I'm involved in this case, I tell you! Let me in! } (*Ad libs.*)

JUDGE: Who's that? What does he want?

LANCE: (*Struggling.*) Judge Rinderbrust—please! I've got to talk to you!

JUDGE: (*Beckoning.*) Come up here. (*Severely.* LANCE *crosses* L. *of* C.) Look here, you, you're in a court of law. What do you mean, creating this uproar?

LANCE: I want to testify for the defendant, Your Honor—
JUDGE: Have you got any new evidence?

LANCE: (*Emotionally.*) Your Honor, you're making a terrible mistake! This lady's innocent—I've known her for years. She's a distinguished artist . . . a cultivated, refined person. . . .

JUDGE: Don't waste my time with character references! Produce your evidence!

LANCE: I saw the performance, Judge—there was nothing offensive in it! She did a little dance—

JUDGE: (*Raps his gavel—rises majestically.*) Now you listen to me, young fellow. The law explicitly states, *ex parte* and *nolens-volens*, that he who comes into court with clean hands is *sub judice* prejudiced *a priori*. In other words, "*Exceptio probat regulam de rebus non exceptis.*" Once and for all, before I pronounce sentence on the accused—have you any evidence relevant and germane in this matter?

LANCE: (*Produces an envelope.*) I have, Your Honor.

JUDGE: Well, give. Hand it to the clerk of the court. (LANCE *gives envelope to* BAILIFF.) But I warn you, there are no extenuating circumstances in this case. Okay, what does it say?

BAILIFF: (*Takes envelope, extracts checks, reads.*) "Pay to the order of Herman J. Rinderbrust—five hundred thousand dollars. Signed, Octavia Weatherwax."

JUDGE: (*Thwacking gavel.*) Case dismissed!

(APRIL *and* LANCE *react joyfully, dissolve into embrace. As* JUDGE RINDERBRUST *raises his hands in benediction over them, a couple of* PRESS PHOTOGRAPHERS *run on, blaze away at the couple with flash bulbs, as we SEGUE into:*)

ACT TWO
SCENE 6

SCENE: *The Weatherwax Library.*

TIME: *One month later.*

AT RISE: APRIL, *a bride's headdress and veil surmounting her head, stands arm-in-arm with* LANCE, *both their faces set in the strained grimace of the conventional society wedding photograph. The two* PRESS PHOTOGRAPHERS *crouch at opposite angles, aiming their cameras.* OCTAVIA *fidgets impatiently nearby.*

In background, MRS. LAFCADIO MIFFLIN, *a majestic dowager well-boned over the diaphragm, with avian headgear and a froth of ruching at her throat, alertly observes the tableau.*

FIRST PHOTOGRAPHER: Hold it!
SECOND PHOTOGRAPHER: O.K., now—personality! Just one more!

(*Their FLASH BULBS explode.* OCTAVIA *steps between them.*)

OCTAVIA: (*From* R., *moves chair* D.S. *Imperiously.*) All right, gentlemen, that's quite sufficient. You've held up the wedding rehearsal long enough. (*Crosses* D.S. *of couch, moves with* APRIL, LANCE *as they go off.*) Run along, children, it's almost time—I'll be along directly.

(PHOTOGRAPHERS *mumble ad-lib thanks, exit. As* LANCE *and* APRIL *hurry off in opposite directions,* MRS. MIFFLIN *joins* OCTAVIA.)

MRS. MIFFLIN: (*Crosses back of* C. *chair, rubs finger along top of chair for dust.*) Octavia, love. Your daughter-in-law couldn't be more captivating.
OCTAVIA: Oh, Milo and I are enraptured with her.
MRS. MIFFLIN: (*Sits* R. *end of couch.*) And so well-bred for a theatrical person.
OCTAVIA: (*Crosses* L. *end of couch. Tinkly little laugh. Crosses behind couch.*) My dear, that phase of April's was just puppy fat. Started way back when she was a senior in Miss Hewitt's Classes.
MRS. MIFFLIN: I thought you said she was at Foxcroft.
OCTAVIA: (*Crosses* R. *back of couch to* R. *end. Adroitly.*) Both, darling—you know how volatile these girls are nowadays. Well, her mother was determined to send her to Bryn Mawr, of course—family tradition—
MRS. MIFFLIN: Was that Alicia Monkhood who captained the field hockey there in Tucky's year?
OCTAVIA: (*Crosses behind chair, sits chair.*) Oh, no, this was the Scottish branch. They derive from Llewellyn Fitzpoultice, ninth Viscount Zeugma.
MRS. MIFFLIN: (*Nodding.*) Of course. That's where she gets that fair English skin.

OCTAVIA: (*Crosses* L.) And her wilfulness, dear child. Nothing would do— (*Rises.*) but she must run off and join Martha Graham's troupe— (*Pulls* MIFFLIN *up.*) and when Lance saw her at Jacob's Pillow, he naturally fell dead.

MRS. MIFFLIN: (*Crosses* R. *with* OCTAVIA. *Pouting.*) Wretch. I still think you might have shared the secret with your eldest friend.

OCTAVIA: (*Hurried kiss, maneuvering her off.*) You'd have spread it all over Prout's Neck—you know you would.

MRS. MIFFLIN: Shall we see you at the Dingbats' Thursday?

OCTAVIA: No, I believe Milo's tied up that night at the Luxor Baths.

MRS. MIFFLIN: Well, tell him how happy we are for the both of you. (*Fluting as she exits* R.) Good-bye—ee-ee. . . .

(LANCE *and* APRIL *reappear, his demeanor clearly rebellious.*)

LANCE: (*Crosses* R. *of chair*; APRIL *crosses* L. *of couch.*) Gosh, Mater, do we have to go through all this mumbo-jumbo?

OCTAVIA: Indeed you must, and you may as well put a good face on it.

LANCE: But the things that really matter are spiritual—aren't they, April dearest?

APRIL: (*Guardedly.*) Well . . .

OCTAVIA: (*Crosses front of couch.*) Lance, darling, you talk like a sausage. The things that matter are objects one can touch —viz. and to wit, diamonds and furs and blue chip securities. Only we on the distaff side understand that. (*Sits* R. *end of couch.*)

APRIL: (*Crosses front of couch to* L. *of chair and back of couch.*) You sure are cooking on the front burner. I may be horribly naive, but blindfolded in a London fog, I can tell mink from stone marten, and it's all thanks to you, Mother Weatherwax! (*Sits couch.*)

OCTAVIA: (*Graciously.*) I like your spirit, April. My first reaction when our son brought you home to our stylish Park Avenue triplex was that you were a cheap little tramp. Nothing you've done since has caused me to alter that opinion.

APRIL: Thank you, Mother Weatherwax.

OCTAVIA: But what can be keeping Milo?

LANCE: What Milo is that?

OCTAVIA: Why, your father, which he is probably handling the management reins of our far-flung interests.

MILO: (*Entering briskly from* R., *kisses* OCTAVIA'S *hand.*) Wrong as per usual, my pet. A young protégée of mine—a geology student—was showing me some rare stones over at Cartier's.

OCTAVIA: (*Acidly.*) And you totally forgot the surprise we are giving LANCE.

MILO: Applesauce. The relevant documents repose inside this very envelope. (*Extracts same.*) Lance, I hope your creative Odyssey has taught you something.

LANCE: (R. *of chair.*) It did, sir. I found there's an awful lot of prejudice against money. Especially from people that don't have any.

MILO: They should be machine-gunned.

OCTAVIA: Hear, hear!

APRIL: You can say that again!

MILO: I will! They should be machine-gunned. (*Crosses* L. *of* LANCE.) But paradoxically, Lance, you also have a responsibility to them.

LANCE: I don't dig you, Guv.

MILO: It's up to you to stamp out that prejudice tooth and nail. (*Handing him envelope.*) My boy, I've set up a mighty foundation in your name—tax free—to bring culture into every American home.

LANCE: (*Glowing.*) Gee, Dads, me—the final arbiter of truth and beauty!

MILO: You may meet resistance to your concept of what's clean and straight and fine, but if you do, just cram it down their throats.

LANCE: (*Crosses* R. *of* MILO.) Will do, Dad!

MILO: (*Crosses* D.C.) But remember that in this weary old world, there's one value that transcends all others.

(ROXANA DeVILBISS, *in nurse's uniform, enters* R. *bearing fancy baby basket trailing swaddling clothes. She passes it to* LANCE, *who transfers it to* MILO.)

OCTAVIA: Why, Milo, there's a suspicious moisture in your eye.

MILO: Yes, I'll 'fess up to same, hardened cynic though I am.

(*Clears throat.*) Friends, this little bundle of happiness is everybody's joy. We must cherish it—share it with us, won't you?

(*As he tilts basket forward, revealing it crammed with greenbacks, dips into it and starts broadcasting it over* LANCE *and* APRIL *like confetti:*)

CURTAIN

END OF ACT TWO

THE HINDSIGHT SAGA

THREE FRAGMENTS FROM
AN AUTOBIOGRAPHY

The Marx Brothers

ONE OCTOBER evening in the fall of 1931, a few minutes after the curtain had risen on the second act of *Animal Crackers*, a musical comedy starring the Four Marx Brothers, the occupant of the seat adjoining mine, a comely person with a mink coat folded on her lap, suddenly reached through it and twitched my sleeve. I was then, and still fatuously conceive myself to be, a hot-blooded young man; and if I did not respond immediately, there were several cogent reasons. To begin with, the occupant of the *other* seat adjoining mine, whom I had espoused a couple of years before, was holding hands with me, so that I had none left over to twitch back. Furthermore, the custodian of the lady in mink, I had observed during the entr'acte, was a chap with an undershot jaw and a beefy neck, the kind of lout I knew would tolerate no poaching. More important than either consideration, however, was the fact that I was breathlessly and rapturously absorbed in Groucho's courtship onstage of the immortal Margaret Dumont, impersonating a dowager named Mrs. Rittenhouse. It was at least five seconds, accordingly, before I realized that my neighbor was extending a note and gesticulating toward an usher in the aisle to indicate its source. Straining to decipher the message in the half darkness, I grew almost dizzy with exultation. Mr. Marx acknowledged the card I had sent in during the break to express my admiration, and requested me to call on him backstage after the show.

While our meeting was in no sense epochal, it did have an unpredictable consequence, and my forehead, to say nothing of my career, might have been far less wrinkled had I not paid this fortuitous homage. For the half-dozen years preceding, I had been a contributor, in the dual capacity of artist and writer, to *Judge* and *College Humor*. Both these magazines, during my undergraduate days at Brown University, had reprinted drawings I had done for the college periodical, and when faced with the choice of a livelihood, I turned naturally (if naïvely) to comic art. There were vicissitudes that seemed insurmountable at the time, but thanks to a stomach that shrank as they arose, I managed to weather them. About the end of 1928, my work was appearing in some profusion, and Horace Liveright, whose daring as a publisher verged on audacity, brought out a collection of it called *Dawn Ginsbergh's Revenge*. It was a curious little volume, bound in the horripilating green plush called "flock" used to upholster railroad chairs, and as far as one could tell, it had only two distinctive aspects. The title page omitted any mention whatever of an author—I presumably was so overawed at the permanence I was achieving that I neglected to check this detail—and the dust jacket bore a blurb from, coincidentally, Groucho Marx. It read: "From the moment I picked up your book until I laid it down, I was convulsed with laughter. Some day I intend reading it."

To say, therefore, that I had set the Thames on fire by that fateful evening in 1931 would be hardly accurate. The brush and quill were yielding a pittance which I had persuaded the idealistic lady whose hand I held to share with me, and through some legerdemain we had managed to squeeze in two summers abroad on the cheap. But the magazines I worked for were feeling the Depression, and all of a sudden the barometer began to fall. I started receiving a trickle of letters from the bank that soon grew into a cascade. Perhaps, its officials hinted delicately, I would like to transfer to some bank that had facilities for handling smaller accounts. Maybe I didn't need a bank after all, they hazarded, but merely a mattress or a loose brick in the fireplace. A deep cleft, resembling the Rift Valley in East Africa, appeared between my eyebrows about the first of every month. Beyond rending my clothes or dropping an occasional reference to the poorhouse, though, I was careful to conceal my anxieties from my helpmate. Whether she suspected anything from the newspaper recipes I left around the kitchen, cheap but hearty agglomerations of macaroni and tuna fish, I cannot say. If she did, she gave no hint of it.

This was our approximate situation, then, at the moment the summons from Groucho arrived, and it was without any portent that the encounter would be fateful that I hastened backstage after the performance. Once, however, we had exchanged cordialities—a bit awkward for my wife since Groucho was clad only in his shorts—he breezily confessed to an ulterior purpose in his invitation. One of the networks had latterly been entreating the Marxes to appear in a radio series, and he wondered if I could be cozened into writing it. Flattering as I found his esteem, I was frankly overwhelmed.

"I—I wouldn't know how to begin," I faltered. "I've never worked on a radio script."

"Neither has Will Johnstone," admitted Groucho. "He's the fellow we'd like you to collaborate with." He went on to explain; Johnstone, like myself a comic artist and a staff member of the *Evening World*, was the author of "I'll Say She Is," a boisterous vaudeville sketch which the Marxes had amplified into their first Broadway success. "Yes siree," he concluded somberly. "I can't imagine two people worse equipped for the job, but there's one thing in your favor. You're both such tyros you might just come up with something fresh."

It was a dubious basis for any undertaking, and yet, as events proved, his words had a certain perverse logic. Johnstone turned out to be a jovial, exuberant chap in his late fifties, a raconteur with a fund of newspaper stories. We put in a couple of enjoyable sessions that got nowhere, except for a misty notion that the Marxes might be characterized as stowaways aboard an ocean liner. On the day designated to report our progress, the two of us met outside the Astor, resolved to confess our inadequacy and throw in the towel. Luncheon with the troupe was as disorganized as my colleague predicted it would be. Groucho expatiated at length on his stock-market losses, Chico kept jumping up to place telephone bets, and Harpo table-hopped all over the dining room, discomposing any attractive lady who gave him a second glance. Finally, the issue could be postponed no longer, and Johnstone, courageously assuming the burden, divulged the sum total of our conferences. To our stupefaction, it evoked hosannas.

"Listen," said Groucho, after a whispered colloquy with his brothers. "You fellows have stumbled on something big. This isn't any fly-by-night radio serial—it's our next picture!"

Primed for a totally opposite reaction, Johnstone and I surveyed him speechless; we had expected to be pistol-whipped and summarily flung into Times Square, and in our humility, thought he was being ironical. Within the next half hour, the brothers dispelled any doubt of their enthusiasm. Pinioning our arms, they hustled us across the street into the office of

Jesse Lasky, the head of Paramount Pictures. There was a short, confused interval brim-full of references to astronomical sums of money, contracts, and transportation to the Coast, inexplicably for our wives as well. We were to entrain for Hollywood within the week, it was tempestuously agreed, to write the screenplay. The Marxes, scheduled to terminate their Broadway run in a fortnight, were off to London for an engagement at the Palladium, after which they would return to California to shoot our film. When Johnstone and I reeled out into what was now truly the Gay White Way, our faces had the ecstatic, incredulous look of prospectors who had just blundered across the Lost Dutchman Mine.

The delirium of leavetaking for California was, of course, punctuated by the usual untoward incidents that complicate life at such moments. My wife—deliberately, I felt at the time—slipped on an icy sidewalk and fractured her arm, and Johnstone, an undisguised foe of Prohibition, was suddenly disheartened by rumors that applejack was unprocurable in Los Angeles. Solutions materialized for both dilemmas; at the eleventh hour, my consort was able to board the Twentieth Century encased in a cast, and influential friends of Johnstone's mercifully supplied him with three stone crocks of his life-giving ichor. To further restrict our mobility, we took with us our pet of the moment, a large and aggressive schnauzer whose antipathy to trainmen and porters kept the compartment in an uproar. He was eventually exiled to the baggage car, where he ululated for three thousand miles and spread neurasthenia among the postal clerks. Much more awesome than any scenery we saw on the trip, it developed, was Johnstone's creative drive. In less than sixty-five hours, he dashed off fifteen or twenty strip cartoons for his paper, not to mention innumerable water-colors of the sunsets, mesas, and hogans en route. How his hand remained sufficiently steady, considering the roadbed of the Santa Fe and the contents of the three stone crocks, was a mystery. I sometimes lay awake in my berth for as long as two minutes pondering it.

Of all the world's storied thoroughfares, it must be confessed that none produces quite the effect of Hollywood Boulevard. I have been downcast in Piccadilly, chopfallen on the Champs

Elysées, and *doloroso* on the Via Veneto, but the avenues themselves were blameless. Hollywood Boulevard, on the contrary,
creates an instant and malign impression in the breast of the
beholder. Viewed in full sunlight, its tawdriness is unspeakable;
in the torrential downpour of the rainy season, as we first saw
it, it inspired an anguish similar to that produced by the engravings of Piranesi. Our melancholy deepened when the mem
and I took an exploratory walk around the hotel. As we sat in a
Moorish confectionery patterned after the Alcázar, toying with
viscid malted milks and listening to a funereal organ rendition
of "Moonlight in Kalua," the same thought occurred to each
of us, but she phrased it first.

"Listen," she said. "Do we really need the money this much?"

"That's cowardice," I said, vainglorious because I had held
my tongue. "Why, we just got here—you can't judge a place so
fast. Besides, it's raining. It's probably beautiful when the sun
comes out."

"It's no such thing," she retorted. "You're whistling in the
dark, and you know it. It's the Atlantic City boardwalk—a hayseed's idea of the Big Apple. We've made a terrible mistake."

"Oh, we have, have we?" I shouted. Two or three cadavers
near us startled out of their torpor turned to survey me, but
I didn't care. "Well, you're certainly a comfort. Here we are
in the mecca of show business, the paradise everyone dreams
about, with one foot on the golden ladder—"

"Unscramble your metaphors," she interrupted coldly. "This
town's already beginning to affect you."

"Well, you don't have to sprinkle weed killer over our hopes
the first day," I said sulkily. "You could fake a little optimism."

"O.K.," she said, assuming an insincere metallic smile. "No
more crabbing. Maybe it's that dismal hotel room of ours that
got me down—let's go find a cheerful nest somewhere and
start acting like forty-niners."

The bivouac we ultimately settled into, a modest duplex in a
bungalow court, had only one advantage—it was new. Otherwise, it was an unalloyed horror, from its overstuffed suite to
its painted bedsteads, from its portable gas heaters to its garish
dinette. Seated there of an evening over our avocado salads
while the radio tinkled out commercials for high-colonics, cre-
matoriums, and sculptured broadlooms, one had the sense of

living in a homemaker's magazine. After a few days, I could have sworn that our faces began to take on the hue of Kodachromes, and even the dog, an animal used to bizarre surroundings, developed a strange, off-register look, as if he were badly printed in overlapping colors. Our neighbors were the customary hodgepodge—studio technicians, old ladies studying Bahai, bit players, chippies, and all the mysterious lamisters who tenant the Los Angeles substratum. They rarely emerged from their burrows, but once in a while we could hear upraised voices extolling the virtues of various faith healers or laxatives. Country people in general display a preoccupation with their innards bordering on the religious, and in Los Angeles, a metropolis made up of innumerable Midwestern hamlets, it amounted to a fixation. Apart from dry cleaners, saddleries, and stores that eternalized baby shoes in bronze, almost every shop in the district was a health-food depot. I have no figures on the per-capita consumption, in Southern California during the early thirties, of soy bean, wheat germ, and blackstrap molasses, and I am thankful. It was frightening.

At the studio, where Johnstone and I were now daily applying ourselves to the script, another and equally fanciful atmosphere prevailed. The two of us were quartered in a ramshackle warren of tan stucco that housed thirty or forty other scribes. They were all in various stages of gestation, some spawning gangster epics and horse operas, others musical comedies, dramas, and farces. Few of them were writers in the traditional sense, but persuasive, voluble specialists adept in contriving trick plot situations. Many had worked before the advent of dialogue, in silent pictures; they viewed the playwrights, novelists, and newspapermen who were beginning to arrive from New York as usurpers, slick wordmongers threatening their livelihood, and rarely fraternized. My collaborator and I, however, had little time to promote social contacts, for a managerial eye was fixed on us to ensure that the script would be forthcoming on time. Herman Mankiewicz, our supervisor, was a large, Teutonic individual with an abrasive tongue, who had been a well-known journalist and *The New Yorker*'s first dramatic critic. Though he was married into the Hollywood hierarchy, his fondness for cards and good living kept him in a state of perpetual peonage and had made him a sort of Johnsonian figure in the industry. Luckily, his duties as our overseer lay lightly on him. He stressed the fact that we were to proceed as fancy dictated, cynically adding that in any case, the Marxes would keelhaul us.

"They're mercurial, devious, and ungrateful," he said. "I hate to depress you, but you'll rue the day you ever took the assignment. This is an ordeal by fire. Make sure you wear asbestos pants."

Johnstone, whose earlier association with the brothers had left no scars, was inclined to scoff at these sentiments, but several weeks later, an incident occurred that unnerved us both. One morning, we were called to Mr. Lasky's office and shown a cable from the Marxes in London. Stating their disenchantment with us in the most succinct terms, they recommended our instant dismissal and replacement by capable writers. Transfixed, we pointed out to Lasky that nobody thus far had seen a word we'd written. He nodded paternally.

"Don't be upset," he advised, smiling. "Actors, you know—they're all a little unstable. I've already replied. I told them to stick to their vaudeville and we'd worry about the movie end."

Evidently the vaudeville was providing its quota of headaches, because rumors of a very cool reception in England soon drifted back to us. Music-hall audiences were not yet attuned to anarchic comedy, and they saluted the Marxes' whirlwind antics by jeering and pitching pennies onto the stage. Insulated from their problems by a continent and an ocean, however, my collaborator and I continued to peg away at our script. We devised jokes and plot twists so hilarious that we could barely gasp them out to each other; we grovelled with laughter in our lazaret as we invented extravagant puns for Groucho, pantomimic flights and Italian malapropisms for his brothers. Zeppo, the youngest, was never a concern, since he was always cast as the juvenile love interest. His speeches were usually throwaways like "Yes, Father" or song cues on the order of "I think you have the loveliest blue eyes I've ever seen."

Six weeks from the day we had begun work, we were notified that the deadline was looming. The troupe was back in the country and about to converge on Hollywood, and we were to read the screenplay to them, *viva voce*, the following Friday night at the Roosevelt Hotel. We put in some intensive burnishing, though, truth to tell, our handiwork already seemed to us to outshine the Kohinoor. To make it still more acceptable, we decided to salt our pages with as many technical movie phrases as we could, many of which we only half understood. We therefore went over the action line by line, panning, irising down, and dissolving, painstakingly sandwiched in Jackman and Dunning shots, and even, at one point, specified that the camera should vorkapich around the faces of the ballroom guests. Neither of us, of course, had the remotest notion of what this last meant, and it was years before I discovered that it derived from a special-effects genius named Slavko Vorkapich. I still have no idea, between ourselves, whether his technique could be applied with impunity to the human face.

At eight-thirty on the appointed evening, I met Johnstone in the suite reserved for our audition. The onus of reading aloud a 126-page script weighed heavily on both of us, so we flipped a coin and I, to my despair, was elected. Half an hour passed without any sign of the quartet, during which I twice urged my colleague to abandon the whole enterprise and leave by the fire escape, but his dentures were chattering so loudly that he did not hear me. Fifteen minutes later, the first auditors arrived—Papa Marx, the progenitor of the band, accompanied by a fellow pinochle player. Our whiplash, Mankiewicz, turned up next, in company with his brother Joseph, then a rising screenwriter at Paramount. They were followed by Zeppo and his wife, who brought along a stately brace of Afghans they had purchased in England. The dogs had eaten the upholstery of a Packard convertible that afternoon and were somewhat subdued in consequence, but they looked intimidating, and they took up a position near my feet that boded ill. Harpo now strolled in with a couple of blond civilians he had dined with, and close on his heels the Chico Marxes, leading a scrappy wirehaired terrier which immediately tangled with the Afghans. In the midst of the tohu-bohu, Groucho and his wife entered; I supposed that thirteen constituted a quorum and made as if to start, but was told to desist—other guests were due. These, it proved, were three gagmen the Marxes had picked up in transit, each of whom was to furnish japes tailored to their respective personalities. (Zeppo, as indicated earlier, could expect only leavings.) Behind the gagmen came *their* wives, sweethearts, and an unidentifiable rabble I took to be relatives, and last of all several cold-eyed vultures obviously dispatched by the studio. When I counted noses and paws before ringing up the curtain, there were twenty-seven people and five dogs confronting me.

The very apogee of embarrassment, according to Madison Avenue, is to dream oneself in some stylish locale, say Carnegie Hall, clad in a bra other than Maidenform or a supporter not manufactured by Haines. Had I been wearing either or both that night, I could not have experienced worse panic as I stammered forth the setting of our opus. Destiny, whatever its intentions, had never supplied me with forensic gifts, and my only thespian flight theretofore had been a minor role in a high-school pageant based on Pocahontas. The incredible folly of my position, the temerity of a virgin scenarist hoping to beguile a hardened professional audience, suddenly overtook me. I became faint, and the roar of a mighty cataract like the Zambesi Falls sounded in my ears. Stricken, I turned to Johnstone for succor, but cataleptic fear had seized him too; his face, the color of an eggplant, was contorted in a ghastly, fixed smile like Bartholomew Sholto's in *The Sign of the Four*, and I thought for one horrid moment he was defunct.

"Go ahead, man," said a voice I distantly recognized as Groucho's. "Get a move on. As the donkey said, we're all ears."

Short of committing hara-kiri on the spot, there was nothing to do but comply, so, clearing my throat with a force that loosened the sidelights, I continued. I had not proceeded very far before I began to sense a distinct change in the mood of my listeners. At first it was pliant—indulgent, so to speak—and there was an occasional polite ripple. This soon ceased and they became watchful—not hostile as yet, but wary. It was as if they were girding themselves, flexing for trouble they knew was inevitable. Then, by slow degrees, an attitude of sullen resentment stole into their faces. They had been betrayed, lured away from their klabiatsch and easy chairs by a will-o'-the-wisp promise of entertainment, and they grew vengeful. *Some* of them got vengeful, that is; the majority got sleepy, for by then I had stopped inflecting my voice to distinguish one character from another and had settled into a monotonous lilt like a Hindu chanting the Bhagavad Gita. I spared them nothing

—the individual shots, the technical jargon, our colorful descriptions of sets and characters. At times my voice faded away altogether and I whispered endless pages of dialogue to the unheeding air. All the while, Johnstone sat with his eyes fixed alternately on his palms and the ceiling, patently trying to dissociate himself from me. Not once did he or anyone else bid me take respite or a glass of water. The whole room—exclusive of those who were asleep, naturally—was watching a man hang himself with a typewriter ribbon, and not a finger was lifted to save him. When I finally croaked "Fade Out" at the end of my ninety-minute unspectacular, there was no sound except the stertorous breathing of the dogs.

After an aeon, Chico stretched, revolved in his chair, and addressed Groucho. "What do you think?" he growled.

With the deliberation of a diamond cutter, Groucho bit the end off his cigar, and applying a match, exhaled a jet of smoke. "It stinks," he said, and arose. "Come on." As he stalked toward the door, he was engulfed in a wedge of sycophants hissing agreement and post-mortems. In another few seconds, the only occupants of the suite were a pair of forlorn sourdoughs numbed by the realization that the Lost Dutchman Mine was actually fool's gold.

Such was my baptism into the picture business, the glamorous and devil-may-care world of illusion I had envied from childhood. I crept away that night to lick my wounds, convinced that this was Waterloo, that contumely and public disgrace would be our portion forever. Happily, I was wrong; in the scalding light of day, our critics capriciously reversed themselves and decided that traces of our handiwork could be salvaged. It took five months of drudgery and Homeric quarrels, ambuscades, and intrigues that would have shamed the Borgias, but it finally reached the cameras, and the end product was *Monkey Business*, a muscular hit. I read the New York reviews in the most ideal surroundings imaginable—a café terrace at Bandol on the Côte d'Azur, midway between Marseilles and Toulon. A soft inshore breeze stirred my wife's hair, a Chambéry *fraise* waited at my elbow, and the schnauzer snored contentedly at our feet. Far more blissful, though, was the certainty that there wasn't a frosted papaya or a sneak preview within a thousand miles. Even that prince of porcupines, Thoreau, couldn't have asked for more than that.

My own relationship with Groucho was, in a sense, a baffling one. I loved his lightning transitions of thought, his ability to detect pretentiousness and bombast, and his genius for disembowelling the spurious and hackneyed phrases that litter one's conversation. And I knew that he liked my work for the printed page, my preoccupation with clichés, baroque language, and the elegant variation. Nevertheless, I sensed as time went on that this aspect of my work disturbed him; he felt that some of the dialogue I wrote for him was "too literary." He feared that many of my allusions would be incomprehensible to the ordinary moviegoer, whom he regarded as a wholly cretinous specimen.

"What'll this mean to the barber in Peru?" he was wont to complain whenever he came across a particularly fanciful reference. The barber, in his mind, was a prototypical figure—not a South American, but a Midwestern square in Peru, Indiana, whose funny bone the Marxes sought to tickle. Groucho visualized him, exhausted from his day's work and attended by a wife and five children, staring vacuously at the screen and resenting japes he could not understand. I tried to convince Groucho that his comedy was unique, a kaleidoscope of parody, free association, and insult, but he brushed me aside. "That's O.K. for the Round Table at the Algonquin," he said impatiently. "Jokes—that's what I need. Give me jokes."

The producer charged with supervising *Horsefeathers*, as it happened, was the same awesome figure who had guided the destinies of *Monkey Business*, Herman Mankiewicz. The choice, I suspect, was a deliberate one on the part of Paramount's front office, for it needed a tough foreman to ride herd on our anarchical troupe. Mankiewicz, whose stormy Teutonic character and immoderate zest for the grape and gambling have since been well delineated in connection with the authorship of *Citizen Kane*, was a brilliant man, but if he had any lovable qualities, he did his best to conceal them. He had a tongue like a rasp, and his savage wit demolished anyone unlucky enough to incur his displeasure. I myself was the recipient on various occasions, but one, which Groucho delighted to recall many years later, deserves repetition.

On a very hot midday in July, it seemed, Mankiewicz betook himself to a celebrated restaurant in Hollywood named

Eddie Brandstetter's, much frequented by gourmands, where he treated his palate to two whiskey sours and a Gargantuan lunch consisting of lentil soup with frankfurters, rinderbrust with spaetzle, red cabbage and roast potatoes, and noodle pudding, irrigating the mixture with three or four flagons of Pilsener. Then, eyeballs protruding, he lumbered painfully to his car and drove to his office at Paramount. Thrusting aside the handful of messages his secretary extended, he enjoined her not to admit any callers, however importunate, for the next couple of hours and retired into his private sanctum. With the Venetian blinds tightly drawn, he stretched out on a sofa, shielded his face with a copy of the *Hollywood Reporter*, and sank into a blissful snooze.

Barely ten minutes later, he was awakened by a timid, re-peated knocking at the door. Mankiewicz's face, mottled with perspiration and mounting fury, swelled like a sunfish as he sat up, prepared to decapitate whoever had flouted his express orders.

"Who the hell is it?" he shouted. "Come in, damn you!"

Two pale-faced young men, twitching with fright, entered haltingly. They were Arthur Sheekman, a gagman Groucho had imported to assist with his material, and myself, and luck-less as always, I had been nominated to voice our petition.

"I—I'm sorry to intrude," I began, "but the fact is—the truth of the matter—"

"What the devil do you want?" Mankiewicz barked. "Get the marbles out of your mouth!"

"Well, it's like this," I squeaked, moistening my lips. "In this sequence we're working on, we're kind of perplexed about the identity of the Marx Brothers—the psychology of the charac-ters they're supposed to represent, so to speak. I mean, who *are* they? We—we wondered if you could analyze or define them for us."

"Oh, you did, did you?" he grated. "O.K., I'll tell you in a word. One of them is a guinea, another a mute who picks up spit, and the third an old Hebe with a cigar. Is that all clear, Beaumont and Fletcher? Fine," he concluded, forcing a poi-sonous smile. "Now get back to your hutch, and at teatime I'll send over a lettuce leaf for the two of you to chew on. Beat it!"

Nathanael West

I F, IN THE latter half of 1932, you were a Midwestern music student at Juilliard, a fledgling copywriter with a marginal salary, or a divorcée rubbing along on a small alimony, the chances are that you lived at one time or another at the Hotel Sutton on East Fifty-sixth Street. The Sutton was a fairly characteristic example of the residential, or soi-disant "club," hotel designed for respectable young folk pursuing a career in New York. There was nothing in the least clublike about it, and it was residential only in the sense that it was an abode, a roof over one's head. Otherwise, it was an impersonal sixteen-story barracks with a myriad of rooms so tiny that their walls almost impinged on each other, a honeycomb full of workers and drones in the minimum cubic footage required to avert strangulation. The décor of all the rooms was identical—fireproof Early American, impervious to the whim of guests who might succumb to euphoria, despair, or drunkenness. The furniture was rock maple, the rugs rock wool. In addition to a bureau, a stiff wing chair, a lamp with a false pewter base, and an end table, each chamber contained a bed narrow enough to discourage any thoughts of venery. As a further sop to respectability, the sexes had been segregated on alternate floors, but the elevator men did not regard themselves as housemothers, and for the frisky, a rear stairway offered ready access or flight. The waitresses in the coffee shop on the ground floor wore peach-colored uniforms and served a thrifty club breakfast costing sixty-five cents. You had a choice of juice—orange or tomato—but not of the glass it came in, which was a heavy green goblet. The coffee, it goes without saying, was unspeakable.

By definition, the manager of the premises should have been a precise, thin-lipped martinet with a cold eye who slunk around counting towels and steaming open the clientele's mail. In point of fact, he was an amiable and well-spoken young man named Nathanael West, whose major interest was books rather than innkeeping. Since I was his friend and brother-in-law, it was only natural that my wife and I gravitated to his hostel when *Sherry Flip* slid into the vortex. A relative with a surplus of rooms was a mighty welcome spar, and we clung to him gratefully. He fixed up two cubbyholes into the semblance of a suite, for which, unsurprisingly, we paid skeletal rates, and he was quick to apply financial poultices when the wolf nipped at our heels. His nepotism, in a way, was an outgrowth of his situation, for he had been appointed manager by some remote uncle who owned the building. Literary tastes and executive talent rarely go hand in hand, but West, curiously enough, was good at his job. He had charm and a quick sense of humor, as well as an innate sympathy with the problems of his guests. This did not blind him to their deficiencies, nevertheless, and he often confided accounts of eccentric, and indeed clinical, behavior that suggested Dostoyevsky and Krafft-Ebing. He also gave us an insight into the sordid mechanics of operating a metropolitan hotel—the furtive inspection of baggage and letters, the surveillance of guests in arrears, the complex technique of locking out deadheads or impounding their effects, and similar indignities. I presume all of these were perpetuated on us in principle, even though we were kinsmen of the boss, but so subtly that we never caught on.

Had West dreamt of becoming a Conrad Hilton, he would have devoted his spare time to studying cost accounting or new methods of adulterating the coffee. The status of Boniface, however, increasingly irked him. He had never given up the hope of writing professionally, and in such leisure as he could contrive, was working on a second novel. It had its origin in a series of letters shown him several years earlier by a friend of ours, a lady who ran an advice-to-the-lovelorn column on the *Brooklyn Eagle*. For all their naïveté and comic superficialities, the letters were profoundly moving. They dealt with the most painful dilemmas, moral and physical, and West saw in them and their recipient the focus of the story he called *Miss Lonelyhearts*. From its inception to the final version, the book occupied him almost four years. He worked slowly and laboriously; he had none of the facility of the hack writer, the logorrhea with which so many second-rate novelists cloak their shortcomings. He openly disliked the swollen dithyrambs and Whitmanesque fervors of orgiasts like Thomas Wolfe, and the clumsy, unselective naturalism of the proletarian school typified by James Farrell repelled him equally. His chief orientation, as is apparent, was European. Among the Russians, Turgenev, Chekhov, and especially Gogol, with his mixture of fantastic humor and melancholy, appealed to him. He idolized Joyce, considering him, as most of us did, the foremost comic writer in the language, and was strongly attracted to the French surrealists like Aragon, Soupault, and Breton, whose experiments were appearing in *transition*. Along with his avant-gardist flair, there was a deep strain of the conventional in West's nature. He loved custom-tailored clothes—his tailor bills were astronomical—first editions, and expensive restaurants. He fancied himself a Nimrod and fisherman, largely, I often suspected because of the colorful gear they entailed. His taste in women, with whom he tended to be shy, was catholic enough, but he preferred tall, rangy girls who had attended certain finishing schools and universities, the type our generation called snakes. For a brief interval, he even owned a red Stutz Bearcat, until it burst into flames and foundered in a West Virginia gorge. He liked to think of himself as an all-around man.

It is axiomatic that when a couple of bibliophiles meet over a remainder bin, a little magazine always results. During the spring of 1931, West, an inveterate browser, became acquainted with William Carlos Williams at a West Forty-seventh Street bookshop. In a short while their union was blessed by issue— that is to say, the first one of a quarterly called *Contact*, which they coedited with Robert McAlmon. The title page bore the defiant epigraph "*Contact* will attempt to cut a trail through the American jungle without the aid of a European compass," but the undergrowth must have proved too thick, because the editors shortly switched their policy from geography to merit. They extracted essays from Diego Rivera and Marsden Hartley, as well as contributions from e. e. cummings, Erskine Caldwell, George Milburn, and Ben Hecht (and with due modesty, of course, from themselves). The magazine published four or five numbers, and then, stricken by the anaemia that dogs all such enterprises, a total lack of advertising, folded.

Though West was left with bales of unsolicited manuscripts which eventually stoked the furnace, he did get to know a horde of writers during his editorial tenure, and many of them, trading on his largesse, dossed down at the Sutton on their visits to New York. At teatime the lobby frequently took on the air of Yaddo or a book-and-author luncheon. Burly, pipe-smoking poets with thick orange cravats—nobody has yet as-certained why poets affect neckwear that has the texture of caterpillars—stood around swapping metres with feverish lady librarians from the Dakotas; the girl at the newsstand who sold you the sports final, unless you were quick on your feet, would try to read you a quatrain in the manner of Rimbaud. One eve-ning, as I was descending alone in the elevator, the operator, a cretin I was certain I had never seen before, halted his car between floors and turned to me with a businesslike gleam in his eye. I thought he was about to glom my stickpin and leave through the escape hatch, but when he spoke, it was in the rich Stanislavskian cadence of a Group Theatre actor.

"Excuse me, sir," he said deferentially. "The housekeeper told me you had a big hit on Broadway. I'm scripting a play too, on a Biblican theme, but I got stuck in the second act, in the obligatory scene. Could you recommend a good book or construction, or would you advise me to go back to the Bible?"

I advised him, and thereafter used the stairs. Not all the as-piring writers at the Sutton, however, were slated for anonym-ity. Lillian Hellman, whom I had originally met when she was a reader for Horace Liveright and married to Arthur Kober, was holed up there, struggling with her first solo effort, *The Chil-dren's Hour*. A pallid youth on the third floor, named Norman Krasna, hitherto a flack in the Warner Brothers publicity de-partment, was endlessly retyping Hecht and MacArthur's *The Front Page*, hoping to learn something of dramatic structure. His toil eventuated in a clamorous comedy on public relations that left Broadway unmoved but swept him on to Hollywood and affluence. The one writer of celebrity in the establishment was something of a recluse. This was Dashiell Hammett, who, in the pages of magazines like *Black Mask* and four novels, had revolutionized the whole concept of police fiction. Like most innovators, he had reaped small financial benefit from his work and was on a lee shore. He had been living, prior to his arrival in our midst, at an opulent Fifth Avenue hotel where he had run up a whopping bill. Unable to pay it, he was forced, in English parlance, to "shoot the moon" and abscond with as many of his belongings as he could conceal. His knowl-edge of the mentality of house detectives provided the key. A tall, emaciated man easily identifiable in a crowd, Hammett decided to use fat as a subterfuge. He pulled on four shirts, three suits, innumerable socks, two lightweight ulsters, and an overcoat, cramming his pockets with assorted toiletries. Then he puffed out his cheeks, strode past the desk without a glimmer of suspicion, and headed for the Sutton, whose manager was acquiring kudos among literary folk as a Good Samaritan. West, a clotheshorse himself, recognized in Hammett a sartorial genius. He put him on the cuff and staked him to a typewriter and a bottle of beer a day. The upshot, the best-seller called *The Thin Man*, clinched Hammett's reputation.

It was another pen pal of West's, in this same seedy epoch, who sweet-talked him into a venture that addled our brains for years to come. About mid-autumn of 1932, my wife and I began to detect glowing references in her brother's speech to Bucks County, Pennsylvania. He had latterly been weekending there with Josephine Herbst, the novelist, and his accounts of the flora, the architecture, and the natives verged on the rhapsodic. Owing to its remoteness and the paucity of highways, the district was still altogether rural; but the submarginal land and the inroads of the Depression had brought about a wave of farm foreclosures, and property was ridiculously cheap. Inevitably, West conceived a romantic dream of ourselves as country squires. He visualized us cantering on fat cobs through leafy lanes, gloating over our waving fields of alfalfa, the great stone barns decorated with hex signs, and the lowing kine. He saw himself as a mighty shikar stalking through pheasant cover, gun dogs at his heels, clad in all the corduroy vests and bush jackets he had lusted for endlessly at Abercrombie's. Since I was stony at the moment, eroded by debt and hostile to any prospect of becoming a mortgagee, West started a campaign of suasion that was a masterpiece of sophistry. The Revolution, he pointed out, was imminent; how sensible it would be for us, when "La Carmagnole" rang across the barricades, to own a patch of ground where we could raise the necessities of life. Fish and game were so abundant in the Delaware Valley that shad, rabbits, and quail had to be restrained from leaping into the cook pot. If Roosevelt closed the banks as predicted, we could grow our own tobacco, cobble our shoes with tough, fragrant birch bark. He painted a pastoral of the three of us in

our bee-loud glade, my wife contentedly humming as she bot-
tled raspberry jam, he and I churning out an unending stream
of prose. Where the requisite paper would come from, since
we were to dispense with cash, he did not specify. Doubtless he
expected the forest to supply it.

I turned a deaf ear to all such blandishments, but his sister, who was easier to influence, succumbed. One Monday
morning, the two of them returned from a reconnaissance of
the section pale with excitement. They had stumbled across
the ultimate, the *ne plus ultra*, in farmsteads—an eighty-seven-
acre jewel in the rolling uplands bordering the river. Their
voices shook as they described the stone house on a hillside circumscribed by a tumbling creek, the monumental barn above
larger than the cathedral at Chartres. The place, it appeared,
belonged to a left-wing journalist, one Mark Silver, who had
tried to launch a ne'er-do-well brother in the chicken business
there. The brother and other rodents had eaten the fowls, and
Silver, to compound his troubles, was involved with a tigress
in New York who was threatening a breach-of-promise suit. To
enable him to flee to Mexico, which seemed to him an ideal
solution for his woes, he was willing to accept a token payment
for the farm, plus easy installments. In West's view, it was the
biggest steal since the theft of the *Mona Lisa* from the Louvre.

I grudgingly went out with them to see the place, and in
a trice also fell for it. The autumn foliage was at its height,
and the woods and fields blazed with color. In contrast to the
bedlam of New York, the only sound that disturbed the syl-
van hush was the distant chatter of crows in the north forty.
There was an air of permanence, of solidity, about the house
and outbuildings that captivated and reassured. My glasses
steamed over as a series of colored lantern slides flashed before
me—sleigh rides, Hallowe'en parties, sugaring off, sugaring
on, and bringing in the Yule log. We hastened through the
dwelling, exclaiming over virtues like its massive fireplaces and
deep window reveals and conveniently ignoring its drawbacks.
Bathrooms, engineered kitchens, and oil furnaces bloomed in
our overheated imagination; magically, we became a trio of
Paul Bunyans, shearing off porches, cementing cellars, and re-
locating stone partitions. Sound as the house was, we had to
admit that the previous tenants had left it in parlous condition.

The living-room closet was heaped with empty walnut husks, and judging from the pots and dishes on the stove, the residents had departed as precipitately as the crew of the *Marie Celeste*. A tour of the farm buildings disclosed that Silver's brother, following the poultry debacle, had turned his hand to cabinetmaking. The sheds were piled with dozens of modernistic plywood bookcases, striped in bronze radiator paint and hot tropical colors. The monstrous things harassed me for years afterward; whenever I tried to chop them up for fireplace use, the fibrous, springy wood repelled the axe and perforated me with splinters. I eventually made an apocalyptic bonfire of them, nearly burning down the barn in the process.

Several years later, incidentally, I learned that a celebrated colleague had seen the property and its owners, just before we did, under peculiarly harrowing circumstances. George S. Kaufman was being shown some of the real estate available in the neighborhood, Kaufman strenuously protesting the while to his wife that he detested the out-of-doors, that country living was full of pitfalls, and that nobody had ever incurred a hernia in Reuben's. Up at the Silver Farm, as they ascended its winding lane, a lesson in firearms was in progress: Mark Silver, who could not open an umbrella without puncturing someone's lung, was initiating his brother in the mysteries of handling a shotgun.

"They call this the breech," he explained, opening the mechanism. "We place the bullet, or shell, in there. Then we close it, like so, and raising it to the shoulder, aim along the barrel and squeeze here."

He pressed the trigger smartly, unaware that the weapon was still trained on his brother's foot. Simultaneously with the explosion, the Kaufmans materialized as though on cue, just in time to see the hapless brother bite the dust. Silver stared at the casualty, his face contorted in horror, and then bounded up to the arrivals.

"Cain and Abel!" he bellowed, and smote his forehead. "Woe is me—I have slain my own brother!"

Kaufman took off like an impala, and it was a decade before he would consent to enter even Central Park. Had West and I had any such therapeutic experience, we too might have been cured of our obsession; but the poison was circulating in our veins, and a fortnight afterward, in a simple ceremony at the county courthouse, two blushing innocents were married to four score and seven acres. Raising my half of the five-hundred-dollar deposit baffled us until my wife came up with a brilliant expedient. The one piano at the Sutton, she suggested, was quite inadequate for the Juilliard scholars, who required sustained practice. She and I had a baby grand in storage, an heirloom from her family, which we might be willing to sacrifice for a consideration in a worthy cultural cause. Her brother went into some pretty complex double-talk with the owners of the hotel to justify his expenditure of two hundred and fifty dollars, but they ultimately held still for it. After all, as West fluently pointed out, he had single-handedly transformed the joint from a flophouse into an artistic mecca.

For the next couple of months, every ounce of energy the three of us could summon—along with whatever paint, hardware, tools, and furniture West could liberate from the hotel short of downright larceny—went into making the farm habitable. The self-deceit of landowners is proverbial, but we reached new heights; we became artisans as well, installing pumps and plumbing, wiring the house, and even, in a Herculean spurt that left us crippled for weeks, implanting a septic tank. All these furbelows, being makeshift, constantly tended to remind us of our inadequacy. Water pipes we had painstakingly soldered would burst their seams in the middle of the night, with a roar like Krakatoa, and drench us in our beds. Tongues of blue fire licked at our homemade electrical conduits; half the time we reeled about with catastrophic headaches, unaware that the furnace needed escape vents to discharge its burden of coal gas. Each weekend was a turmoil of displacement. Groaning like navvies, we trundled barrows of shale to and fro, unrooted and redistributed trees, realigned fences, and changed the entire topography of the place. The vogue for Pennsylvania Dutch artifacts had not yet become general, and there were quantities of dough trays, dry sinks, horsehair sofas, Victorian wig stands, and similar rubbish available around the county to any fool who confused himself with Chippendale. We invariably did, and spent endless nights in a haze of shellac dust, scraping away at some curlicued gumwood commode to bring out the beauty of the grain.

Spring was upon us with a rush of seed catalogues, and we were about to occupy our demesne and see if we could subsist on tomatoes, when the wheel of fortune took an unexpected spin. The Marx Brothers besought me to go West and fashion another movie for them, *Horsefeathers*, this time in collaboration with Kalmar and Ruby, the songwriters. Somewhat less than radiant at the thought of being sucked into the millrace a second time, I hesitated, but the long financial drought had sapped my resistance. At almost the same time, West's novel *Miss Lonelyhearts* was published to considerable critical acclaim. Its early promise of sales, unhappily, was blasted by the publisher's bankruptcy, and though another firm soon reissued it, the delay was fatal. There was, however, a small silver lining. The film rights were acquired for a handful of lima beans by Darryl Zanuck (who, parenthetically, transmuted it into a tepid comedy), and it was on the proceeds that West decided to chuck his job and devote himself to full-time authorship.

Our farewell to him at the farm, where he was starting to woo his muse with a few Spartan adjuncts like an inkhorn, a 14-gauge shotgun, and a blooded pointer, took place in an atmosphere of mingled resignation and hope. It seemed a cruel irony to be cheated of the rustic joys we had labored to achieve, and yet, if we were ever to enjoy them, a spell in the Hollywood deep freeze was unavoidable. As for West, his mood was jubilant; he was through forever with the hotel business, with pettifogging bookkeepers and commission merchants, with the neurotics, drunks, and grifters he had been called on to comfort and wheedle. He had two tangible licenses to hunt and to fish, and one, invisible, to starve as a free-lance writer. We toasted his future and ours with a gulp of forty-rod, and bidding him Godspeed, turned our faces to the setting sun.

Dorothy Parker

DOROTHY PARKER was already a legend when I first met her in the autumn of 1932. Her bittersweet verses and dialogues, her *bon mots*, and her love affairs had made her a distinctive figure in the group of journalists and playwrights who congregated at the Algonquin for lunch and at Tony's, Jack & Charlie's, and the Stork Club for more extended liquefaction. The way in which we met was not one I would have chosen —in fact, it was a scarifying ordeal—but since we ultimately became friends and neighbors, it is worth narrating if only as indicative of manners and customs in the Prohibition era.

The occasion was a cocktail party given by Poultney Kerr, the bibulous producer of *Sherry Flip*, the revue I had written some sketches for and which was about to begin rehearsal. The show at that point lacked a title, and Kerr, seizing on any pretext for a bash, invited forty or fifty social and theatrical acquaintances to drinks at his office in the hope that someone would come up with a frisky and forceful name for the enterprise. Halfway through the proceedings Mrs. Parker arrived, visibly gassed but dressed to kill in a black confection by Lanvin, a feathered toque, and opera-length gloves. Thirty-nine years old and a very toothsome dish, she immediately made every other woman in the assemblage feel dowdy, and for a moment the sound of their teeth gnashing drowned out the buzz of chitchat. When Kerr introduced us, she straightaway fired off a barrage of compliments likening me to Congreve, Oscar Wilde, and Noël Coward. Inasmuch as my total Broadway output was confined to one sketch in the *Third Little Show*, I thought the praise a mite excessive, but I blushingly accepted the tribute. Having fortified the company with several rounds of malt, Kerr called for silence, explained the purpose of the gathering, and bade everyone don his thinking cap. Needless to say, all heads turned toward Mrs. Parker, who accepted the challenge.

"Let me see," she pondered. "What about *Sing High, Sing Low*? No, that's defeatist. It needs something frothy, sparkling —wait, I know! *Pousse-Café!*"

There was an all but imperceptible ripple, and several willowy young men murmured, "Splendid . . . Yes, definitely . . . Oh, I love it." In the hush that followed, I suddenly became aware of Mrs. Parker's eyes fixed on me with catlike intentness. "What do *you* think of *Pousse-Café*, Mr. Perelman?"

"Great!" I said, striving to put conviction into my tone. "It's gay and—and sparkling, you're right. But it lacks—how shall I say?—punch. I mean, *poose*-café—it's too soft, somehow."

"Oh, really?" she asked, with a slow and deadly inflection. "Well, then, here's something punchier. How about *Aces Up*?"

"*Aces Up*," I mused. "That's marvellous, very good. I just wonder, though, if we can't find something a *tiny* bit sharper, less static . . ."

"Well, goodness me." Mrs. Parker's words dripped sweet poison. "What ever shall we do? Our wrist has just been slapped by the house genius there, who feels that we're a bit dull-witted. Of course, *he's* in a position to know, isn't he, leaning down from Parnassus—"

"Look, folks!" Kerr broke in nervously. "Have another drink. Don't go, it's still early—"

"How privileged we are to have the benefit of Mr. P.'s wide experience!" she overrode him. "How gracious of him to analyze our shortcomings! I wonder, though, if Mr. P. realizes that he's a great big etcetera. Because he is, you know. In fact, of all the etceteras I've ever known—"

Well, fortunately for me, the bystanders who had witnessed the carnage recovered their tongues at this juncture, and the rest of Mrs. Parker's diatribe was lost in the babble. I made my escape, and when Kerr phoned me the next day to apologize for her conduct, I swore that if I ever met the woman again, I'd skewer her with one of her own hatpins. That evening I received a dozen magnificent roses from her accompanied by a note steeped in remorse. It was the beginning of a friendship that survived the next thirty-five years, with intermittent lapses. When my wife and I saw her again on the Coast, she was married to Alan Campbell and from all outward appearances was prosperous. The two worked successfully as screenwriters (and in fact I collaborated with them on a film at M-G-M several years later) and might have continued except that Dottie detested Hollywood. Laura and I, who shared her feeling, spoke often of our place in Bucks County; we tended to become lyrical about the countryside, the farmhouses, and the relative simplicity of life there, and evidently our encomiums had an effect. In time we began to notice the recurrence in Dottie's speech of the word "roots."

"We haven't any roots, Alan," she would admonish him after the fourth Martini. "You can't put down any roots in Beverly Hills. But look at Laura and Sid—they've got *roots*, a place to come home to. Roots, roots."

It was practically foreordained, hence, that a month or two after we settled down at our place, the Campbells suddenly materialized on the doorstep with shining faces. They were surfeited with the artificiality and tinsel of Hollywood, they declared; they wanted a farm near ours and they wanted us to help them find it. Property was still cheap in our area, though farther down the Delaware around New Hope, George S. Kaufman, Moss Hart, and several other playwrights had acquired houses and Bucks County was becoming known as a haunt of writers and artists. Dottie and Alan, however, were imbued with what might be called the creative spirit. Not for them a manor house equipped with creature comforts like bathrooms, stainless steel kitchens, and laundries. They wanted a place that had "possibilities," something they would have fun remodeling. It was clearly an assignment for Jack Boyle.

Jack Boyle was a stage Irishman, straight out of George McManus's comic strip, one of the cronies Jiggs was forever hobnobbing with at Dinty Moore's and incurring Maggie's wrath. He was by way of being a real-estate agent, though he spent a good deal of his time seated on the steps of our local post office telling yarns. In a sense, Jack was one of the most celebrated personages in the district, even if nobody there knew it, for his exploits were immortalized in a book called *The Professional Thief* published by the University of Chicago. He had specialized in stealing furs from department stores, employing a technique that baffled the New York police authorities for years. It was his practice to enter a store, just prior to closing, attired in a balmacaan or similar loose topcoat, and to secrete himself in one of the pay toilets. After the store's watchman had made his rounds, Boyle would hasten to the ladies' fur coat section, select a particularly valuable mink or broadtail garment, and return to his cubicle. Soon after the establishment opened the next morning, he would emerge wearing the loot under his coat and stroll off. The truly extraordinary feature of his caper, though, was that he always turned over the money given him by the fence to a cause he believed in: he was a philosophical anarchist. Eventually betrayed by an informer, he so confused the police with an explanation of his motives that they sent him to Matteawan, but he managed to escape and ultimately, after extended litigation, to beat the rap. Thereafter, he had changed his venue to our township, where he trucked an occasional load of wood to Greenwich Village or negotiated the sale of a farm.

It was a lead-pipe cinch that anyone with so colorful a background would appeal to Dottie, and the two instantly hit it off. A couple of days thereafter, Laura and I accompanied the Campbells on an inspection tour of several farms that Boyle listed. The second one we saw was such a plum that had our friends hesitated, we ourselves would have snapped it up. The central portion of the house, its two lateral wings, and the summer kitchen extending from it were all built of field stone. Three enormous Norway maples shaded the residence on its north side; on the south was an apple orchard in full bloom. About fifty yards distant stood a stone barn slightly smaller than Aeolian Hall. The dwelling and its outbuildings, reached by a long lane that guaranteed privacy, lay on a gently rolling southern slope of one hundred twenty acres, and the asking price was four thousand five hundred dollars. As Boyle quoted the figure and all our jaws dropped in unison, he raised his hand.

"A word of advice before you grab it, friends," he told the Campbells. "I think you ought to see the inside first. It needs —well, it needs a little attention."

Even with his warning, none of us was prepared for the actuality. The interior of the house was in an appalling state; floors had rotted out in places, revealing the cellar below, fragments of plaster hung from the ceilings, woodwork gave way at the touch. A disused incubator for baby chicks was balanced crazily in the largest room, and a thick film of poultry feathers and cobwebs shrouded everything. It seemed incredible that the ruin was inhabited, yet, said Boyle, an old Ukrainian couple had been living there several years and cultivating a few fields, thanks to the generosity of the owners.

There is a specially insidious form of self-deception afflicting house hunters wherein they confuse themselves with Hercules, equal to any Augean stable they encounter, and the Campbells promptly succumbed to it. They ran around envisioning the rooms a clever architect could fabricate out of the shell, the baths and bedchambers and butler's pantries necessary for country living, and in all conscience we did nothing to disillusion them, for the prospect of having Dottie as a neighbor was a stimulating one. It did not occur to us that we had taken on the role of midwives, that the Campbells expected us to accouche the birth of their dream house, and that we would be called upon to provide sympathy and counsel—to say nothing of anodynes like Martinis—for the manifold problems plaguing them.

The next few months were a caution. The pair installed themselves at an inn near Doylestown where they groaned through all the legal complexities of acquiring their place, choosing an architect, and approving his plans. Infatuated with him at first, they fell out of love with him in short order; he was stodgy, unimaginative, old-fashioned. The Ukrainians, who had been given notice to vacate, turned obstinate; they refused to adapt themselves to the new owners' timetable and hung on, maddening Alan beyond measure. He turned in desperation to Jack Boyle, who pointed out, reasonably enough, that the old people had chickens they were preparing to market, standing crops not yet ready for harvest.

"That's *their* problem," Alan retorted passionately. "Don't they realize it's costing Dottie and me seven hundred and fifty dollars a week to stay away from Hollywood?"

SELECTED LETTERS

To Edmund Wilson

Paris
September 2, 1929

Dear Wilson,

Your good letter fell like manna on the American Express Company. I wanted to see you before I left but my feet were awash in lilies of the valley and my head bowed down with tons of bridal net. In a word, I was being married. And you should have heard the pretty squeals of my bridesmaids as I threw them my bouquet of fresh cucumbers with Russian dressing! It was a veritable fairyland.

Well, the book is out and, one hears, has sold out its first printing. I cannot say much for the jejune advertising— "Priceless $2.00"—"This book does not stop at Yonkers"— and suchlike, but what would you, as they say here. So far I haven't seen any reviews except a bushel of whimsy from the *Charleston Gazette* which reveals the fine Italian hand of H.L. I was somewhat peeved to note that Liveright had omitted all my drawings, a little dedication I had prepared, and had turned the thing out in a generally cheap fashion. But the usual plaintive cries of a beginner can't have much interest. Let them apply their Rivington Street methods as long as they sell the damn thing.

The usual flock of compatriots lounge before the Dome, the Rotonde, and the Select; the Coupole, the new and garish cafe here, houses all nationalities, just one big family under their berets. We spent several weeks at a place called Bandol on the Mediterranean which Phil and Sally Wylie recommended and had a good time in spite of some of the fellow-countrymen. The *Republic* sails from Cherbourg the 21st of the month with us below hatches, and it will not be long before you will be having dinner with us. Please bear my regards to Gilbert Seldes and Mrs. Seldes and stroll down Broadway for me some evening.

Sincerely,

To I. J. Kapstein

92 Grove Street
New York City
October 9, 1930

Dear Kap,

Can't either one of us smear a little medicated ointment on that large chancre in the groin of Life—no hitting below the parables, mind you—and start the balls rolling again? This Hatfield-McCoy stuff is boloney. Why should I shoot you from ambush? I would hardly recognize you, I haven't seen you in so long, and even if I did shoot, I'd probably bump off your brother Johnny, he must be older than you by this time. Throw away your Krag-Jorgenson and take off your beard, Floyd Collins, I know you.

I often feel that after all Life is only a stage and we are all only players, here to speak our brief piece and then bow off at the command of the Great Showman. Only in this case, I am not a player, I am one of the piccolo-players in the pit, and piccolo-players are notorious sons-of-bitches. For one thing, I am s.o.b. enough not to have got together enough coin to be able to live permanently in Europe, instead I bake my nuts in Sodom here and no Proust to chronicle me or even hand me a glass of poisoned water if I were dying in the street. You know how the elderly Yid ladies put it: *Darf men hauben kinder?* Or *darf men gayan in collitch?* Of course, college is valuable in making contacts, do not you often feel this, my Armenian friend?...Speaking of that lousy mutton-smelling race, a swell girl friend of ours who unfortunately is compelled to make a living in Paris and thus is far away tells this gag: Party of people sitting around in front of the Dome, one of the usual Armenian rug-peddlers pestering everybody in the group to buy his carpets. Too tiresome, my dear. Finally one gent more bored than the rest lifts his conk from a glass of mixed schmaltz and pernod and says: "I'll tell you, fella, *The Green Hat* was o.k., but that last book of yours was LOUSY." Build your own blackout....I'll never forget that Armenian line of yours which went "Come up my room—coffee-cake?"

The babe and I have settled down with our schnozzles to the grandstand at 92 Grove Street for the winter and are wondering what's delaying the wolf, he should have arrived a week or so ago. Myself, I am through with *Judge*, free-lancing for *College Humor* and trying to write a skit for the Marx Bros. to play picture-houses with in the middle west. Between these various things we manage to eke out bread and eke. The bread is mouldy and the eke worse, but we always have enough to visit the Fifth Avenue Playhouse and see *In Gay Madrid* with Ramon Novarro, a short film dealing with the way the sea anemone catches its prey, and a Fox newsreel for Sept. 14th showing gigantic fires in Fall River and waves demolishing the breakwater at Short Ass, Massachusetts.

Well, Hime, you pitch the next inning. Paint me a word-picture of life under the elms, how soon are you going to scram from that place and join our breadline? Or have you got a novel in you, as they say at Liveright's quite seriously. Sometime when I get a week off I am going to sit down and write you a letter telling you about that place. I can match you bastard for bastard you'll name at Knopf's.

Ever the Staten Island wonder girl,

To Groucho Marx

14 Washington Square North
New York City
April 7, 1943

Dear Groucho,

Your initial broadcast reminded me that I was long overdue on a reply; and not to wear out my welcome, thank you for that splendid bit of sewage about Leo (Sunshine) Fon-a-Row and a lot of laughs (spelled "laffs") on the Blue Ribbon show. By now you have probably seen John Hutchens' piece in the radio section of last Sunday's *Times*, which shows that your fans are still legion. I really thought you goaled them and especially loved the business of playing straight to yourself on puns like "aria."

I have been tied up since mid-January on a musical with Ogden Nash and Kurt Weill, which we finished the end of this past week. Nash and I did the book (based on a short story by F. Anstey, who was the editor of *Punch* back in the Eighties), and Ogden's now finishing up his lyrics for Weill's music. It's the story of a small schnückel of a barber who accidentally brings a statue of Venus to life, and it has turned up a lot of pretty funny and dirty complications. The music and lyrics thus far (about ⅔ finished) are grand, and we're dickering with several leading women currently. Rehearsals start about August 1st...All this happened as I was concluding work on the revue; I have six of the seven sketches finished for that, and the present design is to do it in the fall.

Otherwise the usual routine; I've been doing a piece every other week for the *Satevepost* and random *New Yorker* things, though the musical crowded out the latter lately. Also, just to make everything really giddy, I've been taking a course in bacteriology in my spare time, and if you need a fast Wassermann any time this spring, mail me the bottle. I'm putting up posters in subway washrooms after June 1st: "MEN: why worry? See Dr. Morty Perelman, night or day—no more expensive than any quack."

The theater here is blooming, everything's a hit and the wise guys, who have never been known to be right, claim business will hold up right through the summer. As you probably know, *Franklin Street* is being rewritten as a musical by George Kaufman and Gus Goetz, with prospective tunes by Rogers and Hammerstein. To judge from the reception of *Something for the Boys* and *Oklahoma*, it's a musical year. It's also a Mankiewicz year, to judge from the news we get here. I saw an issue of the *Journal-American* containing a photo of Mank chained to a harness bull, in which our jolly friend looked like a member of the Kid Dropper arson ring.

Well, cuddles, my best to yourself and all the pretty girls on the bridle path, and let's know the news. Did you, or are you still planning to, make *The Heart of a City*? And are you getting much? In fact, what about a scholarly little monograph on "Muff Memories of an Old Trouper"?   Love,

To Frances and Albert Hackett

Shelbourne Hotel
Dublin
August 14, 1949

Dear Frances and Albert,

Dublin on a Sunday afternoon in mid-August is so close to being buried alive that I had better not chill your blood with any further description. There are 4,238 churches within one mile of where I'm sitting (sorry, where I'm *afther* sitting), and that part of the population which isn't macerating itself inside them is closeted in the pubs. This morning the children and I walked miles through the slums—and O'Casey was being photographic in *Juno and the Paycock*—to find something called the Bird Market, which turned out to be a dozen louse-ridden canaries. That constitutes the total amusement facilities of this place. They don't even have the opportunity as they once did of sitting around and slandering the English, now that they have achieved their independence.

I believe that Laura wrote you way back there in Bali sometime around early April, since which time, as you see, we have crawled a considerable distance across the intervening continents. About the middle of April or thereabouts, we took off for Bangkok. The trip around Celebes and the Moluccas had been wonderful, and Bali itself even more so. I managed to squeeze in an all-too-short excursion into the Banda Sea on a 30-foot motor schooner to the island of Banda Neira, which used to be the center of the Dutch nutmeg trade in the 17th Century. It was a remarkable experience from every angle, including the fact that I probably got malaria there, but anyway, to get on with the narrative, we landed up in Bangkok plumb in the middle of their summer heat and had ourselves a month of really gruelling weather. Our original plan, to spend a while there, soon got itself amended for a whole lot of reasons—political instability, the kids' schooling, and changes in the scheme for the *Holiday* series. We flew out in mid-May, crossing India and the Middle East and stopping off at Istanbul, which we all thought was an extremely colorful and agreeable place. (Incidentally, such furniture, general antiques, jewelry, and curios in the Grand Bazaars there as to drive you out of your senses.) From there, on to Rome— a week's stay and a most fantastic reaming, inasmuch as the Romans are killing off the golden American goose with complete contempt for the eggs. And then to Beaulieu, twenty minutes' drive from Nice, where we sat down for six weeks of work and recuperation. This was a thoroughly first-rate part of the trip. It was not cheap by any manner of means; I don't think there is such a thing as a moderate, and at the same time good, hotel to be found in Europe any longer, but the Hotel Metropole there was situated smack on the Mediterranean, the food was good, and the staff by and large was cordial. They were nice not only to us but to Tong Cha, which prejudiced us in their favor. Tong Cha, I should explain quickly, is a mynah bird I bought in Bangkok. I always wanted to own one and now (if the pension I left him at in Paris is doing right by him) I hope to import him into the States when we return at the end of September. He is an extremely well-favored specimen—formerly the property of a Chinese fire-cracker store in Siam—with glossy, purple-and-black iridescent plumage, primrose-yellow wattles, a beak like a candy corn, and an extensive repertory of Chinese and Siamese words. . . . *Gracula javanensis* is his technical classification, if Albert wishes to look him up in that pocket manual. Although commonly regarded as savage and unapproachable, this one is Trilby to my Svengali, and one of the more nauseating sights is to see me stroking his wings and muttering little heartbroken cries of affection.

By the time we got ready to leave Beaulieu, our various tropical ailments had vanished. These, incidentally, were fairly extensive; Abby had had a lingering case of jungle boils, I'd had the possibly-malaria and something called Singapore ear, a spectacular fungoid malady, and Adam drew a particularly tenacious case of tropical ulcer of the leg, which demanded protracted and complex treatments at Nice. We moved out of Beaulieu with twenty pieces of hand luggage and first went to Marseilles to intercept six trunks which had come by water from Singapore. We repacked all this and shipped it on to Paris, flew up there and spent five days, and flew on to London. Here we picked up a British sports car I bought, and after two weeks started a tour of southern England. We've spent the larger part of the time since at a truly dreary spot called Sidmouth in Devon, advertised to us as a delightful seaside resort and as stuffy as they come. Since I worked most of the time there, I didn't take the punishment the rest of the troupe did, but it was bad enough. England is very depressing these days, there is hardly any food and less liquor and no sweets and no fun and the future looks grimmer than ever. Meat is unheard-of, eggs rare, butter very strictly rationed, sugar scarce, etc., etc. Our progress after Sidmouth, therefore, was chiefly a matter of whizzing through handsome scenery—Herefordshire, Shropshire, and up to Liverpool, from which we flew over here to do some eating. Fortunately, the latter is available without any trouble. We have been ramming protein into our gullets three times a day; steaks of the most handsome proportions are very cheap, bacon and butter plentiful, and lots of candy, even if it isn't up to our standards at home. We expect to leave here this coming Wednesday, that is, in three days, flying back to Liverpool, where we'll pick up the car and drive down through Derbyshire to Oxford for two days, then spend a day or two in Surrey, and leave England from the east-coast port of Harwich by a Danish steamer across the North Sea to Esbjerg. Thence by road to Copenhagen for about a month and driving down through the western zone of Germany, Holland, Belgium, and to Paris for a final week before embarking on the *De Grasse* September 29th.

I haven't forgotten that when we parted, I promised to give you the dope on what our trip through the East Indies was like, whether it was feasible for yourselves and the like. As to whether it was enjoyable or not, it was easily, far and away, the high spot of either of the trips I've made. I recommend it unreservedly, and Laura agrees with me without qualification. You must understand that we were something of a curiosity there; we were the first tourists who'd come through since the war and I don't believe any have come through since. . . . I think, to belabor the point, that it is an absolutely unique experience, and I honestly believe that we all got more out of it than we anticipated in our rosiest dreams. You will forgive me for sounding ecstatic, but I am only echoing Al Hirschfeld's estimate of Bali when I say that it's the closest thing to Paradise on earth. And, far from being spoiled by tourism, it hasn't been touched in the slightest degree.

Well, girls, I'd better cease this panegyric before the saliva spoils my only remaining clean shirt. The kiddies are off seeing *Sorrowful Jones*, a Bob Hope epic, in some theater on O'Connell Street and if I stop now, Laura and I just have time to sneak down for afternoon tea in the lobby. That means bread-and-butter sandwiches, frosted cakes, and Irish county families muttering "Divil a bit." We think of you all the time and wish you'd write. Considering how long it's taken us to do so, you'd be justified in waiting six months before replying, but it would be very nice to get the gossip from Sepulveda and Westwood. . . . Love and kisses from us all, and up the rebels.

Yours ever,

To Abby Perelman

39½ Washington Square South
New York City
April 15, 1954

Dear Abby,

Sorry I haven't had a chance to write before this, but I've been knocking my brains out on the African stuff for the magazine, and what with interruptions, only just completed the first in the series. Trying to get the complex picture there on paper is just no fun, especially in a piece that begins a series.

Your postcard about *Crime and Punishment* didn't surprise either Laura or myself; it's a most depressing book no matter how young or old, how high or low, one is, and that goes for all of Dostoievsky. I wouldn't have let you read it if I could have prevented it. Of course, it's a great book, but you must realize life isn't necessarily that bleak. For all the woe implied in the lives of those characters, you only have to look about you to see that people can enjoy themselves and laugh and rise above their adversities. Dostoievsky was writing about a group of people in a period of history when there wasn't too much to laugh about—and yet, in another remarkable book called *Dead Souls*, another Russian writer named Nicolay Gogol wrote some very funny pages indeed about the gloomy Slav soul. (Not, by the way, that I'd advise you to read that either, at this point. Even their comic writers are fairly gloomy people.) The Russians have produced some wonderful writers, and when you're next in the country, you could profitably read a little of Turgenev's *Sportsman's Sketches* and bits of Maxim Gorky. However, I repeat, all these men and Tolstoy too were writing about a historical period full of tyranny and oppression in a country full of people who take themselves very seriously. I think that if you'll switch over to Booth Tarkington (be sure and reread *Seventeen*, will you?) and Mark Twain, you will agree with me that life needn't be as heavy-hearted an affair as *C. & P.* suggests. You say in your postcard "What's wrong with me? It deeply affected me." The answer is that nothing is wrong with you because it deeply affects everyone. I told you once, I think, about how people start betraying all the symptoms of T.B. after they read Thomas Mann's *The Magic Mountain*, and I think I also told you that our friend Kurt Wiese, who'd once had a touch of the disease, even took to bed with a temperature after reading it. This should illustrate the power of suggestion that words have when they're used by experts. But there are all kinds of experts, and when George Ade is at his best, or Don Marquis, or any really good comic writer, you can be as deeply moved by laughter as you can by misery. Take the advice of an old broody type—namely, the undersigned—who has learned the hard way, and put aside this sort of literature for the time being. It's all right in small doses, but it's only one side of the picture and should be taken at long intervals.

Laura and I returned to the country after you took off, as you remember, and had a good week there. The weather was everything one could have hoped for, and the afternoon we walked up to the woods was just what both of us needed. Perhaps Laura mentioned it when she wrote you, but we found masses of daffodils and grape hyacinth in bloom around the tumbledown foundation of the old Charity Sumpstone house. Somehow this touched us both, and I think it has a significance for all of us. Seventy-five years ago or more somebody planted a few clumps of daffodil and hyacinth around that house. Except for a few stones balanced on end, which another winter or two will topple over, there is no sign that man ever went that way, but every spring nature produces a brief and lovely memorial.

The only other memorials that are in any way eternal are great works of art—the really first-rate music, painting, sculpture, writing—and they give us the same sense of gratification. And the reason, the paramount reason, for education such as you're getting is merely to enable you to know where to find and to appreciate these first-rate things in life. Whenever you tend to feel low, darling, and to wonder about the meaning and the direction of life, remember that there *are* compensations, and great ones, for the difficult times. I think about the sunrises we saw together off Celebes aboard the *Kasimbar*, the terraced rice fields in Bali, the temples in Bangkok, the harbor of Hong Kong with the coolies dressed in those shaggy straw cones dripping with rain, the Taj Mahal at dawn as Al and I saw it for the first time, the island of Prinkipo off Istanbul and the wisteria blooming over those Turkish cafés along the Bosphorus, the rhinos and elephant moving in on the salt-lick at Treetops, the great gorge at Murchison Falls, the papyrus reeds along the Albert Nile with the hippo peering out at our launch—these are some of the things we've been lucky enough to be part of. And, just as important, all the witty and diverting and eccentric and charming people like Benchley and Al Hirschfeld and Dorothy Parker and Somerset Maugham and so on endlessly. Nobody can possibly regard life as futile or depressing when he has experienced the things and known the individuals—not only celebrities, but all kinds of people—who crisscross the daily existence. . . .   Love,

To Leila Hadley

Brown's Hotel
London
August 21, 1955

Darling,

The past five weeks have been so chaotic that I seem to have lost all sense of time, place, and identity, and if this letter appears slightly deranged, just chalk it up to the hysteria that envelops everything concerned with Mike Todd plus exhaustion, a second-hand Olivetti, and the remains of a dramatic head-cold. . . . As it worked out, I was in New York about eight days, just time enough to work like a navvy in 96-degree temperatures. Then Todd, who meanwhile had flown to Spain to supervise a bull-ring sequence being prepared at a town called Chinchón 40 miles from Madrid, decided that I ought to fly over to be on hand for it; he thereupon flew back to New York, pulverized a series of directors' meetings set up for him, and collecting me, his lawyer, and a couple of other appendages, flew back. This—as near as I can recall—was on August 9th. The journey over was a trancelike experience, divided up between Mike's puttering with the dialogue I'd hastily written for our London scenes (manfully trying to make it as illiterate as possible) and his playing gin rummy with the rest of the party. By skilful arranging, we succeeded in missing our Madrid connection by ten minutes. This gave him a splendid opportunity to rush us all to the Dorchester, where a suite had been emptied of the King of Trans-Jordan or somebody so that Mike could place five or six international phone calls and dispatch thirty or forty cables to all parts of the world. In between, he chartered a small eight-passenger aircraft called a Dove, into which we were all piled together with quantities of roast chicken and box lunches, and we took off on as bumpy a 3-hour trip to Bordeaux as ever recorded in the annals of aviation. After a Gargantuan lunch absorbed at top speed, we zoomed forward again over the Pyrenees and got in late at night, disrupting the entire Spanish customs. The next four or five days consisted of frequent visits to Chinchón, dramatic conferences and arguments with his director, John Farrow—who has since quit the picture, taking most of his technical staff with him—dinner-parties with potent Spanish types, matadors, and French film tycoons, and such a mélange of intrigue, gossip, and back-stairs knifing as you can't imagine. The actual bullfight stuff at Chinchón was very colorful; Luis Miguel Dominguín, the matador whose pants have often been perilously ripped by Ava Gardner, dispatched three undersized bulls with considerable élan, and one of our three leads, Cantinflas, did what seemed to be an effective comic bullfight. Inasmuch as my sympathies were at all times on the side of the bewildered and brutalized bulls—I'm afraid that my brief stay in East Africa cured me of any neo-Hemingway notions about the beauty of bullfighting and that I take a rigid, pro-animal position—I didn't toss my beret quite as high in the air as my confreres. Anyhow, by Sunday the shooting was completed, Farrow and Todd had dissolved their union, and Todd, loading another half-dozen of us into the Dove, whipped off to Biarritz so that he could subdue the baccarat tables. I left the casino at 1:45 when he was 3 million francs ahead, but thanks to the unvarying law of percentages favoring the house, he was even again by 5:00 A.M. At 9:00, four hours later, we continued on to London, where—by main force—I resisted importunate demands that I hole in at the Dorchester and sneaked off to this fairly quiet roost. It was quiet for almost eighteen hours, and then the London press came scuffling in. I enclose a couple of the dubious end products. Mike's adoration of publicity is such that I have to hold still for a certain amount of this kind of merde. The only consolation is that thanks to Mark Hanna's relentless maneuverings behind the scenes, I am extorting a weekly fee that would cause a brigand to blush, and also there is the negative satisfaction that I haven't yet been asked to pose in my underdrawers.

. . .

To Leila Hadley

513-A Sixth Avenue
New York City
September 16, 1955

Darling,

. . .

. . . The whole *schmier* of five weeks—from Madrid through Paris up to this past Sunday night when we took off for home— was just about as brutal, unnerving, and distasteful as possible, and it gives me great pleasure to report that as of 48 hours ago, I've managed to disentangle myself from Todd's slimy tentacles and return to private life.

Just to get him out of the way, all I need say is that as the days drew on, the psychopathic little bastard reached an absolutely indescribable pitch of dementia, enraging everyone about him and treating the entire organization to such out-bursts of temper and petulance as have rarely been seen out-side children's playgrounds and mental hospitals. He became increasingly fixed on the idea that I had to be at his bidding every hour of the twenty-four, made scenes whenever I tried to get away for lunch—even press luncheons concerned with publicity for himself—rang up Joe Liebling one morning at 1:30 (though he didn't know Liebling) to trace me because I'd been missing for several hours, and altogether qualified himself for admission to a looney bin. He was unable to find any evidence that I wasn't working as contracted, and I suppose that galled him in some twisted way. But there were some lovely high-spots—as, for instance, when he ordered me to run to the wardrobe to fetch a hat-pin for Hermione Gingold prior to a scene we were shooting, etc.—and perhaps one day, when I've cooled off sufficiently, I can use a portion of all this as copy. Anyhow, and only to round off the recital, he at last got around to financial mayhem in the final two weeks and that broke the spell. As soon as I was able to complete my moral obligation of not abandoning the picture on location, I got Mark Hanna to function, and Mark gave it to him in the pit of the stomach, or rather the pit of the pocketbook, and that dissolved our ill-starred union. Previous to that, of course, Todd had been painting a rosy future in which I was cast as a coach-dog running at his heels and fulfilling myself as his major-domo in charge of purchasing his cigars. . . .

* * *

. . . Over here, the summer's dying hard—it's school time, your sex is beginning to break out in basic black, and various shows are beginning their out-of-town try-outs. The Hacketts opened last night in Philadelphia—*The Diary of Anne Frank*, upon which they've been laboring these past two years, produced by Kermit Bloomgarden and directed by Garson Kanin. Haven't yet heard reports, but am hoping with every fiber it's the success the Hacketts deserve.

* * *

. . . I expect to be going down to the farm tomorrow for the first time since early July. . . . I'll be in the city pretty constantly hereafter until—God help us all—my lecture tour's scheduled to start sometime after January 1st. I also want to resume working on the musical I started with Nash et al., and —most important of all—get back to doing some *New Yorker* pieces.

.   .   .

. . . Spoke to Jack Goodman this morning but only to say hello; my new book, *Perelman's Home Companion*, is due for publication October 31st and he says the advance sale is very encouraging. . . .   Yours only,

To Betsy Drake

513-A Sixth Avenue
New York City
September 28, 1955

Dear Betsy,

. . . Let me advise you at once that you'd better throw away George Jessel as your standard of all that's most revolting in human behavior. This sinister dwarf who consumed nine weeks of my life has no peer in his chosen profession, which —stated very simply—is to humiliate and cheapen his fellow man, fracture one's self-esteem, convert everybody around him into lackeys, hypocrites, and toadies, and thoroughly debase every relationship, no matter how casual. His enormity grows on you like some obscene fungus; you go to bed in the belief that nothing that happened all day possibly could have, and then, the next morning, it intensifies. Honey, you don't *know*.

.   .   .

. . . I thought that between Irving Thalberg, Hunt Stromberg, and a number of other megalomaniacs—God help me, I almost forgot Zanuck!—I'd worked for, I had seen everything, but this boy is the all-time winner . . . Anyway, to give you some halfway coherent notion of our junket, we spent about five days in Spain . . . a month or so in London, making exteriors and indoor stuff out at Elstree, and a few days in Paris disrupting the French. In addition to usurping his directors' prerogatives—as you may know, John Farrow quit and Todd's now using a young English chap recommended by Noël Coward—Todd interfered in every conceivable department of the production, not excluding my own; indeed, so far as I know, he is now rewriting the picture as he goes along, grinding the crank, building the sets, unnerving the actors, and generally qualifying as an up-to-date Leonardo da Vinci. It's inaccurate to describe his cyclonic conduct as energy or vitality —it's much more a violent frenzy I'm sure the head-shrinkers could classify. His background as a carnival barker, however, aided him in convincing an impressive bunch of actors to string along with his project, and if you ever go to see the picture—or should I say, if it's ever finished this side of ten million dollars —you'll catch glimpses of Noël Coward, Gielgud, Robert Morley, Trevor Howard, A.E. Matthews, Bea Lillie, Hermione Gingold, Glynis Johns, John Mills, Fernandel, Martine Carol, and probably God Almighty himself. . . .

· · ·

. . . Please give my very best to Cary, together with a message that if I can assemble string, paper, and cardboard, I'll ship him a weird little memento I picked up in London. Meanwhile, and with love,   Yours,

To Leila Hadley

Erwinna, Pa.
August 25, 1956

Darling Leila,

· · ·

. . . I'm back here as of yesterday, preparing to take up our prairie-dog existence for an indeterminate period and faced with getting some saleable prose on paper. The Vineyard trip was an indulgence, our exchequer being what it is, but it *was* enjoyable; we stayed at the—don't flinch—Stony Squaw Inn in Gay Head, a small and very pleasant hostelry way out at the very tip of the Island. I can't recall whether we drove up there when you came up; anyway, it's a dramatic combination of

Scottish moorland and precipitous, vari-colored cliffs, sparsely settled by the few remaining members of the Gay Head Indian tribe and their hybrid descendants. Laura, Abby, and I were the only guests for four of our seven days, and during the balance of the time, a self-composed British lady who read Alan Paton's novels while she ate and a pair of young honeymooners were the only other people in view. The place is run by an extremely nice young unfrocked rabbi named Weissberg who's married to an Indian girl; he teaches English in a Cuban high-school in the winter, and spends the summer at the Stony Squaw discouraging potential customers.

We saw a good deal of the Thielens—who, as you know, I like very much—also saw Lilly Hellman a couple of times, and not much of anyone else. Lilly's bought a house in Vineyard Haven, where she's putting the final touches on a musical version of *Candide*, score by Leonard Bernstein, that goes into rehearsal next month. We had a picnic lunch at her beach that was diverting, just the four of us, and were joined later by the young man who's writing the lyrics for her show, a poet named Richard Wilbur whose things have occasionally appeared in *The New Yorker* and who teaches English at Wellesley. . . . A night or two later we again encountered her at a mass beach picnic full of revoltingly smug people. . . . On this occasion Arthur Kober, Lil's ex-husband, was in evidence—fatter, more complacent, and less appealing than ever, and I had ample opportunity to ask myself how on earth I could have borne him in all those houses we shared in Hollywood during the Thirties, and how I could have put up with his ponderous cutie-pie antics. He was busily engaged in pawing La Hellman around the embers, a pursuit it was evident she wasn't deliriously happy about, but there. . . .

•   •   •

. . . Myself, I'm in the initial stages of a possible second job for Mike Todd, necessitated by the pinching financial situation. *Around the World in 80 Days* (which, according to Todd, is the most stupefyingly great colossal superb movie in history) opens October 17th at the Rivoli, and a month later in Moscow, the first picture from here to be shown in Russia since the start of the Cold War. Mike's flying over a planeload of

40 American newspaper publishers for that premiere, and the domestic opening is going to be preceded by such a barrage of publicity in *Life*, *Look*, etc. as you can't imagine. The picture now has a prologue delivered by Ed Murrow, an epilogue laden with gimmicks, and indescribable riches within (quoting Mike, of course—I've seen nothing but the rushes I saw all through last fall). In any case, Todd's made a deal with the Russians to co-produce six pictures, and it's one of the first two on the schedule he's talking to me about. It'll be an English dialogue job, transferring the Russian soundtrack into English I mean to say, to fit the picture, which he wants to retain in its entirety. This is as much as I know at present, and not having seen the film, I can't tell you more other than that he says it's a superb comedy about a travelling theatrical troupe in Russia. I'm due to hear more sometime late next week, if I can catch him between plane jumps. . . .

I haven't said anything thus far about your proposed book title, *Give Me the World*—I like it very much, and like the quotation you drew it from. So does Herman E, to whom I told it. It has a good, and commercially promising, ring. From your labors of typing 220,000 words let all kinds of blessings flow. . . .

.   .   .

Always,

To Leila Hadley

513-A Sixth Avenue
New York City
November 22, 1956

Darling, darling Leila,

.   .   .

. . . [Publishers are] all alike, and the only rule of thumb I know is, get the biggest advance you can (which in turn forces them to try to recoup their investment) and be as demanding of advertising, publicity, etc. as is consonant with your own sense of decency. Publishers regard writers as vain, petty, juvenile, and thoroughly impossible (just as movie producers do—I think I may have once told you Irving Thalberg's classic: "The writer? The writer is a necessary evil"). So there's no use in attempting to be reasonable with them, or trying to prove that you, as a writer, are a person with a sense of dignity who's merely interested in their merchandising your work, a job they very frequently aren't equipped to do by any business standards. Fred Allen told me last year before his death—obviously before, it would have been pretty arresting afterward—that, having long been convinced that book publishing was infantile in its business approach, he contributed the money to support his first book's advertising campaign, his argument being that in show business, you behave like a rooster on a dung-heap and crow endlessly about your wares until the customers take notice. (The publishers contend that you only advertise a book to any extent *after* it's beginning to sell, which is certainly Alice-in-Wonderland thinking.) As a consequence, his book— aided by newspaper advertising, radio appearances, TV plugs, anything he could force the publishers into by a personal and day-to-day harassment—started selling and got into the mild best-seller class. I urge you, when your book appears, to be on the ground and participate in all the Martha Dean, Tex and Jinx, and TV panel merde you can evolve. . . .

·   ·   ·

Your description of the Matterhorn of bills and the general difficulty of Making Ends Meet could subject you to some of the most tedious language you've ever read, and out of regard for you, I'll automatically censor myself. It *is* a murderous process getting by, and I don't know how I do it. And just wait till your chickadees get older and start attending private schools, college, etc. Incidentally and *re* your question "How do you manage two establishments?" kindly recall that it isn't two but *three*—the farm, the apartment, and this office. Three sets of utilities and rents and cleanings and all. Hence, the unimportant fact that all my insurance is borrowed on to the hilt, that we consume every last penny, that there's a respectable Alp of bills, and that I haven't a notion in the world where my tax obligation's coming from at the end of the year, all these parenthetical worries bumble around in the background of my mind waiting to fasten on me just as I'm falling asleep or trying to bestir myself in the morning. It would be nice to report that as a consequence of *Around the World*, these considerations have become academic, but thus far all I have are rosy prospects as yet. The ineffable Irving P. Lazar, who has arisen as the Hollywood end of Mark Hanna, assures me that various deals of mammoth advantage should be consummated soon, and ostensibly Todd still plans to have me work on his next venture. But these—along with a scheme I'm supposed to discuss with John Huston in the next fortnight and a couple of other chimeras—are only vaporous thus far. . . .

Well, I guess I'll have to conclude, Abby having just called to urge me to go up to the Museum of Natural History with her this fine, cold, and sunny afternoon. . . .

With all my heart,

To Paul Theroux

Gramercy Park Hotel
New York City
October 18, 1976

Dear Paul,

•   •   •

My air-mail subscription to the *Times* of London brought me your review of Tom Dardis's *Some Time in the Sun*, by a coincidence a day or so after someone unsuccessfully sought to inveigle me into a radio talk show about it. The honest truth (as opposed to the dishonest truth) is that I now have a snootful about this subject. I'm sick of these innumerable books about Fitzgerald's Sturm und Drang in Hollywood, both by his gossip columnist mistress and the flock of young guys who hope to create reputations by exhuming some tiny phase of his life there. (You may also have read Caroline Moorehead's column in the self-same *Times* stating that Sheilah Graham has another book coming out on further unknown aspects of Scott's life with her.) To what purpose all this crud, anyway? Generally speaking, all the parties concerned (except Agee, who was movie-struck and a determined self-destroyer) worked in

Hollywood because it was the decade of the Great Depression and they couldn't earn a living elsewhere. They none of them made any real money in the Hollywood sense out of it—only the screenwriters on the inside, whose names wouldn't mean a thing to the public, except Ben Hecht's, made the big dough —people like Robert Riskin, Norman Krasna, Harry Kurnitz, Bright & Glasmon. These last were the Roman candles, the Catherine wheels of that epoch of movie writing, and their names now are writ in water. They've been superseded by the Robert Townes (*Chinatown*), Steven Spielbergs, and other infant geniuses who demand and receive $400,000 per script, and who in turn will be replaced in a couple of years by other unrecognizable names. If you want to know who's turning out the present movie feces—i.e., what writers—just read *Variety* for a couple of weeks; I guarantee you won't recognize the name of any writer you ever heard of, even on the *Playboy* level...But just to wrap it all up—I say as I've said for years: if you want to know what writing for the movies is like, just read Raymond Chandler's two pieces on the topic in *Raymond Chandler Speaking*. I think of very few others who have been able to capture the disgust and the boredom of dealing with the Yahoos who run that industry. Their names are no longer Louis B. Mayer, Irving Thalberg, and Darryl Zanuck, but their mentalities are the same, or I should say even baser, because today's tycoons are all agents, ten-per-centers whipped and worn smooth by the hot blast of television...

Ah, well, forgive me for running off at the mouth on this score, it's really brought on by the Tom Dardises and other neo-Joycean Ph.D's rooting around in the Hollywood debris. I suppose I actually *should* have agreed to do that radio tape I spoke of earlier and got all this stuff off my chest.

Re H.P. Lovecraft who you mentioned—I was dimly aware that he was alive and unwell in Providence while I was being forcibly educated there, but what little work of his I came across was in quasi-horror pulps, kind of sub–Edgar Allan Poe stuff, and seemed pretty spurious to me. The only person I ever knew who had any knowledge of him was a spaced-out freak who worked with the Brown Dramatic Society. . . . From what I read in the alumni magazine a couple of years ago, his red corpuscles gave out and he occupies a headstone somewhere in the verdure near Pawtucket. Mention of that part of the world reminds me—you and I never got around, that afternoon at Brown's Hotel, to discussing George V. Higgins and his novels about small-time hoods in southern New England. I enjoyed those—did you care for them?

Pat Kavanagh writes me she'll be coming over shortly before Thanksgiving, and mentions that you've seen each other recently. Give her a pinch in the Sitzfleisch for me—we've been Platonic friends (more's the trouble) for years. All the best for now, and do write again when the spirit moves. Yours ever,

To Paul Theroux

> Gramercy Park Hotel
> New York City
> December 24, 1976

Dear Paul,

Between the constant repetition of "White Christmas" and "Jingle Bells" on station WPAT and the increasing frenzy of Saks' and Gimbel's newspaper ads as these fucking holidays draw near, I have been in a zombie-like state for weeks, totally incapable of rational thought or action. I must have arrived at near-paralysis yesterday afternoon when I was in the 4th-floor lingerie section ("Intimate Apparel") in Saks 5th Avenue. I had just purchased two such intimate garments for gifties to a couple of ladies of my acquaintance, a tall blonde and a somewhat shorter brunette. For the former, I had chosen a black lace chemise in the style known as a teddy back in the Twenties (familiar to you as the scanty garment worn by Rita Hayworth in the war-time pinup). For the shorter brunette, a similar peach-colored job. Both of these real silk, parenthetically, and as I signed the charge slip, I knew that when the bill comes in after January 1st, I would kick myself for my prodigality. Anyway, while the hard-featured saleslady was wrapping them up with appropriate mash-notes to each bimbo, I went upstairs to the men's dept. to buy myself a cheap tie-tack. When I returned for the feminine frillies, I found (a) that the saleslady had forgotten to identify which box was which, and (b) that she had switched the notes. In other words, the blond Amazon would find herself with the brunette's undershirt and some steamy sentiment addressed to the latter, and vice versa. I broke out into a perspiration—it's tropically hot in those department stores anyway—and insisted on the saleslady clawing open the boxes, which meant destroying all the fake holly berries, silver cord, and mish-mash they were entwined in. This of course put her in a foul temper, and meanwhile a waiting queue of customers became incensed. The upshot was a group shot of seven or eight people leering and cackling obscenely as I stood there holding the two chemises and the notes appropriate to the recipients. Given the savoir-faire of Cary Grant I might have risen above it but the only savoir-faire I possess is Oliver Hardy's, and little enough of that.

Other than this, I am well, and better for having read your story "Dependent Wife" in the London *Times* the other day; your description of Ayer Hitam revived my sense of claustrophobia in similar Malaysian locales. . . . Some months ago, when lunching with Caskie Stinnett, who edited *Travel & Leisure* before Pamela Fiori, we got to talking about Ipoh in Malaysia and the grisly Station Hotel there. And he said that once, when he also passed a night there, he saw the most beautiful woman he had ever beheld in his life, a Eurasian, whom he didn't get to meet but who he still dreams about in his lonely island off the Maine coast. This is the kind of fantasy that only three people in the whole world understand—you and I and Caskie Stinnett.

·   ·   ·

Yours ever,

CHRONOLOGY

NOTE ON THE TEXTS

NOTES

Chronology

1904   Born February 1 in Brooklyn, New York, to Joseph Perelman (1875–1926) and Sophie Charren (1883–1964), Russian Jewish immigrants who met in the United States. (Joseph arrived in 1891 and lived on a farm in Connecticut. In the navy during the Spanish-American War, he may have been an engineer aboard the USS *Morro Castle* in the Havana harbor when the USS *Maine* blew up. He became a machinist after moving to New York City, working in Jersey City. Sophie, who arrived in America in 1892, was employed as a garment worker at home until her marriage.) Both parents have strong socialist sympathies and neither practices their religion. They name their son Simeon at birth, but he is quickly renamed Sidney when they realize "Simeon" is a liability for an American boy. Perelman is an only child, though his birth certificate indicates there was an earlier child, "now deceased." Some Yiddish is spoken at home, but he never learns to speak it. In search of better opportunities, the family moves to Providence, Rhode Island, very soon after Perelman's birth to join Joseph's relatives. Joseph opens a dry goods store, which fails. Later he will buy a farm in Norwood, Rhode Island, raising chickens. Over a number of years, this venture, too, fails.

1913–21   Attends Candace Street Grammar School and then Classical High School in Providence. Draws cartoons and studies languages. Goes to many movies, plays, and vaudeville shows in town. Sees the Marx Brothers for first time on stage in 1916. In 1917 wins a nationwide essay contest sponsored by *American Boy* magazine with an entry entitled "Grit," which extols the Paris taxi drivers who shepherded French soldiers to the front at battle of the Marne. In his senior year at Classical in 1920–21 is the editor of the school literary magazine, *The Accolade*, and chairman of the debating society. In fall 1921 enters Brown University. Tuition is paid by his father, borrowing $600 from a cousin. Commutes to campus from home (such students are known as "carpetbaggers").

1922–24   In February 1922 meets Nathan Weinstein, a transfer student from Tufts. Weinstein will soon change his name to Nathanael West. Among the few Jews at Brown, Perelman is not invited to join a fraternity. Helps out his father on the chicken farm and holds various night jobs in stores and at a radiator factory in Providence to pay his expenses. Thinks of becoming a doctor but switches to English when he realizes he is expected to dissect a cat. Draws cartoons with captions for *The Brown Jug*, the campus humor magazine, and *Casements*, Brown's literary journal. Also does set design for two college shows. Publishes his first short piece of comic writing, without accompanying drawing, in the *Brown Daily Herald* during his junior year, signing it with the initials S.J.P. From this point on he will always sign his work using those first two initials. Becomes editor of *Brown Jug* in 1924. Reprimanded by the University for publishing erotically charged material, though such reprimands, which held the possibility of dismissal from Brown, were not uncommon or unique to Perelman's term of editorship.

1925–28   Exits Brown in spring 1925, without a degree, falling three credits short for failing to pass Trigonometry. Immediately accepts a job offer, at a salary of $35 a week, as a cartoonist with *Judge*, a popular long-running humor magazine, which had published several of his drawings while he was still an undergraduate (Harold Ross, later the founder of *The New Yorker*, is a co-editor of *Judge*). First cartoon appears in *Judge* on August 15, 1925. Moves first to Manhattan, living on West Eighth Street with Brown classmate John Richmond, then to Staten Island in 1926. Father dies of cancer on October 2, 1926, at age fifty-one. Returning to Manhattan in 1927, Perelman reconnects with West in January. Takes an interest in West's younger sister, Lorraine Weinstein, who is very close to her brother. In fall 1928 Lorraine enrolls at Pembroke, Brown's sister college, but drops out after one semester when Perelman proposes.

1929   Marriage to Lorraine, now eighteen and calling herself Laura West, on June 20. They honeymoon in France. First book, *Dawn Ginsbergh's Revenge*, published in August by Horace Liveright. It contains forty-nine pieces, mostly culled from Perelman's contributions to *Judge*. Due to a combination of author's and publisher's oversight, no author's name appears on title page. Groucho Marx supplies a jacket blurb: "From the moment I picked up your book until I laid it down, I was convulsed with laughter. Someday I intend reading it." Though it receives few reviews, the book goes through three printings and sells a very respectable 4,600 copies. Perelman later repudiates it and refuses to let it be reprinted.

1930   Leaves *Judge* and takes a job with *College Humor*, a Chicago magazine that publishes work of greater length and sophistication—though he continues to publish in *Judge* as well for another year. With former Brown contemporary Quentin Reynolds, co-authors a novel, *Parlor, Bedlam and Bath*, published by Horace Liveright in the summer. Despite praise from some reviewers, this satire of 1920s sex and high living is a commercial failure, selling only 1,500 copies. Perelman's first piece for *The New Yorker*, "An Open Letter to Moira Ransom," appears in the December 13 issue. Groucho Marx asks Perelman and Will Johnstone to develop a radio script for the Marx Brothers. The basic premise they come up with—stowaways in barrels on an ocean liner—turns, instead, into the foundation for the film *Monkey Business*. Paramount hires Perelman and Johnstone to write the screenplay, giving them a six-week contract for $500 per week each.

1931   In January goes to Hollywood, accompanied by Laura, to begin work on *Monkey Business*. Six weeks later, the first script is savagely rejected. Revisions with contributions by several other writers—with much of Perelman's work still included—are finally approved in the summer. Released in September, *Monkey Business* is a huge hit. Perelman stays on at Paramount to cowrite *Horse Feathers*. Over the next eleven years, he and Laura will return to Hollywood many times, working together as screenwriters (where they could earn a combined $1,000 per week) for major and minor studios, mostly on B pictures or on A pictures that were never made or for which they received little or no credit. Perelman contributes a sketch for a Broadway revue, *The Third Little Show*, which opens in June and runs for 136 performances.

1932   The Perelmans travel in Europe. *Horse Feathers* opens in August. In September Perelman starts writing sketches for *Walk a Little Faster*, a Broadway revue starring Beatrice Lillie, music by Vernon Duke, lyrics by "Yip" Harburg. It opens on December 7 and runs for 119 performances. On December 19 the Perelmans and Nathanael West jointly buy a farmhouse on eighty-three acres in Erwinna, Pennsylvania, from leftist novelist Michael Gold, author of *Jews Without Money*, for $5,500. West nicknames the Bucks County farm, into which they sink much money on repairs, "8-Ball."

1933   *All Good Americans*, a play about American expatriates in Paris, written by the Perelmans, opens in December at Broadway's Henry Miller Theater. Reviews are tepid and it closes after five weeks. It is notable only for the first Broadway appearance of James Stewart, in a small role as an accordion player.

1934   *Paris Interlude*, a movie based on the play *All Good Americans*, is released. The Perelmans get no screenwriting credit. They spend a great deal of time in Hollywood, working on screenplays for various pictures, some unreleased.

1935   Laura has a short affair with Dashiell Hammett, whom both she and her husband have known, through Lillian Hellman, for several years. The Perelmans, whose marriage has been troubled from the start, have both engaged in liaisons, which are largely tolerated when discreet; this one, less so. In September *The Big Broadcast of 1936*, for which Perelman worked on the treatment, is released. During these years he works at many studios, including MGM, where his colleagues and friends include Dorothy Parker and her husband Alan Campbell, Donald Ogden Stewart, Herman Mankiewicz, and F. Scott Fitzgerald.

1936   *Florida Special*, the first movie for which both Perelmans receive screenwriting credit, released in April. Their first child, a son, Adam, born on October 19.

1937   In March relinquishes his rights to both *Dawn Ginsbergh's Revenge* and *Parlor, Bedlam and Bath* to Liveright Publishing in return for dropping their option on his next book. In July *Strictly from Hunger*, a collection of twenty-one pieces from *The New Yorker*, *Judge*, *Life*, and *College Humor*, is published by Random House, with an introduction by Robert Benchley, who proclaims: "Perelman took over the *dementia praecox* field and drove us all to writing articles on economics. . . . Any further attempts to garble thought-processes sounded like imitation-Perelman."

Though the book receives many glowing reviews, its sales, according to publisher Bennett Cerf, are "nothing to brag about." Perelman had received a $300 advance and a year later the book had garnered only an additional $12 in royalties.

1938 Daughter, Abby, born February 9. In March the Perelmans are back in Hollywood, working on two pictures for Paramount: *Ambush*, the tale of a bank robbery—based on a true story—and *Boy Trouble*, a heartwarming melodrama. The Perelmans gain sole screenwriting credit for the former, and Laura gets sole credit for the latter.

1939 *Ambush* and *Boy Trouble* released in January. Both garner solid reviews. Beginning in April, Perelman hosts the radio quiz show *Author! Author!*, in which a panel of celebrity authors spin humorous stories around ideas sent in by listeners. It runs through the summer.

1940 On April 19 Nathanael West marries Eileen McKenney. Perelman is best man. Eileen is the younger sister of Ruth McKenney, whose stories about a carefree young woman living in Greenwich Village with her older sister appear in *The New Yorker* and are gathered into a book that becomes the best seller *My Sister Eileen*. In August Random House publishes *Look Who's Talking*, a collection of twenty-four Perelman pieces gathered from *The New Yorker*, *The New Masses*, and *Broun's Nutmeg* (a short-lived newspaper started by editor Heywood Broun from his home in Stamford, Connecticut). The book sells 2,000 copies in two months, but Perelman grows angry with his publisher for what he sees as a continuing lack of forceful promotion. *The Golden Fleecing*, a movie comedy, with a screenplay by the Perelmans, is released. They also finish writing *The Night Before Christmas*, a farce about bank robbers who take over a luggage store in order to break into the bank next door, which they hope to have produced on Broadway. On December 22, missing a stop sign, Nathanael and Eileen West are killed in a car crash in El Centro, California, the day after the death of F. Scott Fitzgerald. West's death devastates Laura, whose fiercely close attachment to her brother had been palpable and often remarked upon. Perelman becomes the literary executor of West's estate.

1941 *The Night Before Christmas* opens at the Morocco Theater on April 10, but closes after twenty-two performances.

1942   *Larceny, Inc.*, a movie based on *The Night Before Christmas* and starring Edward G. Robinson, is released in May. The film rights garner the Perelmans $30,000, but they do not write its screenplay. In August *The Saturday Evening Post* begins publishing a series of twenty-six articles by Perelman under the title "A Child's Garden of Curses, or the Bitter Tea of Mr. P." It will continue until August 1943.

1943   In February Random House publishes Perelman's new collection, *The Dream Department.* ("Twenty-five of Mr. Perelman's famous prose omelets, dealing with dentistry, ladies' underwear, taxes . . ." *The New Yorker* calls it in a description possibly written by Perelman himself.) It draws largely enthusiastic reviews. *One Touch of Venus*, directed by Elia Kazan, choreographed by Agnes de Mille, with music by Kurt Weill, book and lyrics by Perelman and Ogden Nash, and starring Mary Martin, opens on Broadway on October 7. The play will run for 567 performances before going successfully on the road. A substantial hit, it will give Perelman his first real taste of financial security and allow him to turn down much improved offers for screenwriting jobs, in order to concentrate on writing for the theater. Begins participating in extensive war bond tours, which will last well into 1945.

1944   *Crazy Like a Fox* published. Composed of forty-six *New Yorker* pieces, many gathered from his earlier collections, it becomes a best seller, moving 25,000 copies in a matter of months. In *The New York Times* Eudora Welty calls it "highly complex, deviously organized. . . . more like ju-jitsu than any prose most of us have ever seen." With his great friend and collaborator, caricaturist Al Hirschfeld, Perelman begins writing the book for a musical, *Sweet Bye and Bye*, a lighthearted comedy set in the year 2076.

1945   Spends a good part of the year working on his play and feeling out producers and possible actors. Makes a trip to Hollywood in this regard. Continues crossing the country on bond drives.

1946   *Keep It Crisp* published in August. It includes perhaps the most famous of Perelman's literary parodies, "Farewell, My Lovely Appetizer," his take on Raymond Chandler's prose. It will be Perelman's last new book under the Random House imprint. After great travails, *Sweet Bye and Bye* opens in New Haven on October 10. Though it travels as far as Philadelphia, it never makes it to New York.

1947 Hired by *Holiday* magazine, sets off from San Francisco on February 11, with Al Hirschfeld, on a seven-month trip around the world. Random House learns that Perelman has surreptitiously signed a contract with Simon & Schuster to publish the travel pieces in book form. This ends their nine-year publishing relationship, though *The Best of S. J. Perelman*, a reprint of *Crazy Like a Fox*, plus four other unpublished pieces, is published by Random House's Modern Library imprint later in the year. *Acres and Pains* is published by Reynal and Hitchcock; it comprises twenty-one humor pieces about the exasperations of country life in Bucks County that had first appeared in *The Saturday Evening Post* and the *Country Book* during the war. Crossing the Pacific, Perelman and Hirschfeld begin their journey with visits to Singapore, Hong Kong, and Macao, where Perelman is impressed by Southeast Asian art, of which he will become a keen collector. By October, is back in New York.

1948 In August Simon & Schuster (who will remain his publisher for the rest of his life) releases *Westward Ha!*, based on the *Holiday* pieces, recounting Perelman's experiences aboard ship and in Shanghai, Singapore, Ceylon, India, Egypt, Italy, and France. The book sells more than 60,000 copies, double the sales of any previous Perelman title. Long delayed, the film version of *One Touch of Venus* is released, without any writing contribution by Perelman or Nash. It disappoints at the box office. Perelman meets Leila Hadley, a young woman working as a publicist for cartoonist Al Capp, at a publishing party for *Westward Ha!*. He becomes infatuated and possibly romantically involved.

1949 On January 21, commissioned again by *Holiday* magazine, sails across the Pacific, this time with Laura and the two children in tow. They visit Hawaii, Manila, Hong Kong, Bali, and many points in Indonesia and Indochina, India, Iraq, Turkey, France, the Lowlands, England, and Ireland. They are back in America by early October. In the autumn *Listen to the Mockingbird* published, including his "Cloudland Revisited" series, which had begun appearing in *The New Yorker* the previous year. In it "Mr. Perelman can be seen grappling with nostalgia as he reexamines some red-hot literary hits of the early twenties. Illustrated by Al Hirschfeld," notes *The New Yorker*.

1950   In February adds his name, along with Arthur Miller and
              many other distinguished writers, to an amicus curiae brief
              in support of blacklisted writers John Howard Lawson and
              Dalton Trumbo, whose challenge to their conviction for
              contempt of Congress reaches the Supreme Court. The
              two writers will lose and be sent to jail for a year. *The Swiss
              Family Perelman*, based on the *Holiday* series about his
              second trip around the world, published. Perelman decides
              he wants to divorce Laura and pursue Leila Hadley, who
              has been out of the country traveling for almost two years,
              but she returns deeply in love with a man she met on her
              trip and will soon marry, moving to South Africa with him.
              Nevertheless, Leila and Perelman remain on good terms.
              She will be among his regular correspondents for the rest
              of his life.

1951   Under the title *A Child's Garden of Curses*, Heinemann
              brings out in the U.K. a one-volume edition of three books:
              Crazy Like a Fox, *Keep It Crisp*, and *Acres and Pains*. As
              he had with Random House, Perelman complains about
              Simon & Schuster's lack of promotion for his two most re-
              cent American books: good reviews, modest sales. Agrees
              to switch to Doubleday for his next book, but the deal falls
              through when the publisher leaks the news too soon for
              Perelman's taste and he reneges.

1952   *The Ill-Tempered Clavichord* is published. It includes
              further pieces written under the "Cloudland Revisited"
              rubric, looking back at books and films that captured
              Perelman's fancy in his teens and twenties. His mar-
              riage, which has grown increasingly difficult over the
              years, fueled by his infidelities and Laura's growing al-
              cohol dependency, as well as by their mutual bouts of
              depression, finally unravels to the point where the couple
              agrees to divorce. But on December 12, fifteen-year-old
              Adam Perelman is arrested for attempted robbery in a
              Greenwich Village apartment building and is sent to the
              Cedar Knolls School for Wayward Boys in Hawthorne,
              New York. The crisis leads the Perelmans to put off their
              planned separation indefinitely.

1953   In April the Perelmans give up their long-occupied Wash-
              ington Square apartment and move to their Bucks County
              home full-time. Perelman keeps his writing studio at 513A
              Sixth Avenue near Thirteenth Street. The Perelmans will
              return to Manhattan in 1954. In December Perelman stops

in London on his way to East Africa, where he is to write a series of articles for *The New Yorker* about his adventures with the first "all-girl" safari.

1954   Arrives in Nairobi on January 11. Although Perelman leaves the all-girl safari after a day or two, the African trip produces a series of six articles published in *The New Yorker*. Also in January, Adam escapes from the Cedar Knolls School and flees to Manhattan, where he is arrested again. He is sent to the Elmira (New York) Reception Center for psychiatric evaluation and winds up at a work farm/school.

1955   The Perelmans' marriage deteriorates further. Laura's alcoholism reaches the point where she joins AA. In July Mike Todd hires Perelman to polish the dialogue for a screen adaptation of Jules Verne's *Around the World in Eighty Days* that he is producing. Perelman heads to Hollywood, where he continues to work on the script more extensively. In November *Perelman's Home Companion* published, consisting of thirty-six pieces largely drawn from out-of-print collections.

1956   In February Adam is released from Elmira. In the fall, after a frustrating semester at Pembroke, Abby enters St. John's College in Annapolis, Maryland, where she thrives. On October 17, *Around the World in Eighty Days* is released. It is an enormous success with both critics and moviegoers.

1957   In February *The Road to Miltown* published. Highly praised by critics, it becomes a best seller. At the Academy Awards ceremony on March 27, Perelman wins an Oscar for Best Adapted Screenplay for *Around the World in Eighty Days* (he shares this honor with cocredited John Farrow and James Poe). The film wins five Oscars in all, including Best Picture. He is in demand for film work, but turns instead to TV, writing in the next two years scripts for prestigious series such as *Omnibus* and *The Seven Lively Arts*.

1958   In February a made-for-TV musical adaptation of *Aladdin*, with book by Perelman and music by Cole Porter, is broadcast on CBS. On May 21 Perelman is inducted into the National Institute of Arts and Letters. In the fall *The Most of S. J. Perelman* published, containing ninety-six pieces, including eight previously uncollected, chronologically arranged, in addition to two complete books: *Acres and Pains* and *Westward Ha!*

1959   In January CBS broadcasts "Malice in Wonderland," as part of its *Omnibus* series, with a script by Perelman, based on some of his stories about life in Hollywood. Spends the summer in Rome, joined by Laura and Abby, working on an unproduced screenplay. On August 22 the Bucks County house is broken into; robbers take many pieces from Perelman's Asian and African sculpture collections.

1960   Contracts with Simon & Schuster to write an autobiography, provisionally titled "The Hindsight Saga." Though he works on it sporadically over some years, it will never gather enough momentum to become a book. Begins writing "An Evening with S. J. Perelman," a play based on characters from his humor pieces; it will soon be retitled *The Beauty Part*. Abby graduates from St. John's College and marries the Reverend Winfry Smith, an Episcopalian minister, who was one of her teachers there.

1961   In the summer Laura is diagnosed with breast cancer and has a double mastectomy. In September *The Rising Gorge* published, containing thirty-four pieces, including those about his 1954 safari adventures, "Dr. Perelman I Presume, or Small-Bore in Africa." *The Beauty Part* begins a tryout run at the Bucks County Playhouse, in New Hope, a short drive from the Perelman farm.

1962   After many delays and some last-minute overhauling out of town, *The Beauty Part*, starring Bert Lahr, opens on Broadway on December 26. The timing is inauspicious, opening during the 114-day New York newspaper strike, which began on December 8. Preview audiences and critics are enthusiastic, but the daily newspaper reviews and concomitant ads never run and the weekly and monthly magazine praise arrives too late to save the show.

1963   On March 9 *The Beauty Part* closes after eighty-four performances. Perelman will never complete another play or screenplay. In June goes to London for five weeks as head writer for a travelogue special called *Elizabeth Taylor's London*, which will be the actress's TV debut. Critics pan it.

1964   The Perelmans return to Europe in the summer, dining in London variously with Groucho Marx, T. S. Eliot, and Kenneth Tynan, and then with Charlie Chaplin in Switzerland. They head to Venice, Hungary, Romania, and the Balkans. On October 16 Perelman's mother dies at age eighty-one in Los Angeles, where she had lived for thirty years in a house Perelman bought for her.

1965   In June receives an honorary doctorate of letters from Brown University, from which he had failed to graduate forty years earlier. On December 28, driving down to vacation in Key West, the Perelmans are involved in a head-on collision outside Orangeburg, South Carolina, caused by the other driver swerving into their lane. Both of the Perelmans are injured. Laura remains hospitalized until the end of the year.

1966   At the beginning of the summer, after two burglaries, the Perelmans give up their Manhattan apartment and his writing studio, and move officially to their Bucks County house. In September Perelman's first new book in five years, *Chicken Inspector No. 23*, is published. It contains thirty-three pieces. While it has many favorable reviews, a new note of disapproval enters—namely that Perelman's work fails to address the urgent politics of his time, that the preferred targets of his wit continue to be "such frippery as Dove soap, commercials, his English tailor and ladies who are afraid of mice."

1967   In the spring Perelman and Laura spend six weeks traveling in England and France. Shortly after their return, Perelman enters New York Doctor's Hospital for a prostate operation; he will spend another month convalescing at his Pennsylvania farm. Publishes "Now Silent Flows the Con," in *TV Guide*, a satiric look at making the rounds of TV shows to promote a book, in this case, *Chicken Inspector No. 23*.

1968   In the spring the Perelmans travel to London, then Sligo, Ireland. *Holiday* hires Perelman for another East Africa series but cancels the commission because of the magazine's larger financial difficulties, which will soon cause it to change its editorial focus. Paying for an overseas trip himself, Perelman heads to Europe anyway, visiting England, France, and Switzerland.

1969   Back in a Manhattan sublet in January. In September travels to London with Laura. At the end of the year, asks Laura for a divorce. Unhappy about it, she nevertheless agrees.

1970   The Perelmans return to the United States in January,
          both with flu. Laura fails to recover entirely and dies of
          cancer in a New Jersey hospital on April 10. *Baby, It's
          Cold Inside*, composed of thirty-two pieces, published
          in August. In September Perelman auctions off most
          of the furnishings, collectibles, and memorabilia at the
          Bucks County house, as well as personal items, including
          Laura's clothing. On October 13 sells the property itself
          for $108,000. Complaining about American politics and
          culture, and publicly taking shots at New York and even
          particular people, moves to London on October 21. Soon
          becomes as disillusioned with the English social and polit-
          ical scene as he had been with the American one.

1971   On March 5 sets off from London, heading east, to reen-
          act Verne's protagonist, Phileas Fogg's, eighty-day trip
          around the world, using only Victorian modes of travel. It
          goes well for a time. Unfortunately, setbacks in India lead
          him to fly to most of the remaining places on his itinerary.
          Completes the journey in seventy-six days but is embar-
          rassed by his failure to make good on this challenge.

1972   "Around the Bend in Eighty Days" serialized in six issues
          of *The New Yorker* early in the year. In May, feeling lonely
          and discouraged by British social life and its "smug satis-
          faction," Perelman returns to the United States. In Sep-
          tember, on assignment for *Travel and Leisure* magazine,
          sets off again around the world, through Europe, the Far
          East, and Australia, returning early the following year.

1973   In February improbably goes to Sarasota, Florida, to enter
          a communal living arrangement with playwrights Lillian
          Hellman, Albert Hackett and Frances Goodrich (husband
          and wife), and some young poets. Temperamentally un-
          suited for this life, soon leaves. In March resettles in Man-
          hattan, renting a two-room apartment on the fifteenth
          floor of the Gramercy Park Hotel on the corner of Lexing-
          ton Avenue and East Twenty-First Street.

1974   In October *The Beauty Part* is revived for a limited run at
          An American Place Theatre, a subscription theater in New
          York.

1975   In March *Vinegar Puss* published, containing twenty-two
          pieces, including "Around the Bend in Eighty Days." It
          receives some harsh reviews. There is a growing consensus

that in recent years Perelman's famous wit has become blunted, his subjects formulaic and stale. His work is sometimes rejected by formerly reliable magazines and *The New Yorker* now accepts but "holds in inventory" some of his new pieces. According to his onetime editor Robert Gottlieb, "He still had the manner, but no longer had the charge. His anger and irritation began to dominate his sense of comedy." Also in March Perelman goes off on his sixth trip around the world—Scotland, France, Russia, Greece, Israel, Iran, the Far East, Tahiti; he is gone more than seven months.

1976   Spends the month of February as a Regent's Lecturer at the University of California at Santa Barbara, his one brush with academe. Feeling no rapport with these journalism and creative writing students, complains that the most frequently asked questions are "How does a person get a good agent? How does a person break into writing for television? Could Harpo Marx really speak? Why is *The New Yorker* such a lousy magazine nowadays?" Travels to London in the summer.

1977   *Eastward Ha!*, the record of his sixth trip around the world, published in October. Perelman receives a $15,000 advance; the book sells 20,000 copies. Moves to a more spacious apartment in the Gramercy Park Hotel.

1978   Receives the first Special Achievement medal at the National Book Awards ceremony at Carnegie Hall on April 10 for his "sustained and exceptional contribution to American writing." In September, on assignment from the *Sunday Times* (London), undertakes to retrace—in reverse—the path of the famous 1907 Peking-to-Paris road race. Starting in Paris with two male friends, sets off in his own prized thirty-year-old MG. The trio drive through Central Europe, the Middle East, and twenty-seven days later arrive in Bombay, but because of modern changes in travel routes and new visa restrictions, the travelers have to fly much of the rest of the way. Splitting up with his companions, Perelman arrives in Peking alone. Finds himself unable to write his commissioned articles for the *Times*, the first failure to deliver in his long career.

1979   On October 17 dies alone, of a heart attack, in his apartment at the Gramercy Park Hotel. Coincidentally, this is Nathanael West's birthday. Perelman is cremated on

October 19 and his ashes are buried on his daughter's property in West Hurley, New York.

1981   *The Last Laugh*, a collection of Perelman's final seventeen *New Yorker* pieces, published. Also included are four other pieces that had been intended for his long-postponed, unfinished autobiography, "The Hindsight Saga." They are brief reminiscences of Dorothy Parker, Nathanael West, Groucho Marx, and some reflections on three of his Hollywood screenwriting assignments.

1987   *Don't Tread on Me*, a selection of Perelman's letters, published.

Note on the Texts

This volume contains sixty-two sketches and satires written by S. J. Perelman from the late 1920s to 1965; his play *The Beauty Part* (1963); fragments from his unfinished memoirs, "The Hindsight Saga," published posthumously in the collection *The Last Laugh* (1981); and a selection of Perelman's letters written from 1929 to 1976.

Since the publication of Perelman's first collection, *Dawn Ginsbergh's Revenge* (1929), publishers have been challenged by what to call his sui generis prose pieces. "Twenty-one palpitating pieces" is the language Random House used on the dust jacket of *Strictly from Hunger* (1937). *The New Yorker*, the magazine with which Perelman was most closely associated, called them "casuals." The author's own term was *feuilletons*—literally "little leaves." Perelman wrote more than 450 humorous sketches and satires, nearly all of them first published in magazines prior to their book publication (278 pieces appeared in *The New Yorker* between December 13, 1930, and his death in 1979). He preferred to publish in *The New Yorker* for multiple reasons: he considered it the best possible magazine outlet for humorous writing, it had "respect for the word," and his *New Yorker* editors typically only lightly edited his work. In 1937, he entered a contractual arrangement with *The New Yorker* for his feuilletons that suited his lifestyle: "It's the only thing I enjoy doing in any kind of writing and if I can combine self-indulgence with an occasional check, who's to say me nay." In addition to *The New Yorker*, his work appeared in more than a dozen other magazines, including *Judge*, *College Humor*, *The Saturday Evening Post*, *Holiday*, and *Travel and Leisure*.

Perelman gathered his sketches and satires in twenty-one volumes during his lifetime, and two further collections appeared within five years of his death. In 1948 *Westward Ha! Or, Around the World in Eighty Days* was published by Simon & Schuster, ending a nine-year relationship with Random House. Simon & Schuster remained Perelman's American publisher for the rest of his life (see also page 527 in this volume). Beginning with *Keep It Crisp* (Heinemann, 1947), most of Perelman's collections were published in England, where he had a reputation as America's greatest humorist. He continued to publish his collections primarily with Heinemann until that relationship soured. In a letter of July 13, 1961, he complained about the shoddy production of a 1959 Reprint Society volume, *The Best of S. J. Perelman* ("the straw-that-broke-the-camel's-back"), which had been published by arrangement with Heinemann. Subsequently, he published his books in England with several London publishers, but he appears to have been as little involved in the production of those books as he was with the Heinemann volumes. The texts of the pieces printed here are taken from their first American book publications, as indicated in the list that follows, which also reports their original magazine appearances (where it has been located).

From *Dawn Ginsbergh's Revenge* (New York: Liveright, 1929): "Puppets of Passion: A Throbbing Story of Youth's Hot Revolt Against the Conventions"; "Those Charming People: The Latest Report on the Weinbloom Reptile Expedition," *Judge*, December 29, 1928.

From *Strictly from Hunger* (New York: Random House, 1937): "Scenario," *Contact*, February 1932; "Strictly from Hunger," *Life*, September 1934; "The Love Decoy"; "Waiting for Santy: A Christmas Playlet," *The New Yorker*, December 26, 1936.

From *Look Who's Talking* (New York: Random House, 1940): "Frou-Frou, or the Future of Vertigo," *The New Yorker*, April 16, 1938; "Captain Future, Block That Kick!," *The New Yorker*, January 20, 1940; "Midwinter Facial Trends," *The New Yorker*, January 16, 1937.

From *The Dream Department* (New York: Random House, 1943): "Counter-Revolution," *The New Yorker*, March 21, 1940; "Beat Me, Post-Impressionist Daddy," *The New Yorker*, November 21, 1942; "A Pox on You, Mine Goodly Host," January 4, 1941; "Bend Down, Sister," November 7, 1942; "Beauty and the Bee," *The New Yorker*, September 21, 1935; "Button, Button, Who's Got the Blend?," *The New Yorker*, May 30, 1942; "Swing Out, Sweet Chariot," *The New Yorker*, September 14, 1940.

From *Crazy Like a Fox* (New York: Random House, 1944): "A Couple of Quick Ones: Two Portraits."

From *Keep It Crisp* (New York: Random House, 1946): "Hell in the Gabardines," *The New Yorker*, May 2, 1945; "Farewell, My Lovely Appetizer," *The New Yorker*, December 16, 1944; "Hit Him Again, He's Sober," *The New Yorker*, January 8, 1944; "Physician, Steel Thyself," *The New Yorker*, March 2, 1946; "Take Two Parts Sand, One Part Girl, and Stir," *The New Yorker*, July 8, 1944; "Sleepy-Time Extra," *The New Yorker*, May 20, 1944; "Amo, Amas, Amat, Amamus, Amatis, *Enough!*," *The New Yorker*, May 8, 1943; "Send No Money, Honey," *The New Yorker*, January 6, 1945.

From *Acres and Pains* (New York: Reynal and Hitchcock, 1947): Chapter One, published as part of the "Curses" series, *The Saturday Evening Post*, August 22, 1942; Chapter Twelve, published as part of the "Curses" series, *The Saturday Evening Post*, April 10, 1943.

From *Listen to the Mocking Bird* (New York: Simon & Schuster, 1949): "Don't Bring Me Oscars (When It's Shoesies That I Need)," *The New Yorker*, March 13, 1948.

From *The Swiss Family Perelman* (New York: Simon & Schuster, 1950): "Rancors Aweigh," *Holiday*, October 1944; "Mama Don't Want No Rice," *Holiday*, January 1950; "Columbia, the Crumb of the Ocean," originally published as "The Java Sea, Through a Jaundiced and Bloodshot Eye," in *Holiday*, March 1950; "Whenas in Sulks My Julia Goes," originally published as "Our Author's Portable Matriarchy Fearlessly Braves the Miniscule Perils of Bali and Bangkok," in *Holiday*, August 1950.

From *The Ill-Tempered Clavichord* (New York: Simon & Schuster, 1952): "Cloudland Revisited: Why, Doctor, What Big Green Eyes You Have!," *The New Yorker*, September 30, 1950; "Chewies the Goat but Flicks Need Hypo," *The New Yorker*, March 31, 1951; "Salesman, Spare that Psyche," *The New Yorker*, November 11, 1950; "The Song Is Endless, but the Malady Lingers On," August 5, 1950; "A Girl and a Boy Anthropoid Were Dancing," *The New Yorker*, January 12, 1952; "Cloudland Revisited: Rock-a-Bye, Viscount, in the Treetop," *The New Yorker*, December 23, 1950.

From *The Road to Miltown* (New York: Simon & Schuster, 1957): "Cloudland Revisited: When to the Sessions of Sweet Silent Films . . . ," *The New Yorker*, August 2, 1952; "No Starch in the Dhoti, S'il Vous Plaît," *The New Yorker*, February 12, 1955; "Cloudland Revisited: The Wickedest Woman in Larchmont," *The New Yorker*, October 18, 1952; "Swindle Sheet with Blueblood Engrailed, Arrant Fibs Rampant," *The New Yorker*, June 4, 1955; "Cloudland Revisited: I'm Sorry I Made Me Cry," *The New Yorker*, November 8, 1952; "Sorry—No Phone or Mail Orders," *The New Yorker*, July 18, 1953; "Next Week at the Prado: Frankie Goya Plus Monster Cast," *The New Yorker*, March 26, 1955; "You're My Everything, Plus City Sales Tax," *The New Yorker*, December 12, 1953.

From *The Rising Gorge* (New York: Simon & Schuster, 1961): "Eine Kleine Mothmusik," *The New Yorker*, August 13, 1960; "Where Do You Work-a, John?," *The New Yorker*, June 7, 1958; "Portrait of the Artist as a Young Mime," *The New Yorker*, January 28, 1961; "This Is the Forest Primeval?," *The New Yorker*, July 17, 1954; "Impresario on the Lam," based on "Say a Few Words, Georgie," published in *Holiday*, September 1952; "Revulsion in the Desert," *The New Yorker*, July 23, 1960.

From *Chicken Inspector No. 23* (New York: Simon & Schuster, 1966): "Are You Decent, Memsahib?," *The New Yorker*, August

28, 1965; "Tell Me Clear, Parachutist Dear, Are You Man or Mouse?," *The New Yorker*, December 25, 1965; "Sex and the Single Boy," *The New Yorker*, May 8, 1965; "A Soft Answer Turneth Away Royalties," *The New Yorker*, April 7, 1960; "Hello, Central, Give Me That Jolly Old Pelf," *The New Yorker*, December 21, 1963; "The Sweet Chick Gone," *The New Yorker*, June 3, 1961; "Nobody Knows the Rubble I've Seen/Nobody Knows but Croesus," *Venture*, August 1965.

From *Baby, It's Cold Inside* (New York: Simon & Schuster, 1970): "Three Loves Had I, in Assorted Flavors," *The New Yorker*, March 22, 1969; "Be a Cat's-Paw! Lose Big Money!," *The New Yorker*, July 26, 1969; "Moonstruck at Sunset," *The New Yorker*, August 16, 1969.

The Beauty Part, Perelman's two-act comedy, a satire of American art and commerce, opened on December 26, 1962, at New York's Music Box Theatre and closed three months later after only eighty-four performances. Its failure on Broadway was due at least in part to the unfortunate timing of a New York City newspaper strike, which prevented favorable notices and advertisements from reaching the public (see also page 530 in this volume). The idea for the play, Perelman was fond of saying, came to him one day when he was riding the elevator of Manhattan's Sutton Hotel: the operator stopped the car between floors and announced, "I'm having trouble with my second act." "It's a cultural upsurge," Perelman explained in a 1963 interview with *Newsweek*, "the big move on the part of everyone for expression." The play had a trial run at the Bucks County Playhouse in New Hope, Pennsylvania, in the summer of 1961 before its Broadway debut. Perelman worked assiduously on the play for the next year and a half, putting the play through numerous revisions. The text presented here is that of the original acting edition, published by Samuel French in 1963.

In 1960, Perelman entered an agreement with Simon & Schuster to publish his memoirs, which he never finished. The author intended to call the book "The Hindsight Saga," a playful allusion to *The Forsyte Saga*, John Galsworthy's series of novels and interludes. Four self-contained fragments from "The Hindsight Saga" were included in the posthumous collection *The Last Laugh*, published by Simon & Schuster in 1981 and in London by Methuen the following year. Three of those fragments are presented here: "The Marx Brothers," "Nathanael West," and "Dorothy Parker." "The Marx Brothers" and "Nathanael West" appeared as excerpts from *The Last Laugh* in *Esquire* magazine, respectively as "Going Hollywood with the Marx

Brothers" (September 1981) and "My Brother-in-Law" (June 1981).
This volume prints the 1981 Simon & Schuster texts.

The texts of the letters selected for this volume are taken from *Don't Tread on Me: The Selected Letters of S. J. Perelman* (Viking, 1987), edited by Prudence Crowther. In her preface, Crowther notes that "Perelman was as fastidious in his correspondence as in his pieces. . . . Most of the letters are neatly typed." Crowther has corrected obvious typographical errors, occasionally regularized spelling and punctuation, and made cuts that she thought were necessary or that the Perelman Estate or others had requested. Smaller cuts are indicated in the text by spaced ellipses (ellipses without spacing are Perelman's own). Larger cuts, of a paragraph or more, are indicated by a space break and three centered dots. For a more detailed explanation of the textual policies guiding *Don't Tread on Me: The Selected Letters of S. J. Perelman*, readers should consult Crowther's preface.

This volume presents the texts of the original printings chosen for inclusion here, but it does not attempt to reproduce features of their design and layout. The texts are presented without change, except for the correction of typographical errors. Spelling, punctuation, and capitalization are often expressive features and they are not altered, even when inconsistent or irregular. The following is a list of errors corrected, cited by page and line number: 8.23, pleateau.; 19.25, seepy; 38.10, contretempts; 48.26, Montfried; 52.6, relunctantly; 62.28, Answers,; 105.32, shoulder's.; 108.20, Bergmann."; 111.20, jar.; 129.13, know; 135.33, Rosellini.; 142.5, side idolatry; 162.25, Christians; 168.25, Hennessey,; 193.33, Bulitude; 202.31, brontossaurus,; 204.13, speak,; 249.9, Packy; 252.37, times; 256.5, *Guglhupfe*,; 259.33, rendering; 279.9, LaRocque; 300.35, Hennessey,; 345.2, employe; 359.22, Sneden's; 376.1, beningnly.; 380.29, Zasu; 387.7, Days; 393.35, herd; 409.34, Gaugin; 414.34, Pollacks,; 414.34, Lipschitzes,; 424.25, Goodard; 430.3, the "The; 431.21. *Pick*; 457.36, dignfied.; 458.32, gentleman; 463.3, Grahame's; 463.4, head.; 482.5, his of situation,; 485.40, pastorial; 488.32, change; 489.15, transmutted; 489.25, jubiliant; 494.18, were.

Notes

In the notes below, the reference numbers denote page and line of this volume (the line count includes headings). Biblical quotations are keyed to the King James Version. Quotations from Shakespeare are keyed to *The Riverside Shakespeare*, ed. G. Blakemore Evans (Boston: Houghton Mifflin, 1974). For further biographical background than is provided in the Chronology, see Dorothy Hermann, *S. J. Perelman: A Life* (New York: Putnam, 1986) and *Don't Tread on Me: The Selected Letters of S. J. Perelman*, ed. Prudence Crowther (New York: Viking, 1987).

SKETCHES AND SATIRES

3.19   Old Mould] Cf. Old Gold cigarettes.

3.25–26   *I burn my chandelier . . . the night . . .*] Cf. "Figs from Thistles: First Fig" by Edna St. Vincent Millay (1892–1950). The entire poem reads: "My candle burns at both ends / It will not last the night; / But ah, my foes, and oh, my friends— / It gives a lovely light!"

4.2   Firpo] Luis Ángel Firpo (1894–1960), Argentine boxer who fought the ferocious heavyweight champion Jack Dempsey for the title on September 14, 1923. Knocked down seven times in the first round, Firpo managed to rally briefly, trapping his opponent against the ropes and knocking him out of the ring, stunning the crowd. Dempsey, however, recovered and won the bout.

4.7   yellow jack] Yellow fever.

4.21   momzer,"] Yiddish (slang): bastard; illegitimate offspring.

4.25   Ludwig Baumann] Founder, with his brother Albert, of Ludwig Baumann & Company, a flourishing Manhattan furniture emporium.

4.38   estancias in the Banda Oriental] An *estancia* (Spanish) is a large plot of land for farming or raising cattle in Latin America and the southwestern United States; "Banda Oriental" refers to the territories east of the Uruguay River and north of Río de la Plata that comprise modern Uruguay.

5.14   Barbizon school."] French painters who worked in a realist mode during the heyday of the Romantic movement in the 1830s, and continuing into the 1870s. They often gathered in the village of Barbizon near the Fontainebleau Forest, south of Paris. While landscape was their primary subject, painters like Jean-François Millet often depicted scenes of peasant labor and domestic life.

5.40   mocky] A derogatory term for a Jew. Not used so here, exclusively, but that resonance is pointedly there.

7.21   Leblang] Possible reference to Joseph Leblang (1874–1931), also known as Joe Broadway, a Jewish Hungarian immigrant turned Broadway entrepreneur, credited with introducing the concept of discount Broadway tickets to the public in 1894. He became the clearinghouse for excess tickets from many theaters, selling tickets by phone and by mail as well. Eventually, he bought the George M. Cohan Theater and produced his own shows.

8.12   traps and snares?] Clearly, things to avoid, but also types of drums.

8.15   oboes never do work] Cf. "hoboes."

10.10   Cudjo] Cudjo Kazoola Lewis (c. 1841–1935), the third-to-last-known survivor of the Atlantic slave trade between Africa and the United States. In 1927 Lewis was interviewed by Zora Neale Hurston, then a graduate student in anthropology. The next year she published an article, "Cudjoe's Own Story of the Last African Slaver."

11.2   wilderness were paradise enow] Last line of Quatrain XII of *The Rubaiyat of Omar Khayyam*, translated by Edward Fitzgerald. In the 1889 edition the translation reads: "A Book of Verses underneath the Bough, / A Jug of Wine, a Loaf of Bread—and Thou / Beside me singing in the Wilderness— / Oh, Wilderness were Paradise enow!"

11.24   Vorkapich] Slavko Vorkapich (1894–1976), Serbian-born Hollywood cinematographer, celebrated for his innovative use of montage, specialty camerawork, and trick photography.

11.27   Alexandra Petrovna's] Alexandra Petrovna (1838–1900), Grand Duchess of Russia, a great-granddaughter of Emperor Paul I of Russia, and the wife of Grand Duke Nicholas Nikolaevich of Russia, the elder.

12.18   hog-butcher to the world] Cf. opening line of the poem "Chicago" by Carl Sandburg (1878–1967), which reads "Hog Butcher for the World."

12.22   Ufa] The German film studio UFA (*Universum-Film Aktiengesellschaft*). Founded in 1917 as a direct response to foreign competition in film, it flourished during the Weimar period and became synonymous with high-quality film production. Directors such as Fritz Lang, Ernst Lubitsch, and F. W. Murnau worked there. Among its most notable films were *Metropolis*, *The Last Laugh*, and *The Blue Angel*.

12.25   Hays office] The informal name for the censorship arm of the Motion Picture Producers and Distributors of America, founded in 1922 to improve the image of Hollywood after a number of scandals in the film colony, and to forestall government censorship. Former postmaster general and Republican stalwart Will Hays (1879–1954) was its first president. The "Hays Office" initiated a blacklist, inserted morals clauses into actors' contracts, and in 1930 developed the Production Code, which detailed what was morally acceptable on the screen.

13.3 Powell-Loys] Movies that could have featured the acting team from the popular *Thin Man* series, William Powell (1893–1984) and Myrna Loy (1905–1993).

13.38–39 For love belongs . . . free.] Cf. "The Best Things in Life Are Free," a 1927 song written by Buddy DeSylva and Lew Brown (lyrics) and Ray Henderson (music). The last lines of the lyric are "And love can come to everyone / The best things in life are free."

14.1 *Strictly from Hunger*] Slang: Of poor quality.

14.4 reefer] Double-breasted men's jacket.

14.21 dreaming spires] In his poem "Thyrsis" Matthew Arnold (1822–1888) calls Oxford "the city of dreaming spires," because of the striking architecture of the university buildings.

15.33 B.B.D. & O.] The acronym actually stands for the powerful advertising agency Batten, Barton, Durstine and Osborn.

17.5 Lyle Talbot] American actor (1902–1996). Talbot was a handsome leading man and second lead on stage and in early sound films, playing suave and sometimes sinister characters. He had a long continuing career as a character actor.

17.6 *suttee*] A ritual once practiced in India in which a widow throws herself onto her husband's funeral pyre.

17.34 Will Hays] See note 12.25.

18.6–7 sent . . . into Coventry.] British expression meaning to ostracize someone, usually by refusing to speak to them or socialize with them, acting as if they don't exist.

18.37 Lloyd Pantages] American actor (1907–1987) who appeared in a single movie, *Dante's Inferno*, in the uncredited role of a drunken sailor. The 1935 film, starring Spencer Tracy, takes place in a carnival that features scenes from Dante's Hell.

19.6 Threadneedle Street] London location of the Bank of England and, until recently, the London Stock Exchange.

19.15 Sheik Lure] An imported perfume scent in solid form, advertised as "for both sexes." It came in a small ruby transparent case that a man could keep "in his vest pocket." One fingertip application on the skin could "last for days."

19.18 kümmel] Sweet, colorless liqueur flavored with caraway seed, cumin, and fennel.

19.31   cubebs] Cigarettes made from the dried fruit of *piper cubeba*, a plant indigenous to Java and Sumatra. It has been used for both spiritual and medicinal purposes. Edgar Rice Burroughs, who was fond of smoking cubeb cigarettes, whimsically said that if he had not smoked so many cubebs, there might never have been *Tarzan*.

23.16–17   Warren William] American actor (1894–1948), whose career flourished in the early 1930s. While he occasionally played sympathetic roles, his stock-in-trade was more unscrupulous characters: ruthless businessmen, crafty lawyers, and charlatans. For this reason he was known in Hollywood as "The King of Pre-Code."

23.32   gink] Slang: a foolish or contemptible person.

24.5   Hoffenstein] Perelman may be referring to Samuel Hoffenstein (1890–1947), fellow Hollywood screenwriter in the 1930s. Hoffenstein's screenwriting credits include *Dr. Jekyll and Mr. Hyde*, *Love Me Tonight*, *Design for Living*, and *Laura*. Naming an "ivy-covered" college building after him may have been a lovely—or devilish—gesture on Perelman's part. Two other such halls of learning are so named in "The Love Decoy": Schneider and Lapeedis, but the identities of their honorees have proven elusive.

28.1   *Waiting for Santy*] Cf. *Waiting for Lefty*, a 1935 play by American dramatist Clifford Odets (1906–1963). Consisting of a series of related vignettes, the entire play is framed by a meeting of cab drivers who are planning a labor strike.

29.14   *"Cohen on the Telephone."*] A comedy monologue first recorded in London in 1913, it was released on cylinder, 78 rpm disc, and eventually as a sound-film short. Cohen is trying to ask his landlord to send someone to make repairs, but his thick Jewish accent leads to a series of verbal misunderstandings and puns. For example: "Hello! This is your tenant Cohen . . . YOUR TENANT COHEN. . . . No, NOT Lieutenant Cohen."

29.19   Camp Nitgedaiget!] 250-acre resort founded in 1922 by the United Workers Cooperative Association. Located between Cold Spring and Beacon, New York, it had close connections with the Communist Party and offered respite, outdoor activities, entertainment, and sometimes housing to members of the working class. It was abandoned in the early 1950s. *Nitgedaiget* is Yiddish for "No worries."

31.2   Mermaid Tavern] Tavern on Cheapside in London during the Elizabethan period. The Fraternity of Sireniacal Gentlemen, a drinking club, met there on Friday nights. Among its members were Ben Jonson, John Donne, Francis Beaumont, and John Fletcher.

31.6   yellow-backed novels.] Cheap paperbacks in mustard-colored wrappers, sometimes with sensational or salacious content.

32.2–3 Nicky de Gunzburg . . . Noailles] Nicholas de Gunzburg (1904–1981), French-born editor of such magazines as *Town & Country*, *Vogue*, and *Harper's Bazaar*. Lady Abdy (1897–1993), née Iya de Gay, Russian-born actress and fashion model. Marie-Laure (Vicomtesse) de Noailles (1902–1970), French artist and patron of the arts, notably associated with Cocteau, Dalí, Buñuel, and Poulenc.

32.6–7 Garbo . . . retreat?"] Cf. a scene in the movie *Camille* (1936). Armand was played by Robert Taylor (1911–1969).

32.14 Marquis of Carabas!"] Fictitious nobleman/master, invented by the cat, in the fairy tale *Puss in Boots*.

34.1 *Captain Future*] Science fiction hero—a space-traveling scientist and adventurer—introduced in a namesake pulp magazine that ran from 1940 to 1944.

34.13–14 Buck Rogers . . . Mongo or Dale Arden] Buck Rogers, the twenty-fifth-century space-traveler hero of novels, a syndicated comic strip, a television series, and movies. Mongo, the planet threatening to collide with Earth in the *Flash Gordon* comic strip, and where many of the ensuing adventures are set. Dale Arden, the female space adventurer and love interest of Flash Gordon.

34.18 slippered pantaloon] A man of advancing years and weakening faculties. See Jaques's "Seven Ages of Man" speech in *As You Like It*, II.vii.157–59: ". . . The sixth age shifts / Into the lean and slipper'd pantaloon, / With spectacles on nose and pouch on side."

34.20 Ming] Ming the Merciless, archvillain and nemesis of Flash Gordon.

34.20–21 Holland rusk] Brand of dried biscuit or twice-baked bread, sometimes used as baby teething food.

34.28 merry-andrew] A person who entertains others with comic antics, a public clown.

36.18 *vieux jeu*] French: literally "old game"; old-fashioned, no longer done.

37.3 Dink Stover] Protagonist of Owen Johnson's 1912 novel *Stover at Yale*, which recounts how Dink navigates the social structure and social pressures of the college. F. Scott Fitzgerald called the novel "the textbook" of his generation.

37.14 *Kaffeeklatsch*] German: informal gathering for coffee and conversation.

38.9 beezer] Boxing slang: nose.

41.15 Hays office] See note 12.25.

41.37 the rams] Slang: a drunken state.

42.14–15 Hercule Poirot . . . Inspector Lestrade] Poirot, the brilliant, elegant, mustachioed, fictional Belgian detective created by Agatha Christie. He appears in thirty-three novels, two plays, and more than fifty short stories published from 1920 to 1975. Inspector G. Lestrade, the determined but conventional Scotland Yard detective who consults Sherlock Holmes on many cases. Lestrade initially finds Holmes "too cocksure" and Holmes finds Lestrade "out of his depth."

44.12 Peace of Breda] Treaties between England and its adversaries—France, the Dutch Republic, and Denmark-Norway—signed in the Dutch town of Breda in 1667, ending the Second Anglo-Dutch War.

47.27 *Lin Yutang*] Chinese inventor, linguist, novelist, philosopher, and translator (1895–1976). His informal but polished style in both Chinese and English made him one of the most influential writers of his generation.

48.1 *Beat Me . . . Daddy*] Music slang. In hip circles, "Beat me, Daddy, eight to the bar" was an instruction to the drummer (or piano player) to double the tempo to a boogie beat.

48.6 Messrs. Loew and Lewin] David L. Loew (1897–1973) and Albert Lewin (1894–1968) ran the production company that adapted W. Somerset Maugham's *The Moon and Sixpence* to the screen in 1948. Loew was the son of Marcus Loew, owner of the Loew's theater chain and president of Loew's, Inc., the parent company of the Hollywood studio Metro-Goldwyn-Mayer. Lewin was a successful Hollywood director and screenwriter.

48.15–16 George Sanders] Russian-born British actor (1906–1972) frequently cast as the cad. He won the Best Supporting Actor Oscar for his portrayal of Addison DeWitt in *All About Eve* (1950).

48.26 D. de Monfreid] George-Daniel de Monfreid (1856–1929), a French painter and art collector.

49.3 *pascudnick*] Yiddish: a nasty or contemptible person.

49.11 "Poi,"] Primary traditional staple food in the native cuisine of Hawaii, made from the underground stem of taro, mashed and cooked.

53.9 Dinty Moore's] Irish eatery located at 214 West Forty-Sixth Street, New York City, in the heart of the Broadway theater district. Opened in 1914 by James Moore under his own name, it became a popular dining spot (and watering hole) for playwrights, actors, and gamblers. Moore changed the name to Dinty Moore's, following the appearance of an Irish pub owner of that name in the comic strip *Bringing Up Father*, (also known as "Maggie and Jiggs") whose creator, George McManus, frequented James Moore's establishment.

53.13–14 George S. Kaufman and Moss Hart] Two of the finest popular Broadway playwrights of their era, noted for the comedies they created during their ten-year collaboration of the 1930s, among them *Once in a Lifetime*, *You Can't Take It with You*, and *The Man Who Came to Dinner*. When not collaborating with Hart, Kaufman (1889–1961) wrote or cowrote *Of Thee I Sing*, winner of the Pulitzer Prize; *Dinner at Eight*; *The Solid Gold Cadillac*; and, for the Marx Brothers, *The Coconuts* and *Animal Crackers*. When not collaborating with Kaufman, Hart (1904–1961) wrote the book for the musical *Lady in the Dark* and screenplays for *Gentleman's Agreement* and the 1954 *A Star Is Born*.

53.15   Schrafft's] A chain of high-volume, moderately priced New York restaurants connected to the Schrafft's food and candy business of Boston. Schrafft's was known for an air of gentility typical of the upper-middle-class home. The first Schrafft's restaurants were opened in the first decade of the twentieth century. By 1937 there were forty-three locations, mainly in New York City, with a handful of locations in other northeastern cities.

53.27   Brian Aherne!"] British actor (1902–1986) who often portrayed elegant, cultured, educated men.

54.12–13   Nick Kenny . . . Sonja Henie] Nick Kenny (1895–1975), syndicated newspaper columnist, song lyricist, and writer of light verse. Jack Benny (1894–1974), master comedian, successful on stage, radio, television, and in movie theaters the world over. James Rennie (1889–1965), Canadian stage and film actor, married to Dorothy Gish. Sonja Henie (1912–1969), Norwegian figure skater and three-time Olympic champion, who parlayed her celebrity into a decade-long American film career in lighthearted romantic comedies, which featured her skating talents.

54.15   Jim Thorpe . . . Jay Thorpe] Native American Jim Thorpe (1887–1953) was the 1912 Olympic pentathlon and decathlon champion, as well as a collegiate and professional baseball, basketball, and football player, considered by many to be the greatest athlete of his day. Jay Thorpe opened an exclusive custom clothing store on West Fifty-Seventh Street in Manhattan in the 1920s. It lasted until the 1970s.

54.16   Walter Wanger and Percy Grainger] Wanger (1894–1968) was the head of production at Paramount and later a renowned independent film producer (*Stagecoach*, *Foreign Correspondent*). He is remembered for his track record of making challenging and successful films, and for his 1951 shooting of talent agent Jennings Lang, who was having an affair with Wanger's wife, actress Joan Bennett. He spent four months in jail for attempted murder. Percy Grainger (1882–1961) was an Australian-born composer and arranger, who took a particular interest in folk traditions.

54.16–17   Lou Little . . . Elmer Layden] Born Luigi Piccolo, Little (1893–1979) was a two-time All-American tackle at the University of Pennsylvania. He went on to an illustrious head coaching career, first at Georgetown, then at Columbia University. Layden (1903–1973) was the fullback on Notre Dame's 1924 undefeated, national championship football team, whose backfield was known collectively as the Four Horsemen. Their coach, Knute Rockne, introduced a sudden pre-snap movement, a coordinated shift in the positions of the backfield players, which stymied their opponents.

54.18   Ann Corio] Burlesque house striptease artist and actress (1909–1999). After a long career in burlesque and a short career in B pictures, she starred in a celebration of her art form on Broadway in a 1962 show called *This Was Burlesque*.

55.33   Frank G. Shattuck organization] Shattuck (1860–1937) had nothing to do with casting, per se. He was a Brooklyn candy salesman, the founder of Schrafft's restaurant chain—where actresses might be found eating (or working). See also note 53.15.

56.16   Lindy's] Celebrated New York deli and restaurant founded by Leo "Lindy" Lindemann in 1921. Located in the heart of the theater district on Broadway between Forty-Ninth and Fiftieth Streets, it was famous for its cheesecake. It closed in 1957. A second Lindy's, two blocks farther uptown, closed in 1969.

59.30   Sedormid] Brand name for Apronal or apronalide, a hypnotic/sedative drug.

63.18   George Cable's domain] Novelist George Washington Cable (1844–1925) was noted for his realistic portrayals of Creole life in his native New Orleans. He has been called the first modern southern writer.

65.19–20   Eddy Duchin . . . Eddie Robinson] Edwin Frank Duchin (1909–1951), celebrated pianist on the New York nightclub scene, who played "sweet" music (rather than jazz), a repertoire of slow, romantic songs performed with style and flourish. George Sherwood Eddy (1871–1963), eminent American Protestant missionary and educator. Eddie Cantor, born Isidore Itzkowitz, (1892–1964), a widely popular American comedian, dancer, singer, actor, and songwriter, also known as "Banjo Eyes" for his eye-rolling song-and-dance routines, whose many hit songs include "Makin' Whoopee," "If You Knew Susie," and "Ma! He's Makin' Eyes at Me." Nelson Eddy (1901–1967), classically trained American baritone singer and actor best known for the eight movie musicals he made with actress/soprano Jeanette MacDonald at MGM, among them *Rosie-Marie* (1936), in which Eddy, dressed somewhat comically as a Canadian Mountie, serenades MacDonald with "Indian Love Call." Edward G. Robinson (1893–1973), born Emmanuel Goldenberg, American actor who went from the Yiddish stage to Broadway, then on to a long, successful career as a star in Hollywood movies, epitomizing the charismatic, ruthless gangster, especially in early talkies.

65.35–36   creep a mile for a cup cake.] Cf. advertising slogan for Camel cigarettes: "I'd walk a mile for a Camel."

69.11–12   Morningside Kid] Reference to John Dewey (1859–1952), professor of philosophy at Columbia University from 1904 until his retirement in 1930. Columbia University is located in the Morningside Heights section of Manhattan.

69.13   Middle Temple] One of the four Inns of Court, located in London. (The others are Inner Temple, Gray's Inn, and Lincoln's Inn.) Members of the Inns of Court are the only ones entitled to be called to the English Bar as barristers.

69.14   brier with shag] Pipe with tobacco. The bowls of tobacco pipes are commonly made of briar (or brier) wood. Shag is fine-cut tobacco used to roll self-made cigarettes.

70.30   pile Pelion on Ossa] In Greek mythology Mount Pelion was thought to be home to the centaurs. Two giants attempted to pile it on top of Mount Ossa in order to reach and scale Mount Olympus and destroy the gods. In other words, a great deal of futile labor.

71.1–2   Roselane Ballroom] Cf. the Roseland Ballroom, a spacious venue for dancing, whose first Manhattan location, from 1919 to 1956, was 1658 Broadway at Fifty-First Street. It could accommodate up to 3,000 people and became a destination for the crowds seeking out the best dance bands on the swing and jazz scene. Big band performances—by black orchestras as well as white—were broadcast on the radio: *Live from Roseland*.

71.30   Suzy-Q. . . . shagged and pecked.] Contemporary dance moves: Suzy-Q, a step in which the feet perform alternating cross steps and side steps with swivel action; shag, a two-step with room for lots of improvisation; peck, or pose and peck, hopping forward with hands on hips while pecking with one's head.

72.17   Dun & Bradstreet] Well-known company that provides commercial data, analytics, and insights for businesses.

72.31   Tiz] Powder added to water to give relief to tired feet and soothe corns and bunions. A 1914 ad claims "it's the only remedy that draws out all the poisonous exudations which puff up your feet and cause foot torture." Twenty-five cents a box.

72.39   Garrison finish] Close finish in which the winner comes from behind at the end. Named for Edward "Snapper" Garrison, a nineteenth-century American jockey known for his spectacular come-from-behind wins.

73.1   geeps] Derogatory term used by Italian American and Sicilian American mobsters to refer to newer immigrant Sicilian and Italian mafiosi.

73.5   "shagged and trucked and Suzy-Q-ed] Truck, a shuffling jitterbug step. See also note 71.30.

74.2   ARTHUR KOBER] American humorist, author, press agent, and screenwriter (1900–1975). He was married to the dramatist Lillian Hellman from 1925 to 1932.

74.19   Lincoln Kirstein] Lincoln Edward Kirstein (1907–1996), American poet, impresario, art connoisseur, and cofounder, with George Balanchine, of the New York City Ballet, for which he also served as general director from 1946 to 1989.

74.32   slippered pantaloon] See note 34.18.

75.13   Battle of the Boyne] Fought in July 1690 in Ireland between the forces of James II, who had been deposed in 1688, and those of William of Orange, who had ascended to the British throne. It was the last time two crowned kings of England, Scotland, and Ireland faced each other on the battlefield. William of Orange won a decisive victory, securing the Protestant ascendency in Ireland for generations.

75.33   Seven against Thebes] Third play in Aeschylus's Oedipus trilogy, performed in 467 B.C.E.

75.33–34   I love coffee . . . girls love me.] Cf. "Java Jive," 1940 song that celebrated coffee drinking. Filled with hip slang of the day, the opening lyrics are "I love coffee, I love tea / I love the java jive and it loves me / Coffee and tea and the java and me / A cup, a cup, a cup, a cup, a cup!"

75.37   Marc Connelly] American playwright (1890–1980) who received the Pulitzer Prize for Drama in 1930 for *The Green Pastures*. The play, a retelling of episodes from the Old Testament, was a landmark in American drama—the first with an all-black Broadway cast. A regular presence at the Algonquin Round Table, Connelly was also considered—along with his friends George S. Kaufman and Dorothy Parker—among its wittiest members.

76.1   Teach, Lafitte, Flint] Edward Teach (c. 1680–1718), known as Blackbeard, an English pirate who, with the crew of his forty-gun ship *Queen Anne's Revenge*, terrorized the Caribbean and the Carolinas. Jean Lafitte (c. 1780–c. 1823), French pirate who operated in the Gulf of Mexico and supported American forces, under the command of Andrew Jackson, in their defense of New Orleans in 1814. Captain Flint, a fictional pirate who first appears in Robert Louis Stevenson's *Treasure Island*.

76.10–11   powder-monkey . . . the Shuberts.] Powder monkey, a boy employed on a sailing warship to carry powder to the guns. Klaw and Erlanger, the entertainment management and production partnership of Marc Klaw and Abraham Lincoln Erlanger, based in New York City from 1888 through 1919. The Shuberts, three Shubert brothers who in the late nineteenth century founded the Shubert organization, a theatrical producing company, a major owner of theaters, and a powerful force in American theatrical history.

76.21   Gessler] Fabled fourteenth-century Hapsburg bailiff whose brutal rule in the Austrian-controlled Swiss territories led to the William Tell rebellion. It was Gessler who, according to legend, ordered Tell to shoot the apple off his son's head. Tell later ambushed and killed Gessler—with an arrow.

77.26   Jimmy Durante] American actor, comedian, singer, and pianist (1893–1980). Durante's gravelly voice, Lower East Side accent, comic butchery of the English language, and prominent nose (he was self-dubbed "The Schnozzola") helped make him one of America's most popular personalities.

78.18–19 'Chu Chin Chow.'"] 1916 musical comedy based on "Ali Baba and the Forty Thieves." It ran in London's West End and on Broadway, and was later both a silent picture (with music added) and a 1934 sound film. It was revived on stage in 1940.

81.2 Cameo Kirby] 1909 play coauthored by Booth Tarkington. John Ford directed a silent film version in 1923, starring suave John Gilbert. It also became a sound film.

81.5 Lindy's] See note 56.16.

81.17–18 *The Lobster Is the Wise Guy, After All*] This 1907 song by Theodore Morse and Edward Madden is actually entitled "I'd Rather Be a Lobster than a Wise Guy." The song's last lyrics are "And the more of life I see, / It really seems to me, / that the lobster is the wise guy after all." A lobster was a slang term for someone, perhaps a bit dull, who perseveres and remains steadfast. A wise guy was a slick, impetuous, charmer—easy come, easy go.

82.8 Balaban & Katz] Chicago-based theater corporation that owned a large chain of movie houses throughout the Midwest. It was founded in 1916 by Barney Balaban, his six siblings, and his brother-in-law Sam Katz. Balaban later became the longtime president of Paramount Pictures.

82.27 jehu] Driver of a coach or cab. Derives from Jehu, in the Old Testament, who drives his chariot ferociously in II Kings 9.

82.29 Richard Harding Davis] American journalist, fiction writer, playwright, and the most prominent war correspondent of his day (1864–1916), covering the Spanish-American War, the Second Boer War, and the First World War.

85.6 T.R.B.] Name of the lead column in *The New Republic*, devoted to national and Washington, D.C., politics. Written by many different journalists over the years, it is most closely identified with Richard Strout, who penned the column from 1943 to 1983. As one story has it, using the initials TRB to sign off the column came about as the result of Bruce Bliven, the magazine's editor, having just taken the old Brooklyn Rapid Transit subway into the office and simply reversing the letters.

85.11 Camp Nitgedaiget] See note 29.19.

85.15 White Turkey Town House] Large restaurant on the ground floor of the apartment building at 1 University Place, in New York City, a short walk from Perelman's Washington Square residence. It opened on November 28, 1938.

85.15 Stark Young's] Young (1881–1963), a Mississippi-born writer, playwright, and for many years the drama critic at *The New Republic*. His novel *So Red the Rose*, about the Civil War and its aftermath, was highly regarded at the time of its publication in 1935.

85.36–86.3 Ray Milland . . . Birnam's torment.] Milland (1907–1986), a Welsh actor who became a Hollywood leading man, won the Best Actor Oscar for his performance in Billy Wilder's *The Lost Weekend* (1945), playing Don Birnam, an alcoholic writer who struggles to get and remain sober. The film includes a raw scene of Birnam's battle with delirium tremens.

86.27 Bonnie Brae] The Bonnie Brae Farm for Boys, founded in 1916 by Judge Harry V. Osborne on fourteen acres in Livingston, New Jersey, a place of refuge, training, and education for delinquent and destitute boys and young men.

87.4 Finchley's] A haberdashery catering to affluent men whose tastes ran to English-style clothing. From 1924, it was located in a six-story Tudor-style building on Fifth Avenue between Forty-Sixth and Forty-Seventh Streets in Manhattan. The interior sported a fireplace and a lounge with a piano.

89.17 Fredric March] March (1897–1975) was a noted American actor and two-time recipient of the Best Actor Oscar, first for *Dr. Jekyll and Mr. Hyde* (1932)—an award he shared with Wallace Beery for *The Champ*—then for *The Best Years of Our Lives* (1946). He also had a thriving stage career. March was a staunch supporter of the Democratic Party and contributor to liberal causes. He was a cofounder of the Hollywood Anti-Nazi League, for which he was later investigated by the Martin Dies subcommittee of the House Un-American Activities Committee.

91.1 *Farewell, My Lovely Appetizer*] Cf. Raymond Chandler's novel *Farewell, My Lovely* (1940).

91.11 *Russeks*] Furrier and, starting in 1924, upscale department store on Fifth Avenue at Thirty-Sixth Street in Manhattan. The business, which grew to be a chain, was founded by brothers Frank and Isidore Russek. Frank was the maternal grandfather of photographer Diane Arbus.

92.21 Gristede store] Gristede's, a New York–based supermarket chain founded in 1888.

93.1 gossoon] In Ireland, a youth, especially a serving boy.

93.25 Lloyd Thursday] Cf. Floyd Thursby, Brigid O'Shaughnessy's erstwhile partner-in-crime in Dashiell Hammett's *The Maltese Falcon* (1929).

94.34 jasper] A simple or naive person.

95.3 Heptameron] Collection of seventy-two stories by French princess (sister of Francis I) Marguerite de Navarre (1492–1549), published posthumously in 1558.

95.8 Pee Wee Russell] Charles Ellsworth Russell (1906–1969), the great jazz clarinetist, whose distinctive and unorthodox style (some listeners thought he was playing out of tune) made him a fixture in top bands through the Dixieland, swing, and bebop eras.

98.2–3   Henry James . . . 21 Washington Place] The James family home (renumbered 27 the year after the novelist's birth) was just east of the Square. Perelman lived, over the years, at several addresses on Washington Square north and south.

98.7   Richard Harding Davis] See note 82.29.

98.35   Hall Caine] Sir Thomas Henry Hall Caine (1853–1931), prolific and most highly paid novelist of his day, who tackled in his fiction such subjects as adultery, infanticide, domestic violence, and religious intolerance.

99.1–2   John Barleycorn . . . Walker-Gordon.] John Barleycorn, the personification of the barley grain and, more pointedly, the alcoholic beverages that derive from it, beer and whisky. Walker-Gordon, an innovative, science-based dairy farm founded in 1897 in Plainsboro, New Jersey, known for its wholesome "Certified Milk," tested in its own laboratory.

99.2   *Mens sana in corpore sano.*] Latin: A healthy mind in a healthy body.

99.7–8   Colley Cibber's memoirs] Colley Cibber (1671–1757), British actor-manager, playwright, and poet laureate who published a garrulous but entertaining autobiography, *An Apology for the Life of Colley Cibber, Comedian* (1740). Disliked by many of his contemporaries for his brazen opportunism and sentimental theatrical productions, he was finally immortalized by Alexander Pope, who anointed him King of the Dunces in the revised four-book *Dunciad* (1743).

99.13–14   Mrs. George Washington Kavanaugh] Born Maria Magdalena Muller in Richmond, Virginia, Kavanaugh (1863–1954) was a patron of the Metropolitan Opera, noteworthy collector of expensive, elaborate jewelry and socialite at the center of New York high society, often reported fraternizing with Vanderbilts, Astors, and Dukes. Her name has long faded, but the photographer Weegee captured her for all posterity in his November 22, 1943, image *The Critic.* In it, a shabbily dressed woman (possibly placed there by Weegee) appears to glare in the direction of two gowned, bejeweled, and tiaraed dowagers passing by. Mrs. G. W. Kavanaugh is on the left. Her good friend Lady Decies is on the right.

99.24–25   "Tell it to Sweeney,"] Slang: I don't believe what you say.

100.21–22   Angel of the Crimea] Epitaph given to Florence Nightingale for her nursing work during the Crimean War and, by extension, any heroically compassionate nurse.

100.29   Ariadne?] In Greek mythology, the immortal wife of Dionysus, god of wine. In some tellings Ariadne, a daughter of King Minos of Crete, aided Theseus in his quest to slay the Minotaur and then fled with him aboard his ship. They landed on the island of Naxos, where Theseus abandoned her.

100.40   Gay White Way] Geographically, Broadway in Manhattan between Fortieth and Fifty-Seventh Streets. Figuratively, the theaters along that stretch and along the side streets to the east and west of it. So called for the bright electric lights of the theaters and adjacent businesses and the good times to be had there.

101.12 Jacob "Soldier" Bartfield] Bartfield (1892–1970) was a professional welterweight and middleweight boxer from 1912 to 1923, facing many stiff opponents in the ring but never winning a world title.

101.14 *Stabat Mater*] Thirteenth-century hymn to Mary, portraying her suffering as Jesus's mother during his crucifixion.

101.17 Clyde Fitch] Popular and successful American playwright (1865–1909), who once had five plays running on Broadway at the same time. He was also involved in a collaboration with Edith Wharton to bring her novel *The House of Mirth* to the stage—a critical and commercial flop.

101.23 *The Bohemian Girl.*] English Romantic opera composed by Michael William Balfe with a libretto by Alfred Bunn, and first performed in London in 1843. The plot is loosely based on a Miguel de Cervantes tale, *La Gitanilla*.

101.26 Alt Wien] Café, founded in 1922, in the Innere Stadt section of Vienna.

101.31–32 Gog and Magog] In Celtic lore Gog and Magog are pagan giants. In the Hebrew Bible (Ezekiel 38), Gog is a man, the prophesied enemy of Israel, and Magog is his land of origin. In Genesis 10, Magog is the name of a man and Gog is not mentioned. At some point in the Jewish tradition both Gog and Magog are referred to as men—still Israel's enemies.

103.6 Irish Corn Laws?] Series of measures enacted by Parliament between 1815 and 1846 imposing high tariffs on cereal grains from foreign sources. This protected English growers from competition but left the prices prohibitive for urban dwellers and the rural poor in both Britain and Ireland. The devastations of the Irish famine, finally, led to the repeal of the Corn Laws in 1846.

104.13 *Lady in the Dark*] 1941 Broadway musical with music by Kurt Weill, lyrics by Ira Gershwin, and book by Moss Hart. Starring Gertrude Lawrence and Danny Kaye (whose show-stopping rendition of the patter song "Tschaikowsky" made him a star), it included three dream sequences and introduced the theme of psychoanalysis.

104.19 Sidney Skolsky] Longtime syndicated Hollywood gossip columnist (1902–1983).

105.14–15 George Primrose's Minstrels] Primrose (1852–1919) was a minstrel performer, partnered in a two-act comedy with William H. West.

105.16 Gessler] See note 76.21.

106.6–7 "Stekel] Wilhelm Stekel (1868–1940), Austrian physician, psychologist, and early follower of Sigmund Freud. Stekel did work on dream symbolism and the nature of repression, but in his later years he turned to the study of sexuality itself, including fetishism and perversion.

111.23 Tophet] A term for Hell. In the Hebrew Bible, a place in Jerusalem where practitioners of the ancient Canaanite religion propitiated the gods Moloch and Baal by burning children alive.

113.4 darb] An excellent thing or person.

115.18 Cuba Libres] Cocktail consisting of rum and cola, sometimes adding lime juice, on ice.

117.19 bedirndled] A dirndl was a traditional garment worn by women of southern Germany and Switzerland, consisting of a dress with a tight bodice, featuring an often deep rectangular or round neckline, a wide high-waisted skirt, and an apron. It was modified for the commercial market as everyday off-the-shelf wear, mainly a soft full skirt, pleated and gathered at the waist.

121.1–2 *Amo, Amas . . . Amatis*] Conjugation of the present indicative of the Latin verb "to love."

121.10 Lubitsch] Ernst Lubitsch (1892–1947), legendary movie director working first in Germany and, then, after 1923 in Hollywood, credited with reshaping the narrative style and the look of both silent and sound movies, comedies, and musicals. His use of subtle visual cues to let the audience draw conclusions without need of dialogue or lengthy exposition became known as "The Lubitsch Touch." Among his best-known sound films are *Trouble in Paradise* (1932), *Ninotchka* (1939), and *To Be or Not to Be* (1942).

121.14–17 Nelson Eddy . . . Jeanette MacDonald] See note 65.19–20.

122.5 Nell Brinkley and Leyendecker.] Nell Brinkley (1886–1944), American illustrator and comics artist who created the Brinkley Girl, a feminine, fun-loving working girl (in contrast to the Gibson girl: beautiful but aloof) often portrayed by the illustrator in relationships with handsome gallant suitors. J. C. Leyendecker (1874–1951), painter and the preeminent commercial illustrator of his day, whose "Arrow Collar Man," drawn for the Arrow Shirt Company, appeared in many guises in magazine ads and posters, defining a kind of chiseled, elegant masculinity in the 1920s.

122.25 *bonne bouche*] French: "tasty bite"; a tidbit, an elegant treat.

124.23 *The Perfumed Garden*] Fifteenth-century Arabic sex manual and work of erotic literature, first translated into English (from a French rendering) by Sir Richard Burton in 1886.

124.37 *zäftick*] Yiddish (of a woman): having a round, full, womanly figure; voluptuously proportioned.

125.8 gives him the mitten.] Dismisses or rejects a person. Often said of a lover or suitor, but it can also mean to dismiss a worker; to send someone packing.

125.12–13 Philemon seizes Baucis . . . hammer lock] In Ovid's *Metamorphoses*, Baucis and Philemon are an elderly husband and wife who are the only people in their town to welcome a disguised Zeus and Hera as their guests. As a result, when Zeus decides to destroy the inhospitable town, the couple are allowed to flee the ensuing flood. They request of Zeus that when the time comes for one of them to die, the other would die as well. Upon their death, the couple are changed into an intertwining pair of trees, oak and linden.

125.27 Dutch Cleanser] Brand of pumice-based scouring powder once ubiquitous in kitchens in the United States.

127.8 Leon Leonidoff] Romanian-born choreographer who founded the Isba Russe ballet company. In America he became ballet director at the Capital and Roxy Theaters and later senior producer at Radio City Music Hall, overseeing hundreds of dance extravaganzas during his career.

127.11–12 Greer Garson] Star of stage and screen (1904–1996), particularly known for the eight films in which she was teamed with actor Walter Pidgeon, including *Mrs. Miniver* (1942), for which she won a Best Actress Oscar.

127.14 Brass Rail] Located at 745 Seventh Avenue in Manhattan, the Brass Rail restaurant covered an entire city block between Forty-Ninth and Fiftieth Streets, and spanned five floors. In addition to the restaurant area, there was a café with a full orchestra playing every night, and several bars.

128.1–2 *a groats-worth of wit . . . noddle.*] A groat being a coin of almost no value and a guinea being a coin of substantial value in sixteenth-century England, this expression means "a tiny bit of intelligence ('wit') in a big cranium." *Greene's Groats-worth of Witte, bought with a million of Repentance* was the title of a 1592 pamphlet offered up as written by playwright, poet, and contrarian Robert Greene while he was dying, as repentance for his dissolute life and squandered talents.

129.3–4 heart's deep core?] See William Blake's poem "The Smile" from "The Pickering Manuscript": "And there is a Frown of Frowns / Which you strive to forget in vain, / For it sticks in the Heart's deep Core." See also William Butler Yeats's poem "The Lake Isle of Innisfree," which ends: "I hear it in the deep heart's core."

130.5 *Les jeux sont faits*] French: expression used in casino gambling, e.g., by the croupier at the roulette wheel, to indicate "no more bets." It can also mean reaching a point where there's no going back. Literally "the plays are made."

133.31–32 "St. James Infirmary Blues."] American blues song of unknown origin, which was made famous by Louis Armstrong and Cab Calloway.

134.17 Pecksniff] Seth Pecksniff, a character in Charles Dickens's novel *Martin Chuzzlewit* (1844). A duplicitous manipulator and rascal, Pecksniff thrives on secrecy and snooping while preaching morality.

134.39 Crisco Kid] Cf. the Cisco Kid, whose first appearance, in a 1907 O. Henry story, was as a murderous desperado. But in silent and sound films, comics, radio, and TV, he was always depicted as a gallant *caballero* on the side of law and order along the Texas-Mexico border. Crisco is a brand of shortening used in cooking, made entirely of vegetable oil.

135.20 *Berlin, Year Zero*] Roberto Rossellini's 1948 film was released as *Germania anno zero* in Italian and as *Germany, Year Zero* in English-speaking countries.

135.29 Eric Johnston office] Eric Johnston (1896–1963), president of the Motion Picture Association of America from 1946 until his death, following the tenure of Will Hays. The MPAA's censorship department was tasked to enforce the Production Code established in 1930 and first seriously implemented in 1934, eliminating or modifying, where possible, anything deemed morally or sexually objectionable—anything, in effect, that would create a backlash in public opinion that could jeopardize ticket sales.

136.27 Mr. Burbage,"] Richard Burbage (1568–1619), actor, theater owner, and fellow-shareholder in The Lord Chamberlain's Men (later, The King's Men), Shakespeare's company. Shakespeare wrote most of his greatest tragic parts with Burbage in mind.

136.27–28 Dame Terry] Ellen Terry (1847–1928), renowned English actress of the late nineteenth and early twentieth centuries. She was lauded over the course of three decades for her performances in the great Shakespearean women's roles and, later, for the female leads in the major plays of Shaw and Ibsen.

136.34 *rebozos*] A rebozo is a long flat garment worn mostly by women in Mexico, typically folded or wrapped around the head and upper body to provide shade from the sun. It is also used to carry babies and large bundles.

136.36 *schmoos*] Yiddish: to talk informally, usually in a friendly manner. More commonly spelled "schmooze."

137.6 "Multum in Parvo."] Latin phrase meaning "much in little," "a great deal in a small space."

137.15 trucking shot] More commonly, a tracking shot: in movies, a shot in which a camera is mounted on a conveyance and films while moving.

137.21 shooting through the fire screen] Frequently used example, among technically conservative Hollywood directors, of the silliness of experimental camerawork—placing the camera in a spot where no human point of view was possible. Billy Wilder was known to say, "Who's watching the action through a fire screen? Santa Claus?"

138.20 Jack Armstrong] Character originally created by the General Mills Food Corporation to promote their Wheaties cereal: An "every boy," Jack ate Wheaties and went on adventures around the world. *Jack Armstrong, the All-American Boy*, became a popular radio series (1933–1951) and led to comic books, a movie serial, and a TV series.

138.34 bombardment of Port Arthur] During the Russo-Japanese War (1904–1905), the Japanese navy besieged and heavily shelled Port Arthur, the Russian city and naval base in Manchuria in August 1904. Japan won the siege and the war.

140.9–10   Essex Market Court.] Police court whose premises, built in 1856, were located at the corner of Essex Street and Essex Market Place in lower Manhattan. The court later moved to Second Avenue and East Second Street.

141.28   Threadneedle Street . . . Shanghai Bund] Threadneedle Street, see note 19.6; Shanghai Bund, waterfront area in central Shanghai.

141.34–35   Guy Fawkes . . . infamous Murrel] Guy Fawkes (1570–1606), a member of a group of English Catholics involved in the failed 1605 Gunpowder Plot to blow up the Parliament as part of a wider effort to bring a Catholic monarch to the British throne. Major John André (1750–1780), British army officer and head of its Secret Service in America during the Revolutionary War, who was hanged as a spy by the Continental Army for aiding Benedict Arnold's attempt to surrender the fort at West Point, New York, to the British. John Murrel (1806–1844), a bandit working along the Mississippi River, who twice spent long stretches in prison.

142.24   Hattie Carnegie] Viennese-born fashion entrepreneur (1886–1956) based in New York City from the 1920s to the 1950s.

142.36–37   "*Corpo di Bacco*] Italian: literally "Body of Bacchus." A minced oath, in which rather than offending, by swearing "Body of Christ," the pagan god Bacchus is substituted.

142.40–41   poolroom loafer Hirschfeld . . . last year] Perelman's great friend and collaborator, the caricaturist Al Hirschfeld (1903–2003), accompanied him on a seven-month trip around the world in 1947.

143.2   *Je m'en fiche de Siam.*"] French: I don't care about Siam.

143.14   Norumbega Park?"] Amusement park and recreation area located near Boston, Massachusetts. Its Totem Pole Ballroom became a well-known dancing and entertainment venue for big bands touring during the 1940s.

144.3–4   Lillian Russell balcony."] Russell (1860–1922) was a prominent American actress and singer, admired for her beauty and figure as well as her theatrical talent. Her romantic life was highly publicized: she was married four times and was the mistress of Diamond Jim Brady most of her adult life. "Balcony" is slang for "an ample bosom."

144.31   seven-league boots] In European folklore, a magical character might provide the protagonist with seven-league boots, which would allow the person wearing them to take strides of about twenty-one miles per step, thus speeding up the completion of a difficult task.

144.33   Durbar] Public reception held by an Indian prince or by a British governor or viceroy in India.

145.14   Flents] Brand of earplugs.

146.18   Sir Basil Zaharoff] Greek arms merchant vilified as a merchant of death, and one of the wealthiest men in the world in his lifetime (1849–1936), who often dealt arms to opposing sides in a conflict and was not averse to shipping fake or defective matériel.

146.38 Raines Law] Named after politician John Raines (1840–1909) and passed by the New York State Legislature in 1896, the Raines Law prohibited the sale of alcohol on Sundays (except to guests in hotels). Because of the law's vagaries about what might constitute a hotel and a hotel guest, some saloons were able to add beds, fostering prostitution.

147.6–7 pot-likker] Nonstandard spelling of "pot liquor" in the southern United States. Pot liquor is the liquid left in the pot after boiling greens or beans. It can be reused as stock or a dish in itself, since it is vitamin-rich.

148.1 parasang] Iranian unit of walking distance, equivalent to a league, about three or three and a half miles.

148.37 anopheles mosquito] Mosquito that carries the plasmodium parasite, which causes malaria in humans. It is the bite of the female anopheles that transmits the parasite.

149.4 bêche-de-mer] Sea cucumber, often served boiled or dried in the cuisines of the southwestern Pacific.

149.11 Lapsang Soochong] A black tea originally grown in the mountainous Wuyi region of Fujian province in China.

149.34 Comstock Lode] The first major discovery of silver ore in the United States, the Comstock Lode was discovered in 1859 on the property of Henry Comstock under the eastern slope of Mount Davidson in Nevada (which was then part of the Utah Territory). The rush for the silver mirrored the California Gold Rush ten years earlier.

150.13 *gedämpfte*] German: steamed or stewed.

150.40 Eric Ambler] English author (1909–1998) of thrillers and spy novels, several of them made into films: *The Mask of Dimitrios, Journey into Fear, The Light of Day* (also known as *Topkapi*), to name a few. He also worked as a screenwriter himself (*The Cruel Sea, A Night to Remember*).

151.13 anthropophagi] Greek for "people-eaters." A mythical nation of cannibals living north of Scythia, first described by Herodotus in his *Histories*, Book 4, as *androphagoi*, or "man-eaters." Shakespeare's Othello recounts how he wooed and won Desdemona by telling her of his past hardships, travels, and strange encounters: "And of cannibals that each other eat / The Anthropophagi . . ." (*Othello*, I.iii.143–44).

151.19–20 *Terry and the Pirates*] Action-adventure comic strip created by cartoonist Milton Caniff, which ran from 1934 to 1973 in syndicated newspapers. Terry Lee is an all-American boy who lives in China and thirsts for adventure. He finds constant trouble in the form of the Dragon Lady, the cold, evil queen of the pirates, and her criminal followers. During World War II, Terry grew up and became an American air force pilot and, postwar, worked overseas for the U.S. government.

151.25 Sublime Porte] French translation for the Turkish word *Bâbıâli*, meaning "High Gate," the name for the impressive portal in Constantinople that gave access to the buildings housing all the central government departments of the Ottoman Empire. The term became synonymous with the Imperial government itself.

152.2 *Kochleffel*] Yiddish: a cooking spoon, such as one used in making soup. Figuratively, a person who stirs up trouble; a meddler.

153.6 castle of Otranto] Dark Gothic castle in Horace's Walpole's 1764 novel of the same name. The castle is the scene of strange doings and anguished intrigues about inheritance and bloodlines.

153.13 Russell Birdwell] Birdwell (1903–1977) was one of the most flamboyant and inventive of Hollywood press agents. It was his idea to hire an actress, dressed in widow's black, to put flowers on the grave of Rudolph Valentino on the first anniversary of his death in 1927. This mysterious "Woman in Black" came back each year for decades.

154.25 prahu?"] Type of sailing boat, originating in Malaysia and Indonesia, that may be sailed with either end at the front. It typically has a large triangular sail and an outrigger.

155.7–8 "Brunonia, Mother of Men"] School songs written in celebration of Brown University included "Mother Dear, Brunonia" (1890), with words by Henry R. Palmer. It is likely there was another, similar song entitled "Brunonia, Mother of Men." Perelman attended Brown from 1921 to 1925.

157.13 Hooper ratings] The C. E. Hooper Company was an American company that, starting in 1934, measured radio listenership and then, starting in 1948, television viewership. In 1950, it was bought by the A. C. Nielsen Company, a competitor, which became the ratings giant.

158.26–27 Kay Francis and Paul Henreid] Kay Francis (1905–1968), stage actress and Hollywood star in early Paramount sound films, such as *Trouble in Paradise* (1932) and, after moving to Warner Bros., the studio's highest-paid actress from 1932 to 1936. Paul Henreid (1908–1992), Austrian leading man, immortalized for two Hollywood roles: Jerry Durrance in *Now, Voyager* (his lighting two cigarettes in his mouth at the same time became a fad) and Victor Lazlo in *Casablanca*, both films released in 1942. Francis and Henreid never made a film together.

158.29 aristocratic hauteur Maggie . . . Jiggs] Maggie and Jiggs are the married couple, featured in George McManus's long-running comic strip *Bringing Up Father* (1913–2000). Jiggs, a former hod carrier, has won a million dollars in a sweepstakes but pines for the kind of social and drinking life he previously enjoyed and constantly tries to sneak out to join his old pals.

Maggie, on the other hand, wants to live in accordance with their new wealth, frequently putting on airs in her attempts to do so.

159.14 *enceinte*] French: pregnant.

159.31 *Kaffeeklatsch*] See note 37.14.

161.14 prahus] See note 154.25.

161.32 Borobudur] Ninth-century Mahayana Buddhist temple in Magelang Regency, near the town of Muntilan, in Central Java, Indonesia.

162.3 *coup de main*] French: a sudden, surprise attack.

162.24–25 Charlie Christian] Innovative African American jazz guitarist (1916–1941), influential in both swing bands and the early bebop scene. His skill on the electric guitar, not at the time considered a key instrument, brought fresh sounds to the art form. A member of the Benny Goodman Sextet (1939–1941), Christian died of tuberculosis at the age of twenty-five.

164.6 Lely] Sir Peter Lely (1618–1680), born Pieter van der Faes, a Dutch painter who spent much of his life in England, earning a high reputation as a portrait painter during the reigns of Charles I and Charles II.

164.23 Hirschfeld] The caricaturist Al Hirschfeld (1903–2003), Perelman's friend and collaborator, had traveled to Bali and environs in 1932.

165.9 *rijsttafel.*"] Dutch: rice table. It refers to an elaborate Indonesian meal that can consist of dozens of side dishes, served in small amounts, accompanied by rice prepared in several different ways.

166.1 *Whenas in Sulks . . . Goes*] Cf. Robert Herrick's short poem "Upon Julia's Clothes," the first line of which is "Whenas in silks my Julia goes."

166.13 Chinese Gordon] Nickname for Major General Charles George Gordon (1833–1885), British army officer and administrator who made his military reputation in China putting down the Taiping Rebellion. He was also sometimes referred to as Gordon of Khartoum. Gordon was killed in the Sudan, trying to hold, against orders, a besieged Khartoum against a serious Muslim revolt.

166.20 Cozy Cole] American jazz drummer William Randolph "Cozy" Cole (1909–1981).

166.32 Legong] Balinese dance, characterized by intricate finger movements, complicated footwork, and expressive gestures and facial expressions.

167.30–31 bankrupt . . . Bozo Snyder.] Born Thomas Bleistein, Snyder was a vaudeville and burlesque clown (he had previously worked for the Ringling Bros.). Dubbed "The Man Who Never Speaks," he took the role of Bozo in 1914 as part of a double act in a sketch called "The Piano Movers." Bozo is a silent, shambling figure destined to ridicule and mishap. Snyder continued to perform as Bozo (not to be confused with TV's ebullient clown) until the early 1950s.

168.9 momzer] See note 4.21.

168.34 he jests . . . a wound.] Cf. *Romeo and Juliet*, II.ii.1. Romeo is speaking of Mercutio.

169.6–8 Ivar Kreuger. . . . match king] Swedish engineer, industrialist, and financier (1880–1932) who parlayed a thriving construction business into a fortune in investments. Kreuger controlled more than two-thirds of the world's match production, earning the title "The Match King." Overextended on loans during the Depression, he saw his fortunes begin to unravel, and Kreuger took his own life in Paris in 1932.

169.11–12 generation of vamps . . . Valeska Suratt . . . Clara Kimball Young.] Valeska Suratt (1882–1962), silent film actress who, like Theda Bara, played vamps and exotic characters in most of her eleven movies, all of which are now lost. Clara Kimball Young (1890–1960), silent film actress who mainly played heroines and virtuous women (her casting as a vamp came in real life, when she was accused in a highly publicized divorce case of alienating the affections of film production pioneer Lewis J. Selznick, with whom she was having an affair).

173.24–25 that brave vibration each way free] See the fifth line of Robert Herrick's poem "Upon Julia's Clothes."

174.9 afreets] In Islamic mythology, powerful demons or djinns, often associated with the spirits of the dead.

175.24–25 slippered pantaloons] See 34.18.

175.26 Thuggee] Member of a society of organized assassins in India operating from the thirteenth to nineteenth centuries, part of a fanatic religious group devoted to the Hindu goddess Kali.

175.30 Pecksniff] See note 134.17.

176.15 Pearl White serial.] American actress Pearl White (1889–1938) starred in the popular silent two-reel serial *The Perils of Pauline* (1914), in which the plucky young heroine gets mixed up in dangerous and daring adventures from which she extricates herself.

177.11 dacoits] Members of a band of armed robbers in India or Burma (Myanmar).

177.35 *membrana nictitans*] Transparent or translucent third eyelid, present in some animals, that can be drawn across the eye to protect and moisten it while maintaining vision.

178.19 ginzo] Slang (derogatory): a person of Italian descent.

179.15   highbinders] Members of any of various Chinese American secret societies active primarily from the mid-nineteenth to early twentieth centuries,
often involved in criminal activities such as prostitution, blackmail, and hired
killings.

182.1   *Chewies the Goat . . . Need Hypo*] Cf. the unmistakable compressed
lingo of *Variety*, the Hollywood trade newspaper. The "translation" might be
something like "Concession candy is being blamed, but the movies themselves
need a shot in the arm" if ticket sales are to increase.

182.20   Hawkshaw] A detective. The word derives from the name of the lead
character in a long-running (1913–1947) Sunday comic strip, *Hawkshaw the
Detective*.

184.27–28   Randolph Scott] American actor (1898–1987) who epitomized the
strong, silent cowboy hero in many Hollywood Westerns, though he occasionally and effectively took on roles as more sophisticated urban types.

184.30   Greer Garson] See note 127.11–12.

184.38–39   Karl Dane and George K. Arthur] Dane (1886–1934) and Arthur
(1899–1965) had separate thriving careers as character actors in silent films, but
in the late 1920s they teamed up for a series of silent short film comedies and
a comedy act on the vaudeville circuit.

185.32   Brod Crawford] Broderick Crawford (1911–1986), American stage,
screen, and television actor whose burly looks and gruff, volatile persona led
him to success in both drama—a Best Actor Oscar for *All the King's Men*
(1949)—and comedy (*Born Yesterday*, 1950).

185.39   Charles Coburn] Portly American actor (1877–1961) who played iras-
cible but lovable fathers and grandfathers in dozens of Hollywood movies. He
won a Best Supporting Actor Oscar for *The More the Merrier* (1943).

188.1   *Salesman, Spare that Psyche*] Cf. "Woodman, spare that tree!", the first
line of an 1830 poem by George Hope Morris, commonly anthologized in
collections of poems for children.

188.21   Adam's off ox.] The "off ox" is the ox on the right-hand side of a
paired team, the side away from the human driver of the team, who walks
next to the left-hand ox and therefore becomes familiar with its ways. To be
unfamiliar with Adam's off ox is one step beyond not being able to recognize
the biblical first man. During one of the "never born" sequences in *It's a Wonderful Life* (1946), Nick the bartender uses the expression to emphasize to
George Bailey that he doesn't know him.

189.8   Hope or Skelton] Comedians Bob Hope (1903–2003) and "Red" Skelton (1913–1997).

195.16   Dr. Kildare] James Kildare, a fictional idealistic young doctor created
by author Max Brand in 1936. Dr. Kildare stories quickly moved on to the

screen, starting in 1937, and blossomed into a nine-film MGM series, starring Lew Ayres, in 1938. Amidst the competing claims and personalities surrounding him in the hospital and beyond, Kildare brings his compassion and medical understanding. Dr. Kildare also set off for small screen fame in the 1960s, with a long-running, eponymous television series starring Richard Chamberlain.

202.4 Joyce Hawley] Briefly a Broadway showgirl, Hawley appeared in *The Greenwich Village Follies* for five months in 1925–26. In 1926 she famously posed nude in a tub of champagne (from which men drank) at a party given by the producer Earl Carroll at his Earl Carroll Theater in New York that resulted in a highly publicized Prohibition trial after details of the party were reported in the papers. (Carroll was found guilty of perjury.)

209.29 Barney Oldfield] Pioneering automobile racer (1878–1946). Oldfield's name was synonymous with speed. In 1903, he became the first man to drive a car sixty miles an hour around a circular one-mile track.

211.5–6 pile Pelion upon Ossa] See note 70.30.

211.35 Willie Baxter] Callow teenage protagonist of Booth Tarkington's best-selling novel *Seventeen* (1916).

212.16 Newgate Calendar] Originally a mid-eighteenth-century monthly bulletin of its executions, put out by London's Newgate Prison. The title was quickly appropriated by the publishing world for chapbooks narrating and embellishing the exploits of notorious outlaws and criminals. Later bound into volumes, with the subtitle "The Malefactors' Bloody Register," they were among the most popular books of the late eighteenth and early nineteenth centuries.

215.5–6 Weissmuller."] Johnny Weissmuller (1904–1984), American athlete and winner of five Olympic gold medals for swimming in the 1920s; after his retirement from competitive sports, he became famous for portraying the title character in the Tarzan movies of the 1930s and 1940s.

216.1–2 *When to the Sessions . . . Films . . .*] Cf. first line of Shakespeare's Sonnet XXX.

216.8 Dario Resta's Peugeot] Italian-born British race car driver Resta (1884–1924) won the 1916 Indianapolis 500, as well as many other high-profile races en route to claiming the United States National Driving Championship that year. He died in England, age forty, when his car crashed while he was trying to break the land speed record.

216.12–13 gopher mob] The Gopher Gang was an Irish American mob, centered in Hell's Kitchen, that ran the criminal rackets in a large swath of Manhattan's West Side from the 1890s to World War I. It is unclear whether Perelman is picking up a generic term then in use. The Gopher Gang did employ younger apprentice gangs to do some of their dirty work—one dubbed "The Baby Gophers."

220.13–14 Louise Fazenda] American film actress (1895–1962), who appeared mainly in silent film comedies. She retired after appearing in a supporting role in *The Old Maid* (1939).

220.21 Alfred Russel Wallace] British naturalist, explorer, and biologist (1823–1913), best known for independently conceiving the theory of evolution through natural selection; his paper on the subject was jointly published with some of Charles Darwin's writings in 1858.

221.24 Boob McNutt] Clumsy, well-meaning character created by American cartoonist Rube Goldberg (1883–1970) in his long-running comic strip of the same name (1918–1934). Boob tries to perform task after task entrusted to him by other people, but always winds up destroying whatever he touches. Goldberg's famously byzantine contraptions are sometimes featured as part of the chaos.

222.20 Zbyszko hammer lock] Jan Stanisław Cyganiewicz (1879–1967), known by his ring name Stanislaus Zbyszko, was a dominating Polish heavy-weight wrestler in the early decades of the twentieth century, twice heavy-weight champion of the world.

224.1 *Dhoti*] A type of sarong that outwardly resembles trousers; part of the national or ethnic costume of men on the subcontinent of India.

224.9 Julio] Groucho Marx (1890–1977), born Julius Henry Marx.

226.4 *blanchisseur*] French: launderer.

232.19 poll] Slang: the top of the head; the pate.

233.14 H. B. Warner's] English actor (1876–1958) famous in the silent film era for his portrayal of Christ in Cecil B. DeMille's *The King of Kings* (1927). Warner later became a prolific character actor in talkies (Mr. Gower, the druggist, in Frank Capra's 1946 film *It's a Wonderful Life*).

234.14 Golden Hind] English galleon under the command of Francis Drake (c. 1540–1596), best known for its privateering circumnavigation of the globe from 1577 to 1580.

235.16 *blanchisseuse*] French: laundress.

235.39 lotus-eaters] In Greek mythology, inhabitants of an island who eat the leaves of the lotus tree, which induces a blissful lethargy and forgetfulness. In *The Odyssey*, Book IX, Odysseus encounters such a tribe during his return from Troy. See also Alfred, Lord Tennyson's eponymous poem.

236.7 *Heimweh*] German: homesickness.

237.8 tragedies of D'Annunzio] Gabriele D'Annunzio (1863–1938), one of Italy's most esteemed novelists and poets in the three decades leading up to World War I, who also wrote nine plays (tragedies) that rely on D'Annunzio's characteristic high rhetoric, rather than dramatic action.

238.6–7   relief of Lucknow.] The British Residency in the city of Lucknow, India was besieged by mutinous Indian troops in 1857. In the second of two relief attempts made by British forces, the defenders and civilians were evacuated from the Residency, which was then abandoned.

239.21   Fletcherizing] Horace Fletcher (1849–1919) was an American food faddist who proposed that each morsel of food should be chewed thoroughly, even until liquefied, before swallowing, for optimal absorption. Thomas Edison, Mark Twain, William James, and Franz Kafka were among those who took up the practice.

245.27   Jan Peerce's] Jan Peerce (1904–1984), Metropolitan Opera tenor who also recorded popular tunes and sentimental favorites.

247.10–11   Dawn Patrol Barbershop] Located at 816 Seventh Avenue, between West Fifty-Second and Fifty-Third Streets, the so-called Dawn Patrol Barbershop employed ten barbers, and was open from 8:30 A.M. until midnight. It flourished in the 1950s and 1960s. Haircuts cost around two dollars.

247.19–20   "In your beauty . . . Astolat."] In Arthurian legend, Astolat is a legendary town and castle—home of Elaine, "the lily maid of Astolat," as well as of her father, Sir Bernard, and her brothers, Lavaine and Tirre. Tennyson gives it the name "Shalott" in his poem "The Lady of Shalott," whose heroine, Elaine, imprisoned in an island tower, spends her time dreaming of love.

248.27   Fitzpatrick travel talk] Known as "The Voice of the Globe," James A. Fitzpatrick (1894–1980) produced over 300 travel documentary shorts, from 1930 to 1954. Distributed by MGM, they were known collectively as "Fitzpatrick Travel Talks" and focused on the picturesque aspects of the countries visited rather than on people and social customs.

249.9   Packey McFarland] Patrick "Packey" McFarland (1888–1936), American lightweight and welterweight boxer. Despite an extraordinary record—seventy wins, five draws, and no losses—he was unable to secure a match for either world title.

250.13–14   *femme soignée*] French: neat, well-groomed, immaculate woman.

250.14   *vieux jeu*] See note 36.18.

250.28   Worumbo] Textile mill located in Lisbon Falls, Maine, and a clothing brand.

250.35   Danton Walker] Danton Walker (1899–1960), wrote a widely syndicated celebrity and gossip column, "Broadway," for *The New York Daily News*. He trawled the nightclubs in search of tidbits. Earlier, he had briefly been secretary to drama critic and wit Alexander Woollcott and to *The New Yorker*'s founding editor, Harold Ross.

256.4   Rumpelmayer's] A popular European-style tea and pastry café located on the ground floor of the St. Moritz Hotel on the corner of Sixth Avenue and Central Park South in New York City. It opened in 1930 and closed in 1998. Over the years it expanded its service to include lunch and dinner as well.

256.5 *Gugelhupfe*] A yeast-based cake, often including raisins, traditionally baked in a distinctive circular Bundt mold.

256.6 Sir Alexander Korda] Hungarian-born British producer and distributor (1893–1956), one of the founders of the British sound-film industry. Korda established his own film studio, London Films, whose triumphs included *The Private Life of Henry VIII* (1933), *Rembrandt* (1936), *The Thief of Baghdad* (1940), and *The Third Man* (1949), which Korda coproduced with David O. Selznick. He also had a fruitful career as a silent film director in Hungary, Vienna, and Hollywood.

256.12 *Dobos Torte*] Hungarian sponge cake layered with chocolate buttercream and topped with caramel.

258.2 ginzos] See note 178.19.

258.28–31 Titanus Films . . . Lollobrigida as the Duchess of Alba.] After further delays, Titanus made and released this film as *The Naked Maja* (1958), starring Anthony Franciosa as Goya and Ava Gardner as the Duchess of Alba.

260.1 Breen office] The censorship division of the Motion Picture Producers and Distributors of America was headed by Joseph Breen from 1934 to 1954. See also note 12.25.

261.14 Braganzas] Family dynasty that held the monarchial throne in Portugal from 1640 to 1910, and in independent Brazil from 1822 to 1889.

279.9 Rod La Rocque] American actor (1898–1969) whose expressive good looks made him a star of the silent era, although he was able to transition to the talkies.

280.3 Crokinole] Board game, something like shuffleboard in the round, in which small discs are flipped toward a central area in an effort to score maximum points. Opponents try to knock the discs out into lower point areas or off the board.

287.24 Vincent Youmans] American Broadway composer (1898–1946). Among his best-known melodies are "Tea for Two," "I Want to Be Happy," and "More Than You Know."

288.33 King Cole] While Perelman may allude to the character Old King Cole in the British nursery rhyme of the same name or singer Nat "King" Cole, more probably he refers to the talented pitcher (20–4 in 1910) Leonard "King" Cole (1886–1916), who flourished with the Chicago Cubs from 1909 to 1911. Ring Lardner wrote about Cole in several articles for *The Sporting News* and used the material in his "Alibi Ike" stories.

290.1 *This is the Forest Primeval?*] See the opening words of Henry Wadsworth Longfellow's long narrative poem *Evangeline* (1847).

290.10   D'Annunzio] See note 237.8.

290.25   Mildred Natwick] Versatile stage, screen, and TV actress (1905–1994). She was nominated twice for the Tony Award and once for an Oscar as Best Supporting Actress in the role of Corie Bratter's mother in *Barefoot in the Park* (1967).

291.9   Tootal] Brand name for a line of British ties, scarves, and other garments.

291.37–38   Landseer's dogs] Sir Edwin Henry Landseer (1802–1873) was a British artist noted for his paintings of horses, stags, and dogs, the last of which he often depicted as possessing human feelings and qualities. A variety of Newfoundland dog is named for him.

295.20–21   Eleanora Sears] Eleanora Randolph Sears (1881–1968), American tennis champion of the 1910s. She won the United States Women's National Doubles Championship four times, and was also a champion squash player and a prominent competitive horsewoman in show-jumping.

299.31–32   *The Garrick Gaieties*] 1925 musical revue with melodies by Richard Rodgers and lyrics by Lorenz Hart. Their first Broadway hit, it included the still-popular song "Manhattan" ("We'll have Manhattan, / the Bronx and Staten / Island too. . . .")

300.1–2   *cauchemar*] French: nightmare.

300.2   *Sherry Flip*] Perelman tells the story of some failed attempts to give a name to this unproduced revue (to which he made a minor contribution) in his Dorothy Parker reminiscence included in this volume (see pages 490 to 491).

300.31–32   Daniel Frohman] American theatrical producer and manager and film producer (1851–1940).

300.38   Bachrach] Family name of a multigenerational photography business that has photographed celebrities, scientists, politicians, and heads of state since 1868. At its height in 1929, Bachrach Studios had forty-eight locations in the United States.

302.11   ZaSu Pitts] American actress (1894–1963) whose career spanned six decades. She took on the tragic role of her career as Trina Sieppe in Eric von Stroheim's *Greed* (1924). With the emergence of sound, she established a screen persona as a fretful spinster.

302.25   *estocada*] Spanish: the thrust of the sword by the matador into the bull in the final stage of a bullfight, designed to kill the bull.

303.33   George Antheil] American avant-garde composer, pianist, and inventor (1900–1959) whose modernist compositions explored musical, industrial, and mechanical sounds of his time. His *Ballet Mécanique* (1925) was originally scored for sixteen synchronized player pianos to which were added electronic bells, a siren, and three airplane propellers. In 1941, he co-invented and patented, with actress Hedy Lamarr, a system for guiding torpedos to their targets, bypassing enemy radio wave interference through a variable system of signals called "frequency hopping." The technology was not used by the U.S. military during World War II, but in later years, the frequency hopping concept became a building block of spread spectrum technology—the basis for Bluetooth and the wireless phone.

304.5   Jetta Goudal] Dutch American silent film actress (1891–1985) whose career ended prematurely after she successfully sued Cecil B. DeMille for breach of contract when he fired her for being difficult. She retired from acting in 1932.

305.22   Winchell] Walter Winchell (1897–1972), powerful newspaper and radio gossip columnist, New Deal supporter turned Joseph McCarthy supporter and red-baiter, and maker and breaker of reputations, including his own.

305.32–34   Sir Arthur Wing Pinero . . . your turkeys.] English actor turned enormously prolific playwright (1855–1934). He wrote highly successful farces and drawing-room comedies in the 1880s and early 1890s, then turned to drama, where he continued to have some success, but by the second decade of the twentieth century his theatrical fortunes had declined.

307.1   *Revulsion in the Desert*] Cf. T. E. Lawrence's book *Revolt in the Desert* (1926).

307.13   Mario Buccellati] Italian designer of high-end jewelry and watches with retail stores in Milan, Rome, and Florence. In 1954 he opened a New York City store on Fifth Avenue.

308.27   Congreve, Pirandello, and Norman Krasna] William Congreve (1670–1729), English playwright renowned for his comedies of manners, including *Love for Love* (1695) and *The Way of the World* (1700). Luigi Pirandello (1867–1936), Italian playwright, short story writer, and novelist whose expressionistic plays such as *Six Characters in Search of an Author* (1921) and *Henry IV* (1922) transformed twentieth-century drama and explored psychological depths below social realities. Norman Krasna (1909–1984), American screenwriter and playwright as well as a producer and director whose scriptwriting credits include *Mr. & Mrs. Smith* (1941), *White Christmas* (1954), *Indiscreet* (1958), and *Sunday in New York* (1963), the last two based on his own plays.

309.13   Lionel Atwill] English stage and film actor (1885–1946) who worked in America after World War I. He had a variety of leading roles on Broadway in comedies, dramas, and classics, before appearing in horror films in the 1930s and 1940s—*Doctor X, Son of Frankenstein*, and *House of Dracula*—as well as more high-budget pictures, in which he portrayed villainous characters.

310.7   *cafard*] French: melancholia; depression.

315.12   Grossinger's and the Concord] Resorts in the southern part of New York's Catskill Mountains, commonly known as "The Borscht Belt." With hundreds of other resorts in the region, they catered primarily to Jews and flourished from the late 1940s into the 1970s.

315.19–20   *megillah*] Yiddish: a long, involved story or sequence of events.

315.24–25   Columbia Wheel . . . Izzy Herk time] Columbia Wheel, informal name for The Columbia Amusement Company, which arranged burlesque company bookings in American theaters from 1902 to 1927. Gus Sun (1868–1959), booking agent for lower-level vaudeville theaters in the Midwest, beginning in 1906. Isidore Herk (1882–1944), burlesque show manager and producer, whose career began well before World War I and largely ended when his "Burlesque on Broadway" was closed down in 1941.

315.30   shimmy like my sister Kate] See "I Wish that I Could Shimmy Like My Sister Kate," a 1922 up-tempo song, about the "shimmy," a popular dance move in which the body is stationary, but the left and right shoulders alternate moving back and forth. Later, hips got into the action.

316.1   "Irish Justice," . . . "Flugel Street"—] "Irish Justice" was any burlesque sketch that included a judge wielding a pig bladder and striking all and sundry with it (lawyers, defendants, witnesses) to shut them up. "Flugel Street" was any burlesque routine in which a hapless man on a city street has a series of unprovoked, hostile encounters with passersby, after merely asking for directions or minding his own business. Abbott and Costello's famous "Susquehanna Hat Company" routine is a "Flugel Street" routine.

317.9–10   Lennie Lyons] Leonard Lyons (1906–1976), longtime New York newspaper columnist, who covered a whole range of social and political matters, but most often reported on the doings of celebrities from the movie and theater worlds.

317.31–32   *tzimmas*] Yiddish (slang): an uproar; making a mountain out of a molehill.

317.33   Sardi's East] Vincent Sardi, Sr., (1885–1969), opened his famous Broadway theater district restaurant at 234 West Forty-Fourth Street in 1927. In 1958, he opened Sardi's East, serving French food, at 123 East Fifty-Fourth Street. He sold it in 1968.

318.15   *drehdel*] A four-sided top used in a children's game, typically at Hanukkah. Players spin the top, which has a different Hebrew letter on each face. Depending on which letter faces up when the drehdel stops, a token of some kind is given or taken. Adults may play for money. Here, Perelman uses the word to mean something like "the kicker" or perhaps "the unusual spin."

319.12–13   *East Lynne*] 1861 best-selling English novel by Ellen Wood, remembered chiefly for its elaborate, implausible plot centering on infidelity and double identities.

319.16 Albolene] Brand of moisturizing cream.

319.30–31 sun in the morning . . . at night.] See the song "I Got the Sun in the Morning and the Moon at Night" from Irving Berlin's 1946 Broadway show *Annie Get Your Gun.*

320.18 Sol Hurok] Russian-born American impresario (1888–1974) who managed many of the greatest artists in the worlds of classical music and ballet. In 1959 he arranged for the Bolshoi Ballet to come to America for the first time since the Russian Revolution.

320.22 Mary Garden or Schumann-Heink] Mary Garden (1874–1967), Scottish soprano who had a fruitful career in both America and France; Ernestine Schumann-Heink (1861–1936), Austrian-born American contralto noted for her tremendous vocal range.

320.29 Louis Nizer's] Louis Nizer (1902–1994), noted American trial lawyer who was the advocate of choice in many high-profile divorce cases, but also in highly charged cases involving issues of libel and free speech. Nizer represented broadcaster John Henry Faulk in his suit against AWARE, a right-wing organization that falsely accused Faulk of being a Communist. His successful 1957 suit (adjudicated in 1962) augured the end of the blacklist.

323.3–4 Hanson W. Baldwin] Military analyst and author (1903–1991) long associated with *The New York Times.* Baldwin won a 1943 Pulitzer Prize for his coverage of the early days of World War II.

325.3 *figliuolo*] Italian: son.

325.13 *Che riso sardonico!*] Italian: What bitter sarcasm!

325.21 Amy Lowell's] Amy Lowell (1874–1925), prolific poet, proponent of modernism, and an advocate for and practitioner of free verse. To the consternation of poet Ezra Pound, she declared herself an "Imagist" and pushed forward her notion of it in America. She won the Pulitzer Prize for Poetry in 1925, the year of her death.

329.9 Lew Cody] American stage and film actor (1888–1934) who played in silent films and early sound films. He gained notoriety in the late 1910s for playing "male vamps."

335.12 afreet] See note 174.9.

339.35 Karsh?] Yousuf Karsh (1908–2002), noted Armenian Canadian portrait photographer whose images of Winston Churchill and other world leaders, as well as of writers and actors, are still widely reproduced.

343.5–6 Surtees' English sporting squires—] R. S. Surtees (1805–1864), an English comic novelist whose plots revolve around fox-hunting and shooting in northeast England. His most enduring character, Jorrocks, is a rough, coarse, sport-loving cockney grocer, who becomes the squire of Hillingdon Hall.

343.12–13 Newman's *Apologia pro Vita Sua*] The spiritual autobiography of John Henry Newman (1801–1890), English Anglican clergyman who converted to Catholicism in 1845. The book (Latin for "In Defense of My Life") was published in 1864.

346.17 *David Ogilvy*] Ogilvy (1911–1999), a British advertising executive and guru of the art of marketing, was a founding partner of Ogilvy, Benson & Mather, a top New York advertising agency. He wrote the frequently consulted books *Ogilvy on Advertising* and *Confessions of an Advertising Man*.

346.26 *Mr. Gotrox*] Stock character surname for a rich person. Also spelled "Gotrocks."

349.8–10 dog's name? . . . Garryowen] Name of pub owner Barney Kiernan's "mangy mongrel," who chases after Leopold Bloom at the end of Chapter XII of James Joyce's *Ulysses*. There was a real championship Irish red setter by that name in the 1870s.

349.11 gombeen] Term used in Ireland for a shady, small-time businessman or politician who is always looking to make a quick profit, often at someone else's expense, or by accepting bribes.

349.15 Myles na gCopaleen] Irish pen name of Brian O'Nolan (1911–1966), used when he published his satirical columns in *The Irish Times*, beginning in 1940. When O'Nolan published books in English, he chose a different pen name—Flann O'Brien—and turned out several highly regarded comic novels, including *At Swim-Two-Birds* (1939) and *The Dalkey Archive* (1964).

349.39 *resembling Eamon de Valera*] American-born de Valera (1882–1975) was an Irish revolutionary and the first president of the Irish Republic. He was an imposing figure in person, standing six foot three.

351.1 *The Sweet Chick Gone*] Cf. *The Sweet Cheat Gone*, the title of C. K. Scott Moncrieff's English translation of *Albertine disparue*, the sixth volume of Proust's *À la recherche du temps perdu*. Moncrieff takes as his title the last line of Walter de la Mare's poem "Ghost."

351.2–3 Born Free, Ring of Bright Water] Two nonfiction books (and, later, movies), both published in 1960, with animals for protagonists: Elsa the lioness in Joy Adamson's *Born Free*, and Mijbil the otter in Gavin Maxwell's *Ring of Bright Water*.

354.2 *Confidential*] Founded by New York journalist George Harrison, *Confidential* was a leading celebrity gossip magazine, published from 1952 to 1978.

354.32 George Abbott] Abbott (1887–1995) was a theater and film producer as well as a highly sought-after Broadway director, possessing a talent for shaping a show and making it a hit.

354.37–38 agreement . . . with Gerold Frank] American biographer Gerold Frank (1907–1998) was the author of books about the Boston Strangler and

Judy Garland as well as a pioneer of the as-told-to celebrity autobiography. *Zsa Zsa Gabor: My Story* appeared in 1960.

355.21 Sol Hurok] See note 320.18.

355.22 David Susskind] American TV, film, and stage producer (1920–1987), who also hosted a TV talk show (called *Open End* from 1961 to 1966, and *The David Susskind Show* from 1966 to 1986), focusing on crucial and controversial social and political issues of the day. Susskind's openly and self-proclaimed liberal views were often vigorously challenged on these programs by those to both his right and left on the political spectrum.

355.25–26 John Barkham and Virgilia Peterson] John Barkham (1908–1998), American syndicated writer for *Time, The New York Times Book Review, The New York World-Telegram,* and *The New York Post.* Virgilia Peterson (1904–1966), book reviewer for *The New York Herald-Tribune* and *The New York Times,* and host of the TV show *Author Meets Critics* from 1952 to 1954.

355.27 Bernard Geis Associates] Bernard J. Geis (1909–2001) was a New York–based publisher known for publishing and aggressively promoting celebrity memoirs as well as fiction and nonfiction with a modern sexual angle. Jacqueline Susann's *Valley of the Dolls* and Helen Gurley Brown's *Sex and the Single Girl* were both Geis publications. Bernard Geis Associates operated from 1959 to the 1970s.

357.1–2 *Nobody Knows . . . but Croesus*] Cf. "Nobody Knows the Trouble I've Had," African American spiritual from the slavery period, whose lyrics were first published in 1867. The lyrics have varied in many recorded versions, but the most familiar opening lines are "Nobody knows the trouble I've seen / Nobody knows but Jesus."

357.11 Leonard Lyons'] See note 317.9–10.

357.26 Calouste Gulbenkian] British Armenian businessman (1869–1955) who played a major role in making the petroleum reserves of the Middle East available to Western development. He is credited with being the first person to exploit Iraqi oil.

357.32 Maggie and Jiggs] See note 158.29.

358.4 *estancias . . . Porfirio Díaz*] See note 4.38. Porfirio Díaz (1830–1915) was a Mexican general elected president of the country seven times, ruling, in effect, from 1877 to 1911. His regime assumed power in the name of reform and the promise of rational technocratic solutions, but his policies favored wealthy landowners, as well as investors, both domestic and foreign.

358.35–36 River Rouge] Ford Motor Company's auto plant on River Rouge, southwest of Detroit, Michigan, was the largest integrated factory in the world when it fully opened in 1928, coming to symbolize both industrial automation at its most advanced and the assembly-line system at its most demoralizing. Attempts to organize a labor union there in 1937 were met with violence.

359.15 *Mammalia ponderosa*] A Perelmanism: large-breasted (women).

359.22 Snedens Landing] Hamlet in Rockland County, New York, along the Hudson River. It has long been a sought-after residence for artists, writers, and actors. E. B. and Katharine White, Noël Coward, John Dos Passos, Orson Welles, and Laurence Olivier rented summer homes there in Perelman's lifetime.

360.16 Andy Devine] Devine (1905–1977) was a large, heavyset American character actor, known for his raspy voice. Cast mainly in Westerns, he typically played slow—and often slow-witted—but lovable hayseeds.

360.31–2 *vitelloni*] Italian (slang): young mischief makers, pranksters.

361.29 Barbara La Marr] American screenwriter turned silent-film star (1896–1926) who earned the moniker "The Girl Too Beautiful." She made twenty-seven films in her short film career, married four times, and died of complications of tuberculosis at the age of twenty-nine.

363.37 Sidney Skolsky] See note 104.19.

365.1 *Three Loves Had I*] Cf. first line of Shakespeare's Sonnet CXLIV.

365.18 *Nymph Errant*] 1933 Cole Porter musical that never had a Broadway run and never became a film. Based on a book considered "too English" for American success, it launched in London's West End, running for 154 performances.

366.16 Nell Brinkley's Adonises] See note 122.5.

367.36–37 Dashiell Hammett's dictum . . . the patter,"] Said of Wilmer Cook, Casper Gutman's two-bit henchman in *The Maltese Falcon* (1929).

368.32 Dion O'Banion and Bugs Moran] Chicago mobsters who ran afoul of Al Capone's syndicate—their sometime partner in crime. O'Banion (1892–1924) was gunned down in his flower shop. George "Bugs" Moran (1893–1957), who died in Leavenworth Prison, was not present at the 1929 Saint Valentine's Day Massacre, in which seven members of his gang were shot and killed.

369.11 *Schlagobers*] German: whipped cream, usually sweetened or flavored, often put into coffee.

369.17–18 *Fifty Million Frenchmen, Lady, Be Good, Roberta, A Connecticut Yankee*] Successful Broadway musicals by Cole Porter, George and Ira Gershwin, Jerome Kern and Otto Harbach, and Richard Rodgers and Lorenz Hart, respectively.

372.24 Lina Cavalieri and Gaby Deslys] Cavalieri (1874–1944) was a gifted American opera soprano, sometimes called by admiring contemporaries "the most beautiful woman in the world." Approaching her fortieth birthday, she published an advice book, *My Secrets of Beauty*. She also created the Institut de

Beauté in Paris and sold her own brand of perfume, "Mona Lina." Gaby Deslys (1881–1920) was a singer and actress, renowned for her beauty.

372.25–26   Jess Willard . . . Count Boni de Castellane.] Jess Willlard (1881–1968), exceedingly tall, powerful American heavyweight boxer who took the championship from Jack Johnson in 1915 and lost it to Jack Dempsey in 1919. Count Boni di Castellane (1867–1932), French nobleman and aesthete remembered for his opulent lifestyle and marriage to nineteen-year-old American railroad heiress Anna Gould, which ended acrimoniously in divorce eleven years later.

377.13–14   Dame Nellie Melba nor Lily Langtry] Dame Nellie Melba (1861–1931), Australian operatic soprano made Dame Commander of the British Empire in 1918 for her spectacular fundraising for war charities during World War I. Lillie Langtry (1853–1929), British American beauty, socialite, and actress who was briefly the mistress of Albert, Prince of Wales, later King Edward VII, and had several highly publicized and scandalous relationships with other men of rank and riches.

378.34–35   Edmund Burke denouncing Warren Hastings] In 1788, Edmund Burke led the prosecution against Warren Hastings, the East India Company's first governor-general, for crimes his administration committed in India. The impeachment of Hastings opened with Burke's four-day-long denunciation before the House of Lords. Hastings was eventually acquitted in 1795.

379.28   Peaches Browning] Peaches (née Frances Belle Heenan) and realestate tycoon Edward "Daddy" Browning became one of the largest media sensations of post–World War I America when in 1926 the two began dating and then married weeks later. The aging Browning admitted to being fifty-one at the time, while Peaches was just fifteen. Six months later, Peaches fled the marriage, resulting in a highly publicized trial. After revelations—including a honking pet African goose kept in the marriage bedroom—Edward was granted a legal separation.

380.29   ZaSu Pitts] See note 302.11.

THE BEAUTY PART

385.1   THE BEAUTY PART] An expression less familiar today than it was in Perelman's lifetime: the most appealing aspect of any situation.

389.29   kreplach] In Ashkenazi Jewish cuisine: small dumplings filled with ground meat, mashed potatoes, or some other filling, usually boiled and served in soup, though they can be served fried as well.

391.10   I felt that in my heart's deep core.] Likely Perelman is misremembering the last line of W. B. Yeats's poem "The Lake Isle on Innisfree," which reads "I hear it in the deep heart's core." The phrase "Heart's deep Core" appears in William Blake's poem "The Smile."

391.16–17 Skull and Bones] One of three secret societies of Yale undergraduate seniors. Its alumni tend to be among the most well-placed and powerful in their fields.

394.20–21 colored gentleman in the woodpile.] Some fact of considerable importance that is not disclosed. Here, Milo Weatherwax employs a cleaned-up version of an expression once common in America and England and in Perelman's lifetime already objectionable. Its origins date back at least to the mid-nineteenth century.

398.4 Old Rabbinical] Brand of kosher wine.

399.9–10 *Mrs. Malaprop*] Aunt who gets mixed up in the schemes of the young lovers in Richard Brinsley Sheridan's 1775 comedy of manners *The Rivals*. She often uses an incorrect word to express herself. The term *malapropism* is derived from her name.

400.3 Airedale] Slang: a fool or a pest.

401.35 *Quien sabe corazon?*] Spanish: Who knows, my love?

402.25 *Christmas Tigers*] A "Christmas Tiger" is someone who does exactly as they're told, without asking questions. Jefferson Smith, young appointed senator in the movie *Mr. Smith Goes to Washington* (1939), is called that, at first, by the Washington press corps, who assume he'll vote as he is instructed.

403.17 *Mesdames Luce and Cowles*] Clare Booth Luce (1903–1987), American playwright (*The Women*), war correspondent, congresswoman, and U.S. Ambassador. She was married to Henry Luce, the media mogul and founder of *Time* magazine and its empire. Fleur Cowles (1908–2009), American writer, advertising executive, editor, and artist, best known as the creative force behind the short-lived, lavish lifestyle magazine *Flair* (1950). Perelman lampooned her in a 1950 *New Yorker* piece, calling her "Hyacinth Beddoes Laffoon." Hyacinth reappears here in *The Beauty Part*.

405.11 Sullivan Law] In reaction to an increase in street crime in New York City, the state legislature passed the Sullivan Act in 1911. The law required licenses for New Yorkers to possess firearms small enough to be concealed. Private possession of such firearms without a license was a misdemeanor, and carrying them in public was a felony.

414.9–10 *KNOCK at door,* HARRY HUBRIS *enters*] The bulk of the rest of this scene is a revision and expansion of Perelman's piece "Portrait of the Artist as a Young Mime," included in this volume.

419.20 zook] In tramp slang, an old prostitute. But here, most likely "women available for sex."

422.30 ambiente] Italian: environment, surrounding space.

423.10 memoirs of Polly Adler?] Adler (1900–1962) ran a celebrated bordello at 215 West Seventy-Fifth Street in Manhattan from 1924 to 1944. Politicians, mobsters, actors, and writers—both male and female—were her patrons. Her book of memoirs, *A House Is Not a Home*, was published in 1953.

429.18   got to be there fustest with the mostest—*vershsteh?*] Cf. military maxim, coined by Confederate general Nathan Bedford Forrest (1821–1877): "Git thar fustest with the mostest." *Vershsteh* is Yiddish for "understand."

434.23   *Vuss?*] Yiddish: What?

438.13   Grace Metalious . . . Mother Goose!] Metalious (1924–1964) was an American popular novelist and author of the 1956 runaway best seller *Peyton Place*. Its depictions of the narrow-mindedness, pruderies, vanities, and hypocrisies of a small New England town—particularly when it came to things sexual—were considered daring for a conventional, mainstream work of fiction at the time.

439.28   *schluss*] Yiddish: enough, finished, a done deal.

441.6   momzer] See note 4.21.

442.20   *Edith Cavell*] British nurse (1865–1915) who, working in German-occupied Belgium during World War I, treated the wounded of both sides. The Germans accused her of aiding the escape of British soldiers—a charge she admitted to. She was convicted of treason and, despite international protest, executed by firing squad. Her execution became fodder for the Allied propaganda against German brutality.

453.14–15   sweetest little head . . . Helen Twelvetrees.] Twelvetrees (1908–1958) was an American actress, whose fresh appealing looks led to her appearance in a series of "women's pictures" in the early 1930s. She was often cast as the girl fighting for and suffering over the wrong guy.

454.13–14   *Major Hoople cough.*] Amos B. Hoople costarred with his wife Martha in the comic strip "Our Boarding House," which first appeared in 1921 and ran until 1981. Martha competently runs the boardinghouse while her retired-army-major husband lounges about, bragging, telling stories, and inventing get-rich-quick schemes. When annoyed or provoked (or caught in a lie), the Major issues a cough-like "Harrumph!"

456.24   Kefauver and McClellan] Estes Kefauver (1903–1963), U.S. senator from Tennessee who headed the 1950 Senate committee investigating organized crime. The hearings were televised live. He went on to head a 1954 Senate subcommittee investigation into the impact of certain kinds of comic books on juvenile delinquency. Senator John McClellan of Arkansas (1896–1977) chaired the 1957 U.S. Senate committee probing "improper activities in labor and management," which found clear links between organized labor and organized crime.

457.9–10   David Susskind] See note 355.22.

458.23   restore men's souls] Cf. Psalm 23:3.

459.10   Alta Yenta] Yiddish: old female busybody, gossip, chatterbox.

459.20   wog] Derogatory term for a person from the Indian subcontinent —though like most such terms, boundaries always expand. In this case, to someone who is not Caucasian.

461.9–12   *ex parte . . . non exceptis.*"] Perelman means all of this to stand as judicial double-talk, using Latin legal terms. *Ex parte*: "out of the party of," thus signifying "on behalf of," or a matter in which both parties are not present. *Nolens-volens*: willing or not. *Sub judice*: under judicial consideration and therefore prohibited from public discussion elsewhere. *A priori*: coming before in time, order, or importance. *Exceptio probat regulam de rebus non exceptis*: an exception proves that a rule exists.

463.2–3   Martha Graham's troupe—] Graham (1894–1991) was one of the founders of the modern dance movement in America and one of its most original choreographers. The Martha Graham Dance Company was founded in 1926.

463.9   Prout's Neck—] Coastal peninsula in southern Maine with a thriving and prosperous summer community. Artist Winslow Homer had a studio there.

THE HINDSIGHT SAGA

469.2–4   October evening in the fall of 1931 . . . *Animal Crackers*] Perelman's dating of the encounter that led to his working on the screenplay of *Monkey Business* is confused. *Monkey Business* was released on September 16, 1931, and *Animal Crackers*—the Marx Brother's last Broadway show—closed on April 6, 1929. Either Groucho proposed the radio-script project more than two and a half years earlier than Perelman suggests or he broached it under different circumstances. The Perelmans arrived in Hollywood in January 1931. Likely, the Groucho/Perelman/Johnstone radio-script pitch meeting in New York occurred in the fall of 1930.

473.9   Alcázar] Palace in Seville, Spain, originally built by the Moors in the tenth century. Later rebuilt by Christian kings during the Reconquest.

473.11   "Moonlight in Kalua,"] Romantic 1921 song composed by Jerome Kern (1885–1945) with lyrics by Anne Caldwell (1868–1936). The lovelorn singer dreams of nights in Hawaii, remembers past nights of bliss, and pines for the return of the lover to "Kalua."

474.7   Bahai] Religion established in 1863, teaching the essential worth of all religions, and the unity of all people. It originally developed in Persia and parts of the Middle East.

474.35   Herman Mankiewicz] American drama critic, screenwriter, and playwright (1897–1953) who shared an Oscar with Orson Welles for the screenplay for *Citizen Cane* (1941). Mankiewicz was associate producer of *Monkey Business* (1931) and *Horsefeathers* (1932) at Paramount Studios.

476.7   Dunning shots] Carroll Dunning developed a process for getting a special effect by superimposing one image on another. The Dunning Process used painted background mattes shot with foreground live action. *King Kong* (1933) is an example of a movie using the Dunning Process.

476.8   vorkapich] See note 11.24.

477.20–21   ghastly, fixed smile like Bartholomew Sholto's in *The Sign of the Four*] In the novel by Sir Arthur Conan Doyle, Bartholomew Sholto is killed by a poison dart, which leaves his face thus transformed.

477.35   klabiatsch] A card game.

478.21–22   Lost Dutchman Mine] In folklore of the early West, a lost gold mine located in the southwestern United States.

481.37   *Sherry Flip*] Aborted Broadway revue to which Perelman contributed sketches. See also note 300.2.

482.23–24   Boniface] Landlord or hotel proprietor, after the convivial innkeeper in George Farquhar's play *The Beaux' Stratagem* (1707).

483.7   *transition*] Quarterly magazine of international avant-garde literature and the arts, founded by the American-born Eugene and Maria Jolas in Paris in 1927. Sections of James Joyce's *Finnegans Wake* first appeared there, as did the work of Dadaist and surrealist painters and poets. The magazine ceased publication in 1938.

483.11   Nimrod] In Genesis 10:9, Nimrod is described as "a mighty hunter before the Lord."

483.25   Robert McAlmon] Expatriate American author and publisher (1895–1956) whose Contact Editions promoted the modernist movement in book form, including Ernest Hemingway's *Three Stories and Ten Poems* and Gertrude Stein's *The Making of Americans*. Before McAlmon moved to Paris, he was cofounder with William Carlos Williams of the short-lived but crucial *The Contact Review* in 1920, which published work by Williams, Wallace Stevens, Ezra Pound, H.D., and Marianne Moore.

484.1   Yaddo] Artists' community on a 400-acre estate in Saratoga Springs, New York, that provides living and work space, meals, and time for creative people to work on a current project.

484.22   Arthur Kober] See pages 74 to 79 in this volume.

485.34   "La Carmagnole"] Pointed popular song (authors unknown) that arose during the French Revolution, celebrating the downfall of Louis XVI and Marie Antoinette. It was often accompanied by a wild dance of the same name.

486.1   bee-loud glade] See the fourth line of William Butler Yeats's poem "The Lake Isle of Innisfree."

486.15 Mark Silver] The seller of the Bucks County farm was actually Mike Gold (1894–1967), left-wing journalist and author of the proletarian novel *Jews Without Money.*

487.3–4 *Marie Celeste*] American merchant ship that was found adrift and deserted off the Azores in 1872—cargo intact, personal belongings of the crew untouched.

487.20 Reuben's] New York Jewish delicatessen started by Arnold Reuben in 1908. It had several locations, moving from Park Avenue to Broadway to East Fifty-Eighth Street. It lays claim to being the deli where the Reuben sandwich was created, though that claim has been regularly challenged. Aaron Reuben sold the business in the mid-1960s, though it continued under his name until it closed in 2001.

489.30 forty-rod] Cheap, strong whiskey.

490.6–7 Tony's, Jack & Charlie's . . . Stork Club] Tony's was a speakeasy located on West Forty-Ninth Street, established in 1920 by former waiter Tony Soma. Writers (including members of the Algonquin Roundtable) as well as Broadway show people and gangsters frequented it. Cousins Jack Kreindler and Charlie Berns opened their West Forty-Ninth Street speakeasy in 1922. Like Tony Soma, they sold out to John D. Rockefeller in 1929 to make way for Rockefeller Center. The Stork Club was perhaps Manhattan's most famous nightclub, a symbol of glamorous "café society" from the 1930s to the 1950s.

490.28 *Third Little Show*] Revue that ran for 136 performances on Broadway in 1931.

492.25–27 George McManus's comic strip . . . Maggie's wrath.] See notes 53.9 and 158.29.

493.8 Matteawan] Matteawan State Hospital for the Criminally Insane, established in 1892. It is located in Dutchess County, New York.

493.24 Aeolian Hall] Concert hall located at 29–33 West Forty-Second Street in Manhattan. The 1,100-seat hall opened in 1912 and closed in 1926. It hosted the world premiere of George Gershwin's *Rhapsody in Blue* in 1924.

SELECTED LETTERS

497.1 *Edmund Wilson*] Arguably the leading American literary critic of his day, Wilson (1895–1972) was at the time of this letter associate editor of *The New Republic.*

497.12 the book is out] *Dawn Ginsbergh's Revenge* (1929), Perelman's first.

497.22 Rivington Street methods] Street on New York's Lower East Side, an immigrant area characterized by its poverty and rough manners.

497.28 Phil and Sally Wylie] Philip Wylie (1902–1971), prolific writer of science fiction and mysteries as well as books on social problems and ecology. His best-known book is *Generation of Vipers* (1943), a catchall condemnation of American society, including American motherhood (the book introduced the term "Momism".) He was married to Sally Ondek. They later divorced.

497.32 Gilbert Seldes] Seldes (1893–1970) was a cultural critic, playwright, and magazine editor. He was also the host of radio and TV programs about the arts in America. His most influential book was *The Seven Lively Arts* (1924).

498.1 *I. J. Kapstein*] Israel James Kapstein (1904–1983), writer and later professor of English at Brown University. He and Perelman met as students at Candace Grammar School in Providence. They both attended Brown and wrote for the college magazines. Kapstein moved to Manhattan in 1926, where he and Perelman briefly shared an apartment in Greenwich Village.

498.13 Krag-Jorgenson] A bolt-action, magazine-fed rifle.

498.13–14 your beard, Floyd Collins] Collins (1887–1925) was an American cave explorer who got trapped in Kentucky's Sand Cave. The seventeen-day attempt to rescue him became a media circus with constant newspaper and radio coverage, food vendors, and souvenir hawkers. (Billy Wilder's 1951 movie *Ace in the Hole*, also known as *The Big Carnival*, is based on this event.) The rescue failed. Perelman's reference to a beard may hint at claims by imposters to be a rescued Collins.

498.24–25 *Darf men . . . in collitch?*] Yiddish: Should one have children or should one go to college?

498.35 *The Green Hat*] Fast-paced, best-selling novel of 1924 by Michael Arlen (1895–1956), British author of Armenian extraction, born Dikran Kouyoumdjian.

499.4 *Judge*] Popular New York–based humor magazine, to which Perelman supplied comic sketches and cartoons during his college years, and which gave him his first job immediately thereafter in 1925.

499.36–500.1 musical with Ogden Nash . . . past week.] *One Touch of Venus*, which opened at New York's Imperial Theatre on October 7, 1943, and closed on February 10, 1945, after 567 performances.

500.2 *Punch*] Long-running British humor magazine published from 1841 to 1992 and from 1996 to 2002. The weekly magazine enjoyed its peak circulation in the 1940s.

500.9–10 on the revue] Never produced.

500.28 Mankiewicz] See note 474.35.

500.31 Kid Dropper arson ring] Nathan Kaplan (1891–1923) was a New York gangster specializing in extortion and "labor slugging," sending a gang to provide muscle to either side in a labor dispute. He got the nickname "Kid Dropper" from his early days running a "drop swindle," where a mark picks up a wallet filled with counterfeit money and gets relieved of his own in the process.

501.1 *Frances and Albert Hackett*] Enormously successful American husband-and-wife writing team. Frances Goodrich (1890–1984) and Albert Hackett (1900–1995) wrote award-winning plays (*The Diary of Anne Frank*) and screenplays (*The Thin Man, Seven Brides for Seven Brothers*) in a collaboration that lasted thirty-four years.

501.19 Laura wrote you way back there in Bali] The subject of a great deal of this letter is the Southeast Asian portion of the Perelman family's 1949 trip around the world, described in *The Swiss Family Perelman* (1950).

502.26 Trilby to my Svengali] In George Du Maurier's 1895 novel, *Trilby*, a young Irish girl by that name is transformed into a great singer by the charismatic Svengali, using hypnosis. Unable to perform without Svengali's help, Trilby becomes entranced and controlled by him.

502.31 Abby] The Perelmans' daughter (b. 1938).

502.33 Adam] The Perelmans' son (1936–2013).

504.12–13 Sepulveda and Westwood] Sepulveda Boulevard and Westwood Boulevard in West Los Angeles.

504.15 *Abby Perelman*] See note 502.31.

504.21–22 African stuff for the magazine] Six pieces—based on Perelman's recent trip to Africa—that would be published in *The New Yorker* in 1954 and 1955 under the group title "Dr. Perelman I Presume: Or Small-Bore in Africa."

504.24 piece that begins a series.] "This Is the Forest Primeval?" appeared in the July 17, 1954, issue of *The New Yorker*, and appears in this volume as well.

506.13 Al] Caricaturist Al Hirschfeld (1903–2003), who went to India with Perelman as part of their 1947 trip around the world, chronicled in *Westward, Ha!*

506.17 Treetops] Tree-house lodge in Kenya, built on stilts. Safari-goers could stay there, viewing the wildlife moving below, and sleep overnight. Perelman did this on his 1954 trip to East Africa and wrote about it in "Dr. Perelman, I Presume: Or Small-Bore in Africa."

506.27 *Leila Hadley*] Hadley (1925–2009) was working as cartoonist Al Capp's publicist when she met Perelman at a party in 1948. Perelman became quickly infatuated and considered divorcing his wife to pursue the relationship. Hadley married someone else in 1953, and went on to a career in public relations and travel writing. Still, Perelman and Hadley remained close, mainly as correspondents, until his death in 1979.

506.34–35 hysteria that envelops everything . . . Mike Todd] Perelman had exasperating experiences with mercurial producer Mike Todd (1909–1958) while working on the screenplay for *Around the World in Eighty Days*. Perelman and his co-writers shared a 1956 Oscar for the screenplay.

508.15 Mark Hanna's] Mark Hanna (1899–1958) was Perelman's literary agent, beginning in the late 1940s.

508.25 *schmier*] Yiddish: spread. Often, something lightly spread.

510.3 musical . . . Nash et al.] Perelman and Ogden Nash were working on a musical set in East Africa to be called "White Rhino," with Hermione Gingold as its star. Nothing came of it.

510.6 Jack Goodman] Goodman (1909–1957) was editor-in-chief at Simon & Schuster, Perelman's American publisher beginning in 1947.

510.10 *Betsy Drake*] American actress and writer (1923–2015). She was married to Cary Grant from 1949 to 1962.

510.16–17 George Jessel . . . human behavior.] George Jessel (1898–1981) was a legendary Jewish American actor, comedian, and producer in vaudeville, in silent films, and on Broadway. In private life, the four-time-married Jessel was caught up in several public domestic scandals, one including firearms.

510.17–23 sinister dwarf . . . obscene fungus] Perelman refers to Mike Todd. See note 506.34–35.

511.2 young English chap] Michael Anderson (1920–2018), whose work on *Around the World in Eighty Days* took him from respected director of British films to sought-after director for high-budget international productions.

513.18–19 *Give Me the World* . . . quotation you drew it from.] Hadley quit her New York public relations job in 1952 and took her six-year-old son on a trip around the world. Her book was published in 1958. The title comes from Yeats's epigraph to *The Wanderings of Oisin*, which Hadley uses for her own book's epigraph as well: "'Give me the world if Thou wilt, but grant me an asylum for my affections.' *Tulka*."

513.19 Herman E] Herman Elkon (1904–1983), diamond dealer living in New York, and a friend of Perelman's.

514.8 Fred Allen] Allen (1894–1956) was a comedian and star in vaudeville, on stage, and especially on the radio. He published two volumes of autobiography: *Treadmill to Oblivion* and *Much Ado About Me*.

514.32 this office.] Perelman rented a separate work space at 513-A Sixth Avenue, between Thirteenth and Fourteenth Streets, for decades, only giving it up in 1966.

515.8–9 Todd still plans . . . next venture.] At some point before his death in 1958, Todd—according to Perelman's reminiscences in "The Hindsight Saga"—met with him for a fruitless discussion about doing a script for a film based on *Don Quixote*. Whether this is the venture Perelman mentions here is not entirely clear.

515.16 *Paul Theroux*] American travel writer and novelist (b. 1941) whose books include *The Great Railway Bazaar*, *Saint Jack*, and *The Mosquito Coast*.

515.22–27 *Some Time in the Sun* . . . Fitzgerald's Sturm und Drang in Hollywood] In addition to F. Scott Fitzgerald, Tom Dardis's 1976 book dealt with the Hollywood years of William Faulkner, Nathanael West, Aldous Huxley, and James Agee.

517.3–5 George V. Higgins . . . New England.] Higgins (1939–1999) was a Boston-based journalist and U.S. prosecutor who turned to writing tough, realistic crime novels set mainly in and around Boston. His first, *The Friends of Eddie Coyle*, remains his bestknown.

517.6 Pat Kavanagh] Perelman hired Kavanagh (1940–2008) to be his British literary agent in 1977, two years before his death.

*This book is set in 10 point ITC Galliard, a face designed
for digital composition by Matthew Carter and based
on the sixteenth-century face Granjon. The paper is acid-free
lightweight opaque that will not turn yellow or brittle with age.
The binding is sewn, which allows the book to open easily and lie flat.
The binding board is covered in Brillianta, a woven rayon cloth
made by Van Heek–Scholco Textielfabrieken, Holland.
Composition by Dianna Logan, Clearmont, MO.
Printing by Sheridan Grand Rapids, Grand Rapids, MI.
Binding by Dekker Bookbinding, Wyoming, MI.
Designed by Bruce Campbell.*

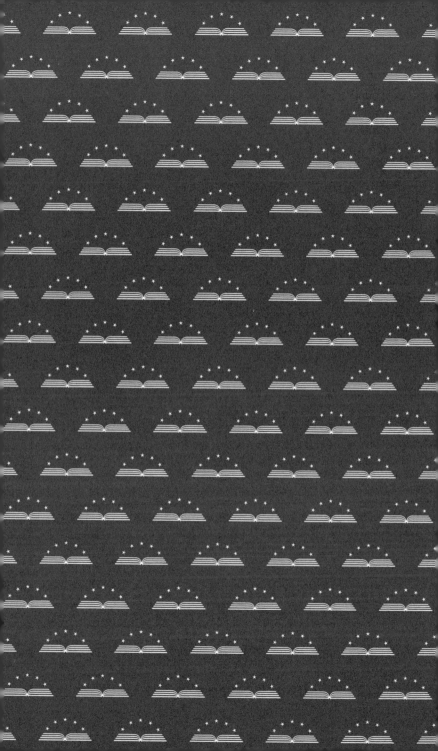